BEHIND THE LINES

BEHIND THE LINES

W.E.B. GRIFFIN

G. P. PUTNAM'S SONS

New York

G. P. Putnam's Sons
Publishers Since 1838
200 Madison Avenue
New York, NY 10016

Behind the Lines was written on Compaq DeskPro XL566 and Laptop 486 computers using
MicroSoft *Microsoft Word For Windows 6.0 and MasterWord* software and printed on an AST
Research, Inc., TurboLaser/PS Printer.

Design by Jennifer Ann Daddio

Library of Congress Cataloging-in-Publication Data

Griffin, W. E. B.
Behind the lines / W. E. B. Griffin.
p.   cm. — (The corps ; bk. 7)
ISBN 0-399-14086-7
1. United States.   Marine Corps—History—Fiction.   2. United
States—History, Military—20th century—Fiction.   3. World War,
1939–1945—Fiction.   I. Title.   II. Series: Griffin, W. E. B.
Corps ; bk. 7.
PS3557.R489137C68   bk. 7   1995b   95-32133 CIP
813'.54—dc20

Printed in the United States of America
6   7   8   9   10

This book is printed on acid-free paper.   ∞

THE CORPS is respectfully dedicated to the memory of
Second Lieutenant Drew James Barrett III, USMC
Company K, 3d Battalion, 26th Marines
Born Denver, Colorado, 3 January 1945
Died Quang Nam Province, Republic of Vietnam, 27 February 1969
and
Major Alfred Lee Butler III, USMC
Headquarters 22nd Marine Amphibious Unit
Born Washington, D.C., 4 September 1950
Died Beirut, Lebanon, 8 February 1984
And to the Memory of Donald L. Schomp
A Marine fighter pilot who became a Legendary U.S. Army
Master Aviator
RIP 9 April 1989
"Semper Fi!"

NOTE TO THE READER

Probably the best-known Marines who served with great distinction behind the enemy's lines with the Office of Strategic Services (OSS) during World War II are Major Peter Ortiz (who was decorated with *two* Navy Crosses and named a member of both the French Legion d'Honneur and the British Order of the British Empire for his valor); Sergeants Jack Risler and Fred Brunner; Gunnery Sergeant Robert LaSalle; and Captains Sterling Hayden (the actor) and Peter Devries (the writer).

There were others. . . .

BEHIND
THE
LINES

I

A Ford pickup truck turned off the Mariveles-Cabcaben "highway" into what was officially called "The Headquarters Area" but known universally as "Little Baguio." The area held, in flimsy tropical buildings, the main ordnance and engineer depots and General Hospital #1, as well as the collection of buildings that housed the various offices of Headquarters, U.S. Army Force, Luzon.

The truck had seen better days. Its fenders were crumpled, its windshield was cracked, and the bright crimson paint of its former life as a utility vehicle for the Coca-Cola Company of Manila showed in twenty places through a hastily applied coat of Army olive drab. On the truck bed were a footlocker, a folding wooden cot, a battered leather suitcase, and half a dozen five-gallon gasoline cans.

In a few moments, it pulled up beside the building identified by a battered sign as the Commanding General's.

A tall, just this side of heavyset man got out of the truck and started to walk toward the building. He was wearing mussed, sweat-soaked khakis, high-topped shoes, and a web belt from which was suspended a Model 1911 Colt .45 ACP pistol. He stopped and returned to the truck, snatched a khaki overseas cap from the seat and put it on. On the cap was the gold leaf of a major. There was no insignia of any kind on his khaki shirt. He rubbed the red stubble on his cheeks.

I need a shave. To hell with it.

He entered the open-sided building and walked past a collection of desks toward the building's rear, stopping before the desk of another major of about the same age. On the desk, an ornately carved triangular nameplate—a remnant of better times—carried the crossed rifles of infantry, a major's leaf, and the legend "Marshall Hurt."

A moment or so later, Major Hurt looked up.

"Fertig," he said. "What can I do for you?"

"I was sent for," Fertig replied.

"Oh, yes. I'd forgotten," Hurt said.

They didn't particularly like each other. Hurt was a professional soldier, Wendell Fertig a reservist. A year before, Hurt had been an underpaid captain and Fertig a successful—and wealthy—civil engineer.

Hurt stood up from his desk and went deeper into the building. A minute later he returned.

"The General will see you now," he said, and nodded toward the rear of the building.

Fertig nodded, walked to an open door, then stood there and waited to be noticed by Major General Edward P. King, Jr., the Commanding General of Luzon Force. King, a stocky fifty-eight-year-old artillery man from Atlanta who wore a neatly cropped full mustache, was at that moment standing before a sheet of plywood on which a large-scale map of the Bataan Peninsula had been mounted.

Fertig both liked and admired General King. He had known him socially before the war—indeed, General King had played an important role in the direct commissioning of Fertig as a Captain, Corps of Engineers, U.S. Army Reserve.

And right now he felt very sorry for him. Fertig didn't pretend to know much about the Army, but he knew enough to understand that the worst thing that could happen to a career officer was to suffer defeat.

The map of Bataan General King was studying was clear proof that not only was he suffering defeat, but the defeat was very shortly going to be total and absolute. It didn't matter that King was going to be defeated by a well-equipped, battle-hardened Japanese force that outnumbered King's poorly equipped, starving, "Filamerican" force four or five to one; he was about to lose, and that was all that mattered.

A minute or so later, General King glanced at the door, noticed Fertig, and waved him inside.

"Wendell," he said.

"General."

"Could you see the map, where you were standing?"

Fertig nodded.

"I'm afraid it won't be long," King said. "You know how we are defining effectives these days, Wendell?"

Fertig shook his head, no.

"An effective soldier is one who can carry his weapon one hundred yards without resting and be capable of firing it after he has gone the one hundred yards. Fifteen percent of our force is effective âs of yesterday. The percentage is expected to decline."

Fertig nodded.

"I had several things on my mind when I sent for you," General King said. "For one thing, I wanted to hear from you, personally, that we are prepared to destroy our ordnance and other stocks."

"Everything is prepared for detonation, General. Redundantly, in terms of both hardware and personnel. In other words, each blow site has been doubly wired, and there are two locations from which the sites can be blown."

King nodded.

"Thank you. Good job. A young lieutenant came up with a means to destroy artillery that somehow didn't occur to the authors of the Field Manuals. You simply shove powder bags down the tube ahead of the charge, or the round, and then fire it."

"I don't suppose the authors gave a lot of thought to destroying our own cannons," Fertig said. "I was going to suggest shoving sandbags down the barrel from the muzzle end. I don't know how it would work with a cannon, but I do know, from painful experience, what happens to the barrel of a Diana-grade Browning when you try to get an ounce and a quarter of Number 6 shot past a lump of mud."

King smiled. It was a memory of better times . . . of a cock pheasant rising from the frozen stubble of a cornfield.

"Secondly, Wendell, I was wondering what to do with you."

"Sir?"

"You've blown up—or arranged to blow up—everything here that has to be blown," King said. "It occurred to me that General Sharp might find some use for your skills."

Brigadier General William F. Sharp commanded, on the island of Mindanao, what was now known as the Mindanao Force of the U.S. Army in the Philippines. From everything Fertig had heard, Sharp's forces had not been subjected to the same degree of attack as the Luzon Force, and so were in much better shape.

In the absence of reinforcements, Sharp's forces were as inevitably doomed as King's, but that defeat was some time off, perhaps as much as two months, and in two months a good deal could happen.

"Yes, Sir."

"Would you be willing to go down there to him?"

"Yes, Sir. Of course."

"Well, we have some small craft that periodically try to get from here to there. There's one leaving at nightfall. I've told Hurt to find space for you on it."

"Yes, Sir."

"Possibly, Wendell, you could make it from Mindanao to Australia. God knows, it would be a waste of your talents to spend the rest of this war in a prisoner-of-war cage.''

"If you think I can be of any use here, General . . .''

"I think we've passed that point, Wendell. And I'm sure General Sharp will be glad to have you. Give him my best regards when you see him.''

"Yes, Sir.''

"That'll be all, Wendell,'' King said. He put out his hand. "You've carried your weight around here. Thank you. See you after the war.''

"It's been a privilege serving under you, Sir.''

Fertig saluted. King returned it.

Fertig did as crisp an about-face movement as he could manage, and then marched toward the door. His throat was tight; he felt like crying.

"Wait a minute,'' General King called after him. Fertig turned.

"I said there were several things on my mind,'' King said. "I forgot one.''

"Yes, Sir?''

King motioned him to approach.

"This used to be done with photographers, with a proudly beaming wife standing by, and would be followed by a drunk at the club at your expense,'' King said. "No clubs, no photographers, and no wife, thank God, but congratulations nonetheless, Colonel.''

He handed Fertig a lieutenant colonel's silver leaf.

"I'll be damned,'' Fertig said.

"Well earned, Wendell,'' King said, and shook his hand. "I'll hold you to the party. In better times.''

"I'll look forward to it, Sir.''

King grabbed Fertig's shoulder, squeezed it, smiled, and then turned away from him.

Fertig left the office and returned to Major Hurt's desk.

"Tell me about the boat,'' he said.

"It's a small coaster,'' Hurt replied. "Be at the pier at Mariveles at half past five. They expect you.''

"Do I need orders, or . . .''

"You're traveling VOCG,'' Hurt said—Verbal Order of the Commanding General. "Technically, you're on temporary duty from Luzon Force to Mindanao Force. We don't have authority to transfer anyone.''

"OK.''

"I'll need your truck,'' Hurt said. "So far as luggage is concerned, one item of luggage.''

"I've got a suitcase and a footlocker.''

"One or the other. Sorry.''

"Well, then, I'll leave the footlocker here with you. For safekeeping.''

Hurt smiled.

"I love optimists," he said. "Sorry, there really is no room on the boat."

"If it's all right with you, Hurt, I'll take the footlocker to one of the ammo dumps. And then bring the truck back, of course. There's some personal stuff in there I'd much rather see blown up than fall into the hands of some son of Nippon."

"May I offer you a piece of advice?"

"Certainly."

"You're a lieutenant colonel now. You don't have to ask a major for permission to do anything."

"I'll try to remember that," Fertig said. He put out his hand. "So long, Hurt. Take care of yourself."

"Yeah, you, too," Hurt said. "And just for the record, I think you deserve that silver leaf."

"If there was anything left to drink around here, I'd think you'd been at it."

"If there was anything left to drink around here, I would be at it," Major Hurt said. "Good luck, Colonel."

"See you after the war, Major."

[ONE]
Headquarters, 4th Marines
Malinta Tunnel
Fortress Corregidor
Manila Bay
Commonwealth of the Philippines
0915 Hours 1 April 1942

Major Stephen J. Paulson, USMC, a slightly built thirty-two-year-old from Chicago, who was acting S-1 (Personnel) Officer, 4th Marines, had been giving a good deal of thought—much of it uncomfortable, even painful—both to his own future and to the future of First Lieutenant James B. Weston, USMC.

Paulson had been a Marine for eleven years, and a Naval Aviator for eight. But he had spent almost two years as an infantry platoon leader before going to Pensacola for flight training. So when push came to shove—by which he meant when the Japanese landed on Fortress Corregidor—he thought he could probably do some good, at least hold his own, as an infantry officer. Not in duties commensurate with the gold oak leaves on his collar points, nor even as a captain, commanding a company. But he remembered enough about leading a platoon to be useful when the Japs came.

On the other hand, in his view, Lieutenant Weston would not. This was not a criticism of Weston, simply a statement of fact. Weston came into The Corps right out of the University of Iowa, went through a sort of boot camp for officers at Quantico, and immediately went to Pensacola for pilot training. He was an aviator, and a pretty good one, but he really wasn't qualified to be a platoon leader.

Not that that would matter to the overall efficiency of the 4th Marines. There were more than enough fully qualified infantry lieutenants and captains around, both among the officers who came to the Philippines when the 4th Marines were moved from Shanghai, and among those—like Paulson himself and Weston—who joined the regiment because they'd been in the Philippines filling billets that no longer existed.

Before the war, Major Paulson had been Aviation Officer on the staff of the Commanding Officer, Marine Barracks, Cavite Naval Station, and had commanded a staff sergeant and a PFC. There had not been much for any of them to do, except on those rare occasions when a carrier with a Marine squadron aboard actually pulled into Cavite. Then there was frantic activity for several days, doing what he could to pry necessary parts and supplies loose from the steel grip of Navy supply officers; arranging for the sick to be admitted to shore medical facilities; and trying for the release from the brig of those Marines who had somehow run afoul of the Shore Patrol in time for them to sail with the carrier.

In those days, he had spent a lot of his ample free time trying to come up with a good reason to ask for a transfer back to flying duties. That was a delicate area. Marine officers are supposed to go where they are sent and do what they are told to do, without complaining or trying to get out of it.

Ordinarily, Paulson would not have tried to get himself out of Cavite. It was a three-year tour, and when it was over, he could expect a flying assignment. But he didn't think the war he considered inevitable was going to wait for him to complete his tour, so he tried to get out of it. He had absolutely no success.

A visiting colonel gave him a discreet word to the wise: Obviously, The Corps had to have someone ashore at Cavite, and he was selected; it was not acceptable behavior for a Marine officer to try to get out of an assignment he didn't like.

Lieutenant Jim Weston's case was somewhat different from his own. After a two-year tour with a Marine fighter squadron, flying Brewster Buffalo F2-As, he had been selected for multiengine training. After transition training, he had been given a six-month assignment to a Navy squadron flying Consolidated PBY-5A Catalina twin-engine flying boats.

The idea was to give him enough time under experienced Navy aviators so that he could return to The Corps and serve as a multiengine Instructor Pilot. That, in turn, meant someone had judged him to be a better-than-ordinary pilot, skilled and mature enough to become an IP . . . and not, as Weston felt, because he hadn't been able to cut the mustard as a fighter pilot.

Three months into his "utilization tour" at Pearl Harbor, the Japanese attacked. Though many of the planes of the Navy squadron to which Weston was attached were destroyed on the ground, Weston flew, as copilot, one of the few remaining Catalinas to Cavite on a courier flight.

The Japanese also attacked Cavite, destroying on the ground other Navy Catalinas, one of which had been flown to the Philippines by a Pearl Harbor–based lieutenant commander. When Lieutenant Weston's Catalina landed at Cavite, the lieutenant commander judged that he could be of far greater value to the war effort back in Pearl Harbor than a lowly Marine lieutenant on loan to the Navy. And when the Catalina took off, he was at the controls and Weston was left behind, "awaiting transportation."

Weston hadn't been in a cockpit since. There were few aircraft of any type left in the Philippines. When it became evident that his chances of returning to flying or of being evacuated to Pearl Harbor were negligible, he was assigned to the staff of the Aviation Officer—Paulson—of Marine Barracks, Cavite.

When Cavite was blown up and left for the enemy, all remaining Marine personnel were transferred to the 4th Marines. Paulson was assigned to the personnel section, relieving a major who had served with the 4th Marines in China and whose infantry expertise could be put to better use, and Weston became his deputy.

In Paulson's view, there was not much left for the Acting Personnel Officer to do but wait for the Japanese to land on Corregidor; whereupon he would order the destruction of personnel records by thermite grenade, grab his rifle, and fight, until the end, as an overage, overranked platoon leader.

There was only one alternative to this course of action, one that Paulson himself could not accept, but which, the more he thought about it, seemed to be a viable course of action for Lieutenant Jim Weston.

Before the war, Paulson came to know a number of Army Air Corps pilots. One of them, an Army Air Corps major—also transferred to ground duty when there were no more airplanes for him to fly—approached him and announced that since the war here was about over and he had no intention of surrendering, he was going to head for the hills and hide out. From there, he would either try to escape to Australia, or maybe even fight as a guerrilla.

"You want to come along, Steve?" he asked.

Paulson gave the offer a good deal of thought before declining. For one thing, it would be AWOL, or perhaps even desertion. Something about that rubbed him the wrong way. The very word "desertion" made him consider that since he still had some contribution to make, even if only as a platoon leader, he would in fact be deserting the enlisted men at a time when they needed him most. Finally, although he didn't like to face the fact, his health was shot. He had some sort of rash whose suppurating sores seemed to grow worse daily. His teeth were falling out. There was no way he could survive running around in the hot, physically debilitating jungles of the Philippines. He would become a burden to whomever he was with.

Weston, however, was another matter. Although Paulson was sure he would try his best, the young pilot would be nearly worthless as a platoon leader. And maybe even worse, he could be a burden to those he was commanding. On the other hand, if Weston could somehow get out of the Philippines, he would be of great use to The Corps. There had been a pilot shortage before the war, and that shortage must, Paulson reasoned, be even more acute now.

And even if Weston couldn't escape from the Philippines, he was young, and—considering the circumstances—in good health. He could probably make himself useful to a guerrilla operation. For one thing, he had a degree in electrical engineering, which meant he probably knew something about radios. Any guerrilla force needed radios.

The final consideration was very simple. If Weston stayed on Corregidor, one of two things was certain to happen: he would be killed, or he would be taken prisoner. It was equally certain that he would be more of a problem than an asset in the final fighting. If he went off into the hills, tried to escape to Australia, he would probably be killed. But he *might* not. He *might* escape. And if he did, he could make a contribution. Or he might be useful to some guerrilla commander (Paulson thought of his Air Corps friend, who one day simply vanished from Corregidor) and make a contribution that way.

On The Rock, the alternatives to death and/or surrender were the subject of many careful, soft conversations between officers. Yet, as close as he and Paulson had become, Weston had never brought the subject up.

Is this, Paulson wondered, *because he's been thinking about it, and is afraid I will order him to forget about it if he mentions it to me? Or because he thinks his duty is clear, to stay here and get killed or become a prisoner? And doesn't want me to think he's even thought about taking off?*

Finally—he later recognized this as one of the most difficult things he'd ever done in The Corps—Paulson brought the subject up to Weston himself, directly and somewhat forcefully. They were discussing Weston's alternatives—as possibilities Weston could choose, one possibility being to try to escape. But then Paulson stopped and changed that from a choice to something close to an order. And Weston accepted it as an order.

Because, Paulson wondered, *he is a good Marine and obeys whatever order he is given, even one that frightens him? Or because he was on the edge of making that decision for himself, and my making it an order made it easier?*

By then—none of this took more than a few days, but things were disintegrating at a rapidly accelerating pace—it was harder and harder to leave the island. The boats, the only means of crossing the two miles of water from The Rock to Bataan, were disappearing . . . partly as a result of enemy action, partly from lack of parts and maintenance, and partly, Paulson suspected, because they'd been "requisitioned" by people who were electing not to surrender when the end came.

There seemed to be proof of that. The boats now carried guards to make sure they completed their intended trips. And getting permission to leave the island for any purpose now required the authorization of a colonel or better.

Solving that was an emotional problem for Paulson, not a practical one. As a paper-pusher, he routinely signed colonels' names to all sorts of documents, including permission authority to leave the island. Sometimes he added his initials to these, sometimes not.

He did not think his memorandum ordering Weston to Bataan on a supply-gathering mission would be questioned. But writing it was still one of the most serious violations of the officer's honor code: *"willfully uttering a document known to be false."*

At 0900, he sent a runner after Lieutenant Weston, whom he had loaned to the Army Finance Officer. Weston and a half-dozen other officers had spent the past three days making lists, in triplicate, of the serial numbers of all the one-hundred-, fifty-, twenty-, and ten-dollar bills in the possession of Army and Navy Finance Officers.

When the lists were completed, the money would be burned, to keep it out of Japanese hands. Attempts would be made to get the lists somehow out of the Philippines.

There's no food, and no medicine, and damned little booze, Paulson thought with bitter amusement, *but the Army and the Navy are loaded with dough.*

"You wanted to see me, Sir?" Weston asked.

Paulson met the eyes of the young, unhealthily thin officer.

"I've decided we should make one more attempt—*you* should make one more attempt—to find the parts for our generator," Paulson said.

"Aye, aye, Sir," Weston replied, trying but not quite succeeding to keep his face expressionless.

"Here's your boat pass," Paulson said, handing him the authorization.

"Yes, Sir."

"And the necessary funds," Paulson went on. "You'll have to sign for them."

"Aye, aye, Sir."

Weston's eyes widened when he glanced into the envelope Paulson handed him. It was a thick stack of crisp, unissued fifty- and one-hundred-dollar bills. Far more money than was necessary to buy generator parts.

"Five thousand dollars," Paulson said. "Inflation seems to have come to this Pacific paradise."

"Yes, Sir," Weston said as he leaned over to sign the receipt on Paulson's desk.

"There's supposed to be a motor pool on shore," Paulson said. "You are authorized, by your pass, to draw a vehicle. You may or may not get one."

"Yes, Sir."

"I've arranged for an interpreter to go with you. He's supposed to be fluent in Spanish. Pick him up at the Headquarters Company CP."

"Aye, aye, Sir."

Paulson had given a good deal of thought about the wisdom of sending an interpreter with Weston. On the one hand, it would reduce any suspicions about Weston's generator-parts-finding mission. On the other, there was no way to predict how the interpreter, a buck sergeant who'd come to the Philippines with the 4th Marines from Shanghai, would react when he found out Weston was not going to return to The Rock.

In the end, he decided in favor of sending the sergeant with Weston. Weston might be able to handle the sergeant. If so, the sergeant, with his knowledge of Spanish, and because he was an Old Breed China Marine, might be very useful when Weston took off.

"And I think you'd better take this with you," Paulson said, taking from the well of his desk a Thompson .45 caliber submachine gun and two extra stick magazines. "You never know when you might need it."

"Aye, aye, Sir. Thank you, Sir," Weston said.

He slung the Thompson's web sling over his shoulder, then put one magazine in each of his trouser side pockets.

"Don't shoot yourself in the foot with that, Mr. Weston," Paulson said, meeting his eyes. "In other words, take care."

"Aye, aye, Sir."

"Move out, Mr. Weston," Paulson said. "Get your show on the road."

Weston said nothing for a long minute. Then he saluted.

Paulson returned the salute and then extended his hand.

"Good luck, Jim," Paulson said.

"Good luck to you, Sir," Weston said. Then he came to attention. "By your leave, Sir?"

Paulson nodded.

Weston made the about-face movement and marched away from Paulson's desk. Paulson watched him go down the lateral tunnel and then turn into the main tunnel. Then he turned his attention to the papers on his desk.

[TWO]
Kindley Field
Fortress Corregidor
Manila Bay
Commonwealth of the Philippines
0920 Hours 1 April 1942

Sergeant Percy Lewis Everly, USMC, had spent most of the morning thinking very seriously about desertion.

Everly, who was twenty-six years old, six feet tall, sharply featured, and weighed 145 pounds, was in charge of a two-gun, water-cooled .30 caliber

Browning machine-gun section of Headquarters Company, 4th Marines. This was set up to train its fire on Kindley Field, a rectangular cleared area toward the seaward end of Corregidor. The area had been cleared years before to serve as a balloon field. Everly had seen that on the map. The map didn't say what kind of balloons it was supposed to serve, whether barrage balloons, designed to interfere with aircraft attacking the island fortress, or observation balloons, from which the tip of the Bataan Peninsula two miles away could be observed.

There had been no evidence of either kind of balloons, although Everly had come across the rusted remains of what could have been a winch for balloon cables.

Everly, in his washed thin khakis, web pistol belt, and steel helmet, looked skeletal. Part of that, of course, was because they were on one-half rations, and everybody had lost a lot of weight. But Everly, who from time to time had been called "Slats," was never heavy, never weighed more than 160 pounds.

The machine guns were set up in bunkers made from sandbags, sand-filled fifty-five-gallon drums, and salvaged lumber. They would probably provide some protection against small-arms fire and even hand grenades, but Everly knew the guns weren't going to get much protection from mortar fire or artillery.

When the field telephone buzzed, Everly took it from its leather case and pressed the butterfly switch.

"Sixteen," he said.

"Everly?" a voice Everly recognized as the company clerk's asked.

"Yeah."

"The first wants you here. Now."

"On my way," Everly said, and put the telephone back in its case.

He had a good idea what the First Sergeant of Headquarters Company, 4th Marines, wanted with him. Because he spoke Spanish, he was in some demand as an interpreter if one of the officers had business on Bataan.

Everly walked, stooping, across the bunker to where Corporal Max Schirmer, a short, no longer plump twenty-three-year-old, was sleeping on a bunk of two-by-fours and salvaged commo wire, and touched his arm.

"You've got it," Everly said when Schirmer opened his eyes. "They want me at the CP."

Schirmer nodded, then sat up and shook his head to clear it. When Everly was satisfied that Schirmer was really awake, he left the bunker and headed up the dirt path toward the Company Command Post.

Everly had been a Marine for almost eight years. If the war hadn't come along, he would have been discharged, at the conclusion of his second four-year hitch, on 25 May 1942. But a whole year before that, on 27 May 1941, when the 4th Marines were still in China, President Roosevelt had proclaimed "an unlimited state of national emergency," one result of which had been the extension of all enlistments in The Marine Corps "for the duration of the emergency, plus six months."

But that had really not meant much to Everly. He liked The Marine Corps, and he could not imagine doing anything but being a Marine. If his enlistment hadn't been extended, he would have shipped over, sewn a second four-years-service hash mark on the sleeves of his uniform, and gone on being a Marine.

The only thing the date 25 May 1942 meant to Everly now was that—unless he did something about it, and soon, and the only thing he could think of doing was to desert—when it came around, and it was going to come around next month, he'd either be dead, or wishing he was dead.

Everly was pretty sure in his mind about three things: (1) Bataan was about to fall; (2) "The Aid" was not coming, at least not in time to do any good; and because it wasn't, (3) soon after Bataan fell, Fortress Corregidor was going to fall.

Bataan was a peninsula on what Everly thought of as the bottom of Luzon Island. It sort of closed off Manila Bay.

Fortress Corregidor was an island in Manila Bay two miles off the tip of Bataan, about thirty miles from the capital of the Philippines, Manila. Maps of Corregidor looked to Everly like the drawings Mr. Hawkings used to make of human sperm on the blackboard at Zanesville High School during what was called "Masculine Hygiene."

Everly graduated from Zanesville High School on 22 May 1934, went into The Corps two days later, and had not been back to Zanesville, or even to West Virginia, since. His father, a coal miner, died when Everly was fourteen, and his mother two years later. Since no relatives were either able or willing to take him in, the State boarded him out for two years with a "foster family." Both the State and his "foster mother" took pains to make sure he understood he would be on his own the minute he was eighteen.

He went to the post office in Wheeling one day in the first weeks of his senior year, intending to Join The Navy and See The World, as the recruiting posters offered. But the Navy wouldn't have him, for reasons he no longer remembered, nor would the Army. But the Marine recruiter said he would accept his application, send it in, and see what happened.

A month later, there was a letter with a bus ticket and meal vouchers. He went back to Wheeling and took a physical examination and filled out some more forms; and two weeks after that, there was another letter, this one from Headquarters, U.S. Marine Corps in Washington, D.C., telling him he had been accepted for enlistment, and that since he was a minor, he would have to have his parents' permission to enlist, form enclosed, signature to be notarized.

He got his "foster father" to sign it and mailed it off. But it came back saying that since Everly was a Ward Of The State Of West Virginia, it would have to be signed by the Responsible Official. That turned out to be the Judge of Probate. The Judge signed the form and told him he thought he was doing the smart thing, shook his hand, and wished him good luck.

Everly left Zanesville the morning after the day he graduated, took the bus to Washington, D.C., was given another physical at the Washington Navy Yard, and was sworn into The Corps that afternoon.

He went through boot camp, and then they loaded him aboard the USS *Chaumont* and sent him to the Marine Barracks, U.S. Navy Base Cavite, outside Manila. That was good duty. The Corps put him to work in the motor pool, where he was supposed to be supervising the Filipino mechanics. But since the Filipinos knew a hell of a lot more about automobile mechanics than he did, what really happened was that they taught him, rather than the other way around.

He also got himself a girl, a short, sort of plump, dark-skinned seventeen-year-old named Estellita, which meant "Little Star" or something like that. Estellita had been raised as a Catholic. Every week she went to confession, because what they were doing—not being married—was a sin, and then to Mass, and then came home and got in bed with him again.

Everly was very careful not to get her in the family way. He had only been an orphan two years before coming into The Corps, but that had been enough to convince him that making a baby that was going to be an orphan because you weren't going to marry the mother would be a lousy thing to do to anybody.

Between Estellita and the little brown brothers in the motor pool, it wasn't long before he was speaking pretty good Spanish. And then he got promoted to private first class, and he considered that things were better for him in The Corps and in the Philippines than they had ever been so far in his life.

Then he got in a fight in the Good Times bar with a sergeant from the Marine Detachment on the battleship USS *Pennsylvania* when she came into Cavite. The sonofabitch was a mean drunk. And when Everly knocked him on his ass the first time he put his hand on Estellita's breast and wouldn't stop, he came back at Everly with a knife, one of those kind that flick open when you press a button. And when the fight was over, both of them were cut, and the sergeant had a broken nose and a busted-up hand, where Everly had stomped on it.

Everly knew the fight wasn't his fault, but he also knew that he was a PFC, and the mean sonofabitch was a sergeant. When they put him before a General Court-martial charged with attempted murder and assault with a deadly weapon upon the person of a superior noncommissioned officer, Everly decided that the other shoe had dropped, the good times were over, and he was going to spend the next ten or fifteen years in the Portsmouth Naval Prison.

But that didn't happen either. They had the court-martial. And he stood up at attention and heard the senior officer, a lieutenant colonel, say that the court, in closed session, two-thirds of its members concurring, had found him not guilty of all the charges and all the specifications.

The next day the Commanding Officer of Marine Barracks, Cavite, called him in and told him that it was his experience in circumstances like this that it was best for everybody if the accused found not guilty was transferred. Then he went on and said Everly could have his choice. He could be reassigned to someplace like San Diego, in the States, or aboard a ship, or—and this is what he would recommend—to the 4th Marines in Shanghai.

So three weeks later, Everly went aboard the USS *Chaumont* when she called at Cavite and rode her to Shanghai, China, where he was assigned to Headquarters Company, 4th Marines, and detailed to the motor pool.

Within a couple of weeks, he could see that being a China Marine was going to be even better duty than Cavite. Not only that, nobody seemed to know about what he did to that mean drunk sonofabitch off the *Pennsylvania*, and about the court-martial. He was sure that Sergeant Zimmerman, who ran the motor pool, didn't know anything about it. And while it seemed likely that somebody—maybe his first sergeant, or his company commander, or maybe even the regimental commander—knew about it, nobody was holding it against him. He really had come here with a clean slate. That made him feel pretty good again about The Corps, and being in The Corps.

He turned twenty-one in Shanghai and signed the papers extending his "until reaching his legal majority or unless sooner discharged" enlistment for a four-year hitch. And then, in May 1938, he shipped over for another four years.

At the time, he thought that with a little bit of luck, he might make corporal during his second hitch. He got himself a Chinese woman, Soo Ling, and she took care of him and taught him to speak some Chinese, enough to say what he wanted to say, and to understand most of everything that was said to him. She even taught him to read and make some of the ideographs, and he took care not to get her in the family way.

And things started to get even better, too. He sometimes thought it was a good thing that mean drunk sonofabitch had come after him with a knife. If he hadn't, he'd still be in the Cavite motor pool.

Just about as soon as he arrived in Shanghai, he was assigned as an assistant truck driver on the regular supply convoys from Shanghai to Peking, where there was a detachment of Marines.

There was at least one supply convoy a month, coinciding with the calling at Shanghai of the USS *Chaumont* or the USS *Henderson,* the Navy transports that endlessly circled the Pacific, bringing replacements and supplies and taking people home. Sometimes there was more than one truck convoy a month, when freight arrived in Shanghai by Navy or civilian freighter.

There was a driver and an assistant driver, both to share the driving and to leave a spare driver in case somebody got sick.

And Sergeant Zimmerman drove a wrecker along. Even so, if for some reason a truck had to be left by the side of the road—even for a couple of hours, because there was no one to drive it and the wrecker already had a truck in tow—by the time they could get a driver to it, there would be nothing left but the frame, and maybe not even that. China was like that.

They drove first to Peking and then to Tientsin, another seaport, where there was a detachment of the 4th Marines, usually stopping over there for two days, and then back to Peking, and then back to Shanghai. Some of the drivers hated getting the duty, because it took them away from the good life in Shanghai. But some liked it, because it was a change of scenery, or women, or both.

Usually Everly was pleased when his name came up on the roster, because it meant a change of scenery. Not women. If something came up, he wasn't going to kick it out of bed, but he thought there was not much point in chasing strange females; you never knew what you might catch, and it was expensive. He was by nature, or perhaps by training, frugal. He had no money in his pockets from the time he became a Ward Of The State until he got his first pay as a Marine; and that left a painful memory.

There was always an officer in charge of the convoys, changing from convoy to convoy, because that was the way things were in The Corps; when there were supplies involved, you had to have an officer in charge. But the officers were ordinarily wise enough to just ride along, leaving the actual running of the convoy to Sergeant Zimmerman.

Zimmerman, who was short, stocky, and phlegmatic, had been in China for six years. He had a Chinese woman, who had borne him three children, and he fully intended to spend the rest of his time in The Corps in China, then retire there and open a bar or something.

Zimmerman was competent and he was fair, and Everly figured him out—and how to deal with him—pretty quick: Zimmerman did what he was told without question and to the best of his ability, and he expected people who worked for him to do the same thing. When Sergeant Zimmerman told PFC Everly to do something, Everly did it, promptly, and to the best of his ability. They got along. On the convoys, they came to spend time together, since neither was interested in chasing women, gambling, or getting shitfaced.

In the spring of 1941, things changed.

A new face appeared when the drivers and assistant drivers were gathered together for a convoy to Peking and Tientsin. Corporal Kenneth R. McCoy. Everly knew him only by sight and reputation. McCoy had quite a reputation.

PFC McCoy had become notorious, and in circumstances not unlike Everly's trouble with the mean drunk sonofabitch off the *Pennsylvania.* In McCoy's case, it was Italian Marines, four of them, who ganged up on him one night when he was on his way back to the barracks.

Killing a couple of Italian Marines was a bigger deal than cutting and stomping on the hand of a Marine sergeant. And when Everly heard they were going to court-martial McCoy, he thought McCoy was almost surely going where he had almost gone, to the Portsmouth Naval Prison.

It wasn't a question of guilt or innocence, Everly reasoned, but rather what was more important: China Marine PFCs were expendable. When one caused trouble—and creating a diplomatic incident was far worse than getting in a knife fight with a sergeant—they got rid of him as quickly as possible.

But that didn't happen. McCoy beat the court-martial. And the next thing you knew, he was promoted to corporal and transferred out of ''D'' Company to work in Regimental Headquarters. McCoy had just completed his first hitch in The Corps, and people just didn't get themselves promoted to corporal after just completing their first hitch.

The scuttlebutt went around that McCoy was really working for Captain Edward Banning, the 4th Marines' S-2 Officer, in Intelligence. The scuttlebutt was that McCoy had been in Intelligence all along.

Making sure that it didn't look like he was putting his nose in where it didn't belong, Everly watched McCoy pretty carefully on that first run to Peking. He noticed a couple of things. For one thing, McCoy not only spoke Chinese like a Chinaman, but had a couple of Japanese military manuals in his rucksack that he obviously could read.

By the time they made three convoy trips to Peking, it was pretty clear to Everly that the officers in charge had gotten the word to do what Sergeant Zimmerman said to do, and that Zimmerman was getting that word from Corporal McCoy.

It was also pretty clear that what McCoy was doing on the convoys was running around spying on the Japanese, identifying units, getting their strength, seeing what kind of weapons they had, and, by spending a lot of time in whorehouses, picking up from the Chinese whores what they had heard from their Japanese customers.

And then, after one trip to Peking, right after they got back to Shanghai, Sergeant Zimmerman and Corporal McCoy disappeared. The scuttlebutt was that they got shipped home, but nobody knew for sure what had happened.

And then, the week after they disappeared, Captain Banning sent for Everly and told him McCoy and Zimmerman had been ordered home. He also told him what McCoy had been doing for him, and that both McCoy and Zimmerman had spoken highly of him. Then he asked him if he would be interested in volunteering to do the same thing.

So Everly volunteered, guessing correctly that Banning was going to give him a lot more expense money than he was going to have to spend, and that it was a good way to make corporal ahead of time. And for a couple of months, he did just that; he made corporal, and managed to put aside nearly a thousand dollars in expense money.

That business had ended when the decision was made to get the 4th Marines and the Navy's Yangtze River Patrol out of China. Captain Banning was assigned to the Advance Party and flown out of Shanghai to the Philippines; and Everly was sent back to the motor pool.

Just before he left, Captain Banning married his Russian girlfriend, which raised him even higher in Everly's opinion. When things got a little tough, a lot of Americans, officers and enlisted and civilians, had just cut their girlfriends—Chinese and Russian—loose to make out as best they could by themselves. Everly couldn't leave Soo Ling to fend for herself, so he gave her all the money he had saved up since he was in China, and the money he'd made working for Banning. Then he told her to check on Mrs. Banning when the Japs came, and if she needed help, to do what she could for her and then go home.

He didn't know what happened to Soo Ling or Captain Banning's wife, either; but he did know what happened to Captain Banning, once he got to the Philippines. Just about as soon as the Marines came under fire, he was too close to an incoming round, and the concussion blinded him, and he wasn't even able to fight.

For a while he was in the hospital, first on Luzon, then here in the Corregidor Hospital tunnel; and then they sent him and some other blind guys out on a submarine.

And Percy Lewis Everly was promoted to sergeant and given the two-gun .30 caliber water-cooled Browning machine-gun section at Kindley Field.

Where, he was convinced, one of several things was going to happen: Once Bataan fell, and the Japanese could bring their artillery to bear on the island, he was going to get killed by Japanese artillery. Or, in the unlikely event that didn't happen, he was going to get killed when the Japanese landed on Corregidor. Or, if he didn't get killed by Japanese artillery, or by Japanese Marine infantry when they landed on Corregidor, he was going to wind up a Japanese prisoner.

He had seen enough of the Japanese in China to know how they treated prisoners. You were almost better off dead than to be a prisoner of the Japs. Everly had seen with his own eyes the Japs using Chinese prisoners for bayonet practice.

The one thing Everly really couldn't figure out was why people—especially senior noncoms and officers—kept talking about "The Aid." "The Aid" could be any number of things—for example, a fleet of B-17 bombers suddenly appearing to bomb the Japs off Bataan and out of the Philippines. Or a fleet of Navy ships, carrying divisions of fully equipped soldiers from the States, to run the Japanese off Bataan and out of the Philippines. Or even a small convoy of transports, bringing food and medicine.

But people kept talking about "The Aid," whatever it meant to them, as if it was really coming and would turn things around.

That was bullshit, pure and simple. If "The Aid"—any kind of aid—was coming, General MacArthur wouldn't have run off to Australia the way he did three weeks before, on 10 March.

Only two things were going to happen to the men in the Philippines, Marines, soldiers, or sailors. They were going to get killed, or they were going to get captured. And getting captured was likely to be as bad as getting killed. Everly had seen people starve to death in China, too, and he didn't think he wanted to die that way, either.

There was one other alternative: take off now, get the hell away from Corregidor and Bataan and Luzon, make your way to one of the other islands, maybe Mindanao, and take off for the hills.

That would be desertion in the face of the enemy, and the punishment for that was death or such other punishment as a court-martial may direct. There had been lectures about that.

The lectures had convinced Everly that he wasn't the only one thinking about avoiding certain death or capture; that people had probably already taken off to do just that. Otherwise, there wouldn't have been the lectures telling them it was not only stupid, but punishable by death or such other punishment as a court-martial may direct.

Everly had learned as a kid, even before he became a Ward Of The State, that the way to really get your teeth kicked in was to hope for something you really wanted. You usually didn't get what you really wanted.

So he didn't let himself think that maybe the reason the first sergeant had sent for him was so that he could serve as interpreter for some officer going off Corregidor onto Bataan. If it turned out to be for some other reason, it would be a real kick in the face.

An officer in the company CP was standing there, a young, skinny first lieutenant with a steel pot on his head, a web belt with a pistol holster hanging from it around his waist, and a Thompson .45 ACP submachine gun slung from his shoulder.

"This is Sergeant Everly, Lieutenant," the first sergeant said.

"Major Paulson tells me you speak pretty good Spanish, Sergeant," the Lieutenant said.

Who the hell is Major Paulson? Oh, the little guy with the bad rash, run-

ning sores all over him. With pilot's wings. We spent two days last week on Bataan looking for parts for some kind of generator. We didn't find any; I could have told him we wouldn't before we left The Rock.

"Yes, Sir."

"We really need those generator parts you and Major Paulson were looking for," the Lieutenant said. "Do you feel up to having another look?"

"Aye, aye, Sir."

"My name is Weston, Sergeant," the Lieutenant said, putting out his hand.

"Yes, Sir," Everly said, shaking it.

"You need anything to take with you?"

"No, Sir," Everly said.

He had with him all he would need. He had his Springfield Model 1903 .30-06 Caliber rifle, with six extra five-round stripper clips; his Model 1911A1 .45 ACP Caliber Colt pistol, and an extra magazine with seven cartridges; two canteens of water; his compass; his first-aid pack; and a small rucksack slung over his shoulder which held two shorts, two skivvy shirts, two pairs of socks, a shirt and a pair of pants, a razor with three decent blades and one brand-new blade, two packages of Chesterfield cigarettes, and a Zippo lighter that wouldn't work until he could find a gas tank to dip it into for fuel.

And the click-open knife the sergeant from the *Pennsylvania* had tried to kill him with. At the court-martial, the sergeant testified that the knife introduced into evidence didn't belong to him, that Everly had come after him with it. When Everly was acquitted, the knife was "returned" to him. The first thing he wanted to do was throw it away; but then he decided maybe he could sell it to someone for a couple of bucks—it was a high-quality knife. But then he realized that he didn't want to sell it, either. So he just kept it hidden in his footlocker in rolled-up skivvy shirts. Later, when he was working for Captain Banning, he started carrying it with him in his pocket, or slipped into the top of his boondockers. He never used it, not even to clean his fingernails, but he kept it sharpened. And every once in a while, he oiled it and made sure that when he slid the button, it flipped open, the way it was supposed to.

"Then why don't we get started?" Lieutenant Weston said.

"Aye, aye, Sir."

The first sergeant didn't say a word; he just looked at Everly.

That old bastard is too smart to believe in The Aid, Everly thought. *He knows everybody on The Rock is fucked. And he knows men, and he knows me. Which means he knows I wouldn't be carrying my rucksack unless I was thinking about not coming back. What does that make me in his eyes? A fucking coward and disgrace to The Marine Corps? Or a lucky bastard who's being given the chance to do something he wishes he could do himself?*

Everly nodded at the first sergeant.

"Take care of yourself, Everly," the first sergeant said.

Everly nodded again, and then followed Lieutenant Weston out of the CP.

III

[ONE]
Mariveles-Morong Highway, Luzon
Commonwealth of the Philippines
1425 Hours 1 April 1942

No vehicles were available for assignment to a lowly lieutenant and his sergeant at the motor pool at Mariveles, at the tip of the Bataan Peninsula.

"You'll have to hitchhike," the Army captain in charge said. "But that's not as bad as it sounds. There's a lot of traffic. Where are you headed?"

"Orion," Lieutenant Weston said. Orion was one of four small towns on the Manila Bay side of the Bataan Peninsula.

"When you leave the compound, turn right," the Captain said. "It's about thirty-five miles. What do you expect to find in Orion?"

"Generator parts."

"Good luck," the Captain said, his tone clearly saying that two Marines had little chance of finding anything in Orion.

"Thank you, Sir," Weston said, and saluted. Everly followed suit, and then courteously waited for Weston to leave the small, frame motor pool office first.

During the short trip from Corregidor on the requisitioned thirty-five-foot Chris-Craft cabin cruiser, there'd been a pleasant breeze; but by the time they'd walked from the Mariveles pier to the motor pool, their backs and armpits were dark with sweat.

At the gate of the compound, a guard shack was manned by two enlisted Army Military Policemen and a captain wearing the crossed rifles of Infantry. He carefully examined the pass (actually a memorandum form, the stockpiled supplies on Corregidor having included six months' supply of printed forms), and, Weston thought, suspiciously.

"Where are you headed, Lieutenant?" he asked.

"Morong, Sir," Weston replied.

The Captain's eyebrows rose questioningly; it was clear he wanted an explanation.

"There was word that some stuff was cached this side of Morong when they evacuated Subic Bay,'' Weston said. ''We thought the generator parts we're looking for could be there.''

He was uncomfortable lying, and he took a quick look at the Old Breed Sergeant from the 4th Marines to see if he had any reaction to his change of destination; Sergeant Everly had heard him tell the motor officer they were headed for Orion. Morong, a small port on the South China Sea, was on the opposite side of the Bataan Peninsula.

Everly's face was expressionless.

''You've got coordinates?'' the Captain asked.

Weston forced himself to smile.

'' 'Two hundred paces due east from an overturned and burned ton-and-a-half,' '' he said, '' 'three point seven miles from Morong.' ''

''There's more than one burned and overturned toñ-and-a-half truck on that road,'' the Captain said.

''Ours not to reason why,'' Weston said with a smile. ''Ours but to . . .''

''Happy hunting,'' the Captain said, waving them through the gate.

There was no traffic headed toward Subic Bay. Weston started walking along the side of the road, remembering when he used to hitchhike in high school and college; he could never understand then—or now—why hitchhikers walked along the road.

There's no way you could walk even a couple miles to where you're headed, so why walk at all? Just wait for a ride.

Everly walked behind him, keeping up with him easily, despite all the equipment he was carrying. Weston decided he would at least walk out of sight of Mariveles before talking to the sergeant. And then when they were out of sight, he decided he would walk a little farther.

He intended to order the sergeant to go back to The Rock, carrying a meaningless message to Major Paulson.

He had just about decided they had gone far enough—being defined as far enough away from Mariveles that if the sergeant became suspicious and said something to the MPs at the gate, he would have twenty minutes or so to find a side road and disappear down it—when the sergeant reported a truck was approaching.

It was a flatbed Ford, driven by an Army corporal. The name of a Manila furniture dealer could still be read under a hastily applied coat of olive-drab paint.

A PFC riding in the cab stepped out and gave Weston his seat, and then climbed in back with Everly. The truck was loaded with bales of empty sandbags, and the driver told him he was headed for a Philippine artillery battalion, then asked him where he was headed.

"I'm looking for a burned and rolled-over ton-and-a-half," Weston replied. "There's supposed to be some stuff cached nearby."

"I was up here this morning," the driver said. "There's a bunch of trucks turned over and burned. How are you going to know which one?"

"I suppose I'll have to check them all out and hope I get lucky," Weston replied.

Fifteen minutes later, on a sharp bend on a deserted stretch of road, the driver slowed and stopped, and pointed out Weston's window. The fire-blacked wheels and underside of an overturned truck were just visible thirty yards off the road, at the bottom of a ditch.

"I guess he missed the turn," the driver said. "At night, no lights, these roads are dangerous as hell."

"Might as well start here, I suppose. Thanks for the ride."

The sergeant was standing by the side of the road looking at Weston by the time Weston got out of the cab.

Weston walked to the side of the road and, nearly falling, slid down into the ditch. After a moment, as if making up his mind whether or not to do so, Everly slid down after him.

Weston pretended to examine the truck, and then walked down the ditch a hundred feet or so. Everly watched him but did not follow. Weston walked back to him.

"Obviously, this isn't the truck," he said.

Everly said nothing.

"I've been thinking, Sergeant," Weston said, wondering if he sounded as artificial as he felt. "We better get word to Major Paulson that chances are we aren't going to find the truck at all."

Everly didn't reply.

"Tell him, of course, that I'll keep looking," Weston said.

"Could I see that Thompson a minute, please, Sir?" Everly asked.

It was not the response Weston expected. And without really thinking what he was doing, he unslung the submachine gun from his shoulder and handed it to Everly. Everly unslung his Springfield '03 and handed it to Weston.

"Sergeant, what are you doing?" Weston asked.

"Lieutenant, I'm trying to figure out what to do about you," Everly said.

"Excuse me?"

"I'm not going back to The Rock, Mr. Weston," Everly said. "I made up my mind about that a couple of days ago. If I ever got off The Rock, I wouldn't go back."

"What are you going to do?"

"I don't really know. Get off Bataan somehow. Go to one of the other islands. Mindanao, probably."

Weston didn't know what to say.

"And I decided I'm going to need this more than you do," Everly added, shrugging the shoulder from which the Thompson was suspended. "Would you give me the extra magazines, please?"

"What do you think you're going to do, even if you make it to Mindanao?"

"I'm not the only one who's decided he doesn't want to surrender," Everly said. "Maybe I can link up with some of the others."

"And do what?"

"I don't know. Maybe do something about the Japs, maybe try to get out of the Philippines. The only thing I know for sure is that I'm not going to find myself a prisoner."

Their eyes met.

"You sure you know what you're doing?"

"The only thing I know for sure," Everly repeated, "is that I'm not going to find myself a prisoner. I seen what the Japs do to their prisoners."

"The reason I was sending you back to The Rock," Weston said, slowly, "is that I had reached much the same conclusion."

"I figured maybe that was it when I heard you bullshit them officers," Everly said.

"I'm a pilot," Weston said. "If I can get to Australia, I can do some good. I'm not doing anybody any good here."

Everly nodded but did not reply.

"Do you have any idea how we can get from here to Mindanao?" Weston asked.

Everly shook his head slowly from side to side. "Except that we're going to need a boat," he said.

"Do you have any idea where we can get a boat?"

Everly shook his head again.

Weston smiled.

"Well, we'll think of something," he said, and held out Everly's Springfield to him. With the other hand, he prepared to take his Thompson back.

"You ever fire a Thompson much, Mr. Weston?"

"Only in Basic Officers' Course," Weston replied. "For familiarization."

"I got a Thompson Expert Bar," Everly said. "Maybe I better keep it." The Expert Bar is one of the specific weapon bars (the others being pistol, rifle, et cetera) attached to the Expert Marksman's Medal.

That's not a suggestion, Weston realized, *nor even a request. It is an announcement that he has taken over the Thompson.*

"If you think that's the smart thing to do, it's all right with me," Weston said, and handed Everly the two spare magazines Major Paulson had given him.

Did I do that because it was the logical thing to do? Or because there is something about this man that frightens me? And I didn't want to—have the balls to—challenge him?

"The way I figure it, we're maybe nine, ten miles from Morong," Everly said. "I don't think it would be smart going into Morong looking for a boat. But maybe we could find something a little out of town, maybe a mile or so. Either side of Morong. There's little coves, or whatever they're called."

"And you speak Spanish," Weston said, thinking aloud.

Everly grunted an acknowledgment.

"And I have five thousand dollars," Weston said, with a touch of enthusiasm in his voice.

Everly quickly dispelled it.

"If we get caught by the Army snooping around, looking for a boat, we better hope your boat pass works."

"You think that's liable to happen?"

"I don't think we're the only ones trying to get away from Bataan," Everly said matter-of-factly. "And what we're doing is desertion in the face of the enemy."

"Is that how you think of it?"

"That's what it is, Mr. Weston," Everly said, and then turned and started up the side of the ditch, back toward the road.

After Weston climbed up after him, Everly had something else to say:

"I think it would be a good idea, Mr. Weston, if we split your five thousand dollars. In case we get separated or something."

Weston didn't like the suggestion, if it was a suggestion. But he took out the envelope and counted out twenty-five hundred dollars and handed it to Everly.

He found a little consolation in the thought that if Everly wanted to steal the money, all he had to do was point the Thompson at him and take it.

"Thanks," Everly said. He removed his canteens from their covers, divided the money into two stacks, shoved it into the canteen cases, and then, with some difficulty, replaced the canteens.

Then he started walking down the road. Weston walked after him, very much aware that he was no longer functioning as a Marine officer in command of an enlisted man. Everly had taken command. It was not a comforting thought.

On the other hand, this Old Breed China Marine seems to know what he's doing. And obviously I don't.

[TWO]

The village on the coast was at the end of a winding dirt road—not much more than a trail. It consisted of no more than fifteen crude houses surrounding a well. The houses were built on stilts, obviously as protection against surf and high tides; some were roofed with galvanized steel, others with thatch.

Weston wondered why they didn't build their houses farther away from the water.

The shoreline was mostly dirt and rocks, onto which boats could have been beached. No boats were in sight, however, and no marks were on the shoreline indicating any had been in there, not only since the last tide, but for a long time.

But Weston, his eyes following his nose, saw fish drying.

There are boats around here somewhere.

There was a cantina.

In the cantina were four tables, perhaps a dozen rickety chairs, and a bar onto which a metal Lucky Strike cigarette advertisement had been nailed. A shelf behind the bar held a dozen glasses and half a dozen empty Coca-Cola bottles. It was tended by a very fat Filipino woman with graying hair and bad teeth.

She eyed them suspiciously.

Weston looked at Everly, waiting for him to speak to the woman. After a moment, it became apparent that Everly was waiting for him to say something to her.

Not because I'm the officer in charge, but because he doesn't want her to know he speaks Spanish. Christ, why didn't I think of that?

Weston gestured that he wanted something to drink.

"No cerveza," the woman said.

Weston knew enough Spanish to understand there was no beer.

He shrugged, hoping she would interpret this to mean he would be satisfied with whatever she had.

"Dinero?" the old woman asked.

He reached in his pocket and laid an American five-dollar bill on the bar. She picked it up, examined it carefully, laid it back down, and walked out of the cantina through a door in the rear. In two minutes she was back with one bottle of Coca-Cola. She opened it and handed it to him. Then she picked up the five-dollar bill and stuffed it in the opening of her dress.

"It's a good thing we're not really thirsty," Everly said, and then indicated with a barely perceptible move of his head that Weston should look behind him.

A small, dark-skinned man had come into the cantina. He was barefoot, and he was wearing a loose-fitting cotton pullover shirt and baggy, ragged cuffed trousers.

"Hello, American buddies," he called from behind the bar. "I speak English. How are you?"

"Hello," Weston said.

"Very bad," the Filipino said. "Goddamn very bad."

"What's very bad?"

"Fucking war," the Filipino said, walking to Weston, putting out his hand, and when Weston took it, shaking it enthusiastically. "Fucking Japons. Bullshit."

"Very bad," Weston agreed.

"Hello, buddy," the Filipino said to Everly.

Everly nodded his head.

"No fucking beer," the Filipino said. "Damn near no Coca-Cola. Fucking Japons."

"Yes," Weston agreed.

"What can I do for you?" the Filipino asked.

"Actually, we're looking for a boat."

"Ha! No fucking boats anymore. You got any money?"

"We're trying to rent a boat to take us off Bataan," Weston said.

"No fucking boats. Japons maybe twenty-five miles away. Next week they be here."

"What happened to the boats that were here?" Weston asked.

"Everybody gone. Except maybe one or two boats hidden."

"We would like to rent one of the boats that are hidden," Weston said.

"Very expensive. Very illegal. Very dangerous. Be very expensive."

"How expensive?"

"Very expensive. Thousand dollars."

"How about five hundred?" Everly said.

"Thousand dollars. No boats left. Fucking war. Fucking Japons."

"All we have is one thousand dollars," Weston said. "And we'll need money when we get to Mindanao."

The slight Filipino looked thoughtful.

"Why you want to go to Mindanao?"

"To fight the Japanese," Weston said.

"Fucking Japons no fucking good. Goddamn. I will ask. But I think man with boat will want thousand dollars."

"If you take us to Mindanao," Weston said, "I'll give you a thousand dollars. Five hundred dollars now, five hundred when we get there."

"I will ask," the Filipino said. "You stay here. Drink Coca-Cola. I will come back."

"When I see the boat, I will give you five hundred dollars," Weston said.

"You stay here. Drink Coca-Cola," the Filipino said. "I come quick."

He left the cantina the way he had come in.

"That was too easy," Everly said softly.

Weston's temper flared.

"You have any better ideas, Sergeant?"

"Your show, Mr. Weston, but if I was you, I'd put all but the one thousand someplace he can't see it."

Weston glowered at him, which didn't seem to faze Everly at all.

"If he does come back, I wouldn't give him the five hundred until we're on the boat," Everly said.

The Filipino came back after fifteen minutes, but he didn't enter the cantina. He stood in the door and motioned for them to follow him.

Everly gestured for Weston to go first.

The Filipino led them down a trail through the thick vegetation for a quarter mile, and then stopped. He pointed toward the water. After a moment, Weston saw faint marks on the muddy, rocky beach which suggested that a boat had been dragged from the water. A moment later, he saw the stern of a boat peeking through the thick vegetation.

"Good fucking boat," the Filipino said. "Carry you to Mindanao. Shit, carry you to fucking Australia."

He left the trail and pushed his way through the vegetation toward the beach.

When they reached the boat, two other Filipinos were there. An older man was dressed like the first, and a stocky, flat-faced young woman wore a thin cotton dress and apparently nothing else.

"They no speak English like me," the Filipino said. "I translate for you."

There was an exchange between the Filipino men.

"He say he want to see money."

"I'll give him the money when that boat is in the water and we're under way," Weston said.

"You no trust me?" the Filipino asked, in a hurt tone.

"When the boat is in the water and we've pushed off," Weston said.

"No go now," the Filipino said, as if explaining something to a backward child. "Must go in dark. Fucking Japons see us if we go now, and maybe fucking U.S. Navy."

Weston wondered if that meant the Navy was patrolling these waters to prevent Americans from leaving the peninsula. *From deserting in the face of the enemy.* He looked at his watch. It was 1735. Darkness should fall soon.

"OK," Weston said. "We'll wait."

"OK," the Filipino said. "Get off beach where nobody can see you."

■ ■ ■

As darkness fell, there was a heavy rain shower, and Weston and Everly found what shelter they could under the hull of the boat. It didn't offer much shelter, though, and they could not help but notice the battered condition of the hull.

It was quite dark when other men appeared. "Their" Filipino motioned them out from under the hull, and when they moved onto the beach, they almost immediately stepped into water. The beach had narrowed; the tide had risen.

The men, using ropes woven from vines, dragged the boat across the beach and got it into the water.

"You give me money now," "their" Filipino said when the boat was bobbing, barely visible, several yards offshore.

When Weston produced the money, the Filipino counted it in the light of a Zippo lighter. The lighter had a USMC insignia. For a moment Weston thought, lightly, that might be a good omen. Then he wondered where the Filipino found the lighter. Lighters were in short supply. There were no more Ship's Stores or Army Post Exchanges, nor stores outside military bases. Good cigarette lighters were in demand; people took care of them.

Where did this guy get the lighter? Steal it from somebody? Offer some other Marine a way off Bataan, then rob him, knowing he couldn't go to the Military Police? Or throw him over the side?

That's paranoid, he told himself. *There's no reason to be suspicious of the Filipino.*

If he'd wanted to rob us, he could have done it in the cantina, or while we were here in the bush, waiting for it to get dark. And we couldn't have done a thing about it. There is *a boat, and absolutely no indication that the Filipino is going to do anything but what he agreed to do, get us off Bataan. What's wrong with you, Jim Weston, is that you're afraid. You're afraid of what you're doing, deserting in the face of the enemy; and you're afraid of getting killed. For Christ's sake, you're supposed to be an officer. Act like one!*

They waded out to the boat, finding themselves in water almost to their armpits, holding their weapons over their heads. When they reached the side of the boat, one of the Filipinos leaned over and took Weston's Springfield from him. Then he reached down for the web belt, with its holstered pistol.

If I hand over the pistol, I'll be disarmed. Maybe they've been waiting for this—to separate us from our weapons.

Oh, for Christ's sake! Stop it! If they wanted to slit our throats, they would have done that on the beach.

He let the Filipino on the boat take the web belt. And then a hand found his in the darkness, and he felt himself being hauled out of the water.

The first thing that happened was his pistol belt and the Springfield were returned to him, which made him feel like a fool.

Everly came aboard a moment later. One of the Filipino seamen took Weston's arm, led them to a small hatch in the deck, and motioned them through it. A match flared, and in its light Weston saw the Filipino lighting a primitive oil lamp, nothing more than what looked like a six-inch piece of clothesline stuck into a bottle of oil. But the flame caught, and the small compartment was dully illuminated. The Filipino handed him the lamp and then left the compartment, closing the hatch after him.

Weston looked at Everly.

"Well, we seem to be on our way," Weston said. Everly did not reply.

Weston saw Everly make sort of a pillow out of his rucksack and then lie down on the deck. Weston had no rucksack, and tried to make himself comfortable without one. But the confinement of the compartment and the curve of the hull made this impossible; his head hung down painfully. Finally, he took off his shirt and rolled it up. This seemed to work.

He heard creaking sounds from outside; and then he had a sense of motion, as if the boat were getting under way.

"Have you got a match, or a lighter?" Everly asked. It was the first time he had spoken.

"Both," Weston replied.

"Why don't you put that lamp out?" Everly said, his suggestion again sounding more like an order. "If we need it, we can relight it. If that lamp spills, lit, there's likely to be a fire."

"Right," Weston said, and blew the flame out. There was an unpleasant-smelling smoke, and the coal on the wick took a long time to die out.

Then the darkness was complete. There was no question now that they were moving. The hull was canted—which forced Weston to readjust his position on the deck—and he could hear the splash and gurgle of water on the hull.

He started to think. The idea that they were going to be robbed and killed no longer seemed credible. He was almost embarrassed that he had had it. But what was real was that he had now deserted. That was a fact. He had deserted in the face of the enemy, in the foul-smelling bilge of a crude Philippine fishing boat. It was not what he had had in mind when he joined The Corps and went through flight school.

He fell asleep trying to put things in order, telling himself he was going to have to stop dwelling on the desertion business. It wasn't as if he was running away to avoid his military duty; what he *really* was doing was *evading capture*, so that he could make his way to Australia and *get back in the cockpit of a fighter* to wage war against the enemy as he had *been trained to fight*.

■ ■ ■

Weston woke in shock and confusion. That immediately turned into terror.

He tried to sit up—a reflex action—and became instantly aware that something—someone—was lying on him. And then whoever was lying on him was thrashing about and making horrible guttural sounds. And then—again without conscious effort—when he tried to push whoever was on top of him off, or to slip out from under him, he realized his hands were slippery.

"Mr. Weston, you all right?" Everly hissed. Before Weston could form a reply, he sensed movement; and then the weight on him lifted.

"What the hell?"

"You all right?" Everly asked again. "Did he cut you?"

"Oh, Christ!" Weston said. "What the hell happened?"

"I cut his throat," Everly said almost matter-of-factly. "*Are* you all right?"

The sonofabitch is annoyed that I didn't answer him quickly enough.

"I'm wet, my hands are wet," Weston said.

And then he realized what made his hands wet and sticky, and was quickly nauseous. Not much came out, but his chest hurt from the effort, and there was a foul taste of bile in his mouth.

"What the hell happened?" he asked, now indignant himself.

"Here it is," Everly said. "I found it."

"Found what?"

"The knife, a filet knife, it looks like," Everly said. Weston felt something pushing at him. "You take it."

"I don't want it!"

"There's three more of them outside," Weston said. "In thirty seconds, they're going to suspect this guy fucked up."

"He tried to kill me?" Weston asked, his brain not quite willing to accept that fact.

"Just be glad he went after you first," Everly said. "If I'd have had to fight the sonofabitch, no telling what would have happened."

"Jesus Christ!"

"Load your pistol," Everly ordered.

"There's shit—there's *blood*—all over my hands."

"Wipe them, for Christ's sake, on your pants. Get your pistol loaded. Quietly!"

Weston slapped his hands against his trousers to wipe off the blood, then somehow managed to get the .45 pistol from its holster. The first time he tried to pull the slide back to chamber a cartridge, his fingers slipped when it was halfway back, and the spring forced the slide forward again without chambering a cartridge.

"Quietly, for Christ's sake!" Everly said. And then, as a flashlight played in the compartment, blinding Weston with its sudden light, he added, "Shit!" A moment later there were half a dozen deafening explosions, each accompanied by an orange flash.

Now everything seemed to move in slow motion.

Weston frantically wiped his fingers on his trousers and felt for the serrations on the rear of the pistol slide. He jerked it back violently. His fingers slipped off, but when the slide moved forward again, he heard—and felt—a cartridge being chambered.

He now recognized the noise. It was the Thompson firing, and it was incredibly loud, painfully deafening. His ears rang, and he felt dizzy. Though he was nearly blinded by the light from the flashlight, he vaguely saw Everly diving for it. Then he covered it with his body, and the light went out.

An orange ball in Weston's eyes faded slowly. After what seemed like a full minute but was probably far less time, he could make out a slightly lighter area in the blackness. This was the hatch to the compartment, he realized— now open. A moment later, he saw the reason the hatch was open: There was a body in it.

He could now make out Everly, not clearly, but clearly enough to see that he was grasping the hair on the head of the body in the hatch. He pulled the head back and cut the man's throat.

"They don't have any weapons," Everly said. "*Guns*. If they did, they would have used them by now. But how the fuck do we get out of here?"

"They'll be waiting for us," Weston said, and immediately felt like a fool.

Everly moved close to the hatch, then rolled onto his back.

"As soon as I'm through the hatch, you follow," Everly ordered. "Come up here!"

Weston moved toward the hatch. When he put his hand to the deck, it slid in what had to be blood. The bile returned to his mouth, but he was able to restrain the impulse to vomit.

He had just reached Everly when Everly fired the Thompson at the side and overhead bulkheads, ten or twelve rounds in two- and three-round bursts. The noise and muzzle flashes were again blinding, deafening, and painful.

When partial sight returned, Weston could see Everly shoving himself through the hatch, still on his back. Additional flashes came from the Thompson. But, with the muzzle outside the compartment, no more painful explosions assaulted his ear.

Weston dove through the hatch the moment Everly had cleared it, then rolled onto his back.

"Shoot the sonofabitch!" Everly ordered.

Weston looked frantically from side to side, and finally saw one of the Filipinos, scurrying aft on all fours.

"Shoot the sonofabitch!" Everly screamed.

Weston held the Colt in both hands, lined up the sights as best he could, and fired. The Filipino seemed to hesitate. Weston shot him again. And again.

"Make sure he's dead," Everly called, somewhat more calmly.

Weston rose to his feet and walked unsteadily aft. The Filipino—he was "their Filipino," the one who'd arranged for the boat, taken the money—was on his stomach, his legs pushing as if trying to get away. Weston did not want to shoot him again. But then, as if with a mind of its own, the hand holding the .45 raised the pistol until it was pointing at the base of the man's skull, and his finger pulled the trigger.

The man's head seemed to explode.

He looked back at Everly in time to see him—far more clearly this time—repeat what he'd done in the compartment. Pulling the man's head backward by his hair to expose his throat, he used a thin-bladed knife to cut deeply into it. Blood gushed out.

Everly dropped the man's head onto the deck. As Weston watched, horrified, Everly ran his hands over the man's body, searching it. He put his hands in the man's pockets and came out with a pocket watch, a key, and some money, all of which he jammed into his own pocket. Finally, he stood up.

"You want to give me a hand here, Mr. Weston?"

"What?"

"Get this sonofabitch over the side. Him and the others."

"You're going to throw him overboard?"

"You want to keep them, Mr. Weston?" Everly asked.

Weston went forward and helped Everly throw the body over the rail. It entered without much of a splash. And when he gave in to the impulse to look over the side, it was nowhere in sight.

Everly was by then already aft, searching the body of "their" Filipino. From it, he took a canvas wallet and a gold locket of some sort the man had been wearing around his neck. He went into the wallet and took from it the five hundred dollars Weston had given the man on the beach. He put the money in his pocket; and then, horrifying Weston, he pulled the man's trousers off.

Everly met his eyes. "We're going to need clothes," he said, adding, "Help me get the bastard over the side."

Weston moved to help him. The body fell backward into the water, and Weston had a quick sight of the man's face, the features obscenely distorted by the .45 bullet. It would remain with him for a long time.

By the time they'd dragged the last two bodies from the compartment, searched them, stripped them, and pushed them over the side, Weston was exhausted, sweating, and breathing heavily. He sat down on the deck, his back against the mast, feeling sick and fighting the urge to throw up.

A few minutes later, Everly came back and sat down beside him.

"No food and no charts," Everly said. "Those bastards had no intention of doing anything but going back where we came from, with our money, and without us."

"Shit," Weston said.

After a while, he became aware that his hands were sticky. He knew why. He pushed himself away from the mast and made his way aft, knelt on the deck, and put his hands in the water. There was no sensation of movement other than a side-to-side rocking motion.

He washed his hands and arms as well as he could, and tried not to think what his chest must look like. Then he pulled himself back in the boat and brushed up against something hard, which moved. After a moment, he realized it was the tiller. There was no life to it, which confirmed his belief that they were sitting dead in the water.

If that's the case, the bodies we put over the side are likely to be floating around right next to us. We have to get out of here.

Where the hell are we?

The flashlight came on, and Everly directed it at the mast. The sail was down, which explained why they were dead in the water.

The light went out. After a moment, there was a creaking sound, and Weston sensed, rather than saw, that Everly was raising the sail. Confirmation of this came a moment later, when he heard the sound of the sail filling. A moment later, he felt a faint suggestion of movement.

He put his hand to the tiller, put it amidship, and felt life come into it.

Everly came aft.

The flashlight came on, and he saw Everly studying a compass.

"We're pointing north," Everly said. "We want to go southeast. You know anything about sailing a boat, Mr. Weston?"

"Only what I learned at camp when I was a kid."

"Can you turn us around, point us southeast?"

"Where are we going?"

"Mindanao," Everly said. "It's five hundred miles or so to the southeast."

"We don't have any food or any water," Weston said.

"There's a bunch of little islands between here and Mindanao. We'll just have to try to get food and water."

"I'll bring us about," Weston said. "Watch the boom. And I think you better give me that compass."

Everly handed him the compass. Weston started pushing on the tiller.

The boat began to turn.

"At least we got our money back," Everly said. "That's something."

And our lives. We're alive, Weston thought, but said nothing.

"Plus what looked like another three, four hundred," Everly added. "I don't think we were the first people these fuckers took for a boat ride."

[THREE]

When the sun came up, they were out of sight of land, alone on a gently rolling sea.

Everly's Marine Corps–issue compass showed them on a southeasterly course. Weston wondered if that were actually the case, or whether steel or iron somewhere on the boat was attracting the compass needle. On the other hand, they were not headed in the *wrong* direction. If the sun rises in the east, and you are headed directly for it, then south is ninety degrees to the right.

Since he was steering somewhat to the right of the rising sun—east and south (in other words, steering southeast), and this corresponded to the compass indications, they were probably headed on a *generally* southeastern course. But they weren't *navigating*. For the moment, of course, that was a moot point, since navigation presumes a destination, and they didn't know where they were going—except in the most imprecise terms, "to Mindanao."

Everly searched the boat as soon as there was light enough for that, but found nothing of value except two cans of pineapple slices and a bottle of Coca-Cola. No charts, no other food, and no water.

He found a bucket, too, and used it to flush the blood from the deck. But cleaning up the compartment where they were hiding, where the Filipinos tried to kill them, was impossible. He could have poured water into the compartment, but there was no way to pump it out.

When a sickly sweet smell began to come from below, Everly closed the hatch and they tried to ignore the odor.

They shared the Coca-Cola and the two cans of pineapple slices.

Weston thought that perhaps it wasn't wise to eat all the pineapple at once. Maybe they should have saved half for later.

Then he decided it didn't make any difference. They had to find more food and water, or they were finished.

By ten in the morning, the heat from the sun grew uncomfortable. Using a foul-smelling piece of worn canvas, they rigged an effective sunshade. But that was too late. They were already badly sunburned.

A few minutes after three in the afternoon, they saw on their left horizon what could be land.

The question was, if it was land, and not their eyes just playing tricks on them, what was it?

It very easily could have been part of the island of Luzon, the far side of the entrance to Manila Bay. The Japanese were supposed to be all over that part of Luzon. Was that true?

Was it worth it to go through everything they'd gone through just to find themselves prisoners of the Japanese . . . even before that would have happened if they'd stayed on The Rock instead of deserting in the face of the enemy?

But the alternative to making for what was probably land on the horizon, Weston decided, was to continue on a course he had very little confidence in, and without food and water. For all he knew, if he kept on his present course, he could very easily be heading out into the South China Sea, with no landfall possible until long after they were dead of dehydration.

Twenty minutes later, they could see enough to know that it was indeed land on the horizon. A half hour after that, they were close enough to make out surf crashing against a solid wall of vegetation. There was no sign of civilization.

It was now getting close to five P.M.

"We don't have an anchor, and we can't get through that surf," Weston said.

"Go to the left. Maybe we'll find something," Everly replied.

As they approached the beach, the western end seemed to recede and then disappear.

"What is this?" Weston asked.

"I think we got a little fucking island," Everly said, pleased.

"Holding two reserve divisions of the Imperial Japanese Army," Weston replied.

Everly looked at him with genuine concern in his eyes.

"Why would you say that, Mr. Weston?" he asked.

"I was making a joke."

"Oh."

The sun was low on the horizon when they finally saw a break in the surf. As they approached it, Weston saw that it was a passage between a very small island and the first island they'd found.

There was still no sign of human life, and the only sounds were the distant rustle of the surf and the waves splashing against the bow of the boat. The war that they had so recently left on Corregidor and Bataan—the smells of burned fuel and supplies, the never-ending muted roar of cannon, the dull crump of explosions—could have been happening at another time on a distant planet.

As they entered the passage between the islands, Weston saw a small beach on the larger island. There was no surf.

"We could try to put in there," he said, as much to himself as to Everly. "I don't know how shallow it is. We're likely to go aground."

"Do we have any choice, Mr. Weston?"

Weston steered for the small beach.

They made it all the way to the shore without scraping bottom. As Everly leapt ashore, carrying a rope with him, Weston decided the current flowing through the passage had scoured it clean of sand.

Tying the boat up was no problem. Trees and thick vegetation came right down to the water. Everly looped the line around a thick, twisted tree trunk. The current pulled the boat against what Weston presumed was the solid rock of the shoreline.

What's going to happen now, he thought, *is that the current is going to batter the hull against the rocks, whereupon we will sink.*

That didn't happen. The current simply held the hull against the rocks with little movement.

Everly heaved himself back aboard.

"There's a goddamned hill, starting right at the trees," he said. "I don't think I could climb it even if it wasn't dark. We'll have to see what happens in the morning."

"There's supposed to be feral hogs on these islands," Weston said.

"What?"

"Wild pigs. Maybe we could shoot one."

Everly's silence made it clear he didn't think that was likely.

"You want to do two-hour watches?" he asked.

"Fine."

"You want to go first, or me?"

"I'll go first," Weston said.

Everly made himself a pillow from some of the clothing he had removed from the bodies, covered himself with the rest, and went to sleep.

In ten minutes, it was so dark Weston had difficulty seeing him.

He sat immobile for perhaps ten minutes, listening to unidentifiable sounds coming from the shore; and then, without thinking about it, he scratched his chest. His skivvy shirt was covered with drying blood.

On all fours, he crawled on the deck, carefully avoiding Everly, until he found the bucket. Then he crawled aft again and stripped. First he carefully rinsed his skivvy shirt and drawers in the water and arranged them on the rail to dry. Then he dipped the bucket into the water, held it over his head, and poured it over his body.

He did this a dozen times—the dried blood had matted his hair together, and didn't want to dissolve—until he was sure he was as clean as he was going to get.

Still naked, he sat down with his legs folded under him. He looked at his watch. The luminous hands told him it was five minutes to eight. He wondered how long it had taken him to find the bucket, do his laundry, and bathe.

Fuck it, I'll count two hours from now. From eight. I'll wake Everly at ten.

He sat there in the dark, his knee touching the web belt with the .45 in its holster, remembering with sudden clarity how the watch had looked when he'd brought it home from the Officers' Sales Store at Pensacola. It was a Hamilton Chronograph, stainless steel. By pressing the appropriate button, he could mark elapsed time of his choice—length of flight; one minute 360-degree turn. Whatever.

It came in a metal box with a spring-loaded cover. It had an alligator strap, and there was a little book of instructions. He wanted one from the moment he first saw it. But it was considered pushy for students to wear one until they had completed Primary Flight and soloed, and stood a reasonable chance to win their wings of gold.

He remembered very clearly the first time he strapped it to his wrist.

On another planet, at another time, when he was a Naval Aviator.

When Weston opened his eyes, Everly, naked, was squatting beside him. It was light. Weston was confused. It shouldn't be light. He woke Everly at ten. Everly therefore should have waked him at midnight. At midnight, it was still dark.

"What's up?"

"I didn't hear a fucking thing for two hours," Everly said. "So I figured, fuck it, why wake you up? And I went to sleep."

"Oh."

"And look what I see when I do wake up," Everly said, and pointed.

Weston sat up.

Two hundred yards offshore was a cabin cruiser.

Adrift, Weston thought. *Not under power.*

"Can you get us over there?"

"I don't know. I can try."

"It's a long way to swim, and there's sharks, I hear, in these waters."

"Let's get the sail up, and we'll see what happens."

Neither put into words what both thought: There was a chance the cabin cruiser would have food aboard. And a compass. And God only knows what else.

What's it doing here? Adrift?

It took them nearly an hour to reach the boat. There was almost no wind, and the current moved both vessels through the passage and into open water as they pursued it.

As they drew closer, they became aware of the sweet stench of corrupting bodies, and then of a horde of flies.

The boat looked like a ChrisCraft 42, but there was no ChrisCraft insignia.

Probably, Weston decided, a local-manufactured boat, using a ChrisCraft as a pattern. Her tailboard read YET AGAIN, MANILA, and a faded Manila Yacht Club pennant flew from her rigging.

The stench grew worse as they approached her. When they were at her stern it was nearly overwhelming.

Everly finally managed to get a hand on her, pulled himself aboard, and then threw Weston a line. The moment he saw Weston had grabbed it, he went to the side rail and threw up.

The line was new, still white.

Weston made the boat fast to the cruiser, and then jumped aboard.

There was evidence that the cruiser had been machine-gunned, probably strafed. He saw bullet holes in the deck, in the bulkheads, and in the glasswork.

The ignition key was in the on position. The fuel gauges showed empty, but Weston pressed the ENGINE START button anyway. The engines turned over, but there was no fuel, and they didn't start.

The flies started to bite. There was nothing he could do about them.

Everly came out of the galley carrying cases of canned food.

"There's even beer," he said. "Fucking flies are eating me alive."

"I wonder what happened."

"Who the fuck knows? What I think we should do is stack everything there by the stern, and then I'll go on the boat and you hand it to me."

They made half a dozen trips into the galley before Weston found the courage to ask the question that was in his mind even before they had come aboard:

"What happened to the people who were on here?"

"If they were alive, they would have come out by now," Everly said.

Weston went into the galley again; and then, forcing himself, he went through it, into the passageway leading to the cabins.

He could not restrain the urge to vomit. When he had stopped heaving, he had difficulty resisting the urge to flee.

But he went into the master cabin. He found two bodies. A gray-haired woman was on the double bunk, her hands folded on her stomach. She was wearing shorts and a knit shirt. The shirt was thick with blood, the blood covered with swarms of flies.

She had been shot in the chest.

The second body was lying on the deck next to the bunk—a man in his fifties; he had shot himself in the temple. A snub-barreled revolver was on the deck beside him.

Weston took a quick look around and fled the cabin.

"Well?" Everly asked when Weston was back on deck.

"There's a . . . a couple . . . back there. It looks as if the woman was killed and then the man shot himself."

"Anything we can use?"

"I didn't look."

Everly gave him a look of contempt and headed for the cabin.

Weston sat down on a cushioned seat against the stern rail and supported his head in his left hand, using the right to wave away the swarming flies.

Everly reappeared carrying blankets. Weston saw that he had the snub-nosed pistol jammed in his waistband, and that he, too, now had a first-class wristwatch. Weston had seen it on the man's body.

"I also found a bunch of *good* fucking charts," Everly said.

"What do you think we should do about the boat?"

"What do you mean, do about it?"

"Burn it, maybe?"

"And call attention to ourselves? The Japs already strafed this boat once. Those were machine-gun bullets in the woman." He indicated the bullet holes in the desk and glass.

"We can't just leave them in there like that," Weston said.

"Yes, we can," Everly said. "We load this stuff on the boat and get the fuck away from here before some other Jap airplane comes this way."

Weston felt anger well up within him, so quickly and so fiercely that he was frightened. He forced himself, literally, to count to ten before he spoke.

"Sergeant, find something to weight the bodies down. Maybe an engine battery. We'll wrap them in blankets and put them over the side."

"Didn't you hear what I said, Mr. Weston, about getting out of here before the Japs come back?"

"Didn't you hear what I said, Sergeant, about finding something to weight the bodies down?"

Everly met Weston's eyes for a long moment.

"The proper response, Sergeant, is 'Aye, aye, Sir.' "

There was another hesitation, shorter, but perceptible.

"Aye, aye, Sir," Sergeant Everly said.

"Where's the charts you said you found?" Weston asked. "I want a quick look at them."

"Over there, Mr. Weston," Everly said, pointing to what looked like a brand-new briefcase. "We also have another three thousand dollars."

"You found a wallet or something?"

"Yes, Sir."

"Names of these people in it?"

"I guess they're their names."

"Don't lose it," Weston ordered. "Someone will want to know what happened to these people."

"Like when we get to Australia?"

"Or when we win the war," Weston said curtly.

Everly smiled.

"Something funny, Sergeant?" Weston said as he felt his temper rise again. Then his mouth ran away with him.

"When I was in the Officers' Basic Course, Everly, I had an instructor, a man like you. As a matter of fact, I recall him mentioning that he was an old China Marine. You know what he told me a Marine was? He said that a Marine was somebody hired by the Government to take bullets for civilians. And that's what we're going to do. We're Marines, and we're going to bury these civilians. If we take a bullet while we're doing it, that's how it will have to be."

Everly continued to smile.

"You think that's funny?" Weston snapped.

"No, Sir, what I was thinking . . ."

"Out with it, Sergeant!"

"That maybe you're not the candy-ass I thought you were at first."

"Well, fuck you, Sergeant!" Weston heard himself say.

"Yes, Sir," Everly said. "I'll go see if I can find some batteries or something."

As Everly said, the charts were good. Within a minute or so, Weston was sure he had found where they were—in the passage between Lubang Island and Ambil Island, to its east. According to the chart, Ambil was uninhabited. To the south, across the Verde Island Passage, was Mindoro.

Now that he had the charts (presuming the boat didn't come apart on them, or Japanese aircraft didn't strafe them, or Japanese vessels didn't intercept them, or, for that matter, they didn't founder in one of the sudden, violent storms for which these seas were famous), he saw a good chance of making it through the inland Sibuyan Sea, and then the Visayan Sea, past the Visayan Islands (Panay, Negros, Cebu, and Bohol) into the Mindanao Sea and to Mindanao.

There was a Waterman pen-and-pencil set in the briefcase. He used the pencil to mark a tentative course, aware, but pretending not to notice, that Everly had brought the bodies onto the deck and trussed them neatly in blankets. Each of them was weighted down with two batteries.

Everly found that a portion of the aft rail of the cruiser could be opened inward. He opened it.

"Anytime you're ready, Mr. Weston," he said.

"I think a word of prayer would be in order, Sergeant," Weston said as he replaced the charts in the briefcase.

Having said that, the only thing he could think of was the Lord's Prayer. He recited it, as Everly stood with his head bowed.

His mind then went blank.

After a long moment, he said, "Into the deep we commit the bodies of our brother and sister departed. Amen."

"Amen," Sergeant Everly parroted.

They pushed the blanket-wrapped bodies through the opening in the rail into the sea.

Thirty minutes later, they cut loose from the *Yet Again* and Weston pointed the bow toward the Verde Island Passage.

He looked back once at the cabin cruiser drifting on the blue water, and was sorry he did.

[FOUR]
Headquarters, 4th Marine Regiment
Fortress Corregidor
Manila Bay, Republic of the Philippines
0415 Hours 6 May 1942

"You know what I know about burning the colors, Paulson?" Colonel S. L. Howard, USMC, who was the senior Marine officer on Corregidor, asked of Major Stephen J. Paulson, USMC, who was acting S-1, 4th Marines.

"No, Sir."

They were perhaps one hundred feet in a lateral tunnel opening off the main Malinta Tunnel. From their lateral, it was perhaps two hundred yards to the entrance to the now sandbagged entrance. The colors, the national flag, and the regimental flag of the 4th Marines were behind Howard's desk, unfurled, their staffs resting in holders.

"Not very much," Howard said. "And I can't even remember where I learned—I must have read it somewhere in a novel—what I do know. I know that it is a disgrace to lose your colors to the enemy, and at the last possible moment before the enemy is to lay his hands on them, it is the duty of the senior officer present to burn them."

"That's how I understand it, Sir."

"I would say we are at that moment, Paulson, wouldn't you?"

"Yes, Sir."

There was no question about that. Two days before, the Japanese assault on Fortress Corregidor had begun, with a massive, unceasing, around-the-clock artillery barrage. Someone had calculated that eleven explosive rounds were landing on the Fortress every minute. That translated to 667 rounds per hour, 16,000 rounds each twenty-four hours.

The Japanese landed on the island the day before, at what was called the "Tail of the Tadpole," and suffered heavy losses. But they kept coming, and it was impossible to throw them back into the sea. To avoid firing on their own men, that portion of the Japanese artillery fire initially directed at the Tail of the Tadpole had shifted, and was now falling on Top Side—the Head of the Tadpole—where the barracks had once stood, and beneath which was the tunnel complex.

Japanese infantry was making its way up from the Tail to Top Side, slowly but irresistibly.

There were approximately 15,000 American and Filipino men and officers defending Fortress Corregidor, very few of whom (approximately one-tenth) had training as infantry soldiers. The vast bulk of American military personnel, except for the regular Corregidor garrison—Coast Artillerymen—were technicians, staff officers, and clerks of one kind or another, who had moved to Corregidor when General MacArthur had moved his headquarters to the Fortress early in the war.

Several hundred of the 1,500 military personnel trained as infantrymen were Marines. The vast bulk of these Marines were members of the 4th Marines, which had come to the Philippines from Shanghai in November 1941, had participated in action against the Japanese on Luzon, on the Bataan Peninsula, and had been ordered to Corregidor. There were also some Marines who had been stationed, prior to the war, at various U.S. Navy installations in the Philippines, then ordered to Corregidor.

The Coast Artillerymen of the Corregidor garrison had done their job, and more than could have been reasonably expected of them. There was ample ammunition for their "disappearing rifles" (which were Coast Artillery cannon that rose on their carriages to fire, and then lowered into a protected position) and for their enormous mortars; and it had been a rare moment in recent days when the roar of American cannon could not be heard, or the concussion of their firing not felt.

But it was not enough to stop the Japanese. And one by one, many of the guns and the gun positions, previously believed impregnable, had been destroyed.

The clerks and technicians, pressed into service as riflemen, had done their duty too, performing it (in the private opinions of many Marines) far better than expected.

But everybody was weak—they had been on half rations for more than six weeks, and half rations had recently been halved again—and exhausted; and they suffered from the ceaseless concussion of incoming Japanese artillery.

"Somehow, I don't like the idea of burning them in here."

"We could carry them outside, Sir."

"Would that be a signal that it's over?" Colonel Howard asked rhetorically, and then, without giving Paulson a chance to respond, changed the subject.

"I took a look at the records yesterday, before ordering them burned," he said. "The personnel rosters. We seem to be carrying an extraordinary number, even under these circumstances, of personnel missing in action."

"Yes, Sir."

"You would know more about this than I would, Major. Would you say some of the missing personnel went—how do I say this?—went missing purposely?"

"If you're asking if there has been an attempt to avoid hazardous service, Sir, I would say no."

"Would you say, then, Major, that some of those Marines those now-burned reports carried as 'missing' absented themselves in the belief that they would thus be able to continue waging war against the Japanese in some other location?"

"I believe that is entirely possible, Sir."

"And how many of those who went purposely missing would you think made it through the enemy lines to someplace where they could indeed continue to fight?"

Major Paulson had a sudden clear mental picture of two Marines: First Lieutenant James B. Weston and Sergeant Percy Lewis Everly.

"There's no way of knowing, Sir. Some, obviously, will have made it. And some, obviously, will have been killed or captured."

"Purposefully absenting oneself, purposely going missing, ordinarily would be something disgraceful. At the very least, even with the best intentions, it could be considered AWOL; at the worst, desertion in the face of the enemy."

"Yes, Sir."

"Right now, Paulson, if I had the opportunity, I think I would go over the hill myself. Burning the colors, hoisting the white flag . . ."

"I thought about it, Sir," Paulson said.

"But you stayed."

"Disobeying an order is hard for me, Sir."

"And for me," Howard said. "How would you propose we do this, Paulson?"

"I've got something," Paulson said, and produced a quart-sized tin can. "I don't know what it is, it's to clean a mimeograph machine. But it's highly combustible. I suggest, Sir, that we pour it on the colors and ignite it. I'll hold the staffs, if you like, or . . ."

"There's enough for both the regimental and national colors?"

"Yes, Sir. And they're silk, Sir. Once they're ignited, they'll burn."

"I don't want to do it in here, in this goddamn tunnel, like a trapped rat," Colonel Howard said. "Would you be willing, Major Paulson, to go with me to the main tunnel entrance?"

"Yes, Sir. Of course, Sir."

Colonel Howard nodded. He stood up and went to the two flags behind his desk. He took the national colors from its holder, held it horizontally, and then twisted the staff until the flag was wrapped around the pole. He handed the furled colors to Paulson. Then he repeated the furling action with the red regimental flag of the 4th Marines.

When he was finished, he preceded Paulson down the lateral tunnel, and then down the main tunnel to the entrance. As they approached the entrance, they could now hear small-arms fire, the solid crack of American .30-06 caliber rifle and light machine-gun fire, and the higher-pitched crack of Japanese small arms.

They made their way past the sandbags.

A Japanese artillery shell whistled in and exploded with a crash that made them both cringe.

"The national colors first, I think, Paulson," Howard said. "They are never supposed to touch the ground."

"Aye, aye, Sir," Major Paulson said.

He held his flagstaff horizontally and twisted the staff so that the flag unwrapped from the staff. Colonel Howard leaned the colors of the 4th Marines against the sandbags, took Paulson's quart can of mimeograph machine cleaning fluid, and carefully poured half on the national colors.

When he tried to ignite it with his Zippo cigarette lighter, it didn't work, and he had to dip into Paulson's pocket for Paulson's Zippo.

The cleaning fluid ignited immediately, quickly igniting the silk material of the flag. But it took longer for the flag to burn than either Colonel Howard or Major Paulson expected. By the time it did burn, the flagstaff was smoldering, and here and there were other small flickers of flame.

Paulson swung the flagstaff like a baseball bat against a concrete abutment, breaking it into two pieces. He picked up the top half, with the gold-plated American eagle, and smashed the eagle against the concrete.

Then he picked up the regimental colors of the 4th Marines, twisted the staff until the flag was unwrapped, and held it out for Colonel Howard to douse with mimeograph cleaning fluid and ignite.

When the colors had burned, he smashed the staff, this time ruining the gold American eagle first, and then breaking the staff.

After that, Colonel Howard and Major Paulson went back into Malinta Tunnel. All other duties assigned to them having been performed, they then picked up their rifles and exited the tunnel to fight as infantry.

IV

The military force that its commander privately thought of as "Weston's Weary Would-Be Warriors" made landfall from Bohol Island at daylight. The commanding officer, First Lieutenant James B. Weston, USMC, in addition to a full beard, wore a wide-brimmed straw hat and a baggy pair of white cotton pants. He was barefoot and bare-chested, and his skin was deeply tanned.

In addition to Sergeant Percy Lewis Everly, USMC, the force consisted of twelve other servicemen. Senior among them was Chief Pharmacist's Mate Stanley J. Miller, USN, who with Seaman First Class Paul K. Nesbit had been the first recruits to the unit.

For two weeks after leaving the *Yet Again* adrift off Lubang Island, Weston and Everly had traveled very slowly and very cautiously, sailing for three or four hours a day and spending the rest hiding. On the afternoon of the fifteenth day, they had come across the Chief and Nesbit in the Sibuyan Sea, drifting in a demasted sailboat. They had left Luzon with the same intention as Weston and Everly: making it to Mindanao and possibly to Australia, meanwhile avoiding capture by the Japanese.

They took them aboard, scuttled their boat, fed them from their dwindling stocks of canned foods from the *Yet Again,* and resumed their painfully slow voyage toward Mindanao.

It took them six months, by far most of it spent on one small island or another, trying to stay alive and out of the hands of the Japanese. On the island of Panay, while moving through the hills in search of food, they encountered a group of five Army Air Corps enlisted men, under Sergeant Allan F. Taylor. Taylor had been sent to search for possible auxiliary landing fields under the command of an Air Corps lieutenant colonel, who had surrendered to the Japanese at his first opportunity, telling his command they could do what they wanted; in the circumstances it was every man for himself. None of the enlisted men had been willing to surrender.

They placed themselves under Weston's command with the understanding that it was their intention to make it to Australia, and that they had no intention of trying to wage a guerrilla war against the Japanese.

The force grew two months later on the island of Cebu by the addition of a sailor and a corporal. The corporal had been one of the few American enlisted men assigned to the 26th Cavalry, which had American officers and Filipino troopers. On Luzon they had decided that between them they had the skills (the sailor knew how to handle a small boat; and the cavalryman, a veterinarian's assistant, knew how to speak Spanish) to make it to Mindanao, and possibly out of the Philippine Islands.

The last three recruits were Marines, Old China Marines, career privates of the 4th Marines, who had been captured and made a valiant effort to escape. Like Sergeant Everly, they were familiar with the practice of the Japanese Army to bayonet their prisoners when feeding or guarding them became a problem—or simply because it seemed like an interesting idea at the time.

Everly knew two of the three. He told Weston that one was a world-class drunk, and the other had a room-temperature IQ but was tolerated in the 4th Marines in Shanghai because when he turned out for Guard Mount he looked like the pictures in the manual. The third had been a clerk in the S-4 (Supply) Office, who was pressed into duty as a rifleman just before the 4th Marines were committed to battle for the first time.

"But don't worry, Mr. Weston. I can handle them, they're Marines."

The 26th Cavalry corporal had an Enfield rifle and twenty-three rounds of .30-06 ammunition. The Air Corps contingent had three Enfields, sixty rounds of ammunition for them, and a .45 Colt 1911A1 pistol with twelve rounds. The Marines had no firearms whatever, but had picked up two machetes and an ax.

The money was just about gone—the five thousand dollars Weston had begun with, plus the four hundred Everly had taken from the murderous Filipinos on the boat, plus the three thousand they had taken from the *Yet Again.* The price of anything was what the market would bear, and simply to have enough simple food to stay alive—rice, fruits, and a rare pig, or fresh ham—had been very costly.

The notion of getting out of the Philippines to Australia now seemed unreal. And Weston privately thought that when they got to Mindanao, it wouldn't be very different from any of the other islands they'd been to. There would be no organized military force to which they could attach themselves. If they found any Americans at all, they would almost certainly be just like themselves, desperately dreaming of getting to Australia but with no real hope of doing so.

They had come to Mindanao because there was no place else to go, and because word had come to them on the grapevine that the Japanese were about to sweep Bohol Island and round up Americans once and for all.

On making port, most of Weston's Weary Would-Be Warriors spent most of the day concealing their two boats, while a reconnaissance party consisting of Sergeant Everly, two of the three Marines, and one of the Air Corps PFCs investigated the area.

When they did not return by nightfall, as Weston had ordered them to, he thought they had probably encountered Japanese. But he wasn't particularly concerned. They had, if nothing else, acquired a demonstrated skill in hiding from Japanese. If they didn't return that night, they'd be back first thing in the morning.

If they had actually gotten into a firefight with the Japanese, it was unlikely that all of them would have been killed or captured. In case there was a disaster, the standing order was for whoever came through the encounter alive to return to "headquarters" and warn the others.

No one came to Gingoog Bay that night, or during the day, or during the next night. And Weston went to sleep about midnight wondering if the ultimate disaster had happened, that everyone had been killed, or, worse for him and the men with him, captured. Given a few hours, the Japanese could force any information a prisoner had out of him. At that moment, the Japanese could be staging an operation to surround him and to make sure that no one slipped out to sea.

At daylight, after Weston decided no one was going to come at first light either, he tried to decide whether to lead a second reconnaissance patrol, leaving Chief Miller in command, or to send Chief Miller on the patrol. The Chief might be a marvelous pharmacist, but he was not a great leader of men. The only thing the Chief would probably be worse at than commanding "the unit" would be leading a reconnaissance patrol.

On top of all that, Sergeant Allan F. Taylor, of the Army Air Corps, was a special problem. Without any justification that Weston could see, he believed himself to be a professional military man on a level with Sergeant Everly. Taylor had been some sort of technician, something between a surveyor and a draftsman. Those skills were not very useful to Weston's Weary Would-Be Warriors.

Weston could not leave Taylor behind to command "the unit," because it was clear that neither the Chief nor the remaining Marine would take orders from him—even if Taylor decided, in his own best interests, to assume command. The same consideration applied to sending Sergeant Taylor to lead the reconnaissance. He knew a little less—which was to say, almost nothing—about how to run a reconnaissance than Weston himself. And it was likely that if he got out of sight (and, as important, out of range) of Weston's Springfield, he would decide that his best interests dictated taking off on his own and getting to Australia.

At that point, Sergeant Everly returned, bringing with him not only everyone he had taken with him, but a Filipino. The Filipino was dressed in dirty, baggy, white cotton trousers and shirt, a U.S. Army campaign hat, and he was carrying an Enfield and a web belt slung around his neck. He looked, Weston thought, like a Mexican bandit.

"Where the hell have you been?" Weston greeted Everly.

"Look at this, Mr. Weston," Everly said, and handed him a sheet of paper.

It was a delinquent tax notice, dated November 8, 1941, from the Misamis-Occidental Provincial Government to a farmer named Almendres Gerardo.

"What the hell?" Weston asked.

"Turn it over, Mr. Weston," Everly said. Weston did so.

OFFICE OF THE COMMANDING GENERAL
UNITED STATES FORCES IN THE PHILIPPINES
MINDANAO-VISAYAN FORCE IN THE FIELD
1 OCTOBER 1942

PROCLAMATION

1. By virtue of the power invested in me, the undersigned, as senior representative of the United States Government and the Philippine Commonwealth, herewith assumes command.
2. A state of martial law is declared for the duration of the war.

BY ORDER OF THE COMMANDING GENERAL

Wendell W. Fertig
Brigadier General, USA
Commanding

DISTRIBUTION:
1. To all commanding officers, USFIP
2. To all Provincial Governors
3. To all Provincial Officials
4. To all Justice of the Peace Courts
5. File

"What the hell is this?"

"I found it nailed to a telephone pole."

"You think it's for real?"

Everly pointed to the Mexican bandit.

"He says he can take us there."

"And you believe him? This thing isn't even printed, mimeographed. It's typed. On the back of a tax-due bill."

"Our luck has got to turn sometime," Everly said. "What have we got to lose?"

[TWO]
Cagayan de Oro
Misamis-Oriental Province
Mindanao, Commonwealth of the Philippines
1225 Hours 10 October 1942

The headquarters of the Military Governor of Mindanao had been established in the prewar combined City Hall of Cagayan de Oro and the Provincial Capitol of Oriental Province.

It was a three-story redbrick building of a vaguely Colonial style, and it was relatively new, built from plans first drawn for the Works Progress Administration in the United States. (The WPA was instituted during the early years of F. D. Roosevelt's presidency, in the belief that government building projects—roads, post office buildings, etc.—would provide employment for the unemployed and "prime the pump" of the depressed American economy.)

A Japanese flag—a red ball on a white background—flew from a flagpole mounted on top of the building. And the flags of the Imperial Japanese Army and the personal flag of a brigadier general, in stands, stood at either side of the main double-door entrance to the building.

A slate-gray 1940 Lincoln V-12 sedan came down what was still MacArthur (after the first General MacArthur) Boulevard and pulled into one of the four reserved parking places in front of the building.

Captain Matsuo Saikaku stepped out of the Lincoln and walked briskly up the shallow flight of stairs to the doors, returned the salute of the somewhat rumpled guard, and entered the building.

Captain Saikaku was twenty-four; and, at nearly six feet and 180 pounds, he was somewhat larger than the average Japanese officer. He was wearing neatly starched and pressed khakis, a tieless blouse and trousers, and well-shined shoes (rather than boots and puttees). A Sam Browne belt held a captured U.S. Army Model 1911A1 Colt .45 ACP pistol in a U.S. Army holster. A large, highly polished chrysanthemum, symbol of Imperial Japan, was attached to the flap of the holster, almost entirely concealing the letters "U.S."

Captain Saikaku was less than pleased with the performance of the Lincoln. It ran roughly at slow speeds and often stalled, but he blamed such things more on the low-quality gasoline he had to use than any design failure of the car. Though Saikaku detested Americans, and most things American, he was willing to acknowledge they produced some fine products—in his view the Colt was a much better weapon than the Japanese Nambu pistol. And they made the finest automobiles in the world. He considered the slate-gray V-12 Lincoln to be one of the best of the best.

He clearly remembered his first encounter with a Lincoln V-12 sedan. It was a 1939 model, but essentially identical to the one he had impressed for his official use from an official—now a detainee—of the First National City Bank of New York office in Cagayan de Oro. It was parked in front of the Foster Waikiki Beach Hotel in Honolulu, where Saikaku was employed as a gardener.

His opinion then and now was that it was both pleasing aesthetically and a mechanical masterpiece. And, he believed, it was a car in keeping with his status. He would have to do something about the way it ran—he had been wondering if aviation gasoline, or a mixture of regular and aviation gasolines, would improve performance—but he was determined to keep the car.

He was aware that Lieutenant Colonel Tange Kisho, who had impressed a Buick Super for his official use, was somewhat annoyed to learn that a Lincoln was a more prestigious car than a Buick Super. Lieutenant Colonel Tange was the senior of the seven Kempeitai officers attached to the Office of the Military Governor of Mindanao, and Captain Saikaku's superior officer. (The Kempeitai—Secret Police—was roughly the Japanese equivalent of the German Gestapo. Although members of the Kempeitai were, in a sense, soldiers, as they came under the jurisdiction of the War Ministry and bore military ranks, they were essentially autonomous and were not directly subordinate to the local military commander.)

Brigadier General Kurokawa Kenzo, the Military Governor, was chauffeured about in a 1940 Cadillac sedan Saikaku had impressed for him from an official of the Dole Pineapple Corporation.

General Kenzo was pleased not only with his Cadillac but with Captain Saikaku's thoughtfulness in finding it for him. It was not the sort of behavior General Kenzo expected from any Kempeitai officer, and especially not from one he knew to be the son of the first cousin of General Tojo Hideki.

Lieutenant Colonel Tange had come into the Kempeitai from the Nagasaki Police Prefecture, and was a reserve officer. Captain Saikaku believed that it didn't hurt at all to remind Lieutenant Colonel Tange that he himself was a regular officer of the Imperial Japanese Army, seconded to the Kempeitai, and a first cousin, once removed, of General Tojo, who was second in power in Japan only to his Imperial Majesty Emperor Hirohito.

Captain Saikaku thought it not unlikely that when his assignment to the Kempeitai Detachment to the Military Governor of Mindanao was over, Lieutenant Colonel Tange would write an enthusiastic efficiency report on him, suggesting that he was highly deserving of promotion.

Lieutenant Colonel Tange occupied the former office of the Mayor of Cagayan de Oro, to the right of the entrance foyer; and General Kurokawa

Kenzo was in the office of the former Provincial Governor, to the left. Saikaku entered Tange's outer office, ignored Tange's sergeant, and walked to Tange's open door.

"Good afternoon, Colonel," he said, saluting with something less than great precision. Then he walked inside and bowed, quickly, from the waist.

"This, Captain Saikaku, has come to my attention," Lieutenant Colonel Tange said. "I would be very interested in your opinion of it."

He handed Saikaku a sheet of paper on which was typewritten Brigadier General Wendell Fertig's assumption of command and declaration of martial law proclamation.

Lieutenant Colonel Tange spoke English, but not as well as Captain Saikaku, who had studied the language for six years and then perfected it while a young lieutenant working for more than a year as a laborer in Hawaii.

"The name is not familiar to me," Tange said. "And, I checked, it is not on the roster of prisoner officers."

"My immediate reaction, Sir, is that it is not what it purports to be," Saikaku said. "I'm sure the Colonel has noticed that it is typewritten, not mimeographed, and that—more important—it is typed on previously used paper."

"If it is not what it purports to be, Captain, what, then, is it?"

"I am guessing, of course, Colonel, and I will of course look into the matter. But my immediate reaction is that this was prepared by a former Army clerk familiar with the form of such a letter, and intended to fool us."

"Why a clerk and not an officer?"

"Officers do not usually know how to typewrite, Sir."

"I don't like it," Tange said. "Could the Americans be setting up some kind of guerrilla force?"

"I respectfully suggest, Sir, that what we should not do is grow excited over this—as whoever prepared this hopes we will do. As the Colonel is well aware, we have had absolutely no indications of guerrilla activity of any kind."

"I don't like it," Tange repeated. "Look into it immediately, if you please, and report what you find. I have not yet discussed this with General Kenzo. When I do, I would like to have something to tell him."

"I will attend to it immediately, Sir."

Twenty minutes later, Captain Saikaku pulled the Lincoln up against a wooden gate set in a brick wall that surrounded a one-floor house on the outskirts of town. He sounded the horn, and a moment later, a soldier swung the gates inward.

The house, previously occupied by a Filipino lawyer and his family, had been impressed into the service of the Kempeitai as a special prison.

Shortly after the American surrender, Captain Saikaku had the junior officers and enlisted men of General Sharp's staff lined up so that he could conduct a personal inspection. Based on his year in Hawaii, he fancied himself a rather good judge of American character.

From these he selected a dozen Americans, four officers and eight enlisted men, on the basis of his judgment that they would turn out to be both knowledgeable and malleable, and then he had them brought to the house behind the wall.

He ordered them stripped and beaten each day for three days. And then, one by one, he examined them again. One of the officers and three of the enlisted men appeared to be properly conditioned, and he ordered their retention. The others were sent back to the POW enclosure.

One of the enlisted men, a somewhat effeminate sergeant from Wisconsin, whom Saikaku suspected of being a sexual deviate, he ordered hung up naked by his heels overnight in the garage of the house behind the wall. In the morning, he ordered an electrical current to be passed through the sergeant's body by means of alligator clips attached to his scrotum and nostrils.

While this was going on, he appeared in the garage, slapped the Japanese soldier applying the electrical current hard enough to knock him off his feet, and ordered the sergeant to be carried into the house and placed in one of the bedrooms.

The next morning, he went to the bedroom and behaved in a very friendly manner to the sergeant, telling him he would do what he could to protect him from the soldiers, but in return the sergeant would have to cooperate with him.

He then left the bedroom and gave orders that the sergeant was to be beaten with switches, not boards, twice a day until further orders. He was to be beaten painfully but not severely, with attention given to the soles of his feet and to his genitals.

Three days later he returned, professed outrage at the beatings, and otherwise behaved in a friendly manner. He then ordered a young Filipino of known deviant tendencies placed in the sergeant's bedroom. He also had the beatings stopped, and he had them furnished with food, rice and chicken and bread, and a case of beer.

The sergeant was thus given a choice. He could choose beatings, starvation, and possibly death, not only for himself but for his newfound friend. Or he could choose confinement under reasonably pleasant conditions. He not surprisingly elected to be cooperative.

"What the hell," he said, "the war's over for me anyway, right?"

■ ■ ■

Captain Saikaku entered the house and went to the sergeant's bedroom.

The sergeant, as always, looked at him with frightened eyes, not sure if Saikaku was going to be friendly.

"Jerry," Captain Saikaku said, "tell me about General Fertig."

The sergeant's eyes showed fear.

"Sir, I don't know . . ."

"Jerry, you promised me you would be cooperative."

"I swear to Christ, I never heard of a General Fertig."

"I would hate to think you were not telling me the truth."

"I give you my word of honor."

"The name means nothing to you at all?"

"Not a thing. I swear it. If it did, I would tell you, you know that."

Captain Saikaku nodded, turned on his heel, and left the bedroom.

After leaving orders that the Filipino boy deviate was to be beaten in the presence of the sergeant, he returned to Lieutenant Colonel Tange's office. Although he would continue looking into the matter, he told him, he was at the moment convinced that Brigadier General Fertig was a figment of some Filipino army clerk's imagination, and there was no cause for concern.

[THREE]
Near Monkayo
Davao Oriental Province
Mindanao, Commonwealth of the Philippines
1615 Hours 11 October 1942

They walked all day, slowly, taking a five-minute break each hour. But the trails through the thick vegetation were steep, in some places slippery, and the heat was debilitating.

And then, all of a sudden, they came out of the jungle, into a clearing.

The Mexican bandit, at whose heels Weston had been walking, stepped aside and pointed at a rather large, thatch-roofed, Filipino house built on stilts.

Sitting in a rattan chair on what could be called the porch of the house sat a tall, sturdy-looking man wearing a khaki uniform. A silver five-pointed star, the rank insignia of a brigadier general, adorned each of his collar points. He was also wearing a red goatee and a wide-brimmed straw hat. A Thompson submachine gun lay at his feet.

"General Fertig," the Mexican bandit said.

Behind him, Weston heard Captain, bringing up the rear of the column, mutter in disgust or disappointment, "Shit!"

"Wait here," Weston ordered.

He walked across the clearing, aware of the General's eyes on him, and climbed the steep stairs—more like a ladder than a flight of stairs—and then walked across the porch to within six feet of the red-goateed man in the chair.

The General met his eyes, but there was no expression on his face.

Weston saluted.

"First Lieutenant Weston, James B., USMC, Sir."

The General returned his salute.

"Have your men been fed, Lieutenant?"

"No, Sir."

"Are there other officers in your party?"

"No, Sir."

"Sergeant!" the General called, raising his voice.

Another Filipino wearing baggy white cotton trousers and a U.S. Army campaign hat came onto the porch from inside the house.

"Sir?"

"See that this officer's men are fed," he said.

"Yes, Sir."

"And when you have done that, please bring us some of the cold pork."

"Yes, Sir."

"Are you a drinking man, Lieutenant?"

The question surprised Weston.

"Yes, Sir."

"And a couple of beers, please," the General said.

"Yes, Sir," the Filipino said.

Fertig met Weston's eyes again.

"Welcome to Headquarters, United States Forces in the Philippines, Lieutenant. Weston, you said?"

"Yes, Sir. Thank you, Sir."

"You will, from this moment, consider yourself and your men under my command."

That announcement made Weston uncomfortable. His imagination shifted into high gear.

What this guy may be—probably is—is a staff officer who went around the bend. He was unable to accept that the Army got the shit kicked out of it, that the Japanese have won the battle for the Philippines hands down. That must have been even tougher to accept for someone of senior rank, with twenty years or so in the service, than it was for somebody like me.

And unable to accept the facts, he's now living out some fantasy where he is still a general, the U.S. Army in the Philippines still exists, and any moment The Aid will appear, galloping to our rescue like the cavalry in the movies.

"Yes, Sir," he said.

"Things are a bit primitive around here at the moment," Fertig said. "We hope to improve on them."

"Yes, Sir."

"Please tell me how you came here, Lieutenant."

"One of my men, Sergeant Everly, Sir, was contacted by one of your men while he was on a patrol. He showed Sergeant Everly your . . ."

"Proclamation?" Fertig asked.

"Yes, Sir. Your proclamation . . . nailed to a telephone pole. He, Everly, brought it to me, and then your man led us here."

"What I was really asking, Lieutenant, was how you came to Mindanao. Presumably, you were formerly assigned to the 4th Marines on Bataan?"

"On Corregidor, yes, Sir."

"And you somehow got off Corregidor and decided that it was your duty not to surrender when Corregidor inevitably fell?"

"Yes, Sir."

Well, at least he knows that we lost Bataan and Corregidor.

Fertig looked at him, obviously waiting for him to continue.

"I was a pilot, Sir," Weston heard himself saying. "I mean, I am an aviator. I was stranded in the Philippines and assigned to the 4th Marines as a supernumerary officer. My commanding officer . . . my commanding officer sent me to Bataan looking for supplies. . . ."

Why is it important to tell this man what really happened? Am I looking for his approval? His forgiveness?

"I was provided with five thousand dollars and a Spanish-speaking sergeant, Sir. I wasn't *ordered* to desert, that was my decision. But I believe Major Paulson hoped I would not return; that I would try to get out of the Philippines, to Australia."

Fertig nodded.

"We attempted to rent a boat," Weston went on. "We found one. And then the Filipinos on the boat attempted to murder us."

"Banditry and piracy have a long history in the Philippines," Fertig said. "What happened?"

"We killed them," Weston blurted, aware of that but unable to stop. "Everly killed the one who was trying to cut my throat, and then we . . . killed the others. And threw their bodies into the sea."

"Where was that?" Fertig replied. He seemed neither surprised nor shocked.

"Right off the Bataan Peninsula, Sir."

"It was just you and your sergeant at first? You picked up the others en route here?"

"Yes, Sir, that's about it."

"You're apparently a resourceful officer, Lieutenant. It must have been difficult to obtain the necessary food and water, and of course the charts, to make a voyage such as you have made. You are to be commended."

"Sir, it wasn't that way," Weston confessed, uncomfortably. "We had neither rations nor charts."

"But?"

"We found a cabin cruiser adrift in the passage between Lubang Island and . . . I can't remember the other island. A little one. Uninhabited."

"Ambil Island," Fertig furnished. "I know the passage. Tell me about the cabin cruiser."

"It was, I think, a locally built copy of a Chris-Craft."

"Did it have a name?"

"Yes, Sir. *Yet Again.*"

The General looked pained. His eyebrows rose, and then he shrugged, in what Weston thought was sadness and resignation.

"You're very observant, Lieutenant," the General said, his voice level. *"Yet Again* was a locally built copy of a Chris-Craft. It belongs—*belonged,* apparently; past tense—to friends of mine. Joseph and Harriet Dennison. He was the Chrysler dealer in Manila. Was there any sign of them, by any chance?"

"In the master cabin, Sir, there were two bodies. A middle-aged couple. The woman was in the bed. She was apparently killed when the boat was attacked by Japanese aircraft. There were bullet holes—"

He was interrupted by a Filipino woman, who thrust at him a plate of pork chunks in rice and some kind of sauce. When he took it, she handed him a fork and a cup, made from bamboo.

"The pork is very nice," Fertig said. "The beer, unfortunately, seems to be proof that a civil engineer and a Navy Chief who don't know what they're doing should not try to brew beer."

Weston wolfed down the pork and rice.

"There's more," Fertig said. "But I would advise waiting an hour or so. When you haven't been eating normally . . ."

"That was fine, Sir. Thank you. It'll hold me for a while."

"You were telling me about what you found on the *Yet Again.*"

Weston tried to remember where he had broken off the story, and then resumed:

"The woman was apparently killed in a strafing attack. The man shot himself in the temple. The boat was out of fuel."

Fertig closed his eyes and said nothing.

Weston took a sip of the beer. It was warm and thick and reminded Weston of a disastrous attempt to make home brew in his fraternity house at college.

"There was canned food aboard, Sir," he went on, "and water. And charts. We took it all and started out for here."

"Leaving everything as you found it aboard the *Yet Again?*"

"No, Sir. I mean we . . . buried the bodies at sea. In blankets, weighted down with batteries. We didn't burn the boat. Everly thought it would attract attention, and I agreed."

"Inasmuch as doing so, under the circumstances, obviously posed a risk to you, it was quite decent of you to . . . bury . . . the Dennisons, Lieutenant."

Weston could think of no reply to make.

"I knew them rather well. Nice people. He was the exception to the rule that you never can trust anyone in the retail automobile business. Mrs. Fertig and I used to see a good deal of them at the Yacht Club."

"You were stationed in Manila, Sir?"

"I was a civil engineer in Manila. I had the foresight to send Mrs. Fertig home when I entered the Army."

"Yes, Sir."

"Though few others—including, sadly, the Dennisons—were willing to face that unpleasant fact, I knew there was no way we could really resist the Japanese when they came here. Roosevelt believes the Germans are the greater threat; our war effort will be directed primarily against them, the Pacific and the Japanese will be a secondary effort. There never was going to be The Aid that everybody was talking about."

"Sir, you said, 'when you entered the army'?"

"I was commissioned as a captain, Corps of Engineers, Reserve. With another chap, Ralph Fralick. He was commissioned a lieutenant, and we spent the early days of the war blowing things up—bridges, railroads, that sort of thing. Interesting experience, taking down in an hour what you had spent months—in several cases, years—building."

"Yes, Sir."

"The last I heard of Fralick, he was a captain, and he had his hands on a forty-foot boat, sail and diesel, and was headed for Indochina. When the end came, I was here. I decided that I did not want to be a prisoner; and since I have a hard head, I decided I could cause the Japanese more trouble by organizing a guerrilla operation here than trying to get out. If I had made it out—and the idea of trying to sail two thousand miles in a small boat to Australia seems iffy at best—I suspected that the Army would have a reserve lieutenant colonel, who is a civil engineer, supervise the construction of officer clubs."

Fertig looked into Weston's eyes.

Then he flipped up one of his collar points with the brigadier general's star pinned to it.

"Would you be wondering, by any chance, Lieutenant, about these?"

"Yes, Sir. I was," Weston said after a moment.

"I've lived in the Philippines a long time, Lieutenant. I know the people, and I know—not as well as I know the Filipinos—the military mind. If I had signed my proclamation 'Lieutenant Colonel, Corps of Engineers, Reserve,' it would have been pissing in the wind. I think you're proof of that, Lieutenant."

"Sir?" Weston asked, confused.

"If my proclamation had announced that Lieutenant Colonel Fertig, CE, USAR, was the senior officer of U.S. Forces in the Philippines, would you have paid any attention to it? To put a point on it, would you have come looking for me?"

"Sir, I was getting pretty desperate. I probably would have come," Weston said uneasily. "At least to have a look."

"And if you found a lieutenant colonel, wearing a straw hat and a goatee, what do you think you'd have done? You'd have gone right back in the bush, perhaps? Avoiding the lunatic?"

Weston shrugged uncomfortably.

That's exactly what I would have done.

"Instead, you didn't see me. You saw that general's star, and that impressed you, right? I might look a little strange in my straw hat and beard, but the cogent fact, right, was that I was wearing a general's star? And you gave me the benefit of the doubt?"

"Yes, Sir."

"Let me give you a little lecture in military law, Lieutenant Weston. Inasmuch as I am what the books call 'the senior officer of the line present,' which means that I am serving in one of the branches of the Armed Forces which engages in combat . . . that includes the infantry, the cavalry, the artillery, the engineers, the air corps, and oddly enough, even the signal corps, but excludes the medical corps, the chaplain's corps, the finance corps, et cetera. . . . You following me?"

"Yes, Sir, I think so."

"Inasmuch as I am a lieutenant colonel of the line, the Congress of the United States, in its wisdom, has given me command over all lieutenant colonels of the line, regular or reserve, junior to me, by date of rank, and every other officer in an inferior grade—a lieutenant commander in the Navy, for example, or, should one wander in here, a full bird colonel of the medical corps. Or, to put a point on it, a Marine Corps first lieutenant who has in fact wandered in here."

"Yes, Sir," Weston said because he could think of nothing else to say.

"My order to you that as of this moment you and your men are under my command is perfectly valid."

"Yes, Sir, I suppose it is."

"You took it a lot easier when you thought I was a brigadier general, didn't you? No question. Just 'Yes, Sir, General'?"

That's not wholly true. But he's made his point.

"Yes, Sir, General," Weston said with a smile.

"I had a Moro silversmith hammer these out for me," Fertig said, flipping one of his silver-starred collar points again, "because the Filipinos I intend to recruit will follow a general. They would not follow a lieutenant colonel. And I did not wish to deliver my little lecture about the small print in military law to every American serviceman I come across."

"I understand, Sir."

"In the absence of any other officer able or willing to assume command of American Forces in the Philippines, I have done so. I'll deal with the subject of my self-promotion with my superior headquarters at some later time."

"Yes, Sir."

"Any questions, Lieutenant Weston?"

"No, Sir."

"That's strange. I thought an intelligent, curious young man like you would be interested to know the current strength of United States Forces in the Philippines."

"Yes, Sir. I am."

"Right now, the officer corps is three officers strong. It consists of myself, and you, and Captain Charles Hedges. He is my chief of staff. At the moment, he's out looking for a radio and mobile rations, which means swine that can be taken along with us under their own power should the Japanese get too close for comfort."

"And enlisted men?"

"Counting the ones that came in with you, sixteen Americans. So far as the Philippine Element of USFIP is concerned, I have eleven commissioned officers and approximately 225 enlisted men. Sometime in the near future, we hope to equip each of the enlisted men with a firearm. At the moment, approximately half are armed with machetes."

"Yes, Sir."

"Reliable intelligence has reached our G-2 Section—which at the moment means me—that there are other small units such as yours who have declined to surrender, here on Mindanao and elsewhere in the islands. Efforts are being made to contact them and place them under the command of USFIP."

"Yes, Sir."

"Reliable intelligence indicates that two such units, with a total strength of 165, are on their way here from Cebu at this moment. More are expected shortly. It is my belief that USFIP will grow rapidly in size, like a snowball rolling down a hill in Vermont."

Weston smiled at the analogy.

"One of our problems is officers," Fertig said. "Of your men, are there any you could in good conscience recommend for a direct commission?"

"Everly," Weston said without hesitation.

"Just the one?"

"Yes, Sir."

"You are authorized to offer him a commission as a second lieutenant, infantry, U.S. Army Reserve. If he accepts, I will swear him in."

"He's what they call an Old Breed Marine, General," Weston said, smiling. "A China Marine. I don't know what he'll think about becoming an Army lieutenant."

Fertig ignored the reply.

"Our second problem is establishing radio communications with Australia. I don't suppose that you are a radioman, or any of your men?"

"No, Sir. But I have a degree in Electrical Engineering."

"Interesting! Fascinating! That would ordinarily be enough for me to name you Signal Officer of USFIP," Fertig said. "But I already have one. Or will shortly, as soon as I commission him. Probably this afternoon, after you have a word with your man Everly. I'll commission them together. He's currently a private soldier named Ball. But he's a radio operator."

There was a disconcerting aura about the whole conversation, at once amusing and frightening. It was simultaneously insane and utterly practical.

It might sound insane, but obviously, this man intends to do exactly what he says he's going to do. And there is a method to his madness.

"When our reinforcements attach themselves to us," Fertig said, "obviously it would be best if they didn't quite understand how recently our officers were commissioned. Or received their assignments in the command structure. Or promoted."

"I take the General's point," Weston said.

"I would hate to think that you were mocking me, Weston."

"No, Sir," Weston replied immediately and sincerely. "That was not my intention, General."

Fertig looked into his eyes again.

"Good. It would be awkward if I thought my G-2, an officer I personally promoted to captain, was mocking me. It would suggest he did not have faith in me."

"Has the General given any consideration to the assignment of Lieutenant Everly?" Weston asked.

"For the time being, he should be your deputy," Fertig said seriously. And then a smile curled his lips. "Maybe between—what was it you said?—an Old Breed China Marine and an airplane-less pilot, we can come up with a half-decent intelligence officer."

"We'll try, Sir," Weston said.

"Do have a razor in your kit, Weston?"

"No, Sir."

"Then you may use mine. I think one bearded officer is enough for USFIP."

"Aye, aye, Sir."

"You may go in my quarters, Captain, and have a shave. And then I suggest you have a word with your man Everly," Fertig said.

"Aye, aye, Sir," Weston said, and stood up. "By your leave, General?"

"That's the first time anyone said 'aye, aye' to me. Nice. You are dismissed, Captain."

Weston saluted, did an about-face, and then walked into General Fertig's quarters.

Inside the house, Weston found, neatly laid out on a rattan table, a round, magnifying mirror in a chrome frame, a leather-covered box holding seven old-fashioned straight razors, a leather strop, a shaving brush, and a wooden jar of shaving soap. The soap was gray, obviously not what originally filled the jar.

There are two ways to look at this, Weston thought, amused. *One way, United States Forces in the Philippines is so fucked up we don't even have soap. On the other hand, USFIP is resourceful enough to make its own soap, and the goateed madman on the porch is confident enough to be worried about the appearance of his officers.*

And since I have never held a straight razor in my hand before, I am liable to die for my country of a slit throat, acquired while I was attempting to set a good example for the enlisted men.

There was a battered aluminum bowl half full of water. He dipped the shaving brush into it, attempted to make suds in the soap dish, and was astonished at his success. The bubbles were gray, but they were bubbles.

He painted his cheek with them and, very carefully, began to hack away at his beard.

Fertig's Filipino sergeant came into the house while he was working on his chin and stood silently watching him while he finished shaving.

Then he handed Weston a campaign hat. Pinned on it were the double silver bars of a captain. They were unquestionably of local manufacture; the marks of a silversmith's hammer were clear.

Weston put on the battered, broad-brimmed hat and looked at himself in the mirror. The hat was several sizes too small. But if he pushed it forward on his head, it would probably stay on, and it even gave him sort of a rakish appearance that he did not find hard to take.

That made him think of something. He went into the baggy pocket of his cotton trousers and pulled out a tied-together handkerchief. In addition to other small items he hadn't needed for a long time, including golden dress-shirt studs, it held a small, gold USMC Globe and Anchor. At one time he'd worn it on a fore-and-aft cap that he had last seen on The Rock.

With some difficulty, he managed to pin The Marine Corps insignia onto the campaign hat, above the captain's bars.

The Filipino sergeant was smiling at him.

"Do you speak English?"

"Yes, Sir."

"Would you take me to my men?"

"Yes, Sir."

Sergeant Everly was sitting with his back against a tree, an empty plate on the ground beside him. Weston thought at first he was asleep, but as he approached, Everly pushed himself away from the tree and looked at him.

Weston gestured with his finger for Everly to join him. The other members of Weston's Weary Would-Be Warriors who had noticed the campaign hat and Weston's now clean-shaven face, looked at them with only mild, even listless, curiosity.

Weston thought he knew their thoughts: *There's no apparent immediate danger. We are being fed. What else could be important?*

"Nice cover, Mr. Weston," Sergeant Everly said, indicating the hat.

"General Fertig gave it to me," Weston replied.

"I never saw a general with a beard before," Everly said evenly.

"He's an engineer officer who decided he didn't want to surrender, and that he did want to make trouble for the Japanese," Weston said, realizing as he spoke that he had decided not to tell Everly that Fertig had promoted himself to brigadier general.

Everly did not respond.

"He knows the islands, speaks Spanish," Weston said. "This whole thing just started. There's apparently at least two groups—of people like us—on their way here."

Everly nodded his head and waited for Weston to continue.

"Under military law, as he is the senior officer of the line in the area, we fall under his command."

Everly nodded again.

"He's made me a temporary captain. He asked me if I thought you could handle a temporary commission as a lieutenant, and I told him I thought you'd make a pretty good lieutenant."

Everly cocked his head when he heard that, and took the time to think it over.

"There were a lot of China Marines in Shanghai who'd served in Haiti, Mr. Weston," he said. "They told me they had what they called the Constabulary down there. A lot of Marine noncoms were officers in the Constabulary. Is this something like that?"

"Something. You would be commissioned into the Army, as an officer of United States Forces in the Philippines."

"Not in The Corps? You're wearing The Corps insignia."

"I don't think General Fertig will object to my wearing The Corps insignia. Or if you or any other Marine wears it. But your commission would be in the Army."

"Sure, Mr. Weston. Why not? I think I could handle it."

"I'm sure you will," Weston said. "Come on, I'll introduce you to the General."

"Can I ask you a question, Mr. Weston?"

"Certainly."

"Is this General Fertig going to be able to do any damage to the Japs?"

"Yes," Weston replied. "I'm sure he is."

I'll be damned. I really believe that.

"We don't have doodly-shit to fight with," Everly said. "What's this general going to do about that?"

"Well, first we have to get organized. You and I are going to be his G-2 section. He's got an Army radio operator whose orders are to find a radio and get in touch with General MacArthur in Australia."

"I did a little work for Intelligence in Shanghai," Everly said.

"You did?" Weston replied, surprise evident in his voice.

"Worked for Captain Banning, the S-2."

Weston searched his mind for a face to go with "Captain Banning," but failed. Yet he judged from the tone of Everly's voice that he was being told the truth.

"Doing what?"

"Keeping an eye on the Japs. Troop strength. Locations of units. Counting artillery pieces and trucks, that kind of stuff."

"Espionage," Weston said without thinking.

"No. More like reconnaissance. I never took off my uniform or anything like that. I never thought I could get away with trying to pass myself off as a Jap."

"I'm surprised," Weston thought aloud, "that they didn't have you working in Intelligence on The Rock."

"I don't think anybody but maybe the Colonel and the exec knew I ever worked for Captain Banning."

"What about Captain Banning?" Weston asked, confused, adding, "I don't remember seeing him on The Rock."

"The first time we came under fire, when the Japs first landed, long before we pulled back to The Rock, Captain Banning got hit. Artillery. He took enough shrapnel so they didn't dare move him right away. So he found himself behind the Jap lines. Then the Army started shelling where he was hiding. Didn't hurt him much, but the concussion got his eyes. Or maybe his brain. Anyway, it made him blind. When they finally got him through the Jap lines and to the hospital on The Rock, he was in pretty bad shape. Finally, they evacuated him on one of the submarines that came to The Rock to take the gold off."

"Christ!" Weston said.

"And I guess he never said anything about me to anybody," Everly said, adding, "He was a hell of a good Marine officer."

From you, that's quite a compliment. I wonder what you think of me?

"I wish I knew more about Intelligence than I do," Weston said. "What I really know is nothing. I'm an airplane driver."

"You'll do all right, Mr. Weston," Everly said. "You learn fast."

I'll be damned. I've been complimented. And I don't think Everly would say that unless he meant it.

"Come on, I'll introduce you to the General," Weston said.

"I never talked to a general before," Everly said as he bent over to pick up his Thompson.

[FOUR]
Headquarters, U.S. Forces in the Philippines
Davao Oriental Province
Mindanao, Commonwealth of the Philippines
0625 Hours 9 October 1942

Breakfast in the Officers' Mess of United States Forces in the Philippines consisted of freshly squeezed pineapple juice, fresh pineapple chunks, and bananas.

Brigadier General Wendell Fertig, sitting at the head of the table, apologized to the members of the mess for not having coffee, bread, eggs, bacon, or ham, but as soon as he acquired a G-4 (Supply) Officer, providing such necessities would be high on his list of priorities.

Present at the table were Captain James B. Weston, Second Lieutenant Percy L. Everly, and Second Lieutenant Robert Ball.

Weston noted that Everly and Ball had also acquired broad-brimmed campaign hats, onto which were pinned brass second lieutenant's bars. And Everly's had a USMC insignia pinned to it. Like Weston himself, Everly had obviously kept his insignia even when it made no sense at all to keep his tattered, worn-beyond-any-utility uniform.

Why is that little piece of metal so important to us? God knows, there are no impressionable blondes around to dazzle with our membership in The Corps. So why is it important to us, in these circumstances, that no one mistake us for soldiers?

Two additional officers appeared at the mess; that is to say, the porch of General Fertig's quarters trembled as someone started up the ladderlike stairs. When they looked, two men appeared. One was dressed like General Fertig, in baggy white cotton shirt and trousers and a crude straw hat. He had a Thompson .45 caliber submachine gun slung from his shoulder.

The second was wearing a battered khaki uniform. The sleeves of his khaki shirt—onto the collar points of which were pinned the railroad tracks of a captain and the crossed flags of the Signal Corps—had been torn off above the elbows, and his khaki trousers had been torn off above the knees. He wore a pith helmet and a web belt, from which hung a .1911A1 .45 automatic in a leather holster green with mildew. He had a 1917 Enfield .30-06 rifle slung from his shoulder. He carried a rucksack—obviously heavy—in his hand.

"Introductions are apparently in order," he said. "Gentlemen, my chief of staff, Captain Charles Hedges. Hedges, this is Captain Weston, a Marine officer who has placed himself and his men—including Lieutenant Everly—under our command. You know Lieutenant Ball."

Hedges wordlessly shook Weston's and Everly's hands.

"General, this is Captain Buchanan," Hedges said. "Late of General Sharp's headquarters."

"I believe I met the Captain," Fertig said.

"Yes, Sir," Buchanan said. "You were a colonel at the time."

"A lieutenant colonel, to be precise," Fertig said, ignoring what could have been an accusation. "How are you, Buchanan?"

"Very well, Sir, thank you."

"Can I offer you some breakfast?"

"Yes, Sir. Thank you."

"Sergeant!" Fertig called, raising his voice. The Filipino sergeant appeared. "Will you get these gentlemen some breakfast, please?"

"Yes, Sir."

"Sit down, please, gentlemen," Fertig said, and then looked intently at Buchanan. "You're aware, of course, that General Sharp was ordered by General Wainwright to surrender his command to the Japanese?"

"Yes, Sir."

"Do I correctly infer by your presence here that you saw it as your duty not to enter into Japanese captivity?"

"Yes, Sir."

"And you are willing to place yourself . . . Are you alone, Captain?"

"No, Sir. I have eight men, Americans, with me."

"Are you willing to place yourself and your men under my command?"

"Yes, Sir."

"Welcome to United States Forces in the Philippines," Fertig said, leaning across the table to shake Buchanan's hand. "After you've had your breakfast, we'll have a private chat."

"Yes, Sir."

"In the meantime—curiosity overwhelms me—what does that bag contain? It seems unusually heavy."

"It's an M94, Sir," Buchanan said. "Device, Cryptographic, M94."

"Enlighten me," Fertig said.

Buchanan put the bag on the table, unfastened the straps, and took from it a small metal box. On the top was a small brass plate.

SECRET

DEVICE, CRYPTOGRAPHIC, MODEL 94
SERIAL NUMBER 145

IT IS ABSOLUTELY FORBIDDEN TO REMOVE THIS DEVICE
FROM ITS ASSIGNED CRYPTOGRAPHIC FACILITY

SECRET

"Things . . . collapsed . . . so quickly, Sir, that I didn't have a chance to destroy this," Buchanan said. "I didn't want the Japs to have the chance to see how it works. They could have, if I had only rendered it inoperable—by shooting it up, or burning it—so I took it with me. With the idea of throwing it into the sea. If I buried it somewhere, and was subsequently captured, the Japanese are very good at interrogation. . . ."

"This thing works?" Fertig asked.

"Yes, Sir."

"Frankly, Captain, I was hoping your heavy bag was laden with twenty-dollar gold coins," Fertig said. "But now . . . this device is literally worth more to USFIP than its weight in gold. Ball, how far away are we from having an operating radio station?"

"If Sergeant Ramirez can get that generator to run on alcohol, maybe we can give it a shot this afternoon, Sir."

"I hate to break up our festive breakfast, gentlemen," Fertig said. "But Captain Buchanan, Lieutenant Ball, and I have some important work to do."

[FIVE]
Headquarters, U.S. Forces in the Philippines
Davao Oriental Province
Mindanao, Commonwealth of the Philippines
1515 Hours 10 October 1942

There being no other pressing official business for them to attend to, both the G-2 of USFIP (Captain James B. Weston) and his deputy (Second Lieutenant Percy L. Everly) had spent most of the day in the USFIP Communications Center (a hastily erected lean-to two hundred yards from General Fertig's quarters) watching the USFIP Signal Officer (Second Lieutenant Robert Ball) and his Chief Radio Operator (Sergeant Ignacio LaMadrid, Philippine Army) attempt to establish radio communication with United States Forces in Australia.

Unlike the others, Sergeant LaMadrid had no previous military service prior to joining USFIP. He was seventeen years old, and in high school when the war came. He was shocked by the defeat of American and Filipino forces by the Japanese, but even more shocked by the brutality the Japanese applied to Filipino prisoners of war—despite Japanese public announcements that Japan and the Philippines were now partners in the Greater Asian Co-Prosperity Sphere.

When he saw General Fertig's proclamation nailed to a telephone pole near his home, he set out to join him. He thought he might be useful. When he arrived he spoke with Captain Hedges. Even though LaMadrid was among the first Filipino volunteers, Captain Hedges did not seem particularly interested in the services of a five-foot-two, one-hundred-and-twelve-pound, seventeen-year-old Filipino who admitted he had never so much as held a firearm in his hands.

And then LaMadrid suggested he might be useful fixing radios; he had been almost halfway through the International Correspondence Course in radiotelephony when the war came.

He was sworn into the Philippine Army as a private shortly thereafter, and promoted to PFC a week later, when he came to headquarters carrying a sound motion picture projector that had been hidden from the Japanese. He said he could probably make a radio transmitter from it.

Captain Hedges informed PFC LaMadrid that if he was successful, he would be a sergeant. USFIP already had a shortwave receiver. If LaMadrid could make a transmitter, and if they could come up with a generator to power both of them, they would have a radio station. That, certainly, was worth sergeant's stripes, even if, at the moment, there were no chevrons in the supply warehouse to actually issue—for that matter, there was no supply warehouse.

A generator had come into being when another Filipino sergeant—this one an actual soldier—managed to make an engine designed to run on gasoline run on alcohol. The alcohol was produced from pineapples and coconuts in a still constructed from salvaged automobile parts.

The transmitter worked. Proof came via the receiver. That was good enough for the Chief of Staff USFIP to make good on the promised promotion to sergeant, with actual chevrons to follow later.

How *well* the transmitter worked was another question, and after almost twenty-four hours of transmitting for three minutes on the hour without a reply, it became a disturbing one.

A message had been encoded with the Model 94 Cryptographic Device. This was then transmitted in five-character blocks, after the address sent in the clear:

MFS FOR US FORCES AUSTRALIA
MFS FOR US FORCES AUSTRALIA
ACNOW BRTSS DXSYT QRSHJ ERASH
POFTP QOPOQ CHTFS SDHST ALITS
CGHRZ QMSGL QROTZ VABCG LSTYE
ACNOW BRTSS DXSYT QRSHJ ERASH
POFTP QOPOQ CHTFS SDHST ALITS
CGHRZ QMSGL QROTX VABCG LSTYE
MFS STANDING BY FOR US FORCES AUSTRALIA
MFS STANDING BY FOR US FORCES AUSTRALIA

The message was tapped out on a radiotelegraph key from Sergeant LaMadrid's International Correspondence Corps Lesson Materials as many times as possible within a three-minute period. Three considerations had determined that length of time. One was the possibility that the Japanese would hear the message and, by a process known as triangulation, locate the transmitter. The second was that the supply of alcohol for the transmitter was in short supply. The third was that if its alcohol fuel damaged the generator, there was no spare.

When there was no reply all day, it seemed logical to assume that despite Sergeant LaMadrid's best efforts, he had been unable to jury-rig a transmitter that would reach the three thousand–plus miles to Australia.

[SIX]
Signal Section
Office of the Military Governor for Mindanao
Cagayan de Oro, Misamis-Oriental Province
Mindanao, Commonwealth of the Philippines
1600 Hours 10 October 1942

When Captain Matsuo Saikaku marched into his office, Lieutenant Hideyori rose from behind his desk, placed his hands, fingers extended and together, against the seam of his khaki trousers, and bowed from the waist.

Hideyori's office formerly belonged to the General Manager of the Mindanao branch office of the Mackay Telephone & Telegraph Company. As he stood up, a large wall clock bearing the Mackay logotype began to strike the hour.

"I understand you have intercepted some kind of radio message?" Saikaku demanded after he had returned the bow.

"Yes, Sir."

Saikaku impatiently put out his hand. Hideyori handed him a sheet of paper.

MFS FOR US FORCES AUSTRALIA
MFS FOR US FORCES AUSTRALIA
ACNOW BRTSS DXSYT QRSHJ ERASH
POFTP QOPOQ CHTFS SDHST ALITS
CGHRZ QMSGL QROTZ VABCG LSTYE
ACNOW BRTSS DXSYT QRSHJ ERASH
POFTP QOPOQ CHTFS SDHST ALITS
CGHRZ QMSGL QROTX VABCG LSTYE
MFS STANDING BY FOR US FORCES AUSTRALIA
MFS STANDING BY FOR US FORCES AUSTRALIA

"That message is being transmitted hourly, Sir, in the twenty-meter band," Hideyori said.

"For how many hours?"

"The first message we intercepted was at ten o'clock this morning, Sir. They send the message repeatedly, for a period of three minutes."

"Do you know from where?"

"No, Sir."

"I was led to believe, Hideyori, that it is within the capability of competent signals people to locate the site of a transmitter by a process known as triangulation. Have I been misinformed?"

"No, Sir."

"Has this triangulation detection process begun?"

"No, Sir. There is some difficulty with two of the trucks, Sir."

"What sort of difficulty?"

"Mechanical difficulty, Sir."

"I really didn't think it would be spiritual difficulty, Hideyori."

"Mechanical, Sir, as opposed to electrical. I have been informed the mechanical trouble will be remedied first thing tomorrow."

"Who told you this?"

"Captain Kuroshio of the Transportation Section, Sir."

"Be so good as to get Captain Kuroshio on the telephone, Hideyori."

"Yes, Sir."

Lieutenant Hideyori sat down, hastily consulted a mimeographed telephone book, dialed a number, spoke briefly with whoever answered, and then handed the telephone to Captain Saikaku.

"Captain Kuroshio is being called to the phone, Sir," he reported.

Saikaku took the telephone and waited, an impatient look on his face, until Captain Kuroshio came on the line.

"This is Captain Saikaku of the Kempeitai," he announced. "Lieutenant Hideyori informs me you are in the process of repairing two trucks. These trucks are required for a Kempeitai operation. Required immediately. I want the necessary repairs to them begun immediately, and continued until the trucks are operating, if that means your mechanics work through the night. Do you understand me?"

He listened to the reply, and then hung up.

"As soon as the trucks are made available to you, Hideyori," he ordered, "I want them manned around the clock. The sooner we locate this station, the sooner we can shut it down."

"Yes, Sir."

"What is your opinion of the message? The code?"

"I don't know what you mean, Sir."

"How soon can I expect to know what message these people are sending?"

"Sir, I took the liberty of sending the message to the Signals Intelligence Branch in Manila, asking them to attempt to decrypt the message."

"You did this on your own authority?"

"Yes, Sir. I believed it to be the thing to do."

"You are to be commended on your initiative, Hideyori," Saikaku said.

"Thank you, Sir."

"Be so good as to inform the Signals Intelligence Branch that there is Kempeitai interest in this message."

"Yes, Sir."

"And inform them that as a suggestion to help in their decryption efforts—you better write this down, Hideyori—that the message may contain the words 'Fertig,' 'Brigadier,' 'General,' and 'U.S. Forces.' Fertig is a name. The other words may be abbreviated.''

''I'm sure Signals Intelligence Branch will be pleased to have your suggestion, Sir.''

''As soon as you have word on your trucks, or from Signals Intelligence, or of any development at all, inform me. Call my office, they will know where to locate me.''

''Yes, Sir.''

''What we have here, Hideyori, is a weed. If we pull it from the earth now, that will be the end of it. If it is allowed to grow, it will become an increasing nuisance.''

''I understand, Sir.''

''One final thing, Hideyori. Have your radio operators on the watch for messages addressed to MFS.''

''I have already ordered that, Sir.''

''Good,'' Saikaku said, then turned and walked out of Lieutenant Hideyori's office.

[SEVEN]
Headquarters, U.S. Forces in the Philippines
Davao Oriental Province
Mindanao, Commonwealth of the Philippines
1815 Hours 10 October 1942

Lieutenant Ball heard through his earphones the sound of the carrier and then a string of dot and dashes.

His heart beating and with tears in his eyes, he wrote down the letters:

```
MFS KFS
MFS KFS
LPORD GHDSG NGFGP JKOWR
DKLHI WRHFS SUHIO SWERI
LPORD GHDSG NGFGP JKOWR
DKLHI WRHFS SUHIO SWERI
KFS CLR
KFS CLR
```

Prior to his attachment to Headquarters, USFIP, Ball had been a radio operator. He recognized the call sign of the answering station.

''That's not Australia. It's a Navy Station. I think Hawaii.''

The message, when decoded, was brief:

STAND BY AT 0600 YOUR TIME

[EIGHT]

Lieutenant Ball erred in part. While KFS was indeed a Navy radio station, it was not in Hawaii, but rather at the U.S. Navy Base, Mare Island, near San Francisco.

And there the radio message had attracted the interest of a veteran chief radioman.

"What the hell is this, Chief?" nineteen-year-old Radioman Third Class Daniel J. Miller, USN, asked, handing it to Dugan. "It's been coming in every hour on the hour in the twenty-meter band. Since yesterday."

The Chief examined the message.

"Whatever it is," he said. "It was encoded on an old Model 94. That second code group means 'Emergency SOI.' "

"What's a Model 94?"

"An old-time crypto machine. They don't use them anymore," the Chief said thoughtfully. "Maybe the Japs captured one on Wake Island or someplace and are fucking with us."

"What's an emergency SOI?"

"It means you don't have a valid signal-operating instruction, so use the Emergency One," the Chief said absently, and then, thinking aloud, "And maybe they ain't."

"Maybe aren't what?"

"Fucking with us."

"Then what the hell is this?" Miller asked.

"I don't know," the Chief said. "But I'm going to find out "

He consulted a typewritten list of telephone numbers taped to the slide in his desk, found the number of the Communications Section of the Presidio of San Francisco Army Base, and dialed it.

"Commo, Sergeant Havell."

"Chief Dugan. Let me speak to Sergeant Piedwell."

"What can the Army do for the Navy?"

"You're always telling me what hot shits you doggies are."

"Statement of fact, Chief."

"If I was to send you something encrypted on a Model 94, could you work it?"

"If I had a Model 94, I could. What's this?"

"You got one, or not?"

"Yeah, there's one in the vault. I saw it last week and wondered what the hell we were still doing with it."

"I'm going to send a fine young man named Miller over there with a message that needs decryption. Out of school, OK, Piedwell?"

"What kinda message?"

"Use the Emergency Code," Chief Dugan said. "Whoever sent this didn't have a valid SOI."

"What's this all about?"

"When I find out, I'll tell you. But in the meantime, just do it, and keep it under your hat, OK?"

"What the hell, why not?"

"Thanks, Piedwell."

Two hours later, Radioman Third Miller was back from the Presidio with a blank, sealed, business-size envelope. When Chief Dugan opened it, he found a single sheet of typewriter paper inside:

WE HAVE THE HOT POOP FROM
THE HOT YANKS IN THE PHILS
FERTIG BRIG GEN

Dugan handed it to Radioman Third Miller.

"What's this mean?" Miller asked.

"It could mean the Japs found a Model 94 and are fucking with us," Chief Dugan said. "And it could mean it's for real."

He refolded the sheet of paper and put it back in the envelope.

"The next time these people come on the air, send them 'Stand by at 0600 your time,' " Chief Dugan said, and stood up. "I'll be back as soon as I get back," he said.

"Where are you going, in case somebody asks?"

"I'm going to tell the Admiral how to run the war," Chief Dugan said.

"I mean, really."

"Chief petty officers never lie, son. Write that on the palm of your hand so you never forget it," Chief Dugan said, put on his jacket and hat, and left the radio room.

"Long time no see, Dugan," Rear Admiral F. Winston Bloomer, USN, said. "You can spell that either 'sss eee eee' or 'sss eee aaa.' Coffee?"

"Thank you, Sir," Dugan said.

The Admiral and the Chief went back a long way, to when the Admiral had been a lieutenant (j.g.) commo officer on an old four-stacker tin-can and the Chief had been a radioman striker.

Dugan handed Admiral Bloomer the envelope, then helped himself to a cup of coffee from the Admiral's thermos.

"OK. What is it?" the Admiral asked.

"Somebody's transmitting that on the twenty-meter band for a couple of minutes every hour on the hour. It was encoded on a Model 94, no SOI."

"A Model 94? They haven't used those for years. Japanese playing with us? They captured one somewhere? Wake Island, maybe? Or in the Philippines?"

"It may be the real thing."

"What do you want to do, Dugan?"

"I want to find out if there is a brigadier general named Fertig."

"In other words, you want *me* to go to Naval Intelligence for you?"

"I've got a pal who can find out for me in a hurry."

"Why does that make me uncomfortable?" Admiral Bloomer asked, adding, "Faster than ONI?"—The *O*ffice of *N*aval *I*ntelligence—"Who does your pal work for, the President?"

"The Secretary of the Navy has an administrative assistant. The administrative assistant has a Chief who works for him."

"And you know where he buried the body, right, Dugan?"

"Bodies, Admiral."

"I don't want to know about this, Dugan. But if you get in trouble, you have my phone number."

"Thank you," Dugan said. "What if I find out something?"

"Yes, please, Dugan. Keep me posted. I hope this is genuine."

"Thank you, Sir."

Radioman Third Miller walked up to Chief Dugan's desk and handed him a sheet of paper.

"This what you've been waiting for, Chief?"

```
U R G E N T

FROM SECNAV
FOR OFFICER COMMANDING
     US NAVY BASE MARE ISLAND
     ATTN: CPO EDWARD B DUGAN, USN

THERE IS NO GENERAL FERTIG IN US ARMY OR USMC

LTCOL WENDELL W. FERTIG CORPS OF ENGINEERS, USARMY RESERVE
REPORTED MISSING AND PRESUMED JAPANESE POW ON BATAAN.

LTCOL FERTIGS NEXT OF KIN WIFE MRS MARY HAMPTON FERTIG,
GOLDEN, COLORADO DOB 11MAY1905

BY DIRECTION SECNAV
HAUGHTON CAPT USN ADMIN OFF TO SECNAV
BY HANSEN CPO USN
```

Dugan read the teletype message.

"What time is it here when it's 0600 in the Philippines?" he asked.

"I don't know, Chief."

"You don't know? My God, Miller, you're a radioman third, you're supposed to know that kind of thing. Find out, and be here when it is."

"You know what time it will be here, right?"

"Of course. I'm a chief."

Dugan stood up and put on his cap and jacket.

"I'll be back when I'm back," he said.

"You're going to tell the Admiral how to run the war again, right?"

"Actually, I'm going over to the Presidio to talk the Army into loaning me their Model 94."

Radioman Third Miller put his fingers to his radiotelegraph key:

```
KFS TO MFS
KFS TO MFS
BY
```

The reply came immediately. Chief Dugan looked over Miller's shoulder as the words appeared on his typewriter.

```
MFS TO KFS
STANDING BY
```

"Send it," Chief Dugan ordered.

Miller took his right hand from the typewriter keys and put it onto the radiotelegraph key.

```
KFS TO MFS
SEND ENCRYPTED MAIDEN NAME FERTIGS NEXT OF KIN AND DATE
OF BIRTH
STANDING BY
```

There was no reply for several minutes.

"They're either encoding it, or we're talking to the Japs, and they're wondering what the hell to do now," Chief Dugan said.

And then there was a reply:

```
MFS TO KFS
JIOQT LPITZ SHDQW JFIUO GMCIT
PSATY SDERJ HQWKM JEWRP AITCD
ITDFS EWNOR HSQIT SDRTP CFENG
JIOQT LPITZ SHDQW JFIUO GMCIT
PSATY SDERJ HQWKM JEWRP AITCD
ITDFS EWNOR HSQIT SDRTP CFENG
MFS BY
```

Chief Dugan ripped the sheet of paper from Miller's typewriter, walked quickly back to his desk, and operated the Model 94 Cryptographic Device he had borrowed from the Army at God only knew what cost in future favors to be repaid.

"Miller," he called, and paused a moment as if he was trying to regain control of his voice. "Send 'We are ready for your traffic.' "

"No shit? It's for real?"

"Belay that. Send 'Welcome to the net. We are ready for your traffic.' "

Chief Dugan reached for his telephone.

"Operator, Chief Dugan. Long Distance Priority Code Sixteen-B. Get me Mrs. Mary Fertig in Golden, Colorado."

Radioman Third Miller, without stopping his tapping on his key, called over his shoulder:

"Chief, you think you should do that without asking somebody?"

"If I ask somebody, they'd likely tell me not to," Chief Dugan said.

Mrs. Mary Fertig came on the line two minutes later.

"Mrs. Fertig, this is Chief Dugan, Mare Island Navy Base."

"Yes?"

"Ma'am, I think we have just heard from your husband. General Fertig?"

"You must be mistaken. My husband is Major Fertig. And he's in the Philippines."

Radioman Miller handed Chief Dugan another sheet of paper, and then hurried back to his typewriter.

"Ma'am," Chief Dugan said, "let me read you something. 'For Mrs. Fertig. Quote. Pineapples for breakfast. Love. End quote.' Does that mean anything to you?"

There was a long pause.

"Yes, that means something. It means my husband is on the island of Mindanao. We used to go there often, to play golf on the Dole Plantation. We always had pineapples for breakfast."

"Yes, Ma'am."

"Is there any way I can get a message to my husband?"

"Yes, Ma'am. A short one. What would you like to say?"

There was another pause.

"Please tell him all is well. And send love."

"Yes, Ma'am. I'll try to get that to him right away. Ma'am, I'm sure some people will be in touch with you. Maybe, when they come to see you, it would be better if you didn't tell them I called you."

"I understand. Thank you so very much, Mr. Dugan."

"That's Chief Dugan, Ma'am. Good-bye, Ma'am."

[ONE]
Office of the Military Governor of Mindanao
Cagayan de Oro, Misamis-Oriental Province
Mindanao, Commonwealth of the Philippines
0900 Hours 13 October 1942

"My General," Lieutenant Colonel Tange Kisho said to Brigadier General Kurokawa Kenzo, "Captain Saikaku has been handling the matter of the clandestine radio station and related matters. With your permission, Sir, I will ask him to brief the General."

General Kurokawa nodded and looked at Saikaku. Instead of rising to his feet as Colonel Tange—and perhaps even General Kurokawa—expected him to do, Saikaku carefully set his teacup on the conference table and slumped back against his upholstered chair. He had decided that it was important to appear relatively unconcerned about the existence of this General Fertig and his radio station, and with Hideyori's inability to locate it.

"My general," he began, "on 10 October, Lieutenant Hideyori's radio operators began hearing a coded message transmitted on the twenty-meter shortwave band. Hideyori brought this to my attention. The message was partly in the clear and partly encrypted. It was addressed to U.S. Forces in Australia.

"At my direction, the message was forwarded to the Signals Intelligence Branch in Manila, together with several suggestions of mine to aid in the decryption process.

"The same day, late in the afternoon, a radio station which we believe to be the U.S. Navy station on Mare Island, California, responded to the station here. That message was also encrypted. There has been a further exchange of messages since then, but let me take this one thing at a time.

"This morning, Signals Intelligence Branch furnished me with their decryption of the first messages. They informed me the encryption was performed on a U.S. Army Model 94 cryptographic machine, two examples of which came into our hands on Luzon.

"The first message, the one Hideyori's operators intercepted, was quite simple. Quote: We have the hot poop from the hot yanks in the phils Fertig brig gen. End quote.''

"So there is a General Fertig?" General Kurokawa interrupted.

"We don't know that for sure, General," Saikaku said. "I'll touch on that in a moment. The body of the message is in American vernacular. 'Hot poop' is a slang expression meaning, roughly, 'fresh information.' 'Hot yanks in the phils' obviously means 'Yankees in the Philippines.' "

" 'Hot Yankees'?" General Kurokawa asked.

"I don't know what that means, General. Possibly it refers to the heat. The reply from California told the station here to stand by—be attentive—at six the following morning. At that time, the California station asked MFS—the call sign of the station here—to furnish them the maiden name—the name of an unmarried woman's father—of Fertig's next of kin—presumably his wife—and her date of birth. This was furnished."

"Obviously, then, there is a Fertig," General Kurokawa said.

"Yes, Sir. A Fertig. Not necessarily a *General* Fertig. I have been looking into this. Nowhere in captured personnel records is there a record of a General Fertig. There is a record of a Major Fertig, believed killed during the Luzon campaign."

"The Americans could have infiltrated this man somehow," General Kurokawa said. "Or it could be—what is the French phrase? A *nom de guerre.*"

"With all respect, Sir, based on the following messages, I have developed a theory. In my judgment, Sir, there was some doubt in the United States about this man's identity. They asked the maiden name and date of birth questions to make him prove who he is."

"And?" General Kurokawa asked impatiently.

"Immediately after the station here furnished the asked-for information, there was a message to Mrs. Fertig. Quote: Pineapples for breakfast. Love. End quote."

"Which you think means what?"

"The Dole Corporation, as I am sure the General knows, had extensive operations on this island. Pineapples and Mindanao have a meaning. I think it is entirely possible that this Fertig fellow has a connection with the Dole Corporation; he very well might be an executive. He was both further identifying himself and telling his wife where he is."

"Presumably, you have inquired into this? I was under the impression that we have detained a number of Americans who worked for the Dole Plantation. Was there a Dole employee named Fertig?"

"I have inquired, Sir, and the inquiries are continuing. We have fairly complete personnel records; the name Fertig does not appear on any of them.

Which brings us to the General's very perceptive theory about a *nom de guerre*. Fertig is a German word meaning finished, or the end, something like that. What we very well may have here is a Dole executive, either from here or one of the other Dole operations in the Philippines, who has assumed the name Fertig. And has undertaken to harass us by announcing that he is a general.''

The General, Saikaku thought, *is not above reacting to flattery. He liked that "very perceptive theory" comment.*

''That seems a possibility,'' General Kurokawa said, ''but I would not recommend that we dismiss the possibility that the Americans have either left behind someone—someone military—to cause us trouble, or sent someone in.''

''No such conclusion has been drawn, General,'' Saikaku said.

''What about the radio station? Where is it?''

''Somewhere in the mountains, Sir,'' Saikaku replied. ''I have learned from Lieutenant Hideyori that location of a radio transmitter is not quite as simple as the Signals people would have us believe.''

''Explain that, please,'' General Kurokawa ordered.

''I defer to Lieutenant Hideyori's expertise, Sir,'' Saikaku said, and waved his hand at the Signals Lieutenant.

Hideyori jumped to his feet, came to attention, and bowed to General Kurokawa.

''Sir, the enemy transmitter is in the mountains. The triangulation location technique requires two—preferably three—truck mounted directional radio antennae. When a signal is detected, the operators rotate the antennae, using a signal-strength meter. That indicates the direction of the transmitting antenna. A line is drawn on a map from the truck antenna in the direction of the transmitting antenna. Each truck does this. Where the lines converge on the map, one expects to find the transmitter.''

''Yes?''

''In the mountains, Sir, it is very difficult to adjust the directional antennae. And the imprecision of the adjustment is magnified by distance. There are very few roads in the mountains which will take our trucks. The distance is great.''

''In other words, Lieutenant, you have not been able to locate the transmitter by triangulation?''

''Yes, Sir. Sir, another problem is that the transmitter is operating only infrequently, not, as in the beginning, every hour on the hour.''

''Find this radio station, Lieutenant,'' General Kurokawa ordered, shutting him off.

Hideyori came to attention again, bowed again, and sat down.

''Has there been other communication between this radio station and the United States?''

''They are not in communication with the Americans in Australia, Sir,''

Saikaku said. "Yes, Sir. They have sent out the names of several of their officers."

"If they have 'several officers,' wouldn't that suggest to you that this is not just one pineapple-company employee harassing us?" General Kurokawa asked sarcastically.

"Sir, we have checked the names against captured records. As you are aware, we do not have personnel rosters before the surrender; the Americans burned those. We have only rosters of personnel who entered captivity. Some of those subsequently escaped. None of the names of the escaped prisoners match those sent by this radio station. It is entirely possible that this man Fertig is transmitting names he has made up, for purposes of deception. And there have been no incidents of anything that might be construed as an attack against our forces. I do not believe," he concluded, "that there is an irregular force, just this man annoying us."

"I devoutly hope you are right, Captain Saikaku," General Kurokawa said. "Thank you all for coming to see me."

[TWO]
Naval Air Transport Command Passenger Terminal
United States Naval Base
Pearl Harbor, Oahu, Territory of Hawaii
0625 Hours 16 October 1942

In his own mind Brigadier General Fleming W. Pickering, USMCR, tended to see himself primarily as a reasonably competent ship's master and businessman—in civilian life he had been the Chairman of the Board of the Pacific & Far East Shipping Corporation—dragged by force of circumstances into situations very little connected with his experience in either commanding a ship or running a Fortune 500 Corporation.

Shortly after the start of the war—like many other top-level corporate executives—he was offered a position at the newly formed Office of Strategic Services. When he arrived in Washington, he found the position offered was not only second-level but would leave him immediately subordinate to a man for whom he had virtually no respect. He furthermore believed this action was less an evaluation of his potential value to the OSS than a gratuitously insulting payback from Colonel William Donovan, head of the OSS. Donovan was a Wall Street lawyer with whom he had had several acrimonious business dealings.

He declined the position—in another acrimonious meeting with Donovan—and then volunteered his services to the United States Marine Corps. Despite the Distinguished Service Cross he had earned in the trenches in France in World War I, the Marines had no place for him, either. About to return to his

San Francisco office, he had a chance meeting with Secretary of the Navy Frank Knox in the hotel suite of their mutual close friend Senator Richardson K. Fowler. Over more than a couple of drinks, he suggested to Knox that after the unmitigated disaster at Pearl Harbor, the decent thing for him to do was resign.

That unabashed candor, and Pickering's reputation in the upper echelons of the American business community, were enough to make Knox realize that Pickering was just the man he needed to be his eyes and ears in the Pacific. If he himself did not intimidate Pickering, Knox concluded, and if Wild Bill Donovan didn't either, no admiral in the Pacific was likely to daunt him; nor, for that matter, was General Douglas MacArthur.

Knox's character assessment had proved valid. On his initial trip to the Pacific—Knox had arranged for him to be commissioned as a Navy Captain—Pickering prepared clear-eyed reports detailing how bad the situation really was. These often differed significantly from the reports Knox had been getting from the admirals at CINCPAC (*C*ommander-*In*-*C*hief, *P*acific) headquarters—which confirmed Knox's fears that he was being told only what the admirals wished him to hear. In addition, Pickering somehow established a strong personal relationship with General Douglas MacArthur. This, in Knox's view, was extraordinary, for MacArthur was not only a notorious loner, but he was surrounded by a group of senior officers—"The Bataan Gang"—who had served with him in the Philippines and regarded it as their duty to keep their Supreme Commander isolated from outsiders.

Knox's pleasure with his selection of Pickering turned out to be short-lived, however. Without any authorization, Pickering sailed with the invasion fleet to Guadalcanal in the Solomon Islands. Shortly after the invasion, there was a message from him expressing, in precise detail, his dissatisfaction with the Navy's role in the invasion. He then further manifested his displeasure by going ashore. Once there, he placed himself at the service of Major General Alexander Archer Vandegrift, the commander of the First Marine Division, and somewhat melodramatically volunteered to perform any duties he might be assigned, if only those of a rifleman.

Inasmuch as the Navy assault fleet had sailed away, leaving the Marines alone on their beachhead—the source of Pickering's contempt—Vandegrift was not able to order the first Navy captain he had ever seen in Marine Corps utilities and carrying a Springfield rifle back aboard a ship with his polite thanks. Shortly afterward, the 1st Marine Division G-2 was killed in combat. By that time, Pickering had so impressed Vandegrift with his intelligence and competence that Vandegrift, short of senior officers, appointed him Acting G-2, until a trained replacement could be sent to the island.

After a month Pickering reluctantly left Guadalcanal, and then only on the direct orders of Secretary Knox, who had ordered the captain of a Navy destroyer making an emergency supply run to Guadalcanal not to leave unless he had Pickering safely aboard. En route to Espíritu Santo, from where Pickering was to be flown to the United States, the destroyer was attacked by a Japanese bomber and her captain killed. Although seriously wounded himself, Pickering assumed command of the destroyer, not because he was the senior Naval officer aboard, but because he believed himself to be the best-qualified mariner aboard—with some justification: he had been licensed as a Master Mariner, Any Tonnage, Any Ocean, at twenty-six.

Pickering's exploits, meanwhile, came to the attention of President Roosevelt, not only through Secretary Knox but also through the Commander-in-Chief, Pacific, who wanted him decorated for his behavior aboard the destroyer, and through Senator Richardson K. Fowler (R., Cal.), Pickering's lifelong friend and the man the President described privately as the "leader of my none-too-loyal opposition."

Roosevelt saw in Pickering the same qualities Knox did. Moreover, he felt a certain personal kinship with him, despite their political differences: Both had sons serving in combat in the Marine Corps. Thus, he overrode the strong, if politely expressed, objections of the Marine Corps establishment and commissioned Pickering a brigadier general, USMC Reserve.

Shortly after that, he was named Chief, USMC Office of Management Analysis. This was done—at Secretary Knox's "suggestion"—primarily because it gave Management Analysis a general officer, essential in the waging of bureaucratic wars in Washington. It also gave him a billet on USMC manning charts. At the same time, it was presumed that Pickering would permit Colonel F. L. Rickabee, a career intelligence officer and the previous Chief, to run things as they had been run. This was an error in judgment. Having been placed in charge, Pickering assumed command.

To everyone's surprise, Rickabee was not outraged. In fact, he seemed delighted with Pickering's leadership. This proved true even after Pickering ignored all advice and ordered, from his hospital bed, the evacuation of two Marines operating a Coastwatcher Station on the Japanese-held island of Buka and were in imminent danger of death either from Japanese action or starvation. The operation was successfully completed before formal objections to it could work their way through the military hierarchy.

"I have something to say," Brigadier General Pickering said softly. Pickering was in his early forties, tall, distinguished looking, and he wore a superbly tailored uniform, the breast of which displayed an impressive array of colored ribbons attesting to his valor both in World War I and the current conflict.

Four Marines turned to look at him: Major Homer C. "Jake" Dillon, USMCR, a stocky, crew-cutted man in his middle thirties; First Lieutenant Kenneth R. McCoy, USMCR, a well-built, lithe, even-featured young man in his early twenties; Sergeant George F. Hart, USMC, a twenty-four-year-old with the build of a circus strong man; and Corporal Robert F. Easterbrook, who weighed 132 pounds, was nineteen years old, and looked younger.

"I want to say thank you," General Pickering said, "to you three"—he indicated the Major, the Lieutenant, and the sergeant—"for the Buka Operation. You carried it off without a hitch. It couldn't have been done without you. You're a credit to The Corps."

"Yeah, we know, Flem," Major Dillon replied. "You really didn't have to get out of bed at this time of the morning to tell us."

Majors do not normally address general officers by their first names, nor mock them, no matter how softly. But the relationship between these two was a bit out of the ordinary. Before they had donned Marine uniforms for the second time in their lives, Jake Dillon, Vice President, Publicity, Metro-Magnum Studios, and Fleming Pickering had been friends.

Pickering shook his head in tolerant resignation, not indignation.

"Shut up, Jake," he said. "I'm serious about this."

"You're embarrassing the Killer," Dillon said, unrepentant, nodding at Lieutenant McCoy. "The next thing you know, he'll be blushing."

"Fuck you, Jake," Lieutenant McCoy snapped unpleasantly.

"You never know when to stop, do you, Jake?" General Pickering said. "You know he hates to be called 'Killer.' "

"Flem, you gave us a job to do, we did it. Leave it at that."

"No, I won't," Pickering said. "As soon as I can find somebody who knows how to fill out the forms, I'm going to do my level best to see that you're all decorated."

"With respect, Sir," McCoy said. "Howard and Koffler deserve a medal, not us."

"The way things are run in The Marine Corps, Lieutenant, generals make decisions like that," Pickering said.

"Yes, Sir."

A loudspeaker went off, harshly but audibly ordering all passengers for the San Diego flight to proceed to the motor whaleboat for boarding of the aircraft.

"Have a nice flight," General Pickering said. "And whether you like it or not, you have my gratitude and my admiration."

He shook hands with McCoy first, and then Dillon. And then he turned to the boyish corporal.

"Easterbrook, you did one hell of a job on Guadalcanal," he said. "Your pictures are probably going to influence this war in ways you can't imagine.

I've told Major Dillon—Jake, listen to me—to make sure the proper people know what you did, and how well you did it.''

Corporal Easterbrook blushed.

Finally, Pickering turned to Sergeant Hart.

"It's not too late to change your mind, George," he said. "You still have a priority to get on that airplane, and you certainly deserve a couple of weeks off."

"No, Sir. I'll go to Australia with you, Sir."

"Try not to fall out of the whaleboat, Jake," General Pickering said, and turned and walked out of the passenger lounge.

"Hart's the one who falls out of boats, General," Dillon called after him.

A 1939 Cadillac Fleetwood with civilian license plates was parked outside the building. Pickering got behind the wheel, started the engine, waited for Sergeant Hart to get in, and then drove off. Five hundred yards down the road, he made a sudden U-turn and headed back to the passenger terminal.

"You never know those damned things are airborne until they're airborne," he said. "Let's wait and see if they really get off."

"Yes, Sir," Sergeant Hart said.

Pickering had several reasons for coming to the Navy base to see the four off. One of them was that he feared that the Navy would ignore their AAAAA travel priority, and give their seats on the plane to some deserving—read high-ranking—Navy officer.

They couldn't do so officially, of course, but in the minds of most people in the Navy, any Marine—not just a lowly corporal—was of far less importance than a fellow sailor with the four stripes of a captain or the solid gold stripes of an admiral on his tunic sleeves. There was far less chance that a "mistake" or an "unfortunate misunderstanding" would occur—leaving an admiral sitting in the seat reserved for Corporal Easterbrook when the plane took off—if the Navy was aware he was being seen off by a Marine general.

Oddly enough, in Pickering's mind, the boyish corporal had the greatest justification for a priority seat to Washington. It was entirely possible that the Secretary of the Navy—for that matter, the President himself—would want to talk to him.

The day before, Major Edward Banning, USMC, had carried still and motion-picture films Easterbrook had shot on Guadalcanal to the States. By now, Banning was either in Washington or soon would be. On his arrival he would brief Secretary Knox and, Pickering believed, the President and his Chief of Staff Admiral William Leahy as well.

A picture was indeed worth a thousand words, and Easterbrook's film showed the situation as it was far better than any thick report could possibly show it. It was impossible to get more than one seat on yesterday's plane, and

Pickering decided it had to go to Banning; Easterbrook obviously was not equipped to handle a briefing.

But there would be questions asked today about specific details of the photographs or 16mm film, if not by Roosevelt, Knox, or Leahy, then certainly by Major General Horace W. T. Forrest, the intelligence officer on the staff of the Commandant of the Marine Corps, by Colonel F. L. Rickabee, of the USMC Office of Management Analysis, and by others. These questions could only be answered by the photographer himself, or possibly by Jake Dillon.

On the other hand, there was no real reason why Lieutenant McCoy had to be rushed to Washington. The polite fiction was that he would be useful in helping Dillon and Easterbrook. But the real reason he was going was that Pickering had decided McCoy had a moral right to a seat on the plane. McCoy—and Hart—had paddled ashore from a submarine onto the enemy-held island of Buka, carrying with them a desperately needed radio and some other supplies for a Coastwatcher team that was supplying information concerning Japanese sea and air movements critical for the battle of Guadalcanal.

The fact that he had accomplished this mission—which included bringing out with him the two Marine Coastwatchers—without firing a shot in no way diminished the enormous risk he had voluntarily taken. While planning the operation, Pickering had privately decided that the operation had one chance in four of succeeding.

In Pickering's mind, if there were forty passengers aboard the huge, four-engine, Consolidated PB2Y-3 Coronado, it was mathematically certain that perhaps ten percent of them—four—were brass hats whose rank, not legitimate importance to the war effort, had gotten them a seat. One of the four could wait a day before going home.

Pickering stopped the Cadillac on a wharf from which much of the carnage the Japanese had caused on Battleship Row on December 7, 1941, could be seen, and got from behind the wheel. Hart followed him to the edge of the pier.

As they saw the whaleboats—three of them—approach the huge seaplane, a Navy officer, a lieutenant junior grade, wearing canvas puttees, a steel helmet, and a .45 pistol suspended from a pistol belt, came trotting down the pier.

We are obviously parked where we are not supposed to park, Sergeant Hart thought, *and driving a civilian car where there are supposed to be no civilian cars.*

The j.g. slowed when he saw the stars on Pickering's epaulettes and collar points.

He saluted.

"May I help the General, Sir?"

"No, thank you," Pickering said, and gestured over the water. "We're just watching to see if the Coronado gets off."

"General, this is a restricted area. There's not supposed to be any civilian vehicles in this area, Sir."

"Is that so?" Pickering replied. "Well, we won't be long, son."

Hart managed to keep his face straight as he watched the Lieutenant decide what he should do about the situation. He was not at all surprised when the Lieutenant decided to do absolutely nothing but fold his arms on his chest and watch as the passengers entered the airplane from the whaleboats.

As soon as the last passenger had entered, the pilot began to start the engines. Before all of them had started, the huge plane began to move. It disappeared around a point of Ford's Island, but the sound of its engines could still be heard.

And then they changed pitch, as the pilot went to takeoff power.

When the Coronado next came into sight, it was airborne.

"Well, unless they threw Jake off when we couldn't see it, I guess they're on their way," Pickering observed. "Let's go, George." He looked at the j.g. "Good morning, Lieutenant."

"Good morning, Sir," the Lieutenant said.

Pickering slipped behind the wheel and drove back toward the passenger terminal. As they approached, another Navy officer appeared, this one in whites. He stood in the middle of the road and raised both arms.

"Uh-oh," Hart said softly, "another one."

Pickering slowed the car and when he reached the Navy officer stopped. Hart saw that the officer, who now saluted, was a commander, and that dangling from the shoulder of his white uniform was the silver cord of an aide to a flag officer.

"Good morning, Sir. You are General Pickering, Sir?"

"That's right. What can I do for you, Commander?"

"Admiral Nimitz's compliments, Sir. The Admiral would be most grateful if you would speak with him, Sir. There's a telephone inside."

"Certainly. I'll park the car."

Admiral Chester W. Nimitz was Commander-in-Chief, Pacific.

Hart followed Pickering back into the passenger terminal, where the aide waited, holding open the door to an office.

"This way, please, General," the aide said, and then made it quite plain with the expression on his face that Hart should remain outside. Hart ignored him. He was under orders to go everywhere that General Pickering went except, Colonel Rickabee had said, into a stall in a head, in which case he was supposed to wait where he could keep an eye on the door.

The aide dialed a number from memory.

"Admiral," he said. "Commander Ussery. Would you please inform CINCPAC I have General Pickering on the line?"

He handed Pickering the telephone.

"Nimitz."

"Pickering, Sir. You wished to speak to me, Sir?"

"How's your health, Pickering?"

"I'm very well, thank you, Sir."

"I didn't expect to see you back here so soon."

"I didn't expect to be back so soon, Sir."

"I appreciate the film you sent me."

"I thought you would be interested, Sir."

"What's your schedule, Pickering?"

"I'm on the 1500 plane to Brisbane, Sir."

"Could you fit an hour or so for me into your schedule?"

"I'm at your disposal, Admiral."

"I think it would be best if you didn't come here," Nimitz said. "Are you free for lunch?"

"Yes, Sir."

"Somewhere private," Nimitz said. "Do you suppose we could meet . . . could I invite myself for lunch at your place?"

"I'd be honored, Sir."

"Noon," Nimitz said. "Would that be convenient?"

"Certainly, Sir."

"I'll make sure the Brisbane plane doesn't leave without you. Thank you, General."

The phone went dead in Pickering's ear.

Pickering looked at Sergeant Hart.

"Shine your shoes, George. CINCPAC is coming to lunch at Muku-Muku."

"Aye, aye, Sir."

Pickering looked at Commander Ussery.

"Would you like me to draw you a map, Commander?"

"That won't be necessary, Sir."

"Well, then, I suppose we'll see you at Muku-Muku at noon."

"Yes, Sir."

[THREE]
Muku-Muku
Oahu, Territory of Hawaii
1150 Hours 16 October 1942

The official vehicle of the Commander-in-Chief, Pacific, was a black 1941 Cadillac Model 62. There was no starred flag officer's plate; instead a blue flag with four silver stars flew from a staff mounted on the right front fender.

Sergeant George Hart was waiting for CINCPAC's arrival on the wide, shaded, flagstone porch of the rambling house overlooking the Pacific. He started down the stairs the moment he saw the car approaching, intending to salute, then open the rear door, then stand to attention while CINCPAC got out, then to close the door after him and follow him up the stairs.

By the time he reached the Cadillac, CINCPAC was already out of the car. Commander Ussery and the driver, a portly chief petty officer, quickly followed him. Hart noticed that the Chief had gotten no farther than the hood of the car before CINCPAC was walking toward him.

Hart saluted.

CINCPAC, a tall, silver-haired man in his fifties wearing a high-collared white uniform, returned the salute, smiling.

"Good afternoon, Sergeant," he said without breaking stride. "Would you be good enough to find the Commander and the Chief something to eat, and do what you can to keep them out of trouble?"

"Aye, aye, Sir," Hart said, as CINCPAC walked past him and up the stairs.

Brigadier General Pickering came onto the porch and saluted.

"Good afternoon, Sir. Welcome to Muku-Muku."

CINCPAC returned the salute, and then put out his hand.

"We gave ourselves an extra ten minutes in case we got lost," CINCPAC said. "I've only been here twice before, and that was a long time ago."

"Well, I'm glad you didn't get lost, Sir."

"You look well, Pickering," CINCPAC said. "Better than I would have expected."

"I'm fine, Sir."

"The way I heard it, the President pulled you out of a hospital bed."

"No, Sir, I was already out of the hospital."

The door to the house was opened by a silver-haired black man in a gray jacket.

"Welcome back to Muku-Muku, Admiral," he said. "I'm Denny. Do you remember me, Sir?"

"Indeed I do, but I'm surprised and flattered that you remembered I've been here before," CINCPAC said.

"May 22, 1939, as the guest of Captain Renner, Admiral," the black man said. "I checked the guest book."

"I don't suppose I could steal you away from General Pickering, could I, Denny?" CINCPAC said.

"Thank you, Sir, but no, thank you."

"Renner has the *Pacific Princess* now, doesn't he?" CINCPAC asked.

"It's the USS *Millard G. Fillmore* now," Pickering said. "I sold her to the Navy, which was wise enough to hire Renner away from me for the duration to skipper her."

"What can we offer the Admiral to drink?" Denny asked.

"If I drink at lunch, I have a hard time staying awake in the afternoon," CINCPAC said. "Having said that, I think a light scotch would go down nicely, thank you very much."

"We're set for lunch on the terrace," Denny said. "If you'll follow me, please?"

He led the way through the luxuriously furnished house to the terrace, on the seaward side of the house. CINCPAC walked to the edge of the terrace and looked down the steep, lush slope. At its end, five hundred yards away, large waves crashed onto a wide white sand beach.

"I've never been here in the daytime before," he said. "I missed that. It's beautiful."

"Yes, it is," Pickering agreed.

"It makes the very idea of war seem all that much more obscene, doesn't it?" CINCPAC asked.

"Yes, Sir, it does," Pickering replied.

CINCPAC met Pickering's eyes. "Are we going to lose Guadalcanal, Pickering?" he asked. "Can Vandegrift hang on?"

Pickering was relieved when Denny appeared with the drinks. It at least delayed his having to answer a question he felt wholly inadequate to answer: whether or not Major General Archer A. Vandegrift's First Marine Division was going to be torn from its tenuous toehold on Guadalcanal.

"Very nice," CINCPAC said, sipping his drink.

"Famous Grouse," Denny said. "Funny name for a whiskey, isn't it?"

"Leave the fixings, please, Denny," Pickering said. "And give me ten minutes' notice when lunch will be ready."

"Ten minutes from when you tell me," Denny replied.

"Admiral?" Pickering asked.

"Ten minutes from now would be fine, Denny," CINCPAC said. He waited until Denny had left them alone on the terrace, and then looked at Pickering again. "Can he, or can't he? A good deal depends on that."

"Admiral, with respect, I am in no way qualified to offer an opinion about something like that."

CINCPAC nodded his head.

"I had a radio early today from Admiral Ghormley," he said. (Vice Admiral Robert L. Ghormley, USN, was Commander, South Pacific, and Senior Naval Commander for the Guadalcanal Operation.) "In it he used the phrase 'totally inadequate' vis-à-vis the forces available to him to resist a major Japanese attack. I think that's going overboard, but I would like to know what Vandegrift really thinks."

"General Vandegrift is a superb officer," Pickering said.

"The feeling around here is that General MacArthur is not doing all he can with regard to reinforcing Vandegrift."

"If that is your perception, Sir," Pickering heard himself say, "I'm truly sorry."

"You don't perceive that to be the case?"

Oh, to hell with it. He asked me. I'll tell him.

"I would suggest that there are people around General MacArthur who believe CINCPAC isn't doing all it can, Admiral."

"You believe that?"

"I'm in no position to make any judgment whatever, Sir."

"Right about now, your Major . . . what was his name? Vanning?"

"Banning, Sir."

". . . *Banning* . . . is presumably briefing Secretary Knox. Which carries with it the unpleasant connotation that he does not trust the reports being sent to him by me."

"I think he wants all the information he can lay his hands on, Sir."

"Do you think it's likely that Secretary Knox will go to the President with the information Banning carried with him?"

"Yes, I do," Pickering replied.

"Do you think General MacArthur shares the opinion of those around him that we're not doing everything we can?"

"No, Sir. I do not."

"When you see General MacArthur, will you give him my personal assurance that I am doing everything I can?"

"I will, Sir, but I don't think it's necessary."

"And assure him that I have absolute faith that he's doing the same thing?"

"Yes, Sir."

"I don't suppose you'd be willing—or are free—to tell me the nature of your current mission to SWPOA?" (*South West Pacific Ocean Area*)

Pickering exhaled audibly.

On one hand, it's none of your business, CINCPAC or not. But on the other, you are CINCPAC.

"General MacArthur, for whatever reasons, has not chosen to receive the emissaries of Wild Bill Donovan. . . ."

"General Donovan, of the Office of Strategic Services?"

"Yes, Sir. General Donovan and the President are old friends. He has complained to the President, and the President has sent me to extol the virtues of the OSS to General MacArthur."

"Do you think you'll succeed?"

"General MacArthur rarely changes his mind. He told me that he doesn't think the good the OSS can do for him is worth what the OSS will cost him.''

''Have you ever wondered, Pickering, why the President, or General Marshall, doesn't simply order Douglas MacArthur to do what he's told to do vis-à-vis the OSS?'' (General George Catlett Marshall was U.S. Army Chief of Staff.)

''I'd heard there was bad blood between Marshall and MacArthur.''

''When MacArthur was Chief of Staff, he wrote an efficiency report on Marshall, who was then commanding the Infantry School at Fort Benning, stating he was not qualified to command anything larger than a regiment.''

''I hadn't heard that, Sir.''

''There's bad blood between them, all right, but that's not the reason I'm talking about. Marshall put a knife in MacArthur's back after he left the Philippines. MacArthur left under the impression he was simply moving his flag and that the Philippines would remain under his command. But the minute he boarded that PT boat, the Army started dealing directly with General Skinny Wainwright, in effect taking him out from under MacArthur's command.''

''I'd heard that story, Sir.''

From El Supremo himself. By admitting that, am I violating his confidence?

''There was a brigadier general on Mindanao, with 30,000 effectives. Fellow named Sharp. They had food and rations, munitions, and they weren't in the pitiable state of the troops on Bataan. When Bataan fell, and then a month later, Corregidor, the Japanese forced Wainwright to order Sharp on Mindanao to surrender. Sharp obeyed Wainwright's order. MacArthur feels, with some justification, that if he had retained command of the Philippines, that wouldn't have happened. He told me it was his plan to use Sharp's people, and matériel, to continue the war, either conventionally or as guerrillas. If he had retained command of the Philippines, he feels, Sharp wouldn't have had to surrender until he at least got a guerrilla operation off the ground and running. And now they want to send somebody not under MacArthur's command in to start guerrilla operations? You have your work cut out for you, Pickering, to talk Douglas MacArthur into agreeing to that.''

''What's the difference who would run it, so long as it's hurting the Japanese?''

CINCPAC looked at Pickering and smiled.

''Of all people, Pickering, I would have thought that you would be aware of the effect of the egos of very senior officers on warfare. And actually, it's a moot point. The surrenders have taken place. Whatever matériel could have been used by a guerrilla operation has either been destroyed or captured, and there's simply no way to get any into the Philippines.''

"What did the Russian partisans do for supplies?" Pickering asked.

"Getting supplies across an enemy's lines is much easier than trying to ship them across deep water," Nimitz said.

"Luncheon, gentlemen," Denny called from the far end of the terrace, "is served."

[FOUR]
The Foster Lafayette Hotel
Washington, D.C.
0005 Hours 17 October 1942

Major Edward J. Banning, USMC, a tall, well-built thirty-six-year-old, fresh from a shower and wearing only a towel, sat on the bed and stared at the telephone. After a full thirty seconds, he reached for it.

He gave the operator a number in New York City from memory.

Maybe, he thought, as he counted the rings to six, torn between disappointment and relief, *she's not home. Away for the weekend or something. Or maybe she's got a heavy date. Why not?*

A woman's voice came on the line, her "Hello?" expressing a mixture of annoyance and concern.

Oh, God, I woke her up.

"Carolyn?"

Why did I make that a question? God knows, I recognized her voice.

"Oh, my God! Ed!"

"Did I wake you?"

"Where are you?"

"Washington."

"Since when?"

"Since about nine o'clock."

"This morning?"

"Tonight."

"I will give you the benefit of the doubt, and believe this is the first chance you've had to call me."

"It really was," he said. "They just left."

"They being?"

"Two bare-breasted girls in grass skirts and a jazz quartet."

"In other words, you don't want to tell me."

"Colonel Rickabee, Captain Sessions, some other people."

I purposely did not tell her the others were Senator Fowler and the Administrative Assistant to the Secretary of the Navy. Was that because of some noble concern with security, or because I am just too tired to get into an explanation?

"Where are you?"

"At the Foster Lafayette."

"Very nice!"

The Foster Lafayette was one of Washington's most prestigious—and inarguably one of its most expensive—hotels.

"You know why I'm here, Carolyn," he said.

Brigadier General Fleming Pickering, USMCR, was married to the only child of Andrew Foster, who owned the Foster Lafayette and forty-two other hotels. Foster had turned over to Pickering a Foster Lafayette suite for the duration; and Pickering had left standing orders that the suite be used by the officers on his staff when he wasn't actually using it himself.

"He's in the Pacific, isn't he?" Carolyn asked innocently. "Is anyone else there with you?"

"Christ, Carolyn, I don't think that's such a good idea," Banning said.

"If the bare-breasted girls in the grass skirts come back, tell them you've made other plans," she said, and hung up.

Banning stared for a moment at the dead phone in his hand, and then put it in its cradle.

"Jesus Christ!" he said, smiling.

The telephone rang.

He grabbed it.

"Major Banning."

"I forgot to tell you something," Carolyn said. "Welcome home. And I love you."

"You're something," he said, laughing.

"With just a little bit of luck, I can catch the one-oh-five milk train," she said, and hung up again.

He put the phone back in its cradle again, swung his feet up on the bed, and lowered his head onto the pillow.

He was almost instantly asleep.

[FIVE]
The Foster Lafayette Hotel
Washington, D.C.
0805 Hours 17 October 1942

When the telephone rang, Carolyn Spencer Howell, a tall, willowy thirty-two-year-old who wore her shoulder-length hair parted in the middle, woke immediately.

She glanced at the man in bed beside her with a sudden tenderness that made her want to cry, and then smiled, anticipating the look on his face when the telephone's ringing finally woke him up.

He slept on, oblivious to the sound.

Finally, she pushed him, at first gently and then quite hard. His only response was to grunt and roll over.

"I never really believed that cutting hair was what Delilah did to Samson," she said aloud. And then made a final attempt to wake him. She held his nostrils shut.

His response was to swat at whatever had landed on his face with his hand. The force of the swat was frightening.

"That was not a good idea," she said, then shrugged and reached for the telephone.

"Hello?"

She looked down at Ed's wristwatch on the bedside table. It was five minutes past eight. She had been with him not quite four hours.

Should I be ashamed of myself for taking advantage of an exhausted man? He didn't seem to mind.

But neither was there any of that postcoital cuddling, of fame and legend. He was sound asleep while I was still quivering.

"Who is this?" a somewhat impatient male voice demanded.

"Who are you?" Carolyn responded.

"My name is Rickabee. I was trying to reach Major Edward Banning."

"He's in the shower, Colonel Rickabee. May I take a message?"

"I'd hoped to see him. I'm downstairs."

"Why don't you give him five minutes and then come up?"

"Thank you," Rickabee said, and hung up.

She hung the telephone up, and then really tried to wake Ed. Tickling the inside of his feet—at some risk—finally worked. After thrashing his legs angrily, he suddenly sat up, fully awake.

"What the hell are you doing?"

"Your Colonel Rickabee is on his way up," Carolyn said.

"Christ! You talked to him?"

"You wouldn't wake up," she said.

"I wonder what the hell he wants?" Banning asked rhetorically, and stepped out of bed. He headed directly for the bathroom.

Carolyn picked up the telephone.

"Room Service, please," she told the operator, and then ordered coffee and breakfast rolls for three.

Ed came out of the bedroom as she was fastening her brassiere.

"Jesus, you're beautiful," he said.

"I ordered coffee and rolls," she said. "Would you like me to take a walk around the block, or what?"

"No," he said. "Don't be silly. You stay."

"I'm not being silly. Is this going to be awkward for you?"

"Don't be silly," he repeated, making a joke of it. "I'm a Marine, aren't I?"

In other words, yes, it is going to be embarrassing for you. But you are either the consummate gentleman, or you love me too much—maybe both—to consciously hurt my feelings. Whichever, Thank You, My Darling!

Almost precisely five minutes later, the door chimes of Suite 802 sounded.

Banning, by then dressed in a khaki shirt and green woolen uniform trousers, opened it to a tall, slight, pale-skinned, unhealthy-looking man in an ill-fitting suit.

He was not what Carolyn expected.

Ed was closemouthed about what he did in The Marine Corps. Even though she told herself she understood the necessity for tight lips, this frustrated Carolyn. But she knew that Ed was in "Intelligence," even if she didn't know precisely what that meant, and that his immediate superior was Colonel F. L. Rickabee, whom he had once described as "the best intelligence officer in the business."

She had expected someone looking like Clark Gable in a Marine uniform. Or maybe an American version of David Niven in a splendidly tailored suit. Not this bland, pale man in a suit that looked like a gift from the Salvation Army.

"Good morning, Sir," Banning said. "I was in the shower."

"So I understand," Rickabee said. He looked at Carolyn.

"Honey," Banning said. "This is my boss, Colonel Rickabee. Colonel, my . . . Mrs. Carolyn Howell."

"How do you do, Mrs. Howell?"

"How do you do?" Carolyn replied, offering her hand.

Rickabee's hand was as she thought it might be. Cold.

Carolyn Spencer Howell was, in the flesh, very much as Rickabee thought she would be. He knew a good deal about her. He was a good intelligence officer.

When Banning first became involved with her, Rickabee asked the FBI for a report on her. And the FBI's New York Field Office turned the investigation over to the Army's Counterintelligence Corps, a move that annoyed Rickabee, although he could not fault the thorough, professional job the CIC did on her:

Carolyn Spencer Howell came from a respected upper-middle-class family. Shortly after graduating *cum laude* from Sarah Lawrence (where she was apolitical), she married James Stevens Howell, an investment banker ten years her senior. Mr. Howell's interest in younger women apparently did not diminish with marriage; and after nearly a decade of marriage, Mrs. Howell caught her husband in bed with a lady not far over the age of legal consent.

As a result of encouragement by his employers to be generous in the divorce settlement—philandering vice presidents do not do much for the image of investment banking—Mrs. Howell became a rather wealthy woman. She took employment in the New York Public Library, more for something to do than the need of income, and there she met Major Ed Banning, and took him into her bed.

So far as the CIC was able to determine, Banning was the only man to ever spend the night in Mrs. Howell's apartment. And Banning, meanwhile, was honest with her, telling her up front that there was a Mrs. Edward Banning, whom he had last seen standing on a quai in Shanghai, and whose present whereabouts were not known.

For Rickabee's purposes, Mrs. Howell was ideal for Banning. So long as he was, in his way, faithful to her, which seemed to be the case, he was unlikely to go off the deep end with a dangerous floozy, or even, conceivably, with an enemy agent. There was talk around, which Rickabee believed, that Ambassador Kennedy's son, the second one, John, had been sent to the Pacific after becoming entirely too friendly with a redhead who had ties with the wrong governments.

"I'm really very sorry to intrude," Rickabee said, meaning it. "And I wouldn't have come if it wasn't necessary. But the thing is, Mrs. Howell, I need about thirty minutes of Ed's time now, and about that much time at half past ten."

"I was just telling Ed that I was going to take a walk around," Carolyn said. "Have a look at the White House, maybe."

"It's raining," Rickabee said. "Walking may not be such a good idea. But if you could read the newspaper over a cup of coffee in the lobby . . ."

"My pleasure," Carolyn said. She smiled and left.

Rickabee waited until the door closed after her.

"Haughton called," he said. "There's a special channel from Brisbane. He's going to bring it by the office."

Captain David Haughton, USN, was Administrative Assistant to Navy Secretary Frank Knox. A "special channel" was a message encrypted in a special code whose use was limited to the most senior members of the military and naval hierarchy—or more junior officers, for example Colonel Rickabee and Brigadier General Pickering, whose immediate superiors were at the top of the hierarchy. Since Pickering was in Brisbane, the special channel was almost certainly from him. The only other person authorized access to the special channel in Brisbane was General Douglas MacArthur, who was the Supreme Commander, South West Pacific Ocean Area. It was unlikely that MacArthur would be sending messages to a lowly Marine colonel.

"Yes, Sir."

"I thought you had better be there, in case something needs clarification."

"Yes, Sir."

"And it's possible that Haughton may want to talk about the Mongolian Operation. If that's the case, I thought it would be better if you were up to date on it, changes, et cetera, since you left."

"Yes, Sir."

"As soon as we're finished with Haughton, you're finished. Take the week I mentioned last night."

"Aye, aye, Sir."

"Do you think you could rustle up some coffee, Ed?"

The door chimes sounded.

Banning opened the door to admit the waiter with the coffee Carolyn had ordered from room service.

"Your wish, Sir," Banning said, chuckling, "is my command. I trust the Colonel will pardon the delay?"

[SIX]
Temporary Building T-2032
The Mall, Washington, D.C.
1045 Hours 17 October 1942

Captain David W. Haughton, USNA '22, a tall, slim, intelligent-looking Naval officer, had called for a Navy car to take him to The Mall, where a large collection of "temporary" frame buildings built to house the swollen Washington bureaucracy during World War I were now occupied by the swollen—and still swelling—bureaucracy considered necessary to wage World War II.

A 1941 Packard Clipper, painted Navy gray, with enlisted chauffeur, was immediately provided. This was not in deference to Captain Haughton's rank—it was said there were enough captains and admirals in Washington to fully man all the enlisted billets provided for on a battleship—but to the rank of his boss.

Captain Haughton, who would have much preferred to be at sea as a lieutenant commander in command of a destroyer—as he had once been—was Administrative Assistant to the Secretary of the Navy, the Honorable Frank Knox.

There were, of course, official automobiles assigned to the Office of the Secretary of the Navy, including two limousines. One of these was at the moment in use by Secretary Knox, and the second was in the Cadillac dealership having a bad clutch repaired. There were also two 1942 Plymouth sedans painted Navy gray. Chief Petty Officer Stanley Hansen, USN, Haughton's chief assistant, regarded one of these as his personal vehicle, and Haughton was reluctant to challenge the Chief's perquisites. And he was reluctant to use the second Plymouth because he regarded it as a necessary spare. The Secretary's limousine—or Chief Hansen's Plymouth—might collapse somewhere.

And finally, he had requested a car from the motor pool for an admittedly petty, selfish reason. It had rained hard all day, and he thought it was unlikely to stop. He correctly suspected that the motor pool would dispatch a car much like the Packard that was in fact sent, a large car, reserved for admirals, and consequently equipped, fore and aft, with a holder for the starred plates admirals were entitled to affix to their automobiles. When an admiral was not actually in his car, the holder was covered.

The Shore Patrol, which patrolled the area of The Mall where Haughton was headed, would, he thought, be somewhat reluctant to challenge an illegally parked Packard with a flag officer's plate holder on it—even if the admiral's stars were covered. He could thus tell the driver to park right in front of Temporary Building T-2032, where he had business to transact with the Marine Corps Office of Management Analysis. This would spare him a long walk in the rain to and from the parking lot where lowly captains were supposed to park.

The Packard pulled to the curb before one of the many identical two-story frame buildings, and the driver started to get out to open Haughton's door.

"Stay in the car, son," Haughton ordered, opened the door himself, and, a heavy black Navy-issue briefcase in his left hand, ran through the rain down a short concrete path to the building and stepped inside into a vestibule.

There was a sign reading "ABSOLUTELY NO ADMITTANCE" on the door to the stairway of the two-floor frame building.

Haughton pushed it open and stepped inside. Inside, there was a wall of pierced-steel planking (interlocking sections of steel, perforated to permit the passage of water, designed for the hasty construction of temporary aircraft runways; it was quickly adopted for a host of other purposes). A door of the same material (closed) and a window (open) were cut into the wall. Through the window, Haughton could see a Marine sergeant armed with a Colt Model 1911A1 .45 ACP pistol, in a shoulder holster, sitting at a desk in his khaki shirt. His blouse hung from a hanger hooked into the pierced steel netting wall. Hanging beside his blouse was a Winchester Model 1897 12-gauge trench gun.

The pierced steel wall and the armed guard were necessary because the Marine Corps Office of Management Analysis had nothing whatever to do with either management or analysis. What the Office of Management Analysis did was clandestine intelligence, and special, clandestine, operations.

The sergeant saw him, recognized him, and stood up.

"Good morning, Sir," he said. "I know the Colonel expects you."

Haughton held out to him a photo identification card.

"Yes, Sir, thank you, Sir," the sergeant said, and pushed a clipboard through the window opening in the pierced-steel planking.

Haughton wrote his name, the time, and "Colonel Rickabee" in the "To

See'' blank on the form on the clipboard and pushed it back. Colonel F. L. Rickabee was Deputy Chief of the Office of Management Analysis.

"Thank you, Sir," the sergeant said, and then pressed a hidden button. When he heard the buzzing of a solenoid, Haughton pushed open the door in the metal wall.

He walked through a second interior door, which gave access to a stairway. He waited for a second buzz of a solenoid, then pushed the door open and started to climb the stairs. Behind him, he heard the sergeant, apparently on a telephone, say, "Colonel, Captain Haughton is on deck."

Haughton went up the wooden stairs two at a time. Beyond a door at the top of the stairs was another pierced-steel wall. Beside it was a doorbell button. As Haughton reached to push the button, the door opened.

"Good morning, Sir," Major Ed Banning said.

When he saw Banning, Haughton was always uncomfortably reminded of his own noncombatant role in the war. On Banning's tunic were half a dozen ribbons, including one whose miniature oak-leaf cluster represented the second award of the Purple Heart, for wounds received in combat. The ribbon representing service in the Pacific Theater of Operations was further adorned with a small black star, indicating that the wearer had not only been in the Pacific but had participated in a battle.

In Banning's case, this was the battle of the Philippines. Haughton had learned—not from Banning, but from Lieutenant Kenneth R. McCoy, who had been there—that Banning took shrapnel from Japanese artillery during the initial Japanese landings. Left behind when American forces retreated, and hiding out behind the enemy lines, he came under American artillery fire, whose concussion blinded him.

He was ultimately led through the enemy lines to a hospital, and finally to the hospital on Fortress Corregidor. From there he was evacuated, with other blinded men, by submarine. His sight inexplicably returned while he was on the sub.

"How are you, Banning?"

"Very well, thank you, Sir. I guess we heard from The Boss?"

Haughton held up the briefcase, which was attached to his wrist by a steel cable and half a handcuff. Then he walked through the pierced-steel planking door, and down a narrow corridor to the end, which held the offices of the Chief, USMC Office of Management Analysis, and his deputy.

The door was opened by Colonel Rickabee, who had changed into a uniform after his breakfast meeting with Banning at the Foster Lafayette. But even in uniform, with the silver eagles of a colonel pinned to his collar points, and even wearing a 1911A1 .45 automatic in a shoulder holster, Colonel F. L. Rickabee, USMC, did not look much like a professional warrior.

"Hello, David. How are you?" Rickabee said, offering his hand.

Haughton wondered if Rickabee really thought the .45 was necessary, or whether he was wearing it to set an example for the others. It seemed highly unlikely that anyone would launch an assault against the Office of Management Analysis—even with its bulging files of TOP SECRET material. And even if that happened, it seemed likely that the pierced-steel doors and the sergeants with their 12-gauge riot guns would at least slow them down enough so that reinforcements could be called up.

"Good to see you, Fritz," Haughton said.

"Little wet outside? Would a cup of coffee be welcome? Or something stronger?"

"Coffee, please."

Banning turned and went down the corridor, obviously in search of coffee. Haughton found the key to his handcuff, and with some difficulty managed to detach himself from the briefcase. Then he worked the combination lock of the briefcase and took from it a manila folder, on which was stamped in inch-high red letters TOP SECRET. He handed it to Rickabee as Banning returned, carrying three steaming china mugs by their handles.

"General Pickering has been heard from," Haughton said, handing the file to Rickabee.

Ten days before, Pickering had left his hospital bed—prematurely, Haughton thought—to undertake a personal mission for the President: Colonel Donovan, the head of OSS, had complained to the President that General Douglas MacArthur had flatly refused to even talk to the man Donovan had sent to run the OSS operation in the Pacific. And Roosevelt had decided that if anyone could solicit MacArthur's cooperation, it was Brigadier General Fleming W. Pickering.

The documents in the TOP SECRET folder Haughton had brought to Rickabee were the first word anyone had heard from Pickering since he had flown back to the Far East.

Rickabee slumped back in his chair and started to read the first of the two messages.

```
T O P   S E C R E T

EYES ONLY—THE SECRETARY OF THE NAVY

DUPLICATION FORBIDDEN
ORIGINAL TO BE DESTROYED AFTER ENCRYPTION AND TRANSMITTAL
TO SECNAV
```

BRISBANE, AUSTRALIA
SATURDAY 17 OCTOBER 1942

DEAR FRANK:

I ARRIVED HERE WITHOUT INCIDENT FROM PEARL HARBOR.
PRESUMABLY, MAJOR ED BANNING IS BY NOW IN WASHINGTON AND
YOU HAVE HAD A CHANCE TO HEAR WHAT HE HAD TO SAY, AND TO
HAVE HAD A LOOK AT THE PHOTOGRAPHS AND FILM.

WITHIN AN HOUR OF WHAT I THOUGHT WAS MY UNHERALDED
ARRIVAL, I WAS SUMMONED TO A PRIVATE—REALLY PRIVATE, ONLY
EL SUPREMO AND ME—LUNCHEON. HE ALSO HAD A SKEWERED IDEA
WHY I WAS SENT HERE. HE THOUGHT I WAS SUPPOSED TO MAKE
PEACE BETWEEN HIM AND ADMIRAL NIMITZ. HE ASSURED ME THAT
HE AND NIMITZ ARE GREAT PALS, WHICH I THINK, AFTER TALKING
WITH NIMITZ AT PEARL HARBOR, IS ALMOST TRUE.

WHEN I BROUGHT UP DONOVAN'S OSS PEOPLE, A WALL CAME DOWN.
HE TELLS ME HE HAS NO INTENTION OF LETTING "DONOVAN GET HIS
CAMEL'S NOSE UNDER THE TENT" AND VOLUNTEERED THAT NIMITZ
FEELS THE SAME WAY. I ALSO SUSPECT THIS IS TRUE. I WILL KEEP
TRYING, OF COURSE, BOTH BECAUSE I CONSIDER MYSELF UNDER
ORDERS TO DO SO, AND BECAUSE I THINK THAT MACA IS WRONG AND
DONOVAN'S PEOPLE WOULD BE VERY USEFUL, BUT I DON'T THINK I
WILL BE SUCCESSFUL.

THE BEST INFORMATION HERE, WHICH I PRESUME YOU WILL ALSO
HAVE SEEN BY NOW, IS THAT THE JAPANESE WILL LAUNCH THEIR
ATTACK TOMORROW.

ADMIRAL GHORMLEY SENT TWO RADIOS (16 AND 17 OCTOBER) SAYING
HIS FORCES ARE "TOTALLY INADEQUATE" TO RESIST A MAJOR
JAPANESE ATTACK, AND MAKING WHAT SEEMS TO ME
UNREASONABLE DEMANDS ON AVAILABLE NAVAL AND AVIATION
RESOURCES. I DETECTED A CERTAIN LACK OF CONFIDENCE IN HIM ON
MACA'S PART. I HAVE NO OPINION, AND CERTAINLY WOULD MAKE NO
RECOMMENDATIONS VIS-À-VIS GHORMLEY IF I HAD ONE, BUT THOUGHT
I SHOULD PASS THIS ON.

A PROBLEM HERE, WHICH WILL CERTAINLY GROW, IS IN THE JUNIOR
(VERY JUNIOR) RANK OF LIEUTENANT HON SONG DO, THE ARMY
CRYPTOGRAPHER/ANALYST, WHOM A HORDE OF ARMY AND MARINE
COLONELS AND NAVY CAPTAINS, WHO AREN'T DOING ANYTHING

NEARLY SO IMPORTANT, THINK OF AS . . . A FIRST LIEUTENANT. IS
THERE ANYTHING YOU CAN DO TO HAVE THE ARMY PROMOTE HIM?
THE SAME IS TRUE, TO A SLIGHTLY LESSER DEGREE, OF LIEUTENANT
JOHN MOORE, BUT MOORE, AT LEAST (HE IS ON THE BOOKS AS MY
AIDE-DE-CAMP) CAN HIDE BEHIND MY SKIRTS. AS FAR AS ANYONE
BUT MACA AND WILLOUGHBY KNOW, HON IS JUST ONE MORE
CODE-MACHINE LIEUTENANT WORKING IN THE APTLY NAMED
DUNGEON IN MACA'S HEADQUARTERS BASEMENT.

FINALLY, MACA FIRMLY SUGGESTED THAT I DECORATE LIEUTENANT
JOE HOWARD AND SERGEANT STEVEN KOFFLER, WHOM WE TOOK OFF
BUKA. GOD KNOWS, THEY DESERVE A MEDAL FOR WHAT THEY DID . . .
THEY MET ME AT THE AIRPLANE, AND THEY LOOK LIKE THOSE
PHOTOGRAPHS IN LIFE MAGAZINE OF STARVING RUSSIAN PRISONERS
ON THE EASTERN FRONT . . . BUT I DON'T KNOW HOW TO GO ABOUT
THIS. PLEASE ADVISE.

MORE SOON.

BEST REGARDS,

FLEMING PICKERING, BRIGADIER GENERAL, USMCR

T O P   S E C R E T

Haughton watched Rickabee's face as he very carefully read the radio-teletype message and then handed it to Banning.

Technically, Haughton thought, not unpleasantly, but simply recognizing the facts, *giving that to Banning to read is a security violation. No matter what kind of a security clearance Banning has, that message, both of these messages, are Eyes Only SECNAV, and that means just what it says. If the Secretary wants to give them to someone else, that's his business. The fact that the Secretary told me to show both radios to Rickabee doesn't mean that Rickabee has any authority to show them to anyone else, even someone like Banning.*

On the other hand, (a) if the Secretary knew about it, he wouldn't say a word. He trusts Rickabee's judgment. (b) Banning isn't just an ordinary Marine Corps major with an ordinary TOP SECRET security clearance. He's cleared for MAGIC, and if an officer is on the MAGIC list, I can't think of any classified material to which he is not authorized access. And (c) after Banning's brilliant—and that's the only word that fits, brilliant—briefing of the President, the Secretary of the Navy, and Senator Fowler on the Guadalcanal situation yesterday, he is one fair-haired boy.

And then, while Rickabee was reading the second radio and Banning was absorbing the first, Haughton had another thought, a wild thought, only peripherally connected to the first:

There are three people in this little room with MAGIC clearances. In all of the world, counting even the cryptographic officers who make the decryptions, and the analysts, there are only forty-two people on that list, as of yesterday.

What is it they say? "A secret is compromised the instant two people know about it." That's probably true. And MAGIC is one hell of a secret. When you have a small, but growing, capability to read your enemy's most secret encrypted messages, the value to the war is literally beyond measure.

And to protect that secret as much as possible, you severely limit the number of people authorized access to it. Some people, obviously, have to be on it. The President; Admiral Leahy, the President's Chief of Staff; the Secretary, and his Army counterpart, the Secretary of War; Admiral Nimitz as CINCPAC; General MacArthur as Supreme Commander SWPOA; and the underlings— those who broke, and are breaking, the codes in Hawaii; the analysts; the cryptographic officers who, using a special code, encrypt the decrypted messages for transmission to Washington and Brisbane; the cryptographic officers and analysts here and in Brisbane; and a very few others—MacArthur's G-2 in Brisbane, Nimitz's Intelligence Officer in Pearl Harbor, and Captain David Haughton, Colonel F. L. Rickabee, and Major Edward F. Banning here. We three underlings have to be on the list because we can't do our jobs without knowing about it. And, of course, Brigadier General Fleming Pickering, for the same reason.

When I read—when was that, a month ago, two?—about the security arrangements for the MAGIC people in Hawaii, I thought it made sense not to permit them to leave CINCPAC without an armed escort. The Japanese might not know about MAGIC, but they almost certainly knew something highly classified was going on.

On one level, the idea of the Japanese kidnapping Naval officers in Hawaii to see what they knew seemed fantastic. But so did the idea of the Japanese launching an aerial attack on Pearl Harbor on 7 December. A lot of unthinkable things happens in war, and even more in Intelligence.

Nimitz was right to provide his MAGIC people with that kind of security. It just made sense. It also made sense to provide Pickering, over his objections, with a Marine bodyguard, an ex–St. Louis police detective. And the brass, of course, were routinely protected. The only people on the MAGIC list who are not protected are Rickabee, Banning, and me.

God, is that why Rickabee is carrying that gun?

Does Banning carry one?

"Banning, may I ask you a question?"

Banning looked up from the radio message.

"Certainly, Sir."

"Everybody else around here is armed to the teeth except you," Haughton said, making it a question.

Banning smiled, stood up, turned around, and hoisted the skirt of his tunic. A 1911A1 .45 Colt was in a skeleton holster in the small of his back.

"In maintaining the hoary traditions of The Corps, Captain," Banning said, as he sat down again. "We of Management Analysis are always prepared to repel boarders."

Haughton laughed, somewhat nervously.

My God, I'm right! The reason these two don't have an armed bodyguard with them is that they consider themselves competent to protect themselves. But the point is they do think there is a sufficient risk that going armed is necessary—even here in Washington.

Does that mean I should get myself a pistol? Christ, I've never been able to hit the broad side of a barn from ten feet with a .45!

Rickabee, who was not known for his genial personality or for his sense of humor, looked up from his radio and glared at both of them.

A moment later, he finished reading his radio and handed it to Banning. Banning handed him the first radio message, and Rickabee handed it to Haughton, who replaced it in the TOP SECRET folder.

Banning started to read the second radio from General Pickering:

```
T O P     S E C R E T


EYES ONLY — CAPTAIN DAVID HAUGHTON, USN
OFFICE OF THE SECRETARY OF THE NAVY


DUPLICATION FORBIDDEN
ORIGINAL TO BE DESTROYED AFTER ENCRYPTION AND TRANSMITTAL


FOR COLONEL F.L. RICKABEE
USMC OFFICE OF MANAGEMENT ANALYSIS


BRISBANE, AUSTRALIA
SATURDAY 17 OCTOBER 1942
```

DEAR FRITZ:

AT LUNCH WITH MACA YESTERDAY, HE JUSTIFIED HIS SNUBBING OF
DONOVAN'S PEOPLE HERE BY SAYING THAT HE HAS A GUERRILLA
OPERATION UP AND RUNNING IN THE PHILIPPINES.

AT COCKTAILS-BEFORE-DINNER EARLIER TONIGHT, I TRIED TO PUMP
GENERAL WILLOUGHBY ABOUT THIS, AND GOT A VERY COLD
SHOULDER; HE MADE IT PLAIN THAT ANY GUERRILLA ACTIVITY GOING
ON THERE IS INSIGNIFICANT. AFTER DINNER, I GOT WITH LT COL
PHILIP DEPRESS—HE IS THE OFFICER COURIER YOU BROUGHT TO
WALTER REED HOSPITAL TO SEE ME WHEN HE HAD A LETTER FROM
MACA FOR ME. HE'S A HELL OF A SOLDIER WHO SOMEHOW GOT OUT OF
THE PHILIPPINES BEFORE THEY FELL.

AFTER FEEDING HIM A LOT OF LIQUOR, I GOT OUT OF HIM THIS
VERSION: AN ARMY RESERVE CAPTAIN NAMED WENDELL FERTIG
REFUSED TO SURRENDER AND WENT INTO THE HILLS OF MINDANAO
WHERE HE GATHERED AROUND HIM A GROUP OF OTHERS, INCLUDING
A NUMBER OF MARINES FROM THE 4TH MARINES WHO ESCAPED FROM
LUZON AND CORREGIDOR, AND STARTED TO SET UP A GUERRILLA
OPERATION.

HE HAS PROMOTED HIMSELF TO BRIGADIER GENERAL, AND APPOINTED
HIMSELF "COMMANDING GENERAL, US FORCES IN THE PHILIPPINES." I
UNDERSTAND (AND SO DOES PHIL DEPRESS) WHY HE DID THIS. THE
FILIPINOS WOULD PAY ABSOLUTELY NO ATTENTION TO A LOWLY
CAPTAIN. THIS HAS, OF COURSE, ENRAGED THE RANK-CONSCIOUS
PALACE GUARD HERE AT THE PALACE. BUT FROM WHAT DEPRESS
TELLS ME, FERTIG HAS A LOT OF POTENTIAL.

SEE WHAT YOU CAN FIND OUT, AND ADVISE ME. AND TELL ME IF I'M
WRONG IN THINKING THAT IF THERE ARE MARINES WITH FERTIG,
THEN IT BECOMES OUR BUSINESS.

FINALLY, WITH ME HERE, MOORE, WHO IS ON THE BOOKS AS MY
AIDE-DE-CAMP, IS GOING TO RAISE QUESTIONS IF HE SPENDS MOST OF
HIS TIME, AS HE HAS TO, IN THE DUNGEON, INSTEAD OF HOLDING
DOORS FOR ME AND SERVING MY CANAPÉS. IS THERE SOME WAY WE
CAN GET SERGEANT HART A COMMISSION? HE IS, IN FAITHFUL
OBEDIENCE TO WHAT I'M SURE ARE YOUR ORDERS, NEVER MORE THAN
FIFTY FEET AWAY FROM ME ANYWAY.

I WOULD APPRECIATE IT IF YOU WOULD CALL MY WIFE, AND TELL HER
THAT I AM SAFE ON THE BRIDGE AND CANAPÉ CIRCUIT IN WATER LILY
COTTAGE IN BEAUTIFUL BRISBANE ON THE SEA.

REGARDS,

FLEMING PICKERING, BRIGADIER GENERAL, USMCR

T O P   S E C R E T

When he finished reading the radio, Banning handed it back to Rickabee, who then handed it to Haughton, who replaced it in the TOP SECRET folder and then replaced the folder in his briefcase.

"The General, I surmise, is in good spirits," Banning said. "What's this business about guerrillas in the Philippines? I never heard anything about that before."

"That's one of the reasons I came over here, to discuss that with you," Haughton said. "On 12 October, the Navy station at Mare Island answered a station that was trying to get a response from Australia. They sent a message—here it is," he interrupted himself and handed Rickabee several sheets of paper stapled together—"encrypted on an obsolete crypto device. The Chief at Mare Island borrowed a crypto device from the Army, and came up with . . . what does it say? *'Here's the Hot Poop From The Hot Yanks, et cetera, Brigadier General Fertig.'* "

"Captain Fertig, according to Willoughby, in Pickering's radio," Banning said.

"How do we know this Fertig is genuine?" Rickabee asked, adding, "How did you come by this information, David?"

Haughton expected the question, but it still embarrassed him.

"The Chief Radioman at Mare Island is a crony of my Chief," he said. "He figured my Chief could check out Brigadier General Fertig. I didn't—if I have to say so—know anything about this."

"He who getteth between two Chiefs will getteth himself run over," Banning said solemnly.

The remark produced a rare smile on Rickabee's face, Haughton noticed.

"My Chief went to the Army and came up with a reserve officer by that name—but not a general—missing and presumed captured in the Philippines. And the vital statistics of his wife. The Mare Island Chief used the vitals to establish they were talking to Fertig."

"Why couldn't they get in touch with MacArthur in Australia?" Rickabee asked thoughtfully.

"At about this time," Haughton said, "my Chief decided I could be told what had happened so far. And I ordered Mare Island to contact SWPOA and relay to them all traffic from Fertig. And I had a message sent to SWPOA confirming that, and that it was our judgment that Fertig was Fertig. SWPOA is now communicating directly with Fertig."

"Repeat:" Rickabee said. "Why couldn't they get in touch with MacArthur in Australia?"

"Because El Supremo, or his minions," Banning said, somewhat nastily, "didn't want to hear from a guerrilla leader in the Philippines after El Supremo had gone on record saying that guerrilla operations in the Philippines 'are impossible at this time,' end quote."

"I think we have to proceed on that same cynical assumption," Haughton said.

"So how are we involved?"

"The Secretary is right now with the President," Haughton said. "He intends to tell him about Fertig. He thinks it's good news—and God knows he needs some—that there is a guerrilla operation. Admiral Leahy will be at the meeting. The Secretary feels that the President will ask Leahy what to do about Fertig, and that Leahy will suggest that you deal with it. At least assess the situation."

Rickabee nodded, and then pointed his finger at Banning.

"Aye, aye, Sir," Banning said, acknowledging that the responsibility had just been delegated.

He wondered how that was going to affect the week off he had been promised. A clear image of Carolyn fastening her brassiere came into his mind.

"After you get back from your week off," Rickabee said.

Christ, is he reading my mind?

"Aye, aye, Sir."

VI

"Douglas," the President of the United States said, "has stated that guerrilla operations in the Philippines are impossible at this time."

"And we all know that Douglas MacArthur is incapable of being wrong, don't we?" the Hon. Frank Knox said, taking his pince-nez off and starting to polish the lenses.

Roosevelt looked up from his wheelchair at the dignified, stocky, well-dressed Secretary of the Navy and smiled.

"Admiral?" the President asked.

"We really know nothing, Mr. President, except that this man Fertig has chosen not to surrender, and that he has a radio," Admiral William D. Leahy said. Leahy, a tall, lanky, sad-faced man, was the former Chief of Naval Operations, and was now serving as Roosevelt's Chief of Staff.

He looked between Knox and the President, who waited for him to continue.

"If we plan to suggest to General MacArthur that he is wrong, I would like to have more facts than we now have," Leahy went on. "I would therefore suggest, Mr. President, that we investigate further. Specifically, that Rickabee's people see what they can find out about Fertig's activities, and what the potential is."

"I suggest the Admiral is correct, Mr. President," Knox said.

"Have you brought this matter to Admiral Nimitz's attention, Mr. Secretary?"

Knox shook his head, no.

"The relationship between Nimitz and MacArthur is at the moment amicable," Leahy said. "I would suggest, Mr. Secretary, if the President believes we should go ahead with this—"

"I think we have a moral obligation here," the President interrupted. "In the absence of an overriding consideration to the contrary, we should go ahead, at least to the point of finding out more about this chap Fertig."

"Yes, Sir," Admiral Leahy said.

"This sort of thing, guerrilla warfare, operating behind the enemy lines, is really in Bill Donovan's basket of eggs," the President said. "But that presumes Douglas's willingness to talk to Donovan's man, doesn't it?"

"Unfortunately," Knox said.

"After Pickering's thoughts on that subject, it occurs to me that if I ordered him to take Donovan's people, the first place Douglas would drag his feet would be in this case."

Knox grunted.

"The result would be a disgruntled Douglas MacArthur, with this fellow Fertig dangling in the breeze? Is that your assessment?"

Leahy nodded agreement, and Knox repeated, "Unfortunately."

"Is there any way around this? To avoid confronting MacArthur?"

Leahy nodded. "I would suggest that it might be best if I sent Admiral Nimitz a Special Channel Personal advising him of what we know so far, and informing him that we are looking further into the matter, and that any support he may be asked to supply be provided with the utmost discretion."

"Don't anger Douglas by not telling Douglas, in other words?" the President asked.

"Yes, Sir."

"General Pickering is with Douglas," the President said thoughtfully.

"I don't think General Pickering has to know that I have communicated with Admiral Nimitz," Leahy said. "If he doesn't know . . ."

"Then it wouldn't slip out in conversation, would it?" the President said approvingly. "Frank, see what information you can develop, as quickly as possible, without annoying Douglas."

"Yes, Mr. President."

"Going off at somewhat of a tangent, Frank," the President said. "I suppose I thought of this because Pickering has a MAGIC clearance. . . ."

"Yes, Mr. President?"

"I have been informed by Churchill that he plans to propose the establishment of a unified China-Burma-India command with Lord Louis Mountbatten named as its supreme commander."

"Yes, Sir?"

"I'm not going to give it to him easily, but in the end, I will have to go along. When that happens, despite the reservations that Admiral Leahy has expressed both eloquently and in great detail—I won't need to hear them again from you, Frank—we are going to have to bring the British in on MAGIC. That means we will have to send to India a liaison officer with a MAGIC clearance, and the necessary communications people."

"General Pickering?" Knox wondered aloud.

"I think we should send Pickering for a visit, when the time comes, yes. But I was thinking of an officer to serve as the MAGIC man on Mountbatten's staff. Think about that, would you? Someone who would not be dazzled by proximity to royal blood?"

Banning, Knox thought immediately. But he said nothing beyond "Yes, Mr. President."

"Thank you for coming to see me, Frank. I know what a brutal schedule you have."

"My privilege, Mr. President," Knox said, aware that he had just been dismissed.

"Keep us up to date on this Fertig fellow, will you, Frank?" the President called as Knox reached the door.

"Yes, Mr. President."

[TWO]

```
T O P    S E C R E T

THE SECRETARY OF THE NAVY
WASHINGTON

VIA SPECIAL CHANNEL
DUPLICATION FORBIDDEN
ORIGINAL TO BE DESTROYED AFTER ENCRYPTION AND TRANSMITTAL

SUPREME COMMANDER SWPOA
EYES ONLY BRIG GEN F.W. PICKERING, USMCR
1515 17 OCTOBER 1942

FOLLOWING PERSONAL FROM SECNAV FOR BRIG GEN PICKERING

DEAR FLEMING:

I JUST CAME FROM A MEETING WITH ADMIRAL LEAHY IN WHICH THE
SUBJECT OF FERTIG AND GUERRILLA RESISTANCE IN THE PHILIPPINES
CAME UP.

LEAHY BELIEVES THAT THE MATTER SHOULD BE INVESTIGATED
FURTHER AND SPECIFICALLY BY OFFICE OF MANAGEMENT ANALYSIS,
AND FURTHER THAT THE FEWER PEOPLE WHO KNOW ABOUT THIS THE
BETTER.
```

HAUGHTON IS WORKING WITH RICKABEE ON THIS AND I WILL KEEP
YOU ADVISED.

BOTH THE PRESIDENT AND LEAHY EXPRESSED THEIR CONCERN
VIS-A-VIS MACARTHUR'S RELATIONSHIP OR LACK OF RELATIONSHIP
WITH DONOVAN'S PEOPLE. THE POINT WAS MADE AND I THINK FAIRLY
THAT THIS (GUERRILLA) SORT OF THING BELONGS IN DONOVAN'S
BASKET.

BEST PERSONAL REGARDS

FRANK

END PERSONAL SECNAV TO BRIG GEN PICKERING

HAUGHTON CAPT USN ADMIN ASST TO SECNAV

T O P   S E C R E T

[THREE]
Office of the Assistant Chief of Staff G-1
Headquarters, United States Marine Corps
Eighth and "I" Streets, NW
Washington, D.C.
0825 Hours 18 October 1942

Colonel David M. Wilson, USMC, Deputy Assistant Chief of Staff G-1 for
Officer Personnel, looked up from his desk to see Master Gunner James L.
Hardee, USMC, standing there with paper in his hands and a smile on his face.
(Master gunner, a rank between enlisted and commissioned status, is equiva-
lent to a U.S. Army warrant officer.)

"I gather there is something in your hand that requires my immediate attention, Mister Hardee?"

"I thought the Colonel would probably be interested in this application for
transfer, Sir," Hardee said.

Wilson put out his hand and Hardee handed him the typewritten letter.

UNITED STATES MARINE CORPS
PUBLIC RELATIONS OFFICE
UNITED STATES POST OFFICE
LOS ANGELES, CALIFORNIA

16 October 1942

FROM: Macklin, Robert B., First Lieutenant USMC

TO: Headquarters USMC
Washington, D.C.
ATTN: MCPER-OP341-B

SUBJECT: Request For Consideration For Special Assignment

1. Reference is made to Memorandum, Headquarters, USMC dated 12 Sept 1942, Subject, "Solicitation of officer volunteers for Special Assignment To Intelligence Duties."

2. The undersigned wishes to volunteer for such duty. The following information is furnished:

(a) The undersigned, a graduate of the U.S. Naval Academy, is an officer of the regular establishment of the Marine Corps, presently on detached service with the USMC Public Relations Office, Los Angeles, Cal.

(b) The undersigned is performing supervisory duties in connection with War Bond Tour II. Previously, the undersigned was a participant (e.g., one of the "Guadalcanal Veterans") in War Bond Tour I.

(c) Prior to this assignment, the undersigned was assigned to the detachment of patients, U.S. Army General Hospital, Fourth Melbourne, Australia, while recovering from wounds suffered in action with the 2nd Parachute Battalion, USMC, on Gavutu during the invasion of Guadalcanal.

(d) Previous to the Gavutu invasion, the undersigned, a qualified parachutist with sixteen (16) parachute jumps, was on the staff of the USMC Parachute School, Lakehurst, N.J.

(e) Prior to the war, the undersigned served with the 4th Marines in Shanghai (and elsewhere in China) in a variety of assignments, including a number that involved intelligence gathering and evaluation.

(f) The undersigned has almost entirely recovered from the wounds suffered during the Guadalcanal campaign, and believes that he could make a greater contribution to the Marine Corps in a Special Intelligence assignment than he can in his presently assigned duties.

Robert B. Macklin

ROBERT B. MACKLIN
First Lieutenant, USMC

Colonel Wilson looked up at Gunner Hardee, then shook his head and smiled in mixed amazement and disgust.

"What the hell are these 'special intelligence' duties he's volunteering for?" Wilson asked.

"We've been levied for two hundred 'suitable' officers for the OSS," Hardee said. "There was a memorandum sent out looking for volunteers."

"Reading this, you might get the idea this sonofabitch is just what the OSS is looking for," Wilson said. "A wounded hero of the Guadalcanal campaign, a parachutist, and even 'intelligence-gathering and evaluation duties in China.' "

Normally full colonels do not offer derogatory remarks about lieutenants in the hearing of master gunners; but Colonel Wilson and Gunner Hardee went back a long ways together in The Corps, and both were personally familiar with the career of First Lieutenant Robert B. Macklin.

Macklin first came to their attention several weeks before, when the Chief of Public Relations asked for his permanent assignment to public relations. The Chief was delighted with Macklin's performance on War Bond Tour One—he was a tall, handsome man, and a fine public speaker, just what Public Relations was looking for.

After reading his records, Colonel Wilson was happy to accede to the request, agreeing at that time with Gunner Hardee that it was probably the one place the bastard couldn't do The Corps much harm.

Lieutenant Macklin, as he stated in his letter, did indeed serve with the 4th Marines in Shanghai before the war. His service earned him a really devastating efficiency report.

Then Captain Edward J. Banning, USMC, wrote that Lieutenant Macklin was "prone to submit official reports that both omitted pertinent facts that might tend to reflect adversely upon himself and to present other material clearly designed to magnify his own contributions to the accomplishment of an assigned mission."

In other words, he was a liar.

Even worse, his 4th Marines efficiency report went on to say that Lieutenant Macklin "could not be honestly recommended for the command of a company or larger tactical unit."

The reviewing officer—Lewis B. "Chesty" Puller, then a major, now a lieutenant colonel on Guadalcanal—concurred in the evaluation of Lieutenant Macklin. Colonel Wilson had served several times with Chesty Puller and held him in the highest possible regard.

Before the war, shortly after being labeled a liar on his efficiency report, an officer would be asked for his resignation. But that was before the war, not now. Macklin's service record showed that when he came home from Shanghai, The Corps sent him to Quantico, as a training officer at the Officer Candidate School. He got out of that by volunteering to become a parachutist.

Macklin invaded Gavutu with the parachutists, as a supernumerary. Which meant that he was a spare officer, who would be given a job only after an officer commanding a platoon, or something else, was killed or wounded.

As his letter stated, Macklin was in the Army's Fourth General Hospital in Melbourne, Australia, recovering from his wounds, when he was sent to the States to participate as a wounded hero in the first War Bond Tour.

Colonel Wilson got the whole story of Macklin's valorous service at Gavutu from someone he'd known years before, with the 4th Marines in Shanghai, Major Jake Dillon. (In those days, Dillon had been a sergeant.)

At the start of the war, in a move which at the time did not have Colonel Wilson's full and wholehearted approval, the Assistant Commandant of The Marine Corps arranged to have Dillon commissioned as a major, for duty with Public Affairs. The Assistant Commandant's reasoning was that The Corps was going to need some good publicity, and that the way to do that was to get a professional, such as the Vice President, Publicity, of Magnum Studios, Hollywood, California, who was paid more money than the Commandant—for that matter, more than the President of the United States. *And wasn't it fortuitous that he'd been a China Marine, and Once A Marine, Always A Marine, was willing to come back into The Corps?*

Colonel Wilson was now willing to admit that Major Jake Dillon did not turn out to be the unmitigated disaster he'd expected. For instance, Dillon led a crew of photographers and writers in the first wave of the invasion of Tulagi, and there was no question they did their job well.

Dillon was responsible for Lieutenant Macklin being sent home from Australia for the War Bond Tour.

"Most of the heroes I saw over there didn't look like Tyrone Power," Dillon said. "That bastard does, so I sent him on the tour."

Dillon told Colonel Wilson that Macklin had managed to get himself shot in the calf and face without ever reaching the beach, and had to be pried loose from the piling he was clinging to, screaming for a corpsman, while the fighting was going on.

"You've got to admire his gall," Gunner Hardee said. "I would have thought he'd be happy to stay in Public Relations."

"I think the sonofabitch really thinks he can salvage his career," Wilson said. "Tell me what would happen next if I endorsed this application favorably."

"Yeah, that would get him out of The Corps, wouldn't it?" Hardee said appreciatively. "But I don't think it would work. The first thing we have to do is get an FBI check on him, what they call a Full Background Investigation. Then we send that and his service record over to the OSS. If they want him, they tell us; and we cut his orders."

"What do you think would happen if his service record turned up missing? I mean, those things happen from time to time, don't they? What if we just got this background investigation on him . . . he probably didn't do anything wrong before he went to Annapolis . . . and his letter of application . . . with service record to follow when available?"

"I think the OSS might be very interested in a Marine parachutist who got himself shot heroically storming the beach on Gavutu."

"And what will happen six months from now when his service record shows up and they see his efficiency report?"

"They might send him back," Hardee said. "But by then, maybe they'll have parachuted him into France or something."

"The true sign of an intelligent man, Hardee, is how much he thinks like you do. Thank you for bringing this valiant officer's offer to volunteer to my personal attention. And have one of the clerks type up a favorable endorsement."

"Aye, aye, Sir."

[FOUR]
Temporary Building T-2032
The Mall, Washington, D.C.
1125 Hours 19 October 1942

There were four telephones on the desk behind the pierced-steel planking wall on the ground floor of Building T-2032. When he heard the ring, Sergeant John V. Casey, USMC, who had the duty, reached out for the nearest one, a part of his brain telling him the ring sounded a little funny.

He got a dial tone, murmured "Shit!", dropped the first phone in its cradle, and quickly grabbed one of the others. And got another dial tone. He dropped that phone in its cradle and grabbed the third. Another dial tone.

"Shit," he repeated, now more amused than annoyed, and reached for the fourth telephone, which was pushed far out of the way. This was the one listed in the official and public telephone books for the Office of Management Analysis. It rarely rang. Hardly anyone in the Marine Corps—for that matter, hardly anyone at all—had ever heard of the Office of Management Analysis. Those people who knew what the Office of Management Analysis was really doing and had business with it had one or more of the unlisted numbers.

Thinking that this call was almost certainly a wrong number, or was from some feather merchant raising money for the Red Cross or some other worthy purpose, Sergeant Casey nevertheless answered the phone courteously and in the prescribed manner.

"Management Analysis, Sergeant Casey speaking, Sir."

"I have a collect call for anyone," an operator's somewhat nasal voice announced, "from Lieutenant McCoy in Kansas City. Will you accept the charges?"

The question gave Sergeant Casey pause. He had no doubt that Lieutenant McCoy was Management Analysis's Lieutenant McCoy; but the last he'd heard, McCoy was somewhere in the Pacific, so what was this Kansas City business? And the immediate problem was that he was calling collect. So far as Sergeant Casey could recall, no one had ever called collect before; it might not be authorized.

What the hell, he decided. *I'll say yes, and let McCoy straighten it out with the officers if he's not supposed to call collect.*

"We'll accept charges, operator."

"Go ahead, please," the operator said.

"Who's this?"

"Sergeant Casey, Sir."

"Can you get Major Banning on the line?"

"He's not here."

"What about Captain Sessions?"

"Hold one, Lieutenant," Casey said, and considered that problem. The Management Analysis line was not tied in with any of the other telephones. He could not transfer the call by pushing a button. He solved that problem by calling one of the other lines, which was immediately picked up upstairs.

"Liberty 7-2033," a voice he recognized as belonging to Gunnery Sergeant Wentzel said. What Sergeant Casey thought of as "the real phones" were answered by stating the number. That way, if the incoming call was a misdial, no information about who the misdialer had really reached got out.

"Gunny, Sergeant Casey. Is Captain Sessions around?"

"What do you want with him?"

"I got a collect call for him from Lieutenant McCoy on the Management Analysis line."

"I don't think you're supposed to accept collect calls on that line."

"I already did."

"He's here, put it through."

"This number don't switch."

"Oh, shit!" Gunny Wentzel said, and the line went dead.

Almost immediately thereafter, Casey heard someone rushing down the stairs, obviously taking them two and three at a time. A tall, lithely muscular, not quite handsome officer in his early thirties came through the door. He was in his shirtsleeves.

Casey handed him the telephone.

"Ken? What did you do, forget the number? Where are you?"

"In Kansas City. Fuel stop. We're on a B-25. They're going to drop us off at Anacostia—"

"Who's we?"

"Dillon and me," McCoy went on. "The pilot said we should be there in about four hours."

"I'll meet you," Sessions said.

"That's not why I called," McCoy said. "I need a favor."

"Name it."

"Could you call somebody for me?"

"Ernie? You mean you haven't called her?"

Ernie was Miss Ernestine Sage, whom Sessions—and his wife—knew and liked very much. She was not simply an attractive, charming, well-educated young woman, but she had the courage of her convictions: Specifically, she had decided, despite the enormous gulf in background between them, that Ken McCoy was the man in her life, and if that meant publicly living in sin with him because he wouldn't marry her, then so be it.

As for McCoy, though he was far from hostile to marriage, or especially to marrying Ernie Sage, he had nevertheless decided—not without reason, Sessions thought, considering what he had done so far in the war, and what the future almost certainly held for him—that the odds against his surviving the war unscathed or alive were so overwhelming that marriage, not to mention the siring of children, would be gross injustice to a bride and potential mother.

"I didn't know when I could get east until now," McCoy said, somewhat lamely. "And now I can't get her on the phone."

"That's kind of you, Killer," Sessions said sarcastically. "I'm sure she was mildly interested in whether or not you're still alive."

"Tell her I tried to call her, and that I'll try again when I get to Washington."

"Anything else?"

"I'll need someplace to stay. Would you get me a BOQ?" (*Bachelor Officers' Quarters*.)

"OK. Anything else?"

"I've got an envelope for the Colonel from the General."

"I'll take it at the airport and see that he gets it. You have a tail number on the aircraft?"

"Two dash forty-three eighty-nine. It's an Air Corps B-25 out of Los Angeles."

"I'll be there," Sessions said. "Welcome home, Kil . . . Ken."

"Thank you," McCoy said, and the phone went dead in Sessions's ear. Sessions put the handset back in its cradle.

"Thank you," he said to the sergeant.

"That was Lieutenant McCoy, and he's back already?"

"Maybe this time they'll let him stay a little longer," Sessions said.

"I guess everything went all right over there?"

"What do you know about 'everything,' Sergeant?" Sessions said, not entirely pleasantly.

"You hear things, Sir."

"You're not supposed to be listening," Sessions said. "But yes. Everything went well."

"Good," Sergeant Casey said.

"You didn't get that from me," Sessions said.

"Get what from you, Sir?"

"You can be replaced, Sergeant. By a woman."

"Sir?"

"They're talking about having lady Marines. You haven't heard?"

"No shit?"

"Scout's honor," Sessions said, and held up his hand, three fingers extended, as a Boy Scout does when giving his word of honor.

"Women in The Corps?"

"Women in The Corps," Sessions said firmly.

"Jesus Christ!"

"My sentiments exactly, Sergeant," Sessions said.

Then he turned and went up the stairs to report to Colonel Rickabee that Lieutenant McCoy would be at the Anacostia Naval Air Station in approximately four hours.

"J. Walter Thompson. Good afternoon."

"Miss Ernestine Sage, please."

"Miss Sage's office."

"Miss Sage, please."

"May I ask who's calling?"

"Captain Edward Sessions."

"Oh, my!" the woman's voice said. "Captain, she's in a meeting."

"Could you ask her to call me in Washington when she's free, please? She has the number."

"Just a moment, please," Sessions heard her say, and then faintly, as if she had covered the microphone with her hand and was speaking into an intercom system: "Miss Sage, Captain Sessions is on the line. Can you take the call?"

"Ed?" Ernie Sage's voice came over the line. "I was about to call you."

"Why?"

"Why do you think? I haven't heard from you-know-who."

"*I've* heard from you-know-who. Just now. He'll be in Washington in four hours."

"Is he all right?"

"Sounded fine."

"The bastard called you and not me."

"He said he tried."

"Where in Washington is he going to be in four hours?"

"He asked me to get him a BOQ."

"Damn him!"

"Where would you like him to be in four hours?"

"You know where."

"Your wish, Fair Lady, is my command. Have you got enough time?"

"I can catch the noon Congressional Limited if I run from here to Pennsylvania Station. Thank you, Ed."

[FIVE]
The Foster Lafayette Hotel
Washington, D.C.
1625 Hours 19 October 1942

"What are we doing here?" Lieutenant Kenneth R. McCoy, USMCR, asked, looking out the rain-streaked windows of the Marine-green Ford as it pulled up last in a long line of cars before the marquee of the hotel.

McCoy's uniform was rain-soaked, and he needed a shave.

"Obeying orders," Captain Sessions said. "I know that's hard for you, but it's a cold cruel world, Killer."

"I asked you not to call me that," McCoy said. His eyes grew cold.

When his eyes get cold, Sessions thought, *he doesn't look twenty-two years old; he looks like Rickabee.*

"Sorry," Sessions said. "As I was saying, Lieutenant, we are obeying orders. General Pickering's orders to Colonel Rickabee, 'there's no point in having my apartment sitting empty. Put people in it while I'm gone,' or words to that effect. Colonel Rickabee's orders to me. 'Put McCoy in the General's apartment,' or words to that effect. And my orders to you, Lieutenant: 'Get out. Go In. Have a shave and a shower. Get your uniform pressed. The Colonel wants to see you at 0800 tomorrow.' Any questions, Mister McCoy?''

"The Colonel said to put me in there?'' McCoy asked doubtfully.

"I am a Marine officer and a gentleman,'' Sessions replied. "You are not doubting my veracity, are you?''

"0800?'' McCoy asked.

"If there's a change, I'll call you. Otherwise there will be a car here at 0730.''

"OK. Thanks, Ed. For meeting me, and for . . . Jesus, I didn't ask. Did you get through to Ernie?''

"I would suggest you call her,'' Sessions said. "I can't imagine why, but she seemed a trifle miffed that you called me and not her.''

"I'll call her,'' McCoy said, and started to open the door.

"You need some help with your bag, Lieutenant?'' the driver asked.

"No. Stay there. There's no sense in you getting soaked, too,'' McCoy said. He turned to Sessions. "Say hello to Jeanne. How's the baby?''

"You will see for yourself when you come to dinner. Get a bath, a drink, and go to bed. You look beat.''

"I am,'' McCoy said, opened the door, and ran toward the hotel entrance, carrying a battered canvas suitcase.

A doorman in an ornate uniform was somewhat frantically trying to get people in and out of the line of cars, but he stopped what he was doing when he saw the Marine lieutenant, carrying a bag, running toward the door.

"May I help you, Lieutenant?'' he asked, discreetly blocking McCoy's passage. It was as much an act of kindness as a manifestation of snobbery. Full colonels could not afford the prices at the Foster Lafayette. It was his intention to ask if he had a reservation—he was sure he didn't—and then regretfully announce there were no rooms.

"I can manage, thank you.''

"Have you a reservation, Sir?''

"Oh, do I ever,'' McCoy said, dodged around him, and continued toward the revolving door.

The doorman started after him, and then caught a signal from one of the bellmen. He interpreted it to mean, *Let him go.*

He stopped his pursuit and went to the bellman.

"That's Lieutenant McCoy,'' the bellman said. "He stays here sometimes. In 802.''

The doorman's eyebrows rose in question.

Suite 802 was the five-room apartment overlooking the White House, reserved for the duration of the war for Brigadier General Fleming Pickering, USMCR.

"He works for General Pickering," the bellman said. "And he's Lieutenant Pickering's best friend."

"*Lieutenant* Pickering?" the doorman asked.

"The only son, and the only grandson," the bellman said. "The heir apparent. Nice guy. Worked bells here one summer. Marine pilot. Just got back from Guadalcanal."

"The next time, I'll know," the doorman said. "Somebody should have said something."

"Welcome to Foster Hotels," the bellman said. "We hope your stay with us will be a joy."

The doorman chuckled and went back to helping people in and out of taxis and automobiles.

Lieutenant McCoy dropped his bag beside one of the marble pillars in the lobby and stepped up to the line waiting for attention at the desk.

A young woman in a calf-length silver fox coat, with matching hat atop her pageboy haircut, rose from one of the chairs in the lobby and walked toward him. She stood beside him. When it became evident that he was oblivious to her presence, she touched his arm. With a look of annoyance, he turned to face her.

"Hi, Marine!" she said. "Looking for a good time?"

A well-dressed, middle-aged woman in the line ahead of McCoy snapped her head back to look, in time to see the young woman part her silver fox coat with both hands, revealing a red T-shirt with the legend MARINES lettered in gold across her bosom.

"Jesus!" Lieutenant McCoy said.

"I'm just fine, thank you for asking. And how are you?"

"Sessions," McCoy said, having decided how Ernestine Sage happened to be waiting for him.

"Good old Ed, whom you *did* call," Ernie Sage said.

"I tried," McCoy said.

Ernestine Sage held up two hotel keys.

"I don't know if I should give you your choice of these, or throw them at you," she said.

"What are they?"

"Daddy's place, and Pick's father's," she said. "Ken, if you don't put your arms around me right now, I *will* throw them at you."

Instead, he reached out his hand and lightly touched her cheek with the balls of his fingers.

"Jesus Christ, I'm glad to see you!" he said, very softly.

"You bastard, I didn't know if you were alive or dead," she said, and threw herself into his arms. "My God, I love you so much!"

After a moment, as he gently stroked the back of her head, he said, his voice husky with emotion, "Me, too, baby."

Then, their arms still around each other, they walked to where he had dropped his bag by the marble pillar. He picked it up and they walked across the lobby to the bank of elevators.

[SIX]
The Bislig-Mati Highway (Route 7)
Davao Oriental Province
Mindanao, Commonwealth of the Philippines
0705 Hours 20 October 1942

The Intelligence Section of Headquarters, United States Forces in the Philippines had developed, through the interrogation of indigenous personnel, certain information concerning enemy activity. Specifically, that each Tuesday morning a convoy of Japanese army vehicles, usually two one-and-one-half-ton trucks, plus a staff car and a pickup truck, departed the major Japanese base at Bislig, on Bislig Bay, on the Philippine Sea for Boston, on Cateel Bay, Baganga, and Caraga.

According to the best cartographic data available (the 1939 edition of *Roads of Mindanao For Automobile Touring,* published by the Shell Oil Company), it was approximately 125 miles from Bislig to Caraga. The road was described by Shell as "partially improved"; and automobile tourists were cautioned that the roads were slippery when wet, and that caution should be observed to avoid stone damage to windshields when following other vehicles.

Indigenous personnel reported that the trucks were laden with various supplies, including gasoline, kerosene, and rations for the small detachments the Japanese had stationed at Boston, Baganga, and Caraga. Each truck was manned by a driver, an assistant driver, and a soldier who rode in the back. The staff car contained a driver, a sergeant, and an officer. And the pickup truck carried a driver, an assistant driver, and two to four soldiers riding in its bed.

This information was personally verified by the G-2, Captain James B. Weston, USMC, and his deputy, Lieutenant Percy Lewis Everly, who walked six hours down narrow paths from Headquarters, USFIP, to the road, watched the convoy pass, made a reconnaissance of the area to determine a suitable place for an attack, and then walked back to Headquarters, USFIP. The return journey, being mostly uphill, and because it was raining, took nine hours.

Among additional intelligence data gathered was that the staff car was a 1940 Buick Limited, seized by the Japanese, and that the pickup truck was a 1939 Dodge requisitioned by the U.S. Army in the opening days of the war and subsequently captured by the Japanese. The Dole Company insignia was still faintly visible beneath the olive-drab paint on the doors.

The information gathered was presented to the Commanding General, USFIP, and various aspects of the operation were discussed with him and officers of his staff.

General Fertig suggested that the Buick was probably the property of the Dole Company, which had provided such a vehicle for the general manager of their pineapple plantation.

"Interesting machine," General Fertig observed. "Not only was it clutchless—they called it 'Automatic Drive,' or something like that; all you had to do to make it go was step on the gas—but it had a little lever, which when flicked flashed lights on the top of the front fenders and in the middle of the trunk, showing the direction you intended to turn. I'm seriously considering getting one after the war."

The pros and cons of an operation against the Japanese convoy were discussed at some length.

Captain John B. Platten, USFIP (formerly Master Sergeant, 17th Philippine Scouts) G-4 (Supply) Officer, stated that while the trucks very likely would contain bags of rice, and possibly other transportable rations, from what he had heard from Captain Weston, the gasoline and kerosene were in fifty-five-gallon drums. Moving them any distance would be difficult. He also pointed out that even with strict fire discipline, any attack would dangerously diminish the very limited stocks of .30 and .45 caliber ammunition available to USFIP, and that it was probable that the Japanese soldiers guarding the convoy possessed limited (no more than, say, twenty or thirty rounds per man) of ammunition for their 6.5mm Arisaka rifles, much of which, it had to be anticipated, would be expended during the attack.

"We're liable to wind up with less ammo and weapons after we hit the convoy than we have now, even counting the weapons we take from the Japs. And the six-point-five is a lousy round, anyway."

"In other words, it is your studied opinion, Captain," General Fertig asked, "that, so to speak, an attack on this convoy would be wasted effort?"

"No, Sir," Captain Platten said quickly. "I mentioned these things so we could plan for them."

"Such as?"

"I suggest, Sir, that we form a group of people whose sole mission it will be to carry the portable supplies—the rice, canned goods, whatever—back here as soon as we lay our hands on them."

"And the nonportable? The gas and kerosene?"

"I suggest, Sir, that we gather together whatever we can lay our hands on that will hold liquid—canteens, water bottles, whatever—and have people to fill them and carry what they can back here with the rations. What we can't bring back, we bury in the jungle, and maybe go back for it later.''

''And the question of having less weaponry subsequent to the attack than we have now? How do we deal with that?''

''Permission to speak, Sir?''

''Certainly, Lieutenant Everly.''

''That Arisaka's not a Springfield, I'll grant you that. But it's more reliable than the Enfields—their extractor is always busting—which is what we mostly have. And the Filipinos can handle the recoil from an Arisaka better than they can from a .30-06. And we know we're not going to get any more .30-06 ammo anytime soon.''

That was a reference, which everyone understood but no one commented upon, to the silence of Headquarters, South West Pacific Ocean Area, in response to repeated USFIP radio requests for the supply of small arms and ammunition.

''Your point, Lieutenant Everly?'' General Fertig asked with either a hint of reproach or impatience in his voice.

''I think we have to kill the Japs before they have a chance to shoot off much of their ammo,'' Everly said. ''Even if that means shooting up the U.S. ammo we have.''

''And how do we do that?''

''First, we stop the convoy by shooting the driver of the Buick. Then, when the trucks are stopped, we kill the soldiers in the backs of them. And finally, we kill the truck drivers and whoever is left over. Every rifleman has a target, and we tell him he don't shoot anybody else until his target is down.''

''I was about to suggest we try to find marksmen,'' Fertig said, ''but I think if we put the question to the troops, every one of them will swear, as a matter of masculine pride, that he is Dead-Eye Dick.''

''Yes, Sir, they will,'' Everly agreed. ''The only thing to do is test them.''

''We don't have enough ammo,'' Captain Platten argued.

''We give them a two-shot test. A head-size target, a pineapple, at one hundred yards. If they can hit a pineapple at a hundred yards, they can hit a Jap in the chest at twenty.''

''Who will . . . take out . . . the driver of the staff car?'' General Fertig asked.

''I will,'' Everly said.

''I always got my three bucks,'' Captain Platten said. ''I'll take out the driver of the pickup. That way he won't be able to turn around and run.''

''Excuse me?'' General Fertig asked. ''What was that you said, 'three bucks'?''

''My Expert Rifleman's pay, Sir,'' Captain Platten said.

"We seem to be getting ahead of the primary question," General Fertig said. "Which is, should USFIP attack the Bislig-Caraga convoy?"

"I don't think we have any choice, Sir—" Captain Hedges began.

"Excuse me, Captain," Fertig interrupted him. "I believe the hoary tradition is that when the commanding officer solicits opinions, the junior of his officers respond first. That way, the juniors are not influenced by the opinions of their superiors."

"Excuse me, Sir," the Chief of Staff of USFIP said.

"Lieutenant Everly?"

"Yes, Sir. The sooner the better."

"Captain Platten?"

"Yes, Sir. Like Everly says."

"Captain Buchanan?"

"Yes, Sir."

"Captain Weston?"

"Yes, Sir."

"Captain Hedges?"

"Yes, Sir. I don't think we have any choice, General. We need the rice and whatever else is edible. We need both gas and kerosene. And the Jap weapons. And it will let the Japs know we're here!"

"Yeah," Everly said, with an intensity that surprised Weston.

Then Weston had a second thought: *Well, now I know where I stand in the pecking order. Ahead of Buchanan and behind Hedges.*

There seemed to be immediate confirmation of this.

"In that case, gentlemen," Fertig said. "We will attack the convoy at our earliest opportunity. Captain Weston will lead the attack."

"I'd like to lead it, Sir," Captain Hedges said.

"You're too valuable around here, Hedges," Fertig said.

"With respect, Sir," Captain Platten said. "I've got more experience in infantry. Nothing personal, Weston."

"I'll tell you this once, Platten," Fertig said. "I considered that, among other factors, before I made my decision. Never again question my orders."

Platten's face tightened, but after a moment he said, "Yes, Sir. Sorry, Sir."

As finally formed, the attack party consisted of the detail commander (Captain Weston) armed with a Thompson .45 caliber submachine gun; three officers (Captain Platten, and Lieutenants Everly and Alvarez) armed with Springfield 1903 .30-06 rifles; and nine enlisted men (two American) armed with Enfield Model 1917 .30-06 rifles.

They were accompanied by a twenty-five-man labor detail under Lieutenant Jose Lomero, late of the 17th Philippine Scouts. Lieutenant Lomero was armed with a .45 ACP Model 1911A1 pistol and an Enfield rifle. Two of his sergeants were armed with the Enfield. The balance of his detail was either unarmed or armed only with machetes. They carried with them the only shovel available to USFIP, and a motley collection of canteens, water bottles, and other vessels, including two small wooden barrels.

The attack party left Headquarters, USFIP, at first light Monday 19 October with the labor detail sandwiched between the armed men. After an eight-hour march through the mountainous jungle, a bivouac was established at what was estimated to be a mile from the ambush site.

A detail under Captain Weston, consisting of Lieutenant Everly, four armed members of the party, and three members of the labor detail, then proceeded to the attack site. Captain Platten remained at the bivouac site to supervise the construction of crude lean-tos and to establish a perimeter guard.

One hundred yards from the highway, the labor detail dug four holes, each large enough for a fifty-five-gallon drum. They next made arrangements to conceal their location by distributing the removed earth over a wide area and selecting foliage that would be placed over the holes once the barrels were placed in them.

Meanwhile, Lieutenant Everly selected both the precise location for the ambush and, insofar as possible, the positions on both sides of the highway from which the convoy would be brought under fire.

The reconnaissance party then returned to the bivouac area, leaving behind two unarmed members of the labor detail, who were wearing native clothing. Should there be any Japanese activity during the night, it was their mission to return to the bivouac area to warn the others.

They were not armed, because it was hoped that if they fell into Japanese hands, they could successfully argue that they were simple Filipino farmers, and because Lieutenant Everly suggested to Captain Weston that not arming the men would remove the temptation to attack the Japanese on their own.

At first light Tuesday 20 October, the bivouac was deestablished, with considerable care given to remove all signs of its overnight occupancy. The entire attack party then resumed the march toward the highway.

By 0645, contact was established with the two men who had been left behind. They reported no activity during the hours of darkness except the intrusion of three small wild pigs, which had been decapitated with a machete and then skinned and gutted.

In total, in Captain Weston's judgment, the pig carci weighed approximately sixty pounds. One of the men who had remained behind overnight was charged with carrying the rations to Headquarters, USFIP, together with a Situation Update for General Fertig.

The labor detail remained approximately two hundred yards from the highway, while the attack party moved into position under the direction of Lieutenant Everly.

At Lieutenant Everly's suggestion, Captain Weston took up a position on the seaward side of the road, near Lieutenant Everly. Captain Platten took up a position approximately one hundred yards away. The balance of the attacking force was placed on both sides of the road, and Lieutenant Everly cautioned each member of the party to remain concealed and not to open fire until they heard the sound of his rifle. They were then to remain aware of the location of USFIP personnel on the other side of the road, so there would be no casualties from USFIP fire. This emplacement was accomplished by 0655 hours.

At approximately 0702, they heard the sound of a truck grinding gears.

Captain Weston at this point retracted the operating rod of his Thompson .45 ACP Caliber submachine gun, took a final look down the road, and then dropped out of sight. Six or eight feet away, he could see Lieutenant Everly, almost entirely concealed by the trunk of a tree and some foliage. He was sitting with his legs crossed under him, leaning forward so that his left elbow touched his knee. All it would take to be in a Parris Island–perfect "Sitting Position for Riflemen" would be for him to put the butt of his Springfield in the small of his shoulder and lower his face to the stock.

A moment later, he did just this; and as Weston heard the sound of vehicles approaching, he saw the muzzle of Everly's Springfield tracking their movement.

And then, without warning, Everly fired. There was a flash of orange at the muzzle, and the sharp—surprisingly loud and frightening—sound of the weapon firing.

The noise was immediately followed by the sound of other weapons firing. Weston got to his feet as quickly as possible. The lead vehicle of the convoy was a four-door Buick convertible, top down, with spare tires mounted in front fender wells. He was surprised to see how close it was to him, and that it was apparently headed directly toward him, as if trying to run him over.

After what seemed like a very long time, the Buick stopped, as its front wheels rolled off the road and further forward movement was impeded. Weston then became aware of the occupants of the vehicle. The driver was now lying against the steering wheel, causing the horn to sound. One of the rear-seat passengers was trying to raise himself off the floor; and the other—an officer—was simultaneously trying to stand up and unholster his pistol.

Everly's rifle fired again. As Weston heard the crack of the weapon firing, he thought he could also hear the whistle of its bullet passing close to him.

Weston raised the submachine gun to his shoulder, got a sight picture, and pulled the trigger, immediately releasing it. He felt the three-round burst recoil against his shoulder. The face of the Japanese officer in the Buick seemed to implode. He sat back and then slid off the seat. The second man in the back of the car suddenly jumped out of the car and started running to the trucks behind him.

Weston raised his Thompson to his shoulder and aimed it. As he was preparing to apply gentle pressure to the trigger, Everly's Springfield fired again, the running man's head seemed to explode, and he fell forward onto his face. His legs and arms twitched.

Weston looked back at Everly, who was now on his feet, pulling the loop of the sling off his arm. He looked at Weston and made an impatient gesture for Weston to return his attention to the road, or,

My God, he wants me to go out there! If I go out there, they'll be able to see me, and shoot me, and I'll be killed!

Oh, shit!

Captain Weston moved out of the foliage, holding the Thompson with one hand. He supported himself on the fender of the Buick and then made what he thought, for a brief moment, was a constructive act. He pulled the body of the driver away from the steering wheel. The blaring of the horn stopped.

There, now they won't be able to hear us!

Jesus Christ! How fucking stupid can I be?

He looked into the rear seat of the Buick. The officer was on the floor, on his back. His eyes were a bloody mess.

I shot him right between the eyes.

I was aiming for his chest.

He moved slowly to the rear of the Buick, then ran to the truck next in line behind it. As he ran, he realized that the intensity of the firing had slowed. And then it stopped entirely.

There was the sound of moaning, and somewhere down the road a man was screaming, and then there was a shot and the screaming stopped.

"Cease fire! Cease fire!" Everly called. Weston turned to see him running up the road. He ran past Weston to the rear of the truck next in line. All of a sudden, he had a machete in his hand, and Weston saw it slash viciously downward.

My God, he's killing the wounded!

And you're acting like a Boy Scout, not like a Marine officer!

What did you expect, that this would be conducted in a gentlemanly fashion, with scrupulous attention to the Geneva Convention?

He made his way through the convoy to the pickup truck at its rear, desperately hoping he would not come across a wounded Japanese and have to kill him.

He did not. Taking their cue from Everly, the Filipinos quickly put their machetes to use, taking care of the problem of the wounded Japanese.

Weston saw a Filipino climb one of the fragile-looking telephone poles lining the road, slash the copper wire with his machete, and then, holding a loose end between his teeth, climb down again.

On the ground, he tugged unsuccessfully to pull the wire from the next pole, cutting his hand in the process, and then shouted angrily in a strange tongue—*Tagalog?* Weston wondered—which caused two other Filipinos to start climbing poles.

Weston started walking toward the head of the convoy again. Now the Filipinos were stripping the Japanese bodies of their weapons, their boots, their ammunition, their bayonets, their leather accoutrements, and their watches, jewelry, and even their spectacles.

The labor detail appeared, and Lieutenant Lomero began to load each man with the supplies and captured weaponry to be carried off. There were more supplies than men, and the attempt to carry off the fuel proved to be a disaster. There was no way to decant the gasoline and kerosene from the drums into the vessels they had brought with them except by putting the drums on their sides and opening the filler hole. More fuel poured onto the ground than into the bottles and barrels and canteens. And the wooden barrels leaked.

Weston returned to the Buick, leaned into the backseat, and finally found the pistol he had seen in the officer's hand.

It looks something like a German Luger, he thought, as he picked it up, then dropped it in horror. *It's covered with blood!*

He forced himself to pick it up again, then to unfasten the officer's belt, which was also slippery with blood. A spare magazine was in a pouch on the holster. He was tempted to throw the belt and the holster away, but decided he was obliged to take it with him. When he tried to strap it around his waist, it was too small, so he looped it around his neck.

He became aware then that the Buick's engine was still running. He reached over and turned the ignition key off and then removed it.

Everly came up to him.

"Anytime you're ready, Mr. Weston."

"Ready for what?"

"Torch the vehicles and go home," Everly said, and nodded toward the rear of the convoy. Two Filipinos were easily carrying one of the now nearly empty fifty-five-gallon gasoline drums. They stopped at the car, obviously waiting for Everly's permission to upend the drum into the car.

"You search him?" Everly asked.

"I got his pistol."

"I noticed," Everly said, and then spoke in Spanish to the Filipinos.

They got in the car, picked up the Japanese officer's body, and slid it over the side of the car. It landed on its face. Everly carefully went through the officer's pockets, coming up with a wallet, some identification papers, and a pocketknife, which he tossed to one of the Filipinos. Then he removed the officer's wristwatch.

"An Elgin," he said, tossing it to the other Filipino. "Do you suppose he bought it in Chicago, or took it away from some American?"

He waited until the Filipino, who was smiling happily, had strapped the Elgin onto his wrist, and then signaled for them to upend the gas drum into the Buick. As the dregs of the drum gurgled onto the red leather upholstery, he took out his Zippo lighter.

"Wait a minute!" he said. "Jesus Christ, how stupid can I be?"

"What?" Weston asked.

Everly shouted something in Spanish and then repeated it in English.

"Get the people with the bottles and canteens back here," he said, and one of the Filipinos said, "Yes, Sir," and ran down the road. Everly turned to Weston. "These fuel tanks are full. All we have to do is cut the fuel lines, and let it run into the bottles."

"Why didn't I think of that?" Weston asked rhetorically.

"Why didn't I?" Everly said.

The translation of that, Weston thought, *is, I didn't expect you to, you're nothing but a useless flyboy I'm stuck with, but I, the professional Marine, certainly should have.*

It took perhaps ten minutes—which seemed to Weston far longer than that—to fill the bottles and canteens from the fuel lines of the Buick and the trucks.

Finally, Everly called, "OK. Torch them!"

He stooped beside a small but growing pool of gasoline spreading from under the Buick.

"You better step back, Mr. Weston," he said.

"Right," Weston said, and took several steps away.

Everly ignited the gasoline and then ran away, grabbing Weston's arm and dragging him into the jungle.

There was a whooshing sound. When Weston looked back, the entire rear half of the Buick was engulfed in flames.

"Sometimes it explodes worse than that," Everly said.

"I suppose," Weston said, somewhat lamely.

"That was a nice head shot you made, Mr. Weston," Everly said. "Right between the eyes. But next time, it might be better if you aimed for the chest."

I am not going to give this sonofabitch the satisfaction of correcting me.

"I knew I could hit him in the head from that distance."

"Yeah, and you did," Everly said, with a touch of what could have been reluctant admiration in his voice. "But it's sometimes better, Mr. Weston, not to take chances."

"Let's get the hell out of here, Everly."

"Aye, aye, Sir," Lieutenant Everly said.

They headed into the jungle. They had gone perhaps fifty yards when Everly had the last word: There was an enormous roar as the fuel tank of one of the trucks exploded.

VII

[ONE]
Office of the Kempeitai Commander for Mindanao
Cagayan de Oro, Misamis-Oriental Province
Mindanao, Commonwealth of the Philippines
1425 Hours 20 October 1942

All but two of the seven officers of the Mindanao Detachment of the Kempeitai were gathered in the office of Lieutenant Colonel Tange Kisho to discuss the outrage on the Bislig-Caraga highway that morning. Present were Tange; Major Ieyasu Matsudaira, his deputy; Captains Matsuo Saikaku and Tokugawa Sadanobu; and Lieutenant Ichikawa Izumo. Lieutenants Okuni Sannjuro and Iemitsu Tokugawa were at the scene of the outrage supervising a ten-man detail searching the area.

Lieutenant Hideyori Niigata, the signals officer, had been summoned in case he might be needed. He was waiting outside Tange's office, sitting on a wooden bench once used by citizens of the Commonwealth of the Philippines seeking audience with the Provincial Governor.

It went without saying that the outrage had to be dealt with immediately and with the greatest severity. The question was how, and with what degree of severity.

Major Ieyasu Matsudaira believed the action to be taken was self-evident. One senior Japanese officer, Major Shimabara Hara, and nineteen other ranks, had been murdered. Therefore, five Filipino males from the surrounding area should be hung in retribution for Major Shimabara's murder—a five-to-one ratio—and thirty-eight Filipinos—a two-to-one ratio—hung in retribution for the other deaths. The arrests should be made today, Major Ieyasu argued, the arrestees interrogated overnight, and the executions carried out first thing in the morning.

Captain Saikaku disagreed with Major Ieyasu, and did so with less tact than Ieyasu expected. Neither Saikaku's disagreement, nor his lack of tact, surprised Lieutenant Colonel Tange.

"It is the policy of the Emperor," Saikaku pontificated, "that we enlist the support of the people here by incorporating them into the Greater Asian Co-

Prosperity Sphere. Hanging forty-odd innocent Filipinos is not the way to do that.''

''Nineteen of His Majesty's soldiers have been murdered, including a senior officer who was a dear friend,'' Ieyasu snapped. ''That cannot go unpunished. Moreover, the attack itself challenges our authority here, and that cannot be tolerated.''

''If we had the people who did this, I would put the rope around their necks myself. I would do so in the square here, with the people watching. But we don't have the people who did this—''

''We know who they are,'' Ieyasu interrupted. ''This so-called 'U.S. Forces in the Philippines.' ''

''No, Sir, we don't know that,'' Saikaku responded. ''That is one possibility.''

''And the others?''

''Simple bandits. Mindanao has a long history of banditry.''

''We found U.S. Army cartridge cases all over the site, for U.S. Army rifles and submachine guns.''

''Which proves nothing. Before we liberated these islands, bandits—many of them members of the Moro tribe—frequently attacked U.S. and Filipino Army units, robbed them, and made off with their weapons. What I am saying is that the execution of forty-odd Filipinos on the questionable premise that they aided U.S. Forces in the Philippines would both unnecessarily antagonize the Filipino population and would lend credence to the idea that U.S. Forces in the Philippines is in fact a military force which threatens us. We don't want that to happen.''

''What makes you so sure U.S. Forces in the Philippines is not 'a military force which threatens us'?'' Ieyasu demanded.

''Well, for one thing,'' Saikaku said, ''we have been reading all their communications traffic with the Americans in Australia. They keep asking for supplies, including such basic items as radios and radio codes; and Australia keeps replying that their requests are being considered.''

''I personally found that interesting, Major Ieyasu,'' Colonel Tange said. ''If this man Fertig—and especially if he were actually a general officer—was sent here, or was left behind when the Americans surrendered, it would seem logical that he would have been provided with both good radios and a cryptographic system.''

''Exactly,'' Captain Saikaku said.

''Perhaps, Captain Saikaku,'' Major Ieyasu said sarcastically, ''you would be good enough to tell us how you would recommend the Colonel deal with this matter?''

''I am sure the Colonel has already decided how to do that,'' Saikaku said smoothly.

"Let's hear what you have to say, Saikaku," Colonel Tange said.

"Sir, I would arrest all the able-bodied males within a five-mile area of the robbery site—"

"Robbery *and murder* site," Major Ieyasu interrupted.

"—robbery and murder site," Saikaku went on. "And subject them to intensive interrogation. A thorough and skillful interrogation, by which I mean there would be no evident marks on their bodies on their release."

"On their release? In other words, before we arrest them, you don't think a 'thorough and skillful interrogation' will come up with anything?"

"I doubt that it will, Major Ieyasu," Saikaku replied. "But I think we have to try. We may find some information, perhaps nothing useful now, but useful to us later. Then we release the prisoners. By arresting them, and then releasing them without serious physical harm, we will accomplish several things. First, we will establish our authority by the very act of arresting them. Second, they will learn—and may be counted on to pass on—just how uncomfortable a Kempeitai thorough and professional interrogation can be. And finally, by releasing them, we will prove that while we are firm, we are just."

"Very interesting," Colonel Tange said. "I wish to consider that at my leisure."

Everyone in the room understood that Colonel Tange's decision would look very much like what Captain Saikaku had suggested—either because that was what he had already come up with on his own, or because Saikaku's ideas seemed to be the best offered. But to make that announcement now would cause Major Ieyasu to lose face.

"You said Lieutenant Hideyori is outside, Captain Saikaku?" Colonel Tange went on. "Has he something to report?"

"No, Sir. I spoke with him at length before I came here. Should the Colonel desire, I am prepared to give a brief report on his failure. I ordered him to be here in case the Colonel, or Major Ieyasu, would like to talk with him personally."

"Let's have the brief report," Tange ordered.

"There have been fewer and fewer communications between Fertig and Australia. I alluded to this before. He asks for supplies; they reply that his request is being considered, and give him a time for his next transmission. The time between such contacts seems to be growing longer.

"This, however, makes Lieutenant Hideyori's efforts to locate the transmitter much more difficult, as Fertig seems to be moving his transmitter after every exchange with Australia. He moves the transmitter within an area thirty miles wide east to west and seventy miles north to south, and always where there are few roads."

"In other words, he's no closer to finding the transmitter than ever?" Colonel Tange asked.

"I regret that seems to be the case," Saikaku replied. "Shall I send for him, Colonel?"

"In your judgment, is he doing everything he should be doing?"

"Yes, Sir. He is."

"Then there's really no point in wasting my time talking to him, is there?"

"I would not think so, Sir."

"Thank you, gentlemen, that will be all," Colonel Tange said. "Major Ieyasu, would you please stay behind?"

[TWO]
Rocky Fields Farm
Bernardsville, New Jersey
1615 Hours 25 October 1942

Miss Ernestine Sage stepped out of her bathroom stark naked, in the process of toweling her hair, having decided it made sense to bathe now, while her father and Ken McCoy were trying to fit in an hour or so of hunting before supper, rather than before she went to bed.

As soon as dinner was over, she intended to announce that she was tired, they all had a busy day tomorrow, and why didn't everybody go to bed?

Thirty minutes after that, she planned to sneak as quietly as possible down the corridor past her parents' bedroom and into the guest bedroom. Ken would not expect her to do that, and it would be a pleasant, if discomfiting, surprise for him. And she had no intention of going back to her bedroom, no matter what his protests.

If her parents heard her, that would be unfortunate. She was not going to lose the opportunity to sleep with her man when she had the chance, no matter what the circumstances. She didn't want to be here anyway; her father had shown up at her apartment in Manhattan early that morning and practically dragged both of them into his car to bring them here.

She glanced idly out the window to see how dark it was, to make sure there was time to finish her toilette before they returned. Her father and Ken were perhaps five hundred yards from the house, walking through the stubble of a cornfield, obviously headed for home. She'd thought she'd have at least half an hour, that they wouldn't return until it was really getting dark.

Oh, God, I hope Daddy didn't say anything to Ken that made him mad!

"Damn!" she said, and increased the vigor of her toweling.

She dressed as quickly as she could, in a brown tweed skirt and a light-green, high-collared sweater, slipped her bare feet into a pair of loafers, quickly applied lipstick, and went downstairs.

She found them in the gunroom. Ken was peering down the barrels of a shotgun. Her father was scrubbing the action of the gun with a toothbrush.

"Home are the hunters, home from the field," she said. "Much sooner than expected."

"It didn't take long," Ernest Sage said, watching with what Ernie knew was discomfort as she went to Ken and kissed him.

Ernest Sage was a slightly built, very intense man of forty-eight, who wore his full head of black hair slicked back with Vitahair. Vitahair was one of the 209 widely distributed products of American Personal Pharmaceuticals, of which he was Chairman of the Board and Chief Executive Officer.

"Tell me," Ernie said.

"We were fifty yards into the first field. Two cocks jumped up. Before I could get my gun up, Ken got both of them."

"He's a Marine, Daddy. What did you expect?"

"He's a hell of a shot, honey," Ernest Sage said. "I'll tell you that."

Ernest Sage did not rise to the top of APP solely because he was the largest individual stockholder in the corporation founded by his grandfather, Ezekiel Handley, M.D. He thought of himself as an ordinarily competent, decently educated individual, who had somehow acquired an ability to get people to do what he wanted them to do, and to like doing it. Or the reverse, to not do what he thought they should not do, and believe that not doing it was the logical and reasonable thing to do.

He had often joked that there were only two people in the world he could not control, his wife and his only child. But even when he said that, he knew he had his wife pretty well under control.

Ernie was the one who did what she wanted to do, and didn't do what she didn't want to do, completely oblivious to the desires and manipulative efforts of her father.

Lieutenant Kenneth R. McCoy, USMCR, obviously confirmed that perception.

Ernest Sage often privately thought that if he compiled a list of undesirable suitors for his daughter's affections, right at the top of that list would be a Marine officer with an unpleasant family background—they didn't have a dime, was the way he thought of it—with only a high school education, whose only prospects were the near certainty of getting himself badly maimed in the war— or more likely killed.

It deeply disturbed him, but didn't really surprise him, when Ernie told him that thirty minutes after she met Ken McCoy she knew she wanted to marry him.

Adding to his difficulties was the fact that he not only admired McCoy but rather liked him. He could not even console himself with the thought that McCoy was after his and his daughter's money. Ernie would marry him at the drop of a hat, he knew, either with his permission or without it. McCoy refused to do that. He thought it would be unfair to leave her a widow, or obliged to spend the rest of her life caring for a cripple.

Since Ernie almost always got what she wanted—because she was willing to pay whatever the price might be—one of the unpleasant possibilities that Ernest Sage was forced to live with was that she would get herself in the family way, either as a bargaining chip to bring McCoy to the altar, or—and with Ernie, this was entirely possible—simply because she wanted to bear his child.

He had discussed this subject with Ernie, and she had pointed out that any illicit fruit of their union would not wind up on public assistance, the annual income from her trust funds being three or four times as much as she was paid by J. Walter Thompson, Advertisers.

Since they were sleeping together—perhaps not here, tonight, because McCoy would object to that; but everywhere else, including a three-month period when they cohabited on a yacht at the San Diego Yacht Club while he was training for what had become the now famous Makin Island raid—the problem of her becoming impregnated was a real one.

He had come to understand that the only reason she did not allow herself to become pregnant was that she was afraid of Ken, or else respected him too much to go against his wishes. And this of course meant that Ken McCoy was doing what he was unable to do as her father, guiding the course of her life.

McCoy came into her life, perversely enough, through the young man Ernest Sage and his wife had hoped for years would become, in due time, her husband. If one ignored his current role as a Marine fighter pilot, with odds against his passing through the war unscathed, or alive, this young man would have headed a list of desirable suitors. He came from a splendid family. His mother, who had been Ernie's mother's roommate and best friend at college, was the only daughter of Andrew Foster, of Foster Hotels International. His father—an old friend whom Ernest Sage could never completely forgive for arranging for the yacht in San Diego, knowing full well what Ernie wanted it for—was Fleming Pickering, now wearing a Marine general's uniform, but previously Chairman of the Board and Chief Executive Officer of Pacific & Far East Shipping.

Ken McCoy and Malcolm S. "Pick" Pickering met and became buddies at Officer Candidate School at the Marine Corps base at Quantico, Virginia. On their graduation, Pick was sowing a few wild oats in a penthouse suite at the Foster Park Hotel on Central Park South—his one semidisqualifying characteristic as the perfect suitor was his proclivity for wild-oats sowing.

Though Ernie unfortunately regarded Pick as a troublemaking brother, she somewhat reluctantly, at her father's urging, went to the party after he told her she was duty-bound to congratulate Pick on his second lieutenant's bar, and to wish him well in pilot training. There she met Ken McCoy, sitting on a ledge, his feet dangling over Fifty-ninth Street.

Fifteen minutes later, they left the penthouse in search of Chinese food in Chinatown.

One of the first things Ernie told her father about McCoy was that he spoke Chinese like a Chinaman.

"Well, they look pretty clean," McCoy said, handing Mr. Sage the shotgun barrels. "But what you really need is some Hoppe's Number Nine. I'll get some for you."

"When he sold me that stuff, the man at Griffin & Howe said it was the best barrel cleaner available," Ernest Sage heard himself say.

Why couldn't I have just said "Thank you"? Am I looking for an excuse to fight with him?

"The best barrel cleaner is mercury," McCoy said matter-of-factly. "Next is Hoppe's Number Nine."

Mercury? What the hell is he talking about, mercury?

"Mercury?"

"You stop up one end of a barrel, fill the barrel with mercury, let it stay a couple of minutes, and then pour it out. Takes the barrel right down to the bare metal. I guess it dissolves the lead, and the primer residue, all the crap that fouls a barrel."

Unfortunately, I suspect he knows what's he's talking about. I will not challenge him on that. There probably is some chemical reaction, vis-à-vis steel, copper, lead, and mercury.

And then he heard himself say, "What you're saying is that the man at Griffin & Howe doesn't know what he's talking about?"

"Not if he said that stuff is best, he doesn't."

"Daddy," Ernie said. "Ken *knows* about guns. Why are you arguing with him?"

"I wasn't arguing with Ken, honey. I was just making sure I understood him correctly." He fixed a smile on his face. "The next step in the sacred traditions of hunting around here is the ingestion of a stiff belt. How does that sound, Ken?"

"That sounds fine, Sir."

Ernest Sage put the side-by-side Parker 12-bore together, and then put it in a cabinet beside perhaps twenty other long arms. He turned and smiled at his daughter.

*I've been around guns all my life, but your Ken knows *about guns*, right?*

"Into the library, honey? Or shall we go in the kitchen and watch your mother defeather the birds?"

"The library," Ernie said. "Mother hates plucking and dressing birds; always prays that you'll never get any pheasant."

"I've never eaten a pheasant," Ken McCoy said.

"Really?" Ernest Page said.

They went into the two-story-high library. The front of what looked like a row of books opened, revealing a bar, complete to refrigerator.

Sage took two glasses and started to put ice in them.

"Yes, Daddy," Ernie said. "Thank you very much, I will have a drink. Whatever you're having."

"Sorry, honey," her father said. "Excuse me. I'm not used to you being a full-grown woman."

"Make her a weak one," McCoy said. "One strong drink and she starts dancing on tabletops."

Sage turned in surprise, in time to see Ernie sticking her tongue out at McCoy.

"Don't believe him, Daddy."

He made the drinks and handed one to each of them.

"What shall we drink to?" he asked. "The fallen pheasants?"

"What about Pick?" McCoy replied. "I feel sorry for him."

"Why do you feel sorry for him?" Sage asked.

"He's going on display on the West Coast right about now."

"I don't understand."

"A War Bond Tour. All the aviation heroes from Guadalcanal. Modesty is not one of his strong points, but I suspect the War Bond Tour will cure him of that."

"Pick is a hero?"

"Certified. Got the DFC from the Secretary of the Navy himself last week."

"I hadn't heard that."

"For doing what he did with you?" Ernie asked. It was a challenge.

"For being an ace. More than an ace. I think he has six kills. Maybe seven."

"What did she mean, Ken, 'for doing what he did with you'? You saw Pick in the Pacific."

"Yes, Sir. I saw him in the Pacific."

"If he got a medal, why didn't you?" Ernie demanded.

"Because I didn't do anything to deserve a medal."

"Huh!" Ernie snorted.

"What exactly is it that you do in the Marines, Ken?" Ernest Sage asked with a smile.

He knew that McCoy worked for Fleming Pickering. He didn't know what Pickering did for the Marine Corps—Pickering had told him he was the general in charge of mess-kit repair—and he thought he probably was going to find out right now.

"Well, right now, I've been trying to make sure that the Navy doesn't steal everybody who speaks an Oriental language from the Draft Board for the Navy; that The Corps gets at least a few of them. I've spent the last week at the Armed Forces Induction Center in New York."

"I mean, ordinarily."

"Whatever General Pickering tells me to do."

"You're his assistant in charge of repairing mess kits, right?"

"Yes, Sir. That's about it."

"You're wasting your time, Daddy," Ernie said. "I live with him, and he won't tell me anything either."

You had to say that, "I live with him," didn't you?

Maintaining a smile with some difficulty, Sage said, "I don't mean to pry, Ken. Would asking you how long you're going to be around be prying?"

"No, Sir. I'll be around a long time, I think. Four, five, maybe even six months."

Well, I suppose, if you're young, and in uniform, five or six months is a "long time."

"And then?"

"They haven't told me."

"And if they had, he wouldn't tell us," Ernie said, adding intensely, "I really hate this goddamn war!"

"You are not too big to be told to watch your mouth, young lady."

"What would you prefer, that I call it 'this noble enterprise to save the world for democracy'?"

"That has a nice ring to it," McCoy said.

"Oh, go to hell!" Ernie said.

Ken McCoy did, in fact, know where he would be going in four to six months—he'd been told the week before; it was classified TOP SECRET. And he had been really impressed with what he would be doing, and with the long-range planning for the war the upper echelons of the military establishment were now carrying on.

The Joint Chiefs of Staff intended to bomb the home islands of the Empire of Japan. Though the islands from which the planes would fly to attack Tokyo and other Japanese cities were now firmly in Japanese hands, the big brass was so sure that the war in the Pacific would see their capture that they had turned their attention to the details.

One of the details was weather information. Without accurate weather predictions—including something called "Winds Aloft," which McCoy had never heard of before last week—long-range bombing of Japan would not be possible.

The ideal place to locate a weather-reporting station would be as close to Japan as possible. Since locating a weather station near Japan was out of the question, the next-best place—for reasons not explained to McCoy—was the Gobi Desert in Mongolia.

Until he had time to think about it, he was genuinely surprised that United States military personnel were presently in the Gobi Desert, which was about as far behind the enemy lines as it was possible to get. Though there were a few soldiers and sailors, the majority of them were United States Marines who had been stationed in Peking and elected not to surrender to the Japanese when the war began. They had made for the Gobi Desert for reasons that were not entirely clear but that certainly included avoiding capture.

They had taken with them a number of ex–China Marines, Yangtze River Patrol sailors, and members of the Army's 15th Infantry who had taken their retirement in China and considered themselves recalled from retirement. There were supposed to be sixty-seven of them.

They had established radio contact through American forces in China, and were now in direct contact with Army and Navy radio stations in Hawaii, Australia, and the continental United States. They were ordered to maintain contact and to avoid capture, but not informed of the plans being made for them.

Once they could be trained in a number of skills, including parachuting, it was planned that an initial reinforcement detachment would be sent to the Gobi Desert. In their number would be radio operators, meteorologists, cryptographers, and other technicians.

Their ability to collect, encrypt, and transmit weather data from the Gobi would be tested, as would the efficacy of predicting weather from the data furnished.

Inasmuch as the personnel in the Gobi were predominantly Marines, and the Marines were part of the Navy, the Navy had been given overall command of the operation. The meteorologists, cryptographers, and communications personnel would be sailors. But the Secretary of the Navy, with the concurrence of the President's Chief of Staff, had given the Marine Corps Office of Management Analysis responsibility for staging the operation.

The Deputy Chief of Management Analysis had in turn named Major Edward Banning as Officer in Charge, with Lieutenant Kenneth R. McCoy as his deputy. Nothing had been said to McCoy, but he knew that Banning held a MAGIC clearance, and thus could not be put in risk of capture, so Banning would not make the mission. He also felt quite sure that he himself would not become Officer in Charge by default; command of the mission would not be entrusted to a lowly lieutenant. Consequently, sometime between now and the time the mission left the United States, a field-grade officer would be assigned.

But between now and then, he knew he would be in charge, turning to Banning only when he ran into a problem he could not handle himself. It would give him, as he had told Ernie and her father, four to six months in the States. And he was sure he could arrange his schedule to spend a good deal of time with her.

Starting, he thought, almost immediately. He was about to go through the Marine Corps Parachutist's School at Lakehurst, New Jersey. While he was there, he could go into New York City every night and every weekend. But he would also have to periodically return to Lakehurst to check on the progress of the others learning how to parachute themselves and their equipment from airplanes.

The thought of parachuting into Mongolia was a little unnerving, but he told himself it was probably a good deal safer than being a platoon leader on Guadalcanal. The real problem with the Mongolian Operation was that once he went in, it would be a long time before he could even think of getting out, perhaps not until the end of the war. But there was nothing he could do about that.

[THREE]
The Congressional Country Club
Fairfax County, Virginia
1 November 1942

Technically, the status of Major James C. Brownlee III, USMCR, at the Office of Strategic Services Reception and Training Station—the pressed-into-service Congressional Country Club—was "Agent, awaiting assignment."

That meant he had successfully completed the training program and passed the "Final Board"—a group of five senior OSS officers who had considered his military background, the comments of his training officers at the Country Club, and then called him in for an hour-long session to finally make the determination whether or not he was the sort of man who could successfully function behind the enemy's lines.

Jim Brownlee, a tall, blond, slender, twenty-seven-year-old who wore spectacles, had always wanted to be a Marine. While at Princeton, he participated in the Marine Corps Platoon Leader's Program, which was rather like the Army's Reserve Officer Training Corps. During the academic year, it exposed young men who thought they might like to be officers to courses with a military application. And then, during summer vacations, it gave them six weeks of intensive training in basic military subjects—"The Three M's," marching, marksmanship, and map reading—at USMC Base Quantico, Virginia, and Parris Island Recruit Depot, South Carolina.

Jim Brownlee intended to apply for a commission in the Regular Marine

Corps; but his eyes did not meet the Marine Corps' criteria for the regular service. Instead, on his graduation from Princeton in June 1937, he was commissioned as a second lieutenant, USMCR. After that, he went through the Basic Officer Course at Quantico, and was released to inactive duty.

He joined Marine Corps Reserve Battalion 14, based in New Orleans, Louisiana, as a platoon leader, even though this meant an overnight train ride—at his own expense—each way once a month from his home in Palm Beach, Florida, for the weekend training program. After two years of service with the battalion, he was promoted first lieutenant.

When he was not training with The Marine Corps, he was Vice President, Domestic Transportation, for the Brownlee Fruit Company (founded by his grandfather, Matthew J. Brownlee). The firm imported bananas—their own production and brokered—from Nicaragua, Honduras, Panama, and El Salvador. His father was currently President, and his older brother, Matthew J. Brownlee III, was Vice President, Production.

What his title meant was that his father had put him to work under an experienced longtime traffic manager, as a way to learn the business. Bananas were off-loaded from Brownlee ships at Port St. Lucie, Florida; Mobile, Alabama; and New Orleans, Louisiana. His job was to ensure the smooth flow of the bananas either to regional distribution centers or to the ultimate retailers.

He liked the challenge of quickly and economically moving vast amounts of bananas—they are, of course, highly perishable—from the off-loading port to their destinations, while keeping them as fresh as possible. At the same time, the intricacies of interstate motor freight laws, tariffs, and the like were rather fascinating.

Since the whole idea was to teach him the business, he also spent a good deal of time in Central America with his brother. Matthew, who was fifteen years older than he was, devoted his attention pretty much equally to showing Jim the plantation operations and trying to prevent him from giving in to what the Episcopal Church terms the sinful lusts of the flesh with dark-skinned native girls.

On 15 October 1940, President Roosevelt ordered the mobilization of Marine Reserve Battalions, which did not surprise Jim Brownlee. On April 9, Germany had occupied Denmark and invaded Norway. The next month, Germany invaded Belgium, the Netherlands, and Luxembourg. British Prime Minister Neville Chamberlain, who had promised "Peace In Our Time," resigned 11 May, and Winston S. Churchill took his place.

What was left of the British Army after the German Blitzkrieg across France was evacuated from Dunkirk on 4 June; and just over a week later, the German Wehrmacht goose-stepped down the Champs Élysées. On 22 June, the French surrendered to the Germans.

In July, a Marine lieutenant colonel who spoke to Jim's reserve battalion in New Orleans brought them up to date on the military picture as the Marine Corps saw it. He mentioned that as of 30 June, the total strength of the USMC was 1,732 Officers and 26,545 Enlisted Men.

He didn't say that the Marine Reserve was about to be mobilized, but he did say that there were obviously not enough Marines in uniform for the present circumstances.

Jim Brownlee reported for active duty with his reserve battalion to Marine Base Quantico, Virginia on 1 November 1940. Within a week of their arrival, the battalion was broken up, and its members were scattered all over the world, wherever Marines were serving.

A Marine Personnel Officer, a major whom Jim correctly suspected was curious how a twenty-four-year-old had become a vice president of a large corporation, questioned him at some length about his duties, and then sent him to see a full colonel, who was the G-4 (Supply) Officer at Quantico.

The Colonel questioned him even more intensively about his knowledge of what the Marine Corps called "Transport." Apparently satisfied with the answers, he told Jim he had been looking for someone with his qualifications, and as of that moment he could consider himself assigned to the G-4 Section as an Assistant Transportation Officer.

Jim's protests that he was trained as an infantry platoon leader were met with the observation that in the Colonel's experience good Marine officers went where they were sent and did what they were told to do, without complaint.

The year between Jim's call to active duty and Pearl Harbor went quickly, and he took a certain satisfaction from his work. He was more than a little surprised to learn how much truck operators serving the Marines had been able to get away with before he laid his expert eye on the invoices they had tendered.

He received during that year three letters of commendation for his official file and a wholly unexpected promotion to captain.

The attack on Pearl Harbor surprised him, for a couple of reasons. For one thing, he did not think the Japanese had the technical capability to strike with such strength at such a great distance. For another, though a surprise attack on the United States was possible, in his view, he thought it would probably come on the Panama Canal, either from the Germans in the Atlantic or the Japanese in the Pacific, or conceivably both.

On 8 December, he applied for transfer to duty with troops. His letter came back within a week, denied. He applied again thereafter on a monthly basis, and on a monthly basis his request was denied. In April 1942, he was promoted major. The ceremony was held in the office of the Commanding General. After offering his congratulations, he said he hoped it would mean the end of the monthly requests for transfer.

In May 1942, a memorandum from Headquarters USMC crossed Major Brownlee's desk. Applications were being solicited from officers for a non-specified duty of an intelligence nature. Preference would be given to those with fluency in one or more foreign languages, and/or who had spent time outside the continental United States.

He submitted his application and promptly forgot about it, sure that it would suffer the same fate as his requests for transfer to duty with troops.

Two weeks later, his orders came through. He was transferred to something called the Office of Strategic Services and ordered to report within forty-eight hours to the National Institute of Health Building in Washington, D.C.

There he was interviewed by another board of officers. This one consisted of three men in civilian clothing; two of them spoke Spanish. At the conclusion of the interview, one of the Spanish speakers shook his hand, offered his name, and said, "Please give my best regards to your brother. But don't tell him where, or under what circumstances, we bumped into each other."

That same afternoon, Jim Brownlee was transported in a Buick station wagon to the former Congressional Country Club to begin training.

The training was difficult, but not nearly so difficult for Major Brownlee as it was for some of his fellow trainees who had entered the OSS directly from civilian life—he had taken pains to keep himself in shape at Quantico and thereafter. Two fellow trainees had never held a weapon in their hands before coming to the Country Club.

As the training proceeded, he began to wonder where he would be assigned. He gradually came to the conclusion that because of his fluency in Spanish, it would either be in Spain or somewhere in South America. In Spain, the policy of the United States Government was to keep Generalissimo Franco, known as "El Caudillo," neutral. If South America, he rather suspected he would be in Argentina, where the military-dominated government was in everything but name an ally of the Germans. It was common knowledge around the Country Club that both the OSS and the FBI were deeply involved in Argentina, Chile, Paraguay, and Uruguay.

There was a decent library at the Country Club, and Jim Brownlee spent many of his evenings trying to learn as much as he could about the history and politics of South America. He felt he would be given an assignment shortly after he completed the training and then got past the Final Board.

That didn't happen. Despite his "Agent, awaiting assignment" status, no assignment was forthcoming. What did happen was that someone in the office realized that he was the senior Marine officer present at the Country Club, and consequently, that administrative responsibility for all Marine Corps personnel assigned to the OSS was logically his.

At first, in what he believed was the interim between the completion of his training and his assignment, he didn't mind at all. For one thing, it gave him something to do, and he rather liked guiding fellow Marines through the rocks and shoals of Country Club training.

But then he began to worry if the same sort of thing that happened to him at Quantico was happening to him at the Country Club. Good administrators were hard to find. And more and more Marines had been accepted by the OSS.

The last thing in the world he wanted was to be sort of a Marine Mother Hen. He wanted to get out on assignment and do something more concrete against the enemy than shepherd other Marines through training. He was no closer now to being what he thought of privately as a "fighting Marine" than he had been at Quantico.

This awareness was made even more painful with the arrival at the Country Club of First Lieutenant Robert B. Macklin, USMC. Macklin was not only a rather handsome man, but his uniform—and his person—were adorned with the symbols of what Jim Brownlee wanted rather desperately to be, a Fighting Marine. Macklin wore the ring of the United States Naval Academy at Annapolis. Colored ribbons on the breast of his well-fitting uniform indicated that he had seen service in the Pacific, and that he had twice been wounded. His face was scarred from one wound; and his slight limp, which he tried but failed to hide, suggested that the wound that caused it had been more severe than the one on his face.

He wore the wings of a parachutist. And when asked, he revealed that he had been wounded with the USMC 2nd Parachute Battalion storming the beach at Gavutu during the invasion of Guadalcanal. Brownlee had heard that the Marine paratroopers at Gavutu were literally decimated—one out of ten Paramarines were killed or wounded.

"I really have only one question, Lieutenant," Brownlee said. "With all the service you've seen, I should have thought by now that you would be at least a captain."

"The Major will note," Macklin replied, demonstrating impeccable military courtesy, "that my service records have been misplaced."

"Yes, of course," Brownlee said. "I'm sure they'll turn up."

Lieutenant Robert B. Macklin devoutly hoped they would not. He was delighted when a master gunner in Officer Personnel at Eighth and "I" informed him that his records were missing but they were going to send him to the OSS anyway, and "hope they turn up."

With a little bit of luck, they wouldn't ever turn up, which meant The Corps would have to "reconstruct" a new set. With just a little more luck, the "reconstructed" records would not contain a copy of the devastating Officer's Efficiency Report he had received from Captain Edward Banning, the S-2 of the 4th Marines in Shanghai.

Lieutenant Macklin had given that efficiency report, and its potential effect on his career, a good deal of thought. Now that he had time to consider it, he was no longer surprised that Captain Edward J. Banning wrote all those despicable—and untrue—things about him. Under the circumstances, Macklin now realized, it was perfectly understandable that he did.

For one thing, while Banning was a career officer, he did not graduate from the Academy. If memory served, Banning went to the Citadel. If not the Citadel, then to VMI or Norwich, one of those quasi-professional private military colleges that for some reason, most likely political, were permitted to commission their graduates into the Regular Service. It was common knowledge that Norwich, Citadel, and VMI graduates were jealous of those who went to Annapolis and West Point, and that whenever the opportunity presented itself, stuck knives into the unsuspecting backs of those who had that privilege.

Furthermore, at the time, Banning's own career was in jeopardy, and he had no one to blame for that but himself. While the Citadel, or wherever he actually went, wasn't the Academy, Banning must have had the opportunity to learn what would be expected of him, in his personal life, as a Marine officer. Teaching potential officers what would be expected of them was one of the major reasons the Army and the Navy sent West Point and Annapolis graduates to serve on the staffs of the private military schools.

Becoming involved, as Captain Banning did, with a Stateless Person, a Russian woman, was conduct unbecoming an officer and a gentleman, in fact, if not in the law. If the war hadn't come along, it would have meant the end of Banning's career, and he must have known that.

Banning, furthermore, should have known better than to become close to an enlisted man, particularly one like Corporal "Killer" McCoy. McCoy was typical of the enlisted men in the 4th Marines, a product of the lower classes, obviously without a decent education. For those people, service in the Marines meant three square meals a day, a cot, and the opportunity to frequently fornicate with the native women.

There are reasons for the line drawn between officers and enlisted men. Banning certainly knew about the line and the reasons for it, and he chose to ignore it. At the same time, it was perfectly clear that McCoy knew all about Banning's Russian mistress—and God only knows what other secrets Banning was hiding. That knowledge gave him a totally unacceptable advantage over an officer.

And then there was the matter of Lieutenant Ed Sessions's support of McCoy's outrageous charges. So far as that was concerned . . . it was, in fact, very disappointing. As a fellow graduate of the Academy, Sessions should have demonstrated at least a modicum of loyalty toward a fellow alumnus when that alumnus was under attack by an enlisted man. But Sessions not only knew that Banning was going to write *his* efficiency report but that Banning had gone off the deep end where Killer McCoy was concerned, and would take his enlisted buddy McCoy's word against anyone else's about what really happened. So he went along.

The usual mechanism to keep personality conflicts out of efficiency reports was their review by a more senior officer. But that failed. Major Puller, the reviewing officer, already overworked preparing the 4th Marines' move to the Philippines, had the choice between believing Banning, whom he knew, and an officer who wasn't in their clique. It was as simple as that.

His subsequent assignment as a mess officer at Quantico was, Macklin knew, a direct result of Banning's efficiency report. That sort of duty does not fall to graduates of the Naval Academy. But he resolved then to do the best job he could.

And then—and he still found this incredible—Corporal Killer McCoy showed up at Quantico as an officer candidate. The only officer candidate in his class from the ranks. The only one who had not spent two weeks in a college classroom, much less taken a degree.

In the matter of his encounter with McCoy at Quantico, Macklin was willing to admit that he made an error in judgment. On the one hand, obviously, he owed it to The Corps to do whatever was necessary to keep such a man from being commissioned. On the other hand, he should have approached the appropriate officer at the school and told him what he knew of McCoy from personal knowledge—information that made the notion of commissioning him an officer absurd on its face.

His personal knowledge would reveal that McCoy was not only insubordinate and untruthful, but the reason he was known in China as "Killer" was that he had become embroiled in a barroom, or brothel, encounter with Italian Marines; he'd stabbed two of them fatally. Some sort of technicality kept him from getting what he deserved—twenty years to life in the Portsmouth Naval Prison. But clearly a man with murderous instincts who wallowed in drunkenness and depravity was not qualified to be a Marine officer.

At the time, however, doing something official did not seem to be the best course of action. His good intentions, his concern solely for the good of The Corps, it seemed at the time, might be misunderstood.

If he had done something official, the question could very well have been raised, "Who is Lieutenant Macklin"? His service records would have probably been examined. And they contained, of course, Banning's efficiency report. Until his performance of duty proved how unjust it was, the less frequently that efficiency report came to light, of course, the better.

And, of course, as an officer and a gentleman, it was beneath him to bear Killer McCoy any ill will. It wasn't, in the final analysis, McCoy's fault that he was in Officer Candidate School. Banning had arranged for that, written him an absolutely unbelievable letter of recommendation.

McCoy belonged in the ranks. In time, under the leadership of other officers, he would probably become a decent sergeant. So the thing to do was to get him back to the ranks. Failing to make it through Officer Candidate School, with his background, was to be expected.

At the Club, he spoke to one of McCoy's tactical officers. Without getting into specifics, he made it quite clear that commissioning Killer McCoy would be a disaster. That officer also believed it ill-advised at the very least to commission a high-school graduate; and he seemed sympathetic to the idea of returning McCoy to the ranks by seeing that he failed Officer Candidate School, if not academically, then in the areas of "potential leadership" and "character."

That probably would have worked. However, at the time it seemed a good idea that there be some failure on McCoy's part on the military aspects of the course. Arranging for McCoy to fail the course's marksmanship requirements seemed a good way to do that.

Such a failure would do McCoy no lasting harm. As soon as he was back in the ranks, he would be given the opportunity to refire the standard course, and he could probably do that. In the meantime, he would be dropped from Officer Candidate School.

But the Post Sergeant Major put his nose in where it properly had no place and challenged McCoy's rifle range scores. McCoy fired again for record, and qualified as High Expert.

Shortly afterward, Macklin was called into the office of Deputy School Commandant, where he was told it would be in his best interests to apply for a transfer. There was no question in Macklin's mind that the Sergeant Major had gone to the Deputy Commandant, carrying tales about what he thought Macklin had been doing in the rifle range butts.

His application for parachute duty was quickly approved. And from there things moved quickly. First, they grew worse with the transfer to the Pacific and the invasion of Guadalcanal. It was only by the grace of God that he wasn't killed during the invasion. Quite literally, he missed death by inches.

But then, in the hospital in Australia where he was sent for treatment of his wounds, things started to get better. He was selected to participate in the First War Bond Tour, as a wounded Guadalcanal veteran. He did so well dealing with the public that on the completion of Tour I, the public relations people asked that he be permanently assigned to supervise Tour II.

The Marines sent on Tour II to encourage the civilian population to buy more war bonds and raise civilian morale were Guadalcanal aviation aces, pilots who had shot down at least five Japanese aircraft. But Macklin did not find these men impressive. He privately decided that most of them were disgraces to the Marine uniforms they wore—they were undisciplined, regarded military courtesy as a joke, and spent most of the tour making unwanted advances to women and drinking themselves into oblivion—and that aviators themselves were highly overrated.

It was one thing to get out of a clean bed and climb into an airplane and fly for several hours, and then possibly—but only possibly—engage in a minute or two of combat, before flying home to a hot meal and a dry bed. It was quite another to do what he had done—or would have done had he not been wounded in the opening minutes of the assault—to make an assault in a landing barge through heavy fire onto an enemy-held beach, to hear the crack of machine-gun fire and the scream of incoming artillery, and then to be called upon to lead men against a determined enemy.

Those introspections had caused him to consider what would happen to him when Tour II was over. Thanks to that damned efficiency report, he was still a first lieutenant. In The Corps, first lieutenants command platoons. While he would of course go where he was sent, and do what he was told to do, the idea of commanding a platoon in the assault of some hostile shore seemed a waste of his professional talents and experience.

He should be a teacher. He had been there. He could make a genuine contribution to The Corps, and probably save some lives, as a teacher, preparing men and officers for what they would find when it was *their* turn to go into combat.

If he just waited for The Corps to order him someplace, it would more than likely be to one of the newly formed divisions, where he would be just one more platoon leader.

He had been trying to think of some way to make the personnel people aware of his unusual talents and experience and the contribution he could thus make—he got so far as drafting several letters—when the memorandum vis-à-vis Special Assignment To Intelligence Duties came to hand.

It seemed to be just what he was looking for. Not only did he have the qualifications and experience—there weren't very many people around who could say they had intelligence-gathering experience in the Orient—but it seemed, with that in mind, that he could be utilized as an instructor. It was clearly a waste of assets to send someone like himself into, so to speak, the lines, when he could make a far greater contribution to the war effort by training others.

When he was so quickly accepted, he thought perhaps his luck was changing. When he learned that his service records had been ''misplaced,'' he felt certain that Lady Luck was finally smiling at him.

[FOUR]
Office of the Assistant Chief of Staff G-1
Headquarters, United States Marine Corps
Eighth and "I" Streets, NW
Washington, D.C.
0945 Hours 2 November 1942

"Good morning, Sir," Master Gunner James L. Hardee, USMC, said to the tall, blond, bespectacled, and lost-looking major. "May I help you?"

"God, I hope so, Gunner," Major James C. Brownlee replied, smiling.

"The difficult takes some time," Gunner Hardee said, "the impossible usually turns out to be impossible."

Brownlee chuckled, and offered his hand.

"My name is Brownlee," he said.

"Hardee, Sir. What can we do for you?"

"I'm trying to get an officer promoted," Brownlee said.

"You and everybody else in The Corps," Hardee said, waving toward a section of his office where two typists, working under the eagle eye of a staff sergeant, were typing mimeograph stencils. "That's just about the end of last week's promotions," he went on. "Tomorrow, we start this week's."

"I'm not in personnel," Brownlee said. "So my ignorance of the process is complete and overwhelming."

"You're not part of our happy family here at Eighth and 'I', Major?"

"No, I'm not," Brownlee said. "Tell me, Gunner, what does it usually take to get a first lieutenant promoted to captain?"

"Well, presuming a first lieutenant can see lightning and hear thunder, isn't under charges, and has twenty-four months in grade—and that's about to drop—it's now nearly automatic."

Hardee gestured again toward the hardworking typists.

"I thought it was probably something like that," Brownlee said. "Gunner, what it is is that I have sort of a responsibility for an officer, a first lieutenant . . ."

"*Sort* of a responsibility, Sir?" Hardee asked, confused.

"The thing is, Gunner," Brownlee said, a little uncomfortably, "I'm with a rather unconventional unit."

"Which one would that be, Sir?" Hardee asked. He was beginning to suspect that he was not going to enjoy this encounter.

"I'm with the OSS, to put a point on it," Brownlee said. "And the chain of command is a little fuzzy in the OSS."

Master Gunner Hardee was not an admirer of the OSS, about which he knew little except that the service records of a couple of hundred officers who had volunteered for it had crossed his desk. Hardee had nearly thirty years in The Corps. So far as he was concerned the officer personnel requirements of The Corps obviously should come first. And with the to-be-expected exceptions to that rule, like that sea lawyer "hero" Macklin a couple of days ago, here they were sending what looked to him like good officers to the OSS at a time when The Corps was up shit's creek without a paddle trying to find officers to staff a Marine Corps that was growing larger than anyone ever thought it would.

"So I hear," Hardee said. "Exactly how can I help you, Major?"

"I'm the senior Marine officer at the OSS reception center," Brownlee said. "Yesterday, an officer, a first lieutenant Macklin . . ."

Oh, shit!

". . . was transferred in. I generally go over the records of people coming into the OSS—Marines, I mean—to make sure everything is shipshape."

"Yes, Sir?"

"And I went over Lieutenant Macklin's records. That's not exactly true. His records have been misplaced. Or possibly lost. Probably at Guadalcanal."

In fact, Master Gunner Hardee knew, the service record of First Lieutenant Macklin, Robert B., USMC, was thirty feet away, filed under the R's, in a file cabinet devoted to those officers "Absent, Sick In Hospital." The reason he knew this to be true was that he himself had put them there, in a place where he—but no one else—could readily lay his hands on them.

"Is that so?"

"I suppose that happens all the time," Brownlee said.

"Yes, Sir. It's not at all unusual."

"This officer is one hell of a Marine, Gunner."

One hell of an asshole of a Marine, is the way I hear it.

"He was twice wounded at Guadalcanal, storming the beaches, during the invasion."

"Yes, Sir."

"As a matter of fact, he was one of the heroes The Corps sent back from over there for the War Bond Tour."

"Is that so?"

"From what you've told me, Gunner, his promotion to captain should have come along by now, more or less automatically."

You and your fucking big mouth, Hardee!

"You think so, Sir?"

"Well, he's got the twenty-four months in grade you mentioned, and then some. And, even though his records have been misplaced, I think we can give him the benefit of the doubt about not being under charges, can't we?"

"I'm sure we can, Sir."

"I had to be in Washington today, Gunner," Brownlee said. "What I'd hoped I would be able to do here is see if we can't find his records and get him promoted, as he deserves."

"As you said, Major, his missing records do pose a problem. I can tell you I'll keep a sharp eye out for them, now that you've brought this to my attention."

"I'd really hate to go to the Inspector General with this, Gunner . . ."

Oh, shit! That's all we need in here, the Inspector General running around trying to do right by this goddamned Marine hero!

". . . because of the administrative problems that would inevitably cause."

"I understand, Sir."

And if I have to "find" this asshole's records, that would mean I would have to send them over to the OSS, where, after one look at this bastard's efficiency reports, they'd boot him out so fast it would take two weeks for his asshole to catch up with him.

And it would also be pretty embarrassing for Colonel Wilson, personally and officially.

"Major, how long are you going to be in Washington?" Master Gunner Hardee asked.

"I'm going to leave about sixteen hundred."

"Do you suppose it would be possible for you to come by here, say, at fifteen hundred? Let me look into this myself and see what I can turn up."

"That would be great!" Major Brownlee said happily. "Thank you very much, Gunner."

"My pleasure, Sir."

As soon as Major Brownlee had left the office, Gunner Hardee went to the R section of the "Absent, Sick in Hospital" file cabinet. He briefly examined a service record it contained, made a note of Macklin's full name and serial number, and then went to the corner of the room where the two typists were preparing mimeograph stencils of last week's promotion list.

He tapped the staff sergeant supervising the operation on the shoulder, and when he turned said, "One more for the captain's list."

"It's already done, Mr. Hardee."

"Do it again."

"Already printed and everything," the staff sergeant pleaded.

"Do it again," Hardee repeated.

"Aye, aye, Sir. Where's the records?"

"I'll take care of his records, you just get his goddamn name on the goddamned orders!"

"Aye, aye, Sir."

When Major James C. Brownlee returned to the office at 1600 hours, Master Gunner Hardee told him that while he had been unable to locate Lieutenant Macklin's records—he was still working on that—he had arranged to deal with the problem of his overdue promotion.

He gave Major Brownlee a copy of the promotion orders, so fresh from the mimeograph machine that the ink was a little wet.

Colonel David M. Wilson, USMC, Deputy Assistant Chief of Staff G-1 for Officer Personnel, never heard a thing about it.

Major James C. Brownlee's belief that master gunners were the people to see when you had a problem was reinforced.

Captain Robert B. Macklin, USMC, was of course delighted to receive his long-overdue—and in his opinion, richly deserved—promotion.

Master Gunner James L. Hardee, who had been on the water wagon for six months, went to a bar in Georgetown that night and got very drunk.

[FIVE]

```
T O P    S E C R E T

SUPREME HEADQUARTERS SWPOA
NAVY DEPT WASH DC


VIA SPECIAL CHANNEL
DUPLICATION FORBIDDEN
ORIGINAL TO BE DESTROYED AFTER ENCRYPTION AND TRANSMITTAL
EYES ONLY—THE SECRETARY OF THE NAVY


BRISBANE, AUSTRALIA
MONDAY 2 NOVEMBER 1942


DEAR FRANK:


I THINK I HAVE GOTTEN TO THE BOTTOM OF WHY EL SUPREMO SHOWS
NO INTEREST AT ALL IN THIS FELLOW FERTIG IN THE PHILIPPINES. I'M
NOT GOING TO WASTE YOUR TIME TELLING YOU ABOUT IT, BUT IT'S
NONSENSE. ADMIRAL LEAHY IS RIGHT, THERE IS POTENTIAL THERE,
AND I THINK RICKABEE'S PEOPLE SHOULD BE INVOLVED FROM THE
START.


I'M GOING TO TELL RICKABEE TO COME TO YOU, IF HE ENCOUNTERS
TROUBLE DOING WHAT I THINK HE HAS TO DO. I SUSPECT HE WILL
ENCOUNTER THE SAME KIND OF PAROCHIAL NONSENSE AMONG THE
```

PROFESSIONAL WARRIORS IN WASHINGTON THAT I HAVE
ENCOUNTERED HERE.

I HAVE BEEN BUTTING MY HEAD, VIS-À-VIS DONOVAN'S PEOPLE,
AGAINST THE PALACE WALL SO OFTEN AND SO LONG THAT IT'S
BLOODY, AND AM GETTING NOWHERE. IS THERE ANY CHANCE I CAN
STOP? IT WOULD TAKE A DIRECT ORDER FROM ROOSEVELT TO MAKE
HIM CHANGE HIS MIND, AND THEN THEY WILL DRAG THEIR FEET, AT
WHICH, YOU MAY HAVE NOTICED, THEY'RE VERY GOOD.

MORE SOON.

BEST REGARDS,

FLEMING PICKERING, BRIGADIER GENERAL, USMCR

T O P   S E C R E T

T O P   S E C R E T

SUPREME HEADQUARTERS SWPOA
NAVY DEPT WASH DC

VIA SPECIAL CHANNEL
DUPLICATION FORBIDDEN
ORIGINAL TO BE DESTROYED AFTER ENCRYPTION AND TRANSMITTAL

FOR COLONEL F.L. RICKABEE
USMC OFFICE OF MANAGEMENT ANALYSIS

BRISBANE, AUSTRALIA
MONDAY 2 NOVEMBER 1942

DEAR FRITZ:

DON'T TELL HIM YET, OR EVEN BANNING, BUT I WANT YOU TO TRY TO
FIND A SUITABLE REPLACEMENT FOR MCCOY FOR THE MONGOLIAN
OPERATION.

PUT HIM AND BANNING TO WORK FINDING OUT ABOUT GUERRILLA
OPERATIONS, BECAUSE I BELIEVE THAT THIS WENDELL FERTIG IN THE
PHILIPPINES IS PROBABLY GOING TO TURN OUT MORE USEFUL THAN
ANYBODY IN THE PALACE HERE IS WILLING TO EVEN CONSIDER. I

SUSPECT THAT THE SAME MENTAL ATTITUDE VIS-A-VIS
UNCONVENTIONAL WARRIORS AND THE COMPETENCE OF RESERVE
OFFICERS IS PREVALENT IN WASHINGTON.

THIS IDEA HAS LEAHY'S BACKING, SO IF YOU ENCOUNTER ANY
TROUBLE, FEEL FREE TO GO TO FRANK KNOX.

IF YOU CAN DO IT WITHOUT MAKING ANY WAVES, PLEASE (A) SEE IF
YOU CAN FIND OUT WHERE MY SON IS BEING ASSIGNED AFTER THE
WAR BOND TOUR AND (B) TELL ME IF TELLING HIS MOTHER WOULD
REALLY ENDANGER THE ENTIRE WAR EFFORT. SHE WENT TO SEE JACK
NMI STECKER'S BOY AT THE HOSPITAL IN PEARL AND IS IN PRETTY
BAD SHAPE.

KOFFLER IS GETTING MARRIED NEXT WEEK, FOR A LITTLE GOOD
NEWS. I DECIDED I HAD THE AUTHORITY TO MAKE HIM A STAFF
SERGEANT AND HAVE DONE SO.

REGARDS,

FLEMING PICKERING, BRIGADIER GENERAL, USMCR

T O P   S E C R E T

VIII

[ONE]
Water Lily Cottage
Brisbane, Australia
0815 Hours 9 November 1942

When he walked into the kitchen of the rambling frame house—the term "cottage," he had decided when he rented the place, was another manifestation of Australian/British understatement—Brigadier General Fleming W. Pickering, USMCR, obviously fresh from his shower, was wearing a pale-blue silk dressing gown that reached almost to his bare feet.

He went to the stove, poured himself a mug of coffee, and then sat on a high stool at the kitchen table. A tall, muscular, deeply tanned man of the same age, wearing a khaki shirt and Marine-green trousers, was already sitting at the table. Something about him suggested illness and/or exhaustion.

For a moment they quietly examined each other without expression.

"Sergeant Stecker," Pickering finally said, "you realize that you and I did not set a good example for the men last night. I trust you are properly ashamed of yourself?"

Lieutenant Colonel Jack (NMI) Stecker, USMCR, who had the previous day flown into Brisbane from Guadalcanal, chuckled. Then he replied slowly, with a smile, "Don't worry about it, Corporal Pickering, I don't think anyone was in any condition to notice."

Pickering looked at his old friend with affection and concern—they had once, a generation before, in a previous war, in France, actually been Sergeant Stecker and Corporal Pickering.

"God, I hope so, Jack. I haven't been that plastered in years."

"I used to think I could handle my liquor," Stecker said.

"That was before we got old," Pickering said.

"Or started drinking with the Coastwatchers. In particular the head Coastwatcher," Stecker said. "I think that is the root of our problem. With the honor of The Corps at stake, I tried to match Commander Feldt drink for drink. That was a colossal error in judgment."

"Well, no real harm done, and I suspect that the newlyweds will remember their reception for a long time."

"Probably not too fondly," Stecker said. "They're nice kids, aren't they? Staff Sergeant Koffler doesn't look old enough to be a father-to-be, or a staff sergeant, or to have done what he did on Buka. And the bride looked a little younger."

"I don't think they come much better," Pickering said. "I was about to ask where the hell the cook is, but on reflection, I'm not sure I'm up to looking a couple of sunny-side-up eggs in the face."

"I have been sitting here wondering whether a little hair of the dog would make me feel better."

"What was your conclusion?"

"I don't want to breathe fumes on the senior Marine officer aboard when I report for duty."

"What?"

"His name is Mitchell. Do you know him?"

Pickering nodded. "Oh, yes, I know Colonel Lewis R. Mitchell," he said, not very pleasantly. "The Special Liaison Officer between CINCPAC and SWPOA. What do you mean, you have to report to him?"

"He's the senior Marine officer at SWPOA. I'm supposed to 'coordinate' with him."

"Fuck Mitchell. Stay away from him."

"I don't see how I can, Flem. Anyway, what have you got against him?"

"Well, for one thing, the minute the pompous sonofabitch showed up here, he tried to tell Eric Feldt how to run the Coastwatcher Organizer, and walked all over Ed Banning in the process. I heard about it, and had Forrest send him a radio telling him in some very plain language to butt the hell out of our business."

Major General Horace W. T. Forrest was Assistant Chief of Staff, G-2, Headquarters, USMC.

Second Lieutenant George F. Hart, USMCR—his chest and biceps straining the material of his skivvy shirt—came into the kitchen.

"Good morning, General," Hart said. "Colonel. I thought I heard something in here."

"What you probably heard was my stomach growling," Pickering said. "George, get on the horn. Present my compliments to Colonel Mitchell, and tell him that I will be 'coordinating' Colonel Stecker's activities at SWPOA. And on your way back in here, bring a bottle of Courvoisier. Colonel Stecker and I require a medicinal dose."

"Aye, aye, Sir."

"And if you feel the need, George, have one yourself. But just one. You're going to help Colonel Stecker move his things from the BOQ here."

"Aye, aye, Sir," Hart said. "Welcome to Water Lily Cottage, Colonel."

Stecker smiled uneasily, but waited until Hart had left the room before speaking.

"I think we had better think about my moving in here, Flem. I don't know what you're doing here . . ."

"For one thing, *I'm* the senior Marine around here, so don't argue with me, Colonel."

". . . except that it's highly classified."

"You don't look like a Japanese spy to me. Just don't ask too many questions, Jack."

"I don't want to be in the way."

"If you would be in the way, Jack, I wouldn't have asked you to move in," Pickering said. "And I need you. With all these kids around, I feel like I'm trapped in a fraternity house. I need someone my own age to keep me company."

Stecker looked as if he was framing a reply.

"Changing the subject, Colonel," Pickering said. "Through the haze, I seem to recall that we discussed guerrilla operations at some time last night. Do you remember what you said? And if so, would you mind repeating it?"

Stecker looked at him in surprise, then thought aloud.

"You're serious, aren't you?"

"Yes, I am. What was it you said about the ratio between the strength of a guerrilla force and conventional forces required to contain them?"

"What I said—and Fleming, I don't regard myself as any kind of an expert on this—"

"How long were you involved, down in the Banana Republics?" Pickering interrupted.

"I did three tours in Nicaragua and two in Haiti. So did a lot of other people. Chesty Puller, Lew Diamond . . ."

"Until somebody comes along with more experience than you have, you're my expert," Pickering said. "Go on, please, Jack."

"What I said was that when The Corps was in Haiti and Nicaragua, we used to say that one guerrilla tied up seven Marines."

"Define a guerrilla for me."

Stecker considered his reply before giving it:

"An armed man who is willing to take a risk to make things difficult for an occupying force."

"Define difficult."

"Anything from ambushing his supply lines, blowing up his supply dumps, denying him the use of roads unless he sends large military forces to guard his convoys, to . . . I don't know quite how to put this, making him look bad, incompetent, ineffective, in the eyes of the native population."

"One guerrilla ties up seven men?" Pickering quoted thoughtfully.

"At least seven. I always thought that it was closer to ten. We outnumbered the banditos in Nicaragua ten to one, and they gave us a lot of trouble."

"What sort of supplies does a guerrilla need?"

"A good guerrilla operation lives off the land. Like the Chinese Communists do. Getting the civilians—without antagonizing them—to provide food and shelter. And intelligence. Paying for it, if at all possible. Aside from that, nothing but the basics, the Three B's—boots, bullets, and beans."

"Is there a racial factor?"

"What do you mean?"

"In the Banana Republics, the guerrillas came from the native population. It was the brown man against white gringos. Is that right?"

"Yes, I suppose it is."

"In the Philippines, what would it be?"

"Oh, I see what you mean. You're asking would the Filipinos support an American guerrilla operation?"

Pickering nodded.

"Fleming, over the years, you've spent as much time in the Philippines as I have."

"I'm asking you."

"Unless American officers did something really stupid—and that's a real possibility—I think seventy-five percent, eighty-five percent of the Filipinos would help an American guerrilla operation."

Pickering nodded.

"Are you going to tell me why you're interested in this?" Stecker asked.

"There's a chap on Mindanao, a reserve officer who chose not to surrender. His name is Wendell Fertig. He's trying to set up a guerrilla operation."

"And?"

"We know he's got some Marines with him. That seems to make it our business. We're looking into what, if anything, we can do for him, and what, if any, good he can really do against the Japs."

"Who's we?"

"Frank Knox, Chester Nimitz, and me. El Supremo doesn't seem to be at all interested."

There aren't very many people around, Stecker thought, *who can so casually refer to the Secretary of the Navy and the Commander-in-Chief, Pacific, by their first names. Or refer, with obviously amused affection, to General Douglas MacArthur, Supreme Commander, South West Pacific Ocean Areas, as "El Supremo."*

I probably should have insisted on obeying my orders, but the truth is, I'm glad he's going to keep this Colonel Mitchell off my back. And, in the final analysis, Flem Pickering is *the senior Marine officer around here; I really don't have any choice.*

Lieutenant Hart returned to the kitchen carrying a bottle of Courvoisier cognac and two crystal cognac snifters.

"Colonel Mitchell's compliments, Sir," he said. "He asked me to tell you that he stands ready to render any assistance to Colonel Stecker requested."

Pickering snorted.

"Shall I pour, Sir?" Hart said, smiling.

"Those snifters are for officers and gentlemen, Hart," Pickering said. "At the moment, what you have is just a couple of badly hung-over old Marines. Just pour about an inch of that stuff into our coffee, will you, please?"

```
T O P   S E C R E T


SUPREME HEADQUARTERS SWPOA
NAVY DEPT WASH DC


VIA SPECIAL CHANNEL
DUPLICATION FORBIDDEN
ORIGINAL TO BE DESTROYED AFTER ENCRYPTION AND TRANSMITTAL


FOR COLONEL F.L. RICKABEE
USMC OFFICE OF MANAGEMENT ANALYSIS


BRISBANE, AUSTRALIA
MONDAY 9 NOVEMBER 1942


DEAR FRITZ:


I DON'T KNOW IF YOU'VE HEARD OR NOT, BUT LT COLONEL JACK NMI
STECKER IS HERE IN BRISBANE. HE WENT TO STAFF SERGEANT
KOFFLER'S WEDDING WITH ME, AS A MATTER OF FACT, AND IS AT
THIS MOMENT MOVING HIS STUFF FROM THE ARMY BOQ INTO MY
HOUSE. HE'S HERE TO SET UP FACILITIES FOR THE FIRST MARDIV
WHEN THEY ARE RELIEVED FROM GUADALCANAL AND BROUGHT HERE
FOR REHABILITATION AND REFITTING. ACCORDING TO STECKER, THEY
ARE IN REALLY BAD PHYSICAL SHAPE; ALMOST EVERYBODY HAS
MALARIA.


STECKER WAS RELIEVED OF HIS COMMAND OF SECOND BATTALION,
FIFTH MARINES, AND IS NOW OFFICIALLY ASSIGNED TO SWPOA IN
SOME SORT OF VAGUELY DEFINED BILLET. I AM UNABLE TO BELIEVE
HE WAS RELIEVED FOR CAUSE, AND STRONGLY SUSPECT THAT IT IS
```

THE PROFESSIONAL OFFICER CORPS PUSHING ASIDE A RESERVIST/UP
FROM THE RANKS MUSTANG TO GIVE THE COMMAND TO ONE OF THEIR
OWN. I CAN'T IMAGINE WHY GENERAL VANDEGRIFT PERMITTED THIS
TO HAPPEN, BUT IT HAS HAPPENED, AND IT MAY BE A BLESSING IN
DISGUISE FOR US.

I HAD A TALK WITH STECKER AFTER THE WEDDING, AND IT CAME OUT
THAT HE HAS HAD EXTENSIVE EXPERIENCE WITH GUERRILLA
OPERATIONS IN THE BANANA REPUBLICS, ESPECIALLY NICARAGUA,
BETWEEN THE WARS. IT SEEMS TO ME THAT IF YOU KNOW HOW TO
FIGHT AGAINST GUERRILLAS, IT WOULD FOLLOW THAT YOU KNOW HOW
TO FIGHT AS A GUERRILLA . . . AND CERTAINLY TO KNOWLEDGEABLY
EVALUATE HOW SOMEONE ELSE IS SET UP, AND EQUIPPED, TO FIGHT
AS GUERRILLAS.

I HAVEN'T SAID ANYTHING TO HIM YET, BUT I KNOW HIM WELL
ENOUGH TO KNOW THAT HE WOULD RATHER BE DOING SOMETHING
EITHER WITH, OR FOR, THIS FELLOW FERTIG ON MINDANAO THAN
ARRANGING TOURS OF PICTURESQUE AUSTRALIA OR USO SHOWS,
WHICH IS WHAT THE CORPS WANTS HIM TO DO NOW. AND THERE IS NO
QUESTION IN MY MIND THAT HIS CONTRIBUTION TO THIS EFFORT
WOULD BE OF MUCH GREATER VALUE THAN WHAT HE IS DOING NOW.
SO I WANT HIM TRANSFERRED TO US, WITH A CAVEAT: HE HAS
ALREADY SUFFERED ENOUGH HUMILIATION (GODDAMN IT, HE HAS
THE MEDAL OF HONOR; HOW COULD THEY DO THIS TO HIM?) AS IT IS,
SO I WANT YOU TO TAKE EVERY PRECAUTION TO MAKE SURE THERE IS
NO SCUTTLEBUTT CIRCULATING THAT HE HAS BEEN FURTHER
DEMOTED BY HIS ASSIGNMENT TO US.

DO IT AS QUICKLY AS YOU CAN, AND I THINK YOU HAD BETTER SEND
MCCOY OVER HERE, TOO, AS QUICKLY AS THAT CAN BE ARRANGED. I
THINK THE SOONER WE GET SOMEBODY WITH CAPTAIN/GENERAL
FERTIG, THE BETTER.

REGARDS,

FLEMING PICKERING, BRIGADIER GENERAL, USMCR

TOP   SECRET

[TWO]
Naval Air Transport Station
Brisbane, Australia
0455 Hours 14 November 1942

First Lieutenant Kenneth R. McCoy, USMCR, was not in a very good mood when the Consolidated PB2Y-3 Coronado splashed down in Brisbane Harbor; a drenching in the whaleboat that carried him ashore made his mood worse; and when he saw Second Lieutenant George F. Hart, USMCR, standing on the wharf, the golden cords of an aide-de-camp hanging from his epaulets, his mood grew worse still.

The sonofabitch hasn't been in The Corps long enough to be a goddamned corporal, and there he stands in an officer's uniform!

The flight from Pearl Harbor in the huge, four-engined flying boat was long and rough. A Medical Corps lieutenant commander got airsick thirty minutes out of Pearl, threw up what looked like the remnants of an entire Hawaiian luau and two quarts of beer all over himself and the deck, and then spent the rest of the flight either moaning, dry-heaving, or rubbing his vomit-soaked uniform in McCoy's face as he made his way—every fifteen minutes—to the head.

Before McCoy boarded the Coronado at Pearl Harbor, he had run into a zealous Navy lieutenant who wouldn't let him get on the airplane—AAAAA priority or not—until his shot record was up to date. McCoy's shot record recorded that he had been injected with every inoculation against every disease known to the Navy Medical Corps. The record itself, however, was in Washington. Ed Sessions had suggested that since he was going to be around for a while, it would make sense to have the contents of the shot record incorporated into all his official records.

Sessions hadn't gotten it back to him when the hurry-up call from General Pickering to go to Brisbane came in.

The idiot at Pearl actually wanted to give him the entire series of inoculations again. But a medical lieutenant commander at the hospital was more reasonable. He gave McCoy ''credit'' for all the shots given Marines in the States, but insisted that McCoy take the series prescribed for people headed for the Pacific and/or South West Pacific Ocean Areas—despite McCoy's protestations that he had been in Australia only the month before, and had had the shots then.

So he suffered from the side effects of half a dozen inoculations—including a left buttock that felt as if it had been bitten by a poisonous snake. He couldn't sit on his sore left buttock without pain, and there was no way, on the pipe-and-cloth seats of the Coronado, to avoid sitting on it.

Before the Coronado took off from Pearl Harbor, there was a long flight on an Army Air Corps B-17 Flying Fortress from San Francisco. He spent that flight making himself as comfortable as possible on a pile of mail sacks.

McCoy climbed out of the whaleboat and then, carrying his bag, made his way up the stone steps cut into the wharf.

Second Lieutenant Hart saluted First Lieutenant McCoy.

There was nothing wrong with the salute. It was crisp and accompanied by a smile.

"Give me your bag, Mr. McCoy," Hart said. "You must be a little weary."

McCoy returned Hart's salute and handed over his bag. Hart picked it up effortlessly—*the sonofabitch really has a build*—and then gestured down the wharf. McCoy looked and saw General Pickering's Studebaker staff car.

"You're cleared through the arrival processing, Mr. McCoy," Hart said. "The General arranged it."

"Thank you," McCoy said, and started walking toward the Studebaker.

There's nothing really wrong with Hart. He didn't ask for that gold bar; and for that matter, I'm the guy who recruited him for General Pickering from Parris Island.

And, oh, shit, I know for a fact he's not a candy-ass. When I told him I was going to leave him alone overnight on the beach at Buka, all he said was "OK." That took balls.

What's wrong around here, McCoy, is you. You've got a bad case of candy-ass yourself. "It isn't fair that I'm back here."

"I don't think the discipline of the entire Marine Corps would collapse if you called me 'Ken,' George."

"That would presume I have forgiven you for leaving me on that beach all by my lonesome, Mr. McCoy. I'm not quite at that point yet."

"Well, in that case, go fuck yourself, Mr. Hart."

"Hey, before I forget it: When you see Koffler, and he thanks you for his wedding present, just say 'You're welcome.' "

"You bought him a wedding present, and said it was from me?"

"Two sets of pajamas, from the Officers' Sale Store."

"How much?"

"Now that you mention it, four-fifty each, plus two bits to have the fly sewn shut on the bride's. Nine and a quarter."

McCoy stopped, took out his wallet, and handed Hart a ten-dollar bill.

"Thanks, George," he said, and then thought aloud: "How did you know you'd get your money back?"

"You ever hear what they say about bad pennies, they keep turning up?"

In other words, you didn't. You're really a nice guy, Hart.

"How's the General?" McCoy asked.

"Ask him yourself," Hart said, and effortlessly waved McCoy's bag toward the Studebaker.

Brigadier General Fleming W. Pickering was in the process of stepping out of the front passenger seat.

"Jesus Christ," McCoy muttered. "It's five o'clock in the morning. What's he doing up at this hour?"

"I think he wants to talk to you before you get out to Water Lily," Hart said. "As a matter of fact, I know he does. He told me."

"I'd welcome you to Australia, Ken," General Pickering said as McCoy came near. "But I'm afraid you'd throw something at me. Sorry about this; it was necessary."

McCoy saluted crisply.

"Good morning, Sir."

"How was the flight?"

"I've had better, Sir," McCoy said.

"You all right? You're walking funny."

"I had a shot where I sit, Sir. It's a little sore. I'll be all right."

"Get in the back, Ken," Pickering said. "I want to talk to you before we get to the cottage."

"Aye, aye, Sir."

"George, take twenty minutes or so to drive us home."

"Aye, aye, Sir."

"I didn't think. Ken, are you hungry?"

"I'm all right, Sir."

"Somehow, I suspect that's not the truth, the whole truth, and nothing but the truth."

"I'm all right, Sir. I can wait until we get to the cottage."

"If you're sure," Pickering said doubtfully. "I'd really like to get this out of the way."

"I'm all right, Sir," McCoy repeated.

"OK, then get in."

A general officer, McCoy thought, is holding the door for me.

There were two reminders that Pickering was a general officer—first when Hart removed the covers from the red-starred general officer's plates on the car, and again when they passed the guard at the gate to the Navy base. He started saluting the car long before they reached the guard shack.

Pickering returned the guard's salute casually, then extended a cigar case to McCoy. McCoy took one.

"Thank you, Sir."

"Cuban," Pickering said. "The Pacific Commerce called here. Unfortunately for her master, I remembered he was a cigar smoker. I pulled rank on him and relieved him of his stock. So he smokes his thumb on the long voyage to San Francisco, and you and I and El Supremo have something to smoke.''

Typical General Pickering, McCoy thought. *If he got cigars from one of his ships, it was because he asked for them politely, not demanded them, and the captain gave him all he had, not so much because Pickering owns Pacific & Far East Shipping, but because the captain, like everybody else I've ever known who works for him, would give him the shirt off his back.*

''Two questions, Ken,'' Pickering said. ''How would you feel about going back to the Philippines? I mean by rubber boat off a submarine?''

''I'm a Marine, Sir. I go where I'm ordered.''

''That's not what I asked.''

''Every time I start feeling sorry for myself, Sir, I remind myself I'm not on Guadalcanal, living in the mud, with people trying to kill me.''

''Are you feeling sorry for yourself right now?''

''I thought I was going to have four or five months in the States.''

''With Ernie, you mean,'' Pickering said. It was not a question. ''How is she?''

''Just fine, Sir.''

She was fine when she put me on the plane, but when Ed Sessions showed up at her apartment with my plane tickets, she lost it. I'd never seen her cry before.

Pickering grunted.

''You coming back must have been tough on her. But she's a tough little lady.''

You didn't see her cry.

''Yes, Sir. She is. I have a package for you—it's in my bag—from Mr. Sage. I was going to send it with an officer courier, but then . . .''

''How do you get along with him?''

''If I were him, I don't think I'd like me, either. Ernie deserves better than this, than me.''

''Better than this, maybe. But if I had a daughter, I wouldn't be laying barbed wire to keep you away from her.''

McCoy chuckled. ''Thank you, Sir.''

''Second question: How do you get along with Colonel Jack Stecker?''

What kind of a question is that? How do I get along with him? He's a light colonel and I'm a first lieutenant. He'll tell me what to do, and I will do it.

''Colonel Stecker is a fine Marine, Sir.''

''And he was a fine buck sergeant in the First World War. My question was, 'How do you get along with him?' ''

''I say 'Aye, aye, Sir' to him a lot.''

"Am I hearing, 'He's a fine Marine, but I don't like him'?''

"No, Sir,'' McCoy replied quickly and sincerely.

"Does the name Fertig mean anything to you?''

"He didn't surrender in the Philippines?'' McCoy asked.

"Right.''

"I picked up on a little about him in Washington,'' McCoy said.

"Right. He's a reserve Army officer, a captain . . .''

The way I heard it, he's a light bird, McCoy thought, but said nothing.

". . . who has a radio, an obsolete code machine, and says he is establishing a guerrilla force. He's got some people with him, including some Marines. El Supremo is a little embarrassed about him—after he announced there was absolutely no possibility of guerrilla activity in the Philippines, this fellow Fertig shows up—but Nimitz, and more important, Leahy and Frank Knox think he may have potential.''

"Yes, Sir.''

"What I want to do is send you and Jack Stecker into the Philippines—specifically, onto Mindanao. You'll take Fertig some supplies, a radio, some codes, medicine, small arms, et cetera.''

"Aye, aye, Sir.''

"But your primary mission will be to evaluate him, the people around him, and his, their, potential. Between you and Stecker, I think you have the experience and the knowledge to come up with some valid answers.''

The last poop I had was that Eighth and Eye was giving Colonel Rickabee a bad time about transferring Stecker to Management Analysis. Did they finally get off their fat asses?

"Yes, Sir.''

"I'm going to have Stecker transferred . . .''

What's he doing, reading my mind?

". . . to us. I asked for him some time ago, got no response, and finally had enough of the feet-dragging at Eighth and Eye, and went right to Frank Knox.''

Well, that ought to get them off their fat asses. But they'll have their knives out for you, and Stecker, and anybody connected with either one of you.

"Yes, Sir.''

"Unfortunately, until he is transferred to us—he's here in Australia to set up for the First Marine Division's refitting and rehabilitation when they're relieved from Guadalcanal—I can't involve him officially. As far as that goes, I haven't even asked him if he'd be willing to go. But I've been pumping his brain and his experience, and Feldt is trying to get an Aussie submarine to take you and the supplies. If that falls through, I think I can get one from the Navy, from Nimitz. When you speak with Stecker, stay off the subject of him going with you.''

"Aye, aye, Sir."

"How soon do you think you could be ready to go?"

"Did you say, Sir, that Colonel Stecker's arranged for the supplies you want me to take in?"

"They're available on twenty-four hours' notice."

I don't want to go to the goddamned Philippines. What I want to do is go home, and put my arms around Ernie, and tell her I'm back and I'm going to be there awhile.

"Then, if we have an Aussie submarine, we can go in twenty-four hours, Sir," McCoy said, and then raised his voice. "Hey, George, you want to go for another rubber-boat ride?"

"No, Sir. Thank you very much just the same, Sir."

"George can't go," Pickering said. "For reasons I can't tell you."

Which means that Hart now has one of these MAGIC clearances I'm not supposed to know about. Just got it. He couldn't have gone along on the Buka Operation if he had had a MAGIC clearance. Banning wouldn't have gone with me to the Gobi Desert, and Hart can't go with me to the Philippines. People with MAGIC clearances are not expendable. Stecker and I don't have them, so we're expendable.

How about giving me a MAGIC clearance, General, so I can't do crap like this? And while you're at it, how about throwing in one for Colonel Stecker?

"Yes, Sir."

"It won't be in twenty-four hours, obviously," Pickering said. "But don't sign any long-term leases, Ken."

"Aye, aye, Sir."

"Take us home, George," General Pickering ordered. "We're done."

"Aye, aye, Sir."

"You sure you don't want to change your mind, George?" McCoy asked. "Maybe this time you won't fall out of the boat."

"Once is enough, thank you just the same, for that sort of thing," Hart said.

"Ken, I said George *can't* go," Pickering said.

"I'm just pulling his chain, Sir."

[THREE]
Water Lily Cottage
Brisbane, Australia
0605 Hours 14 November 1942

Two U.S. Army jeeps, a jeep with USMC markings, and a 1938 Jaguar Drop Head Coupe were parked in front of the cottage when Hart pulled the Studebaker up in front of the wide porch that circled the rambling frame building. Without thinking consciously about it, McCoy identified the vehicles and concluded that just about everybody who lived in Water Lily Cottage was "home."

The Jaguar was the General's personal vehicle, made available to him by its owner, an Australian executive of Pacific & Far East Shipping Corporation. "One of the world's great automobiles," Pickering often declared, "presuming you can get the sonofabitch to start, and if you don't mind a leaking roof."

The Marine Corps jeep was probably Colonel Stecker's. The U.S. Army jeeps, which carried the bumper markings of the SWPOA motor pool, were assigned for the use of the "Dungeon Dwellers": The Dungeon—more formally known as the SWPOA Cryptographic Room—was so called because it was located in the subbasement of the Supreme Headquarters SWPOA Building, behind a creaking steel door, and with walls that oozed condensation.

Within the Cryptographic Room (which was actually a suite) there was another room behind another heavy, always locked steel door. It was a cryptographic section guarding one of the most closely held—and vitally important—secrets of the war, which went by the code name MAGIC.

Navy cryptographers at the Pearl Harbor, Territory of Hawaii, Navy Base had broken many—by no means all—of the Japanese Imperial General Staff and Imperial Navy codes. Not only was the very fact that the codes had been broken classified TOP SECRET, but access to intercepted and decrypted messages was limited to a very few people, personally approved by the Chief of Staff to the Commander-in-Chief, Admiral William Leahy, or by the President himself. The Commander-in-Chief, Pacific, Admiral Chester W. Nimitz, and the Supreme Commander, South West Pacific Ocean Area, General Douglas MacArthur, were on the list. So were Brigadier General Fleming Pickering, USMCR, and Colonel F. L. Rickabee, of the Office of Management Analysis.

McCoy was assigned to the Office of Management Analysis after he was commissioned, and in the course of events learned more than he had any right to know about MAGIC. He did not consciously seek this knowledge, but it was not difficult for him to pick up a fact here and a fact there—it would have been difficult, or impossible, for him not to—and assemble a rather clear picture of MAGIC, and of how USMC Special Detachment 16 (the official unit description for Management Analysis personnel stationed in Australia) were involved with it.

It was clear to McCoy that Major Hon Song Do, Signal Corps, USA, on "Temporary Duty" with Detachment 16, and Second Lieutenant John Marston Moore, USMCR, were far more than a pair of cryptographic officers assigned to handle routine classified material for SWPOA.

Hon, a Korean-American from Hawaii, was not only absolutely fluent in

Japanese, but held a Ph.D. in mathematics from the Massachusetts Institute of Technology. Moore was born in Japan to missionary parents, studied at the University of Tokyo, and was equally fluent in Japanese.

At least once a day, sometimes more often, one or the other of them had a private session with General Douglas MacArthur, and sometimes his Intelligence Officer, Brigadier General Charles Willoughby. They went to these meetings—without leaving the SWPOA Headquarters Building—with a briefcase chained to their wrists, and carrying .45 pistols under their uniform tunics.

Hence, carrying something really secret. What sort of secrets? Secrets that could not be shared with the other general officers at SWPOA; secrets that had to be handled with even greater care than other TOP SECRET material coming into SWPOA; under a classification, MAGIC, that no one was even supposed to talk about.

Hon was a mathematician. Mathematicians broke codes. Hon and Moore were Japanese linguists. By definition, Japanese linguists dealt with the translation of Japanese.

In other words, McCoy correctly concluded, Hon and Moore were reading, translating, interpreting, some kind of highly classified Japanese material. Why highly classified? There would be no strict security involved if all they were doing was reading captured Japanese documents; the more people who knew what the Japanese were doing and thinking, the better.

Unless, perhaps, they were reading intercepted Japanese encrypted radio messages—and didn't want the Japanese to know that their code was broken. That would explain a good many things—why so few people had access to MAGIC material, why anyone who had knowledge of MAGIC was absolutely forbidden to go anywhere where there was any chance at all of their falling into Japanese hands.

Major Hon Song Do, a very large man—tall, muscular, and heavyset— was sitting sprawled on a couch in the living room when General Pickering and Lieutenants McCoy and Hart walked in.

"Welcome home, Ken," he said. He had a thick Boston accent.

He came off the couch with surprising grace for his bulk and offered his hand. His left hand, McCoy noticed, held a briefcase, from which a chain led to his wrist.

"Thank you, Sir," McCoy said.

"Now that you have paid due and appropriate homage to my new and exalted rank, you may revert to calling me 'Pluto,' " Hon said.

"I didn't know Army field-grade officers got up at this time of the morning," McCoy said.

"I haven't been to bed," Pluto said, and then looked at Pickering. "When you have a moment, Sir?"

"I could have come to the dungeon," Pickering said.

They both looked at McCoy.

Whatever is in Pluto's briefcase is none of my business.

"Why don't you show Ken where he'll be sleeping?" Pickering said to Hart.

"Aye, aye, Sir."

Lieutenant Colonel Jack (NMI) Stecker was sitting in one of the wicker armchairs in the bedroom when McCoy came out of the bathroom, a towel around his waist.

"You do get around, Lieutenant, don't you?" Stecker said, smiling. "You're living proof that if you join The Corps, you really will see the world."

"Good morning, Sir."

"How are you, Ken?" Stecker asked, offering his hand without rising out of the chair. "The General said you had some trouble with shots?"

"They gave me one in the tail. I have no idea what it was."

"You all right? Fever? Sweaty? Sick to your stomach?"

"Just a sore tail," McCoy said, touched at Stecker's concern. "The bath made it better."

It's been a long time, McCoy had thought as he soaked in the large, old-fashioned tub, *since I've had a bath*—as opposed to a shower. Here he had no choice. The showerhead was at the end of a long, flexible cable. The moment he lifted it from its cradle and turned it on, it developed a powerful leak, spraying water on the ceiling and over the top of the shower curtain. He quickly turned it off, gave in to the inevitable, and took a bath.

Stecker nodded, then pointed to a table set against the wall. McCoy saw there a silver coffee service and a napkin-covered tray.

"I see you live pretty well around here," Stecker said.

"I'm a nice guy. I'm entitled," McCoy said.

"I'm having a little trouble believing how well," Stecker said. "Under the napkin, your choice of breakfast rolls. And there's real cream in that pitcher. And if you want, for example, ham and eggs—fresh eggs—all you have to do is push that doorbell and someone will come and ask you if you want them over easy or sunny-side up."

"Colonel," McCoy said, smiling. "This is what they call 'the lap of luxury.' You'd be surprised how easy it is to get used to."

Stecker chuckled.

"You want some breakfast, Ken?"

"I'd like some coffee," McCoy said, then walked to the table and poured two cups of coffee, carrying one of them to Stecker.

"The General said something about you setting up for the First Division coming here from the 'Canal?'' McCoy asked, but it was a statement.

"That's what I'm here for,'' Stecker said. "But since the division's movement here is still classified, there's not really much I can do. And since the Army's handling the major logistics, quarters and rations, I really don't know what the hell I'm supposed to be doing.''

"He also told me you were setting up my little operation,'' McCoy said.

"He's decided I'm some sort of an expert on guerrilla operations, which I am not. But what I have been doing is coming up with the supplies—medicine, small arms, and ammo—I think you should take with you. But it's your show, McCoy. I'm just trying to make myself useful. If you don't like what I'm suggesting, or you want something else . . .''

"Colonel, I know less about guerrilla operations than anybody I know. My expertise here is in paddling rubber boats, which is a lot harder than it looks.''

"Hart told me,'' Stecker said, laughing, and then growing serious. "I wanted to talk to you about that. About how we pack the stuff you'll be taking with you.''

"In small packages, nothing that can't be handled by one man,'' McCoy said. "Getting the stuff off the submarine into a rubber boat is tough, and then getting it out of the boat and onto land is harder. Ideally, small, *waterproof* packages that can be handled by one man, and that *float.*''

"Koffler's working on something that may help. You know what plastic is?''

McCoy shook his head, no.

"I was surprised to hear that Koffler's out of the hospital. He's back on duty?''

"Back on duty and married.''

"I heard about him getting married,'' McCoy replied. "The last time I saw him, he looked like death warmed over. And not old enough to even think about getting married.''

"He's the youngest staff sergeant I ever saw,'' Stecker said. "General Pickering promoted him so he'd be eligible to get married. Anyway, his wife has been giving him lots of tender, loving care. Howard's still pretty weak. Apparently, the medicine they give to kill intestinal, and blood, parasites is some kind of poison. Poisons, plural. It hit Howard harder than it hit Koffler.''

"Howard had a nurse girlfriend,'' McCoy said, making it a question.

"He still does, according to Major Hon. But they decided not to get married, because the minute they do, she gets shipped home.''

"Why?''

"Some regulation. It's apparently designed to keep innocent Marines from the clutches of lonely nurses. But speaking of Mrs. Koffler . . . you're having dinner with them.''

"What?"

"She wants to show her appreciation to you and Hart for getting him off Buka."

"I'll pass, thank you, Colonel."

"Is there any reason you couldn't go tonight? I know the General has nothing for you to do then. And he told me he thought a home-cooked meal would be good for you."

"That sounds like an order."

"The General feels sorry for her."

McCoy's eyebrows rose in question.

"You don't know the story?"

McCoy shook his head, no.

"According to the General, Koffler got her . . . in the family way the night before they dropped him on Buka," Stecker said. "That happened to be the night they had a memorial service for her husband, who was killed in Africa."

McCoy's eyebrows rose again, but he said nothing, waiting for Stecker to go on.

"They kicked her out of the Royal Navy . . ."

"Royal Australian Navy," McCoy corrected him, thinking out loud.

". . . when they learned she was pregnant. And her family has . . . Ken, her father wouldn't even come to the wedding. They've just about kicked her out of the family. That's pretty vicious. She's a nice girl, and the General likes her."

"Let the General have dinner with her."

"He already has."

"I wasn't the only one on the Buka Operation. Hart was there. God, Pick Pickering was flying the airplane that picked us up. He and Charley Galloway."

"Young Pickering is somewhere in the States. Galloway is in Hawaii. Hart and you are here, and the General thinks a good home-cooked Aussie meal would do all of you some good."

"What? Roast kangaroo?"

"I knew you would be delighted," Stecker said.

"What were you saying about Koffler and . . . what did you say?"

"Plastic."

"What is it?"

"Have you seen the airtight, waterproof stuff they're packaging equipment in lately?"

McCoy shook his head helplessly.

"That aluminum-backed tar paper?"

"No. Not that. *Plastic.* Hart will tell you all about it over dinner. It'll give you something to talk about."

[FOUR]
Apartment 3C
The Amhurst Apartments
Brisbane, Australia
1915 Hours 14 November 1942

Despite a map General Pickering had drawn for him, it took McCoy a long time to find the Amhurst Apartments, a four-story brick building overlooking the harbor. They were driving the Studebaker President.

"Not bad for a nineteen-year-old staff sergeant," McCoy said to Second Lieutenant George F. Hart, USMCR, as they climbed the stairs to the third floor.

"Jealous?"

"Yeah, I guess I am," McCoy said.

"Just for the record," Hart said as McCoy reached out to punch the doorbell, "I was devoutly hoping you'd be able to talk us out of this."

"Just smile and be nice," McCoy replied.

The doorbell, when pushed, caused a clang. A moment later, the door was opened by Staff Sergeant Stephen M. Koffler, USMCR. Sergeant Koffler was five feet seven inches tall, weighed approximately 130 pounds, and looked two years younger than his nineteen years.

"Good evening, gentlemen," he said, clearly having rehearsed his opening remarks, "please come in."

"Good evening, Sergeant Koffler," McCoy said, and thrust a brown paper bag at him. It contained a bottle of Famous Grouse scotch.

"How are you, Steve?" Hart said, and thrust a somewhat larger brown paper bag at him. It contained two bottles of "a damned nice Aussie Cabernet Sauvignon," as General Pickering said when he intercepted the two of them leaving Water Lily Cottage and handed them both bags.

"Welcome," Mrs. Daphne Koffler said from behind her husband. "Thank you for coming."

"Thank you for having us," McCoy said.

Even in her flat shoes, Mrs. Koffler was an inch taller than her husband. She had hazel eyes and peaches-and-cream skin. She wore her light-brown hair done up in a bun at her neck, and she wore only a light lipstick as makeup.

"We wanted—I especially wanted—to thank you for what you did for Steve. For the both of us."

"For the three of us," Koffler chimed in. His wife blushed.

McCoy found himself looking at Mrs. Koffler's belly. To his embarrassment, she was just starting to show.

"That's not necessary," McCoy said.

"If you hadn't gone into Buka, he'd probably be dead," Daphne Koffler said. "And God only knows what would have happened to me and the baby."

Christ, she sounds like Ernie. Says exactly what's on her mind. And looks you right in the eye when she says it.

"We're Marines, Mrs. Koffler," McCoy said. "We go where we're sent. Steve was sent to Buka, and Hart and I were sent in to get him out. No thanks are necessary."

"Indulge me," she said. "Let me say 'Thank you.' "

"OK. You're welcome. Now can we change the subject? Hart told me we're going to have roast kangaroo. Is that true?"

"No, of course it's not. We're having steak. Pluto brought some from the officers' mess."

McCoy was momentarily taken aback by the casual reference to Major Hon Song Do, and then he remembered Koffler's pregnant wife was in contact with Pluto, as an assistant to Commander Feldt, long before he was.

"Why don't we have a drink?" Staff Sergeant Koffler said.

McCoy saw that Mrs. Koffler looked a little uneasy.

She knows what's going to happen, McCoy thought. *The Boy Sergeant is going to get plastered.* .

I wonder how they got together? Christ, she's older than he is. More sophisticated. What the hell did she see in him?

What the hell does Ernie see in me?

I know two things for sure. Whatever the reason she let him . . . went to bed with him the night before he went to Buka, it's not because she's a slut. This is a nice girl. And her look just now when he offered the drink was of concern for him. She loves him.

Why am I surprised? Because he looks likes a high-school cheerleader?

The drinks Staff Sergeant Koffler provided for his guests were about twice as strong as they should have been.

"Koffler, would you break this one into two? Or three?" McCoy asked. "I would like to be sober when I eat."

Mrs. Koffler looked at McCoy with appreciation. Staff Sergeant Koffler looked at him in embarrassment, as if he had committed a terrible social blunder.

"Koffler, I just got here," McCoy said. "It was a long trip. And Colonel Stecker had me running all day. I can't handle much liquor when I'm tired."

"I was out stealing plastic from the Army all day," Koffler said.

"What's plastic?" McCoy asked.

"I don't know what the hell it's made of, but the Army is wrapping stuff in it. It's waterproof and airtight. Just what you need for the stuff you're going to take into the Philippines."

He went into the kitchen, carrying McCoy's glass.

Jesus Christ, I don't know how this Fertig operation is classified, but it's at least SECRET, and probably TOP SECRET. It should not be casually introduced into conversation.

Well, I doubt if Mrs. Koffler will spread it among the girls over coffee. I'll have a word with him later about talking too much. If he's sober enough later to listen.

Koffler returned with the drink.

"I hope this is better," he said, and turned to Hart. "Can I . . . make yours weaker, Lieutenant?"

"I'll just go slow," Hart said.

"Tell me about plastic," McCoy said.

"Well, it looks like a cross between oilcloth and cellophane," Koffler said. "The first time I saw it was when Pluto got the cryptomachine you're going to take with you from the Army—"

"How many other people know about the Philippine Operation?" McCoy interrupted, a tone of annoyance, or exasperation, in his voice.

"I'm not going to discuss this with the ladies during morning tea, if that's what's concerning you, Lieutenant McCoy," Daphne Koffler said.

McCoy, embarrassed, raised both hands in a gesture of surrender.

"That wasn't . . ."

"Steve thinks he's in the company of friends," Daphne went on firmly, again reminding McCoy of Ernie, "who have the appropriate security clearances. And while his wife no longer has the appropriate clearances, he believes she can nevertheless be trusted to keep her mouth shut."

McCoy looked at her but didn't reply.

"Especially since Steve wants very desperately to go with you," she added.

What did she say? He "wants desperately to go"?

"I don't think that's likely," McCoy said.

"You must know, Lieutenant," Daphne said, "that my husband is a rather determined man."

"You need a radio operator," Koffler argued. "So far the General hasn't come up with anybody. And Pluto already showed me how to operate the crypto machine."

"For Christ's sake, why would you want to go with us?" McCoy asked.

The question obviously discomfited Koffler.

"You just got off of Buka. You just got out of the hospital," McCoy said, warming to his subject. "You just got *married,* for Christ's sake!"

"That's why," Koffler said softly.

"What?"

"I have obligations now. Daphne. And . . . a family."

"And so you want to go running around in the Philippines, hiding from the Japs?"

"I want to be an officer," Koffler said.

McCoy looked at him long enough to see that he was serious, then breathed, "Oh, Jesus!"

"Lieutenant Moore was a sergeant when he came here," Koffler said reasonably. "He went to Guadalcanal, came back, and they made him an officer."

"Moore is a college graduate; he's a Japanese linguist, a cryptographer; and he's twenty-three years old."

Koffler didn't choose to hear the reply.

"Lieutenant Hart came here as a sergeant," he went on. "He went to Buka with you; and when you came back, they made him a lieutenant," he argued.

"Hart is older than Moore," McCoy replied. "Before he came in The Corps, he was a detective. They made him an officer because it makes things easier for the General, not because . . ." The absurdity of Koffler's reasoning, and the determined look on his boyish face, triggered something close to hilarity in McCoy's mind. ". . . not because he fell heroically out of his little rubber boat trying to paddle ashore on Buka Island."

"How did you get *your* commission?" Koffler asked. It was a challenge.

"I went to Officer Candidate School at Quantico, as a matter of fact. With General Pickering's son, incidentally. We spent six months busting our asses—excuse the language, Mrs. Koffler—to get that damned gold bar."

Koffler now looked hurt and embarrassed.

"You want to be an officer, apply for OCS," McCoy said reasonably. "I'm sure the General would recommend you for it. Hell, Koffler, I'll write you a letter of recommendation myself."

"I already looked into that. I can't even apply until I'm twenty-one, for Christ's sake."

"Is that what the regulation says?" McCoy asked.

"Nobody asked me how old I was when I jumped onto Buka," Koffler said.

McCoy could think of no reply to make, and made none.

"Oh, hell," Koffler said, as if finally accepting the logic of McCoy's argument. "But I still want to go with you."

Not if I have anything to say about it, McCoy thought.

"Koffler, give yourself a chance to get your health back. Enjoy your family. Remember that sacred Marine Corps saying, 'Never volunteer for anything.' "

"You volunteered to get Howard and me off Buka," Koffler argued.

"Jesus Christ, you don't know when to quit, do you?" McCoy snapped. "For Christ's sake, Koffler, drop it!"

Koffler shrugged.

McCoy looked at Daphne Koffler in time to see that she didn't like at all the words or the tone of voice he had used on her husband.

"I'm sorry," he said. "Maybe it would be best if I left."

"That would just make things worse," she said. "And you didn't say anything to him I haven't already said. Please stay."

"Fix me another drink, Koffler," Lieutenant Hart said. "And then tell Lieutenant McCoy about plastic."

"Sure," Koffler said.

McCoy met Daphne Koffler's eyes.

"Fix me one, too, while you're at it, please," he said.

She nodded her head, just perceptibly, in approval.

When her husband went into the kitchen, she walked to the couch and sat down beside McCoy.

"Thank you," she said.

"Excuse me?"

"You're wrong about me, Lieutenant," she said. "I married Steve because I love him, not because I'm carrying his child."

"Believe it or not, Mrs. Koffler, I'd already figured that out."

She looked into his eyes again.

"You had, hadn't you?" she said, as if surprised.

He nodded.

"Now that we're all pals," George Hart said, "do you think you two could stop calling each other 'Mrs. Koffler' and 'Lieutenant McCoy'?"

McCoy looked at him.

"Mr. Hart," McCoy said, "second lieutenants should be seen and not heard. Isn't that so, Daphne?"

"I believe that's true, Ken," she replied.

```
T  O  P     S  E  C  R  E  T


SUPREME HEADQUARTERS SWPOA
NAVY DEPT WASH DC


VIA SPECIAL CHANNEL
DUPLICATION FORBIDDEN
ORIGINAL TO BE DESTROYED AFTER ENCRYPTION AND TRANSMITTAL
EYES ONLY—THE SECRETARY OF THE NAVY


BRISBANE, AUSTRALIA
SATURDAY 14 NOVEMBER 1942
```

DEAR FRANK:

WORD JUST REACHED HERE THAT THE BATTLESHIPS WASHINGTON
AND SOUTH DAKOTA HAVE SUNK THE JAPANESE BATTLESHIP
KIRISHIMA, EVEN THOUGH THE SOUTH DAKOTA APPARENTLY WAS
PRETTY BADLY HIT IN THE PROCESS. I'D LIKE TO THINK THAT
ADMIRAL DAN CALLAHAN SOMEHOW KNOWS ABOUT THIS. I WAS
PRETTY UPSET WHEN I HEARD HE WAS KILLED THE DAY BEFORE.
REVENGE IS SWEET.

THE MORE I GET INTO THIS FERTIG IN THE PHILIPPINES
BUSINESS—SPECIFICALLY, THE MORE I HAVE LEARNED FROM LT COL
JACK NMI STECKER ABOUT THE EFFICACY OF A WELL-RUN GUERRILLA
OPERATION—THE MORE I BECOME CONVINCED THAT IT'S WORTH A
GOOD DEAL OF EFFORT AND EXPENSE.

WHERE IT STANDS RIGHT NOW IS THAT A YOUNG MARINE OFFICER,
LIEUTENANT KENNETH MCCOY, WHOM THEY CALL "KILLER," BY THE
WAY, JUST ARRIVED HERE. HE HAS ALREADY MADE THE MAKIN
ISLAND MARINE RAIDER OPERATION, AND WENT ASHORE ON BUKA
FROM ANOTHER SUBMARINE WHEN WE REPLACED THE MARINES
THERE. HE IS AS EXPERT IN RUBBER BOAT OPERATIONS AS THEY
COME, IN OTHER WORDS. HE SEES NO PROBLEM IN GETTING ASHORE
FROM A SUBMARINE OFF MINDANAO.

HE AND STECKER HAVE COME UP WITH A LIST OF MATERIEL THEY
FEEL SHOULD GO TO FERTIG, ESSENTIALLY, AND IN THIS ORDER, GOLD,
RADIOS, MEDICINE, AND SMALL ARMS AND AMMUNITION. BECAUSE OF
THE SMALL STATURE OF THE AVERAGE FILIPINO, BOTH FEEL THAT
THE US CARBINE IS THE PROPER WEAPON. I HAVE THE RADIOS AND
THE CARBINES AND AMMUNITION FOR THEM, AND HAVE BEEN
PROMISED AN ARRAY OF MEDICINES WHENEVER I WANT THEM. I
HAVE ALSO BEEN PROMISED A SUBMARINE, PROBABLY THE USS
NARWHAL, WHICH IS A CARGO SUBMARINE. THE PROMISE CAME FROM
CINCPAC HIMSELF, WHO SHARES MY BELIEF THAT ANY GUERRILLA
OPERATION IN THE PHILIPPINES SHOULD BE SUPPORTED ON
STRATEGIC, TACTICAL, AND MORAL GROUNDS.

I ONLY NEED TWO THINGS MORE: I NEED $250,000 IN GOLD.
ACTUALLY, WHAT I NEED IS A CABLE TRANSFER OF THAT MUCH
MONEY TO THE BANK OF AUSTRALIA, WHO WILL GIVE ME THE GOLD.
THE SOONER THE BETTER.

THE SECOND THING I NEED IS FOR YOU TO GOOSE THE MARINE CORPS
PERSONNEL PEOPLE. THEY STILL HAVEN'T TRANSFERRED LT COL
STECKER TO ME. COLONEL RICKABEE REPORTS THAT HE'S BEEN
GETTING A VERY COLD SHOULDER ABOUT THIS, ALTHOUGH NO
EXPLANATION HAS BEEN GIVEN, AND YOUR NORMALLY INCREDIBLY
ABLE CAPTAIN HAUGHTON HASN'T BEEN ABLE TO GET THEM OFF
THEIR UPHOLSTERED CHAIRS, EITHER. I NEED STECKER FOR THIS.
HE'S AN EXPERT IN GUERRILLA OPERATIONS, AND THIS IS CERTAINLY
MORE IMPORTANT THAN WHAT THE CORPS WANTS HIM TO DO
VIS-A-VIS SETTING UP PROPHYLACTIC FACILITIES AND AMATEUR
THEATRICALS. MCCOY GOING ASHORE ALONE WOULD NOT BE NEARLY
AS EFFECTIVE AS THE TWO OF THEM GOING TOGETHER.

I EARNESTLY SOLICIT YOUR IMMEDIATE ACTION IN THIS REGARD.

BEST REGARDS,

FLEMING PICKERING, BRIGADIER GENERAL, USMCR

TOP   SECRET

IX

[ONE]
Supreme Headquarters
South West Pacific Ocean Area
Brisbane, Australia
1715 Hours 16 November 1942

The two Army Military Policemen on duty at the entrance of General MacArthur's headquarters saluted crisply as Brigadier General Fleming Pickering, USMCR, strode briskly through the door.

Pickering returned their salute with a smile. He walked quickly to the Studebaker President with the letters USMC on each side of the hood and the Marine Corps insignia on its front doors, slid into the driver's seat, and started the engine.

Second Lieutenant George F. Hart, USMCR, the aiguillette of his aide-de-camp status flapping up and down as he ran, slowed as he passed through the door long enough to exchange salutes with the MPs and then broke into a trot to the car, as if afraid he would be left behind.

As soon as Hart was in the car, the Studebaker, with a chirp of its tires, backed out of the RESERVED FOR GENERAL OFFICERS parking space, stopped abruptly, and then, with another squeal of tires, drove away.

The two MPs exchanged glances and small smiles. With the exception of the Marine general, every other general and admiral at Supreme Headquarters, Southwest Pacific Ocean Area, had an enlisted driver for his official vehicle. The driver would jump out of the car when he spotted his general or admiral, open the rear door, stand at attention until the general or admiral had climbed in, close the door, and then, after making sure the aide-de-camp was in the backseat, get behind the wheel and chauffeur his august passenger in the ritual dignity to which he was entitled by virtue of his rank.

Not so General Pickering. Not only did he normally drive himself, but more often than not he wasn't accompanied by his aide-de-camp.

There was more. It was reliably rumored that General Douglas MacArthur called General Pickering by his Christian name. Every other officer was addressed by his rank, except for a very few whom El Supremo honored by addressing them by their last names.

This, and a number of other personal idiosyncrasies—General Pickering did not live, for example, in the quarters provided for the very senior officers, but in a rambling frame house he rented near the racetrack—had not, most of the enlisted men knew, endeared General Pickering to his peers, the other general and flag officers of Supreme Headquarters, SWPOA.

It was therefore perhaps natural for the enlisted men, and many of the junior officers, to look fondly upon General Pickering. Anybody who had most of the big brass pissed off at him couldn't be all bad.

"God*damn* the way these people think," General Pickering said, as he wheeled, entirely too fast, around a corner and headed toward the Closed For The Duration racetrack.

George Hart did not reply. He wasn't sure if he was being spoken to, or whether General Pickering was thinking aloud. But a smile flickered across his lips.

There was a silence of perhaps thirty seconds.

"Fertig was a light colonel when Bataan fell," Pickering said. "Not a goddamned captain."

Lieutenant Hart now deduced that whatever had put General Pickering in his current very pissed-off frame of mind concerned Wendell Fertig. Again, he elected not to reply.

Fertig glanced over at Hart. "That sonofabitch must have known that, George," he said reasonably, "and he should have told me."

"That sonofabitch," Lieutenant Hart correctly suspected, was Brigadier General Charles Willoughby, USA, MacArthur's G-2 (General Staff Officer, Intelligence).

"Yes, Sir," Hart said. "How did you find out?"

"I ran into Phil DePress," Pickering said. "He told me."

Lieutenant Colonel Philip J. "Phil" DePress, who still wore the lapel insignia of the proud, now-vanquished 26th Cavalry—it had been forced to eat its horses before the Philippines fell—had somehow escaped and was now one of MacArthur's staff officers.

Hart met DePress in Washington, three months before, shortly after he went to work for General Pickering. Private George F. Hart, formerly Detective Hart of the St. Louis, Missouri, Police Department, had been recruited from the Marine Corps Recruit Depot, Parris Island, to serve ostensibly as an orderly, but in fact as a bodyguard, to General Pickering, then recuperating from wounds and malaria in the Army's Walter Reed Hospital in Washington.

Colonel DePress, who had been sent to Washington as an officer courier from MacArthur's SWPOA headquarters, showed up in Pickering's hospital room bearing a personal letter from MacArthur congratulating Pickering on his promotion to brigadier general.

At the time, Hart was having more than a little trouble adjusting to the sudden changes in his life. One day he was just one more boot in a basic training platoon. Then he was summoned, late at night, to the Bachelor Officers' Quarters, where a cold-eyed Marine first lieutenant (whom Hart correctly suspected was younger than he was) asked him rapid-fire, but pertinent, questions about his law-enforcement background. Apparently satisfied with his answers and with Hart personally, he offered him an assignment as bodyguard to a General Pickering, adding that General Pickering didn't want a bodyguard.

Two days later, he was in Washington, still wearing his boot's shaven-head haircut, promoted sergeant, and living not in the Marine barracks, but in General Pickering's apartment in the Foster Lafayette Hotel, whose windows looked out across Pennsylvania Avenue onto the White House.

Information was thrown rapidly at him. For instance, he learned that General Pickering was a reservist who had earned the nation's second-highest award for gallantry, the Distinguished Service Cross, as a teenaged enlisted man in France in the First World War, and that, in civilian life, he had been Chairman of the Board and Chief Executive Officer of the Pacific & Far East Shipping Corporation.

Hart had also learned that Pickering was not in the ordinary chain of command in the Marine Corps. He reported directly to Secretary of the Navy Frank Knox. And on a mission to the Pacific for Secretary Knox (not further described to Hart then), he had been on Guadalcanal, where he contracted malaria. Later, aboard a destroyer taking him from the island, he was wounded when the warship was strafed by a Japanese bomber. After her captain was killed, he earned the Silver Star for assuming command of the vessel, despite his wounds.

Hart had heard, of course, of the Marine Raider attack on Makin Island (in which President Roosevelt's son participated); and after what he knew about General Pickering, he was not really surprised to find out that the cold-eyed lieutenant who had "interviewed" him at Parris Island had made the raid. Nor even to find out that the lieutenant—who was in fact three years younger than he was (he was twenty-five)—was the near-legendary "Killer" McCoy.

At the time he met Colonel DePress, Hart was devoutly following the advice of his father—Police Captain Karl J. Hart—that when you're involved in something you don't really understand, keep your eyes and ears open and your mouth shut. Thus, when Colonel DePress came into General Pickering's hospital room, he thought like a cop, and not like a Marine Corps boot promoted far beyond his capabilities to sergeant. And as a cop, trained to read people, he recognized that DePress and Pickering were kindred souls, and that they themselves were both aware of their kinship.

When he came to Australia with General Pickering, he was not surprised that Colonel DePress became one of the very small group of people unconnected with General Pickering's mission who were welcome at Water Lily Cottage.

Not much surprised George F. Hart anymore. Not even when he found himself in a rubber boat with Killer McCoy, paddling ashore onto the Japanese-held island of Buka, nor the gold bars on his collar when the other boots in his platoon at Parris Island were still hoping to make PFC.

He was well aware that his promotion had to do with facilitating General Pickering's mission, and not with his being some kind of super Marine. He was beginning to understand his role as a Marine: In addition to the bodyguard role, it was to make himself as useful as he could to General Pickering. And he liked this role. He had some time ago realized that Pickering was special, and working for him a privilege.

More than that: General Pickering was the only man in his life he admired as much as his father . . . perhaps more than his father, as disloyal as this might sound.

Pickering drove the Studebaker President past the boarded-up racetrack, turned right, and two blocks beyond turned off the street onto the clamshell-paved driveway of Water Lily Cottage.

A Chevrolet pickup truck with Royal Australian Navy markings was among the vehicles pulled nose-in against the porch of Water Lily Cottage. It belonged to Lieutenant Commander Eric A. Feldt, RAN.

Pickering had stopped the Studebaker, pulled on the parking brake, and was halfway up the steps of Water Lily Cottage before Lieutenant Hart could open his door.

When Pickering walked into the room, Feldt and Hon were comfortably sprawled on the rattan furniture with which the cottage was furnished. Hon started to get to his feet, but Pickering waved him back.

"I knew you wouldn't mind if we started without you, Pickering, old sod," Feldt said, raising a glass dark with whiskey. "Particularly since I am the bearer of bad tidings."

"No sub?" Pickering asked, walking to a table holding a dozen or more bottles of liquor.

"Three weeks is the best I could do," Feldt said, "even begging on my knees. Sorry."

"Well, thanks for trying," Pickering said. "It was a long shot anyway."

He picked up a bottle of Famous Grouse scotch whiskey and poured an inch and a half into a glass. Then he turned to Hart.

"You want one of these, George?" he asked.

"No, thank you, Sir. I've got the duty tonight."

"That may be a blessing in disguise," Pickering said thoughtfully, obviously referring to the unavailability of an Australian submarine. "Nimitz may be able to loan us the *Narwhal.*"

"The what?"

"The Navy has two transport submarines. Underwater freighters, so to speak. One of them is the *Narwhal;* I don't know what they call the other one. If we can have it, we could take Fertig a lot more than we could carry on a regular sub."

"You think he'll be willing?" Feldt asked.

"We'll soon find out," Pickering said. "Pluto, send Nimitz a Special Channel Personal, saying we need the *Narwhal,* and where should we plan on rendezvousing with her?" He paused and added, thinking aloud, "Which means we'll probably have to fly them to Espíritu Santo; it would take too much time to bring the *Narwhal* here; which in turn means I'm going to have to fight the Army Air Corps for several tons of space on their transports."

Feldt nodded.

"Yes, Sir," Major Hon said. "Would you like to see the message before it goes out?"

"I have a profound faith in your spelling, Pluto," Pickering said, smiling, "but you better send an information copy to Haughton. I'm sure there are thirty admirals on CINCPAC's staff, with twice as many good reasons why CINCPAC should not let us have the *Narwhal.* I may have to go to Frank Knox about this, and Haughton should have forewarning."

"Yes, Sir," Pluto said. "Haughton but not Rickabee?"

"Ask Haughton to advise Rickabee," Pickering said, and then asked, "Where are they?"

Major Hon pointed to the rear of the cottage.

Pickering took a healthy swallow of the whiskey, then set the glass down beside a row of empty glasses. He then immediately picked it and the empties up with the fingers of one hand. With the other, he grabbed the bottle of Famous Grouse by the neck.

He walked out of the living room and down the corridor to a closed door, and knocked on it with the whiskey bottle.

"Open up!" he ordered.

The door was opened by Staff Sergeant Steve Koffler.

"It's the cocktail hour," Pickering said. "Didn't anyone notice?"

He handed the Famous Grouse to Koffler, and walked to a table in the middle of the room and set the glasses on it. Lieutenant Colonel Jack (NMI) Stecker and First Lieutenant Kenneth R. McCoy were sitting at the table, their uniforms protected by flower-patterned aprons, obviously borrowed from the kitchen. The table held three small rifles, technically U.S. Carbines, Caliber .30, M1, broken down. Pickering saw their trigger group assemblies were also in pieces.

"When you can part with that adorable apron, Jack," Pickering said, "stick these in your pocket."

He tossed a small cellophane-covered package onto the table. It contained two silver eagles, the insignia of a colonel.

"That's a little premature, isn't it?" Lieutenant Colonel Stecker asked, a little uncomfortably.

"The Secretary of the Navy told me, I told General MacArthur; and tomorrow morning at oh eight forty-five, with suitable ceremony, El Supremo will pin those on you."

Stecker shook his head.

"That really wasn't necessary," Stecker said.

"There will be a photographer," Pickering went on. "Elly will soon have a picture of her husband the Colonel, with El Supremo beaming at him, with which to dazzle her neighbors."

Elly was Mrs. Jack (NMI) Stecker.

"I suppose," Colonel Stecker said, reaching for the bottle of whiskey, "that it would be bad manners if I were to say I wish to hell the General had minded his own business?"

"I suppose you've heard the bad news? No Aussie sub?" Pickering asked.

"Feldt told us," Stecker said. He held the bottle over one of the glasses and asked with a gesture if Lieutenant McCoy wanted him to pour.

McCoy held up fingers, indicating that he wanted about an inch and a half.

"Thank you, Sir," he said.

"And will Mrs. Koffler banish you from the marriage bed if you come home smelling of this?" Stecker asked Sergeant Koffler.

"I've got some Sen-Sen, Sir," Koffler said. "A little one, please."

"Now that you've taken those apart, can you put them back together again?" Pickering asked, indicating the carbines. "What are you doing, anyway?"

"Working on the sears," Stecker said.

Pickering was aware that the carbines were almost certainly in perfectly functioning order as they came out of their crates. But he was not at all surprised that Stecker and McCoy felt it necessary to fine-tune them. They were not only Marines, nor even only Marine marksmen—both had drawn extra pay as enlisted men for being Expert Riflemen—but weapons experts.

"I think we can get them back together, General," McCoy said. "And if the Colonel can't, Sergeant Koffler can."

Stecker chuckled.

"And you're determined that's what you want to take with you?" Pickering asked.

"I'd rather take a Garand," McCoy said.

"I thought I'd explained why we . . . why *you* should take the carbines," Stecker said.

"That's not what the General asked, Colonel," McCoy said, smiling at Stecker. "The General asked me what I'd *rather* take. I *will* take one of these, but I'd *rather* take a Garand."

"He was a sea lawyer the first time I ever met him," Stecker said, smiling at Pickering. "Wiseass little China Marine corporal in a handmade uniform. Knew everything. Had Expert medals pinned all over him. But when he went on the KD range, he couldn't hit anything but the butts. It looked like a Chinese fire drill, with all those Maggie's drawers flying." (The KD range was the *k*nown *d*istance small-arms range, while Maggie's drawers was a red flag waved from the target butts to signal a complete miss.)

"Christ." McCoy chuckled. "I forgot about that. Until I figured out what that bastard was doing to me, I thought I was losing my mind."

"Until what bastard was doing what to you?" Pickering asked.

"General," Stecker said, "I know you'll find this hard to believe, but there were a number of officers who didn't think Corporal McCoy should be an officer and a gentleman."

"There was a Master Gunny who didn't think so either, as I remember it," McCoy said.

Before being called to active duty as a reserve officer, Stecker was the senior master gunnery sergeant at Marine Base, Quantico, Virginia.

"I didn't say that," Stecker said. "I said that if by some miracle you got through OCS, you would probably be the worst officer in the history of The Corps. And time seems to have proved me right."

"Are you two going to explain what you're talking about?" Pickering said.

"As I was saying, General, before this impertinent sea lawyer interrupted me," Stecker said, "there was a lieutenant who was sent right up the wall by the prospect of this young man putting on an officer's uniform—"

"Macklin," McCoy interrupted. "Robert B. Macklin. That was the sonofabitch's name!"

"That's the man," Stecker said. "What happened, General, was that he tried to get the sea lawyer here kicked out of OCS."

"Why?" Pickering asked.

"I had a run-in with him in China," McCoy said, "when I was working for Ed Banning. He was—is, if he's still alive, and I suppose it's too much to hope that he isn't—a miserable, lying sonofabitch. Banning wrote him an effi-ciency report that should have gotten him kicked out of The Corps, and would have, if the war hadn't come along."

Whatever happened in China, Pickering decided, *if Ed Banning sided with McCoy, the officer in question was dead wrong.*

Stecker saw the confusion on Pickering's face.

"I didn't know any of this at the time," he explained. "Ken being too proud, or too dumb, to ask for help."

"What was I supposed to say, 'Gunny, this lieutenant doesn't like me, and is being mean to me'?"

"Yeah," Stecker said. "Exactly. That's exactly what you should have done. And told me *why* he didn't like you."

"You would have laughed me out of your office," McCoy said.

"Anyway," Stecker said. "I heard that McCoy wasn't qualifying on the KD range. That didn't seem right, so I went and had a look, and found this Lieutenant Macklin in the pits, scoring McCoy's targets himself. He was scor-ing every third shot as a Maggie's drawers. Then I did some snooping around and got the rest of the story."

"In other words, General," McCoy said, "if it wasn't for the Gunny here sticking his nose in where it didn't belong, I would now be a buck sergeant in some nice, safe mess-kit-repair platoon somewhere."

Instead of, Pickering thought, *getting ready for the third time to climb into a rubber boat and paddle it ashore from a submarine onto a Japanese-held island. First the Makin Island raid, then Buka to get Howard and Koffler out, and now the Philippines.*

"There's a word for someone like you, Lieutenant," Stecker said. "It's spelled ungrateful sonofabitch."

"I didn't think full bull colonels, Colonel, were supposed to swear at inno-cent junior officers like me," McCoy said piously.

"Speaking of sonsofbitches," Pickering said, having decided that it was time to get to what he'd come to tell McCoy. He waited until both Stecker and McCoy were looking at him, and then went on.

"I ran into Phil DePress," he said. "And learned from him that Fertig is a light bird, or was, before he promoted himself."

"How does that make Phil a sonofabitch?" Stecker asked.

"The sonofabitch is the unnamed brigadier general, Army type, on El Su-premo's staff who certainly knew this and elected not to tell me."

"Why not, General?" McCoy asked.

"Aside from his being an all-around sonofabitch, you mean? Here's what I'm thinking. For one thing, Fertig, who came on active duty as a captain, was twice promoted for outstanding performance. By whom? If not by El Supremo himself, then by somebody high up in the palace guard. Two promotions—in what, six months?—means that he was doing an outstanding job.''

McCoy nodded, and made a motion of his hand toward Colonel Stecker. The meaning was obvious. *Here's the proof of what you just said:* When the 1st Marine Division landed on Guadalcanal, Stecker landed on Tulagi—across the channel from Guadalcanal—as a major, commanding 2nd Battalion, Fifth Marines. Shortly after that, he was promoted to lieutenant colonel on Guadalcanal. And earlier today, there was a Special Channel Personal message to Pickering from the Secretary of the Navy. A paragraph of that informed him that Stecker was shortly going to be transferred to Washington, and was promoted to full colonel.

Colonel Stecker took McCoy's meaning, and grew uncomfortable. His promotion and transfer meant that he would not be going into the Philippines. Two things were wrong with that. Personally, he'd rather go to the Philippines than to Washington. He thought he might be of some genuine use there; he wasn't at all sure that would be true in Washington. And secondly, although he would have been happy to publicly announce that Ken McCoy was one hell of a Marine officer, he thought that by sending him in alone to the Philippines, Pickering was placing more responsibility on his shoulders than he should really ask of a twenty-two-year-old.

Pickering nodded. "Precisely," he said. "And Fertig being an outstanding officer does not fit in with the picture El Supremo, and especially Willoughby, want to paint of him now."

"You've lost me, Flem," Stecker said.

"It is their official position that setting up guerrilla activities in the Philippines is impossible. Unless, of course, *they* set them up, at some unspecified time in the future. And here comes this guy, a reservist, who announces that he has recruited people, set up U.S. Forces in the Philippines, and appointed himself as commanding general; then says that as soon as we can get him the matériel to do it with, he will commence guerrilla activities against the Japanese. Since it wasn't their idea, obviously it's bad, and so is this guy. And if he succeeds, he will make Willoughby, and by inference El Supremo himself, look foolish."

"You're not suggesting they hope Fertig will fail?" Stecker asked.

"I think that's a possibility, Jack, that we should keep in mind," Pickering said.

"Did you call Willoughby on this?" Stecker asked.

"You bet I did. He vaguely remembers hearing something about Fertig getting promoted to *major,* but that the records have of course been lost, and officially, they have to consider him as still being a captain."

"Christ," McCoy said in disgust.

"A captain who appoints himself commanding general of anything looks like somebody who may not be playing with a full deck," Pickering said. "Somebody you don't pay a lot of attention to, or more importantly, send arms and ammunition to. It's a hell of a lot different when the fellow is a highly regarded lieutenant colonel."

"According to Phil DePress, Fertig is a good officer," Stecker said.

"And I'm sure he's told Willoughby that," Pickering replied. "Willoughby has selective hearing; he doesn't hear what he doesn't want to hear. But what really bothers me is wondering what else they haven't told me."

"Now I really wish I was going with McCoy," Stecker said. "Particularly with the silver chickens on my collar."

"You know that's out of the question, Jack," Pickering said.

"For the sake of argument, let's say McCoy finds Fertig and decides he's not a lunatic and can do what he says he can do. If they're ignoring what De-Press—one of their own—tells them about Fertig, what makes you think they'll listen to McCoy? *'On such an important matter as this, we can't trust the judgment of a Marine lieutenant.'* "

"That's pretty simple, Jack," Pickering said. "*I* trust McCoy's judgment. And I'm not going to run his report of whatever he finds in the Philippines past Willoughby and company and give them a chance to snipe at it. My recommendation goes right to Frank Knox, who will lay it on Admiral Leahy's desk. Leahy trusts Knox, Knox trusts me, and I trust McCoy. So will the President, I think, once he learns—as I intend that he will—that the Killer was with Roosevelt's son on the Makin Island raid."

Stecker smiled. "OK. But you're not supposed to call him that, you know," he said.

"Sorry, Ken," Pickering said.

"No offense taken, Sir," McCoy said, not very convincingly.

"OK, we're getting down the line. I just told Pluto to message Nimitz at Pearl Harbor asking for the submarine *Narwhal.* I think he'll give it to us. I figure ten days, two weeks on the outside, before we get it."

Both Stecker and McCoy nodded.

"Is there anything else you think you need, Ken? I'm prepared to override the Colonel here if you really want to take a Garand with you."

"No, he's right," McCoy said. "If we're going to equip the Filipinos with carbines, that's what the Americans should carry. And with a little bit of luck, I won't have to shoot anybody anyway."

"I'm glad you brought that up, Ken," Pickering said. "You're not being sent to shoot at the Japanese. I want your honest assessment of Colonel Fertig, and his potential. If you get yourself killed . . ."

"I'll do my very best not to, Sir."

"Back to the original question. Is there anything else you would like to take with you?" Pickering saw McCoy's eyes light up momentarily, but he said nothing. "What, Ken? If I can get it for you, it's yours."

"How about a gunnery sergeant?"

"Anyone in particular?"

"We served together in China, working for Banning. He was on the Makin Island raid. I saw him on Guadalcanal. He was running the weapons shop for VMF-229"—Marine Fighter Squadron 229. "He's an Old Breed Marine. Speaks Spanish, two or three kinds of Chinese, and even a little Japanese. I think he'd be useful. His name is Zimmerman."

What the hell is a man who speaks Spanish, Chinese, and Japanese doing repairing weapons? Pickering thought, more than a little angrily.

"Give me his full name and his serial number, if you've got it, and I'll get right on it," he said, and then had a second thought. "Ken, you're sure he'd volunteer for something like you're going to be doing?"

McCoy smiled at him. *Tolerantly,* Pickering thought. *I just asked a stupid question, and this young man is smiling tolerantly at me.*

"He's an Old Breed Marine, General," McCoy said. "Old Breed Marines don't volunteer for anything. They go where they're told to go, and do what they're told to do."

"I stand corrected, Mr. McCoy," Pickering said. "And if you and this other Old Breed Marine here can get those weapons back together in the next hour or so, I will make amends by taking the both of you out to dinner."

[TWO]
Office of the Assistant Chief of Staff G-1
Headquarters, United States Marine Corps
Eighth and "I" Streets, NW
Washington, D.C.
0915 Hours 17 November 1942

Master Gunner James L. Hardee entered the office of Colonel David M. Wilson, waited until he had the colonel's attention, and then announced that Colonel F. L. Rickabee, Deputy Chief of the USMC Office of Management Analysis, was outside, asking to see him.

Following a hand-delivered, classified SECRET, interoffice memorandum from the Deputy Commandant of The Marine Corps ordering that no personnel actions—read transfers—involving officers assigned to the USMC Office of Management Analysis were to be taken without the specific approval in each instance of Major General Horace W. T. Forrest, Assistant Chief of Staff, G-2, Colonel Wilson and Gunner Hardee had correctly surmised that the Office of

Management Analysis probably had more to do with intelligence than either management or analysis.

They had no idea *what* it had to do with intelligence, and did not consider it their official business to make inquiries. Colonel Wilson had run into Colonel Rickabee at various times during their long service; but with the exception of the time they'd spent as students at the Naval War College, he could not recall ever knowing what Rickabee's assignments had been. Neither were Rickabee's records in the files of the Officers' Branch, Office of the Assistant Chief of Staff, G-1. They had been "borrowed" a long time before by the Office of the Secretary of the Navy and never returned. There had been no reply to two requests for their return.

I haven't seen Rickabee since the War College, Wilson thought as he made a *show him in* wave of his hand to Gunner Hardee.

"How are you, Fritz?" Wilson said, trying to conceal his surprise that Rickabee was in civilian clothing. "Long time no see."

"David," Rickabee replied. "How are you?"

"What can I do for you?"

"I came here looking for Charley Stevens," Rickabee said. "He's out of the office."

Colonel Charles D. Stevens was head of the enlisted branch of the Office of the Assistant Chief of Staff, G-1.

"Charley went down to Parris Island to show some congressmen around."

"He and his deputy, and his deputy's deputy, leaving a young major in charge," Rickabee said. "I didn't want to show him this, so I came to you."

He handed Wilson an obviously decrypted radio message.

"Strange paper, Fritz," Wilson thought aloud, as he felt the unusual, slick paper.

"It burns rapidly," Rickabee said matter-of-factly.

```
T O P   S E C R E T


SUPREME HEADQUARTERS SWPOA
NAVY DEPT WASH DC


VIA SPECIAL CHANNEL
DUPLICATION FORBIDDEN
ORIGINAL TO BE DESTROYED AFTER ENCRYPTION AND TRANSMITTAL


FOR COLONEL F. L. RICKABEE
OFFICE OF MANAGEMENT ANALYSIS
```

BRISBANE, AUSTRALIA
MONDAY 16 NOVEMBER 1942

DEAR FRITZ:

WHILE JACK NMI STECKER'S PROMOTION IS RICHLY DESERVED, IT
MEANS MCCOY WILL BE GOING ON THE FERTIG OPERATION JUST
ABOUT BY HIMSELF. THE MAN WHO SHOULD REPLACE STECKER
OBVIOUSLY IS BANNING, BUT THAT'S OBVIOUSLY IMPOSSIBLE. MCCOY
HAS ASKED ME FOR A CHINESE- AND JAPANESE-SPEAKING GUNNERY
SERGEANT WHO SERVED WITH HIM IN BOTH CHINA PRE-WAR AND WAS
ON THE MAKIN ISLAND RAID WITH HIM.

UNDER THE CIRCUMSTANCES, I THINK MCCOY SHOULD HAVE
WHATEVER HE THINKS HE NEEDS. THEREFORE PLEASE ARRANGE THE
IMMEDIATE REPEAT IMMEDIATE TRANSFER OF GUNNERY SERGEANT
ERNEST ZIMMERMAN FROM VMF-229 (WHICH IS NOW AT EWA,
HAWAII) TO US HERE. DO WHATEVER IT TAKES, AND KEEP ME
ADVISED.

REGARDS,

FLEMING PICKERING, BRIGADIER GENERAL, USMCR

T O P   S E C R E T

E Y E S   O N L Y, S E C N A V

"I'm surprised you showed me this," Wilson said. "It says, 'Eyes Only
SECNAV.' "

"It also says 'do whatever it takes,' " Rickabee said.

"I'm also surprised that General Pickering knows that Jack (NMI) Stecker
was promoted. That was supposed to be kept quiet."

"Yeah, I know. And I know why. And I know that General Pickering
knows about it because the Secretary of the Navy told him."

"What's this 'Fertig Operation'?"

"Sorry, that's classified."

"What do you expect me to do with this?"

"Transfer Gunny Zimmerman."

"For one thing, Fritz, that sort of thing is in Charley Stevens's basket of
eggs. I handle officers. For another, even if Zimmerman was an officer, I
couldn't just order his transfer on the basis of this. Who is this General Picker-

ing, anyway? What makes him think he can just wave his hand and have people transferred?''

''Because what he's doing has a high priority.''

''From whom? What kind of a priority?''

''To stop the flow of bureaucratic bullshit, you're telling me you won't have the gunny transferred?''

Wilson's temper flared.

''What I'm telling you, Colonel,'' he said coldly, ''is that I can't, because I don't have the authority to summarily order the transfer of enlisted men.'' As quickly as his temper had boiled over, it subsided. ''Charley will be back the day after tomorrow. You're going to have to wait until Charley can act on your request. I'm sure his major will decide, correctly, he can't do it on his own authority.''

''Thank you for finding time for me in your busy schedule, Colonel,'' Rickabee said, and marched out of Colonel Wilson's office.

[THREE]
Office of the Secretary of the Navy
Washington, D.C.
1015 Hours 17 November 1942

''Well, look who's here!'' the Secretary of the Navy said, pleasantly, when Colonel Rickabee walked into his outer office, trailed by Captain David Haughton. ''Good morning, Colonel. We don't often see you here.''

''Good morning, Mr. Secretary. I came to see Captain Haughton.''

''Morning, Fritz,'' Haughton said.

''Anything I can do?'' Secretary Knox asked.

''A request from General Pickering that I need some help with, Sir,'' Rickabee said.

Knox's eyebrows rose in question.

Rickabee handed him General Pickering's special channel radio message.

Knox glanced at it and handed it back.

''I saw this at breakfast,'' he said. ''Is there a problem?''

''I had a little trouble with G-1 at Eighth and Eye, Sir. The officer who handles this sort of thing is at Parris Island.''

''Take care of it, David,'' Secretary Knox said.

''Aye, aye, Sir.''

THE SECRETARY OF THE NAVY
WASHINGTON, D.C.

16 November 1942

Lieut. General Thomas Holcomb
Commandant, United States Marine Corps
Washington

By Hand

Dear General Holcomb:

The Secretary of the Navy desires the immediate transfer of Gunnery
Sergeant Ernest Zimmerman, USMC, presently assigned VMF-229, to the
USMC Office of Management Analysis, with duty station USMC Special
Detachment 16, Brisbane, Australia, and further desires that travel be
accomplished by the most expeditious means available.

Respectfully,

David W. Haughton

David W. Haughton
Captain, USN
Administrative Assistant to the Secretary of the Navy

[FOUR]
The White House
Washington, D.C.
1910 Hours 17 November 1942

Admiral William D. Leahy rose quickly to his feet when Secretary of the Navy
Frank Knox came into his office.

"Thank you, Mr. Secretary, for making time in your schedule for me," he
said.

"My time, Admiral, like yours, is the Master's time," Knox said, gesturing toward the closed door to the President's Oval Office.

"Well said, Mr. Secretary," Colonel William J. Donovan said, chuckling.
Donovan, a stocky, silver-haired man in civilian clothing, rose from his red-
leather upholstered chair and offered Knox his hand.

"How are you, Bill?" Knox asked.

"Very well, thank you," Donovan replied, and added, "As a matter of fact, I'm at the moment feeling rather chipper. I think I see a problem on the way to its solution."

"Is that so?" Knox said. "And what problem is that?"

"The intractable Douglas MacArthur," Donovan said.

"The Director, Mr. Secretary, has come up with a suggestion the President feels has considerable merit."

He called Donovan "the Director," Knox thought. Not "Colonel." Is that because Donovan wants it that way, because "the Director" reminds people that he is not just one more recalled World War I colonel but the Director of the Office of Strategic Services—on the level of J. Edgar Hoover of the FBI, who also likes to be called "the Director"?

Or is it because he wants to remind me that Donovan ranks higher in the hierarchy than a lowly colonel? On the other hand, Secretary of War Stimson, who also served in France as a Colonel, likes to be called "Colonel."

The rank structure here is confused, almost certainly because Franklin Roosevelt wants it to be. Admiral Leahy is a serving officer of the Navy. I am Secretary of the Navy. Therefore he is legally subordinate to me. But he is also Chief of Staff to the President. If he were de facto subordinate to me, instead of de jure, this meeting would be held in my office. After he had called Haughton and asked for an appointment.

I am here. Ergo, he speaks with the authority of the President.

"May we speak frankly?" Donovan asked. "Among the three of us."

"Of course," Knox said.

"I am advised by my Brisbane station chief that General MacArthur has not, as of yesterday morning, found time in his schedule to receive him—despite, I am sure, the best efforts of Fleming Pickering."

"You suggested we speak frankly," Knox replied. "I am advised by General Pickering, Bill, that General MacArthur does not want—how did he put it?—'the nose of your camel under his tent.' "

"The President does," Donovan said abruptly.

"The President sent General Pickering over there with express orders to convince General MacArthur that the Office of Strategic Services has a contribution to make to SWPOA."

"He has apparently been unable to do so," Donovan said.

"The word you used to describe General MacArthur a moment ago was 'intractable,' " Knox said. "I have every confidence that General Pickering has done his best to comply with the President's instructions."

"I like Fleming Pickering," Donovan said.

That's not the way I heard it.

"I offered him a job in my shop, you know," Donovan went on. "He declined it."

You offered him a job at the second or third level, which was either stupidity on your part, or vindictiveness. He didn't like the size of the bill you sent him in a maritime case, and told you so in blunt and unmistakable terms. You are not used to being talked to like that; you didn't like it; and when he volunteered for the OSS, you put him in his place.

Which, in the final analysis, was stupidity. He told me the first time I met him that I should have resigned after the debacle of Pearl Harbor. I was smart enough to realize that a man who not only owns, but runs, the second- or third-largest shipping fleet in the world is both accustomed to saying exactly what's on his mind and is wholly unimpressed with political titles.

I put him to work, and his performance exceeded even my high expectations.

"Did you really think, Bill, that Fleming Pickering would be willing to work two or three levels down your chain of command?" Knox asked.

"The President is determined," Admiral Leahy said, trying to change the subject, hoping to avoid a confrontation between the two powerful men, "that General MacArthur will accept the services of the OSS, for the good of the war effort."

"I wonder why the President doesn't simply send him a radio message to that effect?" Knox asked.

"Because he knows, as you know, and I know, that MacArthur would at best pay only lip service to such an order," Donovan replied. "And, at worst, with his judgment questioned, he'd threaten to resign. He did that twice when he was Chief of Staff, you know. And when it became apparent that he was about to lose the Philippines, he announced that he was going to resign his commission and go to Bataan to fight as a private soldier. Our Douglas has a flair for the dramatic."

"The President, Mr. Secretary," Admiral Leahy said, "is reluctant to issue General MacArthur an order that might—from his point of view—question his authority or his judgment to the point where he might . . . respond inappropriately."

Politics again. The carefully nurtured image of the President as Commander-in-Chief would be badly tarnished if any one of his senior generals or admirals resigned in protest. When that senior general was General Douglas MacArthur, the heroic defender of the Philippines, whom Roosevelt had praised so often and effusively, and had awarded the Medal of Honor, the damage would be enormous.

Particularly if MacArthur—still furious that the Philippines had not received supplies, and that General George Marshall had effectively taken command of the Philippines away from him the moment he got on the PT boat to go to Australia—came back and started giving speeches about Roosevelt's military ineptitude.

And MacArthur was fully aware he did not have to obey any orders, from anyone, that he didn't like.

"You said, Bill, you thought you have a solution to the problem?" Knox said.

"I have one that will accomplish what everybody wants," Donovan said.

"One that the President finds very interesting," Admiral Leahy said.

I'm fully aware that you speak with the authority of the President, Admiral, thank you very much. But if this brilliant idea has Presidential approval set in concrete, I would be told about it, not asked.

"Tell me, Bill, what is it you think I want?"

"What the President wants, what Admirals Leahy and Nimitz want, what General Pickering wants."

"Which is?"

"To assist this chap Fertig in the Philippines," Donovan said. "I also suspect that in his heart of hearts, Douglas MacArthur would like to help him, too. But Douglas is worried about two things: He has stated publicly that guerrilla operations in the Philippines are impossible at this time; and he doesn't want to be proved wrong. Even worse than that, from his perspective, he would hate to admit that he was wrong, that this chap Fertig does indeed exist, and *then* have it proved that Fertig is a lunatic—that business of his promoting himself to general is more than a little strange—and that guerrilla operations are indeed not possible. That would make him wrong twice. Douglas MacArthur doesn't like to be wrong at all."

"I'm not sure I follow you," Knox said.

"The first thing I thought, frankly, was to have General Pickering assigned to the OSS. That would solve a good many problems."

"It would also cause some," Knox said. "Speaking frankly, as you suggested we should, not only would General Pickering rather violently object to that, but so would I."

"I made that point to the President, Mr. Secretary," Admiral Leahy said. "It is his feeling that General Pickering should be transferred to the OSS only as a last resort."

"And what are the intermediate steps? The *first* resort?"

Watch it! You're being sarcastic! The fact that I don't like Donovan does not make him a fool. Antagonizing him would accomplish nothing whatever.

"Best case, a team of experts is sent into the Philippines, finds that Fertig is what he says he is, that, with support, he can deliver what he promises to, and once that is accomplished, MacArthur makes the announcement, gets the credit."

"OK. What's the worst case?"

"Fertig turns out to be a disaster, a lunatic, and the team comes out and so reports. That would make MacArthur's statement that guerrilla operations in the Philippines are impossible at this time perfectly accurate."

"Bill, you're not suggesting, I hope, that the OSS take over this operation?"

"Would you have problems with that, Mr. Secretary?" Donovan asked.

"Bill, they're just about ready to go."

"The colonel you were going to send in is no longer available," Donovan said. "Pickering is planning on entrusting the great responsibility of evaluating this man Fertig to a lieutenant."

"Frankly, Bill, I'd like to know how you came by that information," Knox said coldly.

"From Admiral Leahy," Donovan said. "I don't see why that should offend you. For God's sake, we're both on the same side in this war. I heard of that radio station on Mindanao through OSS channels. When I discussed this with the Admiral, he filled in the details of Pickering's involvement."

He's right, damn him. He is the Director of the OSS; he has every right to access to the details of this operation.

"General Pickering has great confidence in that lieutenant," Knox said.

The expressions on both Colonel Donovan's and Admiral Leahy's face made it plain they had little faith in Pickering's judgment on this subject.

And they're right, too. I didn't say anything to Pickering, but I was surprised when he didn't ask Colonel Rickabee for a more senior, more experienced, officer than his Lieutenant McCoy. And he knows there is a problem; otherwise he wouldn't have gotten into the business of arranging for that sergeant to be transferred to go with McCoy. He even referred to Banning, a major, as the man he'd like to send with McCoy.

"All right, Bill, what are you proposing?" Knox asked.

"Among the Marines you have seconded to us are a major and a captain who I want to send in with Pickering's lieutenant," Donovan said.

"How do you suggest that this affect Pickering's role, his authority, and his responsibility in this operation?"

"Not at all. All we'll be doing is providing some assistance," Donovan said smoothly. "They will not reveal their OSS association unless and until the OPERATION WINDMILL is successful. The Major is fluent in Spanish. Good family. They have interests in the Banana Republics and Cuba, and he apparently has spent some time down there. He's a Princeton graduate, a reserve officer . . ."

There are those, Secretary Knox thought, *who believe that OSS stands for Oh, So Social. And it's a fact that Donovan seems to recruit his people from the*

Ivy League, people whose "families have interests" in exotic places. But so what? George Patton's an aristocrat; his aide is Charley Codman of the Boston Codmans. And they're both splendid soldiers. Franklin Roosevelt's son made the Makin Island raid, and by every definition I know, he's an aristocrat. And so, for God's sake, are Fleming Pickering and his son. Why am I so antagonistic toward Donovan?

". . . The Captain's a regular, an Annapolis graduate. He served in China before the war, speaks a little Japanese, which might prove helpful. He was wounded—serving with the Marine paratroops on Tulagi—during the Guadalcanal invasion. I can't see how they could be anything but helpful, Frank."

"Your thinking, obviously, is that if this operation goes well, you've got MacArthur on a spot. How can he be against the OSS if your people worked so well?"

"That's the general idea."

"What will you do, Bill, if MacArthur says, in effect, I still don't want your camel's nose under my tent?"

"Then I'll think of something else," Donovan said.

"May I tell the President how you regard Director Donovan's proposal, Mr. Secretary?" Admiral Leahy asked.

"With these caveats, Admiral, I will go along with Director Donovan: First, that there is no diminution whatever of General Pickering's authority."

"Agreed," Donovan said.

"Which means that General Pickering will have the final say, once he meets these officers, about whether or not they get to go."

"I'm sure General Pickering will be delighted to get them."

"I'm not so sure. You agree that he will have the final decision? About them? About everything?"

"Agreed," Donovan said. "I'm trying to get my nose in Douglas MacArthur's tent, Mr. Secretary, not yours."

"You understand my position, Admiral?"

"Yes, Mr. Secretary."

"Then you may inform the President that I'm willing to sign on," Knox said. And then he thought of something else. "One more thing: The present schedule will not be delayed in any way by the attachment of your two officers."

"As soon as I get back to my office, I will telephone the Country Club, where these two are sitting on their packed bags, and order them to report to Colonel Rickabee at eight o'clock tomorrow morning."

Knox knew what he meant by the Country Club.

"I'll arrange for their air priorities, Mr. Secretary, if Colonel Rickabee encounters a problem," Admiral Leahy said. "And I will advise Admiral Nimitz, with a Special Channel Personal, of the President's interest in this operation. That should ensure a submarine when and where General Pickering needs it.''

Why do I feel I have just been talked into something I shouldn't be doing?

"Thank you, Admiral,'' Knox said.

He got out of his chair and started for the door.

"Here's their names, Frank,'' Donovan said, and handed him a three-by-five-inch card on which two names were typed.

Knox glanced at it.

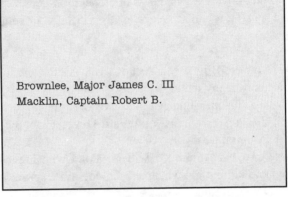

```
Brownlee, Major James C. III
Macklin, Captain Robert B.
```

He recognized neither name.

[FIVE]
Office of the Secretary of the Navy
Washington, D.C.
2105 Hours 17 November 1942

Chief Petty Officer Stanley Hansen, USN, entered without knocking the office of Captain David W. Haughton, USN, Administrative Assistant to the Secretary of the Navy, and laid a single sheet of typewriter paper on his desk.

"The Secretary said I should run that past you, Captain, before I send it,'' he said.

```
T O P    S E C R E T

THE SECRETARY OF THE NAVY
WASHINGTON
VIA SPECIAL CHANNEL
```

DUPLICATION FORBIDDEN
ORIGINAL TO BE DESTROYED AFTER ENCRYPTION AND TRANSMITTAL

SUPREME COMMANDER SWPOA
EYES ONLY BRIG GEN F. W. PICKERING, USMCR
(TIME TIME TIME) 17 NOVEMBER 1942

FOLLOWING PERSONAL FROM SECNAV FOR BRIG GEN PICKERING

DEAR FLEMING:

I JUST CAME FROM A MEETING WITH ADMIRAL LEAHY AND COLONEL
DONOVAN OF THE OSS IN WHICH THE SUBJECTS OF EVALUATING
FERTIG'S GUERRILLA OPERATION AND ITS POTENTIAL AND OSS
OPERATIONS IN MACARTHUR'S SWPOA CAME UP. I BELIEVE THE
MEETING WAS HELD WITH EITHER THE KNOWLEDGE OF THE
PRESIDENT OR AT HIS DIRECTION.

COLONEL DONOVAN, WHOSE DETAILED KNOWLEDGE OF YOUR
OPERATION CAME FROM BOTH HIS OWN SOURCES AND FROM ADMIRAL
LEAHY, PROPOSED THE FOLLOWING AS A MEANS TO OVERCOME
GENERAL MACARTHUR'S RELUCTANCE TO ACCEPT OSS SERVICES.

HE WILL DETAIL TWO USMC OFFICERS PRESENTLY SECONDED TO THE
OSS TO MANAGEMENT ANALYSIS TO PARTICIPATE, UNDER YOUR
COMMAND, IN THE MISSION TO FERTIG. DONOVAN SAYS BOTH AGENTS,
A MAJOR AND A CAPTAIN, ARE HIGHLY TRAINED IN THIS SORT OF
THING. HE MADE THE POINT THAT DESPITE YOUR HIGH REGARD FOR
LIEUTENANT MCCOY, GIVING A YOUNG JUNIOR OFFICER THAT LEVEL
OF RESPONSIBILITY IS ASKING A GOOD DEAL OF HIM. DONOVAN'S
AGENTS WILL NOT REVEAL THEIR OSS CONNECTION UNLESS AND UNTIL
THE MISSION TO FERTIG PROVES SUCCESSFUL.

HAD YOU BEEN ABLE TO MAKE PROGRESS WITH MACARTHUR VIS-A-VIS
SWPOA AND THE OSS AND/OR HAD COLONEL STECKER BEEN
AVAILABLE, OR SOME OTHER SENIOR OFFICER, I MIGHT HAVE
DECLINED DONOVAN'S OFFER TO HELP.

ONCE I AGREED TO IT, LEAHY VOLUNTEERED TO SEND A SPECIAL
CHANNEL PERSONAL TO NIMITZ GUARANTEEING A SUBMARINE WHEN
AND WHERE YOU NEED IT. HAUGHTON WILL COORDINATE TRAVEL
ARRANGEMENTS, ET CETERA, VIS-A-VIS DONOVAN'S PEOPLE, WHO WILL
REPORT TO RICKABEE TOMORROW.

BEST PERSONAL REGARDS

FRANK

END PERSONAL SECNAV TO BRIG GEN PICKERING

HAUGHTON CAPT USN ADMIN ASST TO SECNAV

T O P   S E C R E T

Haughton read it, then glanced at his watch, crossed out TIME TIME TIME, wrote in 2110, and handed it back to Chief Hansen.

"Is he still here?"

"He was when he gave me that, Sir."

Haughton picked up a telephone, which automatically rang a similar instrument on Secretary Knox's desk.

"That Special Channel looks fine, Mr. Secretary," he said when Knox picked up. "May I show it to Colonel Rickabee?"

Chief Hansen could not hear the Secretary's reply.

"Have it sent," Haughton ordered. "But bring that back. I'll take care of burning it."

"Aye, aye, Sir."

Haughton reached for another of the telephones on his desk and dialed a number from memory. It was answered on the second ring.

"Liberty 7-2033."

Although he suspected Rickabee had good reasons for ordering the telephones at the Office of Management Analysis answered in that manner, Haughton was always annoyed when he heard the recitation of the number.

"Captain Haughton for Colonel Rickabee."

"Sorry, Sir, the Colonel is not available at this time."

"Where is he?"

"I'm sorry, Sir, I am not permitted to give out that information."

"Do you recognize my name?"

"Yes, Sir."

"Get in touch with Colonel Rickabee and have him call me. I'm in my office."

"Has the Colonel your number, Sir?"

"I think he does," Haughton said icily, and hung up.

The private line on Haughton's desk rang not more than two minutes later.

"Captain Haughton."

"What's on your mind, David?" Rickabee's dry, emotionless voice asked.

"Something's come up. The sooner we get together, the better."

"Sounds serious."

"It doesn't have to be. Would it be convenient for you to come here?"

"Frankly, no."

"Well, then, where are you?"

"At the Foster Lafayette. General Pickering's suite."

"May I come there?"

"Of course. Banning and Sessions are with me. Will that pose any problems?"

"No. And it will probably spare you having to tell them what this is all about. I'll be there in fifteen minutes."

There was a click, and then a dial tone.

Haughton held the telephone handset in his hand, staring at it in amazement and some annoyance, before placing it in its cradle.

"Colonel Fritz Rickabee, USMC," Haughton said aloud, shaking his head, "having decided that nothing else need be said, hung up."

He picked up the direct line to Knox's desk, intending to ask if the Secretary required anything else of him before he left the office, but there was no answer. Secretary Knox had gone home.

He waited four or five minutes for Chief Hansen to return from the cryptography room with the original of Knox's message, told him "Thank you, Chief, and go home," and then folded the message in thirds and put it in his shirt pocket.

Then, feeling a little foolish, he opened a drawer in his desk, took out a Colt .380 automatic pistol, and, somewhat awkwardly, slipped it into a leather holster on his trouser's belt.

Colonel Rickabee read Frank Knox's Special Channel Personal to Pickering, made a wry face, which could have meant contempt or resignation, and then asked with a raised eyebrow and tilt of his head if he could give it to Banning and Sessions. Haughton gestured with a wave of his hand that he could.

Rickabee knew that something like this would inevitably happen; he had, in fact, seen it coming when the President sent Pickering back to Australia to plead Donovan's case for the OSS to MacArthur.

Rickabee had long ago come to understand that everything in Washington was politics. This meant compromise, sometimes reasonable, sometimes not, between powerful people with different agendas, sometimes noble, sometimes not, and sometimes—as in this case—based on nothing more than personal or professional egos.

Rickabee knew Donovan, and respected him. And he was convinced that Donovan knew as well as he did that the role the Office of Strategic Services envisioned for Europe—which in Rickabee's professional opinion was going to work—simply would not work in the Pacific.

It was relatively easy to parachute agents into France, or Norway, or any of the other countries now occupied by the Germans. Most of the agents would be natives of those countries. They would be fluent in the language, know the country, and have contacts inside the country willing to risk their lives to further the liberation of their countries. Furnished with excellent forged identity documents, an agent fluent in the language could relatively easily lose himself in a sea of other white faces.

The situation in the Pacific was different. A white face seen anywhere in territory occupied by the Japanese would stand out like a flashing lighthouse in a sea of yellow and brown faces, and would be immediately suspect. The English who had been in Singapore and Hong Kong were now in prison camps. So were the Dutch who had been in the Dutch East Indies; and, for that matter, most of the French in French Indochina—the exception being those who could prove their loyalty to Marshal Pétain's German allied government in Vichy.

Rickabee knew the story of Captain Ralph Fralick, who had been commissioned with Fertig in the Philippines. Fralick blew up bridges, railroads, and supply depots in the face of the advancing Japanese on Luzon; and then, rather than surrender, made an incredible journey from Luzon to Hanoi in French Indochina in a fifty-foot boat. On landing in Hanoi, Fralick lined up his forty men and marched them off to report to the French authorities. Salutes were exchanged, and then the French turned Fralick and his men over to the Japanese.

For most of the people in territory now occupied by the Japanese, there would be very little profit in risking one's life, and the lives of one's family, to fight the Japanese . . . especially when the result would not be liberation from occupation, but simply the reinstallation of the British or the Dutch or the French as colonial masters.

There was an exception to this analysis—in Intelligence, there was always an exception—and that of course was the Philippines. Most Filipinos did not hate the Americans who had been running their country since they took it away from the Spanish at the turn of the century. The Filipinos believed—because it happened to be true—that the United States really intended to give their country independence as soon as possible. The Philippine Army fought with great valor against the Japanese invaders, and when further resistance was impossible, they went with their American comrades-in-arms into prison camps.

Meanwhile, the Japanese made the same mistake in the Philippines the Germans made in Russia: They treated the native population brutally; and so they lost any chance of cooperation—or at least docile acceptance of the occupation.

Consequently, American agents sent into the Philippines would have a reasonable chance of obtaining all sorts of assistance from the Filipinos.

But getting them there was going to be a problem, and so was logistics. (Mindanao, closest to Australia, was not the hour or so's flight time away that France and Scandinavia were from American bases in England.) Still, something could be done in the Philippines, and Donovan knew it could.

But that wasn't Donovan's only motive in pushing so hard to be included in Pickering's mission to Fertig, Rickabee believed. He wanted the OSS to be involved worldwide. If the OSS was operational only in Europe, that would diminish its stature, and thus the stature of Colonel William J. Donovan.

Donovan was already engaged in a personal ego war with J. Edgar Hoover of the FBI. On the one hand, Hoover claimed the FBI had sole responsibility for Intelligence and Counterintelligence in the Western Hemisphere. On the other hand, Donovan claimed the OSS had worldwide responsibility for Intelligence, Counterintelligence, and Special Operations—read sabotage and subversion. And—predictably—Roosevelt had declined to make a decision between the two of them. The result was that FBI and OSS agents in Argentina, Chile, Peru, and even Mexico spent more time fighting each other than harming the German, Italian, and Japanese ''Axis.''

In Rickabee's view, not only was Pickering being used as a pawn in this political war, but as soon as he saw the Special Channel Personal, he would know he was being used, and it would bother him a great deal.

He hoped Pickering wouldn't do anything foolish. Certainly, Pickering wasn't a fool, but he was naive in the ways of Washington politics.

Rickabee admired Pickering.

At first, he was willing to admit, his own ego smarted when Frank Knox named Pickering Chief of the Office of Management Analysis. Rickabee had built the organization from scratch over many years, and had run it with some skill and success. He didn't think he needed the advice, much less the supervision, of an amateur like Pickering. He had no choice, however, but to swallow his resentment—consoling himself with the thought that Pickering's flag officer's rank would be useful. In rank-conscious Washington that was important. And Rickabee believed he could control Pickering.

That did not prove necessary. For Pickering immediately made it quite clear that he considered Rickabee the expert, while he himself had some experience in ''a situation like this''—being in charge of someone who knew more than he did. Pickering explained how the death of his father had suddenly elevated him to the office of Chairman of the Board of Pacific & Far East Shipping Corporation when he was still in his twenties.

"All of sudden, Colonel," Pickering said, "I found myself giving orders to the Commodore of Pacific & Far East Shipping Corporation's eighty-one-ship fleet, who was not only old enough to be my father, but under whom I had sailed as a second mate."

"That must have been difficult."

"You're not old enough to be my father, Colonel, but I recognize your experience and expertise. So I hope to build the same kind of relationship with you I had with the Commodore."

It was at that moment Rickabee realized that Pickering understood the subtleties of command.

"While the responsibility for everything that happens is now mine," Pickering went on, "I am perfectly aware that you've been in charge here because you are the most experienced and competent officer available. It would therefore be foolish of me to question your judgment in any but the most extraordinary circumstances."

At the time, Rickabee wondered if Pickering meant what he was saying, or simply pouring oil on potentially troubling waters. It soon became apparent that Pickering meant what he said.

Pickering rarely questioned any of Rickabee's decisions, and only once went against his strongly felt advice. In Rickabee's professional judgment, the effort and the assets required to take Lieutenant Joseph L. Howard, USMC, and Sergeant Stephen M. Koffler, USMCR, off Buka could not be militarily justified.

Pickering overrode that logical conclusion on what he admitted were emotional grounds: He had learned in the trenches in France as an eighteen-year-old that Marines did not leave their wounded behind. He ordered the rescue operation.

This episode taught both men something about the weaknesses of the other. Pickering learned that Rickabee was indeed, where necessary, absolutely ruthless. And Rickabee learned that despite the stars on his uniform, Pickering thought like a Marine sergeant.

The confrontation in no way diminished the respect, and the growing affection, they had begun to feel for each other. A Marine officer charged with clandestine intelligence had to be ruthless. And a Marine general officer's heartfelt concern for the welfare of a junior officer and an enlisted man could hardly be called a character flaw.

"Am I permitted to ask what's going on around here?" Captain Haughton asked.

The coffee table of General Pickering's suite was covered with paper. Also covered with paper was a folding card table and something like a typewriter. After a moment he recognized it as an obsolete Device, Cryptographic, M94.

"Well, for the last half hour or so, Banning has been trying to teach Sessions how to use that thing. Sessions is taking it and some other stuff to Brisbane, where he will teach McCoy how to use it. Until we make the first physical contact with Fertig, take him a decent crypto device—which Sessions will also teach McCoy to use—we have a small communications problem: Where does Fertig think McCoy should get off the submarine? When should he get off the submarine?"

"Yeah," Haughton said thoughtfully. "What other stuff is Sessions taking over there?"

"Banning's been talking to a Navy psychiatrist—"

"Brilliant man," Banning interrupted. "He certified me as sane when I came out of the Philippines."

Haughton chuckled a little nervously, and then Rickabee surprised him.

"That's true, that's true," he said, laughing. "If I'd remembered that, I'd have sent you to another one. Anyway, he's come up with sort of a checklist, things McCoy should look for to see if Fertig might be off the rails."

"I also talked to some people who had guerrilla, counterguerrilla, experience in the Banana Republics," Banning said. "They came up with some material, organizational material, McCoy's going to offer to Fertig."

"How are you going to handle the problem of getting McCoy . . . McCoy and the others ashore and in contact with Fertig?" Haughton asked.

"Well, in the final analysis, that's up to McCoy. What I'm going to recommend is that shortly before we send McCoy and Zimmerman ashore, we will send Fertig a vague message saying to expect visitors—"

"You heard that the Secretary told General Holcomb to arrange that transfer?" Haughton interrupted.

Banning nodded, and went on:

"—to make contact with Fertig. When that's done, Fertig will contact the submarine, which will be lying off shore, with a new code McCoy will have (who'll also have a new crypto device, of course); and he can set up a place where the supplies and gold can be off-loaded from the sub. How they'll get out, and when, is still up in the air."

Haughton nodded.

"Maybe these OSS people will have some ideas," Banning said. "We get them tomorrow?"

"First thing tomorrow morning."

"There may be some trouble getting them over there," Rickabee said. "We laid on only one AAAAA priority, for Sessions. Now we'll need three."

"If you have any trouble, let me know."

"I will," Rickabee said.

"Who are these people? Have you got names?" Banning asked.

"Yes, I do," Haughton said. He dug in his pocket and came up with the three-by-five card Colonel Donovan had given Secretary Knox, and which Knox had passed on to him.

"Brownlee, Major James C. III," he read, "and Macklin, Captain Robert B."

"What was that second name?" Banning asked, incredulously.

"Macklin, Captain Robert B."

"I don't believe this," Banning said.

"You know him?"

"If it's the same guy—and I don't think there's that many Marine officers around named Macklin—yeah, I know him," Banning said. "I sent him home from China with an efficiency report, endorsed by Chesty Puller, that should have seen the sonofabitch kicked out of The Corps."

"Tell me about him," Rickabee said coldly.

Banning delivered a sixty-second précis of the multiple character flaws of Captain Robert B. Macklin, USMC. "I wonder what moron promoted the sonofabitch," he observed bitterly when he was finished.

Rickabee looked thoughtful for a moment.

"Captain Haughton," he said formally, "if it is determined that the officer in question is indeed the one with whom Major Banning is familiar, it will be necessary to inform Colonel Donovan that he is unacceptable to us."

"Christ, Fritz, I don't know," Haughton said.

"If he is the officer with whom Major Banning is familiar," Rickabee repeated, "he is unacceptable to us."

Haughton shrugged.

"How do we find out?"

"Presumably, Banning will recognize him when he reports for duty," Rickabee said.

[ONE]
USMC Office of Management Analysis
Temporary Building T-2032
The Mall, Washington, D.C.
1105 Hours 18 November 1942

Captain David L. Haughton, USN, walked into the office of Colonel F. L. Rickabee, USMC, and handed him a square envelope.

"Sorry, Fritz," he said.

Rickabee opened the envelope and took out the single sheet of paper it contained.

THE SECRETARY OF THE NAVY
WASHINGTON, D.C.

18 November 1942

Colonel F. L. Rickabee, USMC
USMC Office of Management Analysis
Commandant, United States Marine Corps
Washington

By Hand

Dear Colonel Rickabee:

Inasmuch as I have been led to believe that assignment of officer personnel within the Naval Service is my responsibility, I was somewhat surprised to hear from Captain Haughton that you feel that one of the officers being seconded to you from the Office of Strategic Services is "unacceptable."

214 ■ W.E.B. GRIFFIN

> You are directed to carry out the operation in question with the personnel
> assigned to it by me.
>
> No further discussion of this issue is desired.
>
> Sincerely,
>
> *Frank Knox*
>
> Secretary of the Navy

Rickabee looked up at Haughton but didn't speak.

"Out of school, Fritz," Haughton said, "he went right through the roof."

"He doesn't want to risk a confrontation with Donovan," Rickabee said. "Donovan might go to the President, accuse Knox of going back on a deal, and Knox might lose. That's what this is all about."

Captain Haughton did not think it would be proper for him to reply, even though he'd had the same thought when he witnessed Knox's surprisingly angry—and highly unusual—response to Rickabee's request.

"Well, I can always arrange to have the sonofabitch run over by a truck," Rickabee said.

"Don't say something like that, even as a joke," Haughton said.

Rickabee nodded but didn't reply.

Captain Haughton felt a sudden chill.

"For God's sake, Fritz, I hope you were joking."

Rickabee's eyes, cold and expressionless, met Haughton's.

"When Major Brownlee and Captain Macklin reported to me this morning," he said, "I informed them only of what they had Need To Know at this time. Specifically, that tentative arrangements have been made to fly them, this afternoon, to Pearl Harbor, for further transportation to an unspecified location somewhere in the Pacific."

Haughton nodded.

"Captain Macklin assured me that while he was of course willing to go wherever ordered, he nevertheless felt obliged to inform me that not only had he not completed the training course offered by the OSS, but that he had not yet fully recovered from the wounds he suffered at Gavutu."

"Really?"

"Really."

"You will see, won't you, Colonel—personally, I mean—that Captain Macklin makes it safely to the airport?"

"Unfortunately, David, I am one of those people who obeys his orders."

[TWO]
Supreme Headquarters
South West Pacific Ocean Area
Brisbane, Australia
1405 Hours 18 November 1942

Brigadier General Fleming S. Pickering, trailed by Second Lieutenant George F. Hart, passed through the two MP-manned security posts barring entrance to the Cryptographic Facility of Supreme Headquarters, SWPOA, and then walked down an inside corridor to an unmarked steel door leading to the Special Section.

Hart snatched a .38 Colt snub-nosed revolver from under his tunic and rapped three times with the butt on the door. A lighter knock on the thick steel door—with the knuckles, or even with a Zippo lighter or keys or something else metallic—could not be heard inside; it was necessary to make the door ring like a drum.

In a moment, a three-by-five-inch panel in the door screeched open.

"It's me, Pluto," Pickering said.

The panel screeched shut, there was the sound of metal bars sliding out of place, and then the door creaked open. Pickering and Hart entered the small room.

"I didn't expect you, Sir," Major Hon said, pulling his tie into place. He was also wearing a .45 automatic in a shoulder holster. Pickering looked past him. On a table was an open briefcase, to which was attached a chain and half of a set of handcuffs.

"Going somewhere, Pluto?" Pickering asked.

"To see you, Sir," Pluto said, as he closed the steel door behind Pickering and slid the bars back in place.

Pickering waited.

Pluto went to the briefcase and came out with a business-size envelope. He handed it to Pickering.

"That just came in," he said. "I thought you'd want to see it right away."

Pickering tore open the envelope. His lips tightened.

"Somehow, I didn't think you were going to like that," Pluto said.

"Anyone else seen this?"

"No, Sir."

"Nobody but you, Hart, and me does, OK, Pluto?"

"Yes, Sir."

Pickering handed Hart Secretary of the Navy Frank Knox's Special Channel Personal announcing that Colonel Wild Bill Donovan of the OSS—with Knox's blessing—was sending two OSS agents to participate in the Fertig Operation.

Pickering's first reaction—which he immediately recognized as such—was fury.

"God*damn* Franklin Roosevelt," he said, and was immediately sorry. Not for the thought, but for the emotional outburst.

The one thing I cannot afford to do here is lose my temper.

Pluto and Hart looked at him in surprise.

"Am I missing something here?" Hart asked. "Or is that one of the questions I'm not supposed to ask?"

Pickering smiled. "I suppose this will come as a shock to you, as a devout Democrat, George, but our beloved Commander-in-Chief makes Machiavelli seem innocent as Francis of Assisi."

"I never said I was a Democrat," Hart said. "And I still don't understand."

"There are a number—by God, this is Machiavellian!—of factors at play here, George. In theory, President Roosevelt is the Commander-in-Chief, and MacArthur, like every other officer in a uniform, is supposed to obey without question any order received. Roosevelt wants the OSS to start operating in SWPOA. MacArthur wants nothing to do with the OSS. On the surface, the simple solution would be to simply issue the order. That is not going to happen. Why?" he asked rhetorically. "Because Roosevelt has decided that issuing the order would not be in his best interests. Why? Because MacArthur—having made his feelings about the OSS known, through me—is very likely to disobey that order."

"Can he get away with that?" Pluto asked, not sounding very surprised.

"Oh, yes. In two ways. Maybe three. For one thing, he could simply ignore the order. In effect, he's already done that. The way it's supposed to work is that when the desires of the Commander-in-Chief are made known, everybody is supposed to jump through a hoop to see the desires satisfied. MacArthur has not yet found time in his busy schedule to even talk to Donovan's people. That's why I was sent over here this time, to sell Donovan's people to him."

"What's El Supremo got against the OSS?" Hart asked.

"El Supremo doesn't want anything going on in his ballpark that he can't control; and he thinks—probably correctly—that he will not be able to control the OSS because Bill Donovan has the President's ear. This is the proof of that, come to think of it," Pickering said, waving Knox's Special Channel Personal in his hand.

Hart looked confused.

I have no business explaining this to them, Pickering thought. *But on the other hand, Roosevelt and Knox had no right putting me in the middle of their chicanery.*

Another seed of thought appeared in the back of his mind, quickly sprouted, blossomed, and then gave fruit.

Of course, that's what this is all about! Or at least has a hell of a lot to do with it! Roosevelt is one of those people who believe that "If you're not with me, you're against me" nonsense. If I quietly go along with this business, which would mean not telling MacArthur, deceiving MacArthur, then I will have chosen sides, joined Roosevelt's team. His political team, not his military team. When he ordered me over here to try to sell MacArthur on the OSS, as a serving officer, I had no choice but to obey my orders, even though I thought that Donovan's OSS will probably be more trouble here than they're worth, and that Bill Donovan personally is an arrogant, goddamned Democrat New York lawyer and New Dealer.

And Christ knows I tried to sell Donovan's people to El Supremo.

I went to work for Knox to be his eyes and ears over here. While I really think I could be of more use to this war running a shipping operation— God knows I could do a better job of that than three-quarters of those chair-warming admirals in Pearl Harbor—there was a certain value to that. I think I've done some good.

But I did not sign on to be a political errand boy for Knox. Or for Roosevelt. And that's what they're asking me to become.

I'll be damned if I'll go along.

He became aware that both Pluto and Hart were waiting for him to go on.

"When in doubt, Pluto," Pickering said, "tell the truth. Write that on the palm of your hand so you don't forget it."

"Sir?"

"Let me at that phone, George," Pickering said. He squeezed past Hart, picked up a red telephone, and dialed a number.

"Fleming Pickering, Sid," he said into it—telling Pluto and Hart that he had dialed MacArthur's personal number and that Lieutenant Colonel Sidney L. Huff, MacArthur's aide-de-camp, had picked up the telephone—"I would like a few minutes of the Supreme Commander's time at his earliest convenience."

There was a pause.

"No, Sid, squeezing me in for a minute or two at nineteen thirty will not be satisfactory."

There was another pause.

"I'll tell you what you *can* do, Colonel," Pickering said, his voice icy. "You can speak to the Supreme Commander, relay my request to him, and then relay his reply to me."

There was another pause, a longer one.

"Thank you very much, Colonel," Pickering said. "Please inform the Supreme Commander that I'm on my way up."

Hart started to slide the metal bars out of place.

"You wait for me here, George," Pickering said. "Aides-de-camp are not invited to this tête-à-tête."

"Aye, aye, Sir."

"Fleming, my dear fellow," General Douglas MacArthur, Supreme Commander, SWPOA, said, smiling and waving his hand in a *come in* gesture. "Come in, curiosity overwhelms me. Sid said this was an emergency of some kind?"

MacArthur was dressed in his customary washed-soft khakis.

"No, Sir. I said nothing about an emergency. What I told Colonel Huff was that I would be grateful if you could find time for me before half past seven."

"I can always make time for you, Fleming. Sid should have known that," MacArthur said. "Sid, you may leave us."

Huff looked as if he had just been kicked.

Did El Supremo sense that I didn't want Huff to hear what I have to say? Or did he do that to humiliate him and thus placate me? He's just as Machiavellian as Roosevelt, and I better not forget that.

MacArthur waved Pickering into a chair and looked at him expectantly.

Pickering handed him Knox's Special Channel Personal and then sat down.

MacArthur picked up a long, thin, black cigar from an ashtray and puffed on it as he read the message twice. Then he met Pickering's eyes.

"I appreciate your loyalty in showing me this, Fleming."

"General, with all the respect I can muster, loyalty was not my motive."

"Indeed?"

"I did not want you to believe I had any part in this."

"I would have known that without your telling me," MacArthur said. "Whatever terrible things may be said about you around here, no one I know has ever accused you of being devious."

Pickering found himself smiling.

"Among the things that are said about you around here is that you are mounting a supply mission to Lieutenant Colonel Fertig on Mindanao," MacArthur said. "I've been wondering when you were going to discuss this with me."

"More of a reconnaissance mission, Sir," Pickering said. "To see what's really going on with him."

"General Willoughby believes Fertig suffers from delusions of grandeur."

"Yes, Sir, he's made that clear to me."

"I had plans, you know, Fleming, to conduct extensive guerrilla operations against the Japanese—using the matériel and personnel available to General Sharp's Mindanao Force."

"No, Sir, I did not."

"That, and good deal else, went down the toilet when the chain of command became confused. You know what I'm speaking of, of course."

"No, Sir. Not exactly."

"When I was ordered to leave Corregidor by the President, it was my understanding that I was simply moving my flag, not relinquishing my command and its concomitant responsibilities. I conferred with General Sharp on Mindanao—at the Dole Plantation, incidentally, do you know it?"

"Yes, Sir. I was a guest there many times before the war."

"Lovely place. It pains me to think of Japanese boots treading on the verandah of the main house . . . but I digress. I spoke with General Sharp at some length while waiting for the airplane. My orders to him were to hold on, that immediately on my arrival here, I would institute a resupply operation for the Mindanao Force; and, looking to the worst case—if it appeared to him that further organized resistance was not possible—to make provisions, select personnel, and cache supplies and matériel for irregular operations."

"I wasn't aware of that, Sir."

"Oh, yes," MacArthur said. "But the moment that B-17 broke ground at the Dole Plantation airstrip to bring me here, General Marshall began to communicate directly with General Wainwright on Corregidor. General Wainwright naturally assumed the chain of command had been changed, that I had been taken out of it, and that he henceforth would be getting his orders from Washington. Nothing about that was said to me, then or now."

"I wasn't aware of this, Sir."

"Few people are," MacArthur said. "When I arrived here—you were here, Fleming; you know this—I learned that I had been misled vis-à-vis the matériel and troops that would be available to me here. But I kept my word to Sharp. I drew down on the limited matériel here and instituted resupply voyages to Mindanao. Unfortunately, very little got through to him: two small ships containing artillery and small-arms ammunition, and not much else. And then, when George Marshall diverted to Hawaii supply ships already on the high seas to Australia, on the grounds the risk of their loss was too great to bear, I had to terminate my efforts to resupply General Sharp's Mindanao Force—with the greatest reluctance."

"I understand."

"And then, of course, the question became moot. Bataan fell, and then Corregidor. General Homma bluffed General Wainwright. He would not agree to Wainwright's surrender unless Wainwright surrendered *all* U.S. troops in the Philippines. Wainwright had no authority to do that, but he *thought* he did. And, unfortunately, so did General Sharp. As soon as I heard what Wainwright had done, I radioed General Sharp to ignore any orders from Wainwright. But by then, it was too late. General Sharp, as a good soldier, obeyed what he thought were his orders to surrender. As a good officer, he destroyed all the war matériel under his command before hoisting the white flag. All the matériel, Fleming, which could, *should,* have been used to mount a meaningful irregular operation against the Japanese. And the officers who would have commanded such operations, God help them, entered captivity.''

MacArthur paused, took the thin black cigar from the ashtray, relit it carefully, and then met Pickering's eyes.

''At that point I was forced to conclude that the mounting of effective irregular, guerrilla operations against the Japanese in the Philippine Islands was militarily impossible. I so informed General Marshall.''

''Yes, Sir.''

''You do understand the problem here, don't you, Fleming?''

''I'm not sure I take your meaning, Sir.''

''Faith!'' MacArthur said dramatically. ''Faith! At the moment, the Filipino people have not lost their faith in me, in the United States. They *believe* I *will* return. But realistically, that faith is not very deep. It would disappear if we suffered another humiliating defeat at the hands of the Japanese. If, for example, people flocked to this Fertig chap in the belief that he was in fact a general officer of the United States Army. And then, for example, he were to be captured by the Japanese and marched in chains through the streets of Manila and executed as a common criminal. *That* would be playing right into the hands of the Japanese!''

''Yes, Sir.''

Abruptly, MacArthur asked:

''What are you going to do, Fleming, about this obnoxious intrusion of the camel's nose into *your* tent?''

The question surprised Pickering.

''Obey my orders, Sir. See that these people get into Mindanao and then get out.''

MacArthur nodded his head solemnly.

''This headquarters, of course, and myself personally, stands ready of course to render any assistance we can to assist you in the accomplishment of your mission.''

''I can't think of anything I need right now, Sir.''

MacArthur looked at him for a long moment, then nodded his head.

''If something comes up, let me know.''

''Thank you, General.''

"Again, Fleming, I deeply appreciate your loyalty to me. But if there's nothing else?"

"No, Sir. Thank you for seeing me, Sir."

[THREE]
Naval Air Transport Command Passenger Terminal
United States Naval Base
Pearl Harbor, Oahu, Territory of Hawaii
1430 Hours 21 November 1942

The plump, bland-faced officer—his desk plate identified him as Lieutenant (j.g.) L. B. Cavanaugh, USNR, Officer in Charge Passenger Seat Assignment—was simply a typical bureaucrat who had put on a uniform for the duration plus six months, Major James C. Brownlee III, USMCR, thought impatiently.

It was not at all hard for Brownlee to picture Lieutenant Cavanaugh standing behind the Pan American Airways ticket counter in Miami offering the same argument he was offering here:

"I'm sorry, I don't make the regulations, and I have no authority to change them."

Lieutenant Cavanaugh had produced the rules with all the self-righteous assurance of Moses presenting the Ten Commandments on his descent from Mount Sinai: *Here they are, God has spoken, there is no room for argument.*

U.S. Navy Base, Pearl Harbor, T.H., Circular 42-2, "Standing Operating Procedure, Naval Air Transport Command Passenger Terminal," consisted of sixteen mimeographed pages, each protected by a celluloid envelope in a blue loose-leaf binder. From its battered condition, Brownlee concluded that the Lieutenant had found it necessary to produce the regulations frequently.

Section Six, "Conflicting Priorities," took two single-spaced typewritten pages to deal with the inevitability of two or more people showing up at the same time with on-the-face-of-it similar priorities to claim one seat.

The point was that priorities were really seldom absolutely identical, although Lieutenant (j.g.) Cavanaugh was willing to grant that the priorities of Major Brownlee and Captains Sessions and Macklin were more *nearly* identical than was usually the case.

All three carried the highest—AAAAAA—priority classification. Some time ago, Lieutenant (j.g.) Cavanaugh said, an AAAAAA priority would almost have guaranteed a seat on any plane going anywhere. But that had changed, as various headquarters realized the only way to be sure their travelers got on airplanes with the least possible delay was to issue them the highest priority possible.

In consequence of that, authority to issue AAAAAA air-travel priorities had been removed from lesser headquarters. At the present time, only Commander, U.S. Naval Activities, West Coast (COMNAVACTWEST); Commander, U.S. Naval Activities, East Coast (COMNAVACTEAST); CINCPAC (Commander-in-Chief, Pacific); and SWPOA (Supreme Headquarters, South West Pacific Ocean Area) had the authority to issue AAAAAA air-travel priorities. Plus, of course, the U.S. Army Chief of Staff and the Chief of Naval Operations.

Identical AAAAAA priorities issued by the Chief of Staff of the Army and the Chief of Naval Operations had priority over AAAAAA priorities issued by lesser headquarters.

But inasmuch as the AAAAAA priorities issued to Major Brownlee and Captains Sessions and Macklin had all been issued by the Chief of Naval Operations, that was no help in determining who would occupy the one seat available on the Coronado departing Pearl Harbor at 1615 hours for Supreme Headquarters, SWPOA, Brisbane, Australia.

The next selection criteria, given identical AAAAAA priorities issued by the same—or equal-level—headquarters, was the date and time of the issue. And this was the deciding factor here, Lieutenant (j.g.) Cavanaugh announced. Inasmuch as the AAAAAA priority issued to Captain Sessions was dated four days prior to the AAAAAA priorities issued to Major Brownlee and Captain Macklin, Captain Sessions was thus entitled to the seat.

Lieutenant (j.g.) Cavanaugh was deaf to Major Brownlee's argument that the three officers were all on the same mission, that he was by virtue of his rank the commanding officer, and thus had the authority to determine which of the three would travel first, with the others to follow.

"Priorities are not transferable," Lieutenant (j.g.) Cavanaugh said. "Paragraph 14(b)." He indicated with his finger the applicable paragraph.

"Lieutenant," Sessions asked, "what if I was suddenly taken ill? It really is important that Major Brownlee reaches Brisbane before I do."

"You would really have to be sick," Lieutenant (j.g.) Cavanaugh said. "Otherwise that would constitute 'Absence Without Leave With the Intention of Avoiding Hazardous Duty.' All air travel beyond here into the Pacific is considered Hazardous Duty. They'd take you to the dispensary, and you would have to prove you were sick."

He flipped the pages of "Standing Operating Procedure" until he came to the applicable paragraph, then held out the blue loose-leaf binder for them to see for themselves.

"And I can't just voluntarily give up my seat to Major Brownlee?" Sessions asked.

"No, you cannot," Lieutenant (j.g.) Cavanaugh said simply but firmly.

"Have a nice flight, Ed," Major Brownlee said. "I'll see you in Brisbane."

"I'm sorry, Sir," Ed Sessions said.

"It's not your fault," Brownlee said. "This has all come down from Mount Sinai graven on stone."

Sessions chuckled.

"I'll tell you what you might do, Major, if it's really important that you get to Brisbane," Lieutenant (j.g.) Cavanaugh said.

"It's really important."

"You might go out to Hickam Field. The Army's running Flying Fortresses through there to Australia. Sometimes, they can find a ride for people in a hurry. There's no seats on a B-17, of course, and it's a long ride. . . ."

"How would I get from here to Hickam Field?"

"There's a bus from the Main Gate. I think they run every hour on the quarter hour."

"You mind getting on the Coronado by yourself, Ed?" Brownlee asked. "Can you handle all that stuff by yourself?"

He pointed to their luggage. In addition to their clothing, this included the obsolete Device, Cryptographic, M94; the new crypto device—which, to Sessions's surprise, did not seem to have an official nomenclature; four small portable shortwave radios and several spare sets of batteries; and other items which Colonel Rickabee and Major Banning decided, before Brownlee and Macklin showed up, that McCoy might find useful.

Sessions took Brownlee's meaning: While Brownlee might be able to cajole space for himself and Macklin on a Flying Fortress, it was unlikely the Army Air Corps would be willing to carry along several hundred pounds of what looked like his personal baggage.

"I can handle it," Sessions said, and then looked at Lieutenant (j.g.) Cavanaugh to see if he had any objections.

"Let me see your orders again," Cavanaugh said. He studied them carefully, then announced: "No problem. Paragraph 5(b) says, *'and such equipment and accessories as is considered necessary for the accomplishment of the assigned mission.'* I presume all that stuff is necessary?"

"Absolutely," Brownlee and Sessions said at the same instant.

They looked at each other and chuckled. Then Brownlee put out his hand.

"See you in Brisbane, Ed," he said.

"Yes, Sir."

Macklin offered his hand. Sessions pretended not to see it.

But he saw it, Brownlee thought, concerned. *Sessions refused to shake Macklin's hand. And since we reported to Management Analysis, he hasn't said one word to him that was not absolutely necessary. I wonder what that's all about? Resentment that we're going in on what these people thought was their mission? That doesn't sound likely. But there's something.*

[FOUR]
Headquarters, Marine Air Group 21
Marine Airfield
Ewa, Oahu Island, Territory of Hawaii
22 November 1942

Lieutenant Colonel Clyde W. Dawkins, USMC, noticed the staff car parked at the wooden Base Operations building when he passed over the field on the downwind leg of his approach. Dawkins, a tanned, wiry man of thirty-five, who was a career Marine out of Annapolis, commanded MAG-21.

"Now what?" he asked rhetorically, somewhat disgustedly, and aloud, and then turned most of his attention to putting the Grumman F4F-4 Wildcat fighter onto the ground.

He took a closer look at the staff car as he taxied past Base Ops. It was a nearly new Buick Special sedan, and thus was engaged in the transportation of not only a brass hat but a senior brass hat. There were only a couple of Buicks in the hands of Marines in Hawaii, and they were—rank hath its privileges—reserved for general officers.

Dawkins searched his mind but could come up with no reason why a general officer would show up at Ewa on Sunday, unless he was either the bearer of bad tidings or really enraged about something and wished to make his displeasure known personally and immediately to the Commanding Officer of MAG-21.

Dawkins taxied the Wildcat to a sandbag revetment, turned it around so it could be pushed backward into the revetment after refueling, shut it down, and then turned to the paperwork. It had been a test flight, following 100-hour maintenance, and he had found several items that needed either investigation or repair.

He was aware that someone had climbed onto the wingroot, but didn't look up.

"I didn't know they let worn-out old men like you play with hot airplanes like this," a male voice said, causing him to look up into the face of a large-boned, ruddy-faced man in his forties. Without realizing he was doing it—truly a Pavlovian reflex—Dawkins raised his right hand to his eyelid in a salute and simultaneously tried to stand up.

The uniform of the man standing on Dawkins's wing was adorned with both the golden wings of a Naval Aviator and the silver stars—one on each epaulet and one on each collar point—of a brigadier general.

"I think you have to take the harness off before you can do that," Brigadier General D. G. McInerney, USMC, said innocently, as he sort of patted Dawkins's shoulder.

"Yes, Sir," Dawkins said, chagrined. "Thank you very much, Sir."

General McInerney jumped off the wing, then waited until Dawkins unstrapped himself and climbed out of the cockpit. As Dawkins joined him, he extended his hand.

"Good to see you, Sir," Dawkins said. "I thought you were in Washington."

"I got in a couple of hours ago," McInerney said. "How's things, Dawk?"

"There's a lot more creature comforts around here," he said. The last time they were in each other's company, they'd been in a tent at a paved-with-pierced-steel-planking airstrip called "Fighter One" on the island of Guadalcanal in the Solomons.

"Do you know General Forrest, Dawk?"

"I know who he is, Sir."

"ACofS Intelligence," McInerney said. "An old friend. He knew I was coming here, and asked me to do would I could about this."

He dipped into the pocket of his tunic again and handed Dawkins a flimsy carbon copy of an internal USMC memorandum:

TELEPHONE MEMORANDUM

CLASSIFICATION: NONE

DATE AND TIME: 1625 16 Nov 1942

FROM: Commandant, USMC

TO: Maj Gen Forrest

SUBJECT: Gunnery Sergeant Zimmerman, Ernest

SYNOPSIS:

(1) The Commandant has received from SecNav personally SecNav's desire that Gunnery Sergeant Ernest Zimmerman, Serial Number Unknown, USMC, presently assigned VMF-229 be immediately transferred to USMC Special Detachment 16, with duty station Brisbane, Australia.

(2) The Secretary desires that Sergeant Zimmerman's travel to Brisbane be by the most expeditious means, and that he be advised by

> Special Channel Communication of Sergeant Zimmerman's estimated time
> of arrival in Brisbane. The Secretary further desires that the
> Commanding Officer, USMC Special Detachment 16, be similarly advised,
> also by Special Channel Communication.
>
> (3) The Commandant desires that Maj Gen Forrest personally
> accomplish the foregoing as a matter of the highest priority.

"What I would like to do at any time within the next fifteen minutes, Dawk," General McInerney said, "is send a message to General Forrest, telling him that Gunny Zimmerman is on his way to Brisbane."

Dawkins looked distinctly uncomfortable.

"Sir, he's not here."

"Where is he?"

"I think he's on Guadalcanal."

"You *think* he's on Guadalcanal?"

"Sir, he didn't leave the 'Canal when the ground personnel got on the ship."

"Why not?"

"I think Captain Galloway is carrying him as being on temporary duty with the 2nd Raider Battalion."

"You don't know?"

"Big Steve had him—Zimmerman's a Browning expert—transferred from the Raiders to VMF-229 when they were having weapons trouble. When the Squadron was relieved, Zimmerman went back to the Raiders."

"Without orders?"

"I believe it was on Galloway's verbal orders, Sir, with official orders to follow when that became possible."

"Where did you say Galloway is?"

"At Muku-Muku, Sir."

"Where's that?" General McInerney asked, and then, before Dawkins could reply, went on. "You know where to find it?"

"Yes, Sir."

"Get in the car, Colonel," General McInerney ordered. "Curiosity overwhelms me."

A silver-haired, elderly, dignified black man in a crisp white steward's coat walked out onto the flagstone patio of the sprawling mansion on the coast. Five hundred yards down the steep, lush slope, large waves crashed onto a wide white sand beach.

Three people were on the patio, stretched comfortably out on upholstered rattan chaise lounges under a green awning. One was a statuesque, Slavic-appearing blond woman in her forties. Makeup-less, pale-skinned, she had her blond hair piled upward on her head. She was wearing a loose-fitting, gaudily flowered dress, called a "muumuu." Her feet were in woven leather sandals.

One of the men, a good-looking, slim, deeply tanned and brown-haired young man of twenty-six, was wearing swimming trunks and a loose-fitting shirt quite as loud as the lady's muumuu. The other, a large, nearly bald, barrel-chested man in his forties, was wearing stiffly starched Marine khakis, the collar unbuttoned. The collar points held the gold and brown bar of a master gunner, and there were gold Naval Aviator's wings on his chest.

"Captain Galloway," the steward said. "Colonel Dawkins is here to see you. With another gentleman, a general."

"Denny," Charley Galloway said, "I've had a bad week. Do not pull my leg."

The steward raised his right hand, palm outward, to shoulder height as if swearing that he was telling the truth, the whole truth, and nothing but the truth.

"God, Denny, let them in!" Galloway said, rising to his feet. "It wouldn't hurt to bow or something."

Smiling, the steward bowed with great dignity.

"Not to me, not to me, at the General!"

"Your wish is my command," Denny said.

"My God," the woman said anguished. "Look at me!"

Twenty seconds later, Brigadier General D. G. McInerney and Lieutenant Colonel Clyde W. Dawkins walked onto the patio. The master gunner came to a position very much like attention.

"Good afternoon, Sir," Galloway said.

"Ah, Captain Galloway," McInerney said. "And Mr. Oblensky!"

"Good afternoon, Sir," Oblensky said formally.

"Marine Corps legends in their own time!" McInerney went on. "Why am I not surprised to find you two in such an environment of primitive squalor?"

"General, I don't believe you know Mrs. Oblensky?" Galloway said.

"No, but I am genuinely honored to meet you, Commander," General McInerney said, then walked to her and shook her hand.

When she was not playing the role of Mrs. Master Gunner Oblensky, USMC, she was Commander Florence Kocharski, Chief Surgical Nurse, U.S. Navy Hospital, Pearl Harbor. She had been awarded the Silver Star for her valor—"with absolute disregard for her own life"—going aboard a sinking battleship to treat the wounded on December 7, 1941.

"Commander, how's the Stecker boy doing?" McInerney asked.

"He's a long way from well, Sir," she said. "But, considering the shape he was in when we got him, he's doing fine."

"I saw the crash," McInerney said. "It wasn't pleasant."

"Steve told me," she said.

"That's another item on my agenda," McInerney said. "When can I see him?"

She smiled.

"They generally waive visiting hours for general officers, General."

"I meant, when would it be convenient for you and your people?"

"Anytime would be fine, Sir."

"His father and I are old friends," McInerney said. "We were in France together in the last war. And so, incidentally, was our host."

"May I offer the General something to drink?" Galloway asked.

"Hawaiian hospitality, right?" McInerney said. "Goes with the rope of flowers around your neck? Second time today I've had that offer. Colonel Dawkins offered me something to drink, pineapple juice and gin. I was about to accept, and then the Colonel told me you'd put Gunnery Sergeant Zimmerman on TDY to the 2nd Raider Battalion, and I thought I'd hold off until I heard all about that."

"I'm surprised you heard about that, Sir," Galloway said.

"Not as surprised as the Secretary of the Navy is going to be," McInerney said, and handed Galloway the telephone memorandum he had shown Dawkins at Ewa.

Galloway read it and handed it to Oblensky, who read it and winced.

"Permission to speak, Sir?"

"Certainly, Mr. Oblensky," McInerney said.

"The Captain really didn't know much about this," Oblensky said. "I was mostly responsible for this, Sir."

"I'm so carried away with auld lang syne, I may cry," McInerney said.

"Zimmerman was a Raider before we got him, Sir," Galloway said. "He came to me when we were relieved on the 'Canal and said he wanted to go back to the Raiders. I told him to go ahead, I'd fix the paperwork later."

"And why didn't you?" McInerney said.

"I tried, Sir," Galloway said. "I ran into a couple of problems."

"Be specific, Charley. I'm fascinated."

"Sir, the Personnel Officer at Marine Barracks, Pearl Harbor, told me the only way to get Zimmerman into the Raiders was for Zimmerman to apply for them. I couldn't apply for him. They have to be volunteers."

"Did you tell him Zimmerman was already running around behind the Jap lines on Guadalcanal with the Raiders?"

"I didn't think that would be a wise course of action under the circumstances, Sir."

McInerney chuckled.

"So you just decided to sit tight and see what happened?"

"Yes, Sir."

"Something was bound to happen, right?"

"I'm sorry the Secretary of the Navy got involved, Sir. And that you did, Sir."

"So am I," McInerney said.

"I'd love to stay here and have several strong drinks, Charley," McInerney said. "But I have to go find a message center so I can send a radio to General Forrest telling him that Gunny Zimmerman is running around Guadalcanal somewhere."

"Sir, you can call him from here, if you like," Charley said.

"Call, as in telephone call, Charley?"

"The Pacific & Far East Shipping Company Office in Honolulu has a dedicated line to their office in San Francisco."

"And you can use it?" McInerney asked incredulously.

Galloway walked to the wall of the patio and returned with a telephone on a long cord. He dialed a number.

"This is Captain Galloway," he said. "Would you put me through to San Francisco, please?"

He handed the phone to General McInerney.

XI

[ONE]
Naval Air Transport Station
Brisbane, Australia
0625 Hours 24 November 1942

The storm struck as the Consolidated PB2Y-3 Coronado made its final approach. They'd had bad weather all along the route from Hawaii, and their takeoff from the refueling stop at Midway Island was delayed for over two hours by weather. As Captain Edward Sessions, USMC, saw the flashes of lightning, heard the rain drumming on the fuselage, felt the huge plane being buffeted by strong winds, and saw the whitecaps on the water, he thought it entirely likely that having flown literally close to halfway around the world, he was about to get killed on landing.

It had been a long trip. It was 2,269 miles from Washington to San Diego; 2,606 miles from San Diego to Pearl Harbor, Hawaii; and 4,702 from Pearl Harbor to Brisbane—with a refueling stop at Midway Island.

The landing itself was a series of crashes against the water. When they finally stopped, the Coronado rocked sickeningly from side to side, as the pilot taxied it as close as he dared to the shoreline. The storm seemed to worsen by the minute.

A little train of open whaleboats started out through the choppy waters to the Coronado. It required great boat-handling skill to transfer the passengers and cargo (with the exception of the boxes Sessions was carrying, mostly mailbags) into the whaleboats without permitting the boats to crash against the thin aluminum of the seaplane.

By the time the whaleboats made it from the seaplane to the shore, all the passengers were soaked through. On the face of the quai itself, there was a flight of narrow stone steps onto which the passengers had to jump from the bobbing whaleboats.

Sessions was amazed that no one fell into the water, and that he finally managed to heave his personal luggage and the boxes onto the steps without losing anything.

He surveyed the boxes, decided the one carrying the obsolete M94 Cryptographic Device and its replacement was the most valuable, picked it up, and carried it up the stone stairs.

A Marine, a very young one, wearing an Army poncho and a rain-soaked khaki fore-and-aft cap, walked up to him and saluted.

"Captain Sessions, Sir?"

"Right."

"Staff Sergeant Koffler, Sir. If you'll point out your gear, Sir, I'll take care of it. General Pickering's over there, Sir." He pointed to two cars, a Studebaker President and a Jaguar convertible.

"Everything that's on those steps, Sergeant. Thank you," Sessions said, and headed toward the Studebaker.

He was halfway there before his tired mind slipped into gear.

"Staff Sergeant"? Is that what he said? That boy is a staff sergeant? And what did he say his name was? "Koffler"? That's the kid who's been living like an animal under the noses of the Japs on Buka?

As he came close to the Studebaker, the rear door opened, and he stepped in. Brigadier General Fleming W. Pickering extended his hands to take the box from him.

"Hello, Ed, how was the flight?" Pickering said.

"About like that, Sir," Sessions said, waving a hand at the rough water. "Most of the way from Midway."

A hand was thrust at him, and Sessions took it before he saw that it was attached to First Lieutenant Kenneth R. McCoy, USMCR.

"Welcome to sunny Australia," McCoy said.

"If it hasn't melted, I have a letter—actually a little package—from Ernie for you," Sessions said.

"Give it to him now," Pickering said. "You have to go back out in the rain. You're going to staying with us. Which means you and McCoy will go in the Jaguar to the house, while George and I take our guests to the SWPOA BOQ."

"They're not here, Sir. They should be on tomorrow's plane, unless Major Brownlee was able to scrounge a ride on an Air Corps B-17. He was going to try."

"Not that I'm not glad to see you, Ed, but how is it the Major waited while the Captain got to fly?"

"I tried to give him my seat, Sir, but the Navy wouldn't let me."

"You hear that, George?"

"Yes, Sir."

"Drive up to Koffler and tell him to bring Captain Sessions's stuff to the house."

"Aye, aye, Sir."

"Hello, George," Sessions said. "Congratulations on your promotion."

"If I thought I deserved it, Captain, I'd say thank you."

"You wouldn't have it if it wasn't deserved," Sessions said.

Hart started the engine, drove to the edge of the quai, and waited for Koffler to appear. Then he rolled down the window.

"Koffler, nobody else is coming. Bring all of Captain Sessions's gear out to the house."

"Aye, aye, Sir."

Sessions waited until they were under way, then said, "I can't believe that kid is Koffler."

"Don't let that baby face fool you," McCoy said. "He's one hell of a Marine."

"Speaking of Marines," Pickering said. "What do you think of the two OSS Marines?"

"The Major's all right. Nice guy. Bright. Got his head screwed on correctly. Speaks perfect Spanish."

"And the Captain?"

"The Captain is named Macklin," Sessions said evenly.

"Not . . ." McCoy said.

"One and the same, Lieutenant McCoy."

"Shit," McCoy said.

For a moment, Pickering was confused. He was also somewhat surprised at the deep bitterness of McCoy's obscenity. And then he remembered hearing Jack Stecker and McCoy talking about an officer named Macklin. There had been some trouble with him in China, where Banning sided with McCoy against him, and again in Quantico, where Macklin tried to keep McCoy from getting commissioned.

"Is this the same officer you and Jack Stecker were talking about, Ken?" Pickering asked. "The one who gave you trouble on the rifle range at Quantico?"

"I'm still hoping Sessions is pulling my chain," McCoy said. "He has a strange sense of humor."

"I wish I was kidding about this, Ken," Sessions said. "General, this is the officer, using the term very loosely, with whom McCoy, and I, and Major Banning had trouble in China."

"Does Banning know it's the same man? More important, does Colonel Rickabee?"

Sessions went into his tunic and came out with a soggy envelope.

"Colonel Rickabee asked me to give you this, Sir," he said.

It was a glossy photograph of the abrupt note Secretary Knox had sent Rickabee.

After he read it, his first reaction was that Knox must have written it in anger, and that was uncharacteristic of him.

Was Knox boiling because Rickabee had the audacity to object to this man Macklin? Or is there something else?

Well, Frank Knox can tell Rickabee *he doesn't "desire" any "further discussion" of this, but he can't tell* me *that. Just as soon as we get to the house, I'll call Pluto in the dungeon and tell him to send Knox a Special Channel Personal. If Banning, Sessions, and McCoy all think this man is no good, so far as I'm concerned, it's three strikes and he's out!*

"May I keep this, Ed?" Pickering asked politely.

"Of course, Sir."

"Let me think about this."

By the time they reached Water Lily Cottage, he'd had time to control his temper, consider his options, and choose one. It was so simple that he was a little afraid of it. He decided to say nothing now. He'd ask a few more questions and have a couple of cups of coffee and a cigar before finally making up his mind.

"Did I understand you to say, Ed, that Major Brownlee strikes you as a competent officer?" Pickering asked conversationally.

"Yes, Sir. First class. And he impressed Colonel Rickabee the same way, Sir."

"Really?"

"Yes, Sir," Sessions said. "We had a hurry-up briefing session with some Philippine experts from ONI, and the Colonel sat in on it. He quickly came to the same conclusion I did, that Brownlee should have been the briefer, rather than the briefee. The Colonel told me to find out who in G1 had sent Major Brownlee to OSS instead of to us, and have him shot."

"That good, eh?" Pickering chuckled.

Fascinating!

Captain Ed Sessions had heard references to "the cottage." So he was not surprised when Hart pulled the Studebaker up against the verandah of a rambling frame house, and Pickering announced, "Here we are, Ed. Our home away from home."

But he was surprised at the size of the place, and then even more surprised when the rear door of the Studebaker was pulled open by a plump, gray-haired, motherly woman in her late fifties, who was wearing a flowered dress and a frilly apron. She held an enormous umbrella over her head.

"Welcome to Australia, Captain Sessions," she said, and thrust two more umbrellas into the backseat.

Pickering sensed Sessions's surprise.

"Captain Sessions, this is Mrs. Hortense Cavendish," he said, laughter in his voice. "She's in charge around here. You disobey her at your peril."

Inside Water Lily Cottage, Sessions found that a hotel-like buffet of scrambled eggs, sausages—"They call those bangers, Ed," McCoy offered helpfully—ham, and three kinds of biscuits and toast was laid out in a large dining room.

"God, war is hell, isn't it?" Sessions asked.

"Since I went through boot camp," Pickering said solemnly, "I have always disagreed with the Marine Corps belief that you need practice to be miserable and hungry."

Over breakfast, Pickering explained that when he first came to Australia, MacArthur's SWPOA Headquarters was in Melbourne.

"So I rented a house," he said, "presided over by Mrs. Cavendish. By the time El Supremo moved his headquarters here, Mrs. Cavendish had concluded that if it were not for her, all of us, in unwashed clothing and needing haircuts, would die of starvation in unmade beds. So she signed on for the duration, and came up here when I rented this place."

"Some people have all the luck," Sessions said.

"She has a husband and two sons in the service," Pickering went on, the timbre of his voice changing. "One each Royal Australian Army, Navy, and Air Force. All in Africa."

"Oh," Sessions said.

When he finished his breakfast, Pickering lit a cigar and then somehow summoned Mrs. Cavendish. Sessions heard the dull ring of a bell and decided there must be a button on the dining-room table, or else the floor.

"Can I bring something else, General?" Mrs. Cavendish asked.

"Would you please make a fresh pot of—"

"It's already through," she interrupted.

"And then leave us for a while? And if Koffler is out there, send him home."

"Certainly, Sir."

Sessions desperately wanted to climb into bed and the shower, and not necessarily in that order; but he knew that would have to wait until Pickering finished whatever he had in mind. Pickering puffed thoughtfully on his cigar until the coffee was delivered and the buffet and dirty dishes removed.

"Are you going to want me for this, Sir?" McCoy asked, starting to rise out of his chair.

"Stick around, Ken, and you, too, George."

McCoy lowered himself back into his chair and reached for the silver coffeepot.

"One more time, Ed," Pickering said to Sessions. "Both you and Ricka-bee are favorably impressed with Major Brownlee?"

"Yes, Sir. I suppose you could say he's everything Captain Macklin is not."

"I would have liked to make the judgment on my own," Pickering said. "But your opinion, and Colonel Rickabee's, is the next-best thing. And I want this in place before they get here. You said tomorrow morning, right?"

"Yes, Sir. They had seats on today's plane. But maybe sooner, if Major Brownlee was able to get the Army Air Corps to carry them on a B-17."

"OK. The participation of the OSS—which means Major Brownlee and Captain Macklin—in the mission to have a look at General Fertig and his guerrilla operation has been directed. That's a given. That poses certain problems, but also resolves some."

"Yes, Sir?"

"For one thing, it may solve the radio operator problem. Against my better judgment, I agreed to let Koffler go with McCoy." He looked at McCoy and saw in his eyes that he didn't like that at all. "He's a hell of a radio operator, Ken. And there is apparently some way one radio operator can recognize another radio operator. I think they say every operator has 'a hand' that's unlike anyone else's."

McCoy exhaled audibly and shrugged his acceptance of that. That was valuable. If the Japanese captured the new encryption device, and they attempted to send deceptive information—for example, ordering the submarine to appear at a location where it would find a Japanese destroyer waiting for it—the receiving operator would be immediately suspicious if the correctly encrypted message was not in Koffler's hand.

"I have discussed this mission with General MacArthur, including the participation of the OSS," Pickering went on. He saw the surprise in Sessions's eyes. "That surprises you, Ed?"

"Yes, Sir," Sessions said.

"Because you believe that Colonel Donovan, and for that matter Secretary Knox, and for all we know, the President himself, would prefer that General MacArthur had no knowledge of OSS participation until the mission is over?"

"Yes, Sir. I saw the Special Channel Personal from Secretary Knox to you, Sir. With respect, Sir, they seemed to spell that out pretty clearly."

"I'm just a simple civilian in uniform, Captain Sessions, a former enlisted man. If it was bad judgment on my part to make the Supreme Commander, SWPOA, aware of a mission contemplated for execution within his area of responsibility, and if this comes to the attention of Secretary Knox—I don't give much of a damn whether Bill Donovan likes it or not—then the Secretary will have to take the action against me that he deems appropriate."

"Yes, *Sir*," Sessions said.

"General MacArthur graciously offered any assistance he personally and Supreme Headquarters, SWPOA, can provide to help me in the execution of this mission. And I intend to ask him for a qualified high-speed radio operator. It seems entirely likely to me that among those who escaped from the Philippines, there should be such a person, probably a senior noncommissioned officer who also speaks Spanish, and thus would be even more highly qualified than our own Staff Sergeant Koffler."

Pickering now saw approval in McCoy's eyes.

"I have also decided to remove Lieutenant McCoy from the roster of officers who will participate in this mission. I have several reasons for so doing, which I am of course prepared to defend to Secretary Knox. For one thing, there is the consideration of space available on the submarine. The fewer personnel, obviously, the more medical supplies the initial party can take with them. And finally, Lieutenant McCoy is not only the junior of the officers, but he has not been able to avail himself of the splendid training Bill Donovan provides for his agents."

"General," Ed Sessions said, smiling broadly, "at the risk of sounding like a toady, may I say that I wholeheartedly agree with the General's reasoning?"

"Yes, you may," Pickering said, chuckling, and then turned to McCoy.

"You have any problems with this, Ken?"

"Three, Sir," McCoy said immediately, surprising Pickering.

"OK," Pickering said, making a *let's have them* gesture with his hand.

"From personal experience, and I think Captain Sessions will go along with me on this, Macklin is a hell of a load to put on this major's shoulders."

Sessions's smile vanished.

"Captain Macklin has to go, Ken," Pickering said. "That's out of my hands."

McCoy nodded, then said, "Zimmerman. It's a dirty trick to play on Zimmerman."

"Christ!" Sessions said. He had not thought of Zimmerman.

"First of all," Pickering said, "no one seems to know where Gunny Zimmerman is, except with the 2nd Raider Battalion somewhere behind the Jap lines on Guadalcanal. It's entirely possible that he won't arrive in Australia until after this mission has been mounted. And if he does show up, it is entirely possible that he will be suffering from malaria. I have been informed that seventy-odd percent of the First Marine Division has it. And if that's true, he will of course require hospitalization, and for a month or six weeks. By then the mission will have been mounted."

McCoy shrugged and nodded, and then went on. "Fertig. Sending Macklin seems to be a dirty trick to play on him."

"I've thought about that. That's out of my hands, too. Anyway, if Major Brownlee is as good as Sessions and Rickabee seem to think, he should be able to handle Captain Macklin. Anything else?"

"No, Sir," McCoy said.

"You're not getting out of hazardous service, Ken, if that's what you're thinking. As soon as we do—*you* do—everything possible to ensure that Major Brownlee has everything he needs, and this mission is under way, I'm going to send you back to the States to rejoin the Mongolia Operation."

"Aye, aye, Sir," McCoy said.

"OK," Pickering said. "Unless anyone has something else, that's it. You get some sleep, Ed, you obviously need it. And you, Ken, start doing what has to be done to help Major Brownlee."

[TWO]
Water Lily Cottage
Brisbane, Australia
1305 Hours 24 November 1942

"This thing is really primitive, isn't it?" Major Hon Song Do, Signal Corps, USA, said wonderingly, as he examined the Device, Cryptographic, M94 on the dining-room table.

Sitting around the table were Colonel Jack (NMI) Stecker, Major Hon, Captain Edward Sessions, First Lieutenant Kenneth R. McCoy, Second Lieutenant John Marston Moore, and Staff Sergeant Stephen M. Koffler. Everyone was equipped with a pad of notepaper, pencils, and a coffee cup and saucer. In the middle of the table were two silver coffeepots.

McCoy was puffing—blowing smoke rings—on a thin, black cigar. Hon thought it was a symbol—unconscious on McCoy's part—of where he stood in the estimation of General Pickering. Good cigars were in very short supply in Australia. Pickering had obtained two dozen boxes of first-class, long, thin, black Philippine cigars from the master of a Pacific & Far East freighter that had called at Brisbane. They were being smoked by the Supreme Commander, SWPOA, General Pickering himself, and First Lieutenant K. R. McCoy.

"You really never saw one of them before, Sir?" Captain Edward Sessions, USMC, asked, surprised.

"Not even in a museum," Pluto replied. "And you can—what is it you jarheads say, McCoy, 'belay'?—*belay* that 'Sir' business."

"Watch that 'jarhead' business, Major!" Colonel Stecker said sternly, but with a smile.

"Screw you, Major Dogface, Sir," McCoy said.

Stecker laughed out loud.

"OK," Pluto said. "Just to set the priorities. The expert here is Koffler, since he has been on the receiving end of a homemade SOI before." (A *S*ignal *O*perating *I*nstruction specified which one of a large number of available codes was to be used at specific times and dates.)

"I don't know what you're talking about, Pluto," Stecker said. "What's a 'homemade SOI'?"

"In any SOI," Pluto said, "it is presumed both parties to the encryption processes have access to the same symbols. . . ."

"Symbols? What symbols?" McCoy asked, confused.

"When 'A' equals 'X,' 'A' is the symbol for 'X.' OK?"

"Got it."

"Colonel," Pluto said, "to resume the answer I was giving before being so rudely interrupted by Lieutenant McCoy: Before we sent McCoy and Hart into Buka, we had to presume (a) that the Japanese were intercepting the radio traffic between here and Buka; (b) that the SOI that Koffler was using was no longer secure; and it followed, that (c) the Japanese were decrypting our traffic. It followed from that that if we used the existing SOI to inform Buka when and where we were going to land McCoy and Hart on Buka, we would also be informing the Japanese. So we had to get Koffler a new SOI—which meant a homemade SOI."

"How did you do that?" Stecker asked.

Hon waved at Second Lieutenant Moore.

"We devised a simple code, Colonel, using symbols known to both us and the Coastwatchers on Buka, but not to the Japanese," Moore explained. "Specifically, we used some—rather intimate—biographical data."

"And that worked, Koffler, right?" Pluto asked.

"It worked. We had a hell of a hard time figuring some of it out, but it worked."

"What does that mean, 'intimate biographical data'?" Stecker asked.

"Take a look at these, Colonel," Moore said, as he dug in his briefcase and came up with a thin sheaf of three-by-five-inch cards.

He walked around the table to Stecker and laid the cards before Stecker. Koffler got up and went to Stecker; and after a moment, so did McCoy and Sessions. A moment later they were all looking over Stecker's shoulder.

"The first card is the first paragraph of the message we sent to Koffler," Moore explained. "We used the old code, because we didn't want to admit to the Japanese we knew they had broken it."

> USE AS SIMPLE SUBSTITUTION X JULIETS NAME X ROMEOS NAME X
> WHAT SHE THOUGHT HE HAD WHEN THEY MET X NAME OF TEST X RE-
> SULT OF TEST X

"What's this Romeo and Juliet business?" Stecker asked.

Pluto turned from helping himself to a cup of coffee.

"As we understood it, Colonel," he said, dry amusement in his thick Boston/MIT accent, "the great romance between Lieutenant Howard—Romeo—and Juliet—Lieutenant (j.g.) Barbara Cotter, of the Navy Nurse Corps—began at the Navy Hospital, San Diego, when he went for a blood test. The Marine Corps wanted to make sure he did not have syphilis before they made him an officer. Since Miss Cotter, to whom he went to be tested, did not at first know the purpose of the Wasserman test, she treated him accordingly. As a social pariah, so to speak. But Love At First Sight triumphed in the end."

Stecker laughed.

"Really?"

"We believed it was an occasion he would remember," Pluto said.

"What you do for simple substitution," Moore went on, "is write the symbols, without spaces, in a line." He exposed the second three-by-five card. "Under a line of numbers from which the decimal digit after the first nine digits has been dropped."

> 123456789012345678901234567890123456678
> BARBARAJOSEPHSYPHILISWASSERMANNEGATIVE

"OK," Stecker said.

"Card Three is the simple substitution encrypted message," Moore said, and flipped it over.

> 18X19X09X37X11
> 15X23X08X09X11
> 01X02X03X04X05
> 06X07X23X31X05

"Card Four shows the decryption," Moore said, and flipped the last card over. "It was obviously of a personal nature."

```
18x19x09x37x11
I   l   o   v   e
15x23x08x09x11
y   a   j   o   e
01x02x03x04x05
b   a   r   b   a
06x07x23x31x05
r   a   a   n   a

10x23x28x32x10
S   A   M   E   S
35x38x37x38x01
T   E   V   E   B
02x12x13x30x38
A   P   H   N   E
```

"So I see," Stecker said, smiling.

"What we're going to try to do here today is set up the same sort of thing to communicate with General Fertig," Pluto said. "So that we can let him know to expect the people from the OSS, and possibly—General Pickering wants to talk about this to Commander Feldt and Colonel DePress before he decides—when and where they will land from the submarine."

"OK," Stecker said.

"There's an additional problem here," Pluto said. "We only have 'intimate' personal data on General Fertig himself. We have virtually nothing on the Army officers with him. Not only were their records apparently destroyed at the time of surrender, but any dependents are now either dead or interned. In any event, they are not available to help—as Mrs. Fertig is in Colorado. In the presumption that the Japanese will break our simple substitution rather quickly, we are reluctant to use more of General Fertig's personal data than we absolutely have to. If we do, the Japanese will be able to build a dossier on him we don't want them to have."

"What about the Marines?" Stecker asked.

"We have their names . . ." Pluto said.

"Right here," Moore chimed in, dipping into his briefcase again.

". . . but they're not of much use," Pluto continued. "With the exception of the pilot, they're all former enlisted members of the Fourth Marines. All unmarried, according to the Marine Corps in Washington, and all of them have listed their official home of record as 'c/o Headquarters, USMC, Washington, D.C.' I found that a little strange."

"You do that, Pluto, if you don't have a home," McCoy said. "Or you have a home you'd just as soon forget."

Hon had the sudden insight that the official records of Lieutenant K. R. McCoy listed 'c/o Headquarters, USMC, Washington, D.C.' as his home of record.

"What about the pilot?" Stecker asked. "They generally keep more extensive records on officers than they do on enlisted men."

"Unmarried," Moore interjected, consulting a sheet of paper. "His parents are dead. He listed his next of kin as an aunt. ONI contacted her. She hasn't seen him in ten years."

"You have the names of the enlisted men?" McCoy asked. "I used to be in the Fourth."

"So did I," Colonel Stecker said, and put out his hand.

Moore handed him two typewritten sheets of paper. He ran his finger down the names on one page, and then turned to the second.

"I know this character," he said. "Professional private. Hell of a Marine twenty-eight days a month. Then forget him for three days until he's blown his pay."

"Do you think he has a family?" Pluto asked.

"No." Stecker chuckled wryly. "And I really doubt if he'd remember me."

He handed the sheets of paper to McCoy.

Almost immediately, McCoy said, "I know this guy. Mean sonofabitch."

"You're sure, Ken?"

"There aren't very many Marines named Percy," McCoy said, and then his memory cleared. "Christ, if I'm right, this guy worked for Banning after I left China." He raised his eyes to Pluto. "How quick could we get an answer from Banning if we asked him?"

"Using the special channel, we can have an answer in twenty-four hours, maybe less," Moore said.

"How often are we in contact with Fertig?" McCoy asked.

"Once a day in the morning," Pluto said. "But I think they monitor all the time. You want to try to call them?"

"I want to ask Banning if this is the same Percy," McCoy said. "And try to talk to . . . Percy."

"I'm sure General Pickering will authorize use of the special channel," Colonel Stecker said.

"You mean now, Ken?" Pluto asked. "Before we go on with this?"

McCoy didn't answer. He walked back to his seat, picked up his pencil, and began to print characters on the pad of paper.

"What are you doing, Ken?" Sessions asked.

McCoy's left hand waved in a *don't bother me now* gesture.

Pluto looked at Stecker, who shrugged and held both hands palm up in a *let's see what he's up to* gesture.

Two minutes later, McCoy pushed the pad to Pluto.

"What can you spell with that alphabet, Pluto?" McCoy asked. "The line on top."

Pluto looked at the sheet of paper.

ACDEHILMNOPRSUXY

ABCDEFGHIJKLM
NOPQRSTUVWXY
BFGJKVWY

QUENTIN ALEXANDER MCPHERSON

"There's no 'W,' no 'Y,' " Pluto said

"It's got all the vowels," McCoy argued.

"OK," Pluto said. "Using obvious substitution, 'M' for 'W,' 'U' for 'V,' et cetera, it would be useful."

"Slide me that, please," Colonel Stecker ordered, his curiosity aroused. He read it, then looked at McCoy.

"Who is Quentin Alexander McPherson?" he asked.

Looking quite pleased with himself, McCoy smiled at Stecker.

"I thought of this when you said you'd been with the Fourth Marines, *Gunny* Stecker," he said.

He stood up, put his hands on his hips, thrust out his stomach, and in a harsh guttural mimicry announced, "The next time one of youse swine think youse can ruin *my* VD record by bringing some ay-moral, slant-eyed, diseased, Chinese bimbo into *my* barracks, I will cut yer talleywacker off with a dull bayonet and shove it down yer throat, or my name ain't *Quentin Alexander McPherson.*"

Stecker chuckled.

"Oh, yes," he said. "I remember First Sergeant McPherson."

"If Pluto's Sergeant Percy Everly is *my* Percy Everly," McCoy went on, "the one thing about his service with Baker Company, 1st Battalion, 4th Marines, that he will never forget is First Sergeant Quentin Alexander McPherson. And if he remembers him, he'll remember Zimmerman, too; he made the mistake of taking him on."

TOP SECRET

SUPREME HEADQUARTERS SWPOA
NAVY DEPT WASH DC

VIA SPECIAL CHANNEL
DUPLICATION FORBIDDEN
ORIGINAL TO BE DESTROYED AFTER ENCRYPTION AND TRANSMITTAL

FOR COLONEL F. L. RICKABEE
CHIEF USMC OFFICE OF MANAGEMENT ANALYSIS

BRISBANE, AUSTRALIA
MONDAY 23 NOVEMBER 1942

DEAR FRITZ:

BECAUSE OF A PRIORITY PROBLEM AT PEARL HARBOR, SESSIONS AND
SUPPLIES ARRIVED ALONE THIS MORNING. MAJOR BROWNLEE AND
CAPT MACKLIN EXPECTED HERE ON FOLLOWING PLANE TOMORROW
MORNING. WILL ADVISE.

MCCOY BELIEVES SERGEANT PERCY L. EVERLY WITH FERTIG MAY
HAVE SERVED WITH BANNING IN 4TH MARINES. IF THIS IS SO, IT IS
EXTREMELY IMPORTANT THAT BANNING FURNISH IMMEDIATELY
REPEAT IMMEDIATELY WHATEVER PERSONAL INFORMATION RE:
EVERLY BANNING FEELS MIGHT BE VALUABLE IN ESTABLISHING SOI
OF TYPE USED VIS-A-VIS HOWARD AND KOFFLER.

DESPITE THE HIGH REGARD WITH WHICH EVERYONE IN THE NAVAL
SERVICE SEEMS TO REGARD CAPTAIN MACKLIN, I HAVE BEEN
WONDERING WHY HE IS A CAPTAIN AND MCCOY ISN'T. PLEASE SEE
WHAT YOU CAN DO ABOUT THIS.

REGARDS,

FLEMING PICKERING, BRIGADIER GENERAL, USMCR

TOP SECRET

[THREE]
Headquarters, U.S. Forces in the Philippines
Davao Oriental Province
Mindanao, Commonwealth of the Philippines
0810 Hours 24 November 1942

"Come up, gentlemen, please," Brigadier General Wendell W. Fertig, Commanding General, USFIP, said, making the appropriate gesture with his hand.

He was sitting at a rattan table on the verandah of his headquarters, a thatched-roof building on stilts built against a hill.

Second Lieutenant Robert Ball, the USFIP signal officer, and his chief radio operator, Sergeant Ignacio LaMadrid, Philippine Army, who had been standing near the top of the ladderlike steps to the verandah, climbed the rest of the way up.

Both saluted, and Fertig returned the salute.

"We've got a message from Australia, Sir," Ball said. "It doesn't make a lot of sense."

"They rarely do, do they, Lieutenant?" Fertig said, and put his hand out to take the sheet of paper in Ball's hand.

It appeared to be a carbon copy of a decrypted message, but it was in fact the original. Though two typewriters, eight reams of typewriter paper, and a ream of carbon paper had been acquired—from the basement of the ruins of the burned Manuel Quezon Primary School—for the use of HQ, USFIP, neither had a ribbon. It was consequently necessary to make a paper-carbon-paper sandwich to type anything on the ribbonless machines; the original looked like a carbon.

"It's longer than usual, isn't it?" Fertig said as he began to read.

"Yes, Sir," Ball agreed.

The great bulk of their traffic from Supreme Headquarters, SWPOA, was usually very brief: *Your request being considered,* or various paraphrases, all meaning the same thing. *We're still thinking about whether or not we're going to help you.*

```
GYB TO MFS
USING FULL REPEAT FULL NAME OF FIRST DOG BAKER FOURTH
REPEAT BAKER FOURTH SEND LAST REPEAT LAST NAME MOTOR
SERGEANT MISSIONARY RESCUE CONVOY
GYB STANDING BY
```

"What the *hell* does this mean?" Fertig asked, baffled.

Lieutenant Ball and Sergeant LaMadrid responded with a shrug.

"Sergeant, would you please ask Captains Weston and Buchanan to join us?" General Fertig ordered.

"Yes, Sir," LaMadrid said, saluted, and went back down the ladder.

Captains Buchanan and Weston appeared several minutes later. Captain Buchanan was freshly shaved and was wearing a neat khaki uniform. He had even hemmed the trousers and sleeves where they had been cut off. Captain Weston was wearing a pith helmet with a Marine Corps insignia, baggy and somewhat soiled loose white cotton garments of local manufacture, and a full beard.

"I believe, Sir, they're after a simple substitution code," Buchanan offered. "In other words, if we have the full name they mention, we use that to construct a simple substitution code."

"What name?"

"First sergeants are called First Dogs," Buchanan said.

"That could mean Baker Company of the Fourth Marines, Sir," Weston offered, becoming convinced as he spoke that that was exactly what it meant. "We sent out Everly's name. He was in the 4th Marines."

"Where is he?"

"Not here, Sir. He took a patrol out toward Bunawan."

"And won't be back," Fertig said, chagrined that he had forgotten he had ordered the patrol himself, "until when? Day after tomorrow?"

"No, Sir," Buchanan said. "Not until Friday. 27 November. If everything goes well."

"Can we send a runner after him?" Fertig wondered aloud.

"Yes, Sir, we could," Buchanan said, his tone making it perfectly clear he thought this would be ill-advised.

"OK, where are we?" Fertig asked. "It is your opinion, gentlemen, that we need a code based on a name which might be that of a first sergeant in the Fourth Marines, and that name might, just might, be known to Lieutenant Everly? Because he served with the Fourth Marines?"

"What about the other Marines?" Lieutenant Ball asked.

"They're with Everly," Buchanan said.

"Damn!" Fertig said.

He exhaled audibly, then bent over the rattan table and wrote out the reply of Headquarters, USFIP, to the message from Supreme Headquarters, SWPOA. He wrote using very small letters. When the four reams of typewriter paper from the Manuel Quezon elementary school were exhausted, he had no idea where they were going to get more.

```
MFS TO GYB

REGRET TACTICAL OPERATIONS PRECLUDE RESPONSE TO YOUR 24 NO-
VEMBER MESSAGE PRIOR TO 27 NOVEMBER

COMMUNICATIONS BETWEEN OUR HEADQUARTERS WOULD BE GREATLY
FACILITATED IF SUPPLY OF TYPEWRITER RIBBONS COULD BE INCLUDED
IN NEXT WHICH OF COURSE WOULD BE FIRST SUPPLY SHIPMENT

END
FERTIG BRIG GEN COMMANDING
```

[FOUR]
Signal Section
Office of the Military Governor for Mindanao
Cagayan de Oro, Misamis-Oriental Province
Mindanao, Commonwealth of the Philippines
1305 Hours 25 November 1942

Lieutenant Hideyori rose from behind his desk and bowed as Captain Matsuo Saikaku walked in.

"I would have been happy, Sir, to have brought this to your office."

"Not a problem, Hideyori. This was quicker. I have my Lincoln V-12, you know."

"I called as soon as the decryption came in from Signals Intelligence, Sir," Hideyori said, handing Saikaku a single sheet of paper. "GYB, Sir, is the call sign, one of the call signs of American Headquarters in Australia."

"Yes, so you have told me," Saikaku said, somewhat impatiently.

```
GYB TO MFS

USING FULL REPEAT FULL NAME OF FIRST DOG BAKER FOURTH REPEAT
BAKER FOURTH SEND LAST REPEAT LAST NAME MOTOR SERGEANT MIS-
SIONARY RESCUE CONVOY
GYB STANDING BY
```

```
MFS TO GYB

REGRET TACTICAL OPERATIONS PRECLUDE RESPONSE TO YOUR 24
NOVEMBER MESSAGE PRIOR TO 27 NOVEMBER
```

> COMMUNICATIONS BETWEEN OUR HEADQUARTERS WOULD BE GREATLY
> FACILITATED IF SUPPLY OF TYPEWRITER RIBBONS COULD BE
> INCLUDED IN NEXT WHICH OF COURSE WOULD BE FIRST SUPPLY
> SHIPMENT
>
> END
> FERTIG BRIG GEN COMMANDING

After reading both messages, he asked, "Presumably, this copy is for me?"

"Yes, Sir."

"Did Signals Intelligence offer anything that would make sense of this?"

"No, Sir," Hideyori replied. "All they offered in amplification was that this was encrypted on the same U.S. Army device."

"Has there been anything else?"

"No, Sir."

"Make sure your operators are especially alert on 27 November, Hideyori, for Fertig's reply."

"Yes, Sir. I will."

"And call me, no matter the hour, if there are any developments at all."

"Yes, Sir, I will."

Captain Saikaku got back in his Lincoln and drove to the house behind the wall.

The sergeant and his young Filipino friend were sitting side by side eating a pineapple on their bed—a mattress laid against the wall. They both looked at him with fear in their eyes as they jumped to their feet. As they had been taught to do, they bowed to him from the waist.

"I am having some slight difficulty with American vernacular," Captain Saikaku announced. "Perhaps you will be good enough to assist me."

"Yes, Sir. Of course."

"What does the phrase 'baker fourth' mean?"

In the fear in the sergeant's eyes, Saikaku read his answer before he gave it.

"I don't think I know, Sir."

"What about 'First Dog'?"

The sergeant's eyes again showed fear and incomprehension.

"I don't know, Sir."

"That is unfortunate," Saikaku said. "I thought you were beginning to understand the benefits of cooperation with me."

"Captain, maybe if you showed me that," the sergeant said.

Saikaku carefully creased off the upper portion of the page and then carefully tore it off.

Now there was a sign of relief in the sergeant's eyes.

"I think I know what this means," he said. "They sometimes call the first sergeant of a company First Dog."

"The first sergeant? The senior noncommissioned officer?"

"Yes, Sir. Sometimes that's what they are called."

"Is it disrespectful?"

"Yes, Sir, it is. And baker fourth probably means Baker Company, B Company of the Fourth Something."

"Fourth something?"

"Some kind of a battalion, Sir. Like the 4th Signal Battalion, or the 4th Quartermaster Battalion."

"Were there such units here?"

The fear returned to the sergeant's eyes.

"I don't remember, Sir."

"You don't remember, or you don't want to tell me?"

"If I knew I would tell you, Sir."

"Can you help me with the second part of the message? Were you familiar with any missionary rescue mission?"

"No, Sir. I saw that, Sir, and thought about it. I was in Personnel, Sir. I wouldn't know about things like that. That would be considered an operation, Sir, and Personnel never gets involved."

"I know people, Sergeant, who enjoy playing with your friend. Sometimes, when you have been cooperative, I am motivated to discourage them."

"I'm being as cooperative as I can, Sir, I really am."

He looks, Captain Saikaku thought, *as if he is about to weep. He is an utterly despicable parody of a man.*

"I don't know how I feel about you right now," Saikaku said. "Whether you are being cooperative or not. I will have to think about it."

He turned and walked out of the bedroom. He thought he would order the Filipino deviate to be beaten, but decided against it. The *fear* of a beating, he decided, would probably be more useful than another beating.

He returned to his office and told his sergeant to search through the index of captured American documents and prepare a list of every American or Filipino Army unit designated by the Arabic numeral 4.

[FIVE]

```
T O P    S E C R E T

HQ USMC WASHINGTON

SUPREME COMMANDER SWPOA
EYES ONLY BRIG GEN F.W. PICKERING, USMCR
0705 25 NOVEMBER 1942

VIA SPECIAL CHANNEL
DUPLICATION FORBIDDEN
ORIGINAL TO BE DESTROYED AFTER ENCRYPTION AND TRANSMITTAL

(1) PERCY LEWIS EVERLY FOURTH MARINES WORKED FOR ME
SUBSEQUENT DEPARTURE FROM CHINA OF SESSIONS MCCOY AND
ZIMMERMAN.

(2) EVERLY'S HOMETOWN ZANESVILLE WEST VIRGINIA. SERGEANT
JOHN V. CASEY DISPATCHED ZANESVILLE IMMEDIATELY ON RECEIPT
YOUR MESSAGE TO DEVELOP FURTHER BIOGRAPHIC DETAILS.

(3) BELIEVE EVERLY WILL REMEMBER MAIDEN NAME OF MY WIFE,
LUDMILLA ZHIVKOV.

(4) TRYING TO RECALL FROM MEMORY NAME EVERLY'S CHINESE
WIFE.

(5) REGRET SPARSENESS OF INFORMATION AVAILABLE. MORE WILL
FOLLOW AS DEVELOPED.

BANNING, MAJ USMC

T O P    S E C R E T
```

[SIX]
Naval Air Transport Passenger Terminal
Brisbane, Australia
0715 Hours 26 November 1942

Captain Robert B. Macklin, USMC, was rather pleased that things had turned out as they did, even if it meant his arrival in Brisbane was delayed an additional twenty-four hours.

At Hickam Field, Major Brownlee succeeded in finding space for himself aboard a B-17, one of a flight of seven bound for Australia via Midway Island. But that was only possible because one of the plane's crewmen was taken unexpectedly ill, and the decision was made to continue without him.

There was no space for Macklin, which meant that after he saw Major Brownlee off, he returned to Pearl Harbor and a very nice steak dinner at the Pearl Harbor Officers' Club and a comfortable bed in the BOQ.

When he reported the next morning to the Pearl Harbor Naval Air Transport Passenger Terminal, Lieutenant (j.g.) L. B. Cavanaugh, the Officer in Charge Passenger Seat Assignment, told him there would be an additional delay. The plane on which he was scheduled to fly to Brisbane, Cavanaugh explained, had encountered some really bad weather on the way into Pearl Harbor from Midway. It had been temporarily removed from service so that the amount of damage, if any, it had suffered could be ascertained and if necessary repaired.

The entire passenger roster was therefore set back twenty-four hours, Cavanaugh said. That meant a day on the beach, and another dinner at the Officers' Club—a luau, complete to whole roasted pig—and another night in a comfortable BOQ bed. The only thing wrong with the evening was that the Navy nurse he met at the bar almost laughed at him when he suggested they go to his BOQ—after letting him charm her and feed her drinks for hours, teasing him, rubbing her body against him while they danced.

The next morning, the damage, if any, was apparently repaired, and the Coronado took off on schedule. The seat wasn't all that comfortable, but it was certainly more comfortable than anything the B-17 Flying Fortress had offered Major Brownlee, and the flight was as pleasant as could be. After hearing what had happened two days before to the in-bound Coronado, he had worried about the weather; but there was none. The Pacific was really pacific, with hardly a cloud in the sky on both legs—Hawaii–Midway, and Midway–Brisbane.

After the whaleboats transported them from the seaplane to the quai, and he climbed the stone stairs set in the face of the quai, he was met by a Marine staff sergeant.

He looked like a child, and Macklin wondered what fool of a commanding officer had agreed to his promotion.

"Captain Macklin?" the boy-faced sergeant asked.

"Yes, I am."

"Staff Sergeant Koffler, Sir. If you'll point out your gear to me, I'll get it."

"The two bags with my name on them on the steps. Make sure they don't get away from you."

"No sweat, Sir. The Major's over there, Sir," Koffler said, and pointed.

"What did you say, Sergeant?"

"I said the Major's over there, Sir. In the Studebaker."

"I meant before that. Did you really say 'no sweat' to me?"

"Yes, Sir, I guess I did."

"The correct response to an order, Sergeant, is 'Aye, aye, Sir.' "

"Aye, aye, Sir," Koffler said.

He looked amused.

"Did I say something amusing, Sergeant?"

"No, Sir."

"Then wipe that smile off your face."

"Aye, aye, Sir."

As he approached the Studebaker, a very large Oriental—the largest Macklin could ever remember seeing—in the uniform of an Army Signal Corps major, stepped out of the front passenger seat.

Macklin saluted. The Major made a vague gesture toward his head that only generously could be interpreted as a salute.

"You must be Macklin," the Major said, in a heavy Bostonian accent.

"I am Captain Macklin. May . . ."

"Where's the Major?"

"Excuse me?"

"Where is Major Brownlee?"

"You mean he's not here?"

"If he was here, Captain, I wouldn't have asked where he is," Pluto replied.

"Sir, may I ask who you are?"

"My name is Hon," Pluto said. "Have you any idea, Captain, where Major Brownlee is?"

"With all respect, Sir, I am on a classified mission, and until—"

"I know all about your mission, Captain," Pluto cut him off. "And I asked you where Major Brownlee is."

"Sir, Major Brownlee, to the best of my knowledge, should be in Australia. He was under orders to report to General Pickering."

"Well, I don't think he did, or General Pickering wouldn't have sent me down here in his car to meet him. When was the last time you saw him?"

"In Hawaii, Sir. At Hickam Field. He obtained passage for himself on a Flying Fortress."

"When was that?"

"Three days ago, Sir."

"Before or after Sessions left?"

"Several hours afterward, Sir."

Staff Sergeant Koffler, carrying Macklin's luggage, walked up.

"Steve, how fast is a B-17 compared to a Coronado?" Pluto asked.

"About eighty miles an hour faster. Why do you want to know?"

"Major Brownlee left Hawaii on a B-17 a couple of hours after Sessions, and he's not here yet."

"That doesn't sound right," Koffler said.

"I didn't think so, either."

My God, this Oriental major calls this sergeant by his first name, carries on a personal conversation with him, and seems blissfully oblivious to the fact that he hasn't said "Sir" once to him.

"You are some sort of expert, are you, Sergeant, on aircraft?"

Koffler shrugged modestly.

"Oh, yeah," Pluto said. "Steve is our resident expert. If it flies, he knows how fast and how far. And he's also a pretty good radio operator."

"Tell that to the General, please," Koffler said.

"You're not going, Steve," Pluto said. "Give it up." He turned to Macklin. "You might as well get in, Captain, since Brownlee's not here."

"My orders are to report to General Pickering," Macklin said. "Would you take me to him, please?"

"My orders from General Pickering are to set you up in the SWPOA BOQ. When he wants to see you, he'll send for you."

```
T  O  P     S  E  C  R  E  T


FROM: SUPREME HEADQUARTERS SWPOA
0925 26NOV42
BY SPECIAL CHANNEL


TO: CINCPAC HAWAII
    EYES ONLY—CINCPAC


DUPLICATION FORBIDDEN
ORIGINAL TO BE DESTROYED AFTER ENCRYPTION AND TRANSMITTAL
FOLLOWING PERSONAL FROM BRIG GEN PICKERING TO ADM NIMITZ


DEAR ADMIRAL NIMITZ:


MAJOR JAMES C. BROWNLEE III USMC EN ROUTE USMC SPECIAL
DETACHMENT 16 TO PARTICIPATE IN FERTIG OPERATION BELIEVED TO
HAVE DEPARTED HICKAM FIELD AS SUPERCARGO ABOARD USARMY
AIRCORPS B17 APPROXIMATELY 1830 21 NOVEMBER 1942 HAS NOT
ARRIVED HERE.
```

```
REQUEST ANY AND ALL INFORMATION REGARDING THIS OFFICER'S
LOCATION BE FURNISHED VIA SPECIAL CHANNEL AS SOON AS
POSSIBLE.


RESPECTFULLY PICKERING


END PERSONAL FROM BRIG GEN PICKERING TO ADM NIMITZ


BY DIRECTION:


HON SON DO MAJ SIGC USA


T O P     S E C R E T
```

[SEVEN]
Headquarters, U.S. Forces in the Philippines
Davao Oriental Province
Mindanao, Commonwealth of the Philippines
0705 Hours 28 November 1942

Second Lieutenant Percy Lewis Everly, USFIP, walked down the dirt trail through the bush very slowly, followed by the other nine members of the patrol.

His loose-fitting dirty white cotton blouse and trousers—cut off at the knees—were sweat-soaked and filthy. His calves were bloody where they had been scratched by thorns; flies and other insects were feeding on the suppurating wounds.

He carried a Thompson .45 ACP submachine gun in his hand. The leather straps of three Japanese Arisaka rifles and their leather accoutrements crossed his chest.

Behind him came two Filipino soldiers, carrying between them what at first looked like a body suspended from a pole on their shoulders. It was not a body, but the tunic and trousers of a Japanese soldier, stripped from his body and pressed into use as makeshift bags. The tunic held two five-gallon tin cans of gasoline (a total weight of seventy pounds). In the trousers was an estimated fifty pounds of rice, twenty pounds of Japanese canned goods, perhaps ten or fifteen more pounds of ammunition for the Arisakas, and an even dozen grenades. The load bearers also carried U.S. Army Caliber .30-06 Enfield rifles.

Behind them came three more pairs of what Everly somewhat unkindly thought of as coolies—two more Filipinos and four Marines, also carrying captured food and equipment suspended in Japanese uniforms converted into bags.

How the slight Filipinos managed their loads, Everly had no idea. It seemed to be a matter of pride with them to carry at least as much as the Marines. Bringing up the rear was a Filipino making his painful way using a forked stick as a crutch. He had sprained—Everly suspected broken—his ankle in a fall just before they ambushed the Japanese vehicles. Somehow, he had managed to keep up with the others. They had been walking all night, in the light of a half-moon.

Everly walked up to the small building on stilts that was both the G-2 Section, Headquarters, USFIP, and the quarters he shared with Captain James B. Weston.

He turned and faced his men.

"Just drop that stuff where you are," he ordered. "Somebody'll take care of it. Somebody go get the Chief and have him look at Zappo's leg. Get something to eat and some sleep."

There were nods in acceptance of the orders, but no one responded out loud. They just lowered their loads onto the ground.

Everly looked at the steps leading to the verandah of the house. Although he really disliked doing this—it was a mortal sin for a Marine, permitting weapons to touch the ground—he decided there was no way he could negotiate the stairs loaded down as he was.

He put the butt of the Thompson on the ground, leaning the barrel against his leg, and started to remove the leather straps around his chest. When he had the first one off and tried to lower it gently to the ground, the Thompson fell off his leg.

"Shit!" he said, and angrily pulled the other straps over his head and let the rifles fall. Then he picked up the Thompson and brushed the dirt from it as well as he could.

Then he slowly climbed the ladderlike stairs to the verandah. Captain Weston was not in the "office" or their "quarters," the two rooms into which the house was divided.

"Fuck it," Everly said aloud to himself. "He'll be back."

He walked to his bed (constructed of bamboo poles, with a combination spring and mattress made of woven leaves) and lay down. He lay immobile for a minute or two, then sat up and took his boondockers and socks off. The socks were in tatters, and the sole of the right boondocker would not last much longer; it was about to tear free of the nearly rotten leather.

He lay back down and considered that problem a moment. He had big feet, eleven-and-a-halfs, and so far no Japanese he had come across had feet nearly that big. The Filipinos were well shod, courtesy of the Japanese Imperial Army, but the footgear of all the Marines was just about shot.

They were going to have to find a shoemaker. Or something else would have to be done.

The house shook, signaling that someone was climbing the stairs. Everly didn't move his head, but looked at the open door.

"Welcome home," Weston said.

Everly did not reply. He disapproved of Weston's beard. An officer should be shaved, not wearing a goatee like General Fertig, or a full beard like Weston.

"How did it go?"

"We got some stuff. Including fifteen gallons of gas—"

"I saw that," Weston interrupted.

"And I marked some stuff on a map," Everly said, reaching into his trousers pocket and handing it to Weston. "We didn't lose anybody—Zappo hurt his ankle, it's probably broken—and I am down to twenty-six rounds for my Thompson."

"Good job, Everly," Weston said.

"How about a three-day pass?" Everly said.

Weston chuckled.

"You'd just spend it on whiskey and wild women."

"You better believe it!"

"We had an interesting message from Australia," Weston said.

"What did they say this time? 'Your request under advisement'? For a change?"

"Do you remember the name of the first sergeant of Baker Company, 4th Marines, in China?"

"What?"

"The name of the First Sergeant of Baker Company of the 4th Marines in China. Do you remember it?"

"How could I forget it? That fat fucker was one mean sonofabitch."

"What was his name?"

"It was . . ." Everly began, and then drew a blank, even though he had a very clear mental image of First Sergeant *Whatthefuckishisname?* standing with his hands on his hips, his beer belly straining the buttons of his stiffly starched khakis.

"Shit, I can't remember. I can *see* the sonofabitch. . . . Why do you want to know?"

"Australia wants to use his name in a simple substitution code."

"What for?"

"I have no idea."

"Give me a minute, I'll think of it."

Thirty minutes later, he was still unable to call the name from memory. Although one of the other Marines vaguely remembered the first sergeant of Baker Company, Fourth Marines, no one could come up with his name.

By that time, Captain Weston and Lieutenant Everly had been joined by Lieutenant Ball, Captain Buchanan, and General Fertig.

"I'm sorry, General," Everly said. "Maybe if I stop trying so hard; maybe after I get some sleep . . ."

"The problem, Lieutenant, is that I promised Australia I would respond today," Fertig said.

"General, I'm sorry," Everly repeated.

"Those bastards are probably looking for an excuse to break off contact with us," Weston said, putting into words what was in the minds of everybody in the small room.

"Captain," Fertig said sharply. "Please keep thoughts like that to yourself."

"Sorry, Sir."

"Let's try another tack," Fertig said. "Who would want this information? Why?"

Everybody shrugged, but after a moment Lieutenant Ball said, "Maybe they want to know if Everly is really Everly. I mean, the one who served with the 4th Marines."

"What the hell is the difference?"

"Let's go with Ball's idea. Unless he had also served with the Fourth Marines, who else would know about this first sergeant, and know that Everly would know."

"Anybody in the 4th Marines."

"But this chap is in Australia," Fertig said. "So it would be someone who served with the 4th Marines and did not come to the Philippines when they did."

"The Killer," Everly said.

"What?"

"And he would know about Zimmerman," Everly said, now excited. "It's got to be the Killer."

"Who's the Killer?" Fertig asked.

"Corporal Killer McCoy," Everly said. "He used to work for Captain Banning, who was the S-2 of the Fourth. Him and Zimmerman were pals."

Fertig looked at Buchanan.

"What have we got to lose, General?" Captain Buchanan said.

XII

[ONE]
Radio Room
Supreme Headquarters SWPOA
0910 Hours 28 November 1942

"You've got something for me?" Major Hon Son Do asked, as he entered the crowded room.

"I can't imagine who else it would be for, Major," said Captain Edward D'Allesandro, the somewhat prissy Signal Corps Captain on duty. Captain D'Allesandro had not stopped smarting under the injustice of a system that had suddenly promoted to field grade the Asiatic lieutenant with the mysterious duties that kept him off the duty roster, while he himself had been a captain with outstanding efficiency reports for nearly eighteen months and was still waiting for his promotion.

He handed Hon the message.

"It came in in the clear," Captain D'Allesandro said as Hon read the brief message.

MFS TO GYB

CANNOT RECALL FAT BASTARDS NAME. THE KILLER SHOULD KNOW IT.
REMEMBER THE KRAUTS NAME. DO YOU WANT IT IN THE CLEAR

FERTIG BRIG GEN

MFS STANDING BY

Hon smiled.

"Call them back, please, Captain," he said. "Message is 'Negative Krauts Name in Clear. Stand by.' "

"I think I have the right to know what this is all about," Captain D'Allesandro said. " 'Highly irregular' doesn't begin to cover it."

"You don't have the right to know, Captain," Hon said evenly, and reached for the telephone on the Captain's desk.

"General, this is Pluto," he said, and interrupted himself. "Captain, reply to MFS *now!*"

"Yes, Sir," Captain D'Allesandro said.

"Sorry, I was interrupted. Sir, we've just heard from Fertig. Addressed to the Killer. I suggest, Sir, that you send him and Sessions, and the Model 94 here. I'm in the SWPOA radio room."

Captain D'Allessandro returned from responding to MFS.

"We have an acknowledgment of your message to MFS, Sir."

"Thank you. We will be communicating with MFS some more. I'm going to need either your desk or a table, a typewriter, and several chairs."

"I'm sure the Major is aware that he is disrupting my operation. I'm going to have to bring this to the attention of the SWPOA Signal Officer."

"That's Colonel . . . ?"

"Ungerer, Sir. Colonel Jason Ungerer."

"I suggest, Captain, that you hold off on calling Colonel Ungerer for ten or fifteen minutes. By then, General Pickering will be here, and your boss and my boss can sort this disruption out between them."

[TWO]
Headquarters, U.S. Forces in the Philippines
Davao Oriental Province
Mindanao, Commonwealth of the Philippines
0940 Hours 28 November 1942

"Lieutenant," Sergeant Ignacio LaMadrid said, "Australia's calling."

"I'll go get the General," Lieutenant Ball replied. "He said he wanted to be here when they did."

LaMadrid turned to his key and tapped out: MFS TO GYB GA (*Go Ahead*). Then he put his fingers on his typewriter keyboard and took the incoming message. When he was finished, he tapped out MFS SB (*Standing By*), and then tore the carbon paper sandwich from the typewriter. He laid the bottom sheet, on which the message was legible, on his "desk," then placed a fresh sheet of blank paper under the carbon, arranged it neatly, and fed the fresh sandwich to his typewriter.

Then he read the message from Supreme Headquarters, South West Pacific Ocean Area.

```
GYB TO MFS

USE AS SIMPLESUB Z FIRST NAME BANNING WIFE Z SECOND NAME Z
PERCYS HOMETOWN Z

20 19 18 03 13

09 08 02 09 20

18 17 04 19 20

RPT

20 19 18 03 13

09 08 02 09 20

18 17 04 19 20

MFS SB
```

He had absolutely no idea what it meant; and neither, he quickly learned, did General Fertig, Captain Buchanan, and Lieutenant Ball—except, of course, that Captain Buchanan knew Australia wanted them to use a simple substitution code.

"Ball, go get Captain Weston and Lieutenant Everly," Buchanan ordered. They appeared within minutes, Everly's clean-shaven face and clean, if water-soaked, white cotton blouse and jacket indicating he had been summoned from his toilette in the stream that ran through the command post of United States Forces in the Philippines.

"I think this is intended for you, Lieutenant," Fertig said. "You have any idea what it means?"

"Banning's wife's name is Ludmilla Zhivkov," Everly said almost immediately. "There aren't many people who know that. Killer McCoy would be one of them."

"That sounds Russian," Fertig thought aloud.

"It is," Everly said. "She's a Russian refugee. She didn't get out of Shanghai. Neither did my wife. They're together. That's how I know Milla's name."

"How do you spell it?" Captain Buchanan asked, sitting down at the rattan "desk."

As Everly spelled the name, Buchanan wrote each letter as a large block letter, then asked Everly what his home was, and wrote those letters down in large letters. Above the letters, he carefully wrote numerals above each letter.

```
1234567890123456789012345
LUDMILLAZHIVKOVZANESVILLE
```

"OK, now we have the code. Somebody read out those numbers to me. Slowly."

General Fertig read out the numbers one at a time, moving to stand behind Buchanan as he did so.

When Buchanan was finished, he had this:

```
S   E   N   D   Z
20  19  18  03  09


K   Z   A   U   T
13  09  08  02  09


S   Z   N   A   M
20  09  18  17  04


E   S   Z   Z   Z
19  20  09  09  09
```

"What the hell does that mean?" Fertig asked, bewildered and annoyed.

"General, the 'Z' is a wild card. You'll notice they used 'Z's as sentence breaks in the original message?"

Fertig was ahead of him. "Send . . . Krauts . . . Name," he translated.

"I believe that's 'names,' Sir, plural," Buchanan said.

"Who's the Kraut, Everly?" Fertig asked.

"Zimmerman," Everly said. "What the *hell* was his first name?"

"Not again, Everly, please!" Weston said.

"August," Everly said, and then triumphantly: "No. *Ernest.* Ernest Zimmerman."

"You're sure?"

"Yes, Sir."

"Send them that," Fertig ordered.

It took just over a minute for Buchanan to encode the name and to hand it to Sergeant LaMadrid, with the order, "Just send the numbers, send them twice."

"Yes, Sir," LaMadrid said, and tapped out the reply on his radiotelegraph key:

```
MFS TO GYB

19 09 18 25 20

09 09 05 04 04

19 09 04 17 18
RPT

19 09 18 25 20

09 09 05 04 04

19 09 04 17 18
MFS SB
```

There was an immediate reply from Australia:

```
GYB TO MFS
ACK YR NO 1
SB
```

Sergeant LaMadrid read it aloud—translated it—as it came in: "Acknowledge receipt your message Number One. Stand by."

"What's that message number business?" Fertig asked. "They've never done that before."

"I think until about thirty seconds ago, Sir," Weston said, "Australia thought LaMadrid spelled his name T-O-J-O."

"Here comes another one," LaMadrid said, and this time, as he typed, he called the numbers out loud. Buchanan had already begun the decoding before the numbers were repeated.

He handed it to General Fertig.

```
M   E   L   L   S
04 19 01 06 20
E   E   Z   O   U
25 19 09 14 02
S   O   O   N   K
20 14 14 18 13
```

```
I L L E Z
11 06 07 19 09
```

"What the hell do you suppose 'mells eezou soonk illez' means?" Fertig asked softly.

"Sir," Buchanan said, his voice tight, "I believe it means 'we'll see you soon, signature Killer.' "

He looked over at Lieutenant Everly.

"What do you make of it, Everly?"

"Yes, Sir. I think that's what it means. Zimmerman and the Killer. I'd say it means they're coming in."

"It doesn't say that," General Fertig said.

"What else could it mean, Sir?" Everly asked, and then excitedly added, "Quentin Alexander McPherson. *Fucking* Quentin *fucking* Alexander *fucking* McPherson!"

"What?" General Fertig asked.

"I believe Lieutenant Everly's memory has returned, Sir," Captain Weston said.

[THREE]
Office of the Kempeitai Commander for Mindanao
Cagayan de Oro, Misamis-Oriental Province
Mindanao, Commonwealth of the Philippines
1050 Hours 28 November 1942

"Sir, these messages between Fertig and Australia were intercepted within the past hour," Lieutenant Hideyori Niigata said, and laid a manila folder on Captain Matsuo Saikaku's desk.

When Saikaku finished examining them and looked up at Hideyori, Hideyori added, "They have been forwarded to Signals Intelligence in Manila, Sir."

"And how soon may we expect to have a decryption from them?"

"Sir, there is no way of telling."

"You have advised them, of course, of Kempeitai's interest in this? That this matter is to have a high priority?"

"Yes, Sir, of course. Sir, may I ask how familiar the Captain is with simple substitution encryption?"

"I am always willing, Hideyori, to add to my knowledge."

"The difficulty in decoding simple substitution encryption, Sir, arises because the sender and the receiver have access to information the interceptor does not."

"Explain that, please."

"The Captain will notice that the sender is telling the receiver to use the first and second names of Banning's wife and the hometown of Percy. The receiver will write that information in a line, and then write numbers, from zero one through how many letters there are in the names . . ."

Hideyori saw the confusion on Saikaku's face.

"Sir, perhaps it might be a good idea if I demonstrated?"

"Please do," Saikaku said.

The demonstration took about five minutes. When it was finished, Captain Saikaku was aware of the difficulty the Signals Intelligence people would have decoding the message.

"What this means is that we stand virtually no chance of decoding this message?"

"Oh, no, Sir. The Signals Intelligence people are quite clever, and have developed several techniques that will permit them eventually to decode these messages. But, unfortunately, that's likely going to take some time."

"How much time?" Saikaku asked coldly. "Two days? A week? A month?"

"If I had to guess, Sir, I would say five days to a week."

"Splendid!" Saikaku said sarcastically.

"Sir, I had some thoughts. . . ."

"What kind of thoughts?"

"Sir, I am sure that someone like yourself, an officer of the Kempeitai, almost certainly has already—"

"The one thing you learn in the Kempeitai, Hideyori, is never to give in to the temptation not to turn over the last rock. For it is often under that last rock that you find what you're looking for. Please go on."

"Sir, I have noticed that there seems to be a question of the legitimacy of this General Fertig, and of his U.S. Forces in the Philippines."

"He's a bandit, Hideyori. By definition, bandits are illegitimate."

"Sir, I was speaking of his legitimacy in the eyes of the Americans in Australia."

"Go on."

"I am sure the Captain noticed the next-to-last message."

"What about it?"

"It says, Sir—GYB, the Australian station says—'ACK YR NO 1.' That means 'We acknowledge receipt of your message Number 1.' And then it orders them 'SB'—Stand By. That never happened before. It seems to me, Sir, that it could mean acceptance in Australia that Fertig is who he says he is. In other words, it could be official recognition."

"And, of course, it could mean nothing at all," Saikaku said. "But that was very clever of you, Hideyori. In the future, please give me all of your thoughts.''

"It will be my pleasure, Sir.''

[FOUR]

T O P   S E C R E T

FROM: CINCPAC HAWAII
1615 28NOV42

EYES ONLY—BRIG GEN FLEMING PICKERING USMC

DUPLICATION FORBIDDEN
ORIGINAL TO BE DESTROYED AFTER ENCRYPTION AND TRANSMITTAL

FOLLOWING PERSONAL FROM CINCPAC TO BRIG GEN PICKERING USMC

DEAR FLEMING:

(1) DEEPLY REGRET TO INFORM YOU INFORMATION FROM
COMMANDING GENERAL HAWAII DEPARTMENT USARMY AIRCORPS
INDICATES MAJOR JAMES C. BROWNLEE III USMC DEPARTED HICKAM
FIELD AS SUPERCARGO ABOARD USARMY AIRCORPS B17 TAIL NUMBER
42-455502 DESTINATION MIDWAY. AIRCRAFT ENCOUNTERED
MECHANICAL DIFFICULTIES APPARENTLY RESULT OF SEVERE
WEATHER APPROXIMATELY 250 NAUTICAL MILES NORTHEAST OF
MIDWAY. PERSONNEL ABOARD OTHER B17 AIRCRAFT IN FLIGHT OF
SEVEN REPORT 42-455502 CRASHED AND BROKE UP ATTEMPTING
DITCHING OPERATION IN HEAVY SEAS APPROXIMATELY 0725 HOURS
LOCAL TIME 22 NOVEMBER 1942.

NO SURVIVORS WERE SEEN AT TIME OF DITCHING, AND NAVY AND
USARMY AIRCORPS AIRCRAFT WHICH FLEW TO CRASH SITE WHEN
WEATHER CLEARED 23 NOVEMBER FOUND NEITHER SURVIVORS NOR
CRASH DEBRIS.

(2) COMMANDING GENERAL HAWAII DEPARTMENT USARMY AIRCORPS
HAS DETERMINED B-17 AIRCRAFT 42-455502 ITS CREW AND
PASSENGER PERISHED IN THE LINE OF DUTY 0730 HOURS MIDWAY
TIME 22 NOVEMBER 1942. INASMUCH AS AIRCORPS DOES NOT HAVE

INFORMATION REGARDING MAJOR BROWNLEE'S UNIT, ROUTINE
NOTIFICATION OF NEXT OF KIN, ET CETERA HAS NOT REPEAT NOT
BEEN MADE. PLEASE ADVISE SOONEST HOW YOU WISH THIS TO BE
HANDLED.

(3) REAR ADMIRAL DANIEL J.WAGAM OF MY STAFF DEPARTED PEARL
HARBOR 1625 THIS DATE TO CONFER WITH SUPREME COMMANDER
SWPOA. WHILE IN BRISBANE, HE WILL DISCUSS WITH YOU PROBLEMS
CONNECTED WITH SUBMARINE AVAILABILITY. COMPLIANCE WITH 17
NOVEMBER DIRECTIVE FROM ADMIRAL LEAHY IN THIS REGARD WHICH
I PRESUME YOU HAVE SEEN WILL BE VERY DIFFICULT FOR REASONS
WAGAM WILL MAKE KNOWN TO YOU.

BEST PERSONAL REGARDS CHESTER

END PERSONAL FROM ADM NIMITZ BRIG TO GEN PICKERING

BY DIRECTION:

MCNISH, CAPTAIN USN

T O P   S E C R E T

[FIVE]
Water Lily Cottage
Brisbane, Australia
0610 Hours 29 November 1942

Brigadier General Fleming Pickering found First Lieutenant Kenneth R.
McCoy in the library, sitting before a typewriter at one of the desks, obviously
deep in thought. Or frustration. The long, thin, black cigar in his mouth seemed
cocked at an angry angle.

"Am I interrupting, Ken?" Pickering asked.

In one smooth continuous movement, McCoy rose to his feet, snatched the
cigar from his mouth, and came to something like the prescribed position of
attention.

"Good morning, Sir," he said. He was, Pickering noticed, clean-shaven,
his haircut was perfect, and he was wearing a fresh uniform. "No, Sir."

"Typewriter giving you trouble?"

Pickering had sent Pluto out to buy typewriters for Water Lily Cottage on
the open market, after getting them from the officer in charge of office equip-

ment at SWPOA seemed more trouble than it was worth. The battered Under-
woods Pluto found had cost approximately three times what they had cost new
ten years before. Australia had been at war since 1940. Despite official price
controls, shortages of practically everything but food had driven prices up.

"It's seen better days, Sir."

"I heard the typewriter, the noise, and thought you could probably use
some coffee," Pickering said, holding up a silver coffeepot in one hand and
two coffee cups in the other. And then he told the truth. "I'd like to talk to you,
Ken."

"Yes, Sir?"

"But it will hold. Finish what you're doing."

"This will hold," McCoy said. "It's only a letter to Ernie."

" *'Only* a letter to Ernie'?" Pickering parroted. "That's not important
anymore?"

McCoy reached into his open collar and came out with a round silver me-
dallion on a silver chain.

"I'm writing a thank-you for this," he said. "I really don't know what to
say."

"What is it?"

"It's an Episcopal serviceman's cross," McCoy said. "It was in that package Sessions brought me."

"You're Episcopal?"

"I'm not much of anything. Most people hear McCoy, think it's Irish, and
that I'm Catholic. But I'm Scotch, and that's Presbyterian, and I never had
much to do with them."

"Ernie's Episcopal," Pickering said. "So am I. Would you believe that
Pick sang in the choir, that he was an altar boy?"

"Pick's behind this," McCoy said. "Charley Galloway's girlfriend sent
him one. Pick saw Galloway's on the Buka Operation and decided he wanted
one. He wrote and asked his mother for one. She told Ernie's mother, Ernie's
mother told Ernie, and here is mine. It came in a little red velvet bag with 'Tif-
fany & Company' printed on it."

"Well, I think it's a very nice gesture. It can't hurt, Ken." He paused, and
then went on. "You're not religious? Is that the problem?"

"Oh, I believe in God, I suppose. But I think there's a lot of guys in graves
on Guadalcanal, and in the Philippines, who did a lot of hard praying just
before they were blown away."

"I have my problems with organized religion," Pickering said. "But I'm a
sailor. I don't see how anyone who has counted the stars on a clear night on the
high seas or watched the sun come up in the middle of an ocean can doubt the
existence of a superior power."

McCoy chuckled. "Me either. My problem is that I really don't believe that God is all that interested in Ken McCoy, personally."

"Did you pray when you were hit?" Pickering asked.

McCoy shook his head, no. "But I said 'thank you' when I got back to Washington and Ernie was waiting for me."

"I said 'thank you' when El Supremo told me VMF-229 was relieved on the 'Canal, and that Pick had come through all right. And when you all came back from Buka in one piece."

"Not when you got hit?" McCoy asked.

"You mean this time?" Pickering asked, and then went on before McCoy could reply. "I suppose I did. I probably did. I don't really remember. At my age, you say 'thank you' for other people's lives. I figure I've had my fair share and more."

McCoy looked at him in curiosity.

"I didn't really expect to come back from France," Pickering said. "When I did, when I came out of the trenches for the last time, I figured whatever came afterward would be gravy. And it turned out that way."

"It was bad in France, huh?"

"The artillery was terrible," Pickering said evenly. "Especially when we were moving. But what really terrified me was the poison gas. I watched people die that way. I didn't want that to happen to me. That thought scared me bad."

McCoy nodded his understanding.

"I'm not particularly afraid of dying," McCoy said. "What scares me is dying slowly, hanging upside down on a rope while some Jap uses me for bayonet practice."

"They do that?"

"Sometimes they use their rifle butts to see how many bones they can break before the prisoner dies."

Pickering nodded his understanding.

"You said you wanted to talk to me, Sir?"

The exchange of confidences was over.

"I'm going to have to ask you to go into the Philippines, Ken," Pickering said.

McCoy nodded. "I figured that when I heard we lost the OSS major."

"I think we have to do whatever we can to help Fertig and his people."

"Yes, Sir. I agree."

"I wish the other one had been on the B-17," Pickering said.

McCoy chuckled.

"That thought occurred to me, too, General."

"But he didn't, and . . ."

"I was going to come to you, Sir, and tell you that I thought I better go with them, even before I heard the B-17 went down."

"It's still a volunteer mission, Ken. You don't have to go."

"Who else is there?" McCoy replied.

"Is that why you're having a hard time with your letter to Ernie?" Pickering asked. "You wrote and told her you would be coming home, and now you have to write and tell her you won't be?"

McCoy met Pickering's eyes.

"I was pretty vague about when I was coming home. Getting relieved seemed to be too good to be true."

"I'll have a word with Captain Macklin and tell him who's really in charge."

"I can handle Macklin."

"Have you seen him?"

"No, Sir. I've been avoiding that."

"How are you going to handle him?"

"If I have to, I'll kill him."

Pickering looked into McCoy's eyes.

"It would be awkward if that was necessary."

"I won't, unless I have to."

"Anything I can do?"

"I want Zimmerman, and I don't want Koffler."

"Because it would be unfair to Koffler?"

"Because he wants to be an officer, and I'm afraid he thinks the way he can do that is to be a hero. Heroes get people killed."

"They're working on Zimmerman. There's an admiral coming in today from CINCPAC who wants to talk about the submarine. I don't think we can get one for another week or ten days. Zimmerman certainly should be here by then."

"It'll take me another five, six days to get everything ready anyhow."

"Pluto has been having trouble getting a radio operator from SWPOA. I'm going to El Supremo this morning to ask him personally. I think he'll come through."

McCoy nodded.

"I really hate having to ask you to go, Ken."

"I really hate to go," McCoy said. "But there's no other solution that I can see."

Pickering met McCoy's eyes. They held for a moment, then Pickering nodded and started out of the library.

Over his shoulder, he called, "Tell Ernie I said hello."

[SIX]
Cryptographic Center
Supreme Headquarters, South West Pacific Ocean Area
0905 Hours 29 November 1942

When Major Hon Son Do slid open the tiny steel window in the steel door and saw Brigadier General Fleming Pickering's face, he knew that something had happened that Pickering didn't like at all.

He slid the bars out of place and pulled the heavy door inward.

"I didn't expect to see you here, Sir."

"I have just come from the throne of God," Pickering said. "I humbly requested an audience with El Supremo, and, feeling gracious, he granted me one."

When there was no elaboration on this, Pluto went to one of the two type-writers on the desk and jerked a sheet of paper from it.

"Is this about what you want, Sir?"

Pickering took the sheet of paper from him and read it.

T O P   S E C R E T

SUPREME HEADQUARTERS SWPOA TIME TIME TIME 29NOV42
EYES ONLY—THE SECRETARY OF THE NAVY
VIA SPECIAL CHANNEL

DUPLICATION FORBIDDEN
ORIGINAL TO BE DESTROYED AFTER ENCRYPTION AND TRANSMITTAL
TO SECNAV

DEAR FRANK:

I DEEPLY REGRET HAVING TO INFORM YOU THAT I HAVE JUST
LEARNED FROM ADMIRAL NIMITZ THAT MAJOR BROWNLEE DIED IN
THE CRASH OF AN AIRPLANE AS HE WAS COMING HERE. THESE ARE
THE DETAILS AS I GOT THEM FROM ADMIRAL NIMITZ:

BROWNLEE DEPARTED HICKAM FIELD AS SUPERCARGO ABOARD
USARMY AIRCORPS B17 TAIL NUMBER 42-455502. THE AIRCRAFT
ENCOUNTERED MECHANICAL DIFFICULTIES APPARENTLY RESULT OF
SEVERE WEATHER APPROXIMATELY 250 NAUTICAL MILES NORTHEAST
OF MIDWAY. PERSONNEL ABOARD OTHER B17 AIRCRAFT REPORTED
BROWNLEE'S B17 CRASHED AND BROKE UP ATTEMPTING DITCHING

OPERATION IN HEAVY SEAS APPROXIMATELY 0725 HOURS LOCAL TIME
22 NOVEMBER 1942.

INASMUCH AS NO SURVIVORS WERE SEEN AT TIME OF DITCHING, AND
NAVY AND USARMY AIRCORPS AIRCRAFT WHICH FLEW TO CRASH SITE
WHEN WEATHER CLEARED 23 NOVEMBER FOUND NEITHER SURVIVORS
NOR CRASH DEBRIS, COMMANDING GENERAL HAWAII DEPARTMENT
USARMY AIRCORPS HAS DETERMINED ALL PERISHED IN THE LINE OF
DUTY.

I PRESUME YOU OR DONOVAN WILL HANDLE NOTIFICATION OF NEXT OF
KIN, AND OTHER ADMINISTRATIVE MATTERS.

CAPTAINS SESSION AND MACKLIN AND ALL EQUIPMENT ARRIVED
HERE SAFELY, AND AT THIS TIME IT IS NOT BELIEVED MAJOR
BROWNLEE'S TRAGIC DEATH WILL AFFECT THE MISSION.

BEST REGARDS,

FLEMING PICKERING, BRIGADIER GENERAL, USMCR

T O P   S E C R E T

"Take out the 'Dear Frank' and make it 'Dear Mr. Secretary,'" Pickering
ordered, "and delete the 'best regards.' I don't feel like calling the sonofabitch
by his first name, and I don't want to send him my regards."

"Yes, Sir."

"And send an information copy, Eyes Only, to Admiral Nimitz."

"Yes, Sir."

"Pluto, in one word, what would be your reaction if someone told you that
SWPOA doesn't have a high-speed radio operator they can give us for the Fertig operation?"

"One word, Sir?"

"The one word that came to my mind was 'bullshit,'" Pickering said.

"You got that from El Supremo?"

"Three minutes ago."

"What are you going to do?"

"I'm going to have to send Koffler. What else can I do?"

"I can't see where you have any other options, Sir."

"I had the very unpleasant suspicion when I was in the Throne Room that
very few tears would be shed by El Supremo and his cronies if our guys paddled away from the submarine and were never heard from again."

Pluto decided that any response to that remark would be the wrong one.

"General, what about what Admiral Nimitz said, his 17 November directive about a submarine? From Admiral Leahy?"

"I never heard a word about it," Pickering said. "Until I do, I am forced to draw the conclusion that either Knox or Donovan has decided I don't have the Need to Know."

"I'm sure this Admiral, Wagam, that Nimitz is sending will bring you in on it, Sir."

"I wish I was sure, Pluto," Pickering said. "Well, get those off as soon as you can. I'm going to go out to the house and weep on Jack Stecker's shoulder."

[SEVEN]
Company Grade Bachelor Officers' Quarters
Supreme Headquarters, South West Pacific Ocean Area
1105 Hours 29 November 1942

Captain Robert B. Macklin, USMC, was resting, his back against the headboard of the bed of the sparsely furnished room, half asleep, a three-month-old issue of *The Saturday Evening Post* open on his lap.

Before the war, this BOQ had been a second- or third-rate traveling salesmen's hostelry. He couldn't help making unfavorable comparisons between his room and the mess here with the rooms and mess at the Country Club, which was much nicer than even the hotel rooms and restaurants he'd been in all up and down the West Coast during the War Bond Tours.

Last night at the bar, he had drinks with an Army Chemical Warfare Service captain, and the captain told him the SWPOA Field Grade Officers' BOQs were much nicer than the Company Grade. He knew, because until he was ranked out of it, he had been living in a Field Grade BOQ.

That encounter triggered several lines of thought: First, that when Major Brownlee finally showed up, perhaps he could pull a string or two and arrange for them both to live in a Field Grade BOQ. Second, he wondered how this OSS assignment would affect his own promotion to major. Major Brownlee's quiet word in the right ear had seen his long-overdue promotion to captain come through almost overnight.

Next, Macklin found it hard to believe that whoever was in charge here would actually send him on this Philippines operation. For one thing, he had not really fully recovered from his wounds. For another, he had not gone through the OSS training program, and knew very little of what would be expected of him on such a mission—nor did he yet possess the skills to do whatever it was he'd be required to do.

When that became obvious to whoever was in charge here, he felt he would almost certainly be kept in Australia to receive the necessary training—and to fully recover from his wounds—and would not be sent into the Philippines. It did not seem unreasonable to think that when the OSS force here was eventually augmented, since he was already here, he would be "an old hand," and could take over as a training officer to train the newcomers. It seemed only fair that people who had not been in combat should be sent on missions before those who had seen combat—had been twice wounded in combat—were sent into harm's way again. And he knew that Major Brownlee was concerned with his lack of training and his physical condition—the reason Brownlee took the one available space on the B-17 was that he thought he could take the physical stress of that flight better.

The knock at his door startled him. He sat fully up on the bed.

"Who is it?"

"Colonel Stecker's compliments, Sir," a young American voice replied.

Macklin lifted himself off the bed, opened the door, and peered around it. It was the boy-faced sergeant who spoke so flippantly to him on the quai three days before.

"What is it, Sergeant?"

"Colonel Stecker's compliments, Sir. He sent me to fetch you."

Who in the wide world is Colonel Stecker? That name never came up in any of the briefings.

"Who is Colonel Stecker?"

"Colonel Jack (NMI) Stecker, Captain," the sergeant replied, and then, smiling, added, "The NMI means 'No Middle Initial.' "

"You find that amusing, Sergeant?"

Colonel Stecker is probably General Pickering's deputy or chief of staff, something like that.

"I think it's sort of interesting."

"You 'think it's sort of interesting, *Sir*'," Macklin corrected him.

"Yes, *Sir*."

"I'll be with you shortly," Macklin snapped.

"I'll wait for you in the jeep, Captain," the sergeant said.

Except for his subtly disrespectful attitude, there was nothing he could find in the sergeant's behavior to put a finger on, but his behavior was definitely annoying. He was reminded of the behavior of Corporal McCoy in China, and after a moment he decided that was probably the explanation. McCoy was here, McCoy was an officer, and young enlisted men tended to emulate the behavior of their officers.

He hadn't seen McCoy. He hadn't seen anyone, or heard from anyone, since the Asiatic major dumped him at the BOQ shortly after his arrival. Walking home from the 0800 morning prayer service at St. John's Church that morning, he'd decided that if he didn't hear anything by 1700, he would telephone the OSS people here in Brisbane.

He rather enjoyed the worship service. The familiar hymns and the words of the Book of Common Prayer in a church not unlike his own St. Paul's were rather nice. Afterward, as he waited in line to shake the rector's hand, he chatted with a stocky, well-dressed gentleman with a large mustache, who asked him to join him and his family for Sunday dinner if he had no other plans.

He had no other plans, of course, except to return to the BOQ and wait for something to happen. But he did not think he should run the risk of being away from the BOQ should Major Brownlee suddenly appear. So he declined, telling the kind gentleman that he had duty.

But the encounter had tipped the scales in favoring of calling the OSS station in Brisbane. He had been furnished—and had memorized—their number for emergency purposes. He wasn't sure whether this was an emergency or not, but certainly the OSS would be interested to hear that he had not heard from anyone, most importantly from Major Brownlee, in seventy-two hours.

He checked his reflected image as well as he could in the dim mirror over the washbasin, tugged at the hem of his tunic, and then, carefully locking the door behind him, walked down the long, dark, and narrow corridor of the hotel, down the creaking stairs, across the sparsely furnished lobby, and outside.

The sergeant saw him coming, started the jeep's engine, and waited for him to get in—somewhat impatiently, Macklin thought. It was apparent the sergeant hadn't even considered stepping out of the jeep, saluting, and then waiting for the officer to be seated before getting behind the wheel.

"What is our destination, Sergeant?" he asked as Koffler backed the jeep away from its parking spot.

"We're going out to the cottage, Captain."

"And what is the 'cottage,' Sergeant?"

"Where the officers live, Captain."

If "the officers" live there, why am I living in the Company Grade BOQ?

When they arrived at the cottage, Macklin's first reaction was favorable. It could be something like the Country Club, he decided, a rather nice civilian facility requisitioned for the use of the OSS. That view was reinforced when the sergeant opened the door for him and motioned him inside, past an entrance hall, and into a large, comfortably furnished living room. Two young Marine officers—both second lieutenants—slid their rattan upholstered chairs closer to a coffee table, as a middle-aged woman in an apron—obviously some kind of servant—entered the room carrying a tray on which were a silver coffee set and a plate of pastries.

Both officers looked at him curiously, but neither rose to his feet.

"I am Captain Macklin. To see Colonel Stecker."

"Steve'll tell him you're here, Captain," one of the officers, a tall, good-looking blonde, said.

Steve is apparently this baby-faced sergeant who needs a refresher course in military courtesy. As do both of these young officers.

Macklin saw the Purple Heart ribbon among those on the blonde's tunic; the other second lieutenant's tunic carried the silver cords identifying an aide-de-camp to a general officer.

"Is General Pickering here?" Macklin asked.

"Why don't you sit down and have a cup of coffee and a doughnut?" the aide-de-camp said. "I'm sure Colonel Stecker will be ready for you in a minute or two."

"I asked you if General Stecker was here, Lieutenant," Macklin flared. "I am under orders to report to him."

Lieutenant George Hart looked at Macklin long enough for Macklin to realize he would not get an answer, and to consider his next options. He was not forced to make a decision.

"The Colonel will see you now, Captain," Sergeant Koffler announced. Macklin looked at him. He was standing by an open door. And then First Lieutenant Kenneth R. McCoy came through the door, in the act of stuffing an M1911A1 .45 Colt under his belt in the small of his back. He looked at Macklin, meeting his eyes.

"Captain Macklin," he said.

"McCoy," Macklin responded.

McCoy looked away.

"Anybody want to see how much a lot of gold actually weighs?" McCoy said to no one in particular.

"Yeah, I would," the tall lieutenant said.

"I await my master's call," the aide-de-camp said, "damn it."

"What can I use for wheels?" McCoy asked.

"You better take the Jaguar," the aide said. "The Boss is either going to the Palace to meet some admiral, or I'm going to go to the Palace to bring the Admiral here; and I know the Colonel's going to need his jeep."

"In here, please, Captain," a new voice said. Macklin followed the sound and saw a tall, muscular, tanned full colonel motioning him to enter the room McCoy had just left.

"Yes, Sir," Macklin said.

"Did they offer you some coffee, Captain? Would you like some?"

"That would be very nice, Sir."

"You better take somebody with you, Ken," the Colonel said. "That's a lot of gold. I'd hate to have to tell somebody we lost it in a stickup. And take the Jaguar, not a jeep."

"Gimpy's volunteered to ride shotgun, Colonel," McCoy said, nodding toward the tall second lieutenant.

"Any reason you can't go with them, George?" Stecker asked.

"I'm waiting to see what the Boss wants to do, Colonel."

"You go with them. If the General needs wheels, I'll drive him."

"Aye, aye, Sir."

"Colonel, we're only going to take it from the bank to the dungeon, wrap it, and take it back to the bank," McCoy said.

"It is better to be safe than sorry," Stecker said with a smile. "Write that down, McCoy."

"Aye, aye, Sir."

"OK, Captain," Stecker said. "Get yourself a cup of coffee, and then come in the library."

"Yes, Sir. Thank you, Sir."

As he poured coffee, Macklin understood why McCoy had referred to the tall second lieutenant as "Gimpy." He walked with a visible limp, and was apparently in some pain.

Typical of McCoy. To mock an officer who had suffered honorable wounds in combat. One more reason people like that should not be officers.

Carrying his coffee and a sweet roll in his hands, Macklin went into the library. Colonel Stecker was at the door.

"Take a seat, Captain Macklin," Stecker ordered, and then closed and locked the door behind them. Macklin sat down in an upholstered armchair near the desk. Stecker walked to the desk and rested his rump on it.

"I'm afraid there's been some bad news, Captain," he said. "The B-17 carrying Major Brownlee was forced to ditch at sea near Midway. There were no survivors."

Macklin felt a chill.

My God! If I had been fully recovered from my wounds, I would have been aboard that B-17!

"I'm very sorry to hear that, Sir. Major Brownlee was a fine gentleman, a fine Marine officer."

"So I have been led to believe."

"Officially, that places command of the Fertig mission in your hands," Stecker said.

My God!

"Colonel, may I inquire if the OSS has been notified of this terrible loss?"

"General Pickering notified Secretary Knox, and asked that the information be relayed to the OSS."

"I'm sure they will issue new instructions," Macklin said, half thinking aloud, and only at the last second remembering to add, "Sir."

"Why should they do that?" Stecker asked.

"Colonel, the cold facts are that I am not qualified, in terms of training or experience, or physically—I was wounded at Gavutu with the 2nd Parachute Battalion, and am not yet fully recovered—to command such a mission."

"God," Stecker said, loathing in his voice. "I was half prepared to give you the benefit of the doubt. But you haven't changed at all, have you, Macklin?"

"Sir?"

"Do I look familiar to you, Captain?"

"No, Sir. I don't believe I've previously had the privilege of the Colonel's acquaintance."

"The first time we met was at Quantico, Captain. You were at the time engaged in several slimy schemes to keep McCoy from getting a commission."

"Sir, I have no idea—"

"The second time we met was on Gavutu. I commanded 2nd Battalion, Fifth Marines, during the invasion. I went to the aid station to see some of my men, and the battalion surgeon of the 2nd Parachute Battalion pointed out to me the officer his corpsmen had to pry loose from a pier piling. You were a disgrace to The Corps on that occasion, too, Captain Macklin."

"Sir, the only thing I can say is that the Colonel has been grossly misinformed."

"Shut your lying mouth, Captain," Stecker said, almost conversationally. "Open it again only when I give you specific permission."

He looked at Macklin for a full minute before continuing.

"For a number of reasons that are none of your concern—though they include General Pickering's belief that The Corps has a deep responsibility to do all it can to assist the Marines with General Fertig—the mission will proceed with you as its nominal commander. He has so informed Secretary Knox, and thus the OSS. Actual command of the mission will be vested in Lieutenant McCoy. If I were McCoy, you would not leave the beach in the Philippines alive. Not because of your actions toward him at Quantico, but because a lying coward like you threatens both the lives of the men on this mission and the mission itself. Do I make myself clear, Captain Macklin?"

"Sir, I must protest in the strongest possible terms your characterization of my—"

With a swift, seemingly effortless motion, Stecker leaned down to Macklin, grabbed his necktie, and pulled him half out of the chair.

My God, he's going to spit in my face!

As quickly as he had pulled Macklin from his chair, Stecker shoved him back into it.

"You have one chance of coming out of this mission alive, Macklin," he said, his voice and his temper back under control. "And that is to do exactly what McCoy tells you to do, when he tells you to do it. You are two inches away from me *ordering* McCoy to remove you as a threat to the mission the moment you touch the beach in the Philippines. Do you understand me, Captain Macklin? Answer 'Yes, Sir' or 'No, Sir.' "

"Yes, Sir."

"Sergeant Koffler will now return you to the BOQ. You will stay there, prepared to make yourself available at any time McCoy feels he needs you."

As soon as I get out of here, I'm going to get in touch with the OSS. This is outrageous!

"The proper response to an order, Captain, is 'Aye, aye, Sir.' "

"Aye, aye, Sir," Captain Macklin said.

[EIGHT]
Conference Room II
Supreme Headquarters, SWPOA
Brisbane, Australia
1225 Hours 29 November 1942

Just before noon, Lieutenant Chambers D. Lewis III, USN, appeared, unannounced, at Water Lily Cottage. When the doorbell rang, Pickering was close to it, so he opened it. It was clear from Lewis's face that he was a little surprised that a general officer would open his own door.

"General Pickering?" Lewis asked, and when Pickering nodded, went on, "Admiral Wagam's compliments, Sir. I am the Admiral's aide-de-camp."

"I've been expecting to hear from him."

"Admiral Wagam would be pleased if it were convenient for the General to meet with him at Supreme Headquarters," Lewis said. "General Willoughby has been kind enough to offer accommodations."

"When?"

"Admiral Wagam hopes that it would be convenient for the General now, Sir."

"Why not?" Pickering thought aloud. And then, somewhat annoyed with himself, two thoughts came: First, this was really a summons—if the circumstances were reversed, he would have personally called Nimitz's admiral, he wouldn't have had Hart call him. And second, he didn't like Willoughby putting his two cents in.

He turned and saw Jack Stecker.

"General Willoughby," he explained, "has kindly provided a place for Admiral Wagam and me to meet, and the Admiral sent his aide to fetch me."

"Really?" Stecker replied, both his tone of voice and his face showing that he read the situation exactly as Pickering did.

Pickering turned back to Lewis. "Where exactly are these accommodations, Lieutenant?"

"One of the conference rooms at Supreme Headquarters, Sir."

"Please present my compliments to the Admiral, Lieutenant, and tell him that I'm on my way."

"General, I have a car."

"So do I, Lieutenant," Pickering said. "Jack, is George in the dungeon by now, do you think?"

"Yes, Sir. I would think so."

"Call the dungeon, please, Jack, and ask George to meet me in the lobby."

"Aye, aye, Sir," Stecker said with a smile.

"Right this way, General, if you please," Lieutenant Lewis said to Brigadier General Fleming Pickering, USMC, as he pushed open a door.

Then he raised his hand to block the passage of Second Lieutenant George F. Hart, USMCR, and added, "I believe, Sir, with your permission, that the Admiral would prefer to confer in private."

"Oh, George goes everywhere with me, Lieutenant," Pickering replied. "That way we can both recall who said what to whom in one of these meetings."

It was obvious that Lieutenant Lewis did not like that response. This, Pickering decided, was fine with him, because he did not like what little he had seen of Lewis. The first moment Pickering saw him, he concluded he was a self-important young man; it was not a surprise to see an Annapolis ring on his finger.

"Yes, Sir, of course," Lieutenant Lewis said.

As Lewis held open the door for him, Pickering remembered that he was perversely pleased at Lieutenant Lewis's obvious confusion in Water Lily Cottage. *Who was George, and what was the dungeon?*

Lieutenant Lewis then announced him:

"Admiral, Brigadier General Pickering."

Admiral Wagam rose smiling from his chair at the head of the table. He was a tall, handsome, silver-haired officer in a well-fitting, high-collared white uniform.

"General Pickering," he said, putting out his hand. "Thank you for coming on such short notice."

"I realize that you're a busy man, Admiral," Pickering replied.

But I don't like this. I don't like you sitting at the head of the table; no one has appointed you chairman of this conference. And I don't like being summoned here—no matter how politely your aide phrased it.

"General Willoughby was kind enough to offer us this place for our talk," Wagam said. "He said you have declined the offer of an office at SWPOA?"

"How kind of General Willoughby," Pickering said. "Yes, I did. If I took an office here, I thought it might look as if I were a member of the SWPOA staff." When he saw that Wagam was taken a little aback by the remark, Pickering added, with a smile, "I didn't want to wind up on some SWPOA duty roster. Flag officer of the day, or somesuch."

Wagam chuckled.

"Your precise status is the subject of some conversation," Wagam said.

The two men were evaluating each other.

"So I understand," Pickering said.

The truth was, he liked his first impression of Wagam. This at first surprised him, until he reminded himself that he really liked and admired Admiral Chester Nimitz, for whom Admiral Wagam worked. He doubted that Nimitz would tolerate a fool on his staff for more than sixty seconds.

That triggered the thought, the realization, that he was in a lousy mood. And he knew the reasons for that: He didn't want to send McCoy into the Philippines at all, much less with the albatross of Macklin hanging around his neck. And he didn't want to send Koffler along with him either, even if he had no choice. El Supremo had refused to give him a qualified radio operator.

"I'm just a simple sailor, Admiral, sailing in uncharted waters," Pickering said.

"You're an any-tonnage, any-ocean master mariner, General," Wagam said. "Not a simple sailor. I'm sure that you can navigate safely through any array of rocks and shoals."

Pickering was surprised—and somehow pleased—that Wagam knew that he had spent time on the bridge of a ship.

"When I use somebody else's room, I always worry whether or not there's hidden microphones," Pickering said, now smiling.

Wagam's face showed his confusion. He wasn't sure at first if Pickering was serious or not.

"You think the Japanese have placed a microphone in here?"

"I'm not sure about the Japanese," he said, and switched to a thick but credible German accent. "But the *Germans*"—he pronounced it *Cher*-mans—"you haff to vatch out for dem."

Wagam had picked up on the smile. He smiled back. Despite the English-sounding name, General Charles Willoughby had a Germanic background, and sometimes spoke with a perceptible German accent.

"Do you really?" Wagam said.

If Charley Willoughby does have a microphone in here—and I wouldn't put it past him, come to think of it—that should ruin his whole day, Pickering thought, pleased.

"Der Chermans," Pickering went on, "they are not too schmardt, but dey are *thorough!*"

Wagam laughed out loud.

"Would the Admiral be kind enough to join me for lunch at a place where I know there are no microphones?"

"Yes, of course. Thank you."

"George, call out to the cottage and tell Mrs. Cavendish four for lunch as soon as we get there."

"Aye, aye, Sir."

"I'll drive the Admiral in the Studebaker, and you bring Lieutenant Lewis with you," Pickering ordered, and then had another thought. "And I think it would be a good idea to drop by the dungeon and ask the Killer to join us. Would that pose a problem?"

"No, Sir. They're just about through, General."

"Tell him to leave the gold there, and then take it back after lunch."

"Aye, aye, Sir."

"Admiral Nimitz told me to be careful if General Willoughby asked about OPERATION WINDMILL," Admiral Wagam said when they were in the Studebaker, "but do—"

"About operation what?" Pickering interrupted.

"OPERATION WINDMILL," Wagam replied, surprise in his voice, "the mission to Fertig."

"I never heard it called that before," Pickering said. "Where'd you get that?"

"It was in Admiral Leahy's Special Channel Personal to Admiral Nimitz," Wagam said, "in which he said that if we can't provide the kind of a submarine you want—in support of OPERATION WINDMILL—and when you want it, he'll want to know our reasons."

"Nimitz's Special Channel Personal to me suggested there was a problem with the submarine."

"Not from your position, General, but from ours. My orders are to explain the problem to you, and pass on Admiral Nimitz's thoughts on the subject, and then to give you whatever you think you need."

Pickering grunted.

"I was about to ask if you really thought there might be a microphone in that conference room," Wagam said.

"Charley Willoughby," Pickering replied, "is not only about as smart as they come, and a thoroughly competent intelligence officer, but is also fiercely loyal to General MacArthur. That's fine for SWPOA and El Supremo, but sometimes it gets in my way."

" 'El Supremo'? Is that what you call him?"

"Only behind his back," Pickering said.

Wagam laughed.

"We have a personal connection, General," he said.

"We do?"

"My nephew, Lieutenant David Schneider, USMC, flew with VMF-229 on Guadalcanal."

"Did he come out all right?" Pickering asked.

"With five kills, a DFC, and some injuries to his legs when he barely made it back to Henderson Field in a pretty badly shot-up Wildcat. He is now recovered."

"My boy—thank God, luck was with him—wasn't injured," Pickering said. "Well, they're both out of it now, at least for a while. An old pal of mine, General McInerney—"

"I know Mac," Wagam interrupted.

"—told me The Corps plans to use those kids as instructors, hoping they can pass on what they learned the hard way to the new kids."

"He told me the same thing," Wagam said. "And that the two of you were in France together. That's how I knew about your son."

"Small world, Mac, me, and Colonel Jack (NMI) Stecker. At the time we were young enlisted men foolish enough to believe we were in the war to end war forever."

"Me, too," Wagam said. "My contribution to World War I was commanding a couple of three-inchers welded precariously to the superstructure of a freighter. I used to worry about my Naval career, now that there wasn't going to be another war. I was afraid I would never get to be a commander, much less an admiral."

The two men looked at each other for a moment.

"Admiral, would there be any problem having Jack Stecker and the Lieutenant who's going into the Philippines—his name is McCoy—sit in on our little chat?"

"I was going to suggest that my aide sit in," Wagam said. "He's a submariner. He made three trips to Corregidor before it fell. He's suggested that he go along on this operation to see if he could be useful."

Pickering, you've just done it again. Another of your brilliant, snap judgments of character is one hundred eighty degrees off course.

"Fine with me," Pickering said.

"And the OSS people?"

"There's only one of them, and I'll tell you about him later," Pickering said.

Mrs. Cavendish removed the luncheon plates from the dining-room table, brought in two pots of coffee, and left, closing the door softly behind her. General Pickering and Admiral Wagam were at opposite ends of the table. Lining the sides were Colonel Jack (NMI) Stecker, Captain Ed Sessions, Lieutenants McCoy and Hart, USMC, Lieutenant Lewis, USN, and a last-minute addition General Pickering sensed upset Lieutenant Lewis's concept of Naval propriety, Staff Sergeant Steve Koffler.

The Navy's wrong about the way they treat—and think about—their enlisted men, Pickering thought when he saw the shock on Lewis's face after he told Koffler he wanted him present at the meeting. *And I wonder where it started? In the merchant marine, just about every master, every chief engineer, first goes to sea as an apprentice seaman, or an apprentice wiper. The ones with brains and ambition, the ones willing to accept responsibility, are encouraged to think about getting out of the forecastle. The Navy chains the forecastle port shut.*

"The problem, gentlemen, I should say problems," Admiral Wagam began, "are these: CINCPAC has available one submarine designed to carry cargo, the *Narwhal.* She is currently undergoing engine refit, and some other modifications, at Pearl. The operative word there is 'one' cargo sub. Her value to the Pacific fleet goes without saying." He paused, and then went on. "There is a shortage of standard boats as well. We've taken some pretty bad losses, and the sub fleet isn't half as large as we would like. We really can't afford to lose any more."

"Tell us what Admiral Nimitz thinks we should do," Pickering interrupted.

"All right," Wagam said. "And I am in agreement . . . not only because I work for Admiral Nimitz, but because I've given this problem a good deal of thought. First of all, the risk posed to the *Narwhal* in this operation is unacceptable, in my opinion."

"We need a submarine," Pickering said. "What do you suggest?"

Wagam did not reply directly.

"As I understand it," he said, "we do not have secure communication with Fertig, and will not have until we put ashore the first personnel and their communications equipment. Until we do that, until Fertig and his people can communicate directly, and securely, both with a submarine and with radio stations here and elsewhere, we have no reason to assume that the sub can safely surface, much less discharge cargo, off Mindanao. It's entirely possible that the moment the conning tower breaks water, it will come under shore-based artillery fire.''

''We plan to go in at night, Admiral,'' McCoy said.

''There are both artillery illuminating rounds, and aircraft parachute flares available to the Japanese, Mr. McCoy,'' Admiral Wagam said reasonably.

''Let's hear what you would like us to do, Admiral,'' Pickering said, a touch of impatience in his voice.

''OK. A new boat, the *Sunfish,* can be made available for OPERATION WINDMILL—''

''Excuse me?'' Captain Sessions asked.

''OPERATION WINDMILL is what somebody in Washington is calling this operation,'' Pickering replied. ''I'm sure that sooner or later someone would have remembered to tell us.''

''As in tilting at windmills, like Don Quixote?'' Sessions asked.

''I think that's a good guess, Ed,'' Pickering said. ''Go on, please, Admiral.''

''The *Sunfish* can be made available to you at Espíritu Santo as of 10 December. *If* that decision is made today, or no later than tomorrow. She is a standard submarine. This means she is not capable of carrying all the cargo you intend to take with you, even with half of her torpedoes removed.''

''Looking the gift horse in the mouth, Admiral, why are you willing to give us a new submarine?'' Pickering asked.

''Because this cruise for her would also serve as a shakedown voyage,'' Wagam said. ''Our experience has been that losses of submarines, from enemy action or other causes, are disproportionately larger when a boat is making its first combat patrol.''

Stecker snorted.

''In one sense, Colonel,'' Wagam said, now a little coldly, ''you're right. CINCPAC would rather risk the *Sunfish* than the *Narwhal.* For one thing, the loss of the *Sunfish* would not be as damaging as the loss of the *Narwhal.* There are other Gato-class submarines in production. There are no *Narwhal*-class submarines on the way.''

''What are the 'disproportionate' losses of submarines on their first combat patrol?'' Pickering asked.

''Eighteen percent,'' Wagam replied.

''One in five doesn't make it back? God, I had no idea it was that bad!'' Pickering replied, visibly shocked.

''CINCPAC's thinking,'' Wagam said, ''is that the *Sunfish* could make its first combat patrol with a lesser risk of loss than a full combat patrol would entail—despite the hazards incident to surfacing a thousand yards off an enemy-held shore for the hour or so it would take to off-load your men. That would both put your men ashore and get *Sunfish* back to Pearl with the experience of a first combat patrol under her belt. On the return voyage, after the off-loading, she could continue her patrol with the available fuel and half her normal complement of torpedoes."

"Jack?" Pickering asked.

"I see their reasoning," Stecker said thoughtfully. "But I don't like cutting the material we want to take to Fertig. Correct me if I'm wrong, Sir, but you want to give us the space normally taken up by half of the torpedoes normally carried?"

"Correct."

"And if the *Sunfish* carried no torpedoes at all?" Pickering asked.

He directed the question to Admiral Wagam, but Stecker answered:

"We would still be able to carry only about half of what we could take on the *Narwhal,* right?"

"That is correct," Wagam said.

"Which means we could carry only *one-quarter* of what we planned to carry on the *Narwhal,*" Pickering said.

"Correct," Wagam said.

"That's not very much," McCoy said, thinking out loud.

"I ask you to consider this," Wagam said. "There would be room for the communications and cryptographic equipment, a certain amount of small arms and ammunition, medical supplies, and most important, I would suggest, the gold. All of which, I suggest, should convince Colonel Fertig—"

"We think of him as 'General' Fertig," Pickering interrupted.

"—should convince *General* Fertig," Wagam corrected himself, "that help is on the way."

"When?" Pickering asked.

"CINCPAC has directed me to tell you that you have his personal word that, once secure communications have been established, a supply mission, using the *Sunfish,* will have the highest priority."

"*The* highest priority? Or *a* high priority?" Pickering asked.

"The. Absolutely, The."

"But I have that already, don't I?" Pickering said.

"Yes, General," Wagam said. "You do."

"Ken, you're the one going in," Pickering said. "What do you think?"

"Sir, I'm a little over my head talking about something like this."

"I'll decide that," Pickering said. "What do you think? What's wrong with what they're proposing?"

McCoy cocked his head to the side, as if gathering his thoughts, then wondering if he dared offer them.

"Nothing against the Navy, Admiral," he said finally. "They did a hell of a job putting us onto Makin and then getting us off."

"You were on the Makin raid?" Wagam asked.

"Yes, Sir."

"Drop the other shoe, Lieutenant," Wagam said. "We 'did a good job at Makin, but'?"

"This is going to be the *Sunfish*'s first patrol," McCoy said. "Whoever's running the submarine, by definition, and understandably, is going to be a little nervous. We're in the middle of going ashore. There is a sign that the Japs are onto us . . ."

"And you don't want to be left floating around in a rubber boat between the shore and a submarine in the process of submerging, right?" Pickering finished for him. "OK, Admiral. We haven't addressed that. How do we know the crew of this new sub will be up to doing what they'll have to do?"

"I'm going to give Lieutenant McCoy the benefit of the doubt that he's not questioning the courage of the *Sunfish*'s crew—"

"Permission to speak, Sir?" Lieutenant Lewis interrupted.

Admiral Wagam visibly did not like being interrupted. But after flashing his aide a withering look, he said, "Certainly, Lewis."

"McCoy, would it allay your reservations if an officer were aboard the *Sunfish* who was experienced in making runs like the one we're talking about and was also fully aware of CINCPAC's personal interest in this mission?"

"We're back to that, are we, Chambers?" Admiral Wagam asked.

"Back to what?" Stecker asked.

"Lieutenant Lewis feels he could make a far greater contribution to the war by going on this mission than by opening doors for me," Wagam said. "Is that about it, Chambers?"

"Yes, Sir."

"Mr. Lewis is a submariner, Mr. McCoy," Admiral Wagam said. "Before he came to work for me, he was on three missions to Corregidor."

"What I'm thinking, Ken," Pickering said, "—and I don't want to question the courage of the sub crew either, Admiral—is that knowing—"

"That my aide is aboard," Wagam interrupted, "with orders to report to CINCPAC personally when, and under what circumstances, the *Sunfish* left Lieutenant McCoy and party, might keep them on position until they absolutely had no choice but to leave or be sunk?"

"No offense, but that's what I was thinking," Pickering said.

"I also know a little something about how to launch rubber boats from submarines, Mr. McCoy," Lewis said.

"How are you at paddling one of them?" McCoy asked.

"Probably a little better at it than you are," Lewis said. "I can also walk and chew gum at the same time."

McCoy laughed.

"You can't be *too* smart," McCoy said. "It sounds to me like you're volunteering."

"You are volunteering, Chambers," Admiral Wagam said. "You understand that?"

"Yes, Sir. I understand."

Wagam looked at Pickering.

"Have we an understanding, General?"

"Ken?" Pickering asked.

"If General Fertig is what he says he is, we're going to need the *Narwhal*," McCoy replied. "I'd rather see her surface a month from now, two months from now, and be able to unload a couple of tons of equipment, than take a chance on losing everything now—which would also blow our chances to help Fertig for a long time."

Pickering nodded.

"We have an understanding, Admiral," he said.

"Lieutenant Lewis, from this moment, you are detached until further orders to OPERATION WINDMILL," Wagam said.

"Aye, aye, Sir."

"Can you really, Lewis?" McCoy asked.

"Can I really what, McCoy?"

"Chew gum and walk at the same time?"

"Presuming the ground is reasonably level," Lewis replied.

I'll be damned, Pickering thought. *McCoy likes him. And vice versa. I wonder what Sessions thinks of him; I'll have to ask.*

"Ed," he said. "You'll take care of Lewis? Find him a place to stay, et cetera? There's no more room here, unfortunately."

"My pleasure, Sir," Sessions said.

"Colonel Stecker and I are now going to take the Admiral on a tour of Brisbane's famed tourist attractions," Pickering said. "Starting with the Gentlemen's Bar at the Maritime Club."

"If Commander Feldt calls, General, shall I tell him where you are?" McCoy asked.

"By all means, Mr. McCoy," Pickering said. "Commander Feldt is one nautical experience that I'm sure the Admiral, despite his long career, has not yet experienced."

"Feldt?" Wagam asked. "The Coastwatcher man?"

"Right," Pickering said. "As a matter of fact, Ken, see if you can get Feldt on the horn and ask him to join us. And if Colonel DePress calls, ask him to join us, too . . . if he calls. I hope he does, but do not call him; I don't want Willoughby to accuse me of arranging secret meetings with somebody on his staff."

"Aye, aye, Sir."

[NINE]

"Captain," Lieutenant Lewis said to Sessions almost as soon as Pickering, Wagam, and Stecker were out the door, "don't we know each other?"

"You're '40, right?"

"Right," Lewis asked, immediately understanding that Sessions meant the class of 1940 at the United States Naval Academy, Annapolis. He was unable to keep himself from looking at Sessions's hand. There was no Annapolis ring.

"Thirty-nine," Sessions said. "I think we had a class in steam generation together."

"And then the Navy wouldn't take you and you had to join the Marines?"

"Why do I think we're going to have trouble with this swab-jockey?" McCoy asked.

"They start out all right, Ken," Sessions said. "But then they send them down in submarines, and all that pressure squeezes their brains."

"Can I go home, Mr. McCoy?" Staff Sergeant Koffler asked. "Or are you going to need me for something?"

"My compliments to Madame Koffler, Sergeant Koffler," McCoy said. "Take a jeep. Then call Pluto about 2100 and see if Gimpy has a way home from the dungeon. The General does not, repeat does not, want him driving himself. If he needs a ride, you drive him. And we'll see you at 0800."

"Ken," Lieutenant Hart said, "I'll go fetch Gimpy."

"You stay loose to drive the General. If Feldt shows up at the Gentleman's Bar, they'll probably need somebody to drive them."

"Right," Hart said. "Sorry, Koffler."

"No problem, Mr. Hart," Koffler said, and turned to McCoy. "Aye, aye, Sir."

McCoy waited until Koffler had left the dining room, and then opened a drawer in a sideboard, took out a bottle of scotch, and held it up in a gesture of asking if anyone else wanted a drink.

Interesting, Lewis thought, *the sergeant asked* Lieutenant *McCoy for his orders, not* Captain *Sessions. And McCoy gave the orders; and McCoy, not Sessions, announced the cocktail hour.*

"Yes, please," Lewis said.

"Me, too," Sessions said.

"Thank you very much," Hart said.

Hart took a tray of glasses from the sideboard. McCoy splashed whiskey into four of them, announced that only feather merchants used ice, and raised his glass.

"Welcome aboard, Swabbie," he said.

"Thank you," Lewis said.

"It will at least teach you something that every Marine learns in boot camp," McCoy said.

"I already know how to tie my shoes, Mr. McCoy." Lewis said.

"I was thinking about never volunteering for anything," McCoy said.

"You volunteered, Ken," Sessions said. "Pickering told me."

"Knowing you're the only guy available to do the job is not the same as volunteering," McCoy replied.

"That's splitting hairs."

"I have to go, and you know it," McCoy said.

"Can I ask a question?" Lewis asked.

"Depends on the question, whether you get an answer," McCoy said.

"What about the OSS?"

"I'm deeply ashamed to confess the sonofabitch is a classmate of mine," Sessions said; and then, seeing McCoy had held up his hand like a traffic policeman, said, "What, Ken?"

"The General told me I was not to discuss that subject with the Navy until he brought it up with the Admiral. I think that includes you."

"OK," Sessions said.

"Do I look like a Japanese spy, or what?" Lewis asked.

"In that white uniform, you look more like a Good Humor man, I'd say," McCoy said. "Next question?"

It was said jokingly, but Lewis knew that he was not going to learn anything more about the man from the OSS from either Sessions or McCoy.

"Tell me about 'Pluto' and 'Gimpy' and the 'dungeon,' " he said.

"The dungeon is the Special Channel place, inside the SWPOA Comm Center," McCoy said. "Unless you've got a MAGIC clearance, you can't get in there. We're not even supposed to know about it. Pluto, otherwise known as Major Hon Son Do, Signal Corps, USA, runs it. Gimpy is Lieutenant John Marston Moore, USMCR, who forgot to duck on the 'Canal and as a result limps. He works for Pluto. They live here; you'll meet them. Next question?"

"Everybody lives here but the OSS man?" Lewis asked.

"Next question?" Sessions said.

"If I really wanted ice for the drink, where would I find it?" Lewis asked.

XIII

[ONE]
Gentlemen's Bar
The Maritime Club
Brisbane, Australia
1825 Hours 29 November 1942

"Nice place," Admiral Wagam said to General Pickering, looking around the comfortably elegant room, furnished with dark-maroon leather couches and chairs, its paneled walls holding discreetly lighted oil portraits of men in merchant marine uniforms and sailing ships under full sail.

An elderly, white-jacketed waiter appeared immediately as Pickering, Stecker, and Wagam sat down.

"Good evening, gentlemen," he said.

"Are you a scotch drinker, Admiral?" Pickering asked. Wagam nodded.

The waiter delivered glasses, a soda siphon bottle, a bowl of ice cubes, and a bottle.

"We'll pour, thank you," Pickering said, and when the waiter left them, did so.

He picked up his glass.

"How about to 'Interservice Cooperation'?" he asked.

"How about 'The Corps'?" Admiral Wagam said. "Jack NMI and Fleming, I give you The Corps."

They sipped their drinks.

"The Navy," Stecker said, and raised his glass again.

"How about to the kids we're sending off on OPERATION WINDMILL?" Pickering said. "God protect them."

"Hear, hear," Wagam said.

"Before we get really carried away," Stecker said. "Are there any unanswered questions? Have we done everything we can?"

"I've got a question," Wagam said, "about the OSS involvement."

"Apparently," Pickering said, "Colonel 'Wild Bill' Donovan got the President to order Frank Knox to order me to include two OSS agents in the Fertig operation. Which Donovan, apparently, has decided to name OPERATION WINDMILL. When my deputy in Washington, Colonel Rickabee—"

"I know Fritz," Wagam said.

"When Fritz learned the identity of one of the agents, and was reliably informed what a—for lack of more forceful words—miserable sonofabitch he is, and protested to Knox, he got a nasty note saying in effect that the OSS, including the sonofabitch, goes on the mission, and no further discussion is desired."

"Ouch," Wagam said. "I suppose it's too much to hope that the agent who was lost—"

"The good one is the one who went down with the B-17," Pickering said. "Jack had a word with this chap—he's a Marine captain named Macklin—and made it clear to him that McCoy is in charge of the mission, even if he is only a first lieutenant."

"I'll have a word with Chambers Lewis before I go back to Pearl," Wagam said, "and make sure he understands that."

"I think that would be a very good idea," Pickering said. "Thank you."

"I was very impressed with McCoy," Wagam said.

"He's a very impressive young man. And he has the experience. He made the Makin raid, and he ran the operation when we replaced the Marines with the Coastwatchers on Buka. There's no question he should be in charge."

"And we're working on getting a Marine Raider to go along, a master gunnery sergeant who was with McCoy on the Makin raid," Stecker said. "I think he'll show up in time."

"If you don't mind my saying so, Fleming," Admiral Wagam said carefully, "there is one thing wrong with McCoy. At least for your purposes."

"And what would that be?" Pickering said coldly.

"He's only a first lieutenant. I somehow don't feel that General MacArthur will change his opinion about Fertig based on the judgment of a lowly first lieutenant."

"The original plan was that Jack was going on the mission," Pickering said. "He has guerrilla experience in the Banana Republics."

"What happened?"

"The incoming Commandant of the Corps decided he needed him in Washington," Pickering said.

Stecker looked uncomfortable.

" 'Incoming Commandant'?" Wagam asked, surprised. "I hadn't heard that. Who? Vandegrift?"

"You didn't hear that from me," Pickering said. "And changing the subject, you're right. McCoy's rank is going to pose some problems. I'm wide open to suggestion."

"Send somebody out right away who's been with Fertig all along, the higher ranking the better. I mean, on the *Sunfish.*"

"That makes a lot of sense," Stecker said.

"OK, we'll do it," Pickering said. "Presuming McCoy can find somebody to send."

"I really wish I could go," Stecker said.

"You're too old and decrepit, Jack," Pickering said, and reached for the bottle.

[TWO]
Naval Air Transport Passenger Terminal
Brisbane, Australia
0715 Hours 30 November 1942

Lieutenant Chambers D. Lewis, USN, was not surprised when Brigadier General Fleming Pickering and Colonel Jack (NMI) Stecker showed up to see Admiral Wagam off. But he was a little surprised when Captain Ed Sessions, at the wheel of a jeep, drove up as the Pearl Harbor–bound *Coronado,* two of its four engines running, began to taxi away from the tie-down buoy.

Pickering—about to get into the Studebaker staff car with Stecker—changed his mind and walked up to Lewis as Sessions drove up.

"Everything go all right, Ed?"

"McCoy's all set up, and I've got Lewis the room right next to Macklin, but the telephone's going to take some time," Sessions replied.

Macklin? Lewis wondered. *Why does that name ring a bell? There was a guy at the Academy by that name. That would be too much of a coincidence.*

"Maybe Pluto knows somebody in the Signal Corps," Pickering said. "I'll work on it."

"Yes, Sir."

"Lewis, Sessions is going to set you up in the BOQ."

"Yes, Sir."

"Did Admiral Wagam have a chance to discuss the . . . who's in charge of arrangements . . . for this mission?"

"Yes, Sir. I'm to take my orders from Lieutenant McCoy."

"If you've got any problems with anything, bring them to either Colonel Stecker or me."

"Yes, Sir. Thank you, Sir."

"I hope you brought some bathing trunks with you," Pickering said.

"Sir?"

"I got some for him, Sir."

"Well, then, I'll see you both later at the cottage. Have fun."

"I'll try to see that he does, Sir," Sessions said.

Pickering walked to the Studebaker.

"How's your head?" Sessions asked when Lewis slid into the jeep beside him.

"I am a Naval officer, Captain. Naval officers know how to hold their liquor. What gets The Marine Corps up at this early hour? And what was that about swim trunks?"

"First, we're going to get you settled in the BOQ, and next we're going to show you—or maybe you'll show us—how to get heavy and awkward objects down a curved, wet, and very slippery surface into rubber boats. And then you're going to practice paddling a rubber boat overloaded with heavy and awkward things around the harbor. And presuming you don't drown today, you'll do it again tonight, or before daylight tomorrow."

"Really? Where are you going to get a curved and slippery surface?"

"McCoy found an old coastal freighter that went belly-up at a pier," Sessions replied. "He rented it for a week from the Aussies."

"What do you mean, 'rented it'?"

"When he asked if he could use it, the owners said, 'Certainly, and exactly how much were you thinking of paying?' "

"I don't think you're kidding."

"I'm not. Anyway, he and Koffler and Hart have been over there since daylight, setting things up. I hope you remember how to swim?"

"Are you involved in this exercise?"

"No. I'm not going on the mission, therefore I don't have to practice. But I thought I would watch. With a little bit of luck, the OSS might drown himself."

"You've really got it in for this guy, don't you?"

"Let's say it wouldn't break my heart if he did drown this morning."

"You going to tell me why?"

"What did your admiral tell you?"

"He said McCoy's in charge, and to conduct myself accordingly."

"If that's all he said, then one of two things is true. Either the General didn't tell him about the OSS, which means that I can't tell you; or he did tell him, and your admiral decided he didn't want to tell you, which also means I can't tell you."

"If you hate this guy so much, why don't you just drown him?"

"I think that's probably been considered. If anyone had asked me, I would have voted 'yes.' "

Sessions reached into the back of the jeep, dipped his hand into a musette back, and came out with a pair of blue swimming trunks.

"Don't let it be said the Marine Corps never gives the Navy anything," he said as he handed them to Lewis.

"General Pickering used the name 'Macklin,' " Lewis said, making it a question. "The OSS officer's name."

"That's his name."

"I think I may know him."

"I don't think so," Sessions said.

"Why not?"

"If you knew him, you'd try very hard not to let anybody know," Sessions said.

Chambers Lewis examined the swim trunks. According to a Royal Australian Navy label on the inside waistband, they were four inches too large, and they did not have a built-in jockstrap.

"They don't have a jockstrap."

"They're *Navy* trunks," Sessions said. "Sailors have no balls, and therefore a jockstrap is unnecessary."

"Screw you, Captain Sessions."

But you're right. Some sailors don't have balls. This *sailor in particular doesn't have balls.*

Lieutenant Chambers D. Lewis, USN, Annapolis '40, had been forced to the conclusion that there was serious question whether he had the balls—the intestinal fortitude, the courage, however more politely the condition might be phrased—to wear the uniform he was wearing, to represent himself as an officer of the Naval Service.

He was also alive, he believed, because he was a coward.

The first indication that he was equipped with something less than the necessary balls came—as one hell of a surprise—shortly after he reported to the Submarine School at New London, Connecticut, six months after he graduated from the Naval Academy.

During an orientation ride on a fleet submarine before beginning their training, Lieutenant Commander Thomas B. Elliott, USN, Annapolis '32, gave them a little talk, explaining that the makeup of some people simply disqualified them for the silent service. These individuals had nothing to be ashamed of, Lieutenant Commander Elliott said, any more than they should be ashamed of having blue eyes, or red hair. It was the way God had issued them.

The Navy's intention with the orientation ride was to save both the Navy and the individual whose makeup was such that he couldn't take submarine service time and money by sending him back to the surface Navy now—and without any sort of stigma attached—before the lengthy and expensive training began.

That, Ensign Chambers D. Lewis knew, was bullshit pure and simple. Any officer who couldn't handle being in a submarine shouldn't be in the Navy at all. And certainly a notation on a service record that an officer who volunteered for submarine training, and was accepted, and then left New London within a week of his arrival would be tantamount to stamping the record in three-inch-high letters, COWARD. Cowards not only deservedly enjoy the contempt of non-cowards, but are unfit to command men, which is the one basic function of a Naval officer.

Lewis remembered very clearly the first time he heard a submarine skipper give the order to "take her down." He had nightmares about it, waking up from them in cold sweats.

He was standing not six feet from the skipper when he heard that command. And the moment the Klaxon horn sounded, and the loudspeakers blared, *"Dive! Dive! Dive!"*, he was bathed in a cold sweat, virtually overcome by a mindless terror. For a time he thought his heart stopped and that he was going to faint. He remembered little else about his first voyage beneath the sea except that he was aware they were under it; that just a foot or two away the sea was doing its best to break through the flimsy hull and crush and smother everyone inside, including him.

Lieutenant Commander Elliott gave them another little chat after they tied up back at New London—and Lewis had a clear picture of Elliott, too. He looked competent and professional, everything an officer, an officer of the silent service, was supposed to be.

He wanted to emphasize, Lieutenant Commander Elliott told them, that absolutely no stigma would be attached if anyone decided now that the submarine service was not for them. To the contrary, it was their duty to make their uneasiness known, to save themselves and the Navy a good deal of difficulty down the line. The lieutenant commander went on to say that he knew of a dozen young officers who had the balls to speak up, and were now doing very well elsewhere in the Navy, in both the surface Navy and in Naval Aviation.

He would be in his office from 1900 until 2200 that night, Lieutenant Commander Elliott said. If anyone wished to speak with him regarding a release from the silent service, they should come see him. Anyone who did so would be off the base within two hours, and there would be absolutely no stigma attached to their transfer. He would also be in his office for the same purpose every Saturday morning from 0800 until 1100, so long as they were in training.

Ensign Lewis talked himself out of seeing Lieutenant Commander Elliott that night by telling himself that the mindless terror he experienced on the dive was an aberration, an isolated incident that would not be repeated, and that it would be the highest folly to throw away his Naval career—and the tough four years at Annapolis that preceded it—because of one incident, an aberrational incident that would not be repeated.

And he got through the rest of his training at New London in much the same way, one week at a time, telling himself that this Saturday he was going to bite the bullet and see Lieutenant Commander Elliott and tell him that he'd tried, he just didn't have the balls to be a submariner.

And every Saturday morning he decided to wait just one more week. He came closest to seeing Commander Elliott after the Momsen Lung training. The training itself—you're inserted at the base of the famous water-filled tower, you put the lung in place, and then you make your way up a knotted rope to the surface—didn't bother him as much as what it implied:

Submarines, and thus the submariners aboard them, would inevitably get in some kind of trouble, and an attempt to escape from a disabled, and doomed, submarine would be necessary. In Lewis's opinion, there was little chance that the Momsen Escape Procedure would work as well in combat as it did in New London—if it worked at all. If an enemy depth charge caused sufficient damage to a submarine to leave her without power, her crew might as well kiss their asses good-bye.

The various possibilities of dying aboard a submarine ran vividly through his imagination at New London, and later at Pearl, and on patrol, and now in Australia.

He graduated fifth in his class, and after an initial evaluation cruise aboard the *Cachalot,* a 298-foot, 1,500-ton submersible of the Porpoise class operating out of Norfolk, Virginia (SUBFORATL), he was transferred to SUBFORPAC at Pearl Harbor, and assigned to the *Remora,* another Porpoise-class submarine.

By then he had, he thought, his terror under control. At the same time, he came up with a solution to his no-balls dilemma. If he applied for Naval Aviation while aboard the *Remora,* no action would be taken until he completed his assignment. His records would show that he was relieved to transfer to Naval Aviation, not because he quit. And completing his tour, holding his terror under control while he did so, would solve the moral question of whether he had enough balls to remain a Naval officer.

He was on patrol, a long way from Pearl Harbor, when the Japanese struck on December 7. *Remora* immediately went on the hunt for Japanese vessels. She found six, and fired a total of fourteen torpedoes at them. Of the fourteen, nine missed the target—they ran too deep, something was wrong with the depth-setting mechanisms. Of the five which struck their targets, only one detonated—something was wrong with the detonators.

When the *Remora* returned to Pearl Harbor, the crew were sent to Waikiki Beach Hotel for five days' rest and recuperation leave. He spent the five days drunk in his room, not just tiddly, plastered, happy, but fall-down drunk.

He made four more patrols. After each of them he drank himself into oblivion. And then there was a fifth patrol, the last—of three—that the *Remora* made to Corregidor to evacuate from the doomed fortress gold and nurses, and, on one of them, a dozen men blinded in the war. He woke up after that drunk in the hospital at Pearl Harbor with his head swathed in bandages. He had been found, they told him, in his hotel bathroom, where he had apparently slipped in the tub and cracked his head open. He had been unconscious for four days and had lost a good deal of blood. And it had been decided that his medical condition precluded his return to sea until there was time to determine the extent of the concussion's damage to his brain. The *Remora*, he was told, had sailed without him.

The memory of his enormous relief that he didn't have to go out on her again, the shame that he was not sailing with his shipmates because he'd gotten fall-down drunk, made him literally nauseous. He was sorry they found him before he'd bled to death.

Rear Admiral Daniel J. Wagam appeared in his hospital room three days later. There was good news and bad news, Admiral Wagam said. The good news was that he had been declared fit for duty; there was no permanent damage from the concussion. The bad news was that his aide had been promoted, and therefore he needed another aide. And unfortunately, Lieutenant (j.g.) Chambers D. Lewis, USN, not only met the criteria the Admiral had set for an aide, but was available.

"Sir, with respect, I would prefer to go back to sea."

"So would I, Mr. Lewis," Admiral Wagam said. "But unfortunately the Navy feels I am of more use behind a desk, and I have decided you will be of more use working for me. They're going to discharge you tomorrow. Move into quarters, take seventy-two hours, and then report to me at CINCPAC."

"Admiral, I don't know if you know why I'm in here."

"Officially, you slipped in the shower. Leave it at that, Mr. Lewis. You are not the first officer who had far too much to drink than was wise."

Despite the terrible temptation, Lewis did not so much as sniff a cork on his seventy-hour liberty. Afterward, he reported to Admiral Wagam at CINC-PAC as ordered.

Six weeks later, it was officially determined that the *Remora*, two weeks overdue for refueling at Midway, was missing and presumed lost with all hands at sea.

The next day, Chambers D. Lewis was promoted lieutenant.

It therefore followed, in Lewis's mind, that if he were not a coward, he would not have gotten stinking, fall-down drunk in the Waikiki Beach Hotel, he would not have cracked his head, he would have gone on another patrol aboard *Remora*, and he would now be dead.

He went to Admiral Wagam and asked to be returned to submarine service. The Admiral made it rather clear he thought the request was expected, and rather childish, and denied it.

"And please, Chambers, do not make a habit of making such requests again and again in the belief you can eventually wear me down. If I get tired of hearing them, you'll wind up at Great Lakes training boots, not going back to the submarines. I need you here; you're good at what you do. You *are,* whether you think so or not, doing something useful to the Navy."

But it was different, of course, when OPERATION WINDMILL came up. OPERATION WINDMILL was important to the Navy, because it was important to CINCPAC. Because of his experience, he would be more useful to the Navy aboard the *Sunfish* representing Admiral Wagam (and thus CINCPAC) than he would be carrying Wagam's briefcase and answering his telephone.

If he had not volunteered to go aboard the *Sunfish,* he could not have looked at himself in the mirror.

[THREE]

After giving the matter a good deal of thought, Captain Robert B. Macklin, USMC, finally decided that going to the OSS Brisbane Station chief was the wise thing to do, even if the Station Chief was not happy to learn of the problem.

That was to be expected, Macklin concluded. The Station Chief—he did not know his name, and it was not offered—was certainly going to be upset to learn of the death of Major Brownlee, both as a human matter and because Brownlee's loss would adversely affect the mission.

It was also understandable that the Station Chief was upset to learn that Macklin himself was not qualified by training or experience to step into Brownlee's shoes—not to mention his physical condition. And on top of that, it was necessary to inform him of the situation vis-à-vis himself and Stecker, Sessions, and McCoy.

If he were the Station Chief, Macklin decided, he would have been as upset as the Station Chief was; and in the circumstances, he would have done what the Station Chief almost certainly did, seek guidance from superior headquarters. In this case, that of course meant going directly to OSS Headquarters in Washington for direction.

The station must certainly have some sort of high-speed communication link with Washington, Macklin theorized, perhaps even a shortwave radio system with no other purpose. It should be possible, in extraordinary circumstances like these, to get an answer from Washington in twenty-four hours, perhaps in even less time.

Thus, when the knock came at his door, it was perfectly reasonable to assume that it was either a summons to the telephone at the end of the corridor, or that it would be someone from the OSS, perhaps the Station Chief himself.

He opened the door and found himself looking at a tall, good-looking Naval officer wearing submariner's dolphins on the breast of his khaki shirt and the twin silver bars of a full lieutenant on his collar points.

"Hello, Bob," Lieutenant Chambers D. Lewis, USN, said, putting out his hand. "Long time no see."

It took a moment for Macklin to make the connection, to remember the Lieutenant as a midshipman at the Academy, to remember that they had served together on a Court of Honor matter that had seen three midshipmen dismissed in disgrace.

"Lewis, isn't it?" Macklin asked. "Lewis, *Chambers D.?* '40?"

"Right," Lewis said. "May I come in?"

"Of course," Macklin said, and pulled the door fully open.

I knew there would be an immediate response.

"I'll be damned," Macklin said, offering his hand. "I expected someone, but the last person in the world I expected was you."

"I'm a little surprised to be here myself," Lewis said.

He dipped his hand in Sessions's musette bag and came out with a pair of swimming trunks.

"These are for you," he said. "From Ed Sessions."

Macklin looked at them suspiciously.

"No jockstrap," Lewis said.

"What are they for?"

"We're about to practice loading things into rubber boats," Lewis said. "Sessions is waiting downstairs."

My God, maybe he's not from the OSS!

"Lewis, exactly what are you doing here?"

"More or less the same thing you are," Lewis said.

"I'm here on a classified mission," Macklin said. "For the OSS."

"OPERATION WINDMILL," Lewis said. "So am I."

"Then you *are* in the OSS?"

"No. Actually, I'm from CINCPAC."

"I don't understand," Macklin said. "What's your connection with OPERATION WINDMILL? Who told you about it? It's highly classified."

"Admiral Wagam," Lewis said. "Of CINCPAC. I'm his aide. I'm being sent along to see if I can make myself useful."

He's not OSS. He just made that perfectly clear.

"How do you mean 'useful'?"

"To make sure the submarine goes where it's supposed to go, and stays there as long as necessary."

"There may not be a submarine," Macklin said.

"Oh, there'll be a submarine, all right," Lewis said, chuckling. "You can bet on that."

"Things have happened," Macklin said. "I'm not at all sure how much of any of this I'm in a position to tell you. But I can tell you this much: This mission may be scrubbed. Should be scrubbed."

"What sort of things have happened?"

"I really don't know if I should be talking about this to you," Macklin said.

"You're worried, am I cleared for this? The answer is yes. If you have a question about that, check with Captain Sessions."

"He's one of them."

"One of who?"

"I'm not qualified to lead this mission, you know," Macklin said. "The man who was supposed to lead it, who was qualified to lead it, crashed at sea."

"Major Brownlee. I heard about that. Sorry."

"He was a good man, a fine officer. I was his deputy."

"Well, unless they send somebody to replace him, it looks like you will have to take his place."

"Not only am I not qualified to lead this mission, but I haven't fully recovered from my wounds. I've reported this to the proper authority, and they said they'd be in touch. That's who I thought you were. My replacement."

"No," Lewis said. "A reinforcement, maybe, but not a replacement."

"It's not, you understand, that I'm trying to get out of anything; it's simply that I don't have the training to lead a mission like this."

"According to Sessions, one of Pickering's Marines, Lieutenant McCoy, is going to lead it."

"McCoy is a first lieutenant, and I'm a captain. The responsibility will be mine."

"I don't think so," Lewis said. "Not if competent authority—and General Pickering is certainly a competent authority—places someone else in command."

Macklin looked at him with fresh interest.

"That would be so, wouldn't it? If I am formally relieved of command, then I no longer can be held responsible, can I?"

"I wouldn't think so," Lewis said. "Listen, Macklin, I don't know what's going on between you and Sessions and the others, and I don't think I want to know. All I know for sure is that until further orders, I'm taking my orders from General Pickering. My orders from him are to do what Sessions tells me, and Sessions is waiting downstairs for us."

"There is no reason for you to become involved in this, Lewis. It's an OSS matter. The OSS will deal with it."

"Sessions is waiting for us," Lewis said.

I have no choice but to go along with this until the OSS acts.

"I would be grateful, Chambers, if you were to keep the conversation we have just had between us."

"Certainly. Are you about ready to go? Would you like me to wait down-stairs?"

"I'll be right with you," Macklin said. "Just give me a minute."

This man is a coward, Chambers D. Lewis thought. *What is it they say? "It takes one to know one."*

[FOUR]
Office of the Director
Office of Strategic Services
National Institutes of Health Building
Washington, D.C.
0830 Hours 3 December 1942

L. Stanford Morrissette was a fifty-five-year-old Yale-trained attorney who had left his San Francisco law firm and his three-hundred-thousand-dollar an-nual income to serve for an annual stipend of one dollar as OSS Deputy Direc-tor, Special Projects. Though he had a good deal of respect for Colonel William J. Donovan, the Director of the OSS, he was not awed by him.

Moreover, in his view Donovan was in error vis-à-vis what he privately thought of as "the Pickering/Fertig mess." Morrissette happened to know Fleming Pickering rather well—his firm had done a good deal of business with Pacific & Far East Shipping—and thought that Donovan had made a monumental error in refusing Pickering's services almost a year before. He also believed that if Fleming Pickering was unable to convince General Douglas MacArthur of the value of the OSS to his SWPOA operation, no one could.

And he believed that Donovan's clever little plan to circumvent MacAr-thur by sending OSS agents to participate in Pickering's Fertig mission—with-out asking Pickering—was very liable to blow up in his face. *And* to cause trouble somewhere down the pike.

One did not cross someone like Fleming Pickering. Donovan should be smart enough to recognize this, Morrissette believed, and didn't.

Morrissette walked past Donovan's secretary to his open door. In his judg-ment, Donovan's secretary, like doctors' and dentists' receptionists, had as-sumed to herself entirely too much of her employer's prestige. Morrissette did not like to be a supplicant before her desk for permission to seek The Great Man's attention.

"When you have a moment, Bill," Morrissette said. "There's something I think you should see."

Donovan's eyes showed annoyance when he looked up from his desk, but a moment later, his face broke into a charming Irish smile.

"Unlike some people around here, you rarely waste my time, Mo. Come in. What have you got?"

Morrissette walked to Donovan's desk and laid a long sheet of teletypewriter paper on it.

"This just was decrypted," he said.

"Let me see," Donovan said.

```
T  O  P      S  E  C  R  E  T


URGENT URGENT


BRISBANE NUMBER 107
0900GREENWICH2DEC42


FROM        CHIEF OSS STATION
            BRISBANE AUSTRALIA


TO          DIRECTOR OSS
            NATIONAL INSTITUTES OF HEALTH BLDG
            WASHINGTON DC


SUBJECT     OPERATION WINDMILL


(1) YOUR MESSAGE NUMBER 403 0845 GREENWICH 31NOV42 RE LOSS
BROWNLEE RECEIVED 0715GREENWICH 2DEC42 XXX THIS STATION
NOT REPEAT NOT PREVIOUSLY ADVISED OF INCIDENT BY OSS LIAISON
OFFICER SWPOA XXX OSS LIAISON OFFICER SWPOA ADVISES YOUR 403
RECEIVED BY SWPOA 1905GREENWICH 31NOV42 XXX DELAY IN
DELIVERY TO OSS BRISBANE ATTRIBUTED TO QUOTE LARGE VOLUME
OF CLASSIFIED TRAFFIC REQUIRING DECRYPTION ENDQUOTE XXX
SITUATION POINTS OUT ABSOLUTE NECESSITY THIS STATION BE
AUTHORIZED ACCESS TO SPECIAL CHANNEL COMMUNICATIONS
FACILITIES FOR URGENT TRAFFIC XXX


(2) UNDERSIGNED HAD BEEN INFORMED OF BROWNLEE LOSS 1615
LOCALTIME 29NOV42 AS FOLLOWS:


A 1440 LOCAL TIME 29NOV42 MACKLIN TELEPHONED EMERGENCY
CONTACT NUMBER AND REQUESTED IMMEDIATE CONFERENCE WITH
STATION CHIEF XXX DUTY OFFICER SUGGESTED RENDEZVOUS POINT
XXX MACKLIN REFUSED TO LEAVE HIS SWPOA BOQ STATING HIS LIFE
```

WAS IN DANGER XXX DUTY OFFICER UNABLE TO CONTACT
UNDERSIGNED DISPATCHED AGENT TO MACKLINS BOQ XXX

B 1550 AGENT CONTACTED UNDERSIGNED AND STRONGLY
RECOMMENDED PERSONAL VISIT TO MACKLIN AT BOQ XXX
UNDERSIGNED MET WITH MACKLIN AT BOQ 1615 LOCALTIME XXX
FOUND HIM IN HIGHLY EXCITABLE STATE XXX DURING MEETING
MACKLIN:
          1 STATED HE HAD BEEN INFORMED OF BROWNLEE LOSS
BY COLONEL JACK NMI STECKER USMC AT APPROXIMATELY 1130
LOCALTIME 29NOV42 XXX STECKER INFORMED HIM THAT BRIGGEN
PICKERING INTENDED TO CONTINUE OPERATION REGARDLESS XXX
          2 STATED THAT HE HAD REQUESTED TO SEE PICKERING
AND THIS REQUEST WAS DENIED XXX
          3 STATED THAT HE THEN INFORMED STECKER THAT HE
DID NOT FEEL QUALIFIED TO LEAD OPERATION BECAUSE OF LACK OF
TRAINING AND ALSO BECAUSE HE HAS NOT FULLY RECOVERED FROM
WOUNDS SUFFERED AT GAVUTU XXX
          4 STATED THAT STECKER HAD THEN TOLD HIM THAT
ALTHOUGH MACKLIN WOULD BE SENIOR OFFICER MISSION WOULD
ACTUALLY BE UNDER COMMAND OF FIRST LIEUTENANT K R MCCOY
USMCR WHO HE SAID WAS QUOTE KNOWN AS KILLER MCCOY
BECAUSE HE HAD BRUTALLY KNIFED TO DEATH FOUR ITALIAN
MARINES IN INTERNATIONAL SETTLEMENT IN SHANGHAI IN 1941
ENDQUOTE XXX
          5 STATED THAT HE HAS HAD TROUBLE IN PAST WITH
BOTH STECKER AND MCCOY AND THAT BOTH WERE FORMER ENLISTED
MEN CONSPIRING AGAINST HIM TO RUIN HIS NAME AND PROFESSIONAL
REPUTATION XXX
          6 STATED THAT STECKER HAD THREATENED TO HAVE
MCCOY KILL HIM AS SOON AS MISSION LANDS AT DESTINATION XXX

(3) INASMUCH AS COLONEL STECKER WAS UNKNOWN TO UNDERSIGNED
DISCREET INQUIRIES WERE MADE OF COLONEL LEWIS R MITCHELL
USMC SPECIAL LIAISON OFFICER BETWEEN CINCPAC AND SWPOA XXX
MITCHELL ADVISES THAT ALTHOUGH HE DOES NOT KNOW NATURE OF
PICKERING STECKER RELATIONSHIP HE KNOWS STECKER WHO WON
MEDAL OF HONOR IN WWI IS HIGHLY REGARDED BY MAJ GEN A A
VANDEGRIFT OF US FIRST MARINE DIVISION UNDER WHOM HE
COMMANDED BATTALION IN GUADALCANAL INVASION XXX MITCHELL
STATES THAT FROM PERSONAL KNOWLEDGE LIEUTENANT MCCOY IS
HIGHLY REGARDED BY BRIGGEN PICKERING AND THAT STECKER TOLD
HIM THAT MCCOY PARTICIPATED IN MARINE RAIDER OPERATION ON
MAKIN ISLAND

(4) IN VIEW OF THE FOREGOING AND OF UNDERSIGNED PERSONAL
BELIEF THAT SOMEHOW MACKLIN SLIPPED PAST PSYCHIATRIC
EVALUATION BOARD VIS-A-VIS STABILITY IT IS STRONGLY
RECOMMENDED THAT MACKLIN NOT REPEAT NOT BE ALLOWED TO
CONTINUE AS MEMBER OF OPERATION WINDMILL AND THAT HE BE
RELEASED FROM OSS AS UNSUITABLE XXX

(5) UNDERSIGNED RECOMMENDS IN STRONGEST POSSIBLE TERMS THAT
SUITABLY TRAINED AND THOROUGHLY EVALUATED REPLACEMENT
FOR MACKLIN BE SENT AS SOON AS POSSIBLE XXX IF THIS IS
IMPOSSIBLE THREE (3) AGENTS HERE ARE MARGINALLY QUALIFIED
AND WOULD PROBABLY VOLUNTEER IF ASKED XXX

(6) FOR YOUR GENERAL INFORMATION MITCHELL ALSO ADVISED THAT
PICKERING CONFERRED WITH REAR ADMIRAL WAGAM OF NIMITZ
STAFF 29NOV42 PRESUMABLY IN RE AVAILABILITY OF SUBMARINE
XXX TIME IS THEREFORE PROBABLY OF ESSENCE TO FIND
REPLACEMENT FOR MACKLIN XXX

WATERSON
STATIONCHIEF BRISBANE

T O P   S E C R E T

Donovan finished reading and raised his eyes to Morrissette's.

"Well?" he asked.

"What do I do about this, Bill?"

"Aside from finding the idiot who sent this idiot Macklin to Brisbane, you mean? Or are you asking me what we should do to him before we fire him? How about nailing his balls to that large oak tree beside the first tee at the Congressional Country Club? With a rusty nail, of course."

"What do we do about Captain Macklin?"

"What would you suggest, Mo?"

"(a) That we Urgent Radio Waterson telling him to go to Pickering and tell him that Macklin has been relieved and a replacement is on the way and (b) get a replacement on the way."

"We can't do that, Mo," Donovan said.

"Why not?"

"What you will do, Mo, is Urgent Radio Waterson and tell him to keep his opinion of Captain Macklin to himself. The last thing I want Douglas MacArthur to find out is that we sent Pickering this idiot."

"Knowing what we now know about him, you'd rather send Captain Macklin on OPERATION WINDMILL than suffer a little embarrassment? Mistakes happen, Bill. We made one."

"The decision has been made, with the approval of the President, to send two OSS agents on Pickering's mission to Fertig. If we say, 'Hold it a minute, fellows, there's been a minor little mistake here, one of the agents we sent is paranoid,' we're going to look like fools. I don't want to look like a fool before the President, Knox, and MacArthur. Is that so hard to understand?"

"Not to understand, I suppose," Morrissette said. "But to believe. What about the other people on this mission? Have you considered the threat to them, to the mission itself, of taking this man along?"

"Subject closed, Mo," Donovan said. "Having considered everything involved, it is my decision that Captain Macklin goes on the mission. Clear? Send Waterson an Urgent Radio to that effect."

"May I speak frankly?"

"Certainly."

"This stinks, Bill, to high heaven."

"I don't like it any more than you do. It's a question of the greater good."

"What is 'the greater good'?"

"That the OSS operate in the Pacific. I believe, and I hope you do, that we can make a bona fide, substantial contribution to the war effort over there. All we have to do is get around MacArthur standing in our way."

"By doing this? Sending a man like Macklin on a mission? A mission that very possibly will fail because of him?"

"The mission will either be a success or a failure. If it's a success, we will have made the point that the OSS is useful."

"And if it fails?"

"We died trying," Donovan said. "Proving that we are willing to make the sacrifices called for. We'll try again and again until we are successful. What we are *not* going to do is admit that our internal procedures are so sloppy that we actually sent a lunatic like this Macklin on a mission."

" 'We died trying'? 'We are willing to making to make sacrifices'? What's this 'we' business, Bill? We're talking about other men's lives here, not yours and mine."

"That's what war is all about, Mo, other men's lives. When we are permitted to operate in the Pacific, we will save a great many other men's lives."

"And the lives of the people on this mission are the price we pay for the ability to operate?"

"You don't seem to be considering the possibility that the mission will be successful. I'd bet on it. I *am* betting on it. Whatever else might be said about Fleming Pickering, he's not a fool."

"Has it occurred to you that Fleming Pickering, either now, or certainly later, is going to make sure the President knows about this?"

"Let me worry about Fleming Pickering," Donovan said, somewhat impatiently. "Is there anything else, Mo?"

"I'll prepare an Urgent Radio for Waterson," Morrissette said. "A draft, for your signature."

"You can sign it, Mo."

"I can, but I won't," Morrissette said, and turned and walked out of Donovan's office.

[FIVE]
Headquarters, 1st Marine Division
Guadalcanal, Solomon Islands
0945 Hours 4 December 1942

The Sergeant Major of the United States First Marine Division, a large-boned, heavily muscled man who had been a Marine for twenty-six of his forty-three years, pushed open the canvas flap (once part of a tent) that separated the Office of the Commanding General from the rest of the command post.

A tall, dignified man in his early fifties, just starting to jowl, sat on a folding wooden chair before a small table on which sat a U.S. Army field desk. He did not to seem to notice his presence.

"General," the Sergeant Major said respectfully.

Major General Alexander Archer Vandegrift, USMC, Commanding General of the 1st Marine Division and all forces on Guadalcanal, turned and looked over his shoulder. The General was dressed like the Sergeant Major, in somewhat battered and sweat-stained utilities.

"Colonel Carlson, Sir," the Sergeant Major said.

General Vandegrift nodded and made a *let him come in* gesture with his hand.

Colonel Evans Carlson, USMC, Commanding Officer of the 2nd Marine Raider Battalion, pushed the canvas flap out of his way and entered Vandegrift's office as Vandegrift rose to his feet.

Carlson, a large man, was wearing utilities even more battered than Vandegrift's. He carried a Thompson .45 ACP Caliber submachine gun slung from a canvas strap over his shoulder, and he wore a web-harness from which were suspended two canteens, a compass case, a first-aid packet, and a Colt Model 1911A1 .45 ACP pistol.

He looked malnourished and exhausted, Vandegrift thought.

"Colonel Carlson reporting the return of the 2nd Raiders, Sir," he said as he saluted.

The 2nd Raider Battalion had been behind the enemy's lines since 9 November 1942—nearly a month. The Japanese, who had somewhat belatedly come to realize that the outcome of the battle for Guadalcanal would very likely determine the future of the war, had, at a terrible cost in ships, matériel, and life, managed to move reinforcements for the 17th Army ashore at Gavanga Creek.

Despite all the Marines could do to wipe out the force, 3,000 Japanese had broken through the lines and set out through the mountainous jungle toward Matanikau. Carlson and approximately two hundred Marine Raiders had gone after them. They had subsisted on rice, on anything edible they could find in the jungle, and on what they could capture from the Japanese.

"Welcome home, Red," Vandegrift said, crisply returning the salute.

"Sir, I regret to report the loss of sixteen KIA and eighteen WIA" (*Killed In Action; Wounded In Action*).

"None missing?" Vandegrift asked.

"No, Sir. We brought our wounded with us, and marked the graves of the KIA."

Vandegrift nodded.

"Enemy losses were four hundred eighty-eight KIA, Sir. I would estimate time and half that number WIA."

Vandegrift tried not to let his surprise show—nor what he immediately recognized as suspicion. Carlson's Raiders were good Marines, well trained, well equipped, and highly motivated. But Carlson had just reported that his two hundred men had killed more than twice their number of the enemy, and wounded three times their number.

"And you estimate 488 KIA?"

"No, Sir. The KIAs are confirmed. There were that many bodies, Sir."

"Well done, Colonel," Vandegrift said. "I want to hear all about it, of course. But to save you the effort of telling the tale twice, I think it might be smart to wait until the 1300 staff meeting. That all right with you?"

"Yes, Sir. I really need a bath and a change of clothes."

"And, I'm sure, something to eat. Why don't you get a shower and a clean uniform, and come back here and have lunch with me?"

"Thank you, Sir," Carlson said. "I accept, with thanks." He paused, smiled, and went on. "And, Sir, I would also report the return of one AWOL to duty."

Vandegrift frowned.

Carlson smiled. "Gunny Zimmerman, Sir," he said.

"Gunnery Sergeant Zimmerman?" Vandegrift asked. "Of VMF-229?"

"Yes, Sir," Carlson said.

"Tell me, Colonel, how did Gunny Zimmerman wind up with the 2nd Raider Battalion?"

"Well, Sir. He was with the 2nd Raiders from the beginning. He made the Makin Island raid, Sir."

"And then he was transferred to VMF-229?"

"Yes, Sir. They needed a heavy-machine-gun artificer. And Zimmerman's about as good with Brownings as anyone in The Corps."

"So I've heard," Vandegrift said. "And then, when VMF-229 was relieved here, the Gunny somehow missed the ship taking the squadron off the island? Is that about what happened, Carlson?"

"Yes, Sir. That's about it. Zimmerman decided he could make himself useful with us. I'm surprised you know about this, Sir."

What could have been a smile moved around Vandegrift's lips.

"Oh, I heard about it," he said. "A number of people in The Corps have heard about it." He raised his voice and called, "Sergeant Major!"

The Sergeant Major's head appeared in the canvas flap.

"General?"

"Would you run down that paperwork we had on Gunny Zimmerman, please, Sergeant Major?"

The Sergeant Major's head disappeared from the canvas flap. Thirty seconds later, he came through the flap and handed Vandegrift the "paperwork." Vandegrift glanced at it and then handed it to Carlson.

```
S E C R E T

PRIORITY

HEADQUARTERS USMC WASH DC 1535 23 NOV 42
COMMANDING GENERAL 1ST MARDIV

FOLLOWING PERSONAL FROM G2 USMC TO COMMGEN 1ST MARDIV

DEAR ALEX

COMMANDANT AT DIRECTION SECNAV DESIRES IMMEDIATE TRANSFER
G/SGT ERNEST ZIMMERMAN VMF-229 TO USMC SPECIAL DETACHMENT
16 ATTACHED TO SUPREME HQ SWPOA. AIR TRAVEL PRIORITY
AAAAAA AUTHORIZED.

COMMANDING OFFICER VMF-229 ADVISES G/SGT ZIMMERMAN
PRESENTLY SERVING WITH 2ND RAIDER BN. PLEASE TAKE WHATEVER
```

ACTION IS NECESSARY TO PERMIT ME TO ADVISE COMMANDANT THAT
G/SGT ZIMMERMAN IS ENROUTE USMC SPECDET 16 AND ADVISE BY
MOST EXPEDITIOUS MEANS THAT THIS HAS BEEN ACCOMPLISHED.

BEST PERSONAL REGARDS HORACE

END PERSONAL TO COMMGEN 1ST MARDIV

BY DIRECTION:

FORREST, MAJGEN USMC ACOFS G2 HQ USMC

General Vandegrift knew Gunnery Sergeant Zimmerman slightly, but he
knew his type well. In 1939, the total strength of the United States Marine
Corps was 1,308 officers and 18,052 enlisted men, fewer men than were in the
Police Department of New York City. Just about all the officers knew each
other, just about all the enlisted men knew all the officers, and most officers
knew most of the enlisted men, at least by sight.

Gunnery Sergeant Zimmerman was one of the Old Breed. Vandegrift remembered him as a corporal with the 4th Marines in Shanghai before the war.
If there hadn't been a war, he thought, Zimmerman would still be in Shanghai
and still be a corporal. Now there were more than seven thousand officers, and
more than 135,000 enlisted Marines, and Zimmerman was a gunnery sergeant
long before he could have expected to be a buck sergeant.

The Old Breed had been the backbone of the 1st Marine Division here.
Without them, Vandegrift had often thought, the Division might not have been
able to do what it had done.

"And you weren't aware of the Gunny's presence, or absence, of course,
until you were behind the enemy's lines, and there was nothing you could do
about it?" Vandegrift asked. "You don't have to answer that question, Colonel. Marine officers shouldn't lie, and our Constitution prohibits compulsory
self-incrimination."

"Thank you, Sir," Carlson said, smiling. "Sir, what's this all about?"

"You know as much as I do," Vandegrift said.

"General, the reason I mentioned Gunny Zimmerman is that I'd like to
decorate him."

"Put him in for whatever you think he deserves. Offhand, I'd be inclined
to act favorably on any recommendation of yours. What did he do?"

"That's what I wanted to talk to you about, Sir. Nothing in particular, except kill Japanese."

"I don't think I quite understand."

"It's rather hard to describe, Sir. He takes this war personally."

"I don't follow you."

"He doesn't talk much. He's a hard man to draw out. But the way I have Zimmerman figured out is that he was the happiest man in the 4th Marines in Shanghai. He had a Chinese wife. Wife in quotes, because they weren't married. But she bore him three children. They had a small apartment, and were buying a house in her village. What he wanted to do with his life was put in his twenty years, probably making sergeant, maybe even staff sergeant, and then retire to their house in her village. He didn't want much from life; what he had was what he wanted. And then the Japanese came along and ruined it all for him."

"A real China Marine, in other words?"

"Yes, Sir. I think in the back of his mind he believes that as soon as every soldier in the Japanese Army is dead, he can go back to the 4th Marines in Shanghai, and his family, and things will be back to normal. So he kills a lot of Japanese soldiers."

Vandegrift chuckled and shook his head.

"No individual act of great courage, Sir," Carlson said. "But he was always willing to take the point on the march—and he's very good on the point—and he was the happiest when he could assume the prone position, get his sling in the proper position on his arm, and then put rounds into the heads of Japanese at three hundred, four hundred, five hundred yards."

"I see."

"I don't mean to paint him as bloodthirsty, and he's not foolhardy. But he's very very good at killing Japanese. I didn't keep score, but in my mind, there's no question that he killed more Japanese than anybody else on this operation."

"Could you, in good conscience, recommend Gunnery Sergeant Zimmerman for the Silver Star?"

Carlson considered the question before replying.

"Yes, Sir. I get back to saying that there was no one act of spectacular courage. But he went willingly into harm's way just about every day we were out there—sometimes two or three times a day. That adds up, Sir, in my judgment, to more than one act of spectacular bravery."

"So ordered," Vandegrift said. "Get him bathed and shaved and into a clean set of utilities and bring him back here. We'll pin the Silver Star on him, and then you can put him on the next plane to Espíritu Santo."

"Aye, aye, Sir. Thank you, Sir. By your leave, Sir?"

Carlson, having asked permission to withdraw, raised his hand to his temple in salute.

"One more thing," Vandegrift said. "I forgot you were behind the lines and couldn't have heard."

"Sir?"

"We're about through here. On 9 December, next Wednesday, I'm turning the island over to Patch."

"Who, Sir?"

"Major General Alexander M. Patch, U.S. Army, will assume command of Guadalcanal 9 December. The First Marine Division will be sent to Australia for rehabilitation and refitting."

"I hadn't heard," Carlson said. "It's about time."

"Seventy-plus percent of the Division has malaria," Vandegrift said. "The average Marine has lost twenty-two pounds of body weight."

"I didn't realize it was that bad," Carlson said.

"It's that bad," Vandegrift said, and finally raised his hand to return Carlson's salute. "Thank you, Colonel. That will be all."

[SIX]
U.S. Army Air Corps Passenger Terminal
Queensland Air Field
Brisbane, Australia
1715 Hours 6 December 1942

Four U.S. Army ambulances and a complement of medical personnel were waiting for the Army Air Corps C-47 when it taxied up to the terminal. As soon as the wide cargo was opened and an aluminum ladder dropped in place, a doctor, three nurses, and half a dozen medics clambered up the ladder.

The ambulance drivers started their engines, and one of them backed up close to the airplane and opened its rear doors. The first patient came out the door almost immediately, a nurse holding a bottle of blood hovering over the blanket-wrapped body as the litter was carried into the ambulance.

Four minutes passed before the second litter came through the door and was placed in the ambulance. The doors were closed, and the ambulance moved off, to be immediately replaced by a second. Two litter-borne patients were placed in the second ambulance, and two more into the third.

The last litter load was completely covered by a white sheet. It was loaded into the fourth ambulance, and then the doctor and the remaining nurse got in with the body, the doors were closed, and the ambulance drove off.

A stocky, round-faced, tightly muscled, short, barrel-chested Marine in utilities appeared in the wide cargo door. He looked around the airport, dropped a nearly empty barracks bag from the door, and then, carefully, one hand clasping the leather sling of the 1903 Springfield rifle he had slung from his shoulder, climbed down the aluminum ladder.

Lieutenant Kenneth R. McCoy, USMCR, walked up to the Marine and put out his hand.

"I figured you'd be involved in this, McCoy," Gunnery Sergeant Ernest W. Zimmerman, USMC, said. "What the fuck's going on?"

"I need you," McCoy said. "So I sent for you."

"Shit!" Gunnery Sergeant Zimmerman said, and then noticed a Navy lieutenant in khakis walking up behind McCoy. After visibly making up his mind whether or not to do so, he saluted.

Lieutenant Chambers D. Lewis, USN, returned the salute.

"Zimmerman, this is Mr. Lewis," McCoy said.

Zimmerman just perceptibly nodded his head, then briefly and somewhat reluctantly shook Lewis's extended hand.

"Welcome to Australia, Sergeant," Lewis said.

Zimmerman nodded.

"I've gotto piss bad," Zimmerman said. "The fucking relief tube was broke."

"Go behind the airplane," McCoy said. "Nobody'll see you."

Zimmerman nodded, unslung the Springfield from his shoulder, handed it to McCoy, and then walked around the tail of the airplane. Two minutes later, he returned, in the process of buttoning his trousers, and with a look of pleased relief on his face.

"Now what?" he asked.

"We've got to run you past the hospital, and I thought you might be hungry. You want to go to the hospital first, or after?"

"After. What I really would like is a cold beer."

"We've got beer in a bucket in the car," McCoy said, pointing to General Pickering's staff car.

Zimmerman nodded, took his Springfield back, picked up his nearly empty duffel bag, and started to walk to the car.

"What is that, a Studebaker? Where'd you get that?"

"It belongs to General Pickering."

"Who the fuck is he?"

"My boss. Your new boss."

"All I got to wear is what I have on, plus a change of socks and skivvies and a pair of boondockers. My gear is all in Hawaii."

"We can fix that," McCoy said. "We'll get you an issue."

They reached the car.

"The beer is in the back, Ernie, get in the back."

"What about him?" Zimmerman asked, jerking his thumb in the direction of Lieutenant Lewis.

"He will ride in front with Lieutenant Hart," McCoy said.

Zimmerman climbed in the back of the Studebaker, took a bottle of beer from an ice-filled bucket, took a K-Bar knife from the small of his back, opened the bottle and drank deeply, emptying it.

When he finally took it from his mouth, he belched loudly and with obvious satisfaction.

"Welcome to civilization, Gunny," Lieutenant Hart said, a touch of laughter in his voice.

"Who's he?"

"Lieutenant Hart works for General Pickering," McCoy said. "Watch out for him. He used to be a cop."

Zimmerman took another beer from the bucket and flipped the top off expertly with his K-Bar.

"And the swabbie?" he asked, either as if he believed Lieutenant Lewis was deaf and could not hear him, or simply didn't care whether he did or not.

"He's going to give us a ride on a submarine."

"A ride to where?"

"We're going into the Philippines."

"Why?"

"There's an Army officer there, and some guys from the Fourth Marines who didn't surrender. We're going to take them radios, a little gear and medicine, see what kind of help they need, and figure out how to get it to them."

"We? You and me?"

"You and me, a staff sergeant named Koffler, and Captain Robert B. Macklin."

"Macklin? Not the same sonofabitch who tried to fuck us—you and Lieutenant Sessions in particular—in China?"

"One and the same."

"You're working for him?"

"No. He's just going along."

"I'm surprised somebody hasn't shot that bastard by now," Gunnery Sergeant Zimmerman said. He took a long pull at his fresh bottle of beer, and belched again.

"Good beer," he said. "Where are we going now?"

"I thought you could probably use a steak, maybe with fresh eggs. Hart knows a good place."

"What I really could use is a place to take a good dump," Zimmerman said. "How far is this place?"

[SEVEN]
Office of the Military Governor of Mindanao
Cagayan de Oro, Misamis-Oriental Province
Mindanao, Commonwealth of the Philippines
1450 Hours 8 December 1942

"There has been a development in the Fertig matter," Lieutenant Colonel Tange Kisho said to Brigadier General Kurokawa Kenzo, "which we feel should be brought to the General's attention."

General Kurokawa nodded. Lieutenant Colonel Tange turned to Captain Matsuo Saikaku, who handed him a single sheet of paper. Tange handed this to General Kurokawa. He read it, and then looked at Tange, waiting for an explanation.

"As the General can see, Signals Intelligence has broken the simple substitution code used by the Americans in Australia in their last message to Fertig. The message reads, 'We'll see you soon,' signature 'Killer.' "

"And your interpretation of the significance of this, Colonel?"

"After some thought, I have come to believe that Captain Saikaku's interpretation, while it might be in error, is one that we cannot afford to ignore."

"And what is your interpretation, Captain Saikaku?" General Kurokawa asked, somewhat impatiently.

"Sir, I believe we must proceed on the assumption that the Americans will soon attempt to infiltrate Mindanao and make contact with Fertig."

"Expand," Kurokawa ordered.

"It is my analysis, Sir," Saikaku replied, "that Fertig is now accepted by the American command in Australia as legitimate, and that they are now going to attempt to establish physical contact with him."

"For what purpose? And how?"

"If I were the American commander, General, I would first try to get in place a sophisticated communications set. An encryption system that we will not be able to break as quickly as the primitive one they are now using. And, since I don't believe they will be able to send him much in the way of supplies, I believe they will send him gold. And perhaps some medicine and small quantities of small arms and ammunition."

"How? By air?"

"I think by submarine, Sir. I don't believe the risk to American long-range aircraft—what they have available is the Boeing bomber, primarily—would be justified by the amount of cargo they can carry. I also think that they would be unwilling to send a surface vessel, which would almost certainly be detected by our air patrols. That leaves only submarines. As I am sure the General will remember, the Americans used them successfully until almost the day Corregidor fell."

"Where?"

"This of course is a guess, Sir, but I would say somewhere on the eastern shore of the island."

"They are succeeding, aren't they?" General Kurokawa said.

"Sir?"

"In forcing us to divert personnel and equipment to watch for them. That's one of the objectives of irregular forces, to cause their enemy to expend resources they otherwise would not have to expend."

"Yes, Sir, I'm afraid that's true," Saikaku said.

"There must be several thousand miles of shoreline on Mindanao. Obviously, we don't have the aircraft or the people on the ground to patrol every foot of it waiting for a submarine which may or not attempt to put people ashore. So what would you suggest we do, Captain Saikaku?"

"I have given that some thought, General, and Colonel Tange has been kind enough to offer me his counsel. I have prepared a map on which are marked what are in my judgment the ten most likely places where a submarine would attempt to put people ashore. May I show it to the General?"

Kurokawa nodded, and Saikaku laid the map on his desk.

"Very interesting," Kurokawa said after examining it. "But we don't have the forces available to patrol all these beaches."

"I am aware of that, Sir," Saikaku said. "I suggested to Colonel Tange that we patrol these marked areas on a random basis, using aircraft and small—three- or four-man—patrols on the beaches themselves."

"That's the best you can do?" Kurokawa asked, almost sadly.

"Our best hope, General, is the interception and rapid decryption of the message Australia will send to Fertig, telling *him* when and where to expect the submarine."

"Unless, of course, the Americans don't send such a message, and simply put their people ashore to find Fertig by themselves."

"We must accept that as a possibility, General," Tange said. "But still, it is my respectful recommendation that we increase our shore-patrol efforts on the eastern shore."

General Kurokawa considered that for a moment.

"See my Operations officer, Tange, and work out a plan with him. Bring it to me for my approval."

"Yes, Sir."

"And you, Saikaku, make sure that if there is a message from Australia announcing the arrival of a submarine, we intercept it."

"Yes, Sir."

XIV

[ONE]
Water Lily Cottage
Brisbane, Australia
2105 Hours 9 December 1942

Major Hon Son Do, Signal Corps, USA, muttered an obscene and vulgar word not ordinarily in his vocabulary, rose from the paper-cluttered dining-room table, went to the sideboard, picked up a bottle of Famous Grouse, poured an inch and a half into a water glass, and drank it straight down.

Sitting at the table were Captains Robert B. Macklin and Edward Sessions, USMC; Lieutenant Chambers D. Lewis, USN; Lieutenants K. R. McCoy and John Marston Moore, USMCR; and Sergeant Stephen Koffler, USMC. Hon turned to them, met McCoy's eyes, and announced, in his thick Boston accent, "Just between thee and me, Kenneth my lad, when I was recruited to apply the ancient and noble art of cipher to the detriment of our enemy, this was not what I thought they had in mind."

"Why don't we just give up? We've been at this for hours. And all we've come up with is that bullshit," McCoy said, pointing at the typewriter on the table in front of Koffler. "And hand me that bottle when you're through with it."

"The Boss said come up with a way to communicate with Fertig—" Lieutenant John Marston Moore began, to be interrupted by Captain Macklin's bark:

"General officer on the deck!"

Both McCoy and Sessions flashed Macklin a look of mingled disbelief and contempt—this was Water Lily Cottage, not Headquarters, Parris Island. But their response, and that of the others, was Pavlovian: There was the sound of chair legs scraping on the floor as everyone started to rise to their feet and come to attention.

"As you were, gentlemen," Brigadier General Fleming Pickering said as he and Colonel Jack (NMI) Stecker walked into the room. "Keep your seats."

Pickering and Stecker found seats at the table.

"Pass him the bottle, Pluto," Pickering ordered. "And when he's had what I'm sure is a well-deserved taste, he can explain exactly what bullshit it is you've come up with."

"Sorry, Sir, I didn't expect you back so early," McCoy said.

"Obviously," Pickering said. "Colonel Stecker and I just took eleven dollars of El and Madame El Supremo's money at bridge. If you have the bad manners to do that, you are not invited for postgame drinks."

Pluto chuckled, then walked to where Koffler was sitting before a typewriter, jerked a sheet of paper from the platen, added several other sheets to it, and laid them before Pickering and Stecker.

"I'm embarrassed to show you this, Sir," he said. "Koffler just made a clean copy. Most of it's Moore's idea."

"Thanks a lot, Pluto," Moore said.

"I didn't mean that the way it sounded, Johnny, sorry. None of us had any better ideas, Sir. And this just may work."

McCoy snorted.

Pickering read the top sheet of paper, and then handed it to Stecker.

```
Message One
Hour 0000


U   S   E   W   H              USEWH
02 20 19 04 10
A   T   N   A   V              ATNAV
17 09 18 14 21
E   E   W   I   L              EEWIL
19 25 04 05 23
L   F   I   N   D              LFIND
24 09 11 18 03
I   N   H   E   A              INHEA
22 18 10 19 08
V   E   N   A   S              VENAS
12 19 18 08 20
S   I   M   S   U              SIMSU
20 05 04 20 02
B   C   O   D   E              BCODE
09 13 14 03 25
```

"OK, John," Pickering said. "Explain this to me. Start at the beginning, and explain everything carefully. Colonel Stecker and I are old men, and we don't absorb things as quickly as you bright young fellows."

"We were about halfway through this, General," Lieutenant John Marston Moore said, "when Pluto brought up that we have to presume the Japanese (a) are listening to our traffic, and (b) by now have broken the Ludmilla Zhivkov Zanesville simple substitution code, and thus (c) we need another one."

"OK," Pickering said. "So tell me what will the Navy find in heaven?"

" 'If the Army and the Navy ever look on heaven's scene,' " Captain Ed Sessions said, " 'They will find the streets are guarded by United States Marines,' " he continued. "From the Marine Hymn."

"Jesus H. Christ!" Colonel Stecker said, in mingled disbelief and disgust. "That's the best you so-called experts can come up with?"

"Yes, Sir, Colonel Sir," McCoy agreed. "My thoughts exactly."

"With respect, Sir," Pluto said. "Moore said we needed something that any Marine would know and that would not be immediately familiar to the Japanese. This meets that criteria. We tested it on nine of the Marines in Townsville, Joe Howard in the hospital in Melbourne, and Colonel Mitchell at SWPOA."

"Since you obviously couldn't tell them why you were asking, those must have been interesting conversations," Pickering said with a chuckle.

"They were, Sir. But all but one Marine knew—almost immediately— what was meant."

"Who didn't?"

"Colonel Mitchell, Sir," Moore said. "He asked me if I had been drinking, and said that he intended to bring the conversation to your attention."

"It sounds as if you were," Stecker said, pointing to the quart of Famous Grouse in front of McCoy. "How many bottles of that stuff have you people been into?"

"Take it easy, Jack," Pickering said. "If it works, don't laugh at it. OK. We now have a fresh simple substitution code. What's 'Hour 0000' mean?"

"The *Sunfish* will surface thirty minutes after nightfall the day before the landing is attempted, Sir," Pluto said. "And transmit Message One. The clock will start to run—Hour 0000—when receipt of Message One is acknowledged. If you'll look at the second sheet, Message Two?"

"Message One will be transmitted from the *Sunfish?* Is that what you're saying?" Pickering asked, as he read the second sheet of paper.

Message Two
Hour 0200

THEYWILLFINDTHESTREETSAREGUARDEDBYUNITEDSTATESMARINES
12345678901234567890123456789012345678901234567890123
　　　1　　　　　2　　　　　3　　　　　4　　　　　5

K I L L E　　　　　　　　　　　　LILLE
06 07 06 08 03
R A N D E　　　　　　　　　　　　RANDE
18 23 36 40 45

```
R  N  Y  W  I                    RNYWI
49 51 04 05 06
L  L  E  A  T                    LLEAT
07 08 15 23 38
B  E  A  N  S                    BEANS
33 39 43 51 53
T  H  I  R  T                    THIRT
01 02 06 18 21
Y  M  I  L  E                    YMILE
34 47 50 07 15
S  S  O  U  T                    SSUUT
22 46 27 27 38
H  I  S  M  O                    HISMU
02 06 53 47 27
R  N  I  N  G                    RNING
49 51 06 11 26
```

"Lieutenant Lewis suggested, Sir, and we're agreed it's a good idea, that Message One will first be transmitted from the *Sunfish*, and then, when the radio stations here and at Pearl hear it (they will be alerted to listen for it), it will be repeated by them. The greater strength of their signals will more or less guarantee reception by Fertig."

"If Fertig happens to be listening," McCoy said.

"The possibility of course exists, Ken, that they will not be listening," Pluto said. "But I think they will be."

"And if not?" Pickering asked, handing Stecker Message Two. "If you don't get acknowledgment?"

"We'll keep trying—the stations at Pearl Harbor and here, not the *Sunfish*—on an hourly basis, until midnight," Pluto said. "I really think we'll get through."

"And if you do?" Pickering asked.

"Two hours after we get acknowledgment, we send Message Two. That gives them two hours to figure out what the Marine Hymn substitution is."

"Speaking of which," Stecker said. "Will somebody please translate this for me?"

"This is where it really gets far out, Colonel," McCoy said.

"Who is 'Lille'? What is this?" Stecker asked.

"The Marine Hymn substitution code doesn't have a 'K' or an 'O,' Colonel," Moore said. "We are using an 'L' when a 'K' is needed—it's the next letter, and a consonant. Where an 'O' is required, we are using a 'U.' We think the substitution will be self-evident."

"Right," McCoy said sarcastically. "The substitution will be self-evident. These guys are hiding out in the boondocks, and we want to play word games with them."

"If you can't handle the whiskey, McCoy, leave it alone," Pickering snapped. "What we're trying to do here is keep you alive."

He was immediately sorry, not because of his own words (they needed to be said), but because of the look of approval on Captain Macklin's face.

"Message Two, Colonel," Moore said, "reads 'Killer And Erny Will Eat Beans Thirty Miles South This Morning.' "

" 'Eat Beans'? What does that mean? South of what?" Stecker asked. "This doesn't make any sense to me."

"You weren't here, Jack, when Lewis and I went over the charts," Pickering said. "Where's that chart, Pluto?"

"Right here, Sir," Pluto said, and pushed the chart across the table.

"Show him, Lewis," Pickering said.

"Aye, aye, Sir," Lewis said. "Colonel, I suggested to General Pickering that the best place to try to land McCoy and party would be on the east coast of Mindanao."

"I've sailed those interior waters, Jack," Pickering said. "They are not among the best-charted waters in the world. We don't want the *Sunfish* running—submerged—into an uncharted reef or shoal. The waters to the east of Mindanao are safest."

"You'll notice, Colonel," Lewis said, pointing, "the subsurface terrain here. The Philippine Trench, with depths to about 9,000 fathoms, is only about seventy-five miles offshore. The 6,000-fathom curve is sixty miles offshore; the 4,000 curve thirty-five miles offshore; the 2,000 twenty miles offshore; and the 200-fathom curve runs almost along the shoreline."

"I don't know what that means," Stecker said.

"According to Lewis, Jack, a submarine skipper is perfectly happy when he has a hundred fathoms under his keel," Pickering said. "That's six hundred feet. In my experience, and from what Lewis tells me, in the Navy's, when you have fathom curve lines like these, there is little chance of encountering an underwater obstacle."

"Even in a submerged submarine?" Stecker asked.

"We have a two-hundred-fathom depth all along here," Pickering replied. "Twelve hundred feet. If a sub runs at three hundred feet, he's got nine hundred feet under his keel."

"OK," Stecker said.

"Sir, if you will look here," Lewis said, pointing at the chart again, "you will see the two-hundred-fathom curve just about touches the shore at this point, which is thirty miles south of a village fortunately called 'Boston.' "

"Boston? Beans, right?" Stecker asked.

"That's the idea, Sir," Lewis said. "The *Sunfish* can sail, submerged, to within a couple of hundred yards of the coastline and still have at least a hundred fathoms under her keel."

"A couple of hundred yards?" Stecker asked doubtfully. "How are you going to keep from running into the shoreline?"

"SONAR, Sir," Lewis said. "It stands for Sound Navigation and Ranging. The *Sunfish* has it aboard, Sir. She'll know when she's getting in close."

"And you think Fertig will understand this Boston–beans connection?" Stecker asked dubiously.

"We tested that, too, Sir," Pluto replied.

"How?" Pickering asked.

"McCoy and I went to the SWPOA Officers' Club," Sessions said. "We asked ten officers at the bar the first thing that came to mind when they heard the word 'beans.' We got six 'Boston' or 'Boston baked'; and one each 'lima,' 'snap,' and 'navy.' "

"You really did your research, didn't you?" Pickering said, chuckling.

"That's nine," Stecker said. "You said you asked ten officers."

"Now that you mention it, Colonel," McCoy said, "we also got one 'fart.' "

"Six out of ten responses with a Boston connection, Sir," Pluto said, very quickly, "seems more than reasonable. I mean, I think we can presume Fertig will immediately discount 'lima,' 'snap,' and 'navy.' "

"One fart, huh?" Pickering said, and laughed.

"What if you can't get an acknowledgment from Fertig?" Stecker asked.

"There's some argument about that, Sir," Pluto said. "One being that the *Sunfish* should repeat the operation the next day, and the day after that, if necessary. The other argument is to put McCoy and party ashore just before daylight anyway, and attempt to contact Fertig by other means."

"Argument Two came from McCoy, right?" Pickering said.

"Yes, Sir," McCoy said.

"All right, McCoy," Pickering said. "Tell us why you're not happy with this."

"The more complicated something is, the more things can go wrong," McCoy said. "There's too much 'if,' 'if,' and 'if' in this for me. I'd much prefer to do this simply. The four of us go ashore without doing anything to make the Japanese nervous. We find Fertig . . ."

"How are you going to do that?"

"Zimmerman says that the Filipinos will know where he is, and I agree with him. And they will know we've come ashore."

Pickering nodded. "Where is he, by the way?"

"He kept falling asleep, so I sent him home," McCoy replied, and went on. "We'll have good radios and a real code with us. So, as soon as we find Fertig, we get in direct touch with the submarine. It's likely we can do it in five days. I think the sub can hang around that long, surfacing only for a few minutes to listen to the radio. Then we tell the sub where and when to meet us."

Pickering shrugged.

"This is not a democracy, and this is not going to be decided by a vote, but I'd like to hear what everybody thinks about this," he said, and pointed at Koffler. "Starting with you, Steve. We'll work our way up the ranks."

"General, I'm with McCoy," Koffler said. "I don't want a bunch of excited Japs running around looking for us, particularly since we won't know where to hide. And these messages are—no offense, Major, or you either, Mr. Moore—a little screwy."

He is just a boy, not old enough to vote. But on the other hand, he knows more about keeping alive on a Japanese-occupied island than anybody in the room.

"I guess you're next, John, aren't you?" Pickering said.

"I disagree with Steve, about the messages being screwy," Moore said. "Fertig, and the people with him, are desperate. Their minds will be at a high pitch. They're intelligent. I think they will almost immediately comprehend the messages. The great unknown, which worries me, is how quickly the Japanese will be able to decipher both messages. And what that will mean. Steve's 'a bunch of excited Japanese running around' worries me, even if they can't make the Boston bean connection."

That worries me, too.

"Which of you is senior?" Pickering asked, pointing to Lewis and Macklin.

"I believe I am, Sir," Lewis said.

"That makes you next, Captain Macklin," Pickering said.

"Sir, when I'm out of my depth, I try not to offer an opinion," Macklin said in a flat voice.

"Let me put it this way, then. How do you feel about going ashore without our having made contact with Fertig?"

"I'm a Marine officer, General. I'll go where I'm told to go."

He has no interest in any of this. Why is he disinterested? There are two answers to that. Either he has closed his mind to the possibility that he's going to find himself paddling up to an enemy-held shore in a rubber boat, or, and I think this is what it is, he doesn't think he's going.

I can't believe he'd try to miss the boat on this. But stranger things have happened.

"Lewis?"

"General, since I'm not going ashore, I'd rather not offer an opinion," Chambers D. Lewis said.

"Who's right? Pluto or McCoy?" Pickering asked impatiently.

"I would have to align myself with Major Hon, Sir," Lewis said.

"OK. You're next, Ed."

"I think I'd go with Koffler and McCoy, Sir," Sessions said.

"Jack?" Pickering said. "We already know what Pluto thinks."

"McCoy," Stecker said.

Pickering nodded.

This places me in a very awkward position. The people I admire most in this room disagree with me, including the only people who know what it is to be on an enemy-held island, and to have—what did Koffler say?—"a bunch of excited Japs running around looking for them." But they're wrong.

If you put a box around Mindanao, it would be 450 miles on a side. We don't know where Fertig is inside that box, and we certainly can't risk asking him where he is until we deliver to him a code the Japanese can't break in an hour. And if McCoy and his people go ashore and are never heard from again, hell will freeze over before we can mount another mission. MacArthur will consider himself vindicated, and Donovan will gleefully announce that if he had been in charge, the operation would have worked.

"This is what we're going to do," Pickering announced. "We will proceed with what Pluto and Moore have come up with. The *Sunfish* will surface thirty miles south of Boston one half hour after nightfall 23 December. Message One will be sent at that time. *Sunfish* will wait ten minutes for acknowledgment. If no acknowledgment is received, she will submerge. She will resurface at hourly intervals, ten minutes past the hour, the last surfacing to be at 0010 24 December . . ."

"That's Christmas Eve!" Captain Macklin said, shocked.

"Merry Christmas, Sergeant Koffler," McCoy said.

". . . which is, of course, Christmas Eve," Pickering said. "Whether or not there is acknowledgment, the *Sunfish* will surface again thirty minutes before sunrise—which will occur at five twenty-nine—and off-load McCoy, Zimmerman, Koffler, and Captain Macklin. They will carry with them only personal small arms, communications radios, the codes, and a token amount of gold and medicine. The *Sunfish* will remain on the surface until there is word that the landing party has made it safely to the beach . . ."

"Or until a Jap airplane starts dropping bombs on it," McCoy said, "whichever comes first."

"That's quite enough, thank you, from you, Mr. McCoy," Pickering said, but he was unable to restrain a smile. "As I was saying before Charley McCarthy here ran off at the mouth, the *Sunfish* will remain on the surface until the landing party is ashore.'' (A highly popular radio program of the era featured ventriloquist Edgar Bergen, father of actress Candice Bergen, and his dummy, Charley McCarthy.) ''She will then submerge, to resurface for five minutes at two-hour intervals, ten minutes past the hour, during the daylight hours, and from thirty minutes after sunset until thirty minutes before sunrise for a seven-day period. If contact has not been established during that period, she will return to Pearl Harbor. If there is contact between the landing party and the *Sunfish,* or between Fertig, somehow, and the *Sunfish,* we'll play that by ear.''

He looked around the table.

''Any comments, Mr. McCoy?''

McCoy raised both hands palm upward.

''Permission to speak, Sir?'' Captain Robert B. Macklin said.

''Certainly.''

''May I ask, Sir, how you came to the 23, 24 December dates?''

''Show him, Jack,'' Pickering ordered.

Colonel Stecker passed to Captain Macklin a sheet of typewriter paper.

```
T O P    S E C R E T


SPECIAL CHANNEL
FROM: CINCPAC HAWAII
1210 9DEC42


TO: SUPREME HEADQUARTERS SWPOA BRISBANE
EYES ONLY—BRIG GEN FLEMING PICKERING USMC


DUPLICATION FORBIDDEN
ORIGINAL TO BE DESTROYED AFTER ENCRYPTION AND TRANSMITTAL


FOLLOWING PERSONAL FROM CINCPAC TO BRIG GEN PICKERING USMC


DEAR FLEMING:


(1) HAVE BEEN INFORMED SUNFISH WILL COMPLETE FUELING AND
PROVISIONING ESPIRITU SANTO BY 1200 HOURS 10 DEC 1942.


(2) OFFICER COMMANDING NAVAL AIR TRANSPORT COMMAND
BRISBANE HAS BEEN DIRECTED TO MAKE CORONADO PB2Y AIRCRAFT
AVAILABLE TO YOU FOR TRAVEL ESPIRITU SANTO ON ARRIVAL
BRISBANE ETA 0500 10 DEC 1942
```

```
(3) PLEASE PASS TO ALL HANDS ON BEHALF MYSELF AND REAR
ADMIRAL DANIEL J. WAGAM GODSPEED GOOD SAILING AND GOOD
LUCK.

BEST PERSONAL REGARDS CHESTER

END PERSONAL FROM ADM NIMITZ BRIG TO GEN PICKERING

BY DIRECTION:

WAGAM REARADM USN

T O P    S E C R E T
```

"It's about 1,300 nautical miles from here to Espíritu Santo," Pickering said. "Say, seven hours in a Coronado. If it arrives here when it's expected, at 0500 tomorrow, I think we can reasonably expect to get in the air by noon. That would put us into Espíritu no later than 1800. We should be able to load everything aboard the *Sunfish* in an hour or so, and we should be able to sail at first light the day after tomorrow."

" '*We?*' " Colonel Stecker asked warily. "I thought we discussed that."

"Slip of the tongue, Jack. The *Sunfish* will sail, with me standing on the pier, at first light the day after tomorrow, which will be the eleventh. It's 3,200 nautical miles from Espíritu Santo to Boston. Using Lewis's ballpark figures that the *Sunfish* can cruise on the surface at fifteen knots, she should be able to make Mindanao in ten days. That would be the twenty-first. To give us a little slack, I've scheduled her to be off Mindanao on the twenty-third."

He looked around the table.

"Any questions?"

"Sir," Captain Robert B. Macklin said.

"Yes?"

"Nothing, Sir. Excuse me."

"If you've got something to say, Captain," McCoy said, not very pleasantly, "let's hear it."

"Very well, Mr. McCoy," Macklin said. "Since you have the responsibility for this mission, I was wondering, if you have considered my physical condition, how that might adversely affect the mission."

"I watched you paddle the rubber boat, Captain. It looked to me like you could handle that without much trouble. What exactly is your physical condition?"

"Macklin," Colonel Stecker said, even less pleasantly, "if you'd like, we can run you past a doctor and get an official report on your condition."

"I was only thinking of the mission, Colonel," Macklin said. "But I do have one question, Sir."

"Let's have it."

"Has the OSS been kept up on how the mission is proceeding?"

"No," Pickering said. "They haven't."

"Do I have your permission to do so, Sir?"

"I don't see why not. . . ."

"Why don't we just tell them when we come back?" McCoy said.

For some reason, McCoy doesn't like the idea of Macklin getting in touch with the OSS. I can't see what harm it would do, but I think I should indulge McCoy.

"Don't worry about the OSS, Captain Macklin," Pickering said. "As soon as the *Sunfish* puts out to sea, I'll see that Secretary Knox is notified. I'm sure he'll pass the word to Mr. Donovan."

"Thank you, Sir," Captain Robert B. Macklin said.

[TWO]
Water Lily Cottage
Brisbane, Australia
2305 Hours 11 December 1942

First Lieutenant Kenneth R. McCoy, USMCR, pulled the sheet of paper from the typewriter, laid it on the dining-room table, stood up, took a Waterman's fountain pen from his shirt pocket, and scrawled his name at the bottom. Then he picked it up and read what had taken him the better part of an hour to write.

Brisbane, Australia
9 December 1942

Dear Ernie:

Ed Sessions is going to the States the day after tomorrow, and has promised to carry this with him. This will be the last letter for a while, as I've got a job to do someplace where there isn't mail service. That means you don't have to write, either, as I wouldn't get it anyhow.

I can't tell you where I'm going, and I don't know when I'll be back. Please don't put Ed on the spot by trying to get him to tell you. I can't see the necessity for all the secrecy, but Ed is an intelligence type, and they're all a little hysterical about secrets. If they could, intelligence types would classify the telephone book TOP SECRET.

I'll be taking that Episcopal cross, or whatever it's called, you sent here with Ed with me. And the people going with me are first rate Marines.

Actually, I'm sort of looking forward to it. All those native girls in grass skirts and nothing else doing the hula hula, and eating roasted pigs with apples in their mouths, etcetera.

I was thinking a while ago that I met you 20 November last year. That's just a little over a year, even if it seems like much longer. And I remembered that saying, "It's better to have loved and lost than not have loved at all."

I guess what I'm trying to say is that if something goes wrong, not that I think it's going to, I really think I'm still ahead of the game. I never thought I would be lucky enough to get to know somebody like you, much less have you as my girl friend, and to even think that maybe you like me half as much as I like you.

But, let's face it, things sometimes do go wrong. If that happens, what I want you to do is get on with your life. I'm really grateful we had our thirteen months. If it turns out that I do find myself sitting on a cloud playing a harp, that's the way the ball bounced, at least it will have happened doing something I'm good at, and that has to be done. A lot of people get killed doing stupid things like getting hit by a bus walking across a street.

I know Pick will be around for you if something goes wrong, and to tell you the truth, if I had to pick a husband for you, he would be at the head of the list.

Thanks for everything, Baby.

Love,

Ken

He very carefully folded the letter in thirds, found an envelope, and wrote "K.R.McCoy, 1/LT USMCR" in the upper-left-hand corner, "Miss Ernestine Sage, Personal" in the center, inserted the letter, licked the adhesive flap with his tongue, and carefully sealed the envelope.

He looked at the envelope, tapped it against his hand, and exhaled audibly. His eyes fell on the cupboard. He walked to it, opened it and took out a bottle of Famous Grouse, put it to his lips, and took a healthy swallow.

Then he walked out of the dining room, across the living room, and down the corridor to Ed Sessions's room. There was a crack of light under the door. McCoy knocked, waited for a response, and then opened the door and went inside.

Sessions, in pajamas, was about to get into bed. He saw the envelope in McCoy's hand.

"For Ernie?"

McCoy nodded and handed it to him.

"Thanks, Ed."

Sessions shrugged. "You all right, Ken?"

"Yeah, sure," McCoy said, and then asked, "You want to go somewhere and get a drink?"

"Don't tell me there's nothing here?"

"I want to get out of here. I've been in that goddamned dining room since half past four this afternoon."

The last thing in the world I want to do is go somewhere and get a drink; I was also in that goddamned dining room for hours. But he really wants some company.

And this is the first time since I've known him that McCoy has ever asked me for something. I suspect it's one of the few times that Killer McCoy has ever asked anybody, except Ernie, to keep him company.

"Having a drink, or three, is the best suggestion I've heard all day," Ed Sessions said. "Have we got wheels?"

"There's a jeep outside."

"Be right with you."

"God is in his heaven, and all is right with the world," Ed Sessions said as he walked up to Lieutenant Chambers D. Lewis, USN, at the bar of the SWPOA Company Grade Bachelor Officers' Quarters. "The U.S. Navy is nobly doing its duty, holding the bar in place with its elbows."

"I didn't expect to see you two in here," Lewis said. He did not seem especially happy to see them.

I think he's had more than a couple, Sessions decided.

"We're slumming," Sessions said.

"Actually, I was sort of looking for you," McCoy said.

"Oh, were you?" Lewis asked, somewhat coldly. "And are you going to tell me why, Mr. McCoy?"

The very careful pronunciation and exaggerated courtesy of the drunk, Sessions thought, *the belligerent drunk. Christ, why did McCoy decide to come here?*

"Well, you're both a swabbie and an expert on submarines," McCoy said. "I wanted to—"

He was interrupted by the barmaid.

"Gentlemen?"

"Have you got any scotch whiskey?"

"You just got here, right? Otherwise you wouldn't ask."

"Are you trying to tell me you don't have any scotch?"

"In our last shipment from Class VI, there were three bottles. First they take care of the big brass. Then they take care of the field-grade brass. Then they take care of the sergeants. The only people they take care of after us is the corporals and privates, and they aren't authorized any kind of hard whiskey. So what we have is rum, gin, and brandy."

"In that case, my friend and I will have a glass of ice water," McCoy said. "And while we're at it, give the sailor a glass of ice water, too."

The barmaid's shrug indicated that the strange behavior of Yanks no longer came as a surprise to her. She produced three glasses with ice in them, and a stainless-steel pitcher of water.

"Thank you," McCoy said, and produced a quart bottle of Famous Grouse from a cloth bag. "Say when," he ordered, as he began to pour into the first of the glasses.

When he had finished, and water was added, he raised his glass.

"To the United States Navy Submarine Corps, or whatever they call it."

"I'll drink to that," Sessions said.

"Are you two trying to be cute?" Lewis asked.

"No. Not at all," McCoy said.

Lewis took a sip of his scotch.

"You *stole* this from General Pickering, right?" he asked.

"He gave it to me," McCoy said. "His words were I 'was free to help myself to whatever I thought I needed.' Which is more or less what I wanted to talk to you about."

"You found me," Lewis said, with enough of an unpleasant tone in his voice to get through to McCoy. McCoy looked at him curiously.

"Well, I figured you know how things are on submarines, and I know how chickenshit the Navy is about taking booze aboard—"

"You want to take some of that with you?" Lewis interrupted. "Is that what you're after?"

"I was thinking that if I'd been in the boondocks as long as Fertig and his people, a stiff shot of good whiskey would probably taste pretty good."

"I don't think anyone is going to question anything you want to take aboard the *Sunfish,* Mr. McCoy."

"Or the plane from here to Espíritu Santo?"

"Or the plane. You are wrapped, through me, in the protective mantle of CINCPAC himself."

"I was thinking about a case."

"You want to take a *case* of scotch whiskey with you?"

"Why not?"

"Indeed, why not? May I suggest that you wrap it up? So it won't be so obvious that you consider yourself above complying with regulations?"

Sessions looked at McCoy and saw there was no smile on his face, and that his eyes had turned into ice. And then McCoy relaxed, as if he had just realized that Lewis was drunk and should not be held responsible.

"That's already been done," McCoy said. "In some of Koffler's plastic."

"Then I see no problem at all," Lewis said.

"Thanks," McCoy said.

"Would you like to tell me what's bothering you, Lewis?" Sessions asked.

"It shows, does it?" Lewis replied. "That something is bothering me?"

"Has it to do with Macklin?"

"What do you think? I think it's despicable, what you did to him. I never thought I would see a Naval officer so humiliated."

"Am I missing something here?" McCoy asked.

"McCoy doesn't know," Sessions said.

"I don't know what?" McCoy asked.

"Then I hastily offer my most humble and sincere apologies, Mr. McCoy," Lewis said. "Until just now I thought it was your idea."

"What the hell are you talking about?" McCoy said, and the ice was back in his voice and eyes.

"It was General Pickering's idea," Sessions said. "McCoy didn't know anything about it."

"Oh, for Christ's sake!" McCoy said. "What didn't I know about, Ed?"

"Hart showed up here, Mr. McCoy—"

"Knock off that 'Mr. McCoy' shit," McCoy interrupted. "I don't think you're funny."

"Five minutes after Captain Macklin and I got here, *Ken,*" Lewis said, "Lieutenant Hart showed up here. He told Captain Macklin he had orders to stay with him until we were picked up to go to the terminal tomorrow morning, and that Captain Macklin couldn't leave the BOQ, or use the telephone, without Colonel Stecker's express permission."

"Shit," McCoy said. "I was hoping the bastard would go over the hill."

"I think Pickering was one step ahead of you on that," Sessions said. "Right after the meeting broke up and Lewis and Macklin left—and you went to take a leak—Pickering told Moore to relieve Hart in the dungeon; then he told Stecker to call Hart and tell him to go to the BOQ, sit on Macklin, and see that he was at the terminal at 0900 tomorrow."

"*You* don't really think Bob Macklin would have purposely missed the plane, do you?" Lewis challenged Sessions.

McCoy drained his drink, and made another one. "The bartender has just gone off duty," he said. "If you guys want any more, pour your own."

"Because he's Annapolis, you mean?" Sessions replied. "Yes, I do. That sleazy bastard is capable of anything. Including missing a shipment," Sessions said.

"I was sort of hoping he would," McCoy said matter-of-factly. "Christ knows, I don't want to take him with me. Actually I was *counting* on him figuring out some way to get out of going. I wrote my girl that I was taking *good* Marines with me."

Sessions chuckled.

"And once again the wise general officer outwits the junior officer," he said.

"I don't suppose it would do any good if I said I think you two are giving Macklin the short end of the stick?" Lewis asked.

"I trust him about half as far as I can throw him," McCoy said. "Pickering said he hopes I don't have to shoot him, but he didn't tell me I can't. Does that answer your question?"

I wonder, Sessions thought, *if Lewis is capable, drunk or sober, of fully understanding that; that both Pickering and McCoy were seriously discussing the benefits and drawbacks of eliminating, by shooting, an obstacle to the mission who happens to be named Macklin.*

"Has it occurred to you, Ken, that there are people who aren't like you, people who are afraid?" Lewis said, his tone of voice now conciliatory and reasonable.

"What the hell is that supposed to mean?" McCoy said.

"I'm trying to suggest that Bob Macklin is afraid of what's liable to happen on this mission. He's trying hard to get himself under control, and if he hasn't, that's not really his fault. Some people seem to be born with courage, but some people aren't."

"And you don't think I'm scared? Just between you and me, I'm scared shitless about this mission," McCoy said, and then, his voice turning incredulous, "Did you really think I think it's a lot of fun?"

"You don't act as if you're afraid."

"An officer's first duty is to take care of his men. Don't tell me it's any different on a submarine."

"Meaning what?" Lewis challenged.

"If I look scared, then Zimmerman and Koffler get scared, OK? The one thing I can't afford is to have Zimmerman and Koffler thinking they're in the deep shit because their officer is pissing his pants." He looked at Lewis for a moment, and then warmed to his subject. "Or are you trying to tell me the officers on a submarine don't break their asses to make sure the white hats don't see how scared they are?''

"What makes you so sure submarine officers are frightened?"

"They're either scared or mentally retarded," McCoy said. "Don't bull-shit me, Lewis. I've been on two of the goddamned things. The worst part of the Makin raid was getting there and back, in that steel underwater coffin. And the worst part of the Buka Operation was getting there in a submarine. When I saw the Gooney-bird coming in to take us off of Buka, the first thing I thought was, 'Thank Christ, I don't have to get back in that fucking submarine.' ''

"Some of them aren't frightened," Lewis argued.

"OK. In any group of ten officers, you can count on two being stupid. You can also count on those two getting you in trouble. But you were scared. You're too smart *not* to have been scared," McCoy said. "But you were obviously a good enough officer to keep the white hats from seeing it. Otherwise, they would have thrown your ass out of the submarines.''

"The point Mr. McCoy is making, Lieutenant Lewis," Sessions said, "is that what he has against Captain Macklin is not that Captain Macklin has far less then the normal issue of testicles, but that Captain Macklin considers his first duty is to take care of Captain Macklin, and fuck anybody else.''

"That's a pretty harsh judgment, wouldn't you say?''

"I associate myself fully, Lieutenant Lewis, with Mr. McCoy's somewhat obscene, *but right on the fucking money,* assessment of Captain Macklin. I've seen the sonofabitch at work.''

"What would you two say if I told you that I never spent a minute in a submarine that I wasn't afraid?'' Lewis asked, and was immediately horrified to hear what he had blurted.

Neither McCoy nor Sessions seemed surprised to hear the confession.

"Did you let the white hats see it?'' McCoy asked.

"I hope not,'' Lewis said.

"Take it from me, you didn't. If you had, the other officers would have seen to it that you never went down in one again.''

Jesus Christ, Lieutenant Chambers D. Lewis, USN, thought. *Can he be right?*

"May I ask a question, gentlemen?'' Sessions asked. "What the hell are we arguing about?''

"Who knows?'' McCoy said. "Who cares? Slide the bottle over here, will you?''

[THREE]
Office of the Director
Office of Strategic Services
National Institutes of Health Building
Washington, D.C.
0930 Hours 13 December 1942

What could have been a smile crossed the lips of L. Stanford Morrissette, Deputy Director, Special Projects, Office of Strategic Services, as he read the message contained in the manila folder with TOP SECRET stamped across it.

"One moment, please, Colonel, if you don't mind," he said to Colonel F. L. Rickabee, Deputy Chief, USMC Office of Management Analysis, "I believe this should be brought to the attention of the Director."

"My time is your time, Mr. Morrissette," Rickabee said.

Morrissette picked up the receiver of a red telephone—one of three telephones on his desk—and dialed 0.

"Mo, Bill," he said. "Colonel Rickabee, of the Marine Corps, is in my office with something I thought you'd like to see. Can you spare us a minute?"

The reply of the Director was obviously in the affirmative, for Morrissette stood up as he replaced the red handset in its cradle and gestured toward the door.

"He's right down the corridor, Colonel," he said. "I think I should warn you the Director thinks the savages of yore, who killed messengers delivering bad news, had the right idea."

"In my line of work, you get used to that," Rickabee said.

Morrissette opened Colonel William J. Donovan's door without knocking and waved Rickabee in ahead of him.

"Colonel Donovan," he said. "I believe you know Colonel Rickabee?"

"Yes, of course," Donovan said, rising behind his desk and putting out his hand. "I see the chickens, Fritz. Well deserved, and long overdue."

"Thank you, Sir."

"What have you got for me?"

"This, Sir. Captain Haughton, Secretary Knox's assistant, hand-carried this to me this morning, with instructions to make it available to you."

He handed him the manila folder stamped TOP SECRET.

Donovan waved the two of them into the two red leather chairs in front of his desk, sat down, and opened the folder.

TOP SECRET

SUPREME HEADQUARTERS SWPOA 1515 HOURS 11DEC42
EYES ONLY—THE SECRETARY OF THE NAVY WASH DC
        COMMANDER-IN-CHIEF PACIFIC PEARL HARBOR TH

VIA SPECIAL CHANNEL

DUPLICATION FORBIDDEN
ORIGINAL TO BE DESTROYED AFTER ENCRYPTION AND TRANSMITTAL

(1) RADIO FROM BRIGGEN FLEMING PICKERING USMCR REPORTS SSN
SUNFISH DEPARTED ESPIRITU SANTO 0505 LOCALTIME 11DEC1942
CARRYING ABOARD FERTIG CONTACT TEAM. FURTHER DETAILS WILL
BE FURNISHED AS AVAILABLE. SUPREME COMMANDER SWPOA HAS
BEEN ADVISED.

(2) BRIGGEN PICKERING DESIRES CONTENTS THIS MESSAGE BE
FURNISHED COL F. L. RICKABEE USMC OFFICE OF MANAGEMENT
ANALYSIS IMMEDIATELY AND STATES HE HAS NO OBJECTION TO THIS
INFORMATION BEING MADE AVAILABLE TO DIRECTOR, OFFICE OF
STRATEGIC SERVICES:

A. PERSONNEL OF FERTIG CONTACT TEAM ARE AS FOLLOWS:

    MCCOY, KENNETH R FIRST LIEUTENANT USMCR 489657
OFFICER-IN-COMMAND
    ZIMMERMAN, ERNEST W GUNNERY SERGEANT 18909 USMC
DEPUTY COMMANDER
    KOFFLER, STEPHEN M STAFF SERGEANT USMC 504883 USMC
RADIO OPERATOR

B. IN ADDITION, BRIGGEN PICKERING STATED SUNFISH ALSO CARRIED
ABOARD LIEUTENANT CHAMBERS D. LEWIS, USN, AS PERSONAL
REPRESENTATIVE ADM NIMITZ. LEWIS WILL NOT GO ASHORE.

C. IN ADDITION, BRIGGEN PICKERING STATED CAPTAIN ROBERT B.
MACKLIN, USMC, OF OSS QUOTE OPERATION WINDMILL ENDQUOTE
WITH WHICH HE IS NOT FAMILIAR IS ALSO ABOARD SUNFISH AND
MAY GO ASHORE AS OBSERVER. THE DECISION WILL BE MADE AT
TIME OF LANDING BY LIEUTENANT MCCOY BASED ON HIS ASSESSMENT
AT THAT TIME OF MACKLINS POTENTIAL VALUE AND/OR THREAT TO
MISSION.

D. CAPTAIN EDWARD SESSIONS, USMC WILL DEPART BRISBANE FOR
WASH DC VIA PEARL HARBOR AND SAN FRANCISCO 0900 12DEC42
AND IS PREPARED TO BRIEF INTERESTED PERSONNEL ON ARRIVAL.

BY DIRECTION BRIGGEN PICKERING USMCR

HON MAJOR SIGNAL CORPS USA

T O P   S E C R E T

Donovan smiled as he began to read the message. By the time he was finished, the smile was visibly strained.

"First rate, Fritz," he said. "We're moving."

"Yes, Sir."

"This lieutenant, McCoy. And the others. Are you familiar with them?"

"Yes, Sir. They're assigned to us."

Donovan waited until he was sure that he had gotten all he was going to get from Rickabee without prompting, then made a *come on* gesture with his right hand.

"Lieutenant McCoy and Gunny Zimmerman made the Makin Island raid with Captain Roosevelt, Sir. Sergeant Koffler spent some time on Buka with the Australian Coastwatchers, Sir. They're experienced in this type of operation."

"I felt sure General Pickering would select the best available men," Donovan said.

"I think he did, Sir," Rickabee replied.

"You were not familiar with 'OPERATION WINDMILL,' Fritz?"

"No, Sir."

"Our fault, obviously. Sorry. We should have made sure you, and General Pickering, were brought in on that. It is, of course, simply the name we assigned to the Fertig operation."

"Yes, Sir."

"I would be grateful, when Captain Sessions arrives, if he could brief Mr. Morrissette and myself."

"I'll see to it that he does, Sir."

"Have you got anything else for me, Fritz?"

"No, Sir. That's about it."

"Well, thank you for bringing this so promptly to my attention."

"My pleasure, Sir."

"Well, then, Fritz, I won't keep you. Thank you very much."

"Yes, Sir."

"Mo, stick around a minute, will you?" Donovan said.

"Thank you, Colonel Rickabee," Morrissette said, and offered his hand.

"Good morning, gentlemen," Rickabee said.

Donovan waited until Rickabee had closed the door after him and then turned to Morrissette.

"What would you say are the chances that the President has already seen, or will soon see, that goddamn special channel?"

"One hundred percent, Bill. If Frank Knox doesn't show it—hasn't already shown it—to him, I'm sure he'll get it back-channel. Nimitz to Leahy to FDR."

"I don't like to be sandbagged like that. I'll burn Pickering's ass for this."

"For what?

"What do you mean, for what? Did you read that?"

"General Pickering, in compliance with his orders, is making every reasonable effort to include our guy on the mission. He's on the submarine. If he doesn't go ashore, it will be because the officer in charge decides that his presence would pose a threat to the mission."

"Our guy is a captain. This McCoy is only a lieutenant. Our guy should be the officer-in-command."

"This one made the Makin Island raid with Roosevelt's son," Morrissette said. "And if you think Pickering hasn't made sure that FDR knows that, you're underestimating him again."

"Meaning?"

"You'll have a hard time convincing FDR that Pickering's sandbagging you by putting this lieutenant in charge. This lieutenant is a Marine Raider, and Marine Raiders generally—and especially one who was on the Makin raid with young Roosevelt—are the apples of FDR's eye."

"You don't really expect me to take this lying down?"

"Are you asking for advice?"

"Yeah. Advise me."

"Make your peace with Pickering."

Donovan looked at him for a long moment.

"Thank you, Mo," he said. "Is there anything else?"

Morrissette shook his head, no.

XV

[ONE]
Headquarters, U.S. Forces in the Philippines
Davao Oriental Province
Mindanao, Commonwealth of the Philippines
1845 Hours 23 December 1942

It was raining, and Captain James B. Weston, USFIP, stumbled while climbing—and nearly slipped off—the rain-slick ladderlike stairs leading to the quarters of Brigadier General Wendell W. Fertig. He managed not to drop his Thompson submachine gun, but his campaign hat fell into the darkness, and he had to climb back down the stairs and look for it on his hands and knees under the house.

Finally, he gained the porch and walked down it to the door. Hanging over the door as a blackout device was a piece of canvas—reclaimed by United States Forces in the Philippines after six months of service to the Japanese on a captured U.S. Army ton-and-a-half truck.

Someone remembered reading that the light of a candle could be seen from an aircraft on a dark night for seven miles. It sounded a bit incredible, but Headquarters USFIP was in no position to put their incredulity to the test, and General Fertig had ordered blackout curtains over all doors and windows after nightfall, whenever lanterns or candles were alight inside.

Weston pushed aside the blackout curtain and stepped inside. The only light came from one kerosene lamp and three homemade lamps consisting of burning wicks in the necks of Coca-Cola bottles filled with coconut oil; but Weston's eyes, accustomed to the absolute blackness of the night, took a moment to adjust.

After they adjusted, he saw General Fertig behind his desk, and two of the three members of the USFIP Signal Section—Second Lieutenant Robert Ball (signal officer) and Sergeant Ignacio LaMadrid (chief radio operator)—sitting on rattan chairs. Ball and LaMadrid held Coca-Cola bottles containing the getting-better-all-the-time USFIP brewed beer, and four bottles of beer, three of them empty, were on Fertig's desk.

The cocktail hour, Weston thought, *to which I was not invited.*
"You sent for me, Sir?" he asked.

"As our intelligence officer, and, of course, as a Marine, Captain Weston," Fertig said. "I'm sure you are a veritable cornucopia of arcane information vis-à-vis Naval lore."

"Sir?"

I don't think anybody but The General was invited to his cocktail hour.

"Lieutenant Ball, Sergeant LaMadrid, and myself have all been wondering what the Navy expects to find in heaven," Fertig said.

Is he plastered?

"I don't think I understand, Sir."

"I'm disappointed," Fertig said. "I was hoping the answer to that intriguing conundrum would immediately occur to you."

"Sorry, Sir, I just don't understand."

"What occurred to me was that what a sailor would hope to find would be a bevy of naked beauties and real, cold beer, but that doesn't seem to fit. Show that to Captain Weston, would you, please, Lieutenant Ball?"

Ball handed Weston a sheet of paper, its carbon-paper characters hard to read in the dim light.

```
1234567890123456789012345
LUDMILLAZHIVKOVZANESVILLE

U  S  E  W  H
02 20 19 04 10
A  T  N  A  V
17 09 18 14 21
E  E  W  I  L
19 25 04 05 23
L  F  I  N  D
24 09 11 18 03
I  N  H  E  A
22 18 10 19 08
V  E  N  A  S
12 19 18 08 20
S  I  M  S  U
20 05 04 20 02
B  C  O  D  E
09 13 14 03 25
```

"That came in about an hour ago," Lieutenant Ball said.

"A strong signal, Sir," Sergeant LaMadrid amplified, "and it was repeated, two, three times, from both Australia and Pearl Harbor."

"Use what Nave—*Navy*—" Weston read haltingly, "will find in heaven as sim sub code. 'Use what Navy will find in heaven'? What the hell does that mean?"

Jesus, that sounds familiar, Jim Weston thought, and then felt a chill.

" 'If the Army and the Navy,' " he intoned softly, " 'ever look on heaven's scenes, *they will find the streets are guarded by United States Marines.*' "

"Bingo!" Lieutenant Ball said. "That has to be it."

"The Marine Hymn," Weston said. "How long will it take you to decrypt the message using that?"

"About ten minutes," Ball said. *"After* we get the message."

"That's all you've got? You don't have the message?"

"That's all we have," Sergeant LaMadrid said.

"I'm sure there will be more," Fertig said. "And while we're waiting, Captain Weston, would you care for a beer?"

"Yes, thank you, Sir."

The Signal Officer of USFIP, the Intelligence Officer, his deputy, and the Commanding General had considerably more trouble decrypting the number blocks of Message Two when it arrived two hours later.

```
06 07 06 08 03

18 23 36 40 45

49 51 04 05 06

07 08 15 23 38

33 39 43 51 53

01 02 06 18 21

34 47 50 07 15

22 46 27 27 38
```

```
02 06 53 47 27

49 51 06 11 26
```

The highest number used was 53. It was therefore logical to presume that the phrase to use for simple substitution contained fifty-three characters.

```
            STREETSGUARDEDBYUSMARINES

            1234567890123456789012345
```

This was twenty-five characters, although it was possible that the phrase would be repeated twice. They could, Lieutenant Ball said, come back to this later if nothing else seemed to work.

```
       STREETSAREGUARDEDBYUNITEDSTATESMARINES

       12345678901234567890123456789012345678
```

was thirty-eight characters, too short by itself and too long if the phrase was to be duplicated.

```
     THESTREETSAREGUARDEDBYUNITEDSTATESMARINES

     12345678901234567890123456789012345678901
```

was forty-one characters, also too short and too long.

```
        THESTREETSAREGUARDEDBYUSMARINES

        1234567890123456789012345678901
```

was thirty-one characters, also too short by itself, but if used twice, not *too* much longer (sixty-two characters versus the required fifty-three). It was worthy of further consideration. Perhaps the extra nine characters in the repeated phrase would not prove to be important.

Finally, the complete phrase from the Marine Hymn—as precisely as it could be remembered by Weston and Second Lieutenant Percy L. Everly—was tried:

THEYWILLFINDTHESTREETSAREGUARDEDBYUNITEDSTATESMARINES

12345678901234567890123456789012345678901234567890123

It was precisely fifty-three characters. It had to be the substitution phrase. The number blocks of Message Two were decrypted. They made some—not very much, but some—sense.

Lieutenant Percy L. Everly had a stab at it. *"Lille—who the hell is Lille?— and Erny—that has to be Zimmerman—will eat beans—what the hell does that mean?—thirty miles suuth—that could be, probably is, 'south' but south of what?—this murning—this morning."*

"Sir," Sergeant LaMadrid said, "that's 'liller.' With an 'r,' Sir, before the 'and.' "

"Killer!" Lieutenant Everly said. "Goddamn, LaMadrid, you're not as dumb as you look. 'Killer and Erny,' that's what it is."

"Killer and Erny meaning the people you knew, Lieutenant Everly?" General Fertig asked.

"Yes, Sir. China Marines, Sir. Ernie Zimmerman and Killer McCoy."

"Will eat beans thirty miles south this morning?" Weston thought aloud. "The key words are 'beans' and 'thirty miles south.' What the hell can that mean?"

"Beans, beans, beans, lima beans, string beans . . . isn't there a village called 'St. Rose of Lima" or something like that?" Ball asked.

"Yes, there is," General Fertig said. "And there is also a village called Boston on the east coast. Boston baked beans. Weston, for God's sake I hope you still have our one National Geographic Society map of this island?"

"Yes, Sir."

"I suggest you bring it," Fertig said.

"Thirty miles south of St. Rose of Lima is fifty miles from nowhere, up here in the hills," Captain Weston said, using his finger as a pointer on the tattered map. "Thirty miles south of Boston is this little bump sticking into the ocean."

"I believe they call that a 'promontory,' Captain Weston," Fertig said. "How far is that from here?"

Weston measured it with a scrap of paper applied to the legend on the National Geographic Society map.

"Sixty miles, Sir."

"If we are to accept that these two people will be eating beans there this morning, we have to define 'morning,' " Fertig said. "One of two things is true. They are already on Mindanao, and are suggesting this as a rendezvous point. Or they will land there, presumably from a submarine. I think I'd bet on the latter. If this assumption is correct, and we further assume a submarine would prefer to surface no longer than is absolutely necessary, I would suggest 'morning' would mean at first light.''

"My God," Ball said. "Do you really think someone's coming this morning?"

"Are there any arguments to my assumptions?" Fertig asked.

There were none.

"The next question would then seem to be, gentlemen, what are we going to do about it? There is no way we could get anyone from here—you said sixty miles, Weston?"

"Yes, Sir."

"No way we can get anyone to this point," Fertig went on, "sixty miles distant from here by first light. The possibility exists that whoever these people are, they will attempt to make contact with USFIP, fail to do so, and withdraw."

"General, Sir, excuse me?" Sergeant LaMadrid said.

"Yes, Sergeant?"

"I have the motorcycle, General, Sir."

"Shit," Lieutenant Percy L. Lewis said. "I forgot about that."

"Can we get the motorcycle down to the road at night?" Fertig asked.

"More important, is it running?" Weston asked. "Do we have gas for it? Will it make it for sixty miles?"

"It doesn't have a muffler. It'll call every Jap in ten miles," Everly said.

"It has the gasoline," Sergeant LaMadrid said. "And it will go the distance if the oil does not exhaust itself. I will conduct it with great care."

"You're not going, Sergeant," Fertig said. "I can't afford to lose my radio operator."

"I'll go," Weston said immediately.

"Can you ride a motorcycle, Mr. Weston?" Lieutenant Everly asked.

"It can't be that hard," Weston said. "It's only a bicycle with a motor, right? I can ride a bike."

"I'll go," Everly said. "I can ride a motorcycle."

"You'll both go," General Fertig said. "You will both attempt to make your presence known to the submarine, if there is a submarine. If there is a submarine, Captain Weston will remain on the beach to do whatever has to be done, and Lieutenant Everly will get back on the motorcycle to establish contact with the patrol which Captain Hedges will be leading from here, and lead it to the rendezvous point. If there is no submarine, Lieutenant Everly will meet Captain Hedges, who will then return the patrol here. In that circumstance, you will have to get back here by yourself, Weston."

"Aye, aye, Sir."

"We will have to establish, right now, the path of the patrol, and Everly will have to memorize it. It would be best, Weston, if you were unaware of the patrol's route."

"Aye, aye, Sir."

The thinking behind that isn't hard to figure out, Weston thought. *There is a very good chance that I'll be captured. If I don't know the patrol's route, then I can't tell the Japanese, no matter what they do to me.*

"When the patrol leaves, we will relocate Headquarters, USFIP," Fertig said. "If this maneuver proves successful, I will get word of the new location to you. If it doesn't, it won't matter whether you know where we are or not."

"Yeah," Lieutenant Everly said thoughtfully, and quickly corrected himself: "Yes, Sir."

"Captain Weston, would you please give my compliments to Captain Hedges and ask him to join me?"

"Aye, aye, Sir."

"Sergeant LaMadrid, would you please instruct Lieutenant Everly in the operation of your motorcycle, and then, using the new Marine Hymn substitution code, transmit the following message to both Australia and Pearl Harbor: 'We'll bring the hot dogs. Fertig.' "

"Sir," Weston said.

"What is it?"

"May I suggest the message be 'We'll *try* to bring the hot dogs'?"

"Oh, ye of little faith," Fertig said. "Send 'We'll bring the hot dogs,' Sergeant LaMadrid."

"Yes, Sir," Sergeant LaMadrid said.

[TWO]
Approximately 30 miles south of Boston
Davao Oriental Province
Mindanao, Commonwealth of the Philippines
0501 Hours 24 December 1942

It was raining. It had alternated between raining and drizzling all night. The road was slippery and they spilled five times, but suffered nothing more than damaged egos and Christ only knew how much mud and slime forced into the actions of their weapons.

United States Forces in the Philippines, having decreed a state of martial law, had issued an order that all road signs that might be useful to the Japanese be destroyed, removed, moved, obliterated, or otherwise rendered unusable. The Filipinos had carried out the order with an efficiency that disheartened and frustrated Captain Weston. Since they couldn't go into Boston and start counting from there, he needed road markers to tell them how far they were south of Boston.

The next-to-last spill occurred when Weston spotted a nearly concealed concrete mile marker the Filipinos had missed. He applied the brakes too suddenly when he wanted a closer look.

Using Mile Marker 19 as a reference point, they continued 10.0 miles farther down what had been Highway 1. And then, hiding the motorcycle a hundred yards off the road—in a spot where Weston was convinced it would next be seen by archaeologists in the year 1999—they proceeded on foot through the rain-soaked jungle until they heard, but did not see, the surf crashing on the beach.

They then proceeded at approximately a hundred yards' distance from the beach—and the Japanese patrols that might be on the beach—until they reached the tip of what Weston would never forget was called a promontory.

Not without effort, they climbed the tallest trees they could find that might offer a view of the shoreline and ocean, then climbed down again when they could see nothing but other trees. Everly fell the last twenty feet and sprained his ankle. This would pose problems when the time came for him to return to the motorcycle, presuming he could find the motorcycle.

Then, with one hundred yards separating them—if there was a patrol, one of them might stand a chance of escaping—they crawled through the steaming slime to the end of the vegetation, and there took up their vigil.

To protect them both against an inadvertent discharge in case the trigger snagged in the vegetation, Captain Weston had carried his weapon without a round ready to be chambered and fired when he pulled the trigger. Now, his heart leaping, he pulled back the bolt on the Thompson, rolled over on his back, and prepared to fire at whatever was coming through the jungle at him.

"Easy, Mr. Weston," Everly hissed. "Easy does it."

"You scared the shit out of me."

"Did you see the Japs?"

Weston's heart jumped. He shook his head, no.

"Four of them, headed north," Everly said. "A corporal and three privates."

"They've gone?"

Everly nodded.

"Then what's the problem?"

"There's two people out there in a black rubber boat," Everly said.

Weston looked. Visibility was very poor, and the sea very wide, but eventually he saw two men, dressed in black, in a small, black rubber boat, their backs bent to lower their silhouette, paddling slowly through the black water toward the shore.

"Jesus Christ!"

"The Japs may come back, or they may not," Everly said. "Your call, Mr. Weston."

"What do you mean, 'my call'?"

"Do you want to take the chance that they won't come back? If they do come back, they're going to see the boat for sure. If they haven't already seen it, and already started somewhere where they can report it. They didn't have a radio that I could see."

Weston thought the situation over.

"I don't think they're just marching down the beach," Everly went on. "A truck must have put them off down that way." He pointed south. "They'll have a walk on the beach, and the truck will pick them up somewhere down that way." He pointed north. "Unless they climb a telephone pole and tap into the line, which I don't think is likely, they're going to have to go someplace, in the truck, to get on a telephone. Even if they seen the boat, four of them aren't going to do anything; they'd want more people, and they sure as hell are under orders to report something like this."

"Yes," Weston agreed, feeling grossly incompetent.

"So the question is do we want to take them out, in case they seen the boat, or in case they come back? If they do, they damned sure will see the boat. Or are we going to hope we're lucky?"

"I think we had better take them out," Weston decreed, with what he hoped was far more assurance than he felt.

"That means *you'll* have to take them out, by yourself," Everly said.

"Your goddamned ankle!" Weston said.

"I didn't do it on purpose, Mr. Weston," Everly said. "And one of us is going to have to stay here anyway. If those guys in the boat hear shooting, we don't want them paddling back to the sub."

"Shit!"

"Can I make a suggestion?"

"Of course."

"You go after the Japs. If you stick close to the jungle and don't make too much noise, you ought to be able to catch up to them without them suspecting anything. It's going to take those guys in the boat five minutes to make shore. That'll give you enough time to catch up with the Japs, unless they decide to turn around. When the boat makes shore, I'll fire a shot. Then you take out the Japs. They're all bunched up; you should be able to do it easy. And then we'll take it from there."

"Goddamn it, why did they have to patrol this lousy section of beach right now?"

"Things happen that way, Mr. Weston," Everly said.

"How long ago did the Japs go by?"

"You really didn't see them?" Everly asked wonderingly, and then answered the question. "About two minutes ago. They was walking slow. Your ass starts to drag in a hurry, walking through sand."

"I'll take them out when I hear your shot," Weston said. "You make sure whoever's in that rubber boat doesn't leave."

"Aye, aye, Sir."

They rose to their feet and left the protective cover of the jungle. Weston started trotting up the beach, keeping as close to the vegetation as he could.

Within a minute, he realized that Everly was right again. Walking through sand—not to mention trying to run through it—does in fact cause the ass to start dragging in a hurry.

In three minutes, the Japanese came into sight. None of them seemed at all attentive to anything. Weston began to close the distance between himself and them, taking as much solace as he could from the knowledge that his was not the only dragging ass.

When he came out of the jungle, Everly had concealed himself—flat on his stomach—behind a massive outcrop of rock. Suddenly he got to his feet.

The two men were no longer in the boat. After a moment, Everly spotted their heads in the water, and then they began to rise higher and higher from the water, dragging the boat behind them. Finally, they were on the beach. They were dressed in what looked like utilities dyed black, and they had some kind of black grease rubbed on their faces. Even so, one of them looked familiar.

Everly stepped from behind the rock.

"McCoy, is that you?" he called.

"Who's that?"

"Everly."

"Give us a hand with the boat," McCoy ordered.

Everly walked quickly to the edge of the water. Up close, the man with McCoy looked seventeen years old.

"We got a problem," Everly announced.

"What kind of a problem?"

"Four Japs, about five hundred yards down the beach," Everly said. Then he raised his Thompson to his shoulder, raised the muzzle into the air and pulled the trigger. Two shots rang out.

■   ■   ■

Weston had been waiting for the signal. The four Japanese soldiers were walk-ing slowly in a file, not more than twenty yards in front of him. Weston was really surprised that they didn't seem to have any idea that they were being shadowed.

He was carrying the Thompson—with growing difficulty; he was running out of breath—much like a quail hunter carries his shotgun when he expects a covey to flush. He was prepared to fire instantly.

He was aware of the analogy, and the differences. Quail hunters do not usually run through sand; no shotgun he had ever held was nearly as heavy as the Thompson; and quail flush, they do not turn and shoot back.

He had the Thompson to his shoulder and had drawn a sight on the lead Japanese before the first Japanese, hearing the shots, turned in the action of unslinging his Arisaka rifle from his shoulder.

Time seemed to move very slowly.

The first Jap bent his knees and dropped in his tracks. The second and third Japanese in the file fell over forward. The last Japanese, in the act of shoulder-ing his Arisaka, took a four-round burst in the chest and fell over backward.

Weston ran forward to them, the Thompson still at his shoulder. The first and third Japanese showed signs of life. Without really thinking what he was doing, Weston took his Nambu pistol—already carrying a round in the cham-ber—and shot both of them in the head.

A little sanity returned. He felt a twinge of nausea at the sight of the blood and brain matter on the sand.

And then, in a reflex action, Weston stripped each of the bodies of their ammunition, gathered up the Arisakas, and, staggering under the weight, started back to where he had left Everly.

"What the hell . . ." McCoy asked just before they heard the four bursts—three short and one long burst—from Weston's Thompson.

"Captain Weston was waiting for my signal before taking them out," Ev-erly said.

McCoy turned to the kid.

"Koffler, go see if you can help down there," he ordered.

"Aye, aye, Sir," Koffler responded, pulled a Colt .45 pistol from under his dyed-black utilities, and started to run down the beach.

"He's a little young, isn't he, McCoy?" Everly asked as he and McCoy dragged the rubber boat across the narrow beach and into the jungle.

McCoy didn't reply.

"Is it safe enough to bring in a couple more boats?" he asked.

"Your call, McCoy," Everly replied. "I *think* that was all the Japs for right now, but I don't *know* that."

McCoy took a black bag of some kind from the boat, then took a knife, a daggerlike weapon, from a sheath strapped to his arm and sliced at the bag.

Jesus Christ, I'll be a monkey's uncle if that isn't the same knife he used to cut those Italian Marines! Everly thought in wonder.

Then McCoy had a microphone in his hand and was pulling what looked like an automobile antenna out of a black box.

"Coffin, Coffin, Columbus, Columbus."

"Go ahead, Columbus. Read you five by five."

"Coffin, send in two repeat two boats."

"Understand two boats. On the way."

"Who the hell are you talking to, Killer?" Everly asked.

McCoy didn't reply, directly.

"I guess they didn't hear that Thompson," he said. "Otherwise I probably would have been talking to nobody."

Then he touched Everly's arm, and when Everly looked at him, nodded out to sea.

The conning tower of the *Sunfish* rose from the sea. Before her deck broke water, there was activity on her bridge.

Two officers appeared—identifiable by their brimmed caps. And then four or five sailors. A .50 caliber machine gun appeared and was quickly put in its mount. There was the glint of gleaming, belted cartridges as the gun was charged.

The national colors sprouted on a mast, their red, white, and blue suddenly vivid in the early-morning sun against the wet gray of the *Sunfish*. The officers and sailors in the conning tower saluted as the wind whipped the flag straight.

A port in the conning tower burst open and sailors poured out, some to man the four-inch cannon mounted forward, some rushing to open ports in her deck. Two rubber boats suddenly inflated on the *Sunfish*'s deck, and were quickly put over the side.

"Shit!" Everly said, his voice breaking. "Look at that fucking *flag*, will you?"

Weston and Koffler came running back down the beach while the two rubber boats making their way to shore were still a hundred yards offshore.

"Got them all!" Weston reported excitedly, even jubilantly. "We dragged the bodies off the beach."

"Mr. Weston, this is Killer McCoy," Everly said.

"Fuck you, Everly," McCoy snapped.

"McCoy, this is Captain Weston," Everly said.

McCoy, smiling, saluted.

"Lieutenant McCoy, Sir," he said. "Captain, you need a shave."

"I'm Sergeant Koffler, Sir," Koffler said to Captain Weston. "We didn't have time for introductions back there."

"How do you do, Sergeant?" Weston replied formally.

"You're a *sergeant?*" Everly asked incredulously.

"He's a *staff* sergeant," McCoy said, chuckling. "Zimmerman—he's in one of those boats—is a gunny."

Weston looked out to sea and saw the rubber boats and then the *Sunfish,* with her colors streaming proudly from her mast. And then he realized that tears were streaming down his cheeks, and his chest was heaving with sobs he couldn't control.

[THREE]

"Do you have any people with you, Captain?" McCoy asked.

"No. It's just Lieutenant Everly and myself," Weston said.

" *'Lieutenant'* Everly?" McCoy asked.

"The General commissioned me, McCoy," Everly said.

"What were you before the war, Captain?" McCoy asked.

"I was a lieutenant. I'm an aviator," Weston said.

Hearing what he said, he realized that he no longer felt like an aviator. It seemed impossible that he had ever done anything like that.

"You're a Marine officer? A regular?"

"Yes, I am."

"Are there other officers around?" McCoy asked. "Somebody with more rank?"

"Captain Hedges," Everly said. "He's leading a patrol here."

"When will he get here?"

"Two, three days. He has to come sixty miles. Maybe four," Everly said.

"Nobody higher than a captain?"

"That's it, McCoy," Everly said.

"Can you paddle a rubber boat, Captain?" McCoy asked. "I mean, if we can get you into a rubber boat, could you paddle it out to the submarine?"

"I think so."

"How much do you know about Fertig's operation?"

"Here you go, Mr. McCoy," Koffler said, handing him a carbine. "Careful, it's loaded and not locked."

"What the hell is that thing?" Everly asked derisively. And then, "He called you 'Mister McCoy'?"

"You can call me 'Sir,' Percy," McCoy said. "It's a carbine. Fires a real-hot .30 caliber pistol cartridge from a fifteen-round magazine. Good little weapon. We're going to try to bring one hundred of them ashore."

"You know I don't like being called 'Percy,' " Everly said.

"Then don't call me 'Killer,' or I *will* make you call me 'Sir,' Percy."

"Mr. McCoy is a lieutenant," Koffler furnished helpfully.

"You're in charge, here, Mr. McCoy?" Weston asked.

"I am," McCoy said simply. "I asked you how much do you know about Fertig's operation?"

"I'm the G-2," Weston said.

"That OSS guy is in the first boat, Mr. McCoy," Koffler said. "Him and Mr. Lewis."

McCoy turned to look at him. He was peering out to sea through binoculars.

"Give me those," he ordered.

Koffler somewhat reluctantly handed them over.

"Police up that plastic," McCoy ordered. "Jesus Christ, Steve! You know better than to leave stuff like that for the Japs to find!"

"Sorry," Koffler said contritely, and immediately dropped to his knees to pick up the shredded plastic in which the radio, the binoculars, and the carbines had been wrapped.

"What I want you do to, Captain," McCoy said, "is go out in the surf until you're up to your waist. Koffler will go with you. Leave the Thompson. When that first boat gets here, help unload it. The stuff will float, and Koffler will see it doesn't get away. Then get in, and go out to the submarine."

"What for?" Weston asked.

"My orders are to send the highest-ranking officer I can find out with the *Sunfish.* You're it."

"Why? I'm not sure—"

"Don't argue with me," McCoy said coldly. "Just do it!"

"You better do it, Mr. Weston," Everly said.

Weston looked at McCoy, confusion in his eyes. McCoy felt sorry for him.

"I think you're going to brief General MacArthur on what's going on around here," he said with a smile. "I *know* you're going to brief General Pickering."

"MacArthur?" Everly said. "No shit?"

"No shit, Everly," McCoy said. "And, Captain, don't shave off that beard until General Pickering sees it."

Everly still looked confused and hesitant.

"Go, goddamn it!" McCoy said. "By the time you wade through the surf, the boat'll be there."

Weston looked at Everly, who nodded.

"Have a cold one for me, Mr. Weston," he said, and put out his hand.

"Take care of yourself, Everly," Weston said, aware and surprised that he wanted to cry again.

"Yeah," Everly said. He held out his hand for Weston's Thompson submachine gun. Weston gave it to him, then walked to the edge of the water and waded in.

"Where can we stash the stuff we're bringing ashore?" McCoy asked, turning to Everly.

"How much stuff?"

"What's in those two boats for now," McCoy said. "More stuff tomorrow, if we get away with this."

"I think you can forget tomorrow," Everly said. "There's going to be Japs over here sooner or later, and I think sooner."

"Tell me about the Japs," McCoy said.

"Four-man patrol," Everly responded. "I think they got off a truck down there a ways, and were supposed to be picked up by another a couple of miles down that. When they don't show up, I think somebody will come looking for them."

"How much time?"

Everly threw up his hands helplessly.

"If we're lucky, nobody heard the Thompson. That may give us a little more time. If they did, we could have Japs anytime."

"What about stashing this stuff?"

"There's jungle for maybe half a mile from here to the road, in a straight line. Any place between here and the road would be as good as any."

"How far away is Fertig?"

"Sixty miles. But he's moving."

"What do you mean he's moving?"

"He figured maybe one of us would be captured. He didn't want us to tell the Japs if we got captured. If we don't know where he went, we can't tell the Japs."

"Oh, Jesus!"

"But no sweat, McCoy. He'll find us, if the Japs don't find us first."

"What do you think of Fertig?"

"He's a little weird," Everly said. "He's got a little red goatee, and I guess you know he's not a real general. He was a light colonel, I think. But he's smart, and he's got balls."

That's about as close to high praise as Everly is likely to give, McCoy decided.

"OK. Here's the drill. The first thing we do is get Koffler and one of the radios to Fertig. How do we do that?"

"I know where to meet Captain Hedges and the patrol. . . ."

"How many men on the patrol? Enough to carry this stuff?"

"Enough to carry a lot of it. You won't believe how much crap these Flips can carry. But I don't know how many men. Probably fifteen, twenty, anyhow."

"Can a couple of them take Koffler to Fertig? I guess he's got about a hundred pounds of gear."

"I got a motorcycle stashed a ways back," Everly said. "If I can find the sonofabitch. Can we strap what he has to take on the motorcycle?"

"What about Japs on the road?"

"I don't know," Everly said. "And the General didn't say anything, but like I said, he's smart. He'll probably do something the other side of Boston to have all the Japs running around up there."

"Fertig, you mean?"

Everly nodded.

"Or I could carry—what did you say his name is?"

"Koffler."

"—Koffler and his stuff to the motorcycle and wait until tonight to move down the road."

"Your call," McCoy said. "Just keep in mind, getting Koffler and that radio to Fertig is the most important thing right now."

"Just one radio?"

"I got another one here. And there's two more on the sub, if we can get more stuff off."

He looked out to sea. The first boat had reached Koffler and Weston, and Lewis was shoving black plastic-wrapped parcels over the side. Captain Robert B. Macklin, USMC, was kneeling in the center of the boat doing, as far as McCoy could see, absolutely nothing.

The second boat, carrying Zimmerman and two sailors from the *Sunfish,* was approaching them.

The sun was fully up now. If a Japanese patrol boat appeared, or worse, an airplane, the *Sunfish* would be in trouble.

McCoy scanned the horizon, and then the skies, with the binoculars. There was nothing.

Zimmerman's boat passed Lewis's and kept coming.

"If they don't go over the side now, it'll turn over in the surf," McCoy mused aloud.

A minute later, his prediction came true. The boat flipped over on its side, dumping the three men and the stack of plastic-wrapped parcels into the sea.

"Come on, we better get those people some weapons," McCoy said, and led Everly to the boat they had dragged off the beach into the jungle. He reached into the boat, pulled a plastic-wrapped parcel of carbines from it, and slit the plastic.

"That's the knife you had in Shanghai, right?" Everly said.

"So what?"

"Just curious, is all," Everly said.

"Let me show you how this works," McCoy said, picking up one of the carbines. "The safety and the magazine release are here on the trigger assembly. You flip the little lever horizontal to take it off safety. You push the button and the magazine falls out." He demonstrated. "Fifteen shots. You shove it back in until it clicks. Then you work the action—he demonstrated again—and it's ready to go."

"Pistol cartridges, huh?" Everly said scornfully, taking the weapon.

"Hot pistol cartridges. They'd blow up a pistol."

"Will they kill anybody?"

"Yeah," McCoy said. "If you hit him, and he's not five hundred yards away."

"You know that?" Everly asked dubiously.

"I know that. They're not a real rifle, but they're a lot better than a pistol."

"Most people can't shoot a pistol to save their ass," Everly said.

"That's the whole idea," McCoy said.

"You've got ammo, I hope? We're fucking near out of ammo, ours and Japanese. We're making our own fucking bullets from curtain rods, and loading the cases with powder from Jap rounds. I'm down to thirteen rounds for this." He shifted his Thompson on his shoulder.

"There's ammo for these, and a couple of hundred .45 ACP and .30-06 rounds. If we can get it off the sub."

"Grenades? We could really use some grenades."

"Not on this shipment," McCoy said. "Maybe the next."

"Is there going to be another shipment? More submarines?"

"In twenty-one days. *If* we can keep ourselves from getting killed before then," McCoy said. He slit open a second parcel containing four U.S. Carbines, Caliber .30 M1, slung three of them around his shoulder, and started back to the beach.

Lieutenant Chambers D. Lewis, dragging two plastic-wrapped parcels behind him, came out of the water.

"Good morning, Mr. McCoy," he said. "I see the Marines have landed, and the situation is presumably well in hand?"

"You weren't supposed to come ashore," McCoy said.

"I knew how important it was to you that Captain Macklin join your beach party," Lewis said. "And I could not, I found, just go sailing away without proving to you that I could paddle a rubber boat as well as you."

McCoy looked over his shoulder. Macklin was moving as quickly as he could through chest-deep water toward the beach. So far as McCoy could see, he was not towing anything behind him.

And then he laughed. "Oh, Christ, look at that."

Gunnery Sergeant Zimmerman, water streaming off his body, looking very distressed and annoyed, plodded heavily through the sand toward them, dragging four obviously heavy plastic-wrapped parcels. Behind him came the two sailors, each dragging two plastic-wrapped parcels.

"Why didn't you get out of the boat, the way I told you?" McCoy asked.

"I couldn't see how deep the water was, and I didn't want to drown, for Christ's sake. I can't swim!" He recognized Everly. "Hey! What do you say, Everly? How they hanging?"

"Can't complain. McCoy told me they made you a gunny."

"Yeah. How about that? You going to lend a hand with this crap, or just stand there with your thumb up your ass?"

"You may get stuck here," McCoy said to Lewis. "The place is liable to be crawling with Japs anytime now. The Fertig guy—what's his name, Everly?"

"Weston, Sir," Everly said. "Captain James Weston."

He called me "Sir," McCoy realized, surprised. *I'll be damned.*

". . . Captain Weston took out a four-man Jap patrol as we were coming ashore. Everly thinks other Japs will come looking for them."

"That would be best," Everly said.

"Best?" McCoy asked. "What the hell are you talking about?"

"Worst is that they did hear Mr. Weston's Thompson and went off to tell somebody. Best would be if they didn't hear the gunfire, but send a couple of people looking for the first patrol. Better would be we could find the truck they're in—"

"We don't know there's a truck," McCoy interrupted.

"—and take that out, hide the truck and the bodies in the bush someplace where they won't be found for a couple of days. That would make it less likely that the Japs could find the stuff we're going to stash here."

"Or find the truck and take it five miles, ten miles from here," McCoy said thoughtfully.

"Even better," Everly agreed.

"What's wrong with your ankle?" McCoy asked.

"I fell out of a tree and sprained it," Everly said.

"Then how are we going to find the truck?"

"I could get a tree limb, and make a crutch or something."

"You tell me where you think this truck is, Everly, and I'll find the fucker," Gunny Zimmerman said matter-of-factly.

"You're going to have to go with him, Everly," McCoy said. "There's no way around it. We'll get the stuff into the jungle and wait here for you."

"Zimmerman, are those little rifles any good?" Everly asked.

"For what we're going to use them for," Zimmerman said.

"Well, you better give me one, then. All I have is thirteen rounds for the Thompson. Unless . . . Where's that .45 ammo, McCoy?"

"I don't know where it is right now."

"Then hand me one of them little rifles. We don't have much time."

"There is, of course," McCoy said, looking at Lewis, "one other option."

"You want me to go with them? Why not?"

"That's not what I meant," McCoy said, and then, pointing out to sea, went on. "Captain Weston is almost at the *Sunfish*. I could radio them to get the hell out of here the second he's aboard and . . . Maybe that's what I should do."

"The U.S. Navy has gone to considerable expense and effort, Mr. McCoy, to place that vessel where she lies," Lewis said. "I don't think anyone aboard would want to leave until they unload the cargo, or a Jap destroyer appears."

McCoy looked at him thoughtfully.

"Whichever comes first," Lewis added.

"You really are liable to get stuck here with us," McCoy said. "You understand that?"

"I had that unpleasant thought shortly after I got in the rubber boat," Lewis said. "Shall I pass the *Sunfish* the word to start unloading cargo?"

"The radio's right inside the bushes, over there," McCoy said, pointing.

Captain Robert B. Macklin waded the final steps ashore and then threw himself flat on the sand, as if exhausted.

"He hurt, or what?" Everly asked, concerned.

"Fuck him, let him lie there," McCoy said.

"We have to get those boats back into the water," Lewis said, and then bellowed "Macklin!" in a surprisingly loud voice.

Macklin raised his head to look at him, then moved his arms in a helpless gesture.

"Get your ass moving, Macklin, start helping us get the boats back through the surf, or I'll shoot you myself!" Lieutenant Lewis called.

Captain Macklin continued to make gestures implying helpless exhaustion until Lieutenant Lewis took one of the carbines from Lieutenant McCoy, chambered a round, and put the weapon to his shoulder. Then, his strength having miraculously returned, Captain Macklin scurried down the beach, grabbed the line on a rubber boat, and started to drag the boat toward the water.

Lieutenant Everly's eyes grew wide, but he said nothing.

"Were you really going to shoot him?" McCoy asked, a smile on his face.

"I don't know," Lewis said wonderingly. "Fortunately for both of us, neither did he." He then had a second thought. "Why don't we just let him paddle out to the *Sunfish* and go aboard?"

"He stays," McCoy said firmly.

Lewis nodded, turned away, and trotted toward the radio.

"Who's he, McCoy?" Everly asked.

"He's a dog robber for an admiral at Pearl Harbor."

"I meant the asshole on the beach."

"It's a long story, Everly. I'll tell you later," he said.

[FOUR]
United States Submarine *Sunfish*
126° 48″ East Longitude 7° 35″ West Latitude
Philippine Sea
0527 Hours 24 December 1942

"Skipper?" Lieutenant Amos P. Youngman, USN, asked, leaving the second part of the interrogatory—"Do you see that?"—unsaid.

"I see it," Lieutenant Commander Warren T. Houser, USN, replied.

Both Commander Houser and Lieutenant Youngman were on the crowded conning-tower bridge of the *Sunfish,* binoculars to their eyes, alternately watching the rubber boats close to shore and scanning the skies and horizon for signs of Japanese activity.

A passenger in the first rubber boat was returning to the *Sunfish* from the beach—a passenger wearing an old-fashioned, broad-brimmed campaign hat, what looked like dirty white pajamas, and a full, blond beard.

"McCoy said he would try to send a senior officer out," Commander Houser said. "That must be him."

Lieutenant Youngman turned to the Chief of the Boat, who was scanning the horizon through binoculars.

"Chief, make sure we bring that man safely aboard," he ordered.

"Aye, aye, Sir," Chief Buchanan said.

Chief Bosun's Mate Buchanan turned, trained his binoculars toward shore, looked a moment, and then handed the binoculars to a sailor standing in the center of the people crowding the bridge.

Then, moving with surprising agility for someone of his bulk, he disappeared down the hatch in the deck of the conning tower, and a moment later emerged on the deck of the submarine.

By the time the rubber boat reached the *Sunfish,* Chief Buchanan had tied a half-inch line securely around his waist and placed the end into the hands of three sailors on the deck. He had also made a loop in a second length of half-inch line, handed the end to the sailors, and was swinging the looped end in his hand, not unlike a cowboy about to lasso a calf for branding.

"Put the line around that gentleman," he bellowed as he made his way down the slippery, curved hull of the *Sunfish*.

He tossed the line to the two sailors in the rubber boat. Their attempt to grab it failed, and Chief Buchanan, using language not customarily heard in Sunday schools, offered an unkind opinion vis-à-vis the legitimacy of their births.

He retrieved the line and tossed it again. This time the sailor in the aft of the rubber boat managed to snag it.

"Just put that over your head, Sir," he called encouragingly. "And under your arms, and we'll have you aboard in no time."

Captain James B. Weston did as ordered, then lifted himself very unsteadily to his feet and jumped onto the curved hull. He lost his footing, fell flat on his face, and started to slide down the hull into the water.

"Haul away!" Chief Buchanan bellowed.

Captain Weston's descent became an ascent; he was dragged up the hull to the deck, where Chief Buchanan and one of the sailors jerked him to his feet.

"Right this way, Sir, if you please," Chief Buchanan said.

From some long-dormant corner of Weston's memory, Naval protocol suddenly came to life and could not be denied. He shrugged free of Chief Buchanan's arm, faced aft, and saluted.

"Permission to come aboard, Sir?"

Chief Buchanan tried to place his hand on Weston's arm to guide him to the port in the conning tower. Weston, his right hand and arm still raised in salute, pushed him away with his left.

"Permission granted!" a voice called.

Weston followed the sound of the voice and saw a Naval officer's face high on the conning tower. His salute was returned. Weston lowered his arm.

"Escort the gentleman to the wardroom," Commander Houser ordered.

"Aye, aye, Sir."

Weston allowed himself to be led down the deck, and then through a hatch in the conning tower. He found himself in a hot, crowded world of dials and pipes, smelling of oil and sweat, with sailors in work clothing and officers in khaki staring at him with undisguised curiosity.

He was led aft, and then Chief Buchanan pushed aside a green curtain and motioned him inside.

"Someone will be with you shortly, Sir," Chief Buchanan said. "You'll have to excuse me. I've got to get back topside."

"Thank you," Weston said politely.

He walked into the small compartment and turned around. The curtain was back in place, and the Chief gone.

Weston sat down at the small table. On the chair beside him was a copy of *The Saturday Evening Post*. He picked it up.

The curtain parted, and a sailor stepped inside.

"Fresh coffee, Sir," he said. "If there's anything else, just push the button."

He set a tray before Weston. It held a cup and saucer, a silver coffeepot, a pitcher of something like cream, and a bowl of sugar cubes. A small plate held a half-dozen chocolate-chip cookies.

Weston pushed at the cookies with his index finger, then picked one up and took a small bite.

"Are you hungry, Sir?" the sailor asked. "Can I fix you something?"

Weston looked at him without replying.

"Anything from an egg sandwich to steak and eggs, Sir," the sailor said.

"Yes, please," Weston said.

"Which, Sir? The sandwich or the steak and eggs."

"Could I have both?"

"Absolutely," the sailor said, and left.

Weston took another bite of the chocolate-chip cookie, and then thrust the whole thing in his mouth and chewed it very slowly.

He poured coffee into the cup, then sniffed it, then took a sip. It was so hot, it burned his lips. He added cream and a lump of sugar and stirred, then took another sip.

He put another chocolate-chip cookie in his mouth all at once, and then dipped a third into the coffee with cream and sugar.

The curtain opened again as Weston mopped up the juice from the steak with a piece of toast.

It was the officer who had given him permission to come aboard. Weston now saw the golden oak leaves of a lieutenant commander on his collar points and started to rise, as officers of the Naval Service do in the presence of a superior officer.

"Keep your seat," the lieutenant commander said. "Cookie take care of you all right? Is there anything else we can get you?"

Weston shook his head, no, and then said, "Thank you."

"I'm Warren Houser. I'm the skipper."

"Captain Weston, Sir," Weston said. "No—Lieutenant Weston, Sir."

"Which is it, Mr. Weston?" Houser said gently, smiling, offering his hand.

"Captain, U.S. Forces in the Philippines, Sir. First Lieutenant, USMC."

"Welcome aboard the *Sunfish,* Captain."

"Thank you, Sir. What's happening now, Sir?"

"We're discharging cargo."

"Captain, if the Japs don't know you're here, they will shortly. A Jap patrol was on the beach just before the first rubber boat landed. I killed them, but someone's going to wonder where they are, and probably right about now."

"Well, we've come a long way with this stuff, and we'd like to discharge it. I understand you've had a supply problem."

"We haven't had any supplies at all," Weston said simply.

"So we heard," Captain Houser said, and then changed the subject. "As soon as we're finished here, we're going to Espíritu Santo."

"Where, Sir?"

"It's an island. Sort of a forward base. From there, I expect you'll be flown to Australia."

"Yes, Sir."

"If you don't want anything else to eat, may I suggest a shower and a shave? And we'll find some khakis for you. I want to get back to the bridge, so if you'll excuse me, we'll continue our conversation once we're under way. My officers are pretty damned curious."

"I think I'll keep the beard," Weston said. "Lieutenant McCoy said I wasn't to shave it off until General Pickering saw it."

"From what I've seen of him, it would behoove you to do what Lieutenant McCoy told you."

"May I have another cup of coffee? I seem to have drunk all . . ."

"You can have anything on the *Sunfish,* Captain Weston," Lieutenant Commander Houser said, and rang for the messman.

[FIVE]
Approximately 30 miles south of Boston
Davao Oriental Province
Mindanao, Commonwealth of the Philippines
0745 Hours 24 December 1942

Lieutenant Chambers D. Lewis, USN, and First Lieutenant Kenneth R. McCoy, USMCR, were standing just inside the vegetation on the shore. McCoy was holding a carbine, the butt resting on his hip. Lewis had a carbine slung from his shoulder.

The *Sunfish* lay about two hundred yards offshore, her 4.2 cannon and antiaircraft machine guns manned, her colors now hanging limply from the conning-tower mast. She had surfaced just over two hours before.

After McCoy made the decision—feeling the weight of it lying heavily on his shoulders—to take the chance that Everly and Zimmerman could find the Japanese truck—if in fact there was a truck—and get rid of it, there was hectic activity.

Four additional rubber boats were inflated and launched, and manned by sailors—there was no shortage of volunteers from among the *Sunfish*'s crew. They began to ferry plastic-wrapped parcels ashore.

After the first two boats were manhandled back into the water—the surf had diminished since daybreak—they were paddled back to the submarine. The next four boats from the *Sunfish* didn't reach the beach. Their plastic-wrapped parcels were put over the side, and one of the two paddlers went into the water with them. The remaining paddlers paddled the now empty boats back to the *Sunfish*.

That process was repeated four times, so that eventually ten sailors were on the beach or else standing in waist-high water unloading the boats and moving the cargo inland.

It was a far more efficient means to off-load the cargo than they'd been using, but it had not occurred to anyone during the practice sessions in Australia. The idea was Lieutenant Lewis's. After he proposed it, McCoy went along with it, somewhat cold-bloodedly deciding that if the Japanese came submarine hunting with a destroyer, it really wouldn't make a difference whether the *Sunfish* sailors died aboard the submarine or ferrying cargo ashore. He had not really expected they would off-load all the supplies they had brought with them, and now that there was a chance to do that, risking the sailors' lives seemed justifiable.

After they started unloading, one of the sailors, a chubby cook, politely suggested to McCoy that he just let the Navy unload the boats and save his strength. McCoy accepted the offer, wondering whether he agreed to do that because it was the militarily wise thing, or because he would rather have someone else work up a major sweat in the heat and humidity.

He also ordered Koffler to get into the shade and save his strength. As soon as Everly returned—if Everly returned—Koffler was going to have to look for Everly's motorcycle, and then start out to find Fertig. He would need all his strength for that.

How to get everything to Fertig—wherever Fertig was—was going to be a problem, but that could be worried about later. The important thing now was to move the supplies off the beach and into the jungle where the Japanese would be unlikely to find them.

Forty minutes later, Everly came out of the jungle, hopping with surprising speed with the aid of a tree branch used as a crutch. He had both the carbine and an Arisaka rifle slung over his shoulder.

"Found it," he said. "We lucked out. All there was was a sergeant and the driver. Zimmerman cut their throats."

"Where is he?"

"He took the truck south."

"How's he going to get back here?"

"He's only going to take it two miles," he said. "He said that's far enough. Then he's coming back here."

"What's this?" McCoy asked, tapping the stock of the Arisaka. "A souvenir?"

"Until you showed up, McCoy, we got our weapons from the Japs."

"OK. The thing to do now is get Koffler and his radio to Fertig. Can you find your motorcycle?"

"Yeah."

"Koffler!" McCoy called, raising his voice, and Koffler came running up.

The sweat had erased much of the black whatever-it-was that he had had on his face when Everly first saw him. Now he looked even younger.

"Go with Everly, Steve. You know what to do," McCoy said.

"Aye, aye, Sir."

Having completed their final trip to the beach, two of the rubber boats were almost back to the *Sunfish,* carrying with them members of the shore labor party. Before wading a final time into the surf, each of them had shaken hands with the landing party.

The third boat has halfway between shore and the submarine. The fourth had two sailors in it; a third sailor, in chest-deep water, was holding it for Lewis to wade out to it.

Using leafy branches from the jungle as a broom, Captain Macklin was doing what he could to obliterate the evidence of heavy traffic in the sand.

"You didn't have to come ashore," McCoy said, offering Lewis his hand. "I appreciate it. Take care of yourself, Lewis."

"Let me take him back with me, Ken," Lewis said, nodding at Macklin.

"No," McCoy said firmly.

"He's going to cause trouble," Lewis argued.

"Two things. General Pickering wants him here," McCoy said. "And, I realized, so do I."

"Why, for God's sake?"

"I guess the idea of the sonofabitch standing around some O Club bar making it big time with some nurse with stories of being in the Philippines with the guerrillas just pisses me off," McCoy said wryly, and then grew serious. "He's a Marine officer. He was sent here, goddamn it, and he should behave like a Marine officer. If he can't hack it, then he shouldn't be a Marine officer."

"If he threatens your mission, would you really kill him?"

"I hope I don't have to," McCoy said. "But I'm not sending the sonofabitch back."

"I was afraid you'd say that," Lewis said.

McCoy shrugged.

"If you can figure some way to do it without getting your ass in a crack, get word, through Ed Sessions, to my girl that I'm all right," McCoy said.

"Sorry, I can't do that," Lewis said. He walked out of the vegetation to the edge of the water, cupped his hands to his mouth, and shouted, "Boats, take that man aboard and get out to the *Sunfish*. I'm staying ashore."

"Hey, wait a minute!" McCoy called, running out to Lewis.

"You heard me, Boats, shove off!" Lewis shouted.

The two sailors in the rubber boat quickly hauled the one in the water into the boat and startled paddling out to the *Sunfish*.

"Are you out of your mind?" McCoy asked.

"Probably," Lewis said with a smile. "Two things. I don't want you shooting Macklin, and I really don't want to go back aboard that goddamned submarine."

"If I decide I have to take care of him, you're not going to get in my way," McCoy said.

"Understood," Lewis said.

They moved back into the vegetation and watched as the boat reached the *Sunfish,* and as it and the crew were quickly hauled aboard.

"You could still get on the radio and tell them to come get you."

"Too late," Lewis said, and pointed.

The colors were suddenly gone from the mast, and her decks were clear. She began to move very slowly, and very slowly to slip beneath the surface.

"I hope you remembered to bring something to eat," Lewis said.

"Just for the record, I think you've lost your mind," McCoy said. "We've got some Army rations. 'C rations' they call them."

[SIX]
Headquarters, U.S. Forces in the Philippines
In the Field
Davao Oriental Province
Mindanao, Commonwealth of the Philippines
0705 Hours 25 December 1942

The Commanding General had left instructions that he was not to be awakened, unless of course there was an indication the Japanese were nearby. So the first view Staff Sergeant Stephen Koffler, USMCR, had of Brigadier General

Wendell W. Fertig was of a middle-aged man, with a red goatee, rising from his bed. The bed was a piece of canvas laid on the ground beneath an obviously freshly and hastily constructed lean-to.

This apparition was wearing a frayed and mussed khaki shirt, to the collar points of which were pinned silver stars. Matching trousers and a pair of battered boots were hanging from the lean-to roof. The General held a Model 1911 .45 ACP pistol, hammer cocked, and looked somewhat startled.

The first view General Fertig had of Staff Sergeant Koffler was of a boy—an American boy, who looked about seventeen—in dyed-black khakis. His arms and the backs of his hands were black, and his white face was framed in more black, under his hairline, and down his neck. In his hand he was carrying a very small rifle, of a type Fertig had never seen before, and something like a cut-off sword was hanging from his neck on a cord.

The boy came to attention and saluted.

"Staff Sergeant Koffler, U.S. Marine Corps, reporting, Sir."

General Fertig returned the salute.

"Reporting from where, Sergeant?" Fertig asked as he reached up and took his trousers from the lean-to wall.

The boy took some time to consider the question. It seemed to confuse him for a moment.

"From Australia, Sir. General Pickering sent us."

Thank God!

"And who is General Pickering?"

That question also seemed to momentarily confuse him.

"He's a Marine general, Sir. We work for him."

"You landed by submarine?" Fertig asked as he pushed his legs into his still-soggy trousers.

"Yes, Sir. We came off the *Sunfish.*"

"And how many of you are there?"

"Three of us, Sir. Plus an officer from the OSS."

What the hell is the OSS?

'And the name of your commanding officer?"

"McCoy, Sir. Lieutenant McCoy."

They sent a lieutenant? *Well, that certainly establishes our position, doesn't it?*

"And where is Lieutenant McCoy?"

"I left him on the beach with the supplies, Sir. Lieutenant Everly rode me on his motorcycle to where we met Captain Hedges. Captain Hedges sent this guy—he pointed to a Filipino standing to one side—to bring me on the motorcycle to you, and then he took the patrol back to the beach."

"What sort of supplies, Sergeant?"

"Some weapons, Sir, some medicine, other stuff. And the gold, too, of course."

"Gold?" Fertig asked as he pulled on his boots.

"Yes, Sir," Koffler said, and pulled his dyed-black khaki shirt out of his trousers.

Around his waist were two dully gleaming black belts. One formed a tube about two inches wide. The second was narrower, with a package, about five inches square, in the center. Koffler untied the cords that closed the tubular belt and handed it to Fertig. It was a good deal heavier than it looked.

God, is there really gold in here?

Fertig felt what could be coins under the strange, smooth, slippery material. He tried to find an opening.

"If you want to open that, Sir," Koffler said helpfully, "you're going to have to cut it. That plastic can't be torn."

Fertig looked at him.

Koffler ducked out of the cord around his neck and handed Fertig the sword.

"What is 'plastic,' Sergeant?" he asked, taking the sword and testing the blade with his thumb. It was as sharp as a razor.

"I don't really know what it is, Sir," Koffler said. "The Army started packing their radios in it, and we used it to pack the stuff we brought you."

Fertig slit the plastic. A gleaming United States twenty-dollar gold piece fell out.

"We're each wearing a money belt, General," Koffler said. "And there are a couple of bundles back on the beach. There's two hundred and fifty thousand dollars in all."

If they're sending me that kind of money, somebody is taking us seriously.

"And you were sent here to deliver the gold?"

"No, Sir. I was sent here to find you, and when I did, to call Australia."

"We have a radio, but at the moment it's not working. We're on the move, as you can see."

"I've got a radio, General," Koffler said. "I've got two hours' worth of batteries, so if you've got a generator, that would be helpful. But all I really need is some help to string my antenna. I can be on the air in a couple of minutes."

"You're a radio operator, Sergeant?"

"Yes, Sir. That's why General Pickering sent me."

Fertig looked at the Filipino.

"Ask Lieutenant Ball and Sergeant LaMadrid to report to me, would you, please?" he said. He turned back to Koffler. "Lieutenant Ball is my signal officer," he said. "They'll string your antenna for you."

"Yes, Sir. Thank you."

"This is interesting," Fertig said, fingering the sword. "What is it?"

"Lieutenant McCoy told me that when the war just started, some Army asshole—"

He stopped, horrified at what he had just said.

"It's all right, Sergeant. I am perfectly willing to agree that there are a number of assholes in the United States Army."

"Some Army guy sent twenty thousand of them to Australia. They're Cavalry sabers. An Ordnance officer—an *Army* Ordnance officer—cut them down and sharpened them. They make pretty good machetes. Good steel in them."

"I see. And that weapon of yours?"

Koffler handed it to him.

"It's what they call a carbine, General. Sort of halfway between a pistol and a rifle. Fifteen shots. They're good out to about a hundred yards. We brought you a hundred of them. If they got them all off the submarine. They were going to try to unload some more stuff, maybe all we brought, if the Japs didn't show up."

"Interesting weapon," Fertig said, turning it over in his hands.

"Colonel Stecker and McCoy decided it would be smarter to bring carbines than rifles. They're smaller, the ammo doesn't weigh as much, and the Colonel thought that your Filipinos could probably handle them better than rifles."

"Colonel Stecker? Who is he, Sergeant?"

"*Marine* Colonel, Sir. He won the Medal of Honor in the First World War. He was supposed to come in with us, but they're going to make him a general and send him to Washington, so he couldn't."

So at least two people more senior than a lieutenant are involved in this. Thank God!

And then another question occurred to him.

"Did you meet Captain Weston?"

"Yes, Sir."

"Presumably, he is with your lieutenant—McCoy, I believe you said?—on the beach?"

"Yes, Sir. Lieutenant McCoy. No, Sir. Mr. McCoy sent him to Australia on the submarine."

"He did what?" Fertig asked, at first greatly surprised, and then suddenly annoyed. "On whose authority?" he wondered angrily, aloud.

"Mr. McCoy sent him to Australia, Sir," Koffler said. "I guess he figured he had the authority to do that, otherwise he wouldn't have done it."

"I can't wait to meet Lieutenant McCoy," Fertig said.

Lieutenant Robert Ball appeared, sleepy-eyed. He looked at Koffler with undisguised curiosity.

"You sent for me, General?"

"This is Staff Sergeant Koffler of the United States Marines," Fertig said. "He needs some assistance to erect an antenna. He intends to communicate with Australia with it. Would you and Sergeant LaMadrid assist him, please?"

"Yes, Sir," Ball said. He offered his hand to Koffler. "I hope you've got some wire?"

"Yes, Sir. I've cut a straight wire for the twenty-meter band, insulators and everything. It's in one of the parcels."

"And you have a radio?"

"A radio, a key, and enough batteries for two hours. Have you got a generator?"

"It'll take an hour to get it running; it's in pieces."

"Then I guess we better go with the batteries for now," Koffler said. "It won't take long. But I am going to need a generator pretty soon."

With Lieutenant Ball and Sergeant LaMadrid—and halfway through the process, General Fertig—as a fascinated audience, Sergeant Koffler carefully removed the plastic coating from several packages. There were four identical packages, each containing a battery. Others held a neatly coiled roll of copper wire to which were attached ceramic insulators; a receiver; a transmitter; a high-speed telegraphic key; and a small set of headphones.

The receiving and transmitting antennae were quickly erected. Koffler pulled his shirt from his trousers again and untied the second plastic belt.

With all the care of a surgeon, he used his machete to slit open the square package.

"Gotta be careful as hell with this," he explained. "Not only is it printed on what looks like toilet paper, but it's soaked in some chemical that makes it practically explode if you get a match near it."

Inside the package was an oilskin envelope. Koffler opened it, removed a pad of paper, tore the first sheet from it, and carefully tucked it in his pocket. Then he put the pad of paper back in the oilskin envelope, carefully closed it, and looked at Lieutenant Ball.

"This is your new SOI," he said. "You got someplace to keep it where it won't get fucked up, or would you rather I keep it?"

"I'll keep it safe," Ball said, and Koffler handed it to him.

"Lieutenant McCoy's got another copy," he said. "But if we lose both, we're all back up shit's creek."

He took the flimsy sheet of paper from his pocket and read it carefully.

Taking note of the interest of his audience, he then handed it to General Fertig. "I thought it was 'K' and 'P,' but it always pays to check," Koffler said.

MESSAGE 001

PART A - TO BE TRANSMITTED IN THE CLEAR, REPEATED TWICE

OPERATIONAL IMMEDIATE
FROM MXX FOR IMMEDIATE PERSONAL ATTENTION CINCPAC
ALL STATIONS COPY FOR RELAY TO KFS

PART B - ONE OR MORE OF THE FOLLOWING AS APPROPRIATE TO BE TRANSMITTED IN THE CLEAR REPEATED FOUR (4) TIMES

AAA—LANDING PARTY ABORTING MISSION ATTEMPTING RETURN SUNFISH

BBB—LANDING PARTY ASHORE LOST CONTACT WITH SUNFISH

CCC—SUNFISH DETECTED BY ENEMY ASHORE

DDD—SUNFISH DETECTED BY ENEMY SURFACE CRAFT

EEE—SUNFISH DETECTED BY ENEMY AIRCRAFT

FFF—SUNFISH UNDER ATTACK BY ENEMY ARTILLERY

GGG—SUNFISH UNDER ATTACK BY ENEMY SURFACE CRAFT

HHH—SUNFISH UNDER ATTACK BY ENEMY AIRCRAFT

III—SUNFISH BELIEVED DAMAGED

JJJ—SUNFISH BELIEVED SUNK BY ENEMY ACTION

KKK—SUNFISH SAFELY DEPARTED UNDAMAGED

LLL—LANDING PARTY ASHORE SUSPECT DETECTION MOVING INLAND

MMM—LANDING PARTY DETECTED SITUATION IN DOUBT

NNN—LANDING PARTY SAFELY ASHORE NO CONTACT WITH FRIENDLIES

OOO—LANDING PARTY SAFELY ASHORE IN CONTACT WITH FRIENDLIES

PPP—LANDING PARTY SAFELY ASHORE IN CONTACT WITH FERTIG

PART C—TO BE TRANSMITTED IN THE CLEAR, REPEATED TWICE

END

MXX CLEAR

" 'K' and 'P' does have a nice ring to it, doesn't it, Sergeant?" General Fertig said.

"Yes, Sir, it does," Sergeant Koffler said. "Put a match to that, General. We don't need it anymore."

Fertig shrugged, took out his lighter, and applied the flame to the small sheet of paper. There was a flash, a small cloud of smoke, and the paper disappeared.

"I'll be damned," the Commanding General, USFIP, said.

"Now let's see if we can get this sonofabitch on the air," Sergeant Koffler said, and put the earphones on his head.

[SEVEN]
Rocky Fields Farm
Bernardsville, New Jersey
2315 Hours 25 December 1942

When the telephone rang, Miss Ernestine Sage had been standing for ten minutes, in her bathrobe, before the fireplace in the living room, leaning on the mantelpiece, toying with a poker at the vestiges of the fire that had blazed all day. She and her parents had gone to bed over an hour before.

In a transparent effort to cheer her up, her father had kept the house filled with friends on Christmas Eve, and with a dinner for twelve on Christmas Day.

"It's been a long day for everybody," her father had announced, "and getting to bed early won't do anyone any harm."

Unable to sleep, she'd tossed around for a long time, then left the bed, wrapped herself in a bathrobe, and went downstairs. There she'd fixed herself a stiff drink and swallowed deep, then set the glass on the mantelpiece of the fireplace.

She walked quickly to the telephone, feeling sick.

That has to be bad news. Why the hell else would anyone call at this hour on Christmas?

"Ernie?" She recognized the voice of Captain Ed Sessions.

"Oh, no!"

"Oh no, what?"

"Oh no, what the hell do you think? Tell me, Ed. Oh, Christ, *don't* tell me. I don't want this goddamned call."

"Ken's been heard from," Sessions said.

"And?"

"He reached where he was going safely. They all did. An Operational Immediate to Knox, info us, came in just a few minutes ago from CINCPAC. I'm the duty officer here. I got it."

There was no reply.

"I thought you'd like to know," Sessions said, somewhat lamely.

"I'd like to know that you're surprised he got safely where he's supposed to go? Exactly where he got safely to being another of your goddamn secrets. And from which you'll be surprised again if he makes it safely out?"

Captain Ed Sessions, who could think of nothing to say, said nothing.

"Ed, I'm sorry. I had a premonition all day . . ."

"Ken can take care of himself. He'll be all right."

"He said, comforting the near-hysterical female, and knowing goddamned well he doesn't know any more than she does whether or not he'll be all right."

"If I didn't mean that, I wouldn't say it. And you don't sound hysterical."

"The only reason I'm not screaming and pulling out my hair is that it would embarrass my parents," Ernie said. "My father is big on bad form."

"Ernie, Ken's going to be all right."

" 'So how's the baby?' she said, to change the subject."

"Baby's fine. Come down and have a look for yourself."

"I can't do that. I get overwhelmed with jealousy. Ken wouldn't give me one, in case you didn't notice."

"Control your jealousy and come down," Sessions said. "Jeanne would love to have you."

There was a long pause.

"Ed, I'm sorry. I've been a bitch. I very much appreciate the call, and I have no right to jump all over you."

"You can get a little excited, Ernie, but you'll never be a bitch."

"Have you a number for Pick?" she asked.

"He's living in the Peabody Hotel in Memphis, isn't he?"

"I tried there before. No answer."

"I've got his squadron number here someplace. Hold on." She heard the phone being laid down, and then he came back on the line and gave her a number. "Maybe they can help," he said.

She heard another telephone ringing, so she knew he was not trying to get rid of her when he said, "Ernie, I have to go."

"Good night, Ed. Merry Christmas. Thank you. Happy New Year."

"Why don't you come down for New Year's? Think about it," he said, and then the line went dead.

"Newton 4-6761, Newton 4-6761," she repeated over and over until she searched for and found a pencil and could write it down. Then she dialed the operator, said, "Long distance, please. In Memphis, Tennessee, Newton 4-6761"

"Is this call necessary?" the operator asked, in compliance with the government policy to lower the incidence of long-distance calls in order to keep lines free for essential war-connected business.

"No. I'm a Nazi spy trying to tie up the lines so that we'll lose the war," Ernie said.

"Is this call necessary?" the operator repeated.

"Yes, it is."

The phone was answered on the second ring.

"VMF-262, Sergeant Cadman, charge of quarters speaking, SIR!"

"I'm trying to locate Lieutenant Pickering."

"Hold on, Ma'am," Sergeant Cadman said, and she heard the phone being laid down, and then, faintly, "For you, Sir. A lady."

"Lieutenant Pickering."

"Relax, you don't have to marry me, at least right now."

"Well, God, that's a relief. I'm much too young for that sort of responsibility. What's up?"

"What are you doing in—what is that, your office?—at this time of night?"

"Well, before I was summoned to the telephone, I was trying to sleep. I've got the duty."

"You can sleep on duty?"

"There's a cot. What's up, Ernie?"

"Ed Sessions just called. Ken got wherever he went safely. Just where that is being another goddamned secret."

"If they won't tell you where he is, he's probably in the Philippines," Pick Pickering said.

"The Philippines? My God, the Japanese have *captured* the Philippines!"

"On reflection, I don't think I should have said what I just said."

"Well, you can't leave me hanging, damn you!"

"If you insist on swearing at me, I'll never marry you, Ernie."

"Damn you, Pick!"

"I really don't know what I'm talking about. But Dad wrote Mom—and she told me—that he was trying to help some guerrillas in the Philippines—"

"Gorillas? As in King Kong? What are you talking about?"

"*Guerrillas,* with a 'u' and an 'e.' Irregular troops operating behind enemy lines. That sounds right down the Killer's line."

"Oh, my God!"

"Hey, Ernie. Don't underestimate him. He's one hell of a Marine."

"Oh, yeah!" she said sarcastically.

"Ernie, I'd love to chat, but this is an official line, and Little Billy Dunn, my noble squadron commander, is celebrating the joyous Yuletide season by taking our guys up to teach them how to fly in the dark."

"On Christmas Eve, *Christmas Day night?*"

"Some of them shouldn't be trusted with a tricycle, much less a Corsair. He may have to call."

"Billy has people flying tonight?" she asked incredulously.

"Write this down, Ernie. There's a war on."

"And I'm being hysterical, right?"

"You said it, not me. Ken will be all right, Ernie. And if he isn't, at least you get to marry me."

"You sonofabitch, you!" she flamed.

"Now there's my girl, back to normal. Nightie, night, Ernie!"

The line went dead in her ear.

She replaced the phone in its cradle.

"Everything all right, honey?" her father asked.

He was standing behind one of the couches, wearing his bathrobe. His usually slicked-back hair was askew.

"How long have you been in here?"

"I heard the phone," he said.

"It was from an officer who works for Uncle Fleming. He told me that Ken is safely where he's going, but where that is is a big secret. So I called Pick, and Pick says he's probably in the Philippines. Uncle Fleming wrote Aunt Patricia about helping guerrillas in the Philippines, and she told Pick, and Pick said that's probably where Ken is. That's right down the Killer's line, is the way he put it."

"Ken'll be all right, honey," Ernest Sage said gently.

"If one more person says that to me, I'll throw up!" Ernie snapped, and then she ran into her father's arms and wept.

XVI

[ONE]
Headquarters, U.S. Forces in the Philippines
Davao Oriental Province
Mindanao, Commonwealth of the Philippines
0625 Hours 28 December 1942

The first thing General Fertig noticed about the three officers and a Marine sergeant who had come to see him was that they all looked so well nourished, and that their sturdy-looking black clothing and boots were in such good shape.

The second thing he noticed, as they approached his house, was that the two officers wearing the double silver bars of captains stood aside at the foot of the stairs to permit the youngest, and slightest—and most junior, to judge from the single silver bar pinned to his soft cap—to climb up the ladder first.

That has to be Lieutenant "Killer" McCoy, who took it upon himself to order Captain Weston away on the submarine. That young man is about to be put in his place.

The lieutenant saluted as he walked across the porch to Fertig.

"Lieutenant McCoy, Sir, USMC," he said.

Fertig returned the salute.

"And these gentlemen?"

"Lieutenant Lewis, Sir, of CINCPAC," McCoy said. "Captain Macklin of the OSS, and Gunnery Sergeant Zimmerman."

I have no idea what the OSS is, but I'm not going to ask.

"Welcome to U.S. Forces in the Philippines, gentlemen. My name is Fertig." He shook hands with everybody, and motioned for them to sit in the rattan chairs.

"We're a little surprised to find you here, General," McCoy said. "Everly said that you were—on the run?"

"A precautionary measure," Fertig said. "In case the Japanese captured one of my officers. When I learned that didn't happen, we came back home."

"Yes, Sir," McCoy said.

"Just to clear the air, who is in command of this mission?"

"Lieutenant McCoy is, General," Lewis said. "Captain Macklin and myself are observers."

"I understand you took it upon yourself, Lieutenant, to order one of my officers aboard the submarine?"

"Yes, Sir. Acting on orders, Sir," McCoy said.

"And what precisely are those orders, Lieutenant? Do I get to see a copy of them?"

"My orders were verbal, Sir. From General Pickering. They were to find you; to provide you with communications equipment and a Signal Operating Instruction; to bring you a few supplies, including some gold; to evaluate your potential—"

"You consider yourself qualified to evaluate my forces?" Fertig interrupted.

"—and to send one of your senior officers back on the *Sunfish*," McCoy went on. "Sir, it doesn't matter what I think of my qualifications. You're sort of stuck with me."

"Presumably you're on General MacArthur's staff?"

McCoy smiled.

"No, Sir. I'm assigned to the USMC Office of Management Analysis, Sir."

"And you're here to *analyze* my *management,* is that what you're saying?"

"General," Lewis said. "If I may?"

Fertig nodded.

"Among those officers available to General Pickering, Lieutenant McCoy was determined to be the one most familiar with irregular operations. He's done this sort of thing before."

"Conducted guerrilla operations, you mean?"

"Operated behind the enemy's lines, Sir."

"And who is General Pickering? He, presumably, *is* on General MacArthur's staff?"

"No, Sir. He's Chief of the Office of Management Analysis," McCoy said.

"So you're *not* here representing General MacArthur and SWPOA?"

"No, Sir," McCoy said.

"General," Lewis said. "I'm on the staff of CINCPAC. CINCPAC was directed by Admiral Leahy, the President's Chief of Staff, to provide whatever assistance General Pickering required to mount this mission."

And that assistance is three junior officers and a sergeant, apparently.

"I had hoped that what we're trying to do here had finally attracted General MacArthur's interest and concern," Fertig said. "Apparently, that is not the case."

"El Supremo went on record, General," McCoy said, "saying 'guerrilla operations in the Philippines are impossible.' "

Is that what you call him, Lieutenant? El Supremo?

"I presume you are referring to General MacArthur?"

"And you made it worse when you promoted yourself, General," McCoy went on, unabashed.

"I considered that necessary," Fertig said. "I didn't think anyone would pay attention to a lieutenant colonel."

"I believe both General Pickering and Admiral Nimitz understand that, General," Lewis said. "I believe Lieutenant McCoy is trying, Sir, to make you aware of certain problems we all have to deal with."

"I am here, with several hundred courageous men, American and Filipino, living on the edge of starvation, like hunted animals in the jungle, attempting to wage war against the Japanese, and I find myself a humble supplicant, on my knees, begging for the tools to do that," Fertig said. "I confess that from time to time I find myself growing a little bitter."

"May I suggest, Sir," Lewis said, "that first, what you have been doing here has not gone unappreciated, and second, that your supply situation has already begun to change? We've brought some supplies with us—at least a token shipment—and more will very likely follow."

"Depending on a lieutenant's *analysis* of my *management?* Is that what you're saying?"

"Sir, I have reason to believe," Lewis said, "that whatever Lieutenant McCoy's report happens to be, it will be accepted at face value at the highest levels."

"Is that so? What are your reasons for believing that?"

"Sir," Lewis said, "I don't think you have been in a position to know that early on, the President ordered the formation of a special unit within the Marine Corps, the Marine Raiders, something like the British Commandos, with the mission of attacking the Japanese in an irregular manner. In August, ten days after the First Marine Division landed at Guadalcanal, elements of the 2nd Raider Battalion, operating off a submarine, successfully attacked Makin Island."

"Very interesting," Fertig said. "If they could send a submarine to—what did you say?—*Makin Island* in August, why couldn't they send one here?"

"Sir, with respect," Lewis said. "The first indication anyone had that you had established a guerrilla operation here was in early October."

Goddammit! I'm making a fool of myself. What the hell is the matter with me? Why am I being such a horse's ass to these people? Possibly because I am losing my mind. Or because, in some perverted manner, these well-fed, well-shod, self-confident—especially that damned Killer McCoy—young officers anger me.

"As I was saying, Sir," Lewis said, "the Marine Raiders successfully attacked Japanese positions on Makin Island. Lieutenant McCoy and Sergeant Zimmerman were on that operation, General."

"Lieutenant, please don't get the idea that my anger at the powers that be is in any way directed at you," Fertig said. "I am overjoyed to see you here, and fully appreciative of the enormous risks you all took to come here."

"I'm a Marine, General," McCoy said, visibly embarrassed. "I go where they send me."

"If I may continue, General," Lewis said. "Captain James Roosevelt, USMC, the President's son, was also on the Makin Island raid. Captain Roosevelt is known to be another of Lieutenant McCoy's admirers. I submit, Sir, that whatever Lieutenant McCoy has to say about your operation here and its potential will receive a very sympathetic ear from the President."

"I take your point," Fertig said. "I hope to convince you, then, Lieutenant, that what we have here is potentially a very valuable force with which to wage war, and that we are not a motley crew of insubordinate lunatics headed by a self-promoted egomaniac."

"I'm ready to be convinced, Sir," McCoy said with a smile.

"You haven't said anything, Captain," Fertig said to Macklin. "What's your role in this operation? Starting at the beginning, what is the OSS?"

"It's the Office of Strategic Services," Macklin said. "Headed by Colonel William Donovan. It is directly under the President. It is charged with intelligence gathering, sabotage, and guerrilla operations worldwide. I was sent on this mission as an observer. It—"

"MacArthur, and the people around him, don't want anything to do with the OSS," McCoy interrupted. "General Pickering thinks that Colonel Donovan thinks that MacArthur can be forced to accept OSS if somebody from the OSS is in on this operation. Anyway, he was ordered to send Captain Macklin along with us."

And you don't like that at all, do you, Killer McCoy? And from your tone of voice, you don't like Captain Macklin either. I wonder what's behind that?

"Let's get down to business," Fertig said. "In this 'token shipment' of supplies, what exactly have you brought us?"

McCoy reached in the billowing pocket on the side of his camouflage utilities and came out with an oilskin envelope.

"There's a list in there," he said, and chuckled. "You're supposed to sign for them, General. Otherwise, I suppose, they'll start taking them out of my pay."

"The gold will be the most valuable," Fertig said when he'd read the list. "I've been signing IOUs for the supplies, food mostly, we've been able to get from the Filipinos. Money, as someone wise once said, talks."

"El Supremo thinks that matchbooks talk, too," McCoy said, chuckling, and handed Fertig a book of matches. On it was printed, "I SHALL RETURN! MacArthur."

Fertig examined the matches.

"I'll be damned," he said. "Oddly enough, I think these will be very effective."

"We have a case of those," McCoy said, "and we also brought you typewriter ribbons, some uniforms—General Pickering got your sizes from your wife—and a case of scotch. These aren't on the list of stuff you have to sign for."

"Lieutenant," Fertig said, "I am beginning to like you. In time, I may even forgive you for sending Captain Weston off on the submarine."

"I had to do that, General," McCoy said. "And it was a choice between him and Everly. The last time I saw Everly, he was a PFC. PFCs don't rate too high with El Supremo."

"Weston will see General MacArthur?"

"That was the idea, Sir."

"And presumably, after you have *analyzed* my *management* of USFIP, you will report to General MacArthur?"

"I will report to General Pickering, Sir. And then he'll report to General MacArthur. And probably the President."

"You will, then, be evacuated from here?"

"The *Sunfish* is supposed to return for us—and to deliver some more supplies—on 14 January, Sir. There may be a little delay in that. Obviously, she can't surface in the same place again. That's one of the things that will have to be worked out."

"General, I brought charts with me," Lewis said. "Places we feel might be good for a submarine infiltration. We of course don't know what the situation is with the Japanese, but . . ."

"There's a lot of shoreline here. The Japanese can't patrol all of it, all the time. But on the other hand, now they know you're here, I'm sure they'll increase patrol activity, both on the ground and by aircraft. Getting you out of here may be more difficult than getting you in. We have lost the element of surprise."

Fertig waited for this to sink in, then went on.

"The reason I'm curious is that we have some people here—some of my men who are wounded, and whom we can't care for properly, and some American civilians, including some missionary nurses—that I would like to send out with you when you go."

"I think that could be arranged, Sir," Lewis said. "If we succeed in unloading the cargo, there would be room for, say, twenty people. It would be crowded, but . . ."

"I'll make up a list," Fertig said, and then asked, "You mentioned a case of scotch?"

"Yes, Sir."

"Would you gentlemen care to join me in a small libation? I realize the inappropriate hour, but it's been a long time. . . ."

"That would be very nice, General," Lewis said. "Thank you very much. Macklin, would you please go get the General his scotch?"

Without a word, Macklin stood up and went to fetch the scotch.

[TWO]
Office of the Military Governor of Mindanao
Cagayan de Oro, Misamis-Oriental Province
Mindanao, Commonwealth of the Philippines
1450 Hours 29 December 1942

"Let me be sure, Colonel Himasatsu," Brigadier General Kurokawa Kenzo said to the Commanding Officer of the 203rd Infantry Regiment, "that I understand what you're telling me. Your regiment, some twenty-five hundred men, took five days to find your missing patrol's truck?"

"Sir, the General must understand what the terrain is like in that area. It is heavy jungle, there is no—"

Kurokawa held up his hand to shut him off.

"And that when you found the truck," Kurokawa went on, "and the patrol sergeant and the truck driver—with their throats cut—you saw no sign of the missing patrol itself?"

"No, Sir. We have not yet been able to locate the patrol itself."

"How many incidents of guerrilla activity does this outrage make this month in your area of responsibility, Colonel?"

"Twenty-two, Sir."

"And how many Japanese soldiers have been murdered by these bandits?"

"Seven officers and one hundred and sixteen other ranks, Sir."

"Counting the dead sergeant and the truck driver?"

"No, Sir."

"Counting the missing four members of the patrol?"

"No, Sir."

"That would bring the total to one hundred twenty-two other ranks, wouldn't it?"

"We don't know that the members of the missing patrol are actually dead, Sir."

"I suppose it is possible that they are off cavorting in a brothel somewhere, but I don't think that's likely, Colonel, do you?"

"No, Sir."

"And how many bandits have you caught, Colonel Himasatsu?"

"None, Sir."

"Let me state this as clearly as I can, Colonel. The performance of your regiment is not satisfactory."

"Yes, Sir."

"You have two weeks, Colonel, to bring me some results. Otherwise, I will recommend that you be relieved."

"Yes, Sir."

"That will be all, Colonel," Kurokawa said. "Colonel Tange is outside. On your way out, will you be good enough to ask him to come in, please?"

"Yes, Sir," Colonel Himasatsu said. He bowed, turned on his heel, and marched out of the room. Colonel Tange marched in and bowed.

"If the Kempeitai can assist me in dealing with these bandit attacks on our forces, Colonel Tange," General Kurokawa said, "I would be most grateful. I would also solicit any suggestions you might have."

"General, the Kempeitai has thoroughly interrogated close to two hundred Filipinos who might have some knowledge of Fertig's activities. Seventeen of those interrogated died during their interrogation. Unfortunately, I must tell you that I was forced to conclude that those interrogated knew nothing of Fertig's activities before these attacks occurred."

"Then may I respectfully suggest you should interrogate another two hundred Filipinos—four hundred Filipinos, a *thousand* Filipinos—until we find someone who does know something?"

"Further interrogations are under way at this moment, General. I will keep you advised, of course."

"You wanted to see me, didn't you?" Kurokawa said. "I forgot that. I apologize. It was my intention to ask you to see me, and when my sergeant told me you were outside, I assumed it was because I had sent for you. I confess, Tange, this business is upsetting me more and more."

"Yes, Sir. We have heard from Signals Intelligence in Manila, Sir. They have provided me with a decryption of the December 24 messages from Australia to Fertig."

"Anything significant in them?"

"Signals Intelligence believes it was notification to Fertig that an infiltration was to be attempted on the coast, south of Boston."

"How far south of Boston?" Kurokawa asked quietly.

"Thirty miles south. Not far from where Colonel Himasatsu's patrol vanished."

"You heard they found the truck?"

"Just before I came here, Sir."

"So there was an infiltration," Kurokawa said. "A successful infiltration."

"There seems to be additional proof of that, Sir," Tange said. "Signals Intelligence has reported that communication between Fertig and Australia is now being transmitted over a far more powerful transmitter using a new encryption system. By a far more skilled radio telegrapher."

"Does that mean we will no longer be able to decrypt their messages?"

"No, Sir. But it will be more difficult, and hence more time-consuming, to perform the decryptions."

Kurokawa shook his head in resignation.

"There is talk, Tange, that shortly we will no longer have the services of Captain Saikaku available to us. Anything to it?"

"That was another reason I asked you to receive me, General. I thought you would be interested in hearing that Captain Saikaku has been ordered to Tokyo to assume duties on the Imperial General Staff."

"How interesting," Kurokawa said. "He requested such a transfer?"

"My understanding, Sir, is that the orders came from General Tojo's office. Three days after Captain Saikaku requested, and I granted, permission for him to use Kempeitai lines to communicate with his sick mother."

"Do you suppose we dare hope that Captain Saikaku will convey to the Imperial General Staff our difficulty in dealing with General Fertig?"

"Perhaps, General. But I rather think it more likely that once Captain Saikaku arrives in Tokyo, he will quickly forget anything to do with Fertig."

"Yes," General Kurokawa said. "Especially his initial enthusiastic pronouncement that Fertig was a small problem that could be dealt with quickly and effectively."

[THREE]
USFIP Field Hospital #2
Near Compostela, Davao Province, Mindanao
Commonwealth of the Philippines
31 December 1942

USFIP Field Hospital #2 consisted of three thatch-roofed buildings on stilts in a small clearing in the jungle on the steep side of an unnamed hill, accessible only by dirt path. One of the buildings housed the medical staff, which consisted of Lieutenant Stanley J. Miller (formerly Chief Pharmacist's Mate, USN) and his four assistants, Sergeant Waldron Barron (formerly Seaman 2nd Class, USN), and Sergeants Manuel Garcia, Luis Delarocca, and Oswaldo Lopez (late of the Medical Corps, Philippine Army).

The Detachment of Patients was divided, according to the medical judgment of Lieutenant Miller, into two groups. Those who had a reasonable expectation of survival were in Ward #1, and those who did not were in Ward #2.

"Doc, say hello to Mr. McCoy," Second Lieutenant Percy L. Everly said as he and First Lieutenant Kenneth R. McCoy entered Ward #2.

Chief Miller, whose only item of uniform clothing was his now badly tattered brimmed chief petty officer's cap, raised his eyes from the emaciated, sweat-soaked Filipino lying on a crude cot and saw a young man dressed in loose black clothing. He noticed that the young man looked well fed, and was carrying in his hand what looked like a miniature rifle.

He nodded, just barely perceptibly, but did not speak.

"Chief," McCoy said.

"We brought you stuff," Everly said.

"Like what?" Chief Miller asked.

"Rice, a couple of porkers on the hoof, pineapples, and a bottle of booze," Everly said, and handed Miller a bottle of Famous Grouse.

"Jesus Christ, where did you get this?" Miller asked, taking the bottle from him and looking at him wonderingly.

"And this," McCoy said, and handed Chief Miller the rucksack that had been hanging from his shoulder.

Miller carefully laid the whiskey bottle on the bamboo floor, then took the rucksack and opened it. It contained a number of flat parcels packaged in a shiny opaque material strange to Miller. He looked up at McCoy curiously. McCoy was in the process of drawing a knife from a sheath strapped to his lower left arm. He handed the knife to Miller, who slit open one of the plastic-wrapped packages. He reached inside and removed from it a half-dozen flat olive-drab packages approximately 1.5 inches square. After placing all but one back in the plastic package, he examined the one in his hand very carefully.

"You know what this is?" McCoy asked.

"Yeah, I know what sulfanilamide is," Miller said. "How much of it do you have?"

"Two more bags like that with us," McCoy replied. "And another dozen bags back with General Fertig."

"What is that stuff, Doc?" Everly asked.

Miller bent over the patient on the crude cot, carefully pulled a blood-soaked bandage from the Filipino's side, then tore open the olive-drab envelope and sprinkled the white powder it contained on the ugly, obviously infected wound.

"This stuff was invented by a chemist named Roblin—he works for Lederle Laboratories. The original stuff came from the aspirin people, Bayer, in Germany."

"What's it do?" Everly asked.

"It's an antibacterial," Chief Miller said, conversationally. "It kills infection. If it's as good as advertised, it'll keep this guy alive."

"No shit?" Everly asked.

"I never expected to see any here," Chief Miller said. "Where did you come from, Mr. McCoy?" Before McCoy could answer, Miller went on. "Did you bring me anything else?"

"Morphine, field surgeon's kits, Atabrine . . ."

"Jesus Christ! Where did you come from?"

"Off a submarine," Everly replied for him.

"What are you doing here?"

"I need a list of things you need. You get three thousand pounds in the first shipment."

"Christ, I need everything!" Miller said, gesturing around Ward #2.

"You get three thousand pounds in the first shipment," McCoy repeated. "Nothing weighing more than fifty pounds. More later."

"When's the first shipment?"

"The *Sunfish* is due back here 14 January," McCoy said.

"How are they going to know what to bring?"

"You tell me what you want in your three thousand pounds," McCoy said. "That'll be radioed from Fertig's headquarters."

"You ought to see the way they've got that fixed, Doc," Everly said.

Miller looked at him in confusion.

"Everything is on a list of numbers. Like, .45 ammo, one 600-round case, is number 606, or some shit. All they radio is four-dash-six-oh-six, and they'll load four cases of .45 ammo."

"We need your list as soon as possible," McCoy said, handing him a mimeographed list of available medical supplies.

"Christ, Doc, you wouldn't believe what they brought us," Sergeant Waldron Barron, a small, very thin, bony-featured twenty-two-year-old, said, coming into Ward #2. "Bags of rice, *six* fucking pigs!"

"Mr. McCoy also brought some gold," Everly said. "Amazing what stuff comes out of hiding when you start paying with twenty-dollar gold pieces."

"Did you bring any dressings?" Miller asked. "I mean now."

"Standard field compresses," McCoy said.

"Start in here, Barron," Miller ordered. "Take off every bandage. Sprinkle the wound with sulfanilamide . . ."

"With what?" Sergeant Barron asked.

"This stuff," Miller said, taking another envelope from the package. "Watch what I do."

He demonstrated.

"Then put on fresh dressings."

"What is that stuff?"

"It kills infections, or it's supposed to."

"I'll be damned," Sergeant Barron said. "It really works?"

"It's supposed to," McCoy said.

"Christ, is that a bottle of whiskey?" Barron asked, spotting the Famous Grouse.

Miller picked it up and twisted the cap off.

"One drink," he said, handing the bottle to Barron. "And then get to work."

Barron looked at the bottle.

"The guy with the knee wound needs this more than I do, Chief."

"We also have some morphine."

"Then I will have a little taste," Sergeant Barron said, and raised the bottle to his mouth.

[FOUR]
United States Submarine *Sunfish*
161° 27″ East Longitude 5° 19″ West Latitude
Philippine Sea
0505 Hours 4 January 1943

First Lieutenant (Captain, USFIP) James B. Weston, USMC, put his head through the hatch in the deck of the conning tower.

"Permission to come up, Sir?" he called.

Lieutenant Commander Warren T. Houser, USN, took the binoculars from his eyes and looked down at the blond-bearded head.

"If I have told you *oncet,* Mr. Supercargo, I have told you *thrice,* you have the privilege of the bridge."

"Thank you, Sir," Weston said, and came through the hatch.

He was wearing khakis, and, aside from the beard, was indistinguishable from the other three officers on the bridge.

Nine days previously, orders had been transmitted to the *Sunfish:*

OPERATIONAL IMMEDIATE
2105 GREENWICH 25 DEC 1942

FROM CINCPAC
TO SUNFISH

(1) PROCEED AT BEST SPEED CONSISTENT WITH FUEL EXHAUSTION TO COORDINATES SEVEN EIGHT ZERO XXX ONE FOUR NINE. RESERVE

SUFFICIENT FUEL TO SUBSEQUENTLY PROCEED AT NORMAL SPEED TO
COORDINATES SEVEN FOUR FOUR XXX TEN NINE SIX.

(2) COMMENCING 1 JAN 43 ADVISE DURING SCHEDULED CONTACT
ESTIMATED TIME ARRIVAL COORDINATES SEVEN EIGHT ZERO XXX ONE
FOUR NINE.

(3) PREPARE TO TRANSFER SUPERCARGO AT COORDINATES SEVEN
EIGHT ZERO XXX ONE FOUR NINE. FURTHER DETAILS TO FOLLOW.

BY DIRECTION CINCPAC

WAGAM RADM USN

When laid over the chart, coordinates 774 × 096—according to the SOI for the date of reception; they changed daily—were those of Espíritu Santo. It was reasonable to assume that the *Sunfish* would be refueled there.

Coordinates 780 × 149, when laid over the chart, showed an empty expanse of water in the South Pacific Ocean several hundred miles from Espíritu Santo.

To avoid detection by Japanese aircraft and/or surface vessels, the *Sunfish* had traveled submerged during the daylight hours for four days after leaving Mindanao. This permitted a submerged cruising speed, on her four battery-powered 2,085 Shaft Horse Power electric motors, of approximately eight nautical miles per hour. She had surfaced just after nightfall on each of the first four days—bringing very welcome fresh air into her hull—and switched to her four 4,300 SHP diesel engines. While simultaneously recharging her batteries, this had permitted a fuel-economy-be-damned speed on the surface of approximately seventeen nautical miles per hour.

For the last five days, *Sunfish* had run on the surface, prepared to emergency-dive at the sight of anything in the sky or on the horizon. There had been nothing. At 1805 the previous day, she had transmitted her estimated arrival time—0445—to CINCPAC.

Now, having reached coordinates 780 × 149 at 0440 hours, she was running with just enough turns to provide steerageway over a calm and endless sea. Despite what her original orders had said about "further details to follow," none had followed.

The change in the pitch of her engines had brought Captain Jim Weston to the conning tower from the wardroom, where he had been reading every magazine *Sunfish* had aboard.

It was light, but the sun had not yet appeared on the horizon. Lieutenant

Commander Houser had made a command decision—which did not lie lightly on his shoulders—not to man the antiaircraft weaponry, four .50 caliber Browning air-cooled machine guns, or her four-inch naval cannon. Should aircraft appear in the sky, or a warship on the horizon, he felt the greater safety for his vessel lay in crash-diving as quickly as possible. Ensuring that gun crews had made it safely inside would take time.

At the instant the tip of the sun appeared on the horizon, Chief Buchanan, unable to conceal his concern, bellowed:

"Aircraft dead ahead, estimate two miles, two thousand feet!"

Commander Houser turned to his talker, a sailor equipped with a microphone and a headset permitting him to relay orders to and from the conning tower.

"All ahead full, prepare to dive," Houser ordered.

"All ahead full, prepare to dive," the talker parroted, and there was a near-instant roar and billow of smoke from *Sunfish*'s diesels.

"Get below, Mr. Weston, please," Commander Houser ordered calmly, then trained his binoculars on the rapidly approaching speck in the sky.

The aircraft was difficult to see. It was coming in out of the sun, which lay just over the horizon. But Houser could make out that it was a flying boat; he could see the fuselage, from which pontoons dropped, and a high wing.

It's probably a Catalina, he decided. *It would be the ideal aircraft for a mission like this.* A Catalina was a long-range reconnaissance aircraft, easily capable of making a landing in the sea, taking Weston aboard, and taking off again.

And then he felt bile in his mouth.

That sonofabitch has four engines; it's not a Catalina, it's an H8K!!! The Kawanishi H8K, which borrowed many of its design features from the two-engine Catalina, was a four-engine long-range reconnaissance/bomber seaplane. It was faster and more heavily armed and armored than the Catalina.

And my antiaircraft isn't manned! Goddamn it, what was I thinking of when I made that *decision?*

"Emergency dive!" he ordered. "Dive, dive, dive!"

The personnel on the bridge began to drop through the hatch as quickly as they could manage to do so.

The submerging process seemed to be slower than Houser remembered.

The H8K was growing larger by the second. And it was unquestionably on a bomb run. A nice, slow, sure-to-be-accurate bomb run.

And then he saw something that made the situation appear even worse.

The H8K was not alone. Other aircraft were above and behind it, two of them, on the exact same course, smaller planes, almost certainly fighters. At the speed they were moving, they would be in strafing range of the *Sunfish* long before the H8K could drop its bombs. Twenty-millimeter machine-cannon fire would probably sweep the hull, or certainly the conning tower. Houser didn't know how well the conning tower could resist that kind of fire; he did not think it could resist much of it.

And then, as Houser watched, the left wing of the H8K began to emit smoke, almost immediately followed by the yellow glow of an explosion; and a moment after that, the wing crumpled. The H8K turned into the crumpled wing, then began to tumble. It struck the surface of the sea, causing a simultaneous flash and explosion. There was an enormous cloud of black smoke, suddenly cut off as the plane went beneath the water and the fire died.

"Jesus H. Christ," Chief Buchanan said, "talk about the goddamned Cavalry to the rescue!"

Commander Houser had not known that the Chief was still on the bridge. But when he thought about it, he was not surprised. If Buchanan had his way, *he,* not the skipper, would have been the last man to leave the bridge.

"Belay the dive," Houser ordered.

The talker was gone, so Buchanan relayed the order orally, dropping to his knees and shouting down the open hatch. Then he rose to his feet.

"They're dipping their wings, Skipper," Chief Buchanan announced, quite unnecessarily.

"It would appear so," Houser replied.

The aircraft closed quickly. Then, at what the pilots obviously estimated to be the maximum range of a .50 caliber bullet, they turned sharply to the left and right. The maneuver served to turn their wings so that their undersides—and their American identifying insignia—were visible to the personnel in the conning tower.

There were now three people on the bridge. The talker had been the first to return.

Commander Houser turned to him.

"One quarter ahead," he ordered.

"One quarter ahead," the talker parroted.

"Mr. Weston to the bridge," he said.

"Mr. Weston to the bridge," the talker parroted.

Weston immediately climbed through the hatch again.

"I don't know where your coach is, Cinderella," Commander Houser said, "but the outriders are here." He pointed to the two fighters.

The fighters were almost on them, now down on the deck. They were aircraft the like of which Weston had never seen before. Obviously fighters, they were low-wing monoplanes, whose wings seemed to be bent, coming straight out from the fuselage, and then tipping upward.

The plane on the portside flashed past the *Sunfish* with its cockpit canopy open, close enough for Weston to see the pilot. He was a bareheaded, blond young man, earphones cocked jauntily on his head, wearing aviator sunglasses. He smiled as he waved a cheerful hand in greeting.

But more important to Jim Weston, late G-2 of USFIP and onetime Naval Aviator, were the big, bold letters across the aft portion of the fuselage: *MARINES.*

Tears ran down Weston's face and disappeared under his beard.

"Aircraft ninety degrees to starboard, estimate three miles, two thousand feet," Chief Buchanan bellowed. "A great big sonofabitch!"

Before Commander Houser could bring his binoculars to bear on the new aircraft, there was another call.

"Aircraft, dead aft, estimate three miles, two thousand feet. Make that two aircraft. More fighters."

"They're Corsairs," Commander Houser announced, "I didn't know they had them out here," and then faced his talker.

"Make turns for steerageway, prepare to stop engines."

"Make turns for steerageway, prepare to stop engines," the talker parroted.

"Boat crew on deck, prepare to inflate and launch rubber boat," Houser ordered, and then as the talker repeated it, turned to Weston.

"I think that great big sonofabitch, as Chief Buchanan so vulgarly described it, *is* your carriage, Cinderella," he said. "It looks like a Coronado."

"God, look at that," Weston said as a Corsair approaching the *Sunfish* from the rear, flashed past on the deck at what must have been 350 knots, and then soared high in the sky.

"Jim, is there anything you want to take with you?" Houser asked gently.

Weston thought that over for a moment.

"My hat, Sir."

Houser turned to his talker.

"Mr. Weston's campaign hat to the bridge," he ordered.

"Mr. Weston's campaign hat to the bridge," the talker dutifully repeated.

The Coronado, growing larger by the moment, slowed as the pilot lowered his flaps and dropped her closer to the water. Above it, two of the Corsairs circled protectively, as two others rose into the sky at a rate of climb that had Jim Weston shaking his head in awed disbelief.

A tall officer in somewhat mussed khakis pulled Weston out of the rubber boat and through the door in the side of the Coronado. Almost immediately, the engines of the aircraft revved up as the pilot turned into the wind.

Inside were plushly upholstered chairs. After the tall officer in the mussed khakis made sure that Weston was safely strapped into his, he sat down beside him. Weston saw that the passenger compartment was otherwise empty, except for one other officer, a lieutenant commander of the Navy Medical Corps, sitting forward.

"Welcome back to the world, Captain Weston," the tall officer said. "My name is Pickering."

It was only then that Jim Weston saw that the silver insignia on his collar points were five-pointed stars.

"General, it's really lieutenant," Weston said.

"Oh, no, it isn't," Pickering said, and handed him a sheet of paper.

HQ USMC WASHINGTON

VIA SPECIAL CHANNEL

SUPREME COMMANDER SWPOA
ATTENTION: BRIG GEN F. W. PICKERING, USMCR
0905 2 JANUARY 1943

(1) NEXT OF KIN, MRS DOUGLAS WILLIAMS (AUNT) CEDAR RAPIDS IOWA WAS BEEN NOTIFIED OF RETURN TO ACTIVE DUTY OF FIRST LIEUTENANT JAMES B. WESTON, USMC BY THE UNDERSIGNED 26 DEC 1942. THERE MAY BE SOME ADMINISTRATIVE PROBLEMS IN THIS REGARD AS WESTON WAS PREVIOUSLY DECLARED MISSING AND PRESUMED DEAD IN ACTION AND DEATH BENEFITS ETCETERA HAVE BEEN PAID. WILL ADVISE.

(2) FOLLOWING QUOTED FOR YOUR INFORMATION:

EXTRACT, GENERAL ORDER 1 HQ USMC WASH DC DATED 1 JAN 1943

PARA 13.1/LT JAMES B. WESTON, USMC, DETACHED FROM HQ USFIP AND ASSIGNED USMC SPECIAL DETACHMENT 16 WITH DUTY STATION BRISBANE AUSTRALIA.

PARA 14. FOLLOWING OFFICERS PROMOTED TO GRADE OF CAPTAIN, USMCR, WITH DATE OF RANK 25 DECEMBER 1942

MCCOY, KENNETH R USMC OFFICE OF MANAGEMENT ANALYSIS
WESTON, JAMES B USMC SPECIAL DETACHMENT 16

> (3) FOR YOUR INFORMATION, CAPT WESTON IS AUTHORIZED THIRTY
> (30) DAY RECUPERATIVE LEAVE, NOT CHARGEABLE AS LEAVE, AT
> LOCATION OF HIS CHOICE IN CONTINENTAL US AS SOON AS HIS
> MEDICAL CONDITION PERMITS. SECNAV HAS AUTHORIZED AAA AIR
> PRIORITY FOR RETURN TO US VIA PEARL HARBOR.
>
> BY DIRECTION:
> BANNING, MAJ USMC

All four engines of the Coronado began to roar as the pilot shoved the throttles to takeoff power. In less than a minute, they were airborne.

The Navy doctor came aft as the Coronado was still climbing out. General Pickering left his chair and walked forward.

"Good morning, Captain," the doctor said, and then put a stethoscope to Weston's chest, took his pulse, pinched his skin, looked into his eyes, told him to open his mouth, pulled at his teeth, and then patted him encouragingly on his shoulder.

Then he stood up and walked to General Pickering.

Weston considered this a moment, then unstrapped himself and got out of his seat and walked forward.

The doctor stopped whatever he was saying in midsentence.

"If you're talking about me, I'd like to hear it," Weston said.

"Tell him, Doctor."

"You are malnourished," the doctor said. "But you don't have malaria, which is surprising. We'll do some tests, of course, when we reach Brisbane, but I can't see any indications of parasitic infestation, or other illness. And once we get some balanced nutrition into you, I think your gums will firm up quickly; you won't lose any teeth, in my opinion."

"Is that where we're going, Brisbane?"

"Right," General Pickering said. "The fighters will give us cover, these and some others from Henderson Field, until we're out of range of Japanese aircraft."

"Where is Henderson Field?"

"On Guadalcanal, an island in the Solomons," Pickering said, and then added, "My son used to fly Wildcats off Henderson."

"I never saw these before," Weston said, gesturing out the window, where a Corsair flew three hundred feet away.

"They just got here. Corsairs. My son—he's now an IP in the States in them—wrote me that they have the most powerful engine ever put in a fighter.''

"I used to be a fighter pilot," Weston said.

"Used to be?" Pickering said. "An old friend of mine named McInerney told me that flying is like riding a bicycle: Once you learn how, you never forget.''

"I hope that's true," Weston said. "General, do you think it would be all right if I went to the cockpit?''

"I'm sure it would," Pickering said.

Weston started forward, toward a ladder on a bulkhead.

"Captain," Pickering called after him.

"Sir?"

"Do you happen to play bridge?''

"Yes, Sir, I do."

"Fine," Pickering said.

Wondering what that was all about, Weston climbed the ladder and made his way to the cockpit. The pilot—a lieutenant commander—the copilot, and a chief petty officer Weston presumed was the flight engineer, looked at him curiously.

"I like your beard," the pilot said finally.

"I was ordered to keep it," Weston said.

"You ever been up here before?" the pilot asked.

"No, Sir. First time. A million years ago, I flew Catalinas, and before that Buffaloes.''

The pilot turned to the copilot and jerked his thumb upward. The copilot unstrapped himself and lifted himself out of his seat.

"Sit down," the pilot said. "It's supposed to be like sex."

"Sir?" Weston asked, wondering if he had heard correctly.

"Once you learn how to do it, you never forget," the pilot said.

[FIVE]
Quarters of the Supreme Commander
South West Pacific Ocean Area
Brisbane, Australia
1730 Hours 6 January 1943

It is entirely possible that I am dreaming, Captain James B. Weston, USMCR, thought, absolutely seriously, as he examined himself in the mirrored walls of the elevator.

There were four splendidly uniformed Marine officers in the elevator, each wearing crisp, high-collared white summer uniforms. One of them was a brigadier general, whose breast bore an impressive array of ribbons representing his decorations for valor and places of overseas service in two world wars. A second was a full bull colonel, whose breast was similarly adorned, and around whose neck hung the blue-starred ribbon of the highest award for valor awarded by the United States, the Medal of Honor. The third was a second lieutenant of Marines, wearing only five colored ribbons, but also the red and gold aiguillette of an aide-de-camp to a general officer.

The fourth officer was a Marine captain, on whose breast were only two ribbons. One of these was yellow with two narrow red, white, and blue stripes representing the American Defense Service Medal, awarded to all military personnel who had been on active duty before 7 December 1941. A second yellow ribbon, this one with two white-red-white stripes and one red, white, and blue stripe, represented the Asiatic Pacific Campaign Medal, which was awarded to anyone who had served anywhere in the Pacific between 7 December and a date to be announced later.

The fourth officer also wore the gold wings of a Naval Aviator and a full, blond beard.

The elevator door whooshed open.

A master sergeant with olive-colored skin, in stiffly starched khakis, either standing at attention or incapable of slouching, stood outside.

"Good evening, gentlemen," he said in impeccable English. "The Supreme Commander and Mrs. MacArthur are in the study. I believe you know the way, General?"

"Yes, I do, thank you," Brigadier General Fleming Pickering said.

"Está muy acepta aquí, mi Capitán," the master sergeant added to Captain James B. Weston. (You are especially welcome here, my Captain.)

"Gracias, Sargento," Weston replied.

The exchange sort of shattered the dreamlike feeling.

First, he must know that I've been in the Philippines. Second, he spoke Spanish to me. And I understood him, and replied in Spanish without thinking about it. Which means that all the time I spent in the dark with Sergeant LaMadrid, as I tried to perfect his English and he tried to teach me Spanish, was worth it. That makes everything real. Maybe I really am going to meet General Douglas MacArthur.

He followed General Pickering and Colonel Stecker for twenty-five yards down a carpeted corridor. The right half of a double door was open. A white-jacketed orderly, also obviously a Filipino, bowed them inside.

The Supreme Commander was far less splendidly uniformed than his guests. He wore khakis faded and softened by many washings. He had a long, thin, black cigar in his mouth.

"Fleming, my dear fellow!" he said.

"Good evening, Sir," Pickering said. "Mrs. MacArthur . . ."

"Jean, please, Fleming."

". . . You both know Colonel Stecker and Lieutenant Hart. May I present Captain James Weston, USMC, late G-2 of United States Forces in the Philippines?"

Suddenly not at all sure whether this was specified by regulations for such an occasion, Weston saluted.

MacArthur returned it, then put out his hand. When Weston took it, MacArthur put his left hand with his right and squeezed Weston's hand emotionally.

"My wife and I thank you for finding time for us, Captain," he said. "I'm sure that you're anxious to return to the United States, to the bosom of your family and friends. Jean, this is the young officer I've been telling you about."

"Good evening, Captain," Jean MacArthur said, and offered her hand. "How do you do?"

"My wife and I, Captain, as you can certainly understand, are hungry for any word of the Philippines."

"I'll be happy, Sir, to tell you what I can. But that isn't much."

The orderly appeared.

"Will you raise a glass with us, Captain?" MacArthur asked. "Is your physical condition such that . . ."

"They've just given him a clean slate, General," Pickering answered for him. "He's undernourished, of course, but that was to be expected."

"In that case, Captain, what can Manuel fix you?"

"Scotch, please, Sir. Scotch and water."

"Through General Pickering's generosity, we have a more-than-adequate supply of scotch," MacArthur said. "Famous Grouse all around, please, Manuel."

El Supremo hasn't said anything about the beard, Pickering thought. *I'm sure he's noticed it. Is he just being gracious, or indulgent?*

"The beard, I presume, is on medical advice?" MacArthur asked.

There he goes again. I really think El Supremo can read my mind.

"He kept his beard on my orders, actually," Pickering said.

"Indeed?" MacArthur said.

"It occurred to me that Captain Weston would probably find himself being debriefed by one of Colonel Donovan's people," Pickering said. "And I thought—"

"What made you think Colonel Donovan would wish to debrief him?" MacArthur interrupted.

"Just a gut feeling," Pickering said, "and sure enough, shortly after the operation was launched, I received a radio from his deputy—oddly enough an old acquaintance of mine, a lawyer, named L. Stanford Morrissette—asking me to arrange for any of General Fertig's people we brought out to be debriefed by the OSS here as soon as possible.''

The white-jacketed orderly passed around a silver tray holding glasses dark with scotch.

MacArthur raised his glass.

''If I may, gentlemen, three toasts. First, to this valiant young officer, who did what I truly would have exchanged my life to do—disobeyed my orders to seek safety and continued the fight.''

''Hear, hear,'' Pickering said, and the others joined in. Weston looked uncomfortable.

''Second, to the valiant warriors,'' MacArthur said, ''Filipino and American, still in the Philippines.''

''Hear, hear,'' Pickering said again, and they all sipped their drinks.

''And finally, to victory!''

''Hear, hear,'' Pickering repeated a third time. He sipped his drink.

''If I may, General—it seems we left them out,'' Pickering said. ''To General Wendell Fertig, and U.S. Forces in the Philippines.''

''I had, I hoped, included Fertig and his men in my toast,'' MacArthur said, a tone of annoyance in his voice. ''But, by all means, we should toast our irregular forces in the Philippines, and their commander.''

Pickering, restraining the urge to smile, thought: *God, he's magnificent. He's unable to call Fertig "General" but USFIP has instantly become, in the regal sense, "our"—read "my"—"irregular forces."*

MacArthur took a sip from his glass, set it down, and turned to Pickering.

''I heard from your friend Morrissette, too,'' he said. ''Complaining of inadequate communications between the OSS in Washington and here. He asked if there wasn't some special communications channel to which his people could be given access.'' He paused significantly, and smiled. ''I politely replied that the only special communications channel I knew of was controlled by you, Fleming.''

''Then I shall doubtless be hearing from Morrissette again,'' Pickering said.

''And what will you tell him?''

''A wise old friend once told me that the greatest danger involved with the OSS was letting the camel's nose work its way under the tent flap, General,'' Pickering said. ''If the question comes up, I shall keep that wise observation in mind.''

''You are suggesting that you have had personal proof that what this wise, old—but unnamed—friend warned you about the dangers of the intrusive nose of an ugly dromedary was true?''

"I would be very surprised if my wise, anonymous old friend didn't know that already," Pickering said.

"I understand that you took at least one more officer on your operation than you had originally planned for?"

"Just one more, General."

MacArthur chuckled.

"Excuse us, Jean, and gentlemen," MacArthur said. "A private joke between myself and my young but growing wiser friend here." He touched Pickering's shoulder in a gesture of affection and then went on. "So are you going to subject this young man to an OSS debriefing?"

"I don't see how I can avoid it," Pickering said. "Colonel Stecker will take him to see the OSS Station Chief here—"

"Colonel John J. Waterson," MacArthur interrupted. "Class of '22 at West Point. He resigned in 1934, as a passed-over-for-promotion captain. He was commissioned in the reserve in 1939, and called to active duty in September 1941. I rather doubt if he's ever heard a shot fired in anger."

There are several reasons for that little biographical sketch, Pickering thought. *The first being that he wants me to know that Charley Willoughby has done his homework vis-à-vis Waterson—Know Thine Enemy is the first rule for an intelligence officer. And the second is to make sure that I understand that Waterson had something less than a brilliant career when he was in the Army, and is not a* real *warrior, in the sense that El Supremo and Stecker and I—and, for that matter, Weston and Hart—are.*

". . . *Colonel Waterson,* in the morning," Pickering finished.

"Before Captain Weston leaves SWPOA," MacArthur said icily, "I would very much like for General Willoughby to have the opportunity to speak with him. Would that be possible, do you think, Fleming?"

"General Pickering, Captain Weston and I spent two hours with General Willoughby and his people this afternoon," Colonel Stecker said.

That announcement surprised him. He obviously didn't know. I would have thought Willoughby would have come right to him after hearing what Weston had to say.

"Did you really?" MacArthur said, and warmth came back into his voice and eyes. "I wonder why Charley didn't mention that to me?"

Probably, Pickering thought, *now that I think about it, Charley Willoughby didn't come to see you immediately because he knew you would not want to hear what Weston told him, that Fertig has done an amazing job, and that just as soon as we can get some supplies to him, he is going to really cause the Japanese a good deal of trouble.*

"Probably because he's boiling down what Weston had to tell him into a more convenient form, so as not to waste your time, General," Pickering said.

"Yes, of course, that must be it," MacArthur said. He changed the subject. "You were telling us about Captain Weston's beard, that you had ordered him to keep it?"

"Until after he deals with the OSS, General. I thought it might—"

"Impress them with the fact that they are dealing with a warrior?" MacArthur interrupted.

"Well, at least with a Marine whom the fortunes of war have placed where he had more important things to worry about than five o'clock shadow."

"You and I share a sense of humor, Fleming," MacArthur said. "I don't know how Jean feels about it."

"I think his beard is handsome!" Jean MacArthur said.

"My grandfather wore a beard," MacArthur said. "My father, General Arthur MacArthur, Jr., did not. It is family lore that he could not grow one, possibly because at the time of the battle, Missionary Ridge—where he won the Medal of Honor—he was just eighteen years old. Family lore also holds that after he was brevetted colonel—he was then nineteen, the youngest officer ever to hold that rank—he tried to grow one to make himself look older. He failed. Humiliated by that, he was clean-shaven the rest of his life, except for his mustache; and I suppose that I have patterned myself after him in that regard as well."

"*You* would look distinguished with a mustache!" his wife said.

He gave her a look that could have been mild annoyance or amusement, or both, and turned to Jim Weston.

"Captain," he said. "Perhaps an odd question: What did you think, or more precisely, what is your assessment of the reception of the matches by the Filipinos?"

"Matches, Sir?" Weston asked, baffled.

"Yes, matches. Matchbooks."

"Sir, I'm afraid I don't know what you're talking about."

MacArthur turned to Pickering.

"I was led to believe, Fleming," he said coldly, "that matches were among the supplies your people took into the Philippines."

"I don't think Captain Weston saw your matches, General. They probably weren't off-loaded from the *Sunfish* before he was sent aboard. We sent a case, or two cases. I told McCoy to see that at least one case went with the first rubber boat."

"I see."

"Darling," his wife said. "I have some. Should I get them?"

"If you please, if for no other reason than to satisfy Captain Weston's curiosity."

"Dinner is served," the white-jacketed orderly announced.

"It will have to wait," MacArthur snapped. "Mrs. MacArthur is not quite ready. Bring another round of drinks in the meantime."

"Yes, Sir."

The drinks were served before Jean MacArthur returned with a handful of matchbooks. She gave one to Weston, and then, like a hostess serving cookies, gave one to Pickering, Stecker, and Hart.

Weston looked at the matchbook in his hand. On it was printed "I SHALL RETURN! MacArthur."

"It was an idea my psychological-warfare people came up with," MacArthur said. "It rather embarrassed me, but they are supposed to know what they are doing, and I gave in."

"I never saw these before, Sir. But with respect, I think your psychological-warfare people are right."

"How is that, Captain Weston?"

"They're like General Fertig's gold, Sir. Proof that the United States hasn't forgotten them. And they'll drive the Japanese crazy."

"How is that, Captain?"

"The Filipinos think you, and for that matter, your father, are sort of like gods." Major General Arthur MacArthur, General Douglas MacArthur's father, was formerly the Military Governor of the Philippines; he ruled with both wisdom and compassion, and was instrumental in the transformation of the captured Spanish colony into the Commonwealth of the Philippines. "They're not going to use these matches. They'll carry them around like religious relics. And the Japs won't be able to do anything about it."

"Would you explain that?"

"They're killing people they find with arms, or trying to help us; but not even the Japs are going to start killing people over a book of matches. They're still trying to push that 'Greater Asian Co-prosperity Sphere' business. They would lose face doing something brutal over matchbooks."

"Charley Willoughby, General," Pickering said, "seemed to be fascinated with Captain Weston's views about the Japanese philosophy of occupation. And with the principles General Fertig has laid out for his psychological-warfare operations."

"Did he really?" MacArthur said impatiently.

"Yes, Sir," Colonel Stecker said. "I had the feeling that General Fertig was setting that sort of thing up the way General Willoughby would himself."

"Fascinating," MacArthur said. "I will discuss that with him." He turned to Weston.

"And you don't think, Captain, that putting my name on it was going a bit too far? Instead of, for example, the American flag, or crossed Filipino and American flags, something on that order?"

"No, Sir. Without the name MacArthur, all they'd be is matches."

"You see, Douglas?" his wife said. "I told you."

"Well, I don't mind being proven wrong by an expert," MacArthur said.

"Sir, could I ask you for a favor?" Weston asked. "Could I ask you to autograph one of these for me?"

"You would like my autograph, Captain?"

"Yes, Sir. If you would please, Sir."

"Not on a matchbook, Captain," MacArthur said. "But I'll tell you what I will do. If General Pickering will bring you to my office at, say, oh nine hundred tomorrow, I will be happy to give you my autograph. It will be affixed to a document awarding you the Silver Star medal for conspicuous gallantry in action."

"Yes, Sir."

If a medal is well deserved, Fleming Pickering decided, *the circumstances surrounding its award are not really important. And it is probably very cynical of me to suspect that the notion to decorate you for your valor come shortly after you told El Supremo the Filipinos regard him as a god.*

"Douglas, what time did you order dinner?"

"Right now, my love," he said. "Captain Weston, would you do Mrs. MacArthur the honor of taking her in to dinner?"

[SIX]
Office of the Director
Office of Strategic Services
National Institutes of Health Building
Washington, D.C.
0900 Hours 8 January 1943

"I didn't know if you would want to see this or not," L. Stanford Morrissette said, laying a long sheet of teletypewriter paper on the desk of OSS Director William J. Donovan.

"What is it?"

"A synopsis of Waterson's debriefing of the officer who came out of the Philippines on the submarine."

"Why did you think I wouldn't want to see it?"

"There's nothing new in it. All it does is confirm what Lieutenant McCoy has been reporting all along. And McCoy's reports, which you've seen, have much more detail."

Donovan shrugged and pulled the long sheet of teletypewriter paper across the green blotter of his desk and began to read it.

TOP SECRET

URGENT URGENT

BRISBANE NUMBER 138
1500GREENWICH7JAN43

FROM   CHIEF OSS STATION
            BRISBANE AUSTRALIA

TO   DIRECTOR OSS
            NATIONAL INSTITUTES OF HEALTH BLDG
            WASHINGTON DC

SUBJECT   OPERATION WINDMILL

(1) RE YOUR MESSAGE FROM MORRISSETTE FOR HAND DELIVERY TO
GEN MACARTHUR: UNDERSIGNED ATTEMPTED TO DELIVER SAME TO
GEN MACARTHUR. WAS ADVISED BY COL SIDNEY HUFF, AIDE DE
CAMP, THAT SUPREME COMMANDERS BUSY SCHEDULE PRECLUDED
RECEIVING ME. GAVE MESSAGE TO HUFF. HUFF SUBSEQUENTLY
TELEPHONED TO STATE QUOTE ONLY SPECIAL COMMUNICATIONS
CHANNEL WITH WHICH GEN MACARTHUR IS FAMILIAR IS CONTROLLED
BY BRIG GEN FLEMING PICKERING USMC AND ANY REQUESTS FOR ITS
USE SHOULD BE DIRECTED TO HIM ENDQUOTE. UNDERSIGNED THEN
ATTEMPTED TO CONTACT BRIG GEN PICKERING AND WAS INFORMED
THAT HE WAS NOT PHYSICALLY PRESENT IN BRISBANE. REQUESTED
THAT HE CONTACT ME ON RETURN. HE HAS NOT YET DONE SO.
SUBSEQUENTLY LEARNED THAT HE WAS ON ESPIRITU SANTO ISLAND
DIRECTING OPERATION WINDMILL.

(2) UNDERSIGNED WAS CONTACTED 1600 6JAN43 BY COL JACK NMI
STECKER USMC WHO STATED BRIG GEN PICKERING HAD RETURNED TO
BRISBANE BUT THAT HIS BUSY SCHEDULE PRECLUDED HIS MEETING
WITH ME. HE ALSO STATED THAT PICKERING HAD BROUGHT WITH HIM
CAPT JAMES B. WESTON, USMC, WHO HAD BEEN SERVING AS G-2 US
FORCES IN PHILIPPINES AND THAT CAPTAIN WESTON COULD BE MADE
AVAILABLE FOR OSS DEBRIEFING 0800 HOURS 7JAN43

(3) SYNOPSIS OF DEBRIEFING OF CAPTAIN JAMES B. WESTON, USMC,
BY UNDERSIGNED 1005–1240 7JAN43 FOLLOWS:

    (A) WESTON IS MARINE AVIATOR CAUGHT IN PHILIPPINES AT
OUTBREAK OF WAR AND ATTACHED 4TH MARINES ON CORREGIDOR.

WHILE ON A SUPPLY MISSION ON BATAAN PENINSULA, LUZON, WITH SGT PERCY LEWIS EVERLY USMC ON 1APR42 THEY FOUND THEMSELVES BEHIND ENEMY LINES. UNABLE TO RETURN TO CORREGIDOR, THEY DECIDED TO ATTEMPT TO ESCAPE TO AUSTRALIA BY SMALL BOAT.

(B) ON 8OCT42, THEY LANDED AT GINGOOG BAY, MISAMIS-ORIENTAL PROVINCE, ISLAND OF MINDANAO, HAVING BEEN JOINED ENROUTE BY TWELVE OTHER US MILITARY AND NAVY PERSONNEL SEPARATED FROM THEIR UNITS. ON LANDING THEY FOUND NAILED TO TELEPHONE POLE PROCLAMATION ISSUED BY BRIG GENERAL WENDELL FERTIG ANNOUNCING HIS ASSUMPTION OF COMMAND OF ALL US FORCES IN PHILIPPINES.

(C) ON 11OCT42 CONTACT WAS MADE WITH FERTIG NEAR MONKAYO, DAVAO-ORIENTAL PROVINCE. FERTIG INFORMED WESTON THAT HE WAS LTCOL CORPS OF ENGINEERS, RESERVE, AND THAT HE HAD DECLARED HIS RANK TO BE BRIG GEN IN BELIEF THIS WAS NECESSARY TO COMMAND RESPECT OF FILIPINO MILITARY AND CIVILIANS. AT THIS POINT WESTON PLACED HIMSELF AND HIS MEN UNDER FERTIG'S COMMAND. FERTIG APPOINTED WESTON CAPT AND EVERLY 2ND LT IN USFIP. WESTON STATED THAT IT IS FERTIG'S POLICY TO RAISE US OFFICERS WHO PLACE THEMSELVES UNDER HIS COMMAND AT LEAST ONE RANK IN USFIP, AND TO COMMISSION US NONCOMMISSIONED OFFICERS IN USFIP. SIMULTANEOUSLY WESTON WAS NAMED G-2 USFIP AND EVERLY HIS DEPUTY.

(D) DESPITE CRITICAL SHORTAGES OF ALL SUPPLIES AND WEAPONS ACTION AGAINST JAPANESE COMMENCED ALMOST IMMEDIATELY. SHORTAGE OF WEAPONRY SUCH THAT AMMUNITION FOR US .30-06 ENFIELD RIFLES LOCALLY MANUFACTURED USING BRASS CURTAIN RODS FOR BULLETS, LOCALLY MANUFACTURED BLACK POWDER, AND MATCHHEADS FOR PRIMERS. WESTON STATED FERTIG BELIEVED ANY COMBAT ACTION AGAINST JAPANESE WOULD CAUSE FILIPINOS TO ACCEPT HIM AS CG USFIP. WESTON STATED USFIP NOW ALMOST ENTIRELY ARMED WITH WEAPONS CAPTURED FROM JAPANESE.

(E) WESTON STATED THAT AFTER WORD OF INITIAL EIGHT OR TEN COMBAT ACTIONS AGAINST JAPANESE CIRCULATED THROUGHOUT MINDANAO FOLLOWING HAPPENED:

1 US AND FILIPINO MILITARY PERSONNEL WHO HAD EITHER NOT SURRENDERED OR WHO HAD ESCAPED BEGAN TO COME TO HIS HQ

FROM PLACES OF HIDING IN SUCH NUMBERS (WESTON STATES MORE
THAN TWO THOUSAND (2000)) THAT IT WAS IMPOSSIBLE TO EITHER
ARM OR FEED THEM. MOST WERE ORDERED BACK INTO HIDING UNTIL
SUCH TIME AS SUPPLIES BECAME AVAILABLE. OTHERS (PRIMARILY US
AND FILIPINO COMMISSIONED OFFICERS) WERE ARMED AND
DISPATCHED THROUGHOUT MINDANAO WITH ORDERS TO FORM NUCLEI
FOR LATER EXPANSION OF USFIP.

2 FILIPINOS BEGAN TO ACCEPT REQUISITIONS AND
PURCHASE ORDERS ISSUED BY USFIP FOR LATER PAYMENT FOR FOOD
AND OTHER SUPPLIES.

3 A NUMBER OF US CITIZENS (WESTON ESTIMATES 300)
CONTACTED USFIP FOR HELP IN EVADING CAPTURE AND/OR FOR
EVACUATION FROM MINDANAO. IT WAS OF COURSE IMPOSSIBLE TO
HELP THEM, AND THEY WERE ORDERED TO REMAIN IN HIDING FOR
THE TIME BEING. THE NUMBER INCLUDES FIVE (5) MEDICAL DOCTORS
AND ELEVEN (11) NURSES OF VARIOUS MISSIONARY ACTIVITIES. TWO
US MEDICAL DOCTORS AND SIX NURSES HAVE ACCEPTED COMMISSIONS
IN USFIP, WITH UNDERSTANDING THEY WILL BE EVACUATED WHEN
POSSIBLE.

4 JAPANESE ANTI-USFIP ACTIVITY PRESENTLY REQUIRES
DEPLOYMENT OF ESTIMATED 20,000 TROOPS.

(F) WESTON STATES THAT IF SUFFICIENT SUPPLIES OF ALL SORTS
CAN BE MADE AVAILABLE, USFIP CAN ULTIMATELY FIELD 20,000
TRAINED TROOPS. HE AND FERTIG BELIEVE, AS DOES COLONEL
STECKER, WHO HAS GUERRILLA EXPERIENCE IN LATIN AMERICA,
THAT BETWEEN SIX AND SEVEN JAPANESE TROOPS WILL BE REQUIRED
TO ATTEMPT TO SUPPRESS EACH USFIP GUERRILLA.

(G) WESTON BELIEVES THAT CREDIBILITY OF USFIP WILL BE
GREATLY IMPROVED AS RESULT OF SUPPLIES SENT IN OPERATION
WINDMILL, IN PARTICULAR THE GOLD, WHICH WILL PERMIT FERTIG TO
BEGIN TO PAY FOR REQUISITIONS AND PURCHASE ORDERS. HE
SIMILARLY FEELS INTRODUCTION OF CARBINES, UNKNOWN IN
PHILIPPINES BEFORE WAR, WILL PROVE THAT US SUPPLIES ARE
COMING AS PROMISED.

(H) WESTON STATED THAT HE HAS NO KNOWLEDGE OF CAPTAIN
MACKLIN BEYOND THAT HE WENT ASHORE FROM SUNFISH AND
PRESUMABLY ACCOMPANIED MCCOY TO HQ USFIP.

(4) IT IS THE OPINION OF THE UNDERSIGNED THAT WESTON IS
ENTIRELY CREDIBLE AND THAT HIS OPINION OF FERTIG AS BEING
INTELLIGENT, SANE AND COMPETENT SHOULD BE ACCEPTED.

(5) FOR YOUR GENERAL INFORMATION, WESTON WAS DECORATED
WITH SILVER STAR THIS MORNING BY MACARTHUR. ACCOMPANYING
PRESS RELEASE USED PHRASE QUOTE CAPTAIN WESTON WAS
ASSIGNED TO SWPOA'S USFIP ENDQUOTE. WESTON WILL DEPART
BRISBANE BY AIR VIA PEARL HARBOR TOMORROW FOR THIRTY DAY
RECUPERATIVE LEAVE IN US. COL STECKER STATED ANY REQUEST FOR
FURTHER OSS DEBRIEFING IN US SHOULD BE REFERRED TO SECNAV.
WESTON DECLINED TO GIVE HIS ADDRESS ON LEAVE.

WATERSON
STANTIONCHIEF BRISBANE

T O P   S E C R E T

"I'll tell you what this does confirm, Mo," Donovan said. "Your pal
Pickering is thumbing his nose at me."

"I told you it would be wise to make peace with him, Bill," Morrissette
said.

"Who the hell does he think he is, telling Waterson he's too busy to see
him?"

"He thinks he's Brigadier General Pickering, who doesn't work for you."

"He was sent there, for Christ's sake, with specific orders from the President to persuade MacArthur to let us operate."

"*To try* to persuade MacArthur to let us operate," Morrissette said. "If he
were asked, I'll wager he would say he has tried. And he did arrange for Captain Macklin to go along."

"You noticed, of course, there has not been one word from Macklin,"
Donovan said.

"I noticed."

"Which suggests to me that Pickering's Lieutenant McCoy is not giving
him access to the radio. Probably on orders."

"Maybe Captain Macklin has had nothing to say that McCoy hasn't already said."

"The whole idea was to get the OSS involved in this," Donovan said.
"Didn't anyone tell Macklin that?"

Morrissette didn't reply.

"Macklin might as well not be there, for all the good he's doing us,"

Donovan said. "I feel like a goddamned fool when I'm with the President, and Knox briefs him on what we're getting from Pickering, and I don't have a damned thing to say about what I hear from my OSS man on the scene."

"I understand they're sending the *Sunfish* back with more supplies. If we have time to do it, would you like me to send somebody in to replace Macklin?"

"Do whatever you have to do, Mo, to get somebody competent over there—where is there, by the way?"

"What there, Bill?"

"Where they're going to load the *Sunfish,* obviously."

"I don't know. It's half a dozen one way and six the other between Pearl Harbor and Brisbane. Maybe Espíritu Santo."

"Well, find out where and get somebody competent there in time to get on the sub. Somebody senior to Macklin."

"Why is being senior to Macklin important?"

"Because we're not going to replace Macklin, we're going to *augment the OSS element at USFIP.* And if Macklin is the idiot everybody seems to think he is, I don't think he should be in a position to give orders."

"Wouldn't it be easier just to bring Macklin out?"

"That, I suggest, would give people the opportunity to see for themselves what an idiot we sent in. Tell the Navy we want to send three people in."

"Pickering's people, and that aide-de-camp who stayed, are coming out."

"Good," Donovan said. "If that's the case, maybe our people will be able to get on the radio. And let the world know that the OSS is alive and well."

XVII

[ONE]
Naval Air Transport Command Passenger Terminal
U.S. Navy Base, Pearl Harbor, Territory of Hawaii
0625 Hours 10 January 1943

It was raining steadily when the Coronado touched down, but it was a gentle rain, and the landing was smooth, as was the taxiing to the tie-down buoy.

An admiral's barge—far more luxurious than the whaleboats that served as water taxis in Brisbane and Midway—came out to take the passengers off. Carrying so much money—a thousand dollars in twenties—that he'd split it between the bellows pockets of his tunic, Captain James Weston stepped off the barge onto the wharf.

"Captain Weston?"

He saw a Marine officer, a first lieutenant, saluting and smiling somewhat hesitantly at him.

Weston returned the salute.

"I'm Weston."

"Is your name on your bag, Captain?"

"Yes, it is."

A brand-new canvas suitcase jammed with brand-new uniforms was someplace on the airplane. The passengers had been told it would be delivered to them ashore.

"I'll get it," the Lieutenant said. "You go up the ladder. The car's right at the head of the ladder."

The ladder was in fact a wide set of concrete stairs.

At the top was a Plymouth staff car, bearing an uncovered brigadier general's silver star on a red background plate. Weston wondered where his car was. If there was a general sitting in this car, it obviously wasn't the one the lieutenant was talking about.

The back door of the car opened.

"If you're Weston," a voice called to him, "get in."

He walked to the car and stepped in.

"Pickering said you were unusual," the man inside said. "He didn't say that unusual. What's with the beard?"

"I guess I can shave it off now, Sir," Weston said, ill at ease.

"Since you are taking lunch with Admiral Nimitz, I think that would be a good idea," the man said.

He shifted on the seat, and Weston could now see the stars on the collar of his khaki shirt.

"My name is McInerney," the General said, and put out his hand.

"Good morning, Sir."

Brigadier General McInerney handed him a sheet of paper.

"Read that," he said.

P R I O R I T Y

SUPREME HEADQUARTERS SWPOA 1625 HOURS 8JAN43

TO CINCPAC HAWAII

PERSONAL FROM BRIG GEN PICKERING USMCR TO BRIG GEN
MCINERNEY USMC

DEAR MAC:

I JUST LOADED CAPTAIN JAMES B. WESTON ABOARD A PEARL HARBOR
BOUND CORONADO. HE IS ENROUTE TO THE STATES FOR A THIRTY DAY
RECUPERATIVE LEAVE. HE IS A VERY UNUSUAL YOUNG OFFICER WHO
JUST CAME OUT OF THE PHILIPPINES WHERE HE WAS G-2 FOR
GENERAL FERTIG'S GUERRILLA OPERATION. MACARTHUR GAVE HIM A
WELL DESERVED SILVER STAR YESTERDAY.

I WOULD APPRECIATE VERY MUCH ANYTHING YOU CAN DO TO MAKE
HIS PEARL HARBOR STOP AS SMOOTH, COMFORTABLE AND AS BRIEF
AS POSSIBLE.

HAVING SAID THAT I WOULD NOT BE AT ALL SURPRISED IF ADMIRAL
NIMITZ WANTED TO AT LEAST SHAKE HIS HAND WHILE HE'S THERE.
SO PLEASE AS QUIETLY AS POSSIBLE INFORM ADMIRAL NIMITZ OF HIS
ARRIVAL.

BEST REGARDS FLEM

END PERSONAL TO BRIG GEN MCINERNEY

BY DIRECTION BRIG GEN PICKERING USMCR

HART 2ND LT USMCR

"I'll tell you what I can't do," McInerney said. "I can't get you out of lunch with Admiral Nimitz; I can't get you on a plane to the States before tomorrow, and maybe not then; and I can't make it stop raining. Aside from that, the place is yours."

"Thank you very much, Sir. I'm surprised. Overwhelmed."

"General Pickering and I were enlisted men in France in the First World War," McInerney said. "He's one of my favorite people."

"Yes, Sir."

"I'm an aviator, and—did he tell you?—so is his son. He flew Wildcats—made ace, as a matter of fact—on Guadalcanal."

"Yes, Sir, he told me. I'm an aviator, too. Or was."

"Was? Let me tell you something, son. Once you learn how to fly, it's like riding a bicycle. You never forget."

"General Pickering told me that, Sir. As a matter of fact, he quoted you."

"For a nonaviator, he's a surprisingly bright fellow," McInerney said. "Ah, here comes Charley with your bag."

"God, what is this place?" Weston asked as a silver-haired black man in a white jacket opened the door of the Plymouth.

"This is Muku-Muku, Captain," the black man said. "I'm Denny. I sort of take care of it."

"What is it, a hotel?"

"Sometimes, lately, it feels like one," Denny said. "But no, Sir. It's not a hotel. It's where Pacific & Far East Shipping puts up its masters and chief engineers when they're in port, and General Pickering's friends, and Mr. Pick's friends . . . which sometimes seems like the entire U.S. Marine Corps."

McInerney laughed. "Denny, in the case of Mr. Weston, he is here as the personal guest of General Pickering. I am under orders from your boss to make sure his stay in Hawaii is as comfortable as possible."

"Well, then, let's bring him inside, and we'll get to work on that," Denny said. "Have you gentlemen had your breakfast?"

"Charley and I have," McInerney said. "I'm sure he hasn't. But don't feed him too much, Denny, he's going to have lunch with Admiral Nimitz."

"Here?" Denny asked. "This is the first—"

"No. At Pearl Harbor."

"I'm not really hungry," Weston said.

"Well, why don't I have somebody bring everybody coffee and some pastry?"

He led them through the house to the patio, and they took seats around a cast-iron, glass-topped table. Another black man, well into middle life, appeared.

"Would you get the General's guests some coffee and pastry, please?" Denny ordered.

"This place is fantastic!" Weston said.

"Is your razor sharp, Denny?" McInerney asked.

"I wondered about that beard," Denny said. "It's so beautiful I sort of hate to cut it off. Where'd you grow that, Captain?"

"I was in the Philippines," Weston said.

"Recently?"

"Yes, recently."

"And you're *sure* you don't want anything to eat? A small steak, and some eggs?"

"That's tempting."

"You just get out of that chair, and into that one," Denny said, pointing. "And I'll fetch my barber tools, and by the time your beard is gone, your breakfast will be ready."

"Sir?" General McInerney's aide-de-camp said.

"What?"

"The telephone, Sir?"

"God, I forgot about that. Thank you, Charley. Weston, among other things you can do here you can't do anywhere else without a two-hour—or longer—wait is talk to the States. So if there's someone you'd like to call? Your parents?"

"My parents are dead, Sir. I have an aunt . . ."

"Where?"

"In Iowa."

"General," Denny said. "It's none of my business, but it's the middle of the night in Iowa."

"Yes, of course it is," McInerney said. "Well, you can call after lunch."

At 1530, when General McInerney, his aide, and Captain Weston returned from luncheon with the Commander-in-Chief, Pacific, in his personal mess, Captain Charles M. Galloway, USMCR, was on the patio of Muku-Muku.

Captain Galloway was not only surprised to see General McInerney, but more than a little uncomfortable, in part because his uniform was stained with both perspiration and oil, in part because he was caught in the act of drinking during duty hours, and in part because of the manner in which he was drinking, from the neck of a quart bottle of beer.

"Good afternoon, Sir," he said, coming to attention.

"Captain," McInerney said. "Why is it that I suspect your day did not go as well as it could have gone? Because to judge from your uniform, you found it necessary, in direct disobedience of my orders, to repair an engine by yourself? Or perhaps because of the way you are attacking that quart of beer? Or simply because I am a splendid student of human nature?"

"No excuse, Sir," Galloway said.

"Captain Galloway, Captain Weston, is another of the Marine Corps orphans who have found a home away from home here in Muku-Muku. He would be a fine officer if he could only remember to obey orders."

"No, Sir," Galloway said.

"No, Sir?" McInerney said.

"I have not been personally working on aircraft, Sir."

"You are a Marine officer; I will accept you at your word. What have you been doing, rolling around on a hangar deck?"

McInerney saw something in Galloway's face.

"*Why* were you rolling around on a hangar deck, Captain Galloway?"

"Sir, with respect, I decline to answer the General's question."

"Who did you punch out, Charley?" McInerney asked. "And why? We are now out of school."

"Stevenson, Sir."

"And what did Lieutenant Stevenson do to arouse your ire?"

"He said that if I wasn't hiding behind my bars, he'd kick the shit out of me."

"So, of course, you went into the hangar, closed the doors, and took off your bars?"

"Yes, Sir."

"What shape is Lieutenant Stevenson in?"

"He lost a tooth, Sir, and he's going to be sore for a while."

"Did he seek medical attention?"

"Yes, Sir."

"And how did he explain his lost tooth when asked?"

"Big Steve said he told the dentist he walked into a pitot tube."

McInerney turned to Weston.

"Big Steve, Mr. Weston, is Master Gunner Oblensky, an ancient aviator I have known more years than I care to think about," he said, and then turned back to Galloway: "And is Lieutenant Stevenson going to bring this brawl of yours to the attention of the appropriate authorities?"

"I don't think so, Sir."

"Captain Galloway, brawling between officers and gentlemen is something the Naval Service simply cannot tolerate under any circumstances."

"Yes, Sir."

"On the other hand, there is an exception to every rule, and from what I have seen of Mr. Stevenson, having someone knock his tooth out was long overdue. Consider the matter forgotten."

"I wish I could do that, Sir."

"Is there some reason you can't?"

"Isn't losing your temper and punching somebody out an admission you can't lead them?"

"You weren't listening, Charley," McInerney said. "There is an exception to every rule. As long as this doesn't become routine, don't let it worry you."

Galloway looked at McInerney for a long moment, then said, very sincerely, "Thank you, Sir. I'll try not to let it happen again."

"Try?"

"The truth is, General, when I was watching him try to get up—he's not a quitter; it may be his only virtue—I was thinking of several other of my officers I would really like to deck."

"You've had my friendly word of wisdom for the day, Charley. Don't push your luck."

"No, Sir. It will not happen again."

"It better not," McInerney said, and then obviously changing the subject: "I have been a good boy all day, and somewhere in the wide world, I am sure, the sun is over the yardarm. Where's Denny?"

"The *Pacific Merchant* made port at noon and he went down to loot her freezer and liquor locker," Galloway said. "He took Alphonse with him. I think we're in the unusual position around here of having to make our own drinks."

"Charley . . ." General McInerney said to his aide.

"What would you like, Sir?"

"Bourbon, a double, water on the side," McInerney said. "Weston?"

"Scotch, please, water."

"And you may consider yourself off duty, Charley," McInerney said. "Weston, if you want to call the States, just dial nine on the phone in your bedroom. That'll get you the Pacific & Far East switchboard in Honolulu. Tell the operator 'San Francisco,' and when the operator in San Francisco answers, tell her what number you want. If you don't know it, she'll get it for you."

"Thank you, Sir," Weston said. "I don't know the number. It's my aunt."

Weston and Charley left the patio, leaving Galloway and McInerney alone.

"Interesting young man," McInerney said. "Until a few days ago, he was G-2 of U.S. Forces in the Philippines. Working for a self-promoted Army brigadier who's set up, according to what he told Admiral Nimitz at lunch, one hell of a guerrilla operation on Mindanao."

"He's wearing wings," Galloway observed.

"He's an ex-Brewster Buffalo jockey. He flew a Catalina into Cavite and got stranded there. They put him in the 4th Marines, and when things really went sour, he decided he'd rather try to get out than surrender. That took balls."

"How'd he get out?"

"I didn't know about any of this until lunch, but when this Army guy—his name is Fertig—finally got word to MacArthur what he was doing, MacArthur ignored him. Pickering found out about it somehow and sent your friend McCoy in to see what was going on. Nimitz gave him a submarine; Weston came out on it."

"McCoy's still there?"

"McCoy, two other Marines, some guy from the OSS, and Admiral Wagam's aide."

"Admiral Wagam's *aide?*" Galloway asked incredulously.

"He went along to make sure the sub did what was necessary. And then he apparently had to see for himself how the other half lives, went ashore, and stayed. Another exception to the rule, apparently, that if a sailor can't get three square meals a day and a bed with sheets, it's somebody else's war."

"Maybe this guy was lucky," Galloway said. "Most of the Buffalo pilots I knew went down at Midway."

"Yeah," McInerney said softly, and then changed the subject again. "You having trouble with the squadron, Charley? Anything I can do to help?"

"Trouble? Oh, yeah. The basic problem is that most of them are hotshot pilots. They're good, they know they're good, but they don't like it when somebody tells them they're not quite as good as they think they are."

"That's a problem."

"Are we still out of school?" Galloway asked, and when General McInerney nodded, went on. "The trouble I had with Stevenson was that he showed up on the flight line with lipstick all over him, and obviously half in the bag. I don't think he'd been to bed. Correction, I don't think he had any sleep."

McInerney chuckled.

"I had to call him on it," Galloway went on. "There were a half-dozen other hotshots watching. So I restricted him to quarters for a week. That's when he called me a chickenshit hotshot hiding behind my bars. I could have brought charges against him—that would have probably meant a little loss of pay—or reported him to Colonel Dawkins as incorrigible—which would have meant the Colonel would take him off flight status and ship his ass to the First Division, which would have meant the loss of a pretty good pilot and screwed up the First Division. So I took him into the hangar.''

"The only thing wrong with your solution was that he might have whipped *your* ass," McInerney said. "Did you think about that?''

"I thought about that, and so did Big Steve. He came in the hangar with us.''

"Did you need him?''

"No. But it was touch and go for a couple of minutes.''

"Are you letting Big Steve fly, Charley?''

"No, Sir.''

"Why not?''

"Because if I got caught, Colonel Dawkins would transfer him, and he's the only friend I've got in the squadron.''

"Does he understand that? Why you can't look the other way and let him fly?''

"No, Sir.''

"I'll have a word with him. We go back a long way. At one time, he and I were the entire corps of Marine Aviators in Nicaragua.''

"Be careful. He's a very persuasive guy. He's liable to talk you into putting him back on flight status.''

"Not with his heart. He shouldn't even be in uniform. Should I have a word with him?''

"I'd be grateful, Sir.''

"Just between us, Charley, you're doing a much better job with your squadron than a lot of people thought you could.''

"Including you, General?''

"Don't fish for compliments, Captain. It's unbecoming to a Marine officer," McInerney said, and then, very softly, "I wonder why I suspect that Weston's call home was something less than a joyful occasion?''

Galloway followed his eyes. Weston was coming back toward them with a thoughtful, unhappy look on his face.

"Where the hell is Charley?" McInerney asked rhetorically. As if waiting for the cue, his aide appeared pushing a wheeled cart on which were an array of bottles, glasses, and a bowl of ice.

"You have a perfect sense of timing, Captain Weston," McInerney said.

Weston looked at him in confusion.

"Sir?''

"How'd the call go?''

"Aunt Margaret wanted me to understand that she's not in a position to give the government its money back."

"What money?"

"My death benefits," Weston said. "I was reported KIA and the government paid off."

"Did she have anything else to say?" McInerney asked.

"Not much," Weston said.

"Well, fuck her!" Galloway said indignantly.

Weston looked at him and smiled.

"Well, whatever happens about that," McInerney said, "I'm sure they won't take it out of your pay."

"You know what really bothers me?" Weston asked. "All the time I was on Mindanao—even before Mindanao—all I could think of was getting back to the States. And now that I'm actually going, I don't want to."

"Why not?"

"I don't have anyplace to go. I don't know anybody anywhere in the States, and I certainly don't want to go to Iowa."

"You mean that?" McInerney asked.

"Yes, Sir."

"Then stay here. Recuperative Leave orders state to any destination of your choice in the United States. I'm sure that would include Hawaii."

"Where here?" Weston said, obviously interested.

"Here, here at Muku-Muku," McInerney said. "General Pickering would insist on that. And you could keep Charley company, and if you listen with proper awe to his tales of aerial derring-do, he just might teach you how to fly a Corsair. It *is* your intention, I presume, to go back on flying status?"

"You have a Corsair squadron?" Weston asked Galloway, awe in his voice.

Galloway nodded.

"It's one hell of an airplane," he said.

"The only ones I've ever seen were the ones they sent to fly cover when the Coronado took me off the submarine. Christ, they were beautiful!"

Well, that answers my question about whether or not he wants to go back on flying status, McInerney thought. *And I just might be able to arrange it so that Charley has more than one friend in his squadron.*

"Take your time and think it over," General McInerney said. "I don't want to talk you into doing anything you really don't want to do."

"General," Weston said. "There's nothing to think over. I'd kill to get in the cockpit of a Corsair."

[TWO]
Flag Officers' Quarters
U.S. Navy Base
Espíritu Santo
1655 Hours 11 January 1943

''Well, look what the tide washed up,'' Brigadier Fleming W. Pickering said as the screen door to his luxurious—by comparison—Quonset hut temporary quarters opened and Rear Admiral Daniel J. Wagam walked in. ''What brings you to this tropical paradise?'' (Quonset huts are prefabricated portable buildings constructed of corrugated metal that curves down to form walls.)

Pickering was lying on a narrow cot, wearing only his underwear. Wagam crossed over to him and shook his hand.

''You're not going to like this, Fleming,'' Wagam said.

''Not like what?''

Wagam reached into his briefcase and took out a manila folder stamped TOP SECRET and handed it to Pickering.

```
T O P    S E C R E T


THE SECRETARY OF THE NAVY
WASHINGTON


VIA SPECIAL CHANNEL


COMMANDER IN CHIEF, PACIFIC
PEARL HARBOR


0815 9 JANUARY 1943


FOLLOWING PERSONAL FROM SECNAV FOR ADMIRAL NIMITZ


DEAR ADMIRAL NIMITZ:


OSS DIRECTOR WILLIAM DONOVAN HAS REQUESTED OF ADMIRAL
LEAHY TRANSPORTATION OF THREE (3) OSS AGENTS TO AUGMENT OSS
FORCES PRESENTLY OPERATING IN PHILIPPINES AND TO ASSUME
COMMAND OF OPERATION WINDMILL.


IT HAS BEEN DECIDED BETWEEN ADMIRAL LEAHY AND MYSELF THAT
THE MOST EFFICACIOUS MEANS OF ACCOMPLISHING THIS IS TO DELAY
SCHEDULED DEPARTURE OF SUBMARINE SUNFISH ON OPERATION
```

GROCERY STORE ONE UNTIL THE AFOREMENTIONED OSS PERSONNEL
CAN BE CARRIED ABOARD HER.

OSS PERSONNEL WILL DEPART WASHINGTON VIA AIR FOR ESPIRITU
SANTO 1200 HOURS WASHINGTON TIME TODAY.

PLEASE INFORM BRIG GEN PICKERING OF THIS CHANGE TO PLAN OF
OPERATION GROCERY STORE ONE AND REQUEST HIM TO INFORM
COMMANDING OFFICER OF OPERATION WINDMILL TO EXPECT OSS
AUGMENTATION PERSONNEL ABOARD SUNFISH.

COMMAND OF OPERATION WINDMILL WILL PASS TO SENIOR OSS AGENT
ON DEPARTURE FROM PHILIPPINES OF PRESENT COMMANDER.

BEST PERSONAL REGARDS

FRANK KNOX

END PERSONAL SECNAV TO ADMIRAL NIMITZ

HAUGHTON CAPT USN ADMIN ASST TO SECNAV

T O P   S E C R E T

"That sonofabitch!" General Pickering said bitterly, and then corrected himself. "Those sonofbitches, plural!"

"How near is the *Sunfish* ready to sail?" Admiral Wagam asked.

"She's sailing at first light," Pickering said. "She *was to sail* at first light. I was about to put my pants on and go buy Captain Houser a farewell drink and dinner. Christ, Dan, we've already pushed up her ETA to the twentieth. We're not running the Congressional Limited here! Do you know how much planning has gone into finding the place and the right time where she can safely surface?"

"A good deal, I'm sure."

"And it's not just McCoy and Lewis coming out. There's a dozen sick and wounded. . . ."

"Is there any reason she could not sail immediately?" Wagam asked. "Or have sailed an hour ago, before I got here?"

Pickering looked at him for a long minute.

"That would get you in a lot of trouble. It would get us both in trouble, but right now . . ."

"It would not get me in trouble with my boss," Admiral Wagam said.

"As a matter of fact, I don't think he would be at all surprised to get a radio from me saying I arrived here too late to keep the *Sunfish* from sailing, and that imposed conditions of radio silence make it impossible to recall her."

"So that's why you delivered that message in person," Pickering said. It was a statement, rather than a question.

"I'll deny under oath that I said this, but we have here proof that Mac-Arthur's and Admiral Nimitz's worries if Donovan got the OSS nose in the tent have in fact come to pass. The OSS—Donovan—is deciding how operations should be conducted here, and to hell with what the commanders think."

"Knox wouldn't believe that story of you being too late to stop her from sailing. Neither would Leahy," Pickering said.

"I don't think anyone expects them to believe it. With your exception, Fleming, flag officers don't say, 'Fuck you, I won't do it,' when they decide that disobeying an order is the right thing to do."

" 'Gee, I really would have liked to do what you wanted me to, but it just couldn't be done'?"

"Something like that," Wagam said. "How do you want to handle this, Fleming?"

"I'm so goddamned mad right now that any decision I make will be the wrong one."

"Be that as it may . . ."

"Goddamn them!" Pickering said. "Goddamn Donovan!"

"I agree, but it doesn't solve the problem."

"There's really no problem," Pickering said softly. "I took an oath, the operative passages being that I would carry out the orders of the officers appointed over me."

Wagam nodded.

"The departure of the *Sunfish* will be delayed until Donovan's people can be carried into the Philippines aboard her," Pickering said, formally.

"I think that's the reaction Admiral Nimitz expected of you," Wagam said.

"Let me put my pants on, Dan," Pickering said. "And we'll go to the Communications Center and get the word passed. And then we'll pick up Captain Houser at the *Sunfish,* and have several drinks to mark the nonsailing of the *Sunfish* as originally scheduled."

[THREE]

Espiritu Santo Island
0500 12 January 1943

Senator Richardson K. Fowler
Washington, D.C.
By Hand

Dear Dick:

An unnamed friend leaving here in a couple of hours has promised that he will have this in your hands as quick as humanly possible. He has no idea what it says. I regret having to put you on the spot with this, but I can't think of anyone else I can turn to.

I have come to the conclusion that I am doing more harm than good in uniform, and that my potential for doing the war effort more harm is growing like an out of control cancer.

I want to resign my commission, is what I'm saying, and don't tell me it can't be done. The Navy turned young Lieutenant Henry Ford loose to run the Ford Motor Company, and a couple of months ago I ran into a Texas schoolteacher turned Congressman out here. He got himself a Navy commission and got sent out here—maybe you know him, his name was Linton, or Lyndon, or something like that Johnson, great big guy with bad teeth—Anyway, he was on his way back to Congress, so I know that people are getting out of the service "for the convenience of the government."

Yesterday, I was a hair's breadth away from willfully disobeying the orders of the President. That's bad enough, but it gets even worse. I was almost encouraged to do so by a senior Naval officer.

Bill Donovan is without question an unmitigated sonofabitch, but I have come to understand that he was right when he rejected my application for employment. What do I know about Intelligence, clandestine or otherwise, that would entitle me to become one of his Twelve Disciples? Further, what is there in my background that justifies me running around pretending to be a Marine general? What I am is a reasonably competent ship's master, and that's all.

More important, what gives me the right to question the wisdom of orders from Donovan and Admiral Leahy? What the hell am I doing agreeing with MacArthur and Nimitz—as if we're three equals—that "we're" right and the President, Leahy and Donovan are wrong?

I was sent out to pour oil on troubled waters. What I have done is pour gasoline on a smouldering fire. The one thing we absolutely can't afford to have out here is guerrilla warfare pitting CINCPAC and SWPOA against Washington.

Get me out of here, Dick, before I cause any more damage. Pull what strings you have to to allow me to resign quietly, as soon as possible. As soon as possible is defined as "as soon as the people I sent into the Philippines are successfully evacuated." That should be sometime late this month.

Let me go back to Pacific & Far East Shipping and try to make some contribution to this war doing something I know how to do.

I'll owe you.

Fondly,

Flem

[FOUR]
Headquarters, U.S. Forces in the Philippines
Davao Oriental Province
Mindanao, Commonwealth of the Philippines
1045 Hours 13 January 1943

Lieutenant Percy L. Everly walked into the thatched-roof house on stilts that Brigadier General Wendell Fertig had declared to be the Visiting Bachelor Officers' Quarters carrying a stack of khaki uniforms.

"Los Presentos from El General," he announced to McCoy, Lewis, Macklin, and Zimmerman. He pronounced "General" in the Spanish manner, "Hen-eral."

"Is that supposed to be Spanish, Everly?" Lieutenant Lewis asked, chuckling.

"Yes, Sir," Everly said. "Doesn't it sound like Spanish? And special presentos for you, mi capitain, and you, mi gunny," he went on, reaching into his shirt pocket and handing small silver objects to McCoy and Zimmerman.

"I ain't no officer," Zimmerman said, examining the handmade lieutenant's bar in his hand.

"You are here," Everly argued. "El Hen-eral says so. It's not so bad, Ernie. You get used to it."

"I'll be damned," McCoy said, almost to himself, examining the captain's bars in his hand. Word of his promotion had been radioed from Australia, but until now, he hadn't thought much about it. The insignia somehow seemed to make it more official than the radio message had.

And then McCoy looked at Everly. "What's with the khakis? Where'd they come from?"

"Money talks," Everly said. "Bullshit walks."

"Meaning what?"

"Just before Sharp—Mindanao Force—surrendered, they opened the Quartermaster warehouses to the Filipinos," Everly explained. "I guess Sharp figured it was better to give the stuff to the Filipinos than to burn it to keep the Japs from getting it. Or maybe he didn't have time to burn it; they had all sorts of supplies here. Anyway, the Filipinos took this stuff and hid it. They didn't seem to remember where until our guys started passing out twenty-dollar gold coins. We're getting offers of all sorts of stuff now."

"As the man says, *Captain* McCoy," Lieutenant Lewis said. "Money talks, bullshit walks. Phrased somewhat more eloquently, cash equals credibility."

"These is *Army* uniforms," Zimmerman said, in either disgust or disappointment.

"Put it on, and put the bar on it," McCoy ordered. "General Fertig wants Americans to look like officers, and he's right."

"That's not all that's coming out of the bushes," Everly said. "Half an hour ago, a half-dozen civilians, including two female ones, showed up here."

"What's that?" Lewis asked, surprised.

"Americans," Everly explained. "When the Japs started rounding up the civilians, these took off. Now they're coming in."

"What kind of civilians?"

"The ones we have here is ordinary civilians, you know, they worked here for Dole, or Shell Oil. But we got word by runner that some other ones, missionaries, will be here in the next day or two."

"What's Fertig going to do with them?" Lewis asked.

"Send them out with you when the *Sunfish* returns. Captain Buchanan wanted to send them back where they came from, but the General said no."

"How are we going to get a bunch of civilians—" McCoy began, and interrupted himself. "What shape are they in, Everly?"

"Skinny, weak, but they can walk."

"How are we going to get a half-dozen civilians from here to the beach?" McCoy asked.

No one replied.

"The General told Captain Buchanan to spread the word that we can't handle any more civilians right now—not to bring any more here, in other words—but said we have to keep the ones we have for—what was that word, Mr. Lewis?—reasons of *credibility.*"

"Yeah," Lewis said.

McCoy looked at him for amplification.

"American citizens are entitled to the protection of their government," Lewis explained. "Right now, USFIP is the U.S. Government. Fertig can't turn these people away. If he did, the word would quickly spread among other Americans, and thus quickly throughout the island, that USFIP can't help people. No help, no credibility."

"But he did order his USFIP people not to bring any more civilians here, right?" McCoy asked.

Lewis nodded.

"I wonder how many there are," McCoy said.

"Couple of hundred, Mr. McCoy, is what I hear," Everly said.

"My God, if several hundred civilians show up here, not only will it make it difficult, possibly impossible, to conduct our evacuation, but it can't help but attract the attention of the Japanese," Macklin said.

"You was in China," Zimmerman said. "You should know that's what Marines do, protect American civilians."

Captain Macklin visibly did not like being spoken to in such a manner by an enlisted man. But he said nothing.

"Macklin, why don't you go have a look at these civilians?" McCoy ordered. "Take Everly with you. Don't tell them any more than you have to, but tell them how hard—and dangerous—it's going to be to get them from here onto a submarine. Maybe some of them will have second thoughts. And go back where they came from."

"It's worth a shot," Everly said. "But don't get your hopes up, Mr. McCoy."

"In any event, get their names and next of kin in the States," McCoy said. "You know what we need. Koffler can radio it. People in the States are probably worried about these people."

"Aye, aye, Sir," Everly said.

"And speaking of the devil, the communications genius of OPERATION WINDMILL," Lewis said, as Staff Sergeant Koffler walked into the single room of the building from the porch.

"You hear about the civilians?" Koffler asked.

"Just now."

"Where'd the khakis come from?" Koffler asked.

"Courtesy of the U.S. Army," McCoy said. "Everly, have you got a bar for Koffler, too?"

"Yeah," Everly said, and reached into his pocket and came out with another silver lieutenant's bar. He tossed it to Koffler.

"Don't get too attached to that, Steve," McCoy said. "It comes off when we get out of here."

"It'll still look good on my Officer Candidate School application," Koffler said, unabashed. "Highest Rank Attained: First Lieutenant, U.S. Forces in the Philippines.' "

McCoy laughed.

"The only reason you're a first lieutenant, *very* temporary, is that General Fertig decided he had better things to do with gold than make second lieutenant's bars out of it."

"It'll still look good on my application," Koffler said, and then handed McCoy a decrypted message. "I thought you would want this right away."

```
FROM KFS TO MXX
FOR CAPT MCCOY


PART ONE


A - ADVANCE DATE GROCERY STORE PHASE ONE BY FIVE REPEAT FIVE
DAYS


B - CONFIRM TIME AND COORDINATES WHEN DETERMINED


PART TWO


A - PREPARE TO RECEIVE THREE REPEAT THREE OSS OFFICERS WHO WILL
AUGMENT REPEAT AUGMENT PRESENT OSS STAFF


PICKERING BRIG GEN
```

McCoy read it and then handed it to Lewis.

"What's the delay?" Koffler asked. "They didn't say."

"I guess they didn't want us to know, otherwise they would have told us," McCoy replied. "What's the problem, Steve? You get to wear your first john's bar for another five days."

"The problem is that we can't use Site Charley," Lewis said. "There will be Japs all over that area then."

"So where do we go?" McCoy asked.

Lewis took his chart from its oilskin pouch, unfolded it, spread it on the floor, and then knelt beside it. It was a full minute before he replied to McCoy:

"Site George, or Site Mike or . . . Site Sugar," he said. "And the closest of those three is twenty miles further from here than Site Charley."

"Oh, shit," McCoy said.

Movement of any kind through the area was difficult. The temperature and humidity were high, and the terrain steep, uneven, and slippery.

Military efficiency would dictate that those making the journey carry as little individually as possible—a carbine, four fifteen-round clips, a canteen, a change of socks, and dry rations—and that communal property, the carrying of which would be shared, be limited to the absolute essentials: a radio, batteries, a small quantity of ammunition and hand grenades, and emergency medical supplies.

The decision had been made, however, for a number of reasons, to evacuate nine seriously ill and/or wounded personnel who would almost certainly die if they could not receive the attention of a general hospital.

Since they could not walk, they would have to be carried. That meant four bearers for each evacuee. Even by alternating bearers, the pace would be considerably slower than otherwise. And since carrying both a sick man and weapons would be impossible, other bearers would be required to carry the bearers' weapons and food. The larger the party, the greater the risk of detection by the Japanese. That would mean additional bearers to carry additional ammunition and hand grenades in case of a confrontation with the Japanese.

And now there were civilians to be evacuated.

"Did you pick up on that 'augment repeat augment' business, Ken?" Lewis asked.

"What?" McCoy asked, having been dragged back to the present from his consideration of the ramifications of adding an unknown number of civilians in unknown physical condition to the original evacuation party.

"Did you pick up on the word 'augment'?" Lewis asked.

"Yeah. It looks as if Macklin stays, doesn't it?"

"You going to tell him?"

"Not now," McCoy said. "What I'm thinking is that I'm going to let the OSS people tell him on the beach. And I don't want anybody telling the General, either."

"Why not?"

"He's liable to order us to take him with us," McCoy said. "Fertig's got Macklin figured out by now."

[FIVE]
Headquarters, U.S. Forces in the Philippines
Davao Oriental Province
Mindanao, Commonwealth of the Philippines
1045 Hours 26 January 1943

Captain Kenneth R. McCoy, USMCR, and First Lieutenant Percy L. Everly, USFIP, marched erectly into the office of Brigadier General Wendell Fertig and came to attention twelve inches from his desk.

General Fertig looked up at them expectantly. After a very long moment, Captain McCoy saluted. A perceptible period of time after Captain McCoy raised his hand to his temple, Lieutenant Everly did likewise. General Fertig returned their salutes with a casual wave of his right hand in the general direction of his forehead.

"Am I missing something here, gentlemen?" Fertig asked. "It looked to me as if you were making up your mind whether or not you were going to offer me that hoary gesture of recognition between warriors."

"General," Captain McCoy said, "Marines do not salute indoors unless under arms."

"Fascinating. I learn something every day," Fertig said. "I take it that dagger strapped to your wrist falls in the category of 'dagger on arm' rather than anything else?"

"We left our carbines outside, General."

"I was hoping to have a word with you before you left, Ken," Fertig said. "This is as good a time as any."

"General, that's why we're here," McCoy said.

"You looked serious," Fertig said. "OK. Let's have it. What's gone wrong?"

"The thing is, Sir, there's a hundred things that could go wrong. The odds that we can make it to the beach without a half-dozen serious things going wrong aren't very good."

"When you have something unpleasant to say, say it," Fertig said. "You think that your priority is to make it onto the *Sunfish,* and you can't do that with the civilians and the wounded? I have been considering that myself, frankly."

"Everly and I have an idea—" McCoy said, and then quickly interrupted himself. "General, we weren't thinking about not taking the civilians and wounded with us."

"Let's have it," Fertig said.

"The problem is transporting them forty-five miles from here to Site Sugar," McCoy said. "With all the bearers, we'll be nearly a hundred people."

"One hundred two, if memory serves," Fertig said. "Are we back to not taking the wounded and civilians with you?"

"No, Sir, I'm just trying to make the point that I think we have almost no chance of moving that many people, that slowly, that far, without being detected."

"Almost no chance? If you've got a point, Ken, let's have it."

"Can I lay my map on your desk, Sir?"

"One of the things I wanted to talk to you about is that map. Could you leave it with me?"

"Absolutely. We have three. You can have two of those, and I could leave the last one with Everly on the beach."

"OK. What is it you want to show me?"

"Here we are," McCoy said, pointing to the map, "and here is Site Sugar." He pointed to a spot on the coast twenty-five miles south of the promontory off which the *Sunfish* had first surfaced.

"If we leave in the morning, it will take us nine days to make the trip, if nothing goes wrong. Maybe eight. But nine to be safe. That's 5 and 6 February."

"We've been over this," Fertig said.

"We can make it from here to here in a day and a half," McCoy said, pointing to a spot on the coast five miles north of Tarragona.

"And how do you propose to get from there to Site Sugar?"

"Steal a couple of trucks," Everly blurted.

Fertig's eyebrows rose.

"The idea, General, is that instead of using the ninety-odd people as bearers, we use them to delay the Japs."

"You're getting ahead of me, McCoy," Fertig said.

"The Japs are not sending anything out on that highway alone. They send at least three trucks, most often four. We ambush their convoy two miles out of Tarragona. Take the two best trucks, burn the others, and drive here, where the civilians will be waiting. We then *drive* to Site Sugar."

"Thirty minutes after you ambush the convoy, the Japs will know about it, and start after you."

"Every time there's a curve in the road, we will have a guy in the bush. He fires a couple of shots at the lead truck, and then shags ass out of there. We figure the Japs will stop and send out a patrol. That'll take fifteen minutes. They don't find anything—our sniper is long gone—so they get back in the trucks and start after us again. Next curve, another sniper."

"It won't take them long to figure out what you're doing," Fertig said. "They won't stop, they'll just keep going when you shoot at them."

"That's what Everly said," McCoy said. "I think our snipers can take out drivers two times out of three."

"They'll still come after you."

"As long as they don't catch us, let them come. We'll send people to reconnoiter near Site Sugar, and find someplace where we can get rid of the trucks. With a little luck, we'll put them in the woods where they won't be seen, but if necessary, just burn them on the road."

"By this time in your plan, the Japs will have reconnaissance aircraft all over the area. You'd be putting the *Sunfish* at grave risk."

"The *Sunfish* won't be there," McCoy said.

"Excuse me?"

"We'll leave for Tarragona tomorrow, ambush the convoy the next day, if we're lucky, or the day after that, or the day after that. That way we know there will be a convoy to ambush. And then the *Sunfish* comes on 5 February as scheduled."

"And where will the civilians and wounded be . . ." Fertig began. "Of course, at Site Sugar."

"That's the risk, General," McCoy said. "That the Japs will find us at Site Sugar, or near Site Sugar. If the Japs find them there . . . well. But there is less risk of being discovered if we're trying to hide twenty-five people in one place than if we're trying to move 102 people around for days."

Fertig stood up suddenly and left the room. He came back a moment later with a bottle of Famous Grouse and three glasses. He put everything on his desk and started, carefully, to pour the whiskey.

"I have an interest in getting the wounded and the civilians to Pearl Harbor that is not entirely altruistic," he said as he poured. "There will be a certain interest on the part of the press in these American civilians snatched from the claws of the Japanese, and in the brave men grievously wounded fighting the Japanese against terrible odds. Once these people get out, it will not be nearly as easy for certain people to pretend United States Forces in the Philippines does not exist."

He walked to the door, raised his voice, and called, "Sergeant!"

His Filipino sergeant appeared almost immediately.

"Please pass the word that an officer's call will be conducted here immediately," he said.

"Yes, Sir."

He walked back to the drinks and handed McCoy and Everly a glass, then picked up his own.

"Before the others join us," he said, "I think we should raise a glass to your successful evacuation. For the first time, I'm beginning to think we can get away with it."

[SIX]
Headquarters, U.S. Forces in the Philippines
Davao Oriental Province
Mindanao, Commonwealth of the Philippines
1305 Hours 26 January 1943

Captain Kenneth R. McCoy, USMCR, took a U.S. Rifle, Caliber .30-06, Model 1903, from Lieutenant Percy L. Everly, USFIP, held down the catch, and removed the bolt. He put his thumb into the action, raised the muzzle to his eye, and then turned his body until the rays of the sun reflected off his thumbnail and illuminated the interior of the barrel.

"It's pitted," he announced.

"We've been a little short on bore cleaner around here, Mr. McCoy," Everly said.

McCoy examined the bolt.

"What have you been oiling these with, coconut oil?"

"Motor oil," Everly said.

"They're all like this?"

Everly nodded.

"That's it, unless you want to try doing this with a carbine."

"No. We've got to try for headshots, and I don't want to try headshots with a carbine," McCoy said. "I can't believe we didn't think to bring bore cleaner and oil with us."

Everly shrugged, and then McCoy had a second thought.

"But there's something," he said. "You see that thing that holds the sling in the carbine stock? It's an oiler."

"No shit?" Everly asked, impressed.

"Give me that," McCoy said, pointing to a carbine. Gunny Zimmerman handed it to him. McCoy loosened the web sling where it passed through a slot in the stock and took out a two-inch-round metal tube. He unscrewed the top and pulled it off. A metal rod, flattened at the end, was attached to the top. A drop of light-brown oil dropped off.

"Lube oil," he announced.

"I'll be damned," Everly said, impressed.

"Let's get the motor oil, or whatever the hell this gunk is, off the bolts," McCoy said. "And at least lube them right."

With a practiced skill, he began to disassemble the bolt. He looked up and saw the others watching him—Lieutenant Chambers Lewis, USN; Captain Robert B. Macklin, USMC; Gunnery Sergeant Zimmerman, USMC; two former 4th Marines PFCs (now 2nd Lieutenants, USFIP), Oscar Wendlington and Charles O. Pierce; First Lieutenant Claudio Alvarez, late of the Philippine Scouts; and Master Sergeant Fernando Lamar, late of the 26th Cavalry.

"This isn't a goddamn demonstration," he said. "You know how to take a bolt apart. Or should."

The others turned to the other Springfields and began to remove their bolts. They had three battered, intended-for-weapons-cleaning toothbrushes between them—McCoy's, Zimmerman's, and Everly's—and in a few minutes the bolts had been cleaned of the thickened motor oil and lubricated with a thin coat of the finer gun oil from the carbine oiler.

Zimmerman was finished first. He replaced the bolt in his Springfield and worked the action a half-dozen times, finally nodding with satisfaction.

"Ernie, pace off a hundred yards," McCoy ordered. "We'll zero for two hundred yards. We should be shooting at anywhere from fifty to a hundred fifty yards. Trajectory will be pretty flat with two-hundred-yard Zero."

Zimmerman marched off toward the end of the clearing, found a suitable tree, and then marched back toward them, one hundred measured three-foot paces.

McCoy drew a one-inch circle in the center of a piece of typewriter paper with a grease pencil, and then filled in the center.

"Now let's see if these things will shoot into eight inches at a hundred yards," he said.

"We have sixty-eight rounds, period," Everly said, then took from a musette bag four gray cheap cardboard boxes labeled ORDNANCE CORPS U.S. ARMY. TWENTY CARTRIDGES CALIBER .30-06 ARMOR PIERCING and laid them carefully on the ground. They showed signs they'd been wet; the cardboard had shrunk when it dried, and the outline of the cartridges they contained was clearly visible. McCoy picked up one of the boxes, the one that was not full.

He took a black-tipped cartridge from the box and examined it. On the base it was stamped FA 1918.

"Frankford Arsenal, 1918," he announced. "Jesus Christ! They're as old as I am! What makes you think these will fire? They've been water-soaked, God knows how many times."

"There's shellac over the primers," Everly said. "Most of them work fine."

" 'Most of them,' " McCoy said, and then turned to Captain Macklin. "Make some more targets," he said, handing him the grease pencil.

Then he took the target, walked to the tree Zimmerman had selected, and stood for a moment frustrated. Then he took the knife strapped to his left wrist from its sheath and used it to pin the target to the tree.

Then he walked back to the line in the dirt Zimmerman had drawn with the toe of his boondockers and sat down. He unfastened the frogs of the leather sling on his rifle and converted it to a rifleman's sling. He adjusted the sling, twice, until he was satisfied, and then rolled onto his stomach.

By this time, the others had walked up to him. He took three cartridges, loaded them into the magazine, and rammed one into the chamber with the bolt.

He took a long time finding the proper sight picture before touching off the first round. Then he chambered another round, fired, and repeated the process a third time.

"Well, at least they all went off," he said as he rose to his feet and went to the target—removing the sling as he walked. A half-inch above the black circle and two inches to the right of it were three holes in the target. He was able to conceal them with his thumbs held together.

"Not bad," he said.

"You going to fuck with the sights?" Zimmerman asked. "Or do it Kentucky?"

"I don't have two inches to play with, Ernie," McCoy said, and sat down and adjusted the rear sight so that it would move bullet impact two inches to the left.

Then he went back to the firing line, dropped back in the prone position, replaced the sling, and loaded three more cartridges into the magazine. It took him as long as the first time to find what he thought was a satisfactory sight picture, and then he squeezed one off.

This time, the result was only a dull click as the firing pin moved forward against the cartridges' primer.

"Shit," McCoy said bitterly. "And I fired the worst-looking ones first."

He angrily worked the action, ejecting the malfunctioning cartridge. He looked at it in disgust. There was a clear mark where the firing pin had struck the primer. He started to throw it away in anger.

"Don't," Everly said. "We can use the bullet!"

McCoy looked up at him and tossed him the malfunctioning cartridge. Then he rolled back into the prone position, found a satisfactory sight picture, and squeezed the trigger. The cartridge fired, and so a moment later did the third.

He stood up and walked back to the target. Now there were two holes, which he could cover with one thumb, in the grease pencil bull's-eye.

"OK," he said. "Now you, Ernie."

McCoy jerked his knife from the tree.

"How am I supposed to put my target up?" Zimmerman protested.

"You'll think of something," McCoy said. "You're a gunny, right?"

"I'm not going to shoot your fucking knife," Zimmerman said.

"You'll think of something," McCoy repeated.

Zimmerman affixed his target to the tree with a chrome-plated toenail clipper, then walked back to the firing line.

By the time the four marksmen—McCoy, Zimmerman, Wendlington, and Alvarez—had zeroed their rifles, the total stock of CARTRIDGES CALIBER .30-06 ARMOR PIERCING available to USFIP was down to thirty-six. Eight cartridges had misfired.

McCoy did the mental arithmetic—eight failures in thirty-two shots was one in four, twenty-five percent—but said nothing. He was sure the others could count too.

[SEVEN]
Headquarters, U.S. Forces in the Philippines
Davao Oriental Province
Mindanao, Commonwealth of the Philippines
0815 Hours 27 January 1943

"We won't have time to talk this all through again when we get down to the highway," Captain McCoy said, "so this will be the last time. If there's any question, if anybody doesn't know exactly what he's supposed to do, now is the time to ask, not later. So listen up."

McCoy was sitting on—or more accurately, leaning against—the ladder-like stairs to the bachelor officers' thatched hut on stilts. The others, again wearing their dyed-black utilities, were sitting on the ground in a half-circle facing him. Wendlington, Pierce, and the two Filipinos were wearing the spare sets of utilities the landing team had carried with them.

"There are some things we won't know until this happens," McCoy said. "First of all, we won't know how many Jap trucks there will be until Everly comes down the road on his motorcycle. At least two, that's almost for sure, and maybe as many as four or five. If there's only two, that gives us the most trouble, because we need two trucks to move the wounded and civilians. That means we're in trouble if one truck—or both of them—are damaged when we hit the convoy. If both trucks are knocked out, then we call the whole thing off. We grab their weapons and whatever we can get off the trucks and come back here. If one truck is knocked out, we'll make the decision whether to call it off, or try to do with just one truck, then.

"There are four firing teams. Each team has a Springfield and nine rounds. Five in the rifle and four spares, plus two carbines, each with six fifteen-round magazines. I can't say this enough: The less shooting the better, and the one thing we don't want to hit is the trucks.

"There will probably be four Japs in each truck—the driver, somebody riding with him, and two soldiers in the back. The first thing we do is take out the drivers of the first and last trucks. Then the drivers of the trucks in between, and then the guards.

"I'll fire the first shot. Nobody shoots until I do. We can't take the chance that when he hears shooting the driver of the lead truck will step on the gas to get away. As soon as you hear my shot, start shooting. But have a target before you shoot!

"As soon as the trucks are stopped, the riflemen will take a carbine, and we'll go on the road and make sure everybody is dead."

"Don't just drop the Springfields and forget them," Everly interrupted. "I want them on the trucks before we leave!"

"Right," McCoy said. He didn't see any real use for the rifles without ammunition, and if each rifleman fired three shots—and five seemed most likely—before picking up a carbine, there would be four rounds left for each rifle. And Garands, and ammunition for them, would be on the *Sunfish*. But he knew the Springfields were important to Everly, so he went along.

"As soon as we get the trucks rolling," McCoy went on, "Lieutenant Everly will get back on his motorcycle and head off down the road to the wounded and civilians. And to make sure the people on the side of the road know it's us, and not Japanese in the trucks.

"Then we pick up our passengers and go on down the road until Everly stops us. We'll unload the passengers and move them into the jungle. Lieutenant Alvarez's people will then take the trucks further down the road and get rid of them. And then we wait for the *Sunfish*."

He looked around his audience. No one seemed to be paying attention to him.

They're bored, he thought. *This must be the tenth time I've gone through this.*

"Are there any questions?" McCoy asked.

There were no questions.

I think at this point that I'm supposed to say something encouraging. I can't think of what.

"OK," McCoy said. "Let's get this show on the road."

He pushed himself off the ladderlike stairs and picked up his Springfield.

"Good luck, gentlemen," Fertig called from behind him.

I was wondering where he was, and he's been there all the time.

Their eyes met.

"See you after the war, McCoy," General Fertig said.

"Yes, Sir," McCoy said. He raised his hand in salute. Fertig returned it casually. McCoy did an about-face and walked to Master Sergeant Lamar, who was in the process of slinging his Springfield over his shoulder.

Lamar would lead them to the interception site north of Tarragona. Lamar met McCoy's eyes, nodded, turned, and started off. McCoy looked over his shoulder to make sure that Macklin was behind him, and then started off after Master Sergeant Lamar.

[EIGHT]
**1.7 miles north of Tarragona
Davao Oriental Province
Mindanao, Commonwealth of the Philippines
0920 Hours 31 January 1943**

In the professional judgment of Captain Kenneth R. McCoy, if there was going to be a convoy today, it would have been here by now. That meant that there would be no convoy today. That posed problems.

They had been here since shortly after noon on the twenty-ninth. It had rained on and off since their arrival, often in short, intense storms against which the crude shelters they had built offered little protection. They were soaked through each time it rained, and there was no time to get dry. After each rain, the insects came out, and they were all covered with angry welts.

He did not like to consider the effect this was having on the wounded and civilians down the road.

It was possible, of course, that the Japanese would set out from Tarragona at ten, or eleven, or for that matter at half past two in the afternoon, which meant they could not leave their concealed positions on the road and move into the jungle where they could safely make fires. All they could do was wait.

And it was entirely possible that a key element of what now was seeming less and less a clever plan—Everly's riding down the road on his motorcycle to inform them the convoy was on the way—would go awry for a number of reasons, starting with the malfunction of the motorcycle, or a motorcycle accident, to Everly falling into the hands of the Japanese.

He found himself in the uncomfortable position of hoping that Everly had been killed. Better that than falling into the hands of the Japanese. McCoy had seen enough of Japanese techniques of interrogation to know that no man had the ability—courage had nothing to do with it—to deny Japanese interrogators anything they wanted to know.

He was deep in this depressing chain of thought when he heard the faint but unmistakable sound of a motorcycle engine.

Then, behind him, he heard the action of a carbine, and turned to look at Macklin.

"What are you going to do, shoot Everly?" McCoy asked sarcastically, and was immediately sorry.

This is not the time to jump all over Macklin; what I should be doing is reassuring him. I will very likely need the sonofabitch.

Macklin looked at him like a kicked puppy.

"Don't fire that thing until I shoot," McCoy said, then rose to his feet and stood behind a tree that gave him a good look at the road.

Two minutes later Everly appeared, looking from side to side as he rode very slowly down the road.

McCoy stepped from the behind the tree so that Everly could see him.

When he did, Everly cut the motorcycle's engine and coasted up to McCoy.

"They should be about ten minutes behind me," Everly said. "Four trucks. All the guards are in the last truck."

"Go hide the bike," McCoy ordered.

Everly kicked the engine to life. The noise now seemed deafening.

McCoy turned to Macklin.

"Did you hear that? Four trucks? All the guards in the last one?"
Macklin nodded.

"You stay here. I'll pass the word to the others."

Macklin visibly did not like the idea of being left alone, but he nodded his understanding.

McCoy went onto the shoulder of the road. Lieutenant Alvarez, late of the Philippine Scouts, and Lieutenant Lewis, late aide-de-camp to Rear Admiral Wagam, stood up in the positions across the road.

"We heard him," Alvarez said.

"I'm going to pass the word to them," McCoy said, gesturing down the road to where Pierce, Lamar, Zimmerman, and Wedlington were in position, "to take out all the guards as soon as I start shooting."

Alvarez nodded, and McCoy trotted farther down the road.

When he returned to his position, McCoy didn't see Macklin. After a moment, he found him. He was five yards deeper inside the thick jungle than he had to be, in a squatting position behind a large tree.

Resisting the urge to tell him to get back where he had placed him, McCoy walked to him, took the spare carbine and two magazines from him, and went back to the position he had selected for himself.

He put the Springfield sling on his arm, carefully examined his stock of nine cartridges, and loaded into the rifle the five that had the best chance of firing.

The sound of the Japanese truck engines began to be heard just a minute later, far sooner than the ten minutes Everly had predicted. McCoy worked the Springfield's bolt and made sure the safety was off.

The driver of the first truck that appeared was hunched over the wheel, resting both arms on it. The soldier beside him seemed to be sleeping.

McCoy found a sight picture, the front blade of his sight on the Japanese's nose. He took a deep breath, let half of it out, and squeezed the trigger.

The Springfield slammed into his shoulder. Without thinking about it, McCoy chambered another round.

The Japanese driver seemed to jerk erect, then slumped farther over the wheel. The truck continued down the road, not slowing at all. McCoy's front sight found the other, now wide-awake, Japanese, and he squeezed off another round.

Nothing.

Furiously, he chambered a third cartridge and searched for a sight picture. He found one, but just as his finger tightened on the trigger, the head of the second Japanese jerked violently to the side.

Lieutenant Alvarez had also found a suitable sight picture.

McCoy moved his eyes to the second truck. The driver had slammed on the brakes and seemed to be trying to push the steering wheel away from him. McCoy found his nose with his front blade sight and squeezed off a round. The Springfield slammed reassuringly against his shoulder. When he found the Japanese again, he immediately lost that sight picture as the truck veered off the road and slammed into a large tree. McCoy searched for the front-seat passenger, and again, as he tightened his finger on the trigger, his target seemed to explode.

Lieutenant Alvarez, McCoy thought approvingly, *knows how to shoot.*

And then he became aware of many gunshots.

He tore off the Springfield sling and picked up the carbine, chambering a round as he did so.

He heard movement behind him, and turned to see Macklin coming out of the jungle, holding the carbine as a hunter holds a shotgun. He moved past McCoy as if he didn't see him.

McCoy's attention was diverted by a crunching sound, and he looked toward the sound. The first truck had driven off the road and into a tree.

The engine stalled.

McCoy jumped to his feet and ran down the road toward it. Out of the corner of his eye, he saw Chambers Lewis start after him.

They reached the truck at about the same time. Both Japanese were beyond question dead. They rested their carbines against the fender and, with what seemed like an extraordinary amount of effort, pulled both bodies from the truck.

McCoy crawled behind the wheel, put the transmission in neutral, and cranked the engine. After a moment's hesitation, it caught. He and Chambers grinned at one another.

McCoy backed the truck onto the road. Apparently, it was undamaged. He got from behind the wheel and looked back up the road.

Captain Robert B. Macklin, USMC, was moving among the bodies on the road, shooting each one in the head with his carbine.

[NINE]
Site Sugar
Davao Oriental Province
Mindanao, Commonwealth of the Philippines
0001 Hours 6 February 1943

With some difficulty, Captain Robert B. Macklin, USMC, read the luminous hands on his wristwatch. The hour and minute hands pointed at midnight; the second hand clicked past thirty-five seconds.

"Columbus, Columbus, this is Coffin, Coffin," the radio hissed.

"Right on schedule," Captain Macklin whispered.

McCoy ignored him. "Read you five by five, Coffin, go ahead," he said to his microphone. He stood up and shined a flashlight out to sea, two long flashes and then two short ones.

"We have your light," the radio hissed. "What are surf conditions?"

"Your boats can land."

"Give us five, I say again, five, minutes and another light."

"Acknowledge," McCoy said, then let the microphone drop to the length of its cord and looked at his watch.

"Right on schedule," Macklin repeated.

"Right on schedule," McCoy parroted. "Tell the people with the civilians to get them ready to move. Bring them up here in groups of six."

"Aye, aye, Sir," Macklin said.

A moment later, it occurred to him that he did not have to say "Aye, aye, Sir," to McCoy. Despite the peculiar command conditions of this mission, he still outranked him.

But it was not really a cause for concern. This mission was just about over, and it had gone very well. In no time at all, he would be aboard the *Sunfish,* and that would be the official end of the mission.

He wondered what the OSS would do with him now. At the very least, he reasoned, he would be returned to Washington for a debriefing on Fertig and his guerrillas. Considering all he had gone through, a decoration seemed at least possible, and maybe even probable. The only problem was that no one was around to recommend him for one; McCoy certainly wouldn't do it.

But on the other hand, if they decorated Lieutenant Lewis, which seemed probable, and didn't give him one, questions would be asked.

Even that didn't really matter. A decoration would be nice, but what he knew he would be getting for sure would be a remark on his service record that he had been on OPERATION WINDMILL, a top-level, top-secret mission behind enemy lines. And that would effectively put behind him, once and for all, that unfortunate and unfair efficiency report of Banning's.

Even McCoy could not fault his performance of duty on this mission. He had, after all, personally killed eight of the enemy. That was a fact. McCoy couldn't change that fact. Lewis wouldn't stand for that.

The most logical thing to do with him, what he would do himself if he were the officer making the decision, would be to assign him to the Country Club, where he would be of inarguable use in training others for missions of this type. There is nothing like experience. And men are inspired by teachers who have personally done what they are being trained to do.

Eight minutes later, he was back on the beach, accompanied by six of the nine females who would be taken aboard the *Sunfish.* That was the law of the sea, women and children first. First the women, which would take three boats,

and then the other civilians and the wounded. And then they would be paddled out to the *Sunfish*. And that would be the end of it.

"I've got six women with me, McCoy," Macklin said. "The rest will be coming in ten-minute increments."

McCoy pointed out to sea. It took Macklin a moment to find them, but he saw, just barely, what looked like half a dozen rubber boats making their way to the beach.

"Six at once? I'll go back and tell them to send the evacuees up more quickly."

"What I want you to do is stand here and flash the light, just flash it twice, once every thirty seconds," McCoy ordered. "I'll go back and have the evacuees brought up here."

Five minutes later, the first of the boats reached the surf. The others were a short distance behind. Now there was a light flashing, two short flashes, from the *Sunfish*, obviously to guide the rubber boats on their return.

A man wearing dyed-black utilities came wading through the surf. He walked up to Macklin.

"Welcome to Mindanao," Macklin said.

"Who are you?"

"Captain Robert Macklin, USMC, on detail to the OSS."

The man offered his hand.

"Major Al Fredericks, Macklin. I'm the OSS team chief."

"How do you do, Sir?"

"Where's Captain McCoy?"

"With the evacuees, Sir. I have six on the beach, ready for evacuation."

McCoy appeared.

"I'm McCoy," he said. "Who are you?"

"My name is Fredericks. I'm the OSS team chief."

"I'll see you before I leave," McCoy said, shaking his hand. "Right now the priority is to get the evacuees aboard."

"Sorry, it's not," Major Fredericks said.

"Excuse me?"

"I have my orders, Captain. From General Pickering. The first people to go aboard the *Sunfish* are you and Lieutenant Lewis, followed by the other people of your party. I didn't like it at first, but after a while, it makes sense. The purpose of this operation was to get your report on General Fertig. Everything has to fall in line behind that."

"For Christ's sake!" McCoy protested.

"As I understand it, we're both Marine officers," Major Fredericks said. "That being the case, Captain, the proper response to an order is 'Aye, aye, Sir.' "

"Aye, aye, Sir," McCoy said.

"If you think about it, McCoy, that makes sense," Macklin said reasonably. "The priority is to get us out of here."

"Wade out and get in the boat, Captain," Major Fredericks said. "I'll see that the others follow."

"Would you like me to go with Captain McCoy, Sir?" Captain Macklin asked.

"Why? From what I hear, Captain McCoy is the Marine Corps rubberboat expert. He can probably get into a rubber boat without assistance."

"Yes, Sir. Of course. When would the Major like me to go out to the *Sunfish*, Sir?"

"You're not going anywhere, Captain," Major Fredericks said.

"Sir?"

"I wish you were, frankly, Macklin," Major Fredericks said. "Your reputation precedes you. But my orders are to keep you here." He looked at Macklin and then at McCoy. "Are you waiting for something, Captain, or will one direct order to get in a boat be sufficient for you?"

"Take care of yourself, Macklin," McCoy said. He handed Major Fredericks his carbine. "Round chambered, Sir. Safety on."

And then he waded into the surf.

[TEN]

OPERATIONAL IMMEDIATE
FROM SUNFISH
1105 GREENWICH 6FEBRUARY1943

FOR CINCPAC
ALL STATIONS COPY AND RELAY

1 OPERATION GROCERY STORE ONE SUCCESSFULLY COMPLETED 2300
LOCAL TIME THIS DATE

2 OSS AUGMENTATION TEAM SAFELY ASHORE AND IN CONTACT WITH
OSS AGENT ATTACHED TO HQ USFIP

3 SUNFISH HAS TAKEN ABOARD CAPT K.R.MCCOY, USMCR, LT
CHAMBERS LEWIS, USN, GUNNERY SERGEANT ERNEST ZIMMERMAN
USMC AND STAFF SERGEANT STEPHEN KOFFLER USMC. ALL HANDS IN
EXCELLENT SHAPE.

4 SUNFISH ALSO HAS ABOARD NINE (9) U.S. FEMALE CIVILIANS; FOUR

U.S. MALE CIVILIANS AND ELEVEN (11) WOUNDED AND/OR SERIOUSLY
ILL U.S. AND FILIPINO MEMBERS OF US FORCES IN PHILIPPINES. ALL
WILL URGENTLY REQUIRE MEDICAL ATTENTION AT DESTINATION

5 PROCEEDING AS ORDERED.

END

[ELEVEN]

SUPREME HEADQUARTERS SWPOA 2315 6FEB43
VIA SPECIAL CHANNEL

TO NAVY DEPT WASH DC
FOR COLONEL F.L. RICKABEE USMC OFFICE OF MANAGEMENT
ANALYSIS

PLEASE RELAY IMMEDIATELY FOLLOWING TO MISS ERNESTINE SAGE
ADDRESSES KNOWN TO BOTH BANNING AND SESSIONS

DEEPLY REGRET MUST SUGGEST YOU TELEPHONE PICK AND ADVISE
HIM YOU CANNOT MARRY HIM INASMUCH AS CAPT KENNETH R MCCOY
IS ON HIS WAY HOME. MORE DETAILS WHEN AVAILABLE. LOVE UNCLE
FLEMING END

BY DIRECTION OF BRIG GEN PICKERING USMC

HART 2LT USMCR

[TWELVE]

T O P S E C R E T

THE WHITE HOUSE
WASHINGTON

0900 8 FEBRUARY 1943

VIA SPECIAL CHANNEL

GENERAL DOUGLAS MACARTHUR
SUPREME COMMANDER SWPOA

FOLLOWING PERSONAL FROM THE PRESIDENT TO GENERAL
MACARTHUR

MY DEAR DOUGLAS:

I'M SURE THAT YOU WILL AGREE THE FOLLOWING IS SOMETHING AT
LEAST ONE OF US SHOULD HAVE THOUGHT OF SOME TIME AGO. I
WOULD APPRECIATE YOUR GETTING THIS INTO FLEMING PICKERING'S
HANDS AS SOON AS POSSIBLE.

ELEANOR JOINS ME IN EXTENDING THE MOST CORDIAL GREETINGS TO
YOU AND JEAN.

AS EVER,

FRANKLIN

END PERSONAL FROM THE PRESIDENT TO GENERAL MACARTHUR

FOLLOWING PERSONAL FROM THE PRESIDENT TO BRIG GEN PICKERING

MY DEAR FLEMING:

FIRST LET ME EXPRESS MY GREAT ADMIRATION FOR THE MANNER IN
WHICH YOUR PEOPLE CONDUCTED THE OPERATION TO ESTABLISH
CONTACT WITH WENDELL FERTIG IN THE PHILIPPINES AND MY
PERSONAL DELIGHT THAT JIMMY'S COMRADE-IN-ARMS CAPTAIN
MCCOY AND HIS BRAVE TEAM HAVE BEEN SAFELY EVACUATED.
PLEASE RELAY TO EVERYONE CONCERNED MY VERY BEST WISHES
AND GRATITUDE FOR A JOB WELL DONE.

SECOND, LET ME EXPRESS MY CHAGRIN AT NOT SEEING THE OBVIOUS
SOLUTION TO OUR PROBLEM VIS-A-VIS OSS OPERATIONS IN THE PACIFIC
UNTIL, LITERALLY, LAST NIGHT. I WOULD NOT HAVE DREAMED OF
COURSE OF OVERRIDING THE WHOLLY UNDERSTANDABLE CONCERNS
OF GENERAL MACARTHUR AND ADMIRAL NIMITZ THAT THE OSS
OPERATIONS IN THEIR AREAS OF COMMAND WOULD MEAN THE
INTRUSION OF STRANGERS, AND THUS MIGHT INTERFERE WITH THEIR

OWN OPERATIONS. IN THEIR SHOES, I WOULD HAVE BEEN SIMILARLY
CONCERNED.

OUR NEED, OF COURSE, IS FOR SOMEONE WHO ENJOYS THE COMPLETE
TRUST OF BOTH ADMIRAL NIMITZ, GENERAL MACARTHUR, AND
DIRECTOR DONOVAN. I HAD FRANKLY DESPAIRED OF FINDING SUCH A
PERSON UNTIL LAST NIGHT. WHILE HAVING DINNER WITH OUR GOOD
FRIEND SENATOR RICHMOND FOWLER, I WAS STRUCK BY SOMETHING
CLOSE TO A DIVINE REVELATION, FOR I REALIZED THAT HE . . . . .
YOU . . . . . HAD BEEN STANDING IN FRONT OF ALL OF US ALL THE
TIME.

I HAVE TODAY ISSUED AN EXECUTIVE ORDER APPOINTING YOU DEPUTY
DIRECTOR OF THE OFFICE OF STRATEGIC SERVICES FOR PACIFIC
OPERATIONS. I AM SURE THAT GENERAL MACARTHUR AND ADMIRAL
NIMITZ WILL BE AS ENTHUSIASTIC ABOUT THIS APPOINTMENT AS WAS
DIRECTOR DONOVAN. I HAVE FURTHER INSTRUCTED ADMIRAL LEAHY
TO TRANSFER ALL PERSONNEL AND EQUIPMENT OF USMC SPECIAL
DETACHMENT SIXTEEN TO YOU, AND TO ARRANGE FOR THE TRANSFER
OF ANY OTHER PERSONNEL YOU MAY FEEL ARE NECESSARY.

WHILE YOU WILL BE REPORTING DIRECTLY TO DIRECTOR DONOVAN,
LET ME ASSURE YOU THAT MY DOOR WILL ALWAYS BE OPEN TO YOU
AT ALL TIMES. I LOOK FORWARD TO DISCUSSING FUTURE OPERATIONS
WITH YOU JUST AS SOON AS YOU FEEL YOU CAN LEAVE BRISBANE.

WITH MY WARMEST REGARDS

FRANKLIN

END PERSONAL MESSAGE FROM THE PRESIDENT TO BRIG GEN
PICKERING

BY DIRECTION OF THE PRESIDENT

LEAHY, ADMIRAL USN
CHIEF OF STAFF TO THE PRESIDENT

T O P   S E C R E T

AUTHOR'S ENDNOTE

When the U.S. Navy Cargo Submarine *Narwhal,* later in the war finally surfaced off Mindanao to deliver a good many supplies and to evacuate seriously ill Americans, civilian and military, they were greeted by the band of USFIP, in uniform, playing "The Stars and Stripes Forever."

When General Douglas MacArthur was able to finally make good his pledge to return to the Philippines, his troops were greatly assisted in the liberation of Mindanao by the 30,000 trained, uniformed, and armed men, Filipino and American, of U.S. Forces in the Philippines, under the command of Wendell Fertig.

Fertig survived the war, and resumed his successful civilian career as an engineer. He was a familiar sight, and a revered figure, around the Special Warfare Center—home of the Green Berets—at Fort Bragg, N.C.

Although he had commanded more men in combat than does a major general commanding a division, the Army never saw fit to promote him, even in the reserve, beyond full colonel.

His comrade-in-arms (and fellow civil engineer turned demolition expert) in the early days of the war on Luzon, Lieutenant (later Major) Ralph Fralick, successfully escaped from Bataan just before the peninsula fell, taking with him forty of his men. After a harrowing 1,200-mile voyage in an open boat, they arrived at Hanoi, in what then was French Indochina.

Fralick lined up his starving, exhausted, but still-proud troops and marched them to report to the French authorities. Salutes were exchanged, and then the French turned the Americans over to their allies the Japanese. Fralick survived four horrible years of Japanese captivity, and after a brief period in the peacetime Army, also resumed his career as a civil engineer.

To the end of his life he hated all things French.

Major Ralph Fralick died in 1993, and is buried in the U.S. Cemetery at the Pensacola, Florida, Naval Air Station. The author was privileged to know him well, and ultimately to deliver his eulogy.